JO

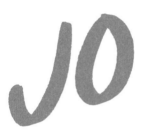

KATHLEEN GROS

JO

AN ADAPTATION OF
LITTLE WOMEN
(SORT OF)

Quill Tree Books
Imprints of HarperCollinsPublishers

HARPER
alley

HarperAlley is an imprint of HarperCollins Publishers.
Quill Tree Books is an imprint of HarperCollins Publishers.

Jo: An Adaption of Little Women (Sort Of)
 For information address HarperCollins Children's Books, a division of HarperCollins Publishers, 195 Broadway, New York, NY 10007.
www.harpercollinschildrens.com

ISBN 978-0-06-287596-9—ISBN 978-0-06-287597-6 (hardcover)

The artist used Photoshop to create the digital illustrations for this book.
20 21 22 23 24 EP 10 9 8 7 6 5 4 3 2 1
First Edition

FOR C

CHAPTER 1

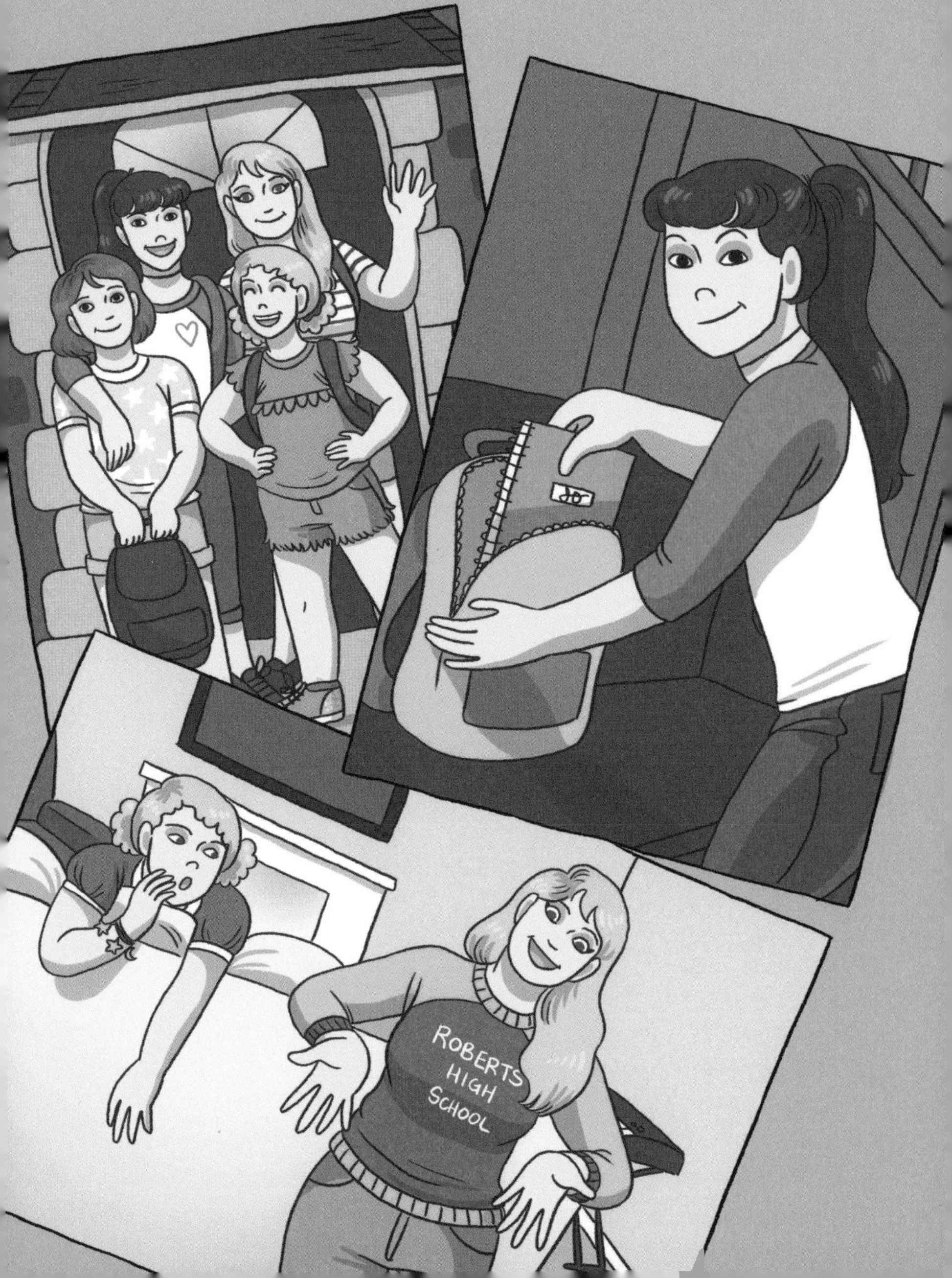
ROBERTS
HIGH
SCHOOL

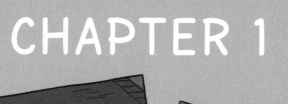

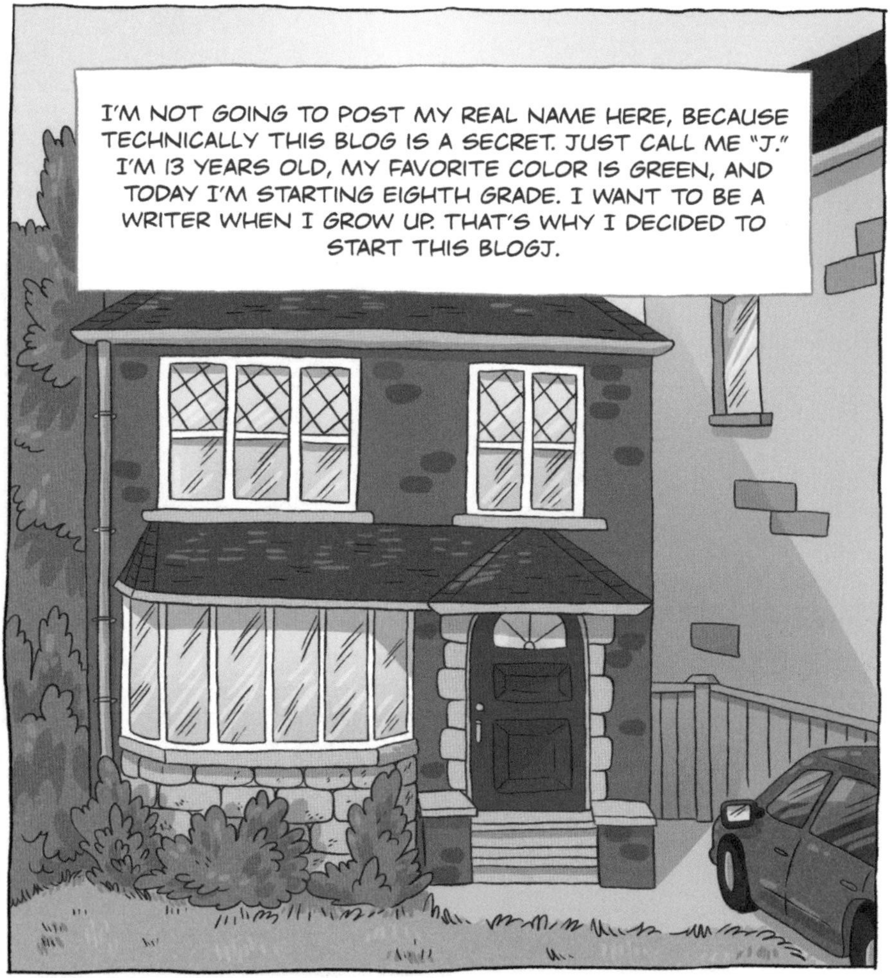
I'M NOT GOING TO POST MY REAL NAME HERE, BECAUSE TECHNICALLY THIS BLOG IS A SECRET. JUST CALL ME "J." I'M 13 YEARS OLD, MY FAVORITE COLOR IS GREEN, AND TODAY I'M STARTING EIGHTH GRADE. I WANT TO BE A WRITER WHEN I GROW UP. THAT'S WHY I DECIDED TO START THIS BLOGJ.

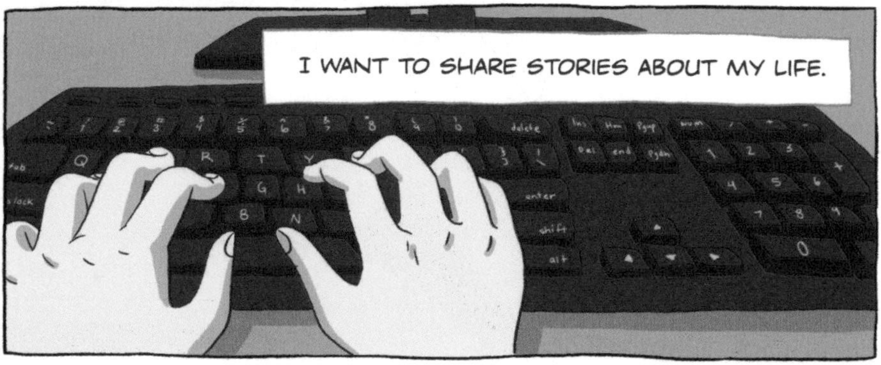
I WANT TO SHARE STORIES ABOUT MY LIFE.

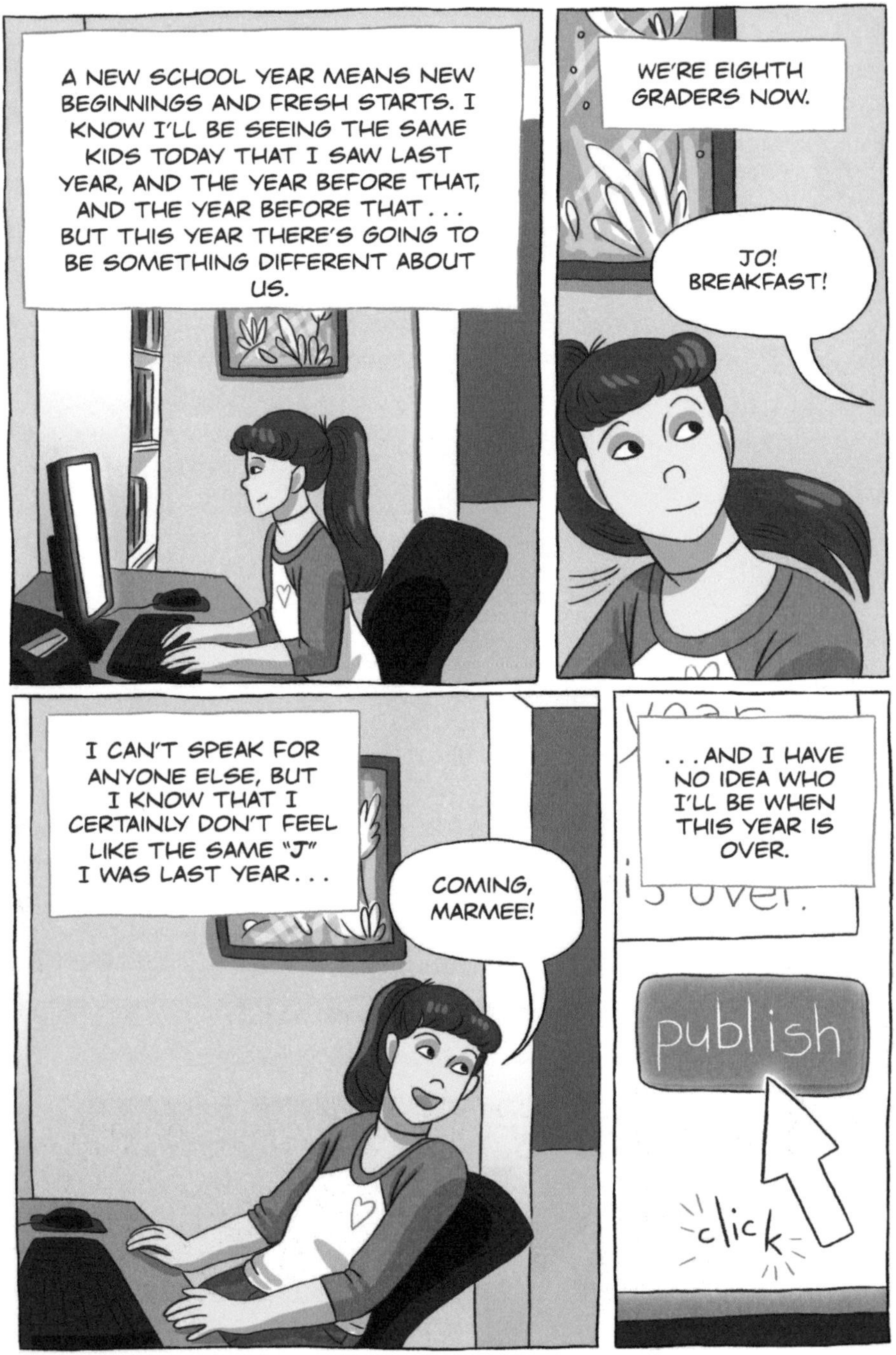
A NEW SCHOOL YEAR MEANS NEW BEGINNINGS AND FRESH STARTS. I KNOW I'LL BE SEEING THE SAME KIDS TODAY THAT I SAW LAST YEAR, AND THE YEAR BEFORE THAT, AND THE YEAR BEFORE THAT . . . BUT THIS YEAR THERE'S GOING TO BE SOMETHING DIFFERENT ABOUT US.
WE'RE EIGHTH GRADERS NOW.
JO! BREAKFAST!
I CAN'T SPEAK FOR ANYONE ELSE, BUT I KNOW THAT I CERTAINLY DON'T FEEL LIKE THE SAME "J" I WAS LAST YEAR . . .
COMING, MARMEE!
. . . AND I HAVE NO IDEA WHO I'LL BE WHEN THIS YEAR IS OVER.
publish
click

I'VE GOT THE EVENING SHIFT AGAIN TONIGHT, GIRLS.

MEG, HONEY, I'VE PUT A CASSEROLE IN THE FRIDGE THAT YOU CAN HEAT UP FOR DINNER. I'LL LEAVE THE INSTRUCTIONS ON THE COUNTER.

MY OLDEST SISTER, M, HAS THE BIGGEST NEW BEGINNING OF ALL OF US. SHE'S STARTING HIGH SCHOOL THIS YEAR. HIGH SCHOOL!

I'M GOING TO MISS SEEING HER IN THE HALLS AND AT LUNCH, BUT IT'LL ONLY BE A YEAR BEFORE I'M IN HIGH SCHOOL WITH HER!

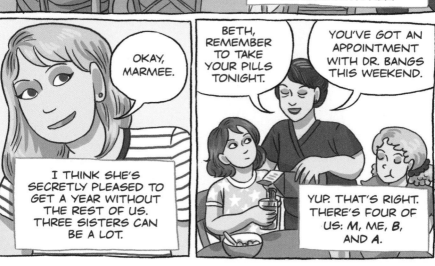

OKAY, MARMEE.

I THINK SHE'S SECRETLY PLEASED TO GET A YEAR WITHOUT THE REST OF US. THREE SISTERS CAN BE A LOT.

BETH, REMEMBER TO TAKE YOUR PILLS TONIGHT.

YOU'VE GOT AN APPOINTMENT WITH DR. BANGS THIS WEEKEND.

YUP. THAT'S RIGHT. THERE'S FOUR OF US: M, ME, B, AND A.

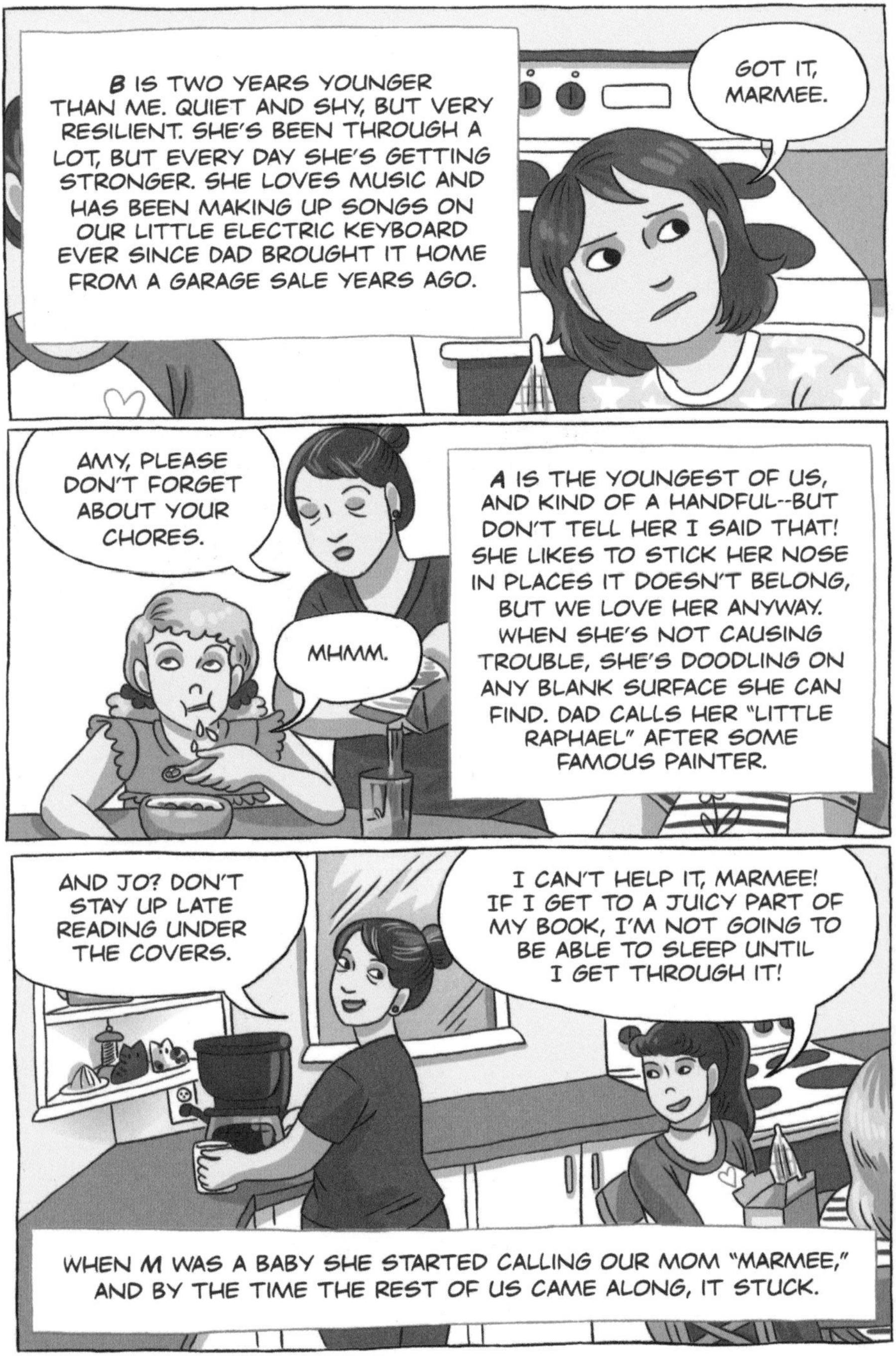
B IS TWO YEARS YOUNGER THAN ME. QUIET AND SHY, BUT VERY RESILIENT. SHE'S BEEN THROUGH A LOT, BUT EVERY DAY SHE'S GETTING STRONGER. SHE LOVES MUSIC AND HAS BEEN MAKING UP SONGS ON OUR LITTLE ELECTRIC KEYBOARD EVER SINCE DAD BROUGHT IT HOME FROM A GARAGE SALE YEARS AGO.
GOT IT, MARMEE.
AMY, PLEASE DON'T FORGET ABOUT YOUR CHORES.
MHMM.
A IS THE YOUNGEST OF US, AND KIND OF A HANDFUL--BUT DON'T TELL HER I SAID THAT! SHE LIKES TO STICK HER NOSE IN PLACES IT DOESN'T BELONG, BUT WE LOVE HER ANYWAY. WHEN SHE'S NOT CAUSING TROUBLE, SHE'S DOODLING ON ANY BLANK SURFACE SHE CAN FIND. DAD CALLS HER "LITTLE RAPHAEL" AFTER SOME FAMOUS PAINTER.
AND JO? DON'T STAY UP LATE READING UNDER THE COVERS.
I CAN'T HELP IT, MARMEE! IF I GET TO A JUICY PART OF MY BOOK, I'M NOT GOING TO BE ABLE TO SLEEP UNTIL I GET THROUGH IT!
WHEN M WAS A BABY SHE STARTED CALLING OUR MOM "MARMEE," AND BY THE TIME THE REST OF US CAME ALONG, IT STUCK.

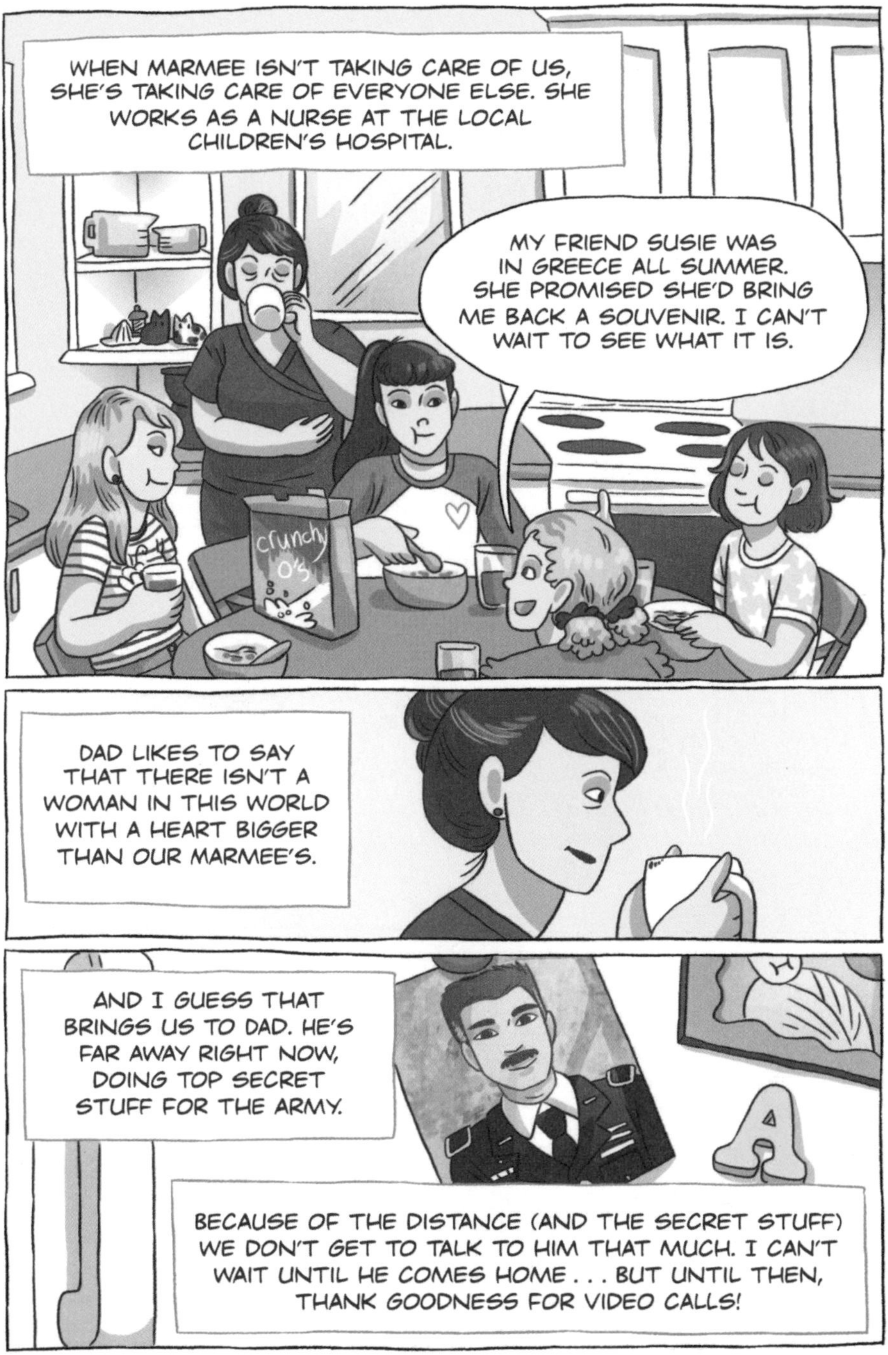
WHEN MARMEE ISN'T TAKING CARE OF US, SHE'S TAKING CARE OF EVERYONE ELSE. SHE WORKS AS A NURSE AT THE LOCAL CHILDREN'S HOSPITAL.
MY FRIEND SUSIE WAS IN GREECE ALL SUMMER. SHE PROMISED SHE'D BRING ME BACK A SOUVENIR. I CAN'T WAIT TO SEE WHAT IT IS.
crunchy O's
DAD LIKES TO SAY THAT THERE ISN'T A WOMAN IN THIS WORLD WITH A HEART BIGGER THAN OUR MARMEE'S.
AND I GUESS THAT BRINGS US TO DAD. HE'S FAR AWAY RIGHT NOW, DOING TOP SECRET STUFF FOR THE ARMY.
A
BECAUSE OF THE DISTANCE (AND THE SECRET STUFF) WE DON'T GET TO TALK TO HIM THAT MUCH. I CAN'T WAIT UNTIL HE COMES HOME . . . BUT UNTIL THEN, THANK GOODNESS FOR VIDEO CALLS!

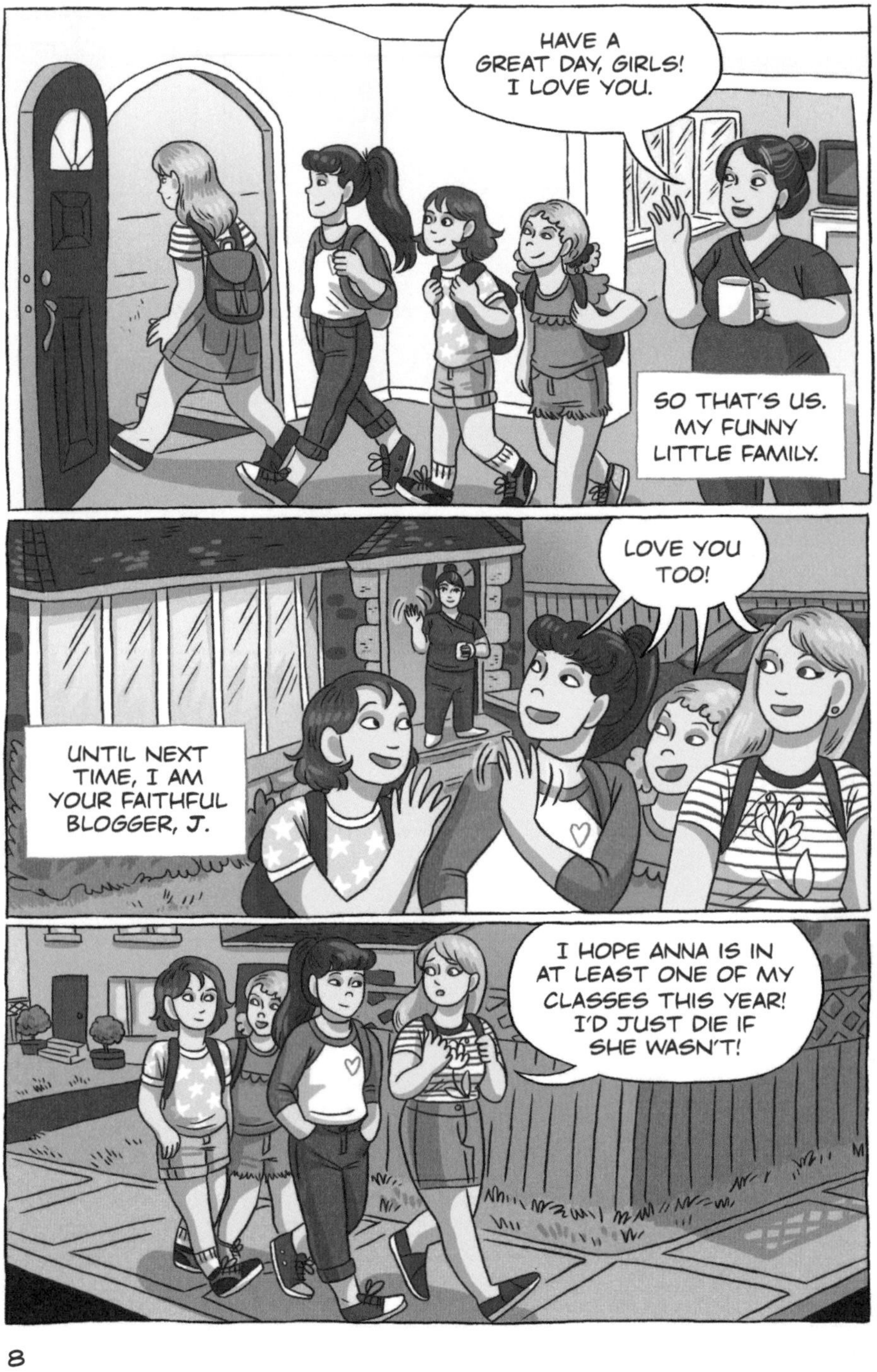
HAVE A GREAT DAY, GIRLS! I LOVE YOU.
SO THAT'S US. MY FUNNY LITTLE FAMILY.
LOVE YOU TOO!
UNTIL NEXT TIME, I AM YOUR FAITHFUL BLOGGER, J.
I HOPE ANNA IS IN AT LEAST ONE OF MY CLASSES THIS YEAR! I'D JUST DIE IF SHE WASN'T!

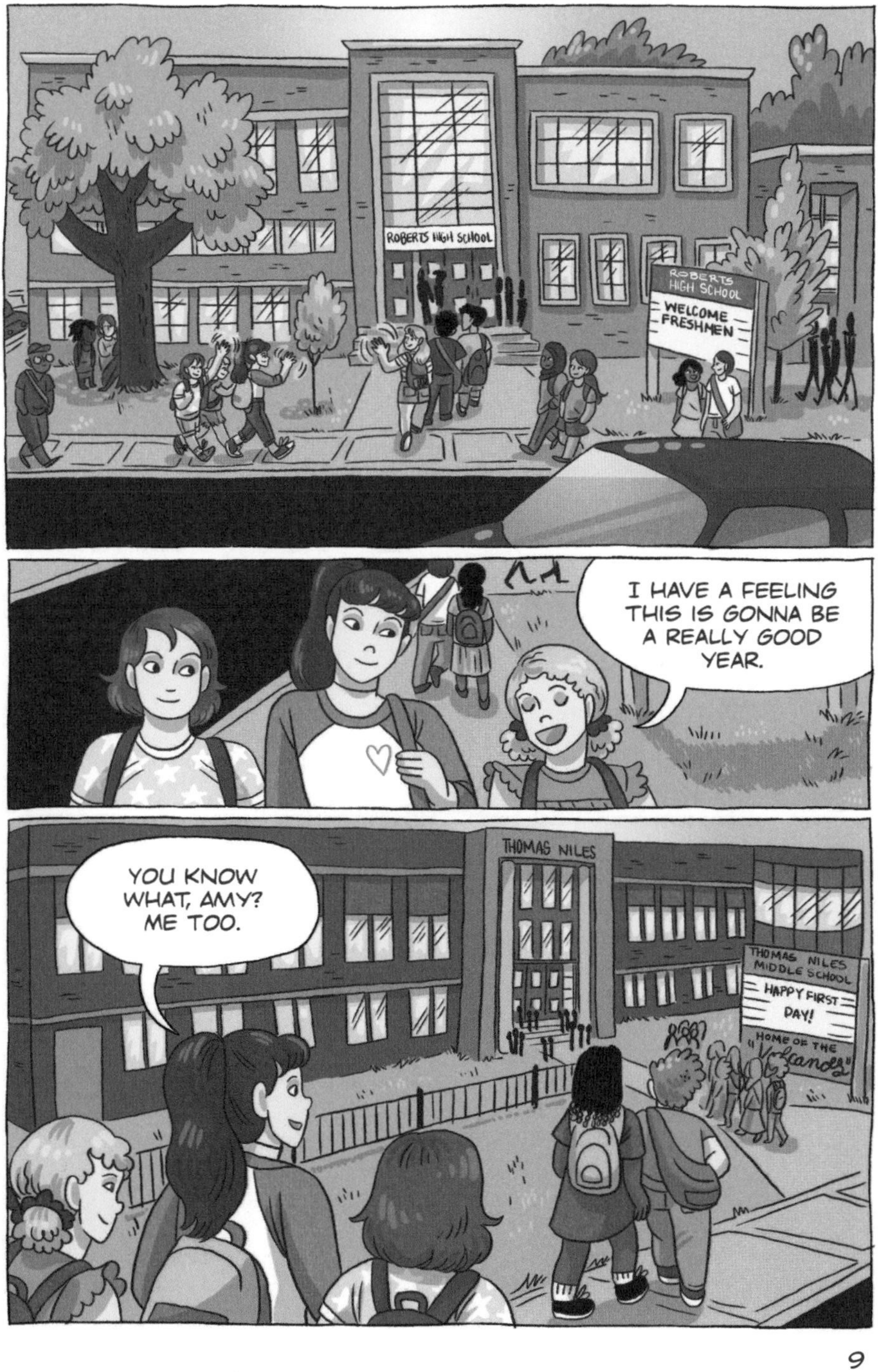
ROBERTS HIGH SCHOOL
ROBERTS HIGH SCHOOL
WELCOME FRESHMEN
I HAVE A FEELING THIS IS GONNA BE A REALLY GOOD YEAR.
THOMAS NILES
YOU KNOW WHAT, AMY? ME TOO.
THOMAS NILES MIDDLE SCHOOL
HAPPY FIRST DAY!
HOME OF THE "Volcanoes"

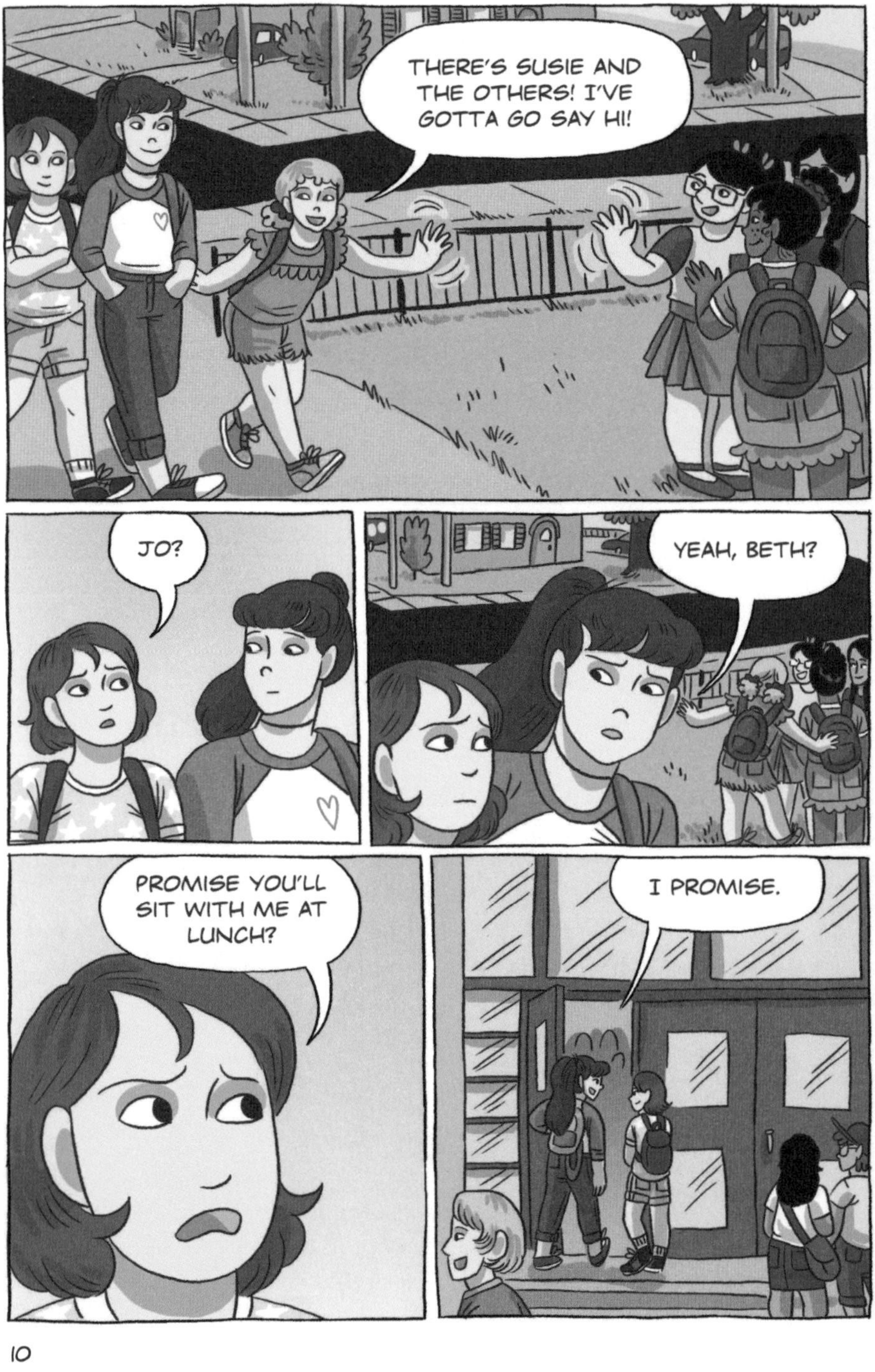

THERE'S SUSIE AND THE OTHERS! I'VE GOTTA GO SAY HI!
JO?
YEAH, BETH?
PROMISE YOU'LL SIT WITH ME AT LUNCH?
I PROMISE.

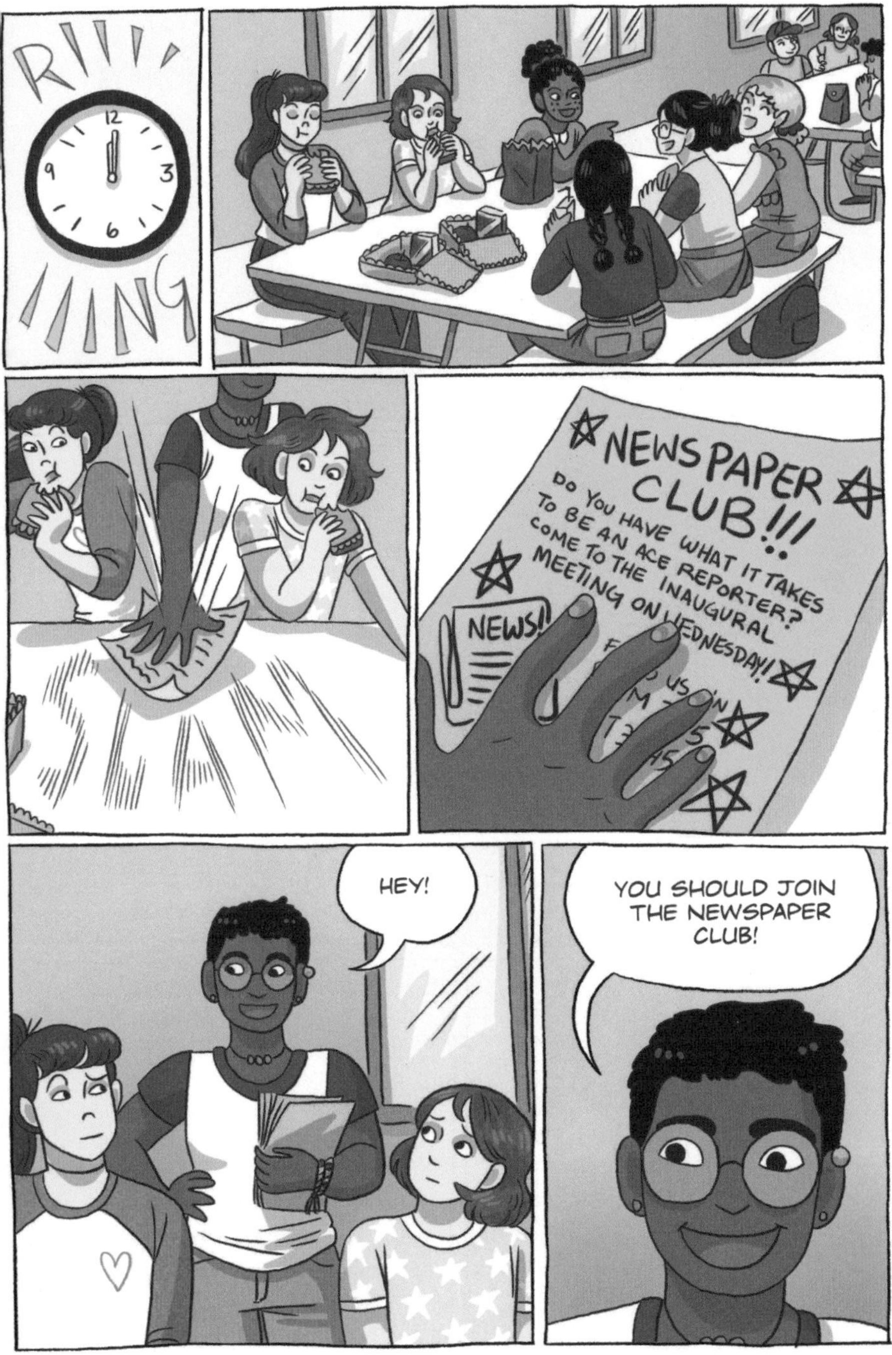
RIIIIIIING
SLAM
NEWSPAPER CLUB!!!
DO YOU HAVE WHAT IT TAKES TO BE AN ACE REPORTER?
COME TO THE INAUGURAL MEETING ON WEDNESDAY!
NEWS!
HEY!
YOU SHOULD JOIN THE NEWSPAPER CLUB!

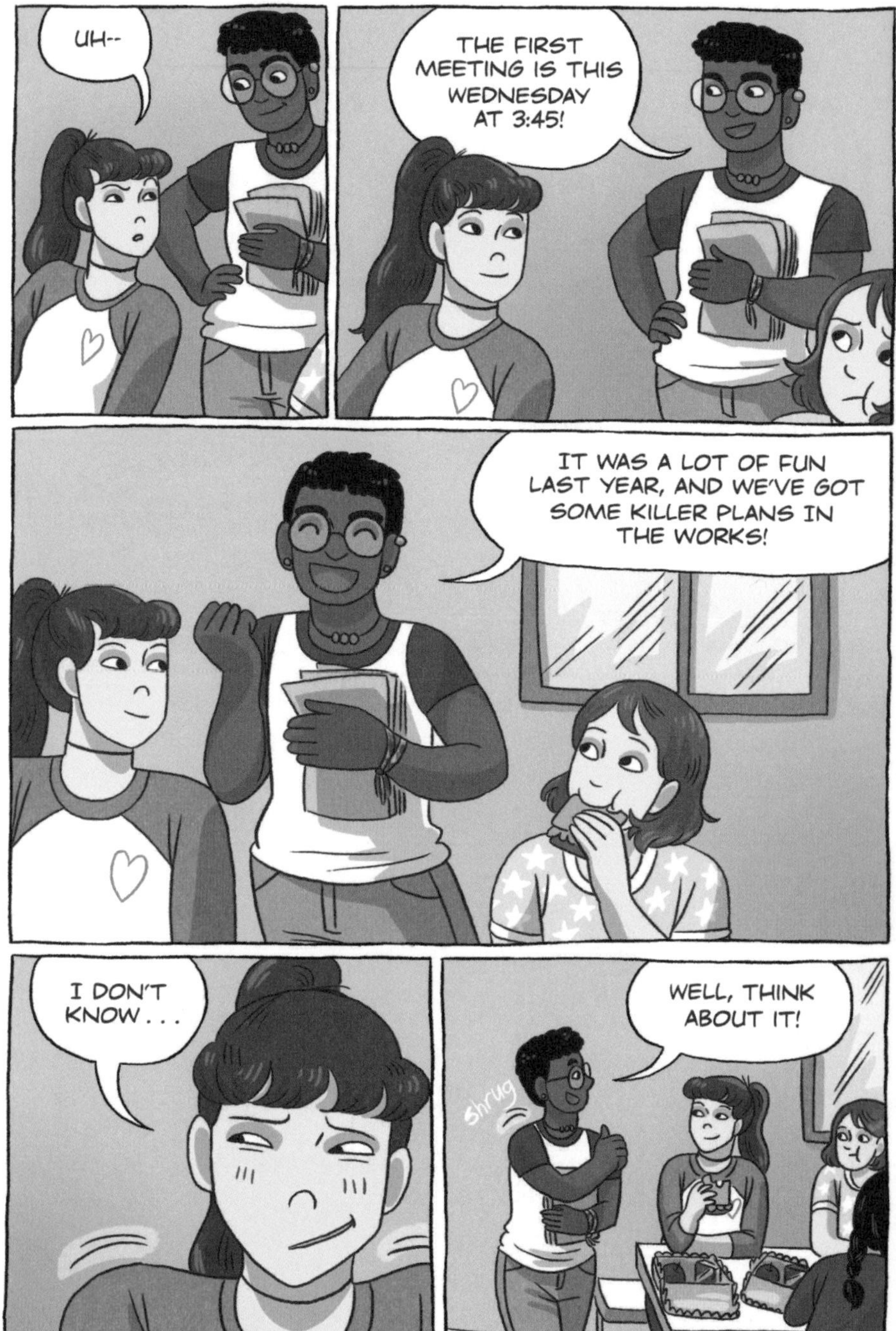
UH--
THE FIRST MEETING IS THIS WEDNESDAY AT 3:45!
IT WAS A LOT OF FUN LAST YEAR, AND WE'VE GOT SOME KILLER PLANS IN THE WORKS!
I DON'T KNOW . . .
shrug
WELL, THINK ABOUT IT!

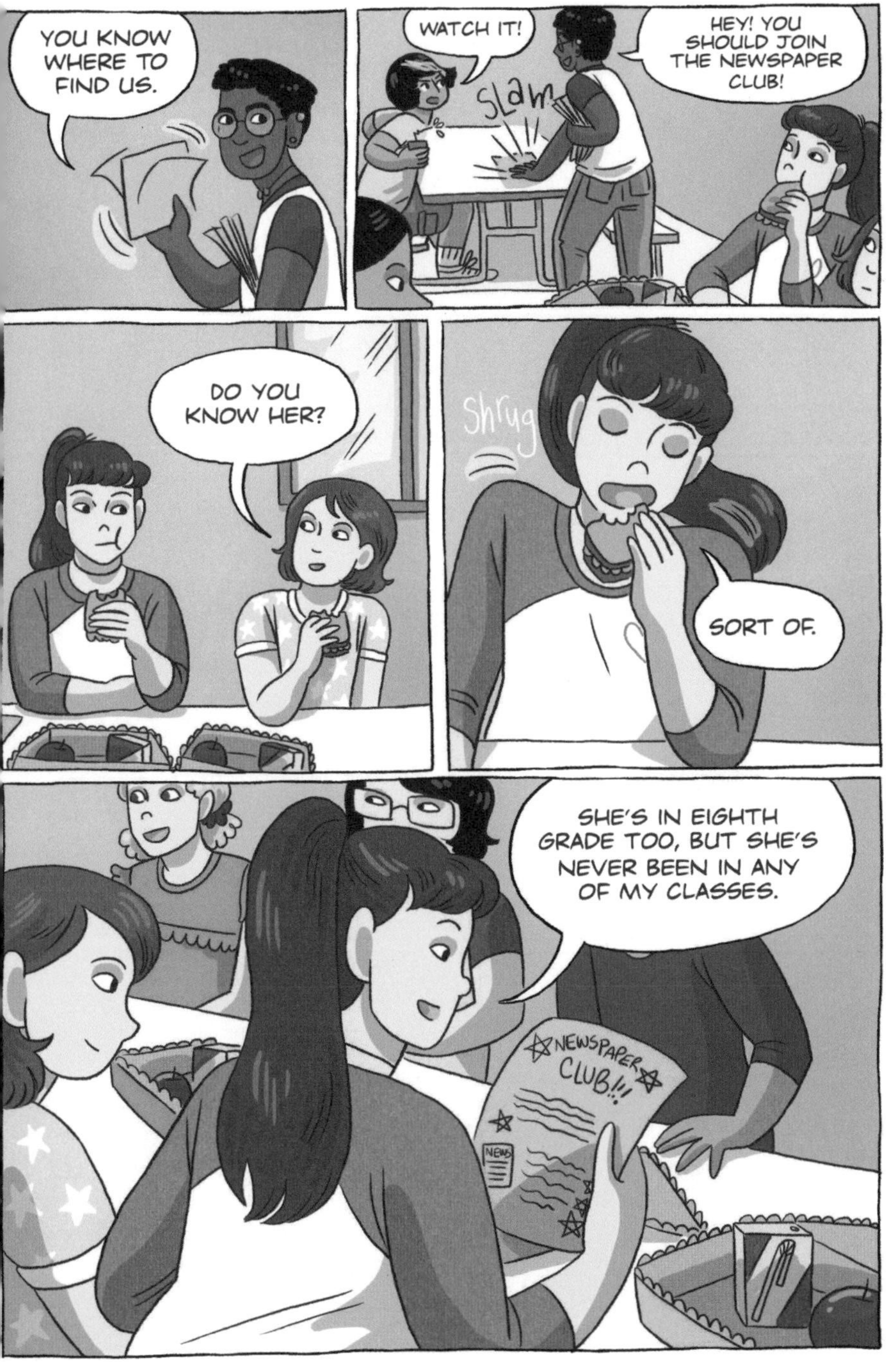
YOU KNOW WHERE TO FIND US.
WATCH IT!
SLAM
HEY! YOU SHOULD JOIN THE NEWSPAPER CLUB!
DO YOU KNOW HER?
SHRUG
SORT OF.
SHE'S IN EIGHTH GRADE TOO, BUT SHE'S NEVER BEEN IN ANY OF MY CLASSES.
NEWSPAPER CLUB!!!
NEWS

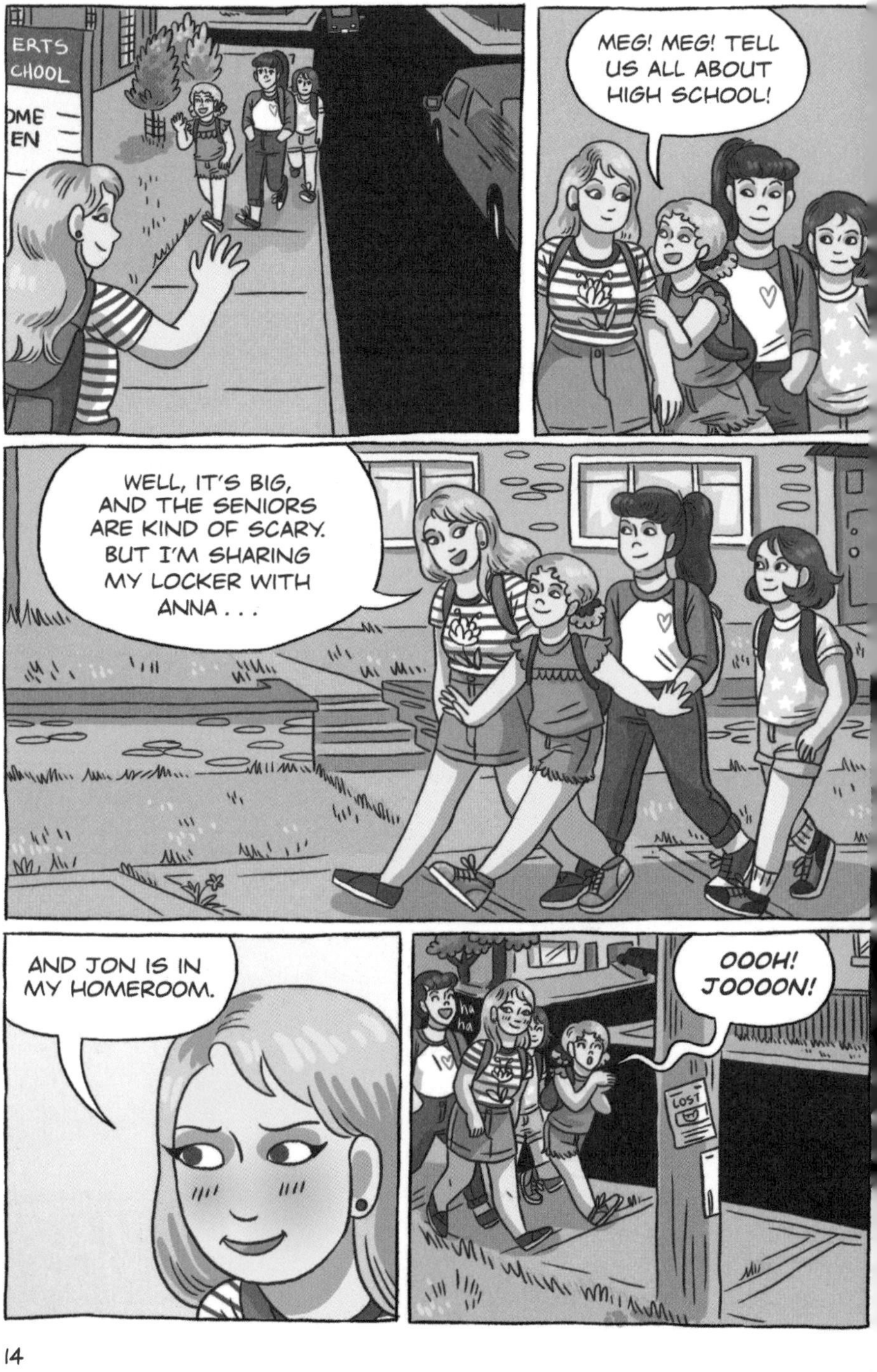
ERTS
CHOOL
OME
EN
MEG! MEG! TELL US ALL ABOUT HIGH SCHOOL!
WELL, IT'S BIG, AND THE SENIORS ARE KIND OF SCARY. BUT I'M SHARING MY LOCKER WITH ANNA . . .
AND JON IS IN MY HOMEROOM.
ha ha
OOOH! JOOOON!
LOST

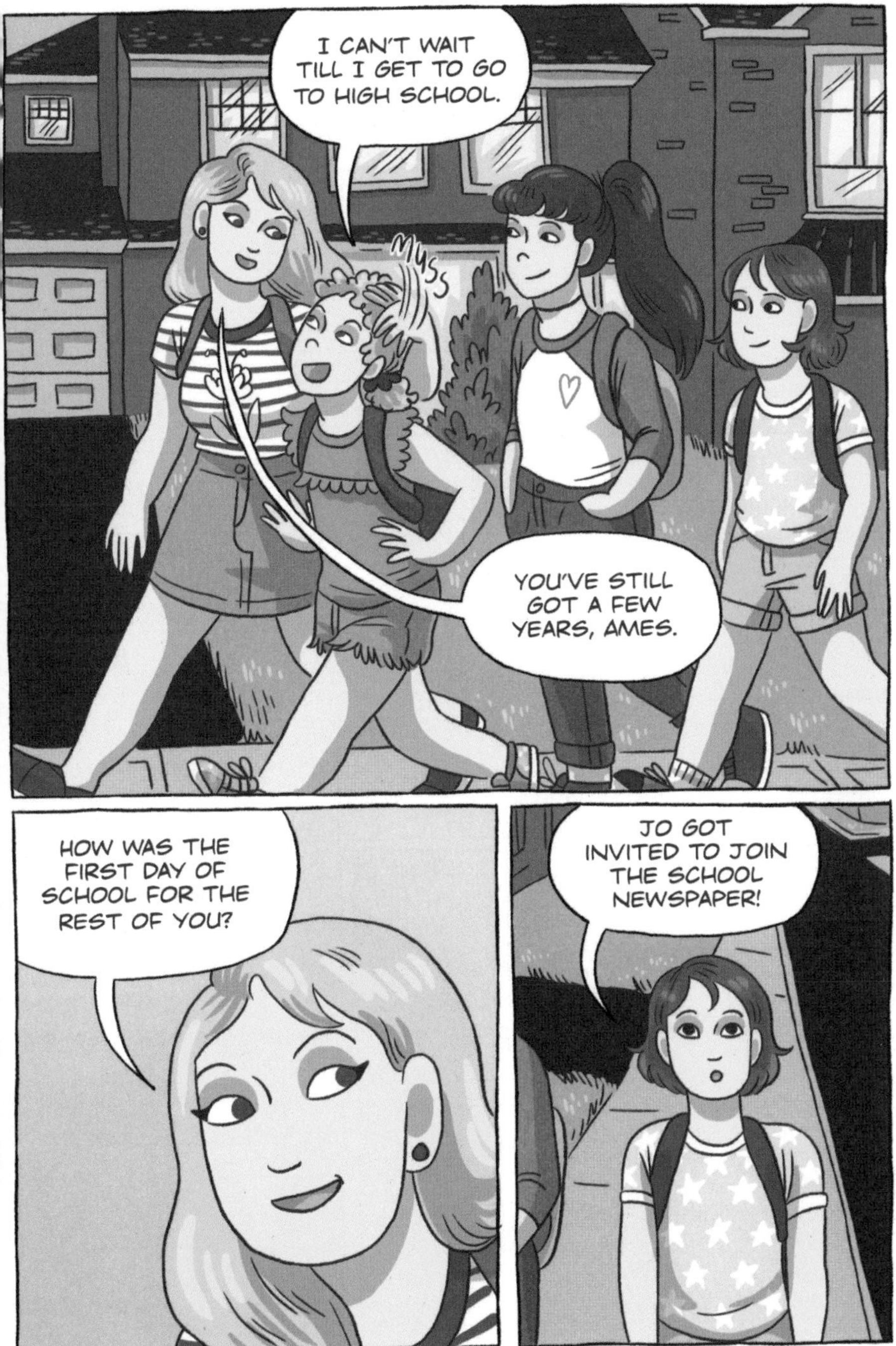
I CAN'T WAIT TILL I GET TO GO TO HIGH SCHOOL.
MUSS
YOU'VE STILL GOT A FEW YEARS, AMES.
HOW WAS THE FIRST DAY OF SCHOOL FOR THE REST OF YOU?
JO GOT INVITED TO JOIN THE SCHOOL NEWSPAPER!

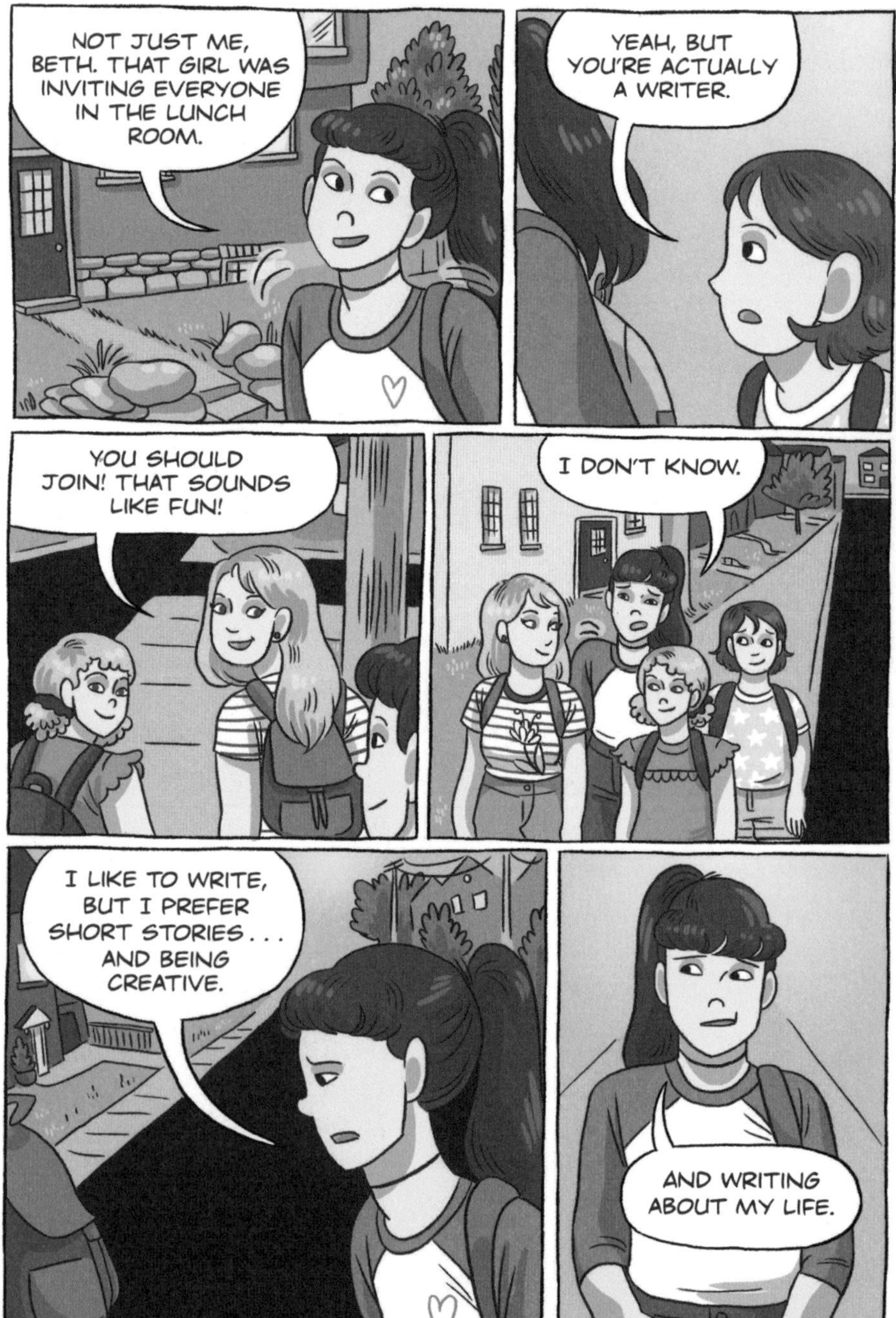
NOT JUST ME, BETH. THAT GIRL WAS INVITING EVERYONE IN THE LUNCH ROOM.
YEAH, BUT YOU'RE ACTUALLY A WRITER.
YOU SHOULD JOIN! THAT SOUNDS LIKE FUN!
I DON'T KNOW.
I LIKE TO WRITE, BUT I PREFER SHORT STORIES . . . AND BEING CREATIVE.
AND WRITING ABOUT MY LIFE.

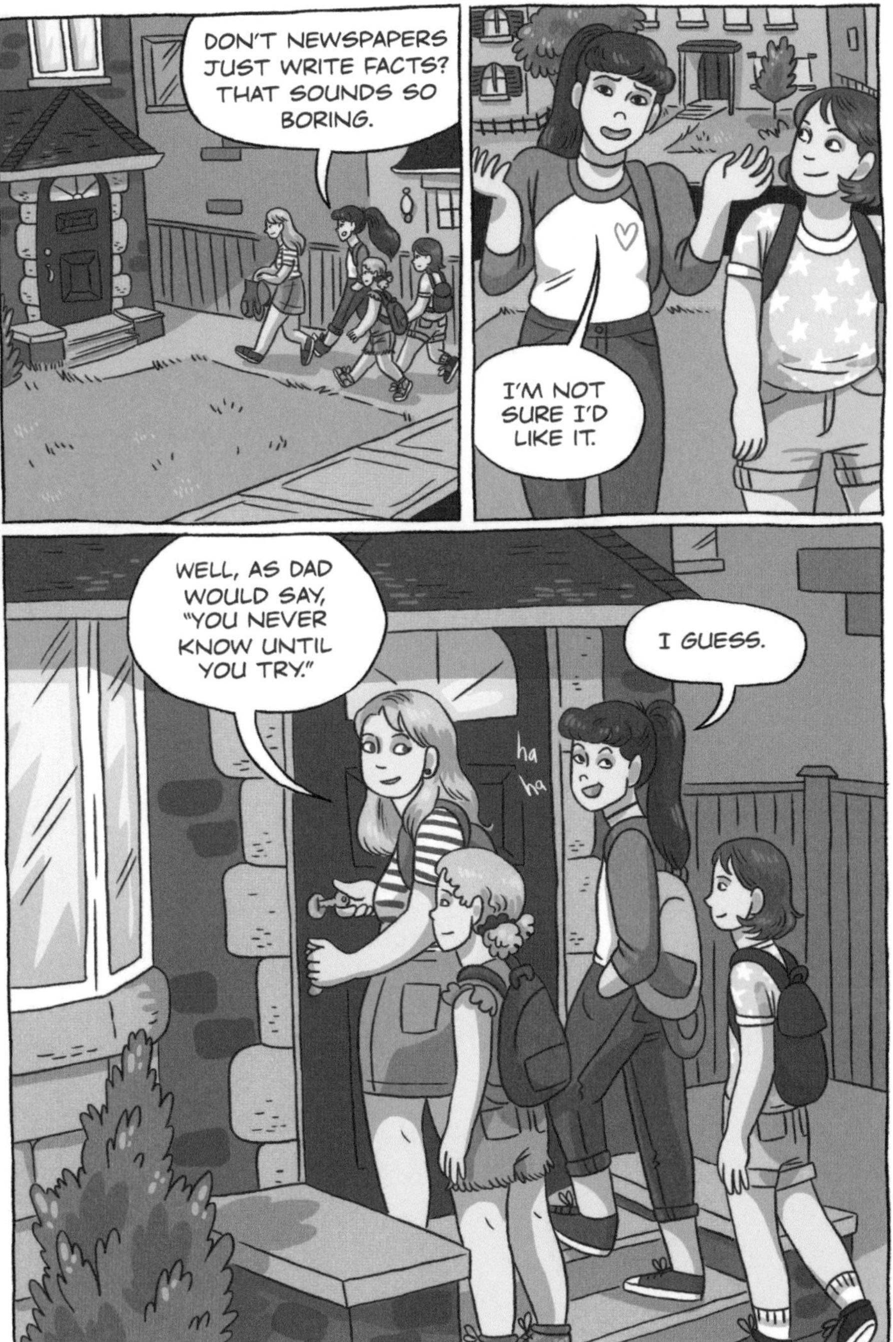
DON'T NEWSPAPERS JUST WRITE FACTS? THAT SOUNDS SO BORING.
I'M NOT SURE I'D LIKE IT.
WELL, AS DAD WOULD SAY, "YOU NEVER KNOW UNTIL YOU TRY."
ha ha
I GUESS.

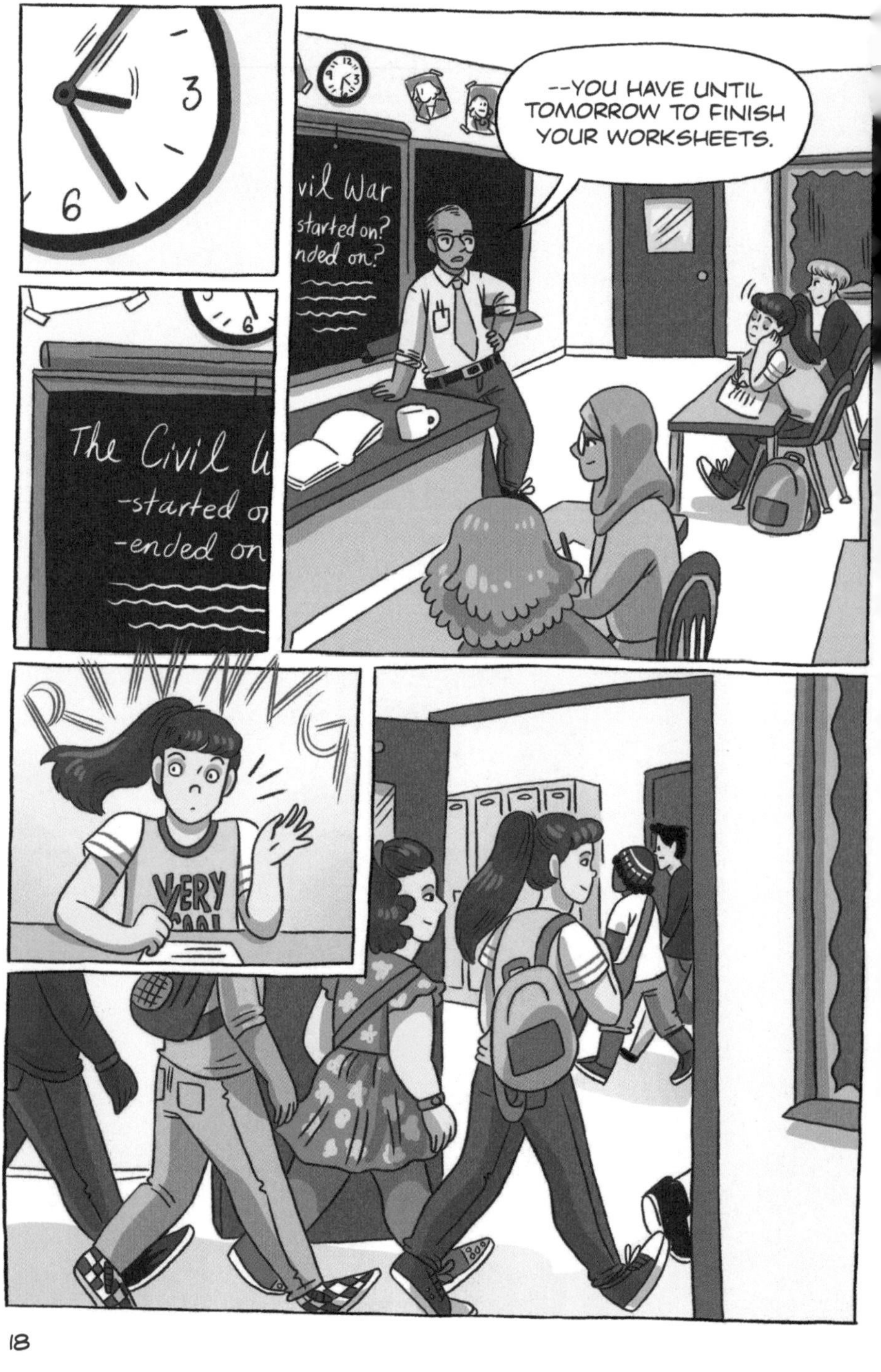
The Civil War
-started on?
-ended on?
--YOU HAVE UNTIL TOMORROW TO FINISH YOUR WORKSHEETS.
RIIIIING
VERY

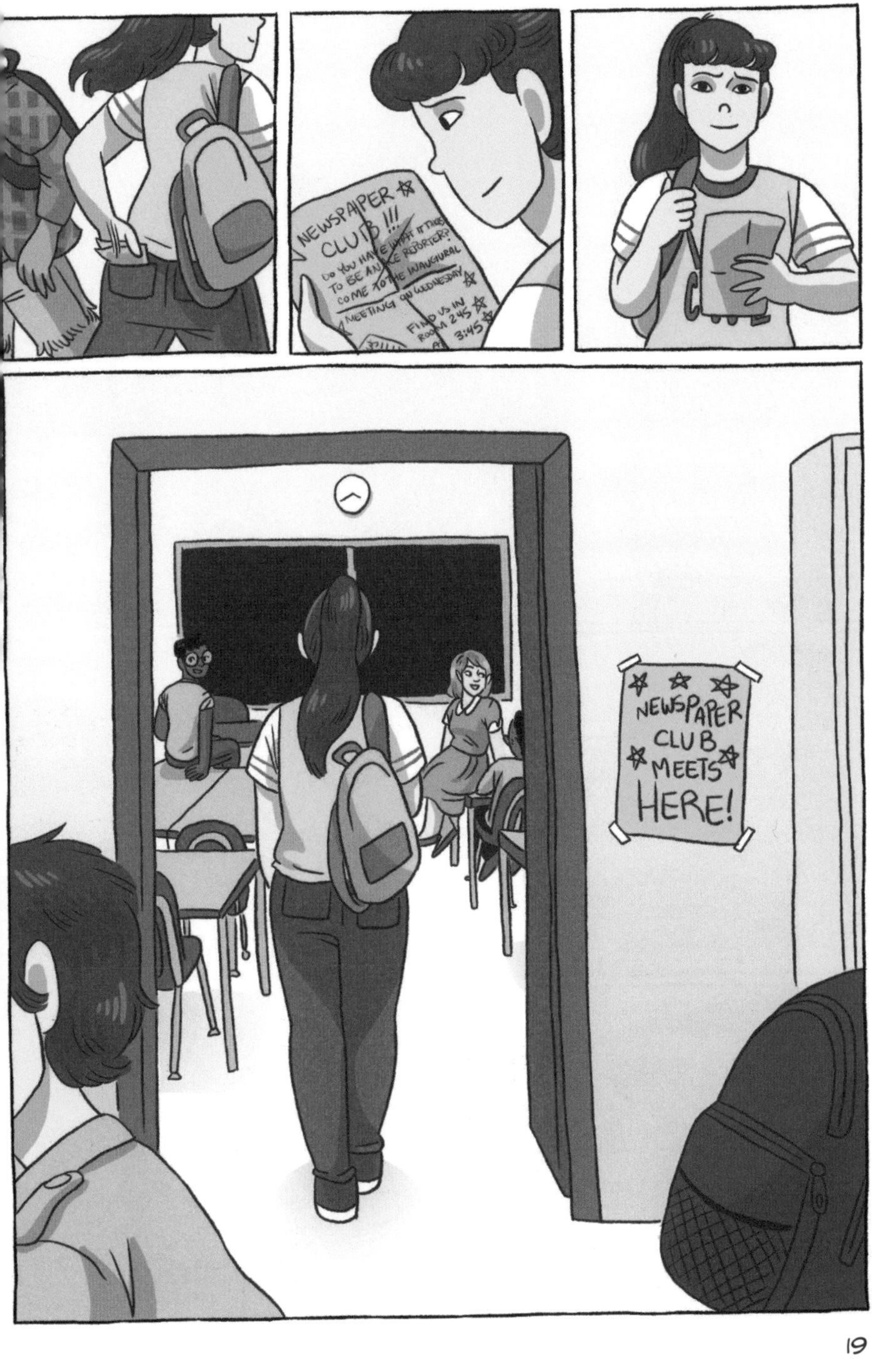
NEWSPAPER CLUB!!!
DO YOU HAVE WHAT IT TAKES TO BE AN ACE REPORTER?
COME TO THE INAUGURAL MEETING ON WEDNESDAY
FIND US IN ROOM 245 3:45
NEWSPAPER CLUB MEETS HERE!

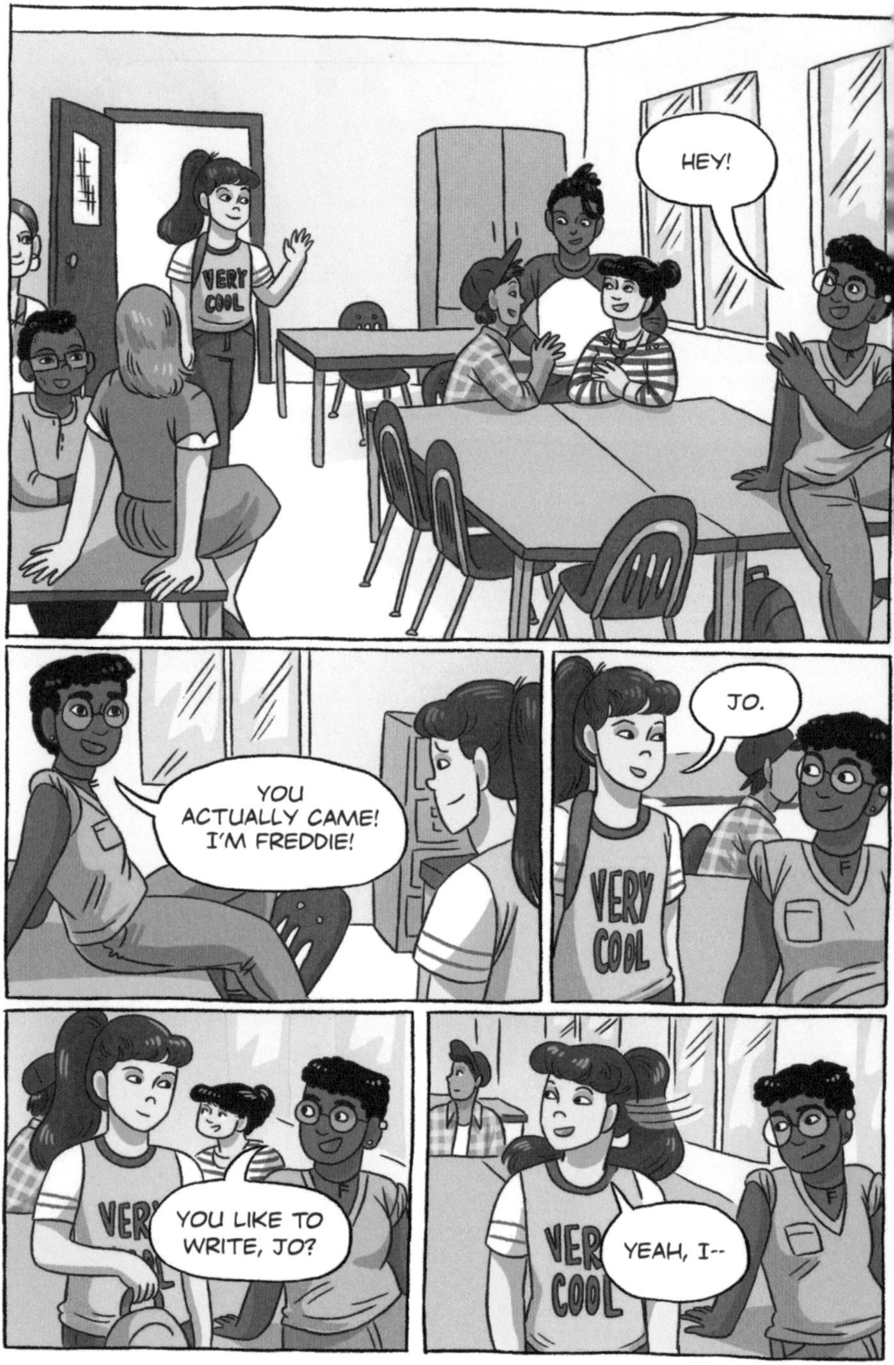
HEY!
YOU ACTUALLY CAME! I'M FREDDIE!
JO.
YOU LIKE TO WRITE, JO?
YEAH, I--

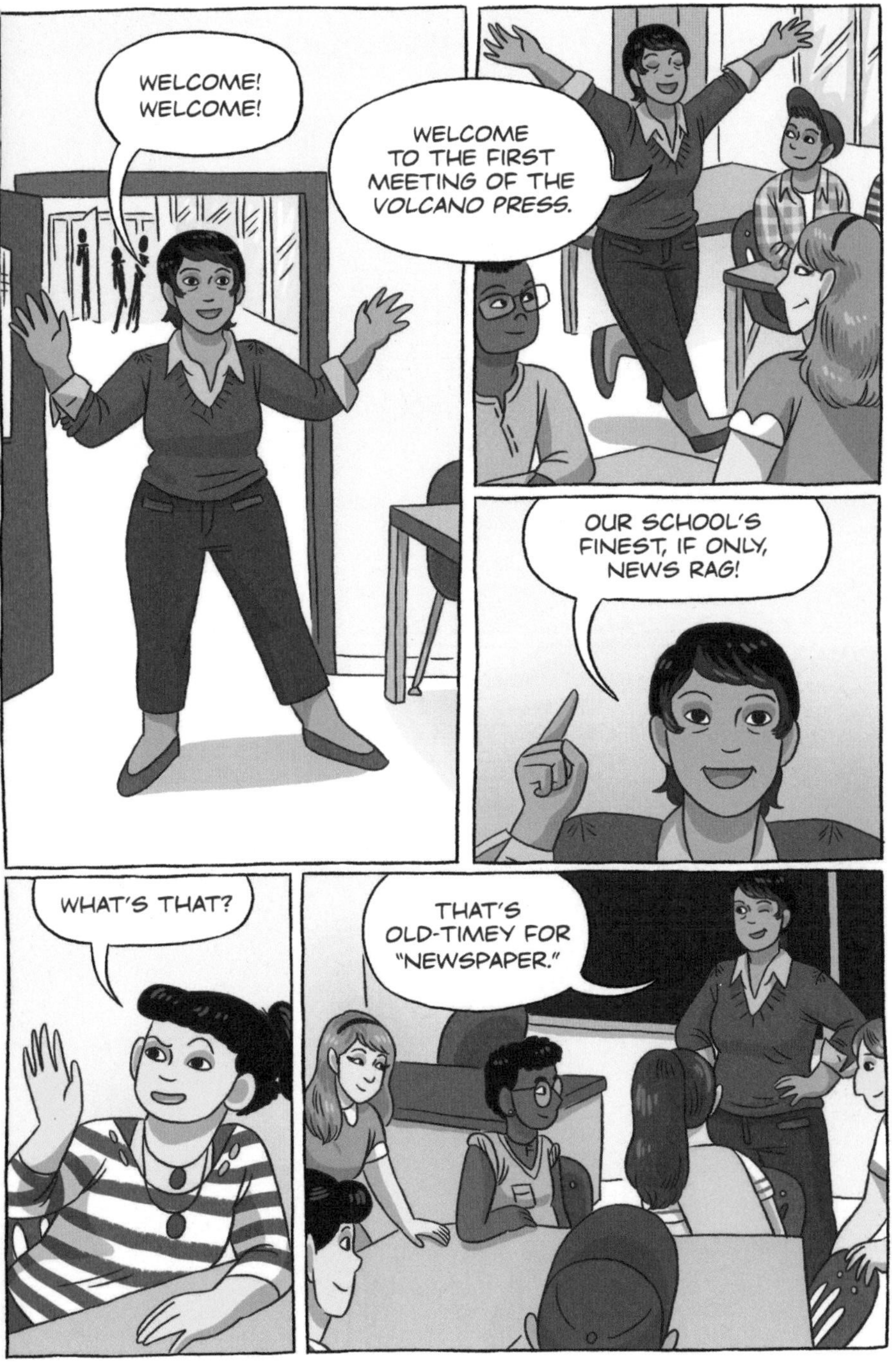
WELCOME! WELCOME!
WELCOME TO THE FIRST MEETING OF THE VOLCANO PRESS.
OUR SCHOOL'S FINEST, IF ONLY, NEWS RAG!
WHAT'S THAT?
THAT'S OLD-TIMEY FOR "NEWSPAPER."

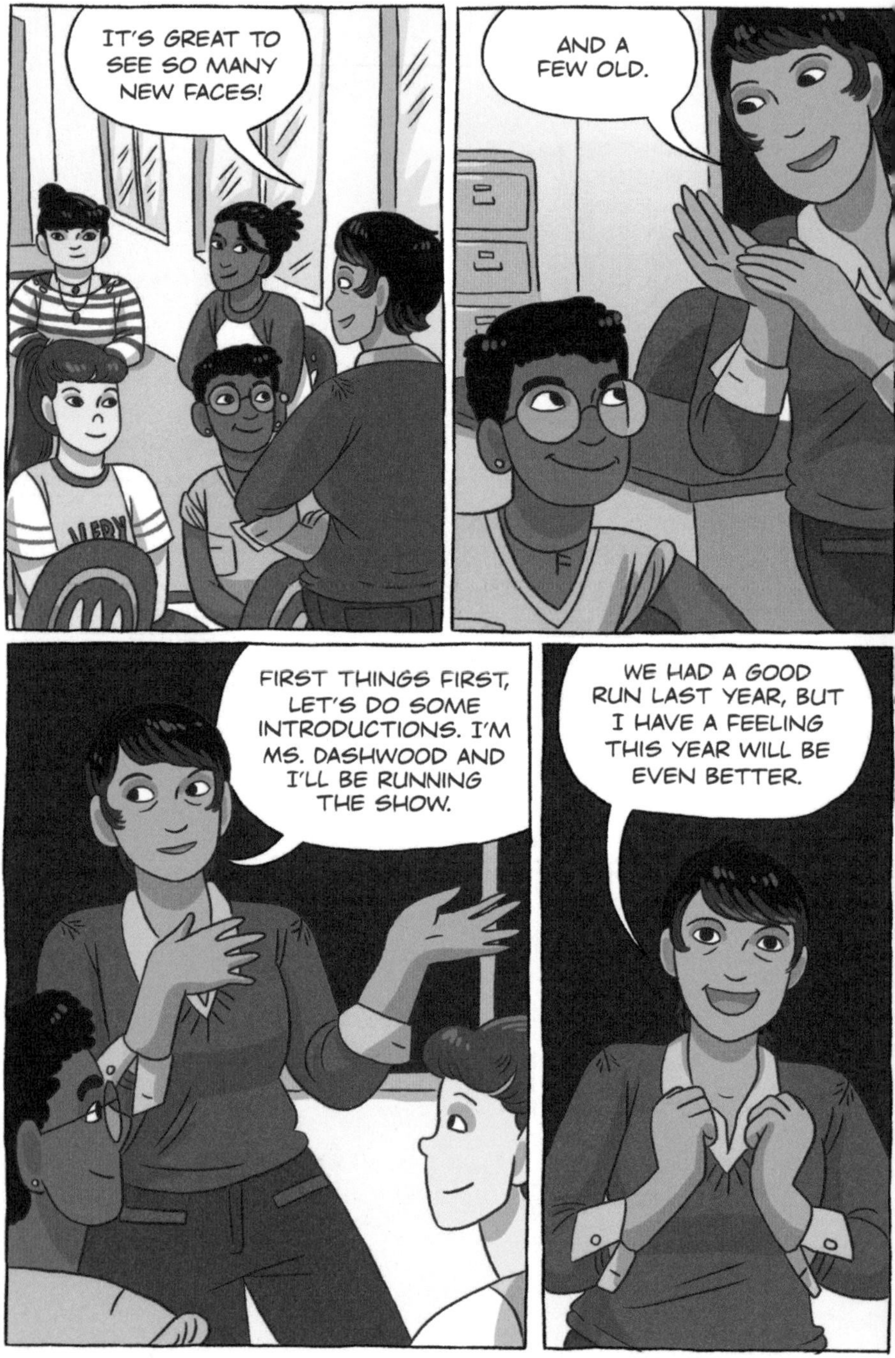
IT'S GREAT TO SEE SO MANY NEW FACES!
AND A FEW OLD.
FIRST THINGS FIRST, LET'S DO SOME INTRODUCTIONS. I'M MS. DASHWOOD AND I'LL BE RUNNING THE SHOW.
WE HAD A GOOD RUN LAST YEAR, BUT I HAVE A FEELING THIS YEAR WILL BE EVEN BETTER.

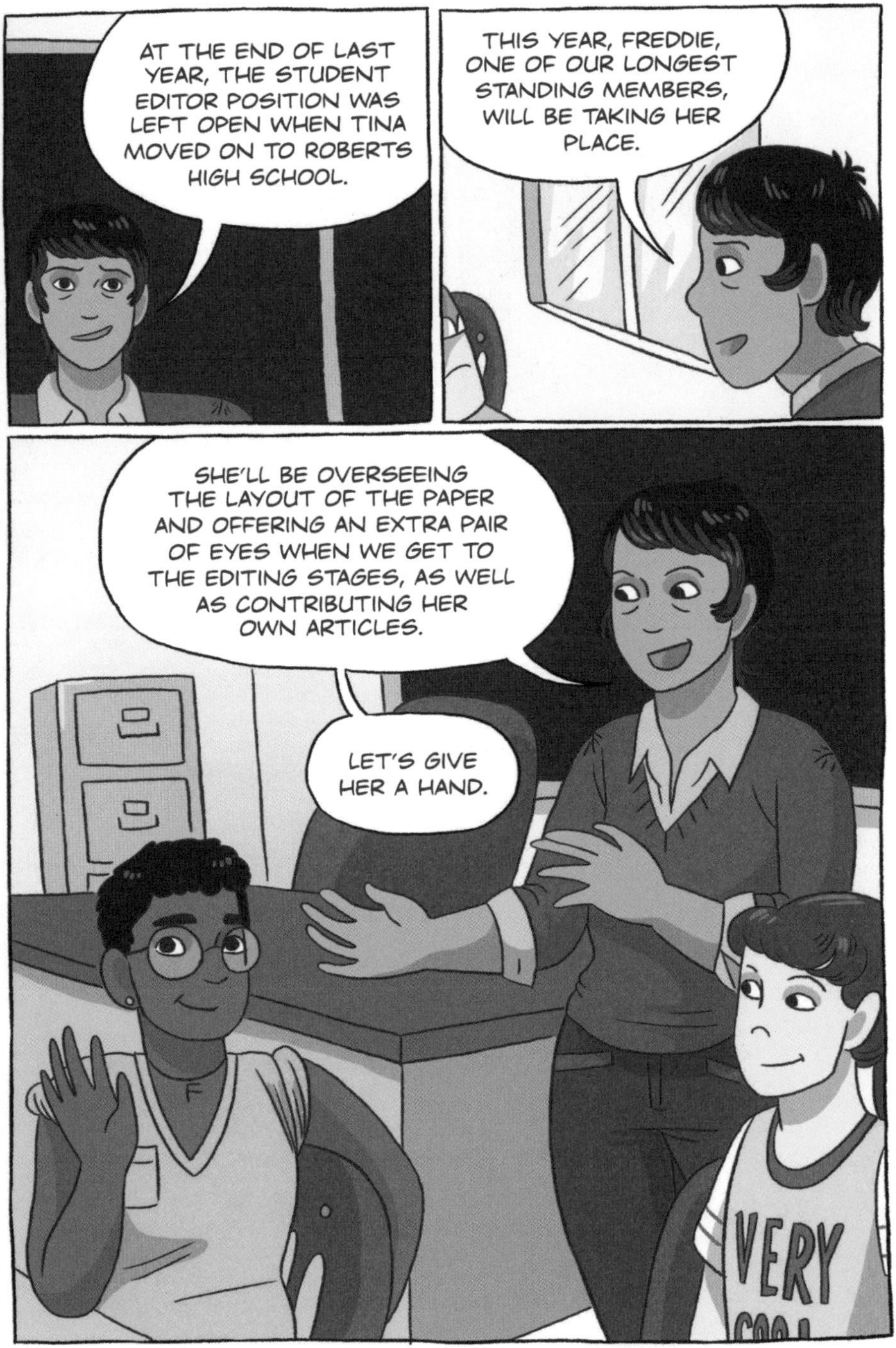
AT THE END OF LAST YEAR, THE STUDENT EDITOR POSITION WAS LEFT OPEN WHEN TINA MOVED ON TO ROBERTS HIGH SCHOOL.
THIS YEAR, FREDDIE, ONE OF OUR LONGEST STANDING MEMBERS, WILL BE TAKING HER PLACE.
SHE'LL BE OVERSEEING THE LAYOUT OF THE PAPER AND OFFERING AN EXTRA PAIR OF EYES WHEN WE GET TO THE EDITING STAGES, AS WELL AS CONTRIBUTING HER OWN ARTICLES.
LET'S GIVE HER A HAND.
VERY

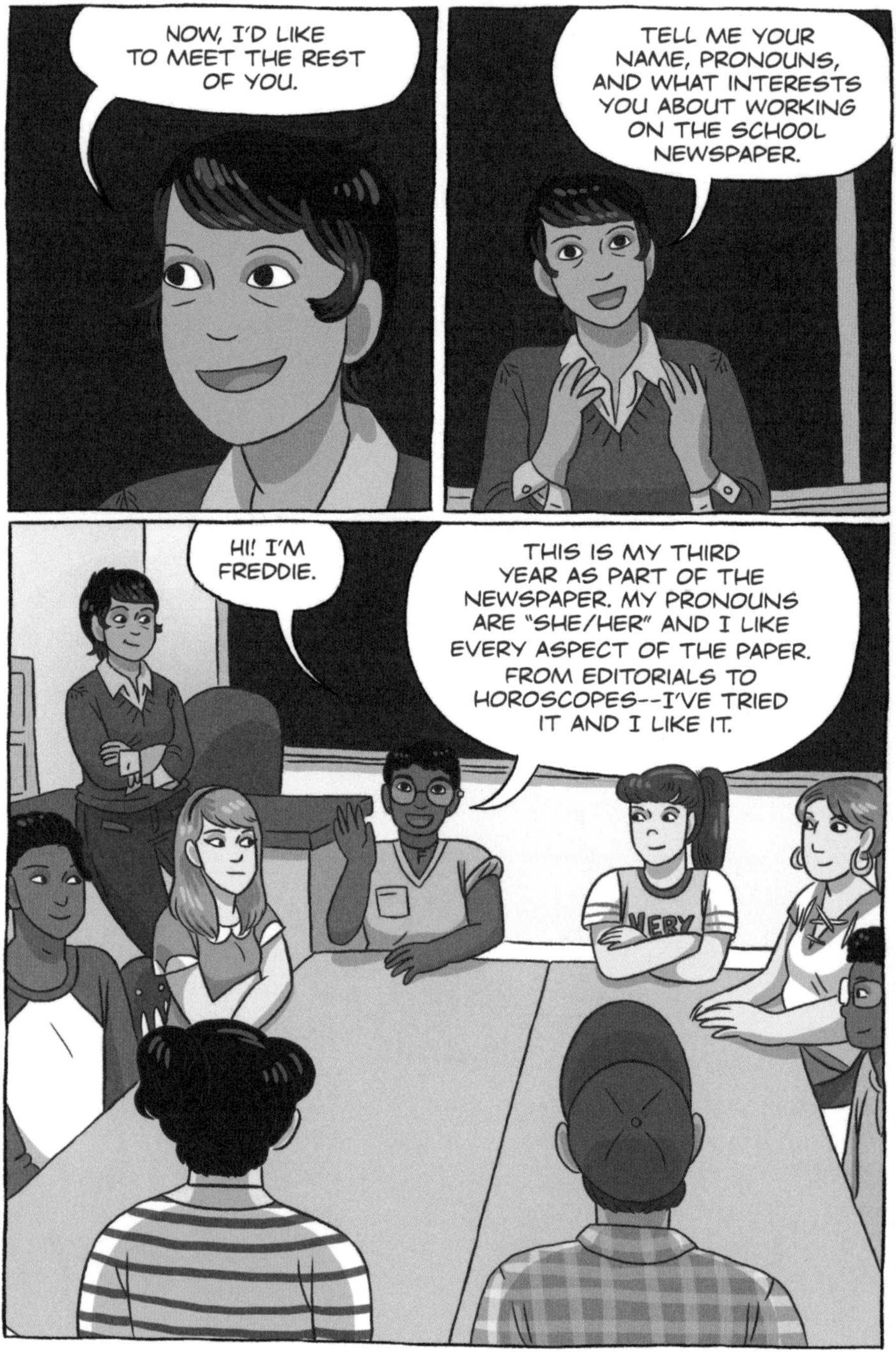
NOW, I'D LIKE TO MEET THE REST OF YOU.
TELL ME YOUR NAME, PRONOUNS, AND WHAT INTERESTS YOU ABOUT WORKING ON THE SCHOOL NEWSPAPER.
HI! I'M FREDDIE.
THIS IS MY THIRD YEAR AS PART OF THE NEWSPAPER. MY PRONOUNS ARE "SHE/HER" AND I LIKE EVERY ASPECT OF THE PAPER. FROM EDITORIALS TO HOROSCOPES--I'VE TRIED IT AND I LIKE IT.
VERY

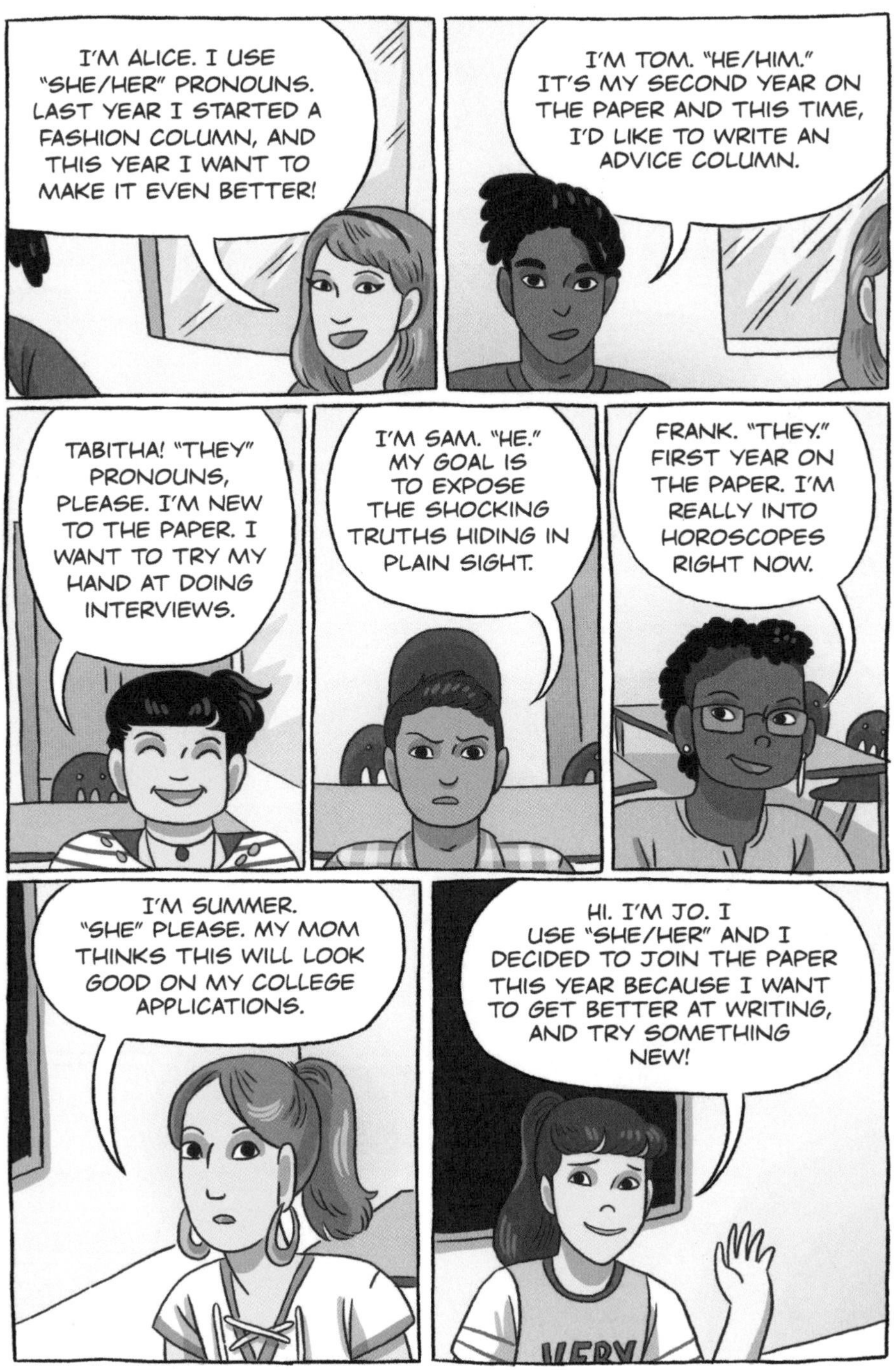
I'M ALICE. I USE "SHE/HER" PRONOUNS. LAST YEAR I STARTED A FASHION COLUMN, AND THIS YEAR I WANT TO MAKE IT EVEN BETTER!
I'M TOM. "HE/HIM." IT'S MY SECOND YEAR ON THE PAPER AND THIS TIME, I'D LIKE TO WRITE AN ADVICE COLUMN.
TABITHA! "THEY" PRONOUNS, PLEASE. I'M NEW TO THE PAPER. I WANT TO TRY MY HAND AT DOING INTERVIEWS.
I'M SAM. "HE." MY GOAL IS TO EXPOSE THE SHOCKING TRUTHS HIDING IN PLAIN SIGHT.
FRANK. "THEY." FIRST YEAR ON THE PAPER. I'M REALLY INTO HOROSCOPES RIGHT NOW.
I'M SUMMER. "SHE" PLEASE. MY MOM THINKS THIS WILL LOOK GOOD ON MY COLLEGE APPLICATIONS.
HI. I'M JO. I USE "SHE/HER" AND I DECIDED TO JOIN THE PAPER THIS YEAR BECAUSE I WANT TO GET BETTER AT WRITING, AND TRY SOMETHING NEW!
VERY

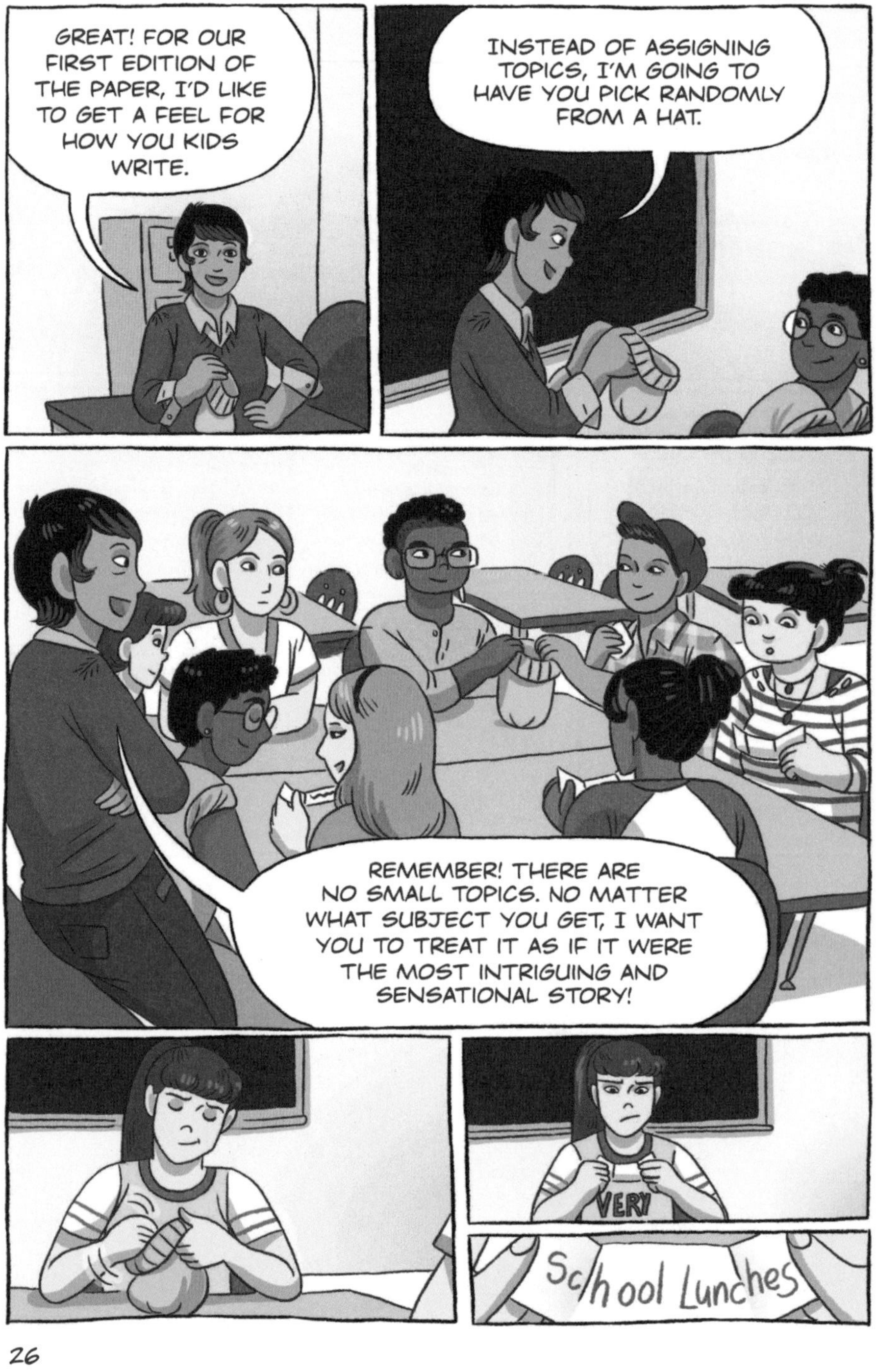
GREAT! FOR OUR FIRST EDITION OF THE PAPER, I'D LIKE TO GET A FEEL FOR HOW YOU KIDS WRITE.
INSTEAD OF ASSIGNING TOPICS, I'M GOING TO HAVE YOU PICK RANDOMLY FROM A HAT.
REMEMBER! THERE ARE NO SMALL TOPICS. NO MATTER WHAT SUBJECT YOU GET, I WANT YOU TO TREAT IT AS IF IT WERE THE MOST INTRIGUING AND SENSATIONAL STORY!
VERY
School Lunches

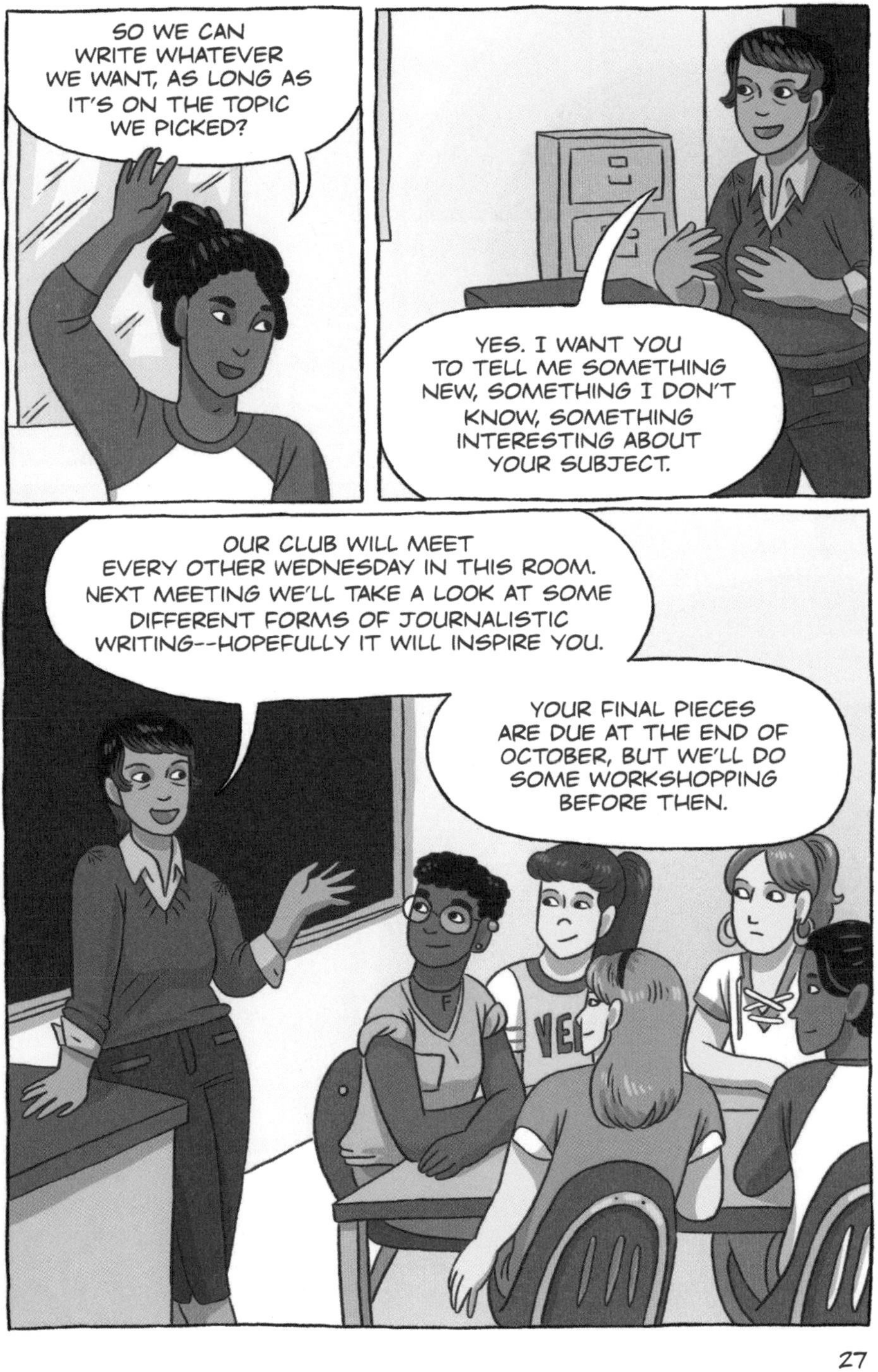
SO WE CAN WRITE WHATEVER WE WANT, AS LONG AS IT'S ON THE TOPIC WE PICKED?
YES. I WANT YOU TO TELL ME SOMETHING NEW, SOMETHING I DON'T KNOW, SOMETHING INTERESTING ABOUT YOUR SUBJECT.
OUR CLUB WILL MEET EVERY OTHER WEDNESDAY IN THIS ROOM. NEXT MEETING WE'LL TAKE A LOOK AT SOME DIFFERENT FORMS OF JOURNALISTIC WRITING--HOPEFULLY IT WILL INSPIRE YOU.
YOUR FINAL PIECES ARE DUE AT THE END OF OCTOBER, BUT WE'LL DO SOME WORKSHOPPING BEFORE THEN.

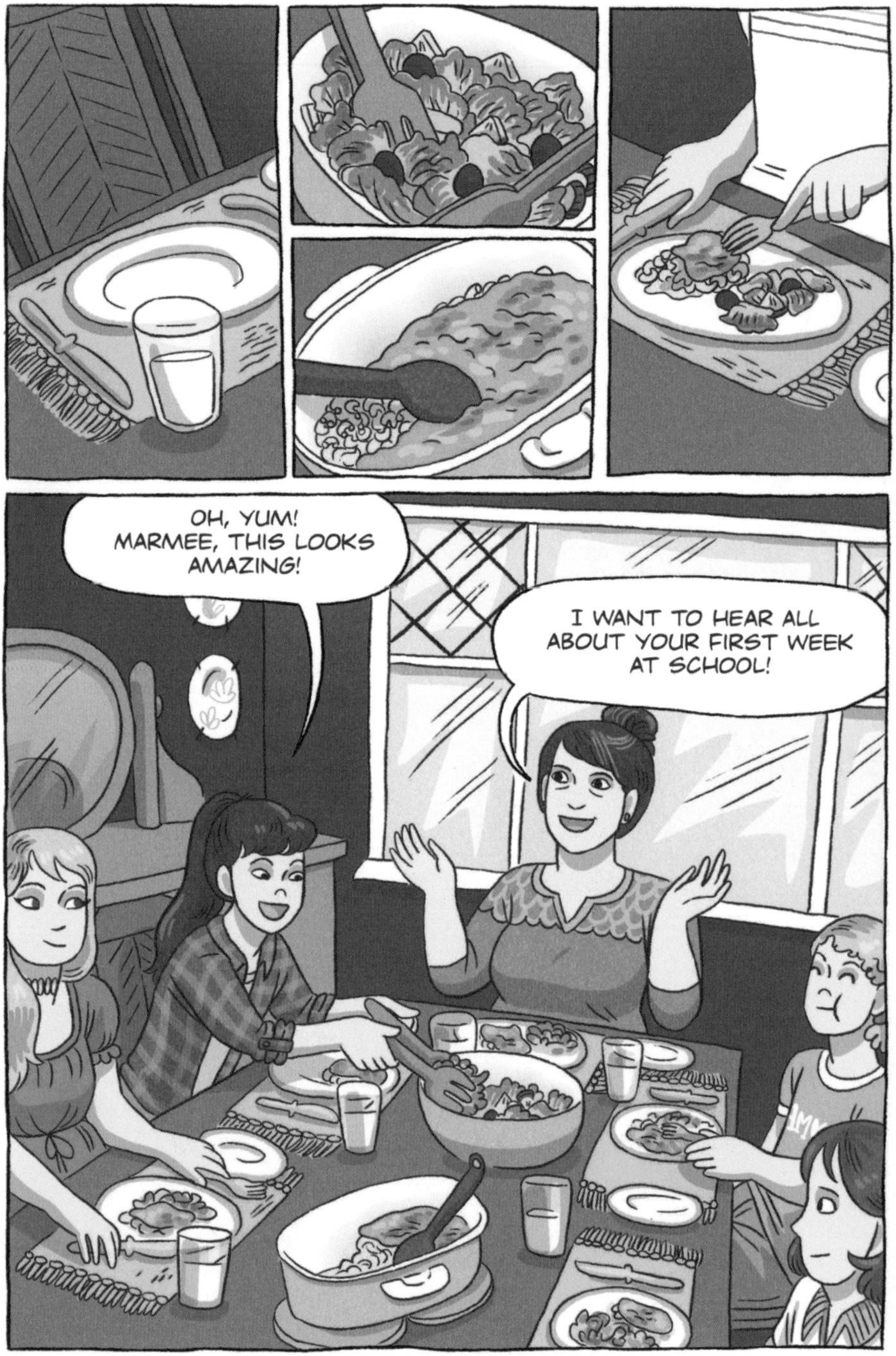
OH, YUM! MARMEE, THIS LOOKS AMAZING!
I WANT TO HEAR ALL ABOUT YOUR FIRST WEEK AT SCHOOL!

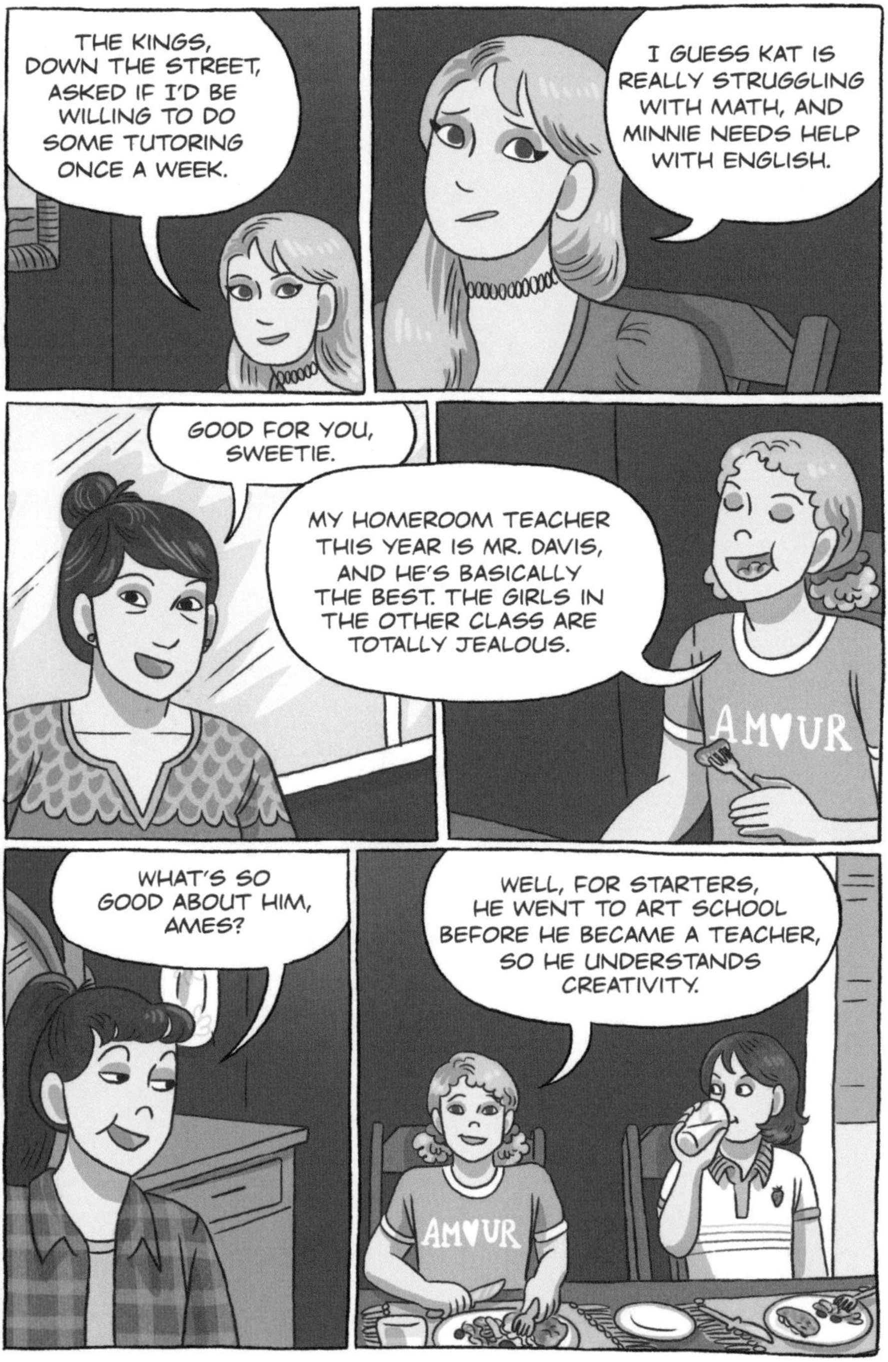
THE KINGS, DOWN THE STREET, ASKED IF I'D BE WILLING TO DO SOME TUTORING ONCE A WEEK.
I GUESS KAT IS REALLY STRUGGLING WITH MATH, AND MINNIE NEEDS HELP WITH ENGLISH.
GOOD FOR YOU, SWEETIE.
MY HOMEROOM TEACHER THIS YEAR IS MR. DAVIS, AND HE'S BASICALLY THE BEST. THE GIRLS IN THE OTHER CLASS ARE TOTALLY JEALOUS.
AMOUR
WHAT'S SO GOOD ABOUT HIM, AMES?
WELL, FOR STARTERS, HE WENT TO ART SCHOOL BEFORE HE BECAME A TEACHER, SO HE UNDERSTANDS CREATIVITY.
AMOUR

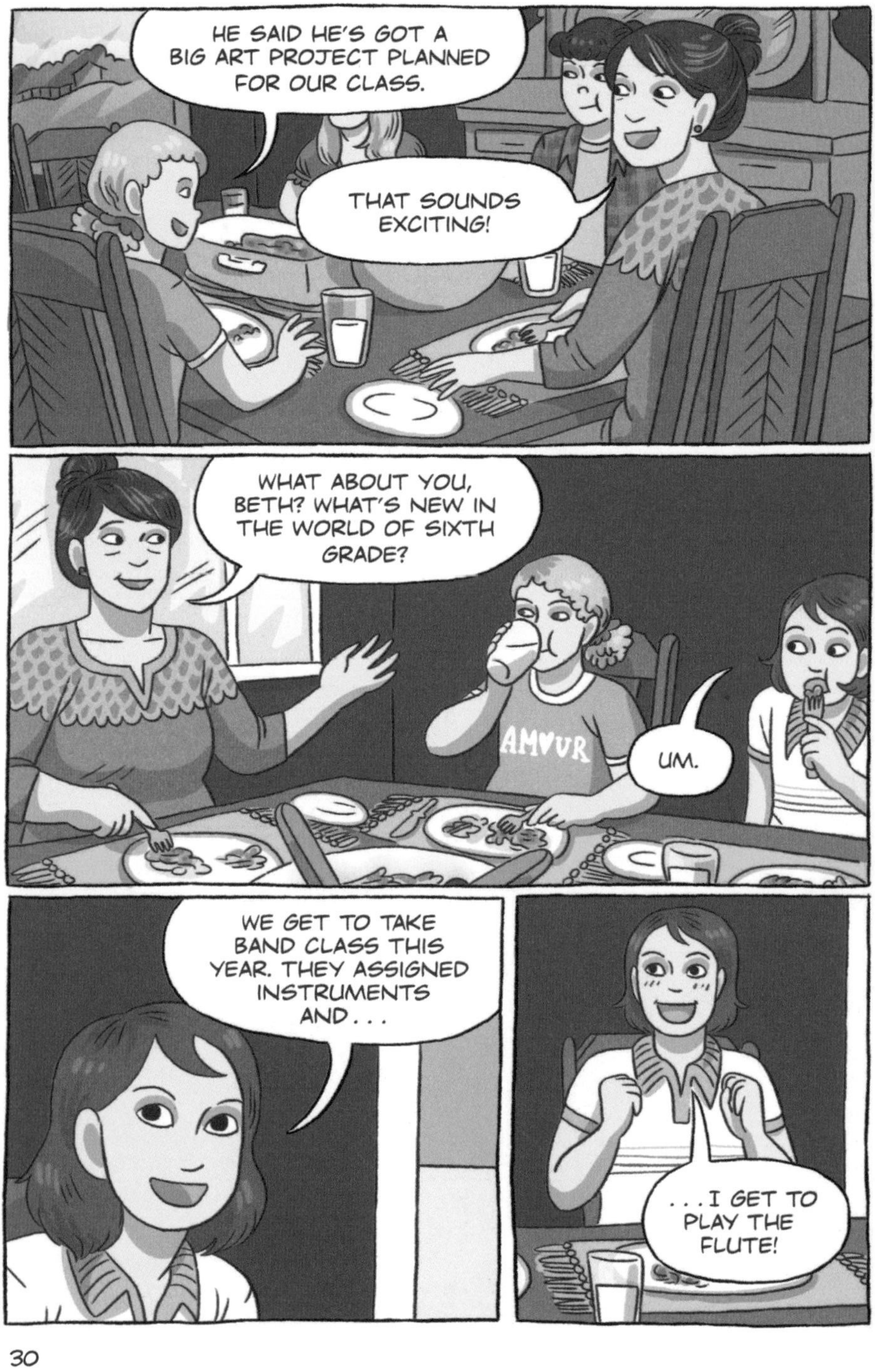
HE SAID HE'S GOT A BIG ART PROJECT PLANNED FOR OUR CLASS.
THAT SOUNDS EXCITING!
WHAT ABOUT YOU, BETH? WHAT'S NEW IN THE WORLD OF SIXTH GRADE?
AMOUR
UM.
WE GET TO TAKE BAND CLASS THIS YEAR. THEY ASSIGNED INSTRUMENTS AND . . .
. . . I GET TO PLAY THE FLUTE!

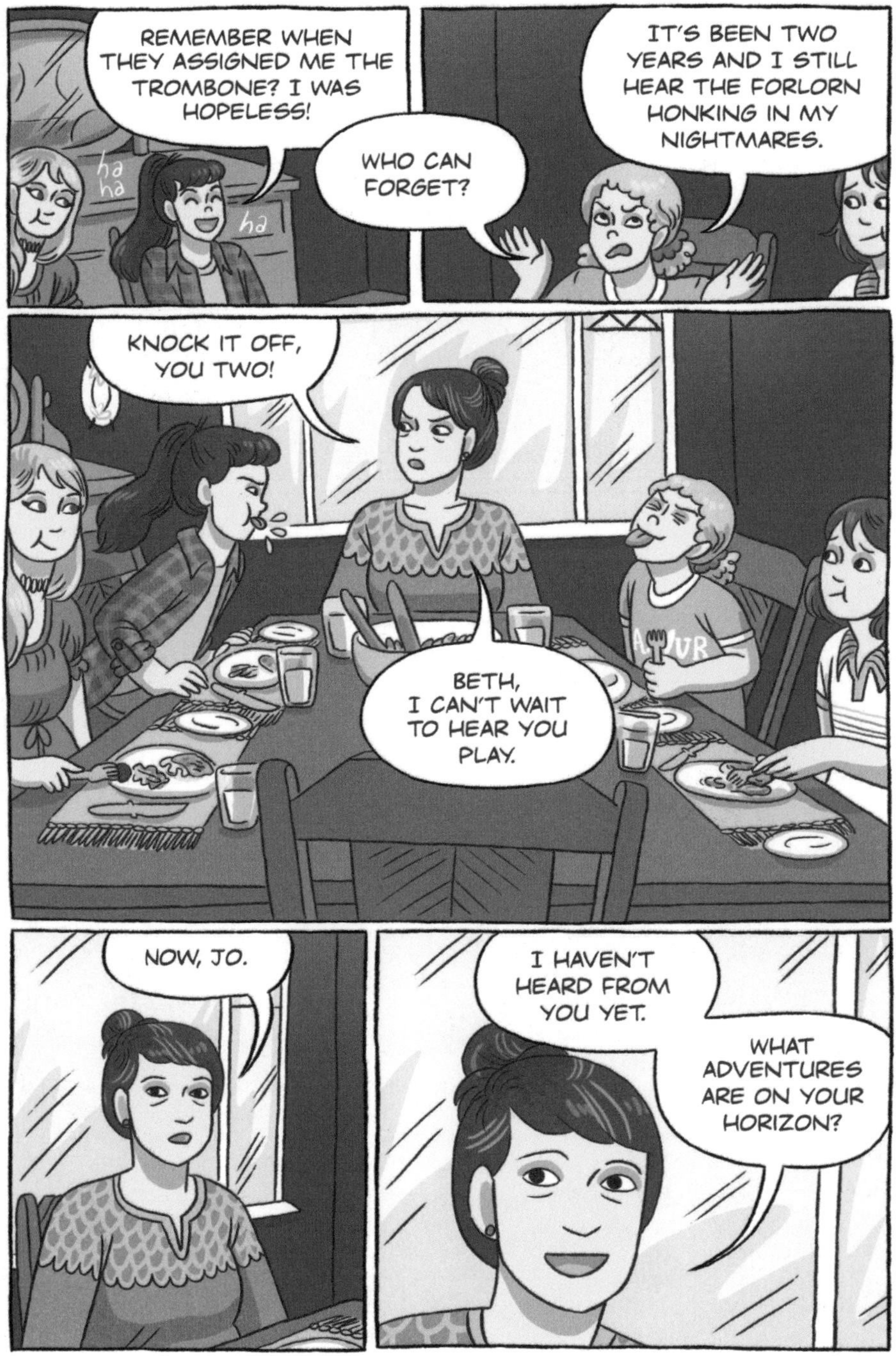
REMEMBER WHEN THEY ASSIGNED ME THE TROMBONE? I WAS HOPELESS!
ha ha
ha
WHO CAN FORGET?
IT'S BEEN TWO YEARS AND I STILL HEAR THE FORLORN HONKING IN MY NIGHTMARES.
KNOCK IT OFF, YOU TWO!
BETH, I CAN'T WAIT TO HEAR YOU PLAY.
NOW, JO.
I HAVEN'T HEARD FROM YOU YET.
WHAT ADVENTURES ARE ON YOUR HORIZON?

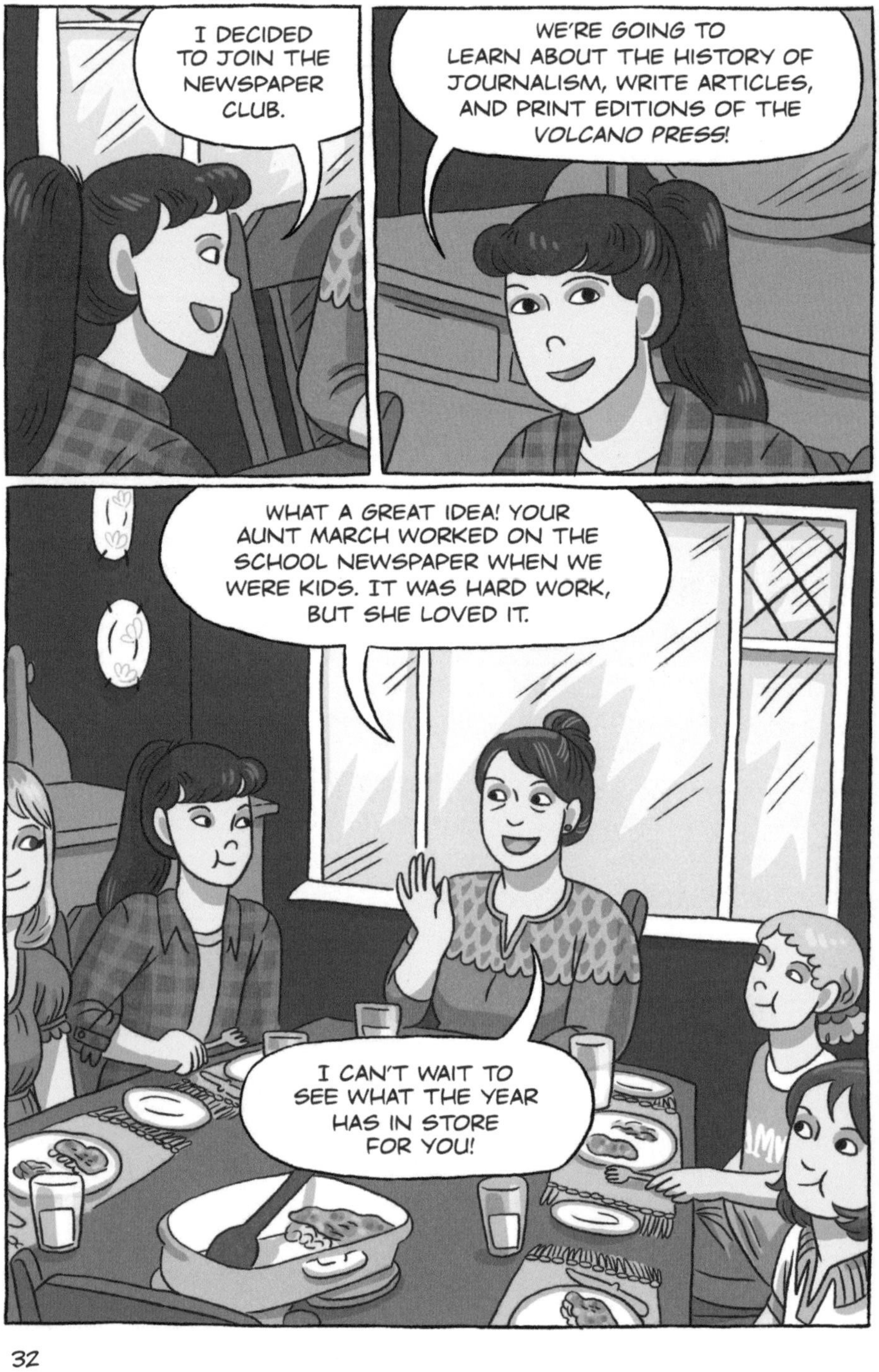
I DECIDED TO JOIN THE NEWSPAPER CLUB.
WE'RE GOING TO LEARN ABOUT THE HISTORY OF JOURNALISM, WRITE ARTICLES, AND PRINT EDITIONS OF THE *VOLCANO PRESS*!
WHAT A GREAT IDEA! YOUR AUNT MARCH WORKED ON THE SCHOOL NEWSPAPER WHEN WE WERE KIDS. IT WAS HARD WORK, BUT SHE LOVED IT.
I CAN'T WAIT TO SEE WHAT THE YEAR HAS IN STORE FOR YOU!

CHAPTER 2

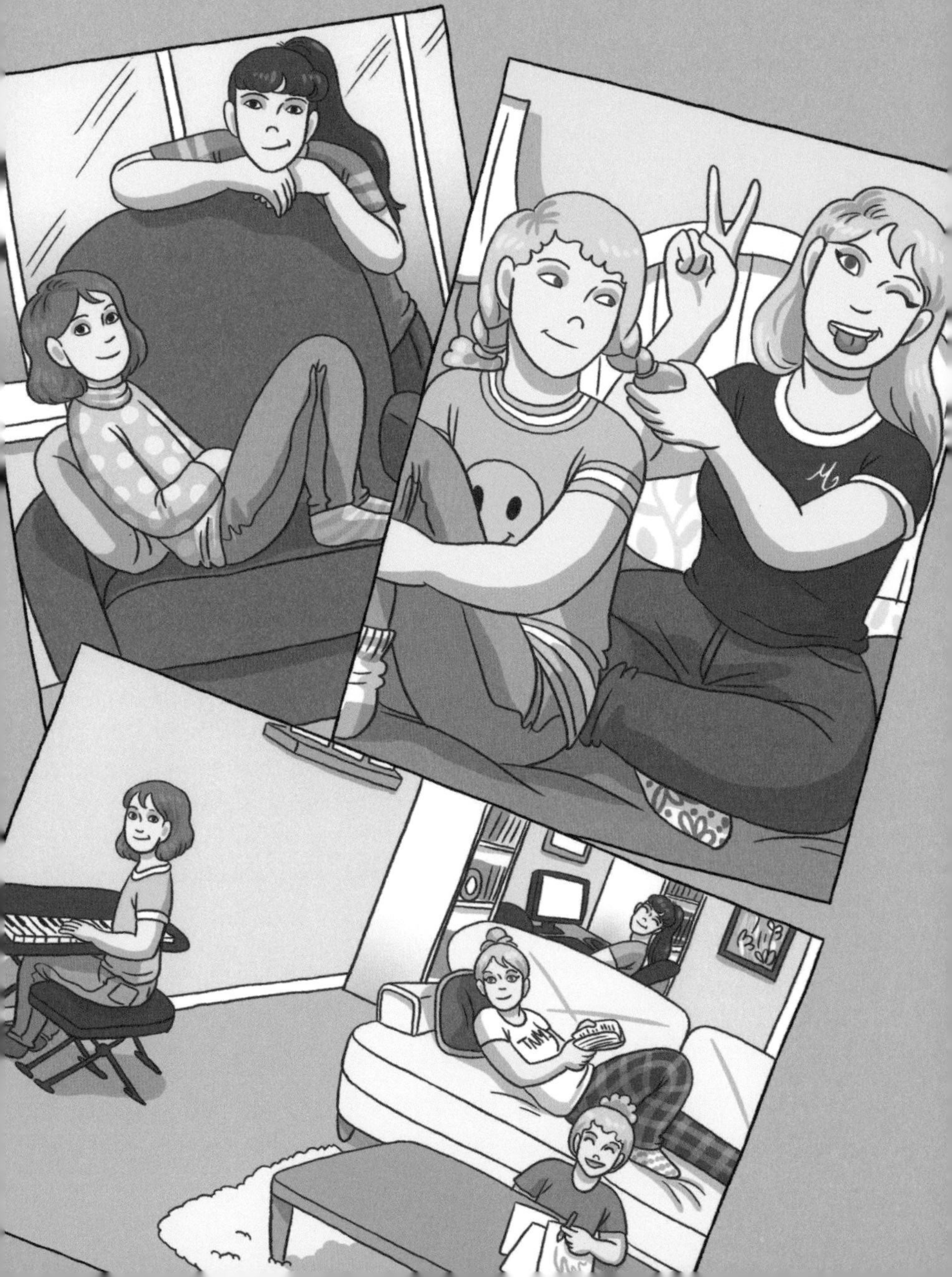

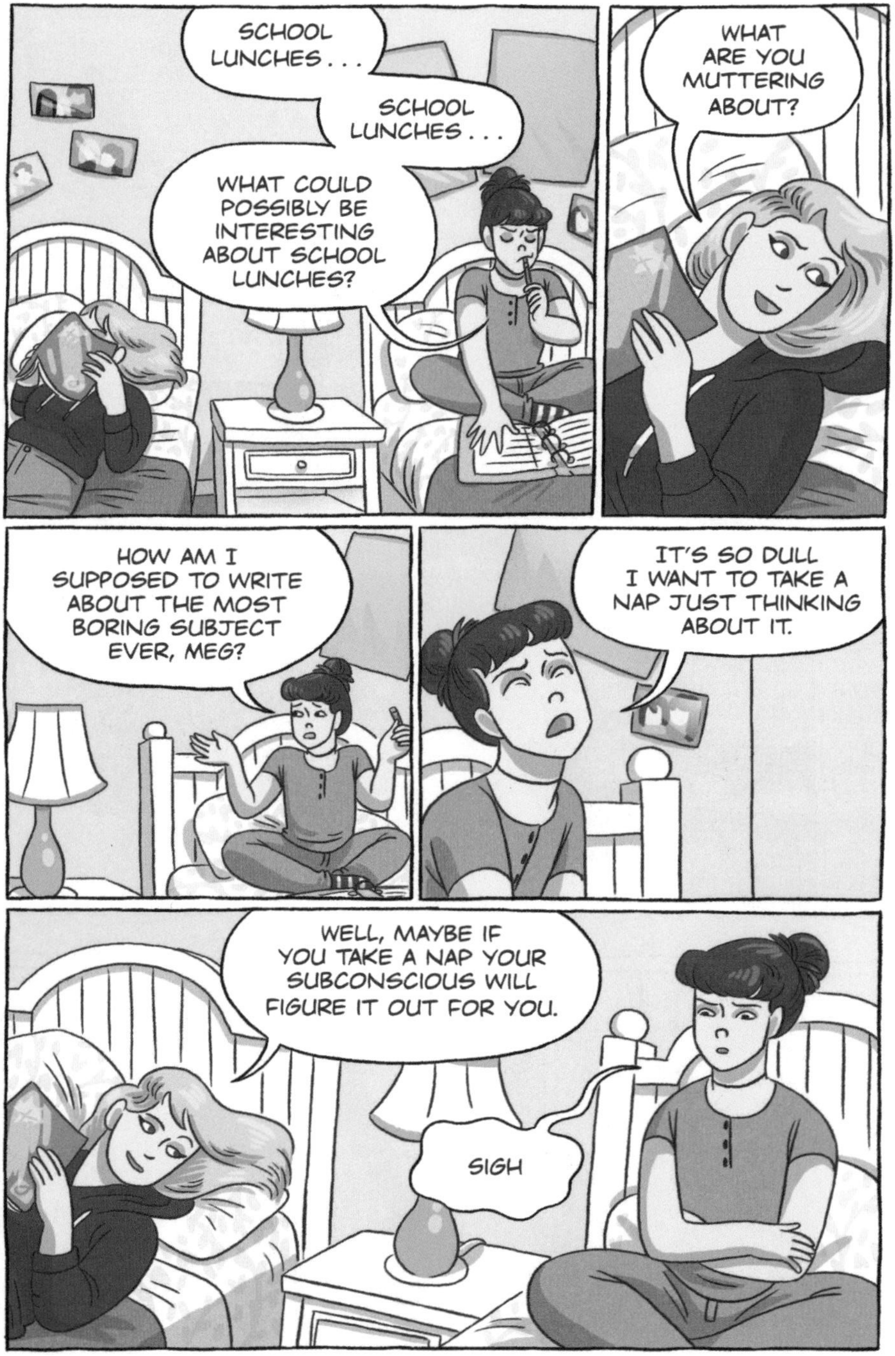
SCHOOL LUNCHES . . .
SCHOOL LUNCHES . . .
WHAT COULD POSSIBLY BE INTERESTING ABOUT SCHOOL LUNCHES?
WHAT ARE YOU MUTTERING ABOUT?
HOW AM I SUPPOSED TO WRITE ABOUT THE MOST BORING SUBJECT EVER, MEG?
IT'S SO DULL I WANT TO TAKE A NAP JUST THINKING ABOUT IT.
WELL, MAYBE IF YOU TAKE A NAP YOUR SUBCONSCIOUS WILL FIGURE IT OUT FOR YOU.
SIGH

HI. ME AGAIN. J.

I SAID WHEN I STARTED THIS BLOG THAT I WANTED TO BE A WRITER, AND I DO, BUT LATELY I'VE BEEN WONDERING IF I'M CUT OUT FOR IT.

WHAT ARE YOU WORKING ON?

JUST THIS ARTICLE FOR THE PAPER.

minimize

Click

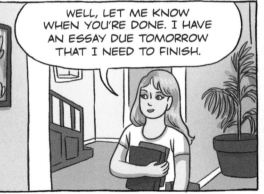

WELL, LET ME KNOW WHEN YOU'RE DONE. I HAVE AN ESSAY DUE TOMORROW THAT I NEED TO FINISH.

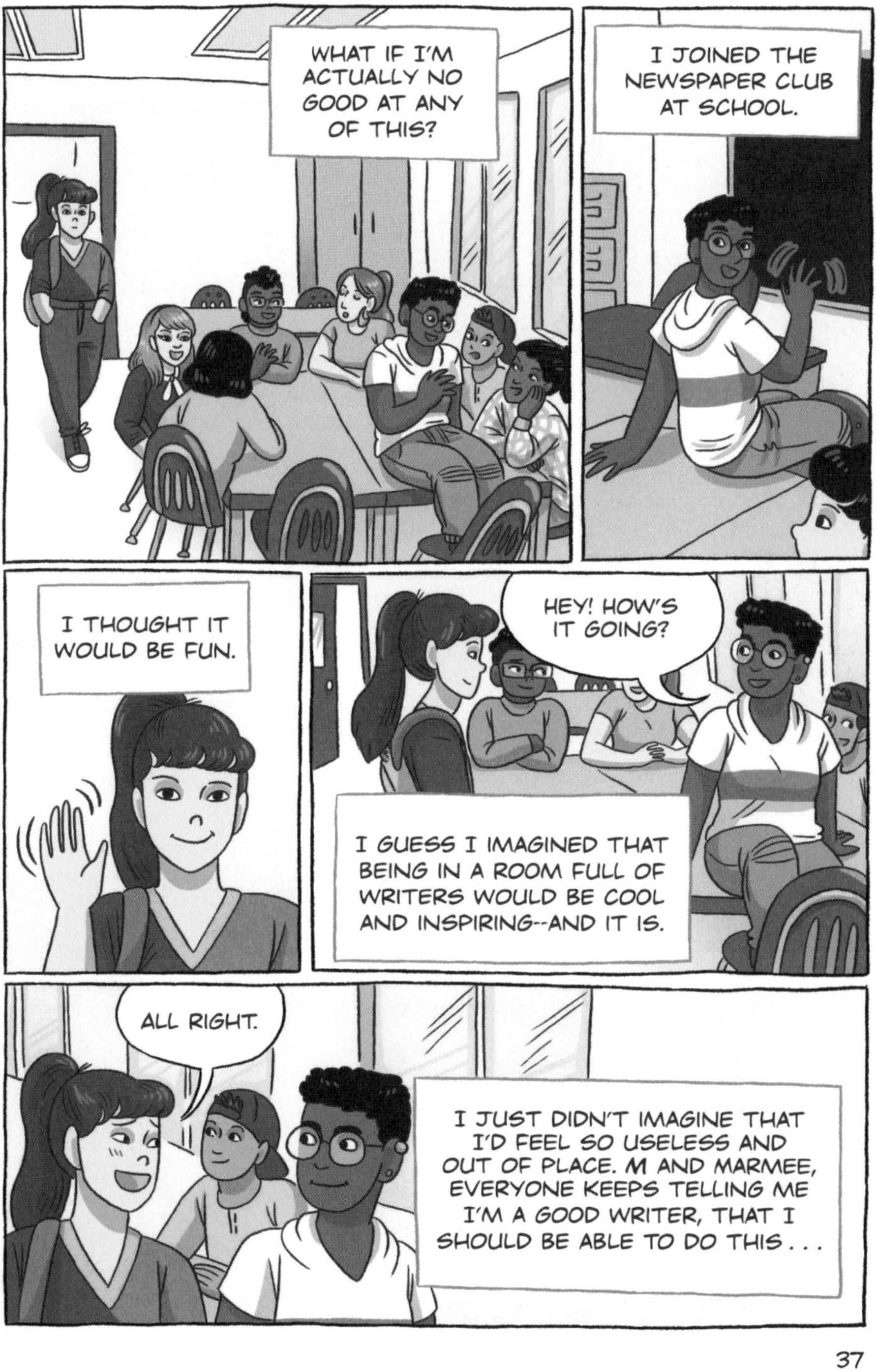
WHAT IF I'M ACTUALLY NO GOOD AT ANY OF THIS?
I JOINED THE NEWSPAPER CLUB AT SCHOOL.
I THOUGHT IT WOULD BE FUN.
HEY! HOW'S IT GOING?
I GUESS I IMAGINED THAT BEING IN A ROOM FULL OF WRITERS WOULD BE COOL AND INSPIRING--AND IT IS.
ALL RIGHT.
I JUST DIDN'T IMAGINE THAT I'D FEEL SO USELESS AND OUT OF PLACE. M AND MARMEE, EVERYONE KEEPS TELLING ME I'M A GOOD WRITER, THAT I SHOULD BE ABLE TO DO THIS . . .

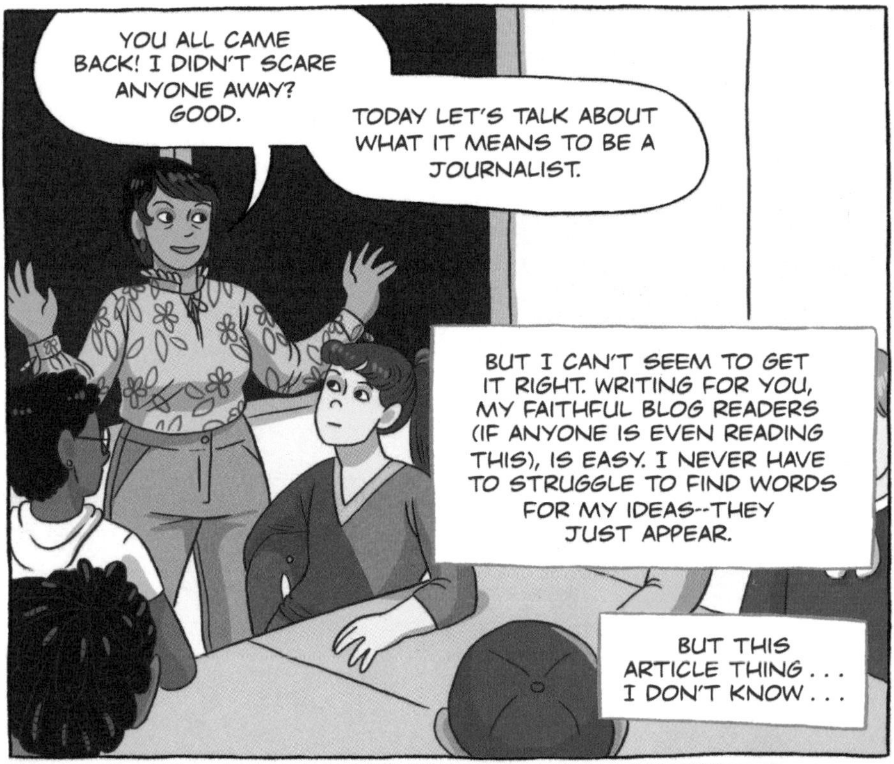
YOU ALL CAME BACK! I DIDN'T SCARE ANYONE AWAY? GOOD.
TODAY LET'S TALK ABOUT WHAT IT MEANS TO BE A JOURNALIST.
BUT I CAN'T SEEM TO GET IT RIGHT. WRITING FOR YOU, MY FAITHFUL BLOG READERS (IF ANYONE IS EVEN READING THIS), IS EASY. I NEVER HAVE TO STRUGGLE TO FIND WORDS FOR MY IDEAS--THEY JUST APPEAR.
BUT THIS ARTICLE THING . . . I DON'T KNOW . . .

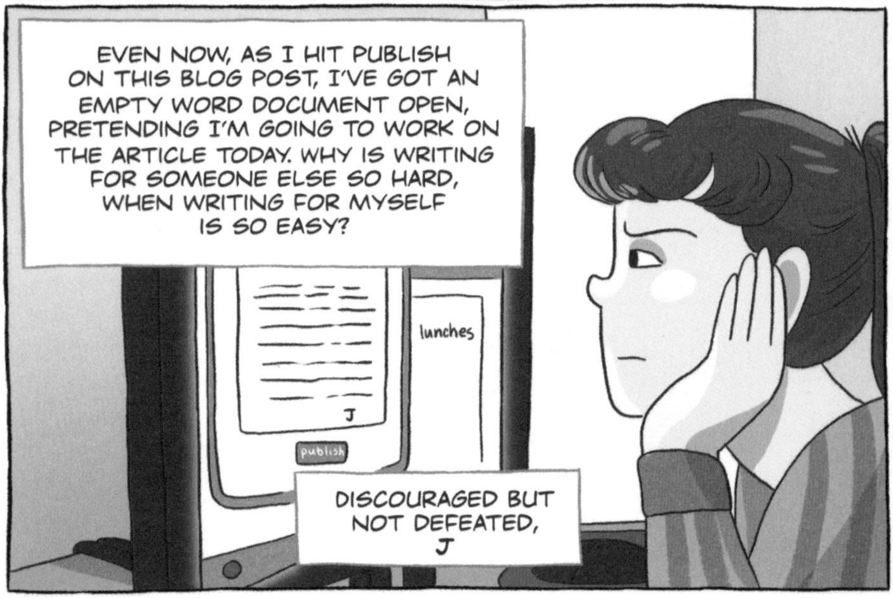
EVEN NOW, AS I HIT PUBLISH ON THIS BLOG POST, I'VE GOT AN EMPTY WORD DOCUMENT OPEN, PRETENDING I'M GOING TO WORK ON THE ARTICLE TODAY. WHY IS WRITING FOR SOMEONE ELSE SO HARD, WHEN WRITING FOR MYSELF IS SO EASY?
lunches
J
publish
DISCOURAGED BUT NOT DEFEATED, J

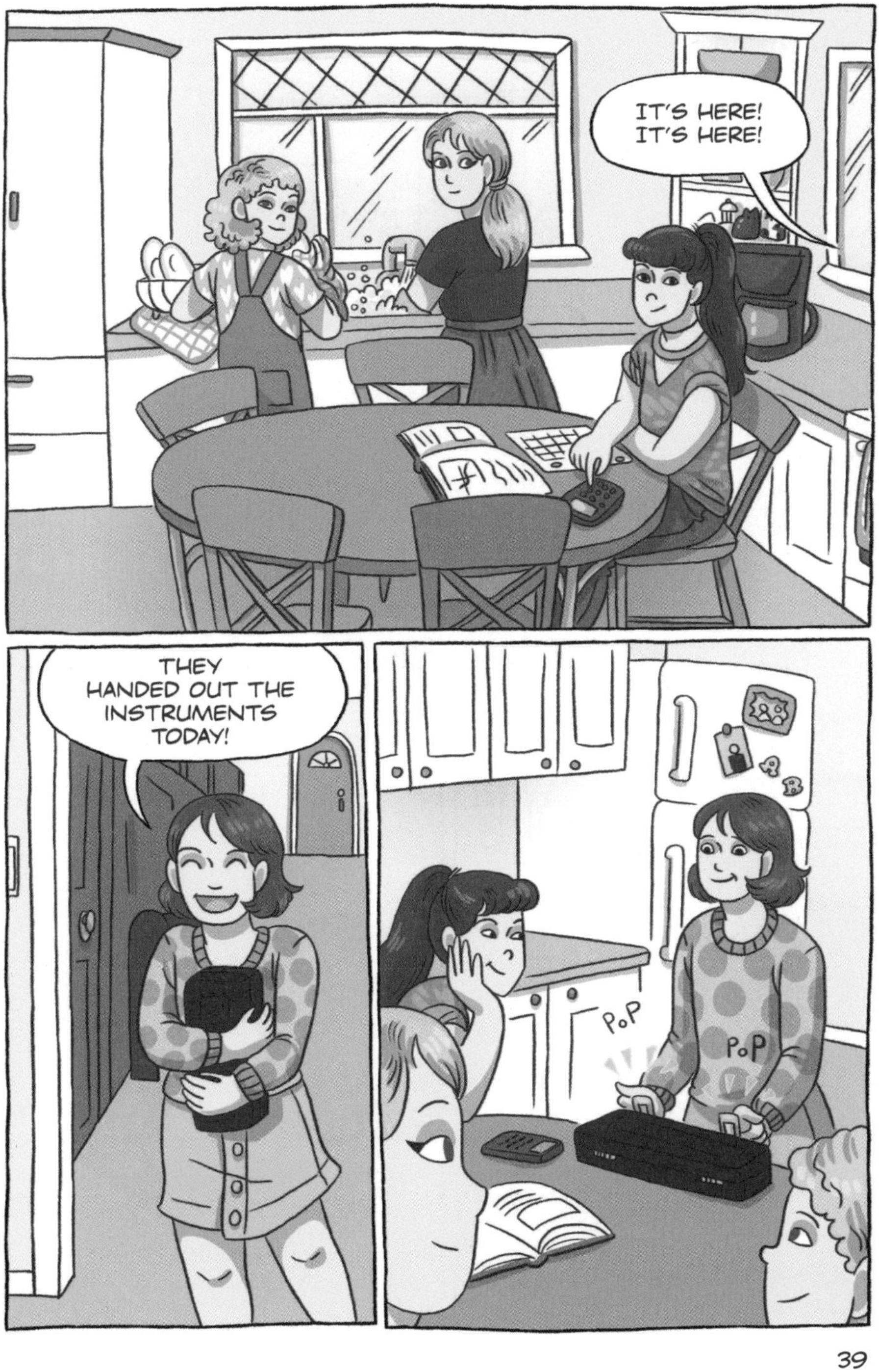
IT'S HERE! IT'S HERE!
THEY HANDED OUT THE INSTRUMENTS TODAY!
POP
POP

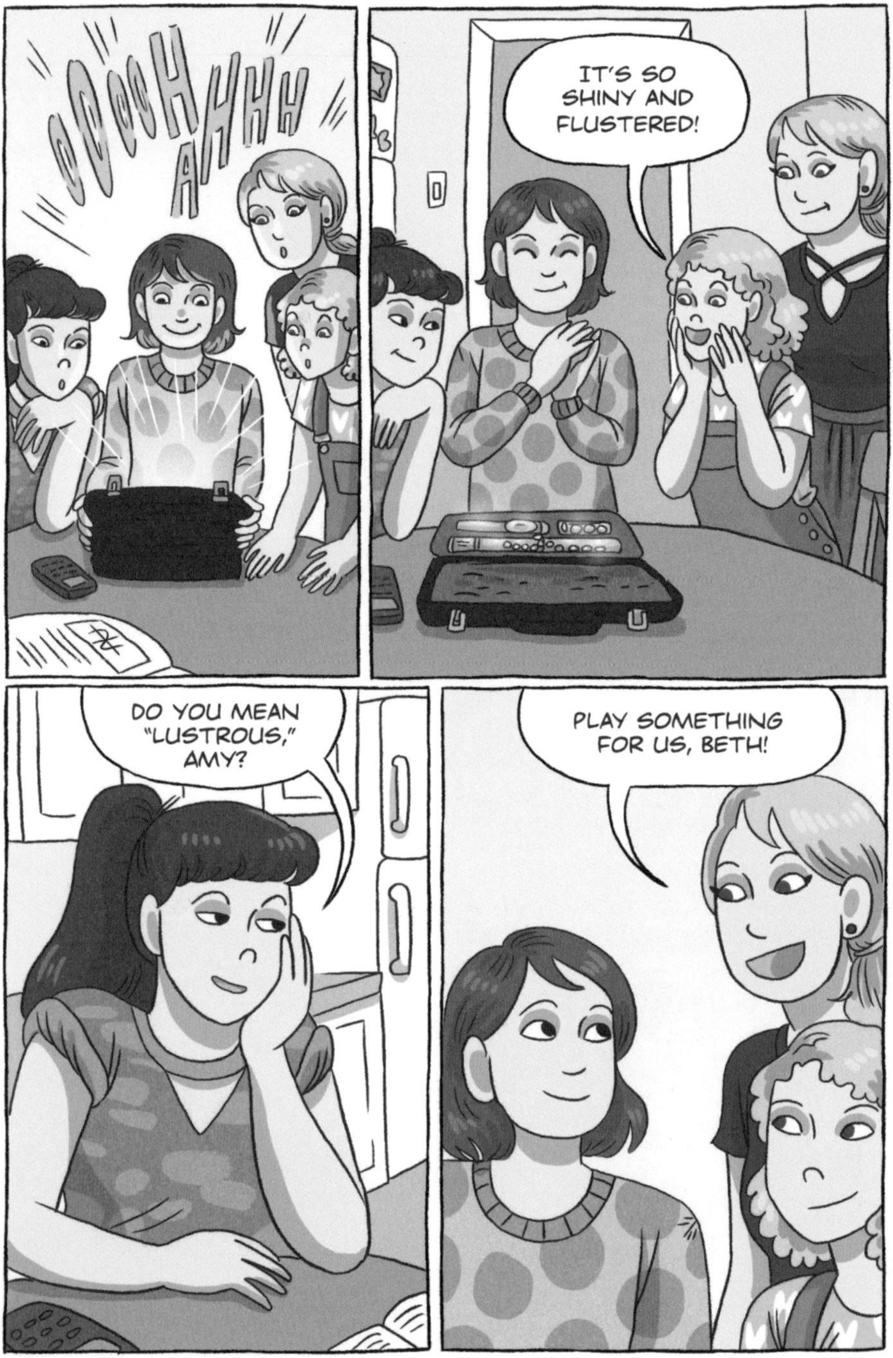
OOOOHAHHH
IT'S SO SHINY AND FLUSTERED!
DO YOU MEAN "LUSTROUS," AMY?
PLAY SOMETHING FOR US, BETH!

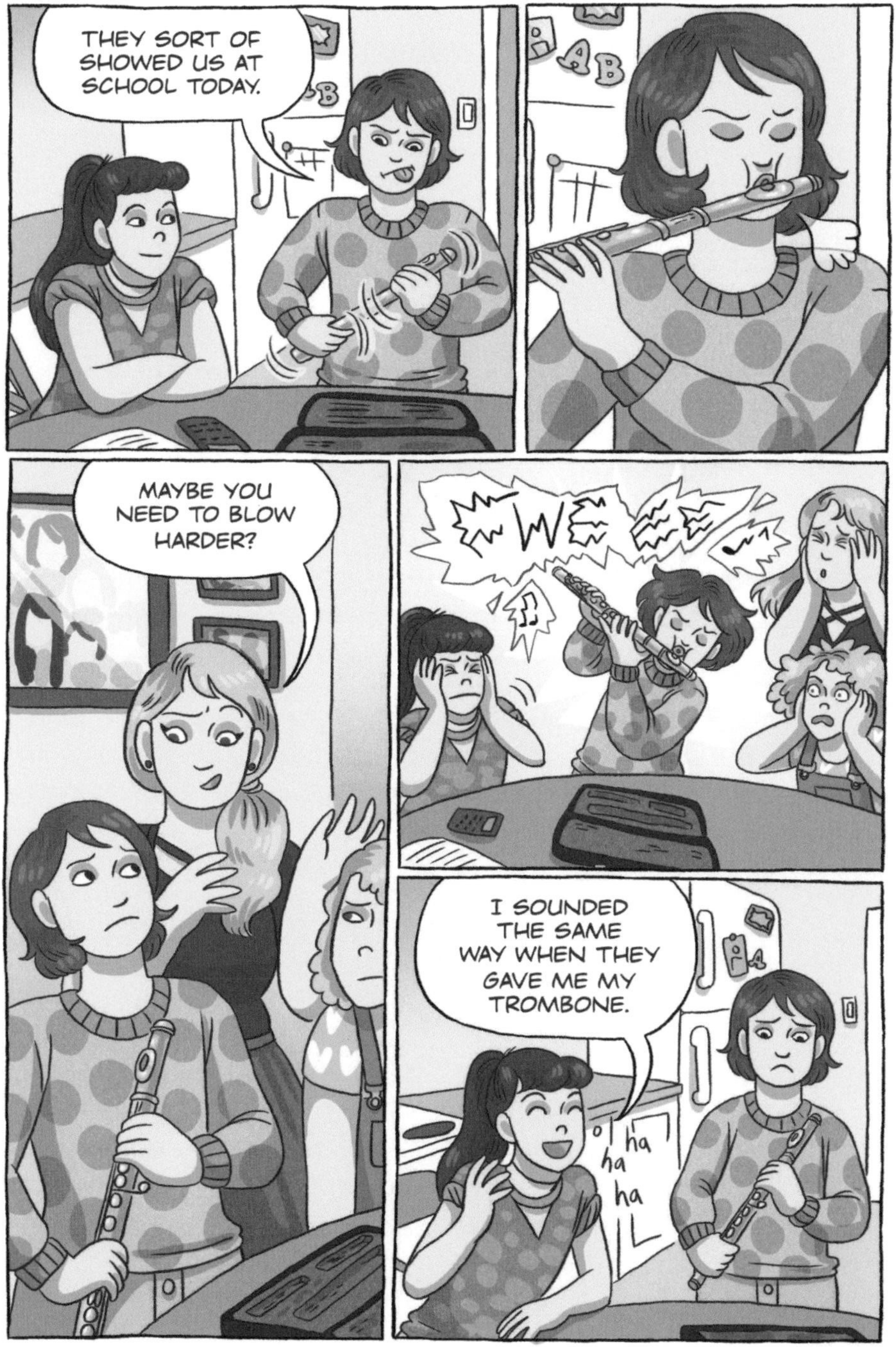
THEY SORT OF SHOWED US AT SCHOOL TODAY.
MAYBE YOU NEED TO BLOW HARDER?
WEE
I SOUNDED THE SAME WAY WHEN THEY GAVE ME MY TROMBONE.
ha ha ha

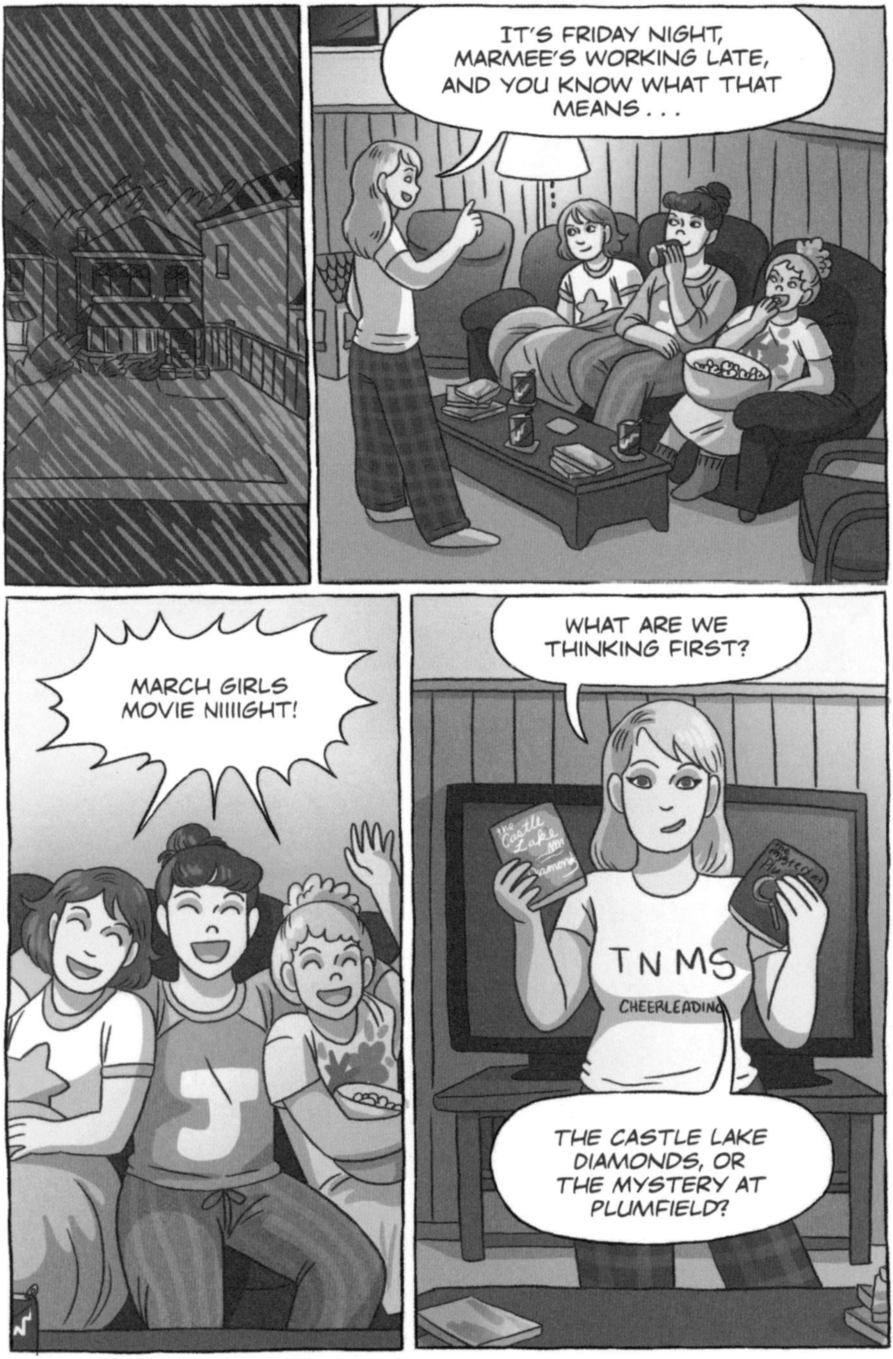
IT'S FRIDAY NIGHT, MARMEE'S WORKING LATE, AND YOU KNOW WHAT THAT MEANS . . .
MARCH GIRLS MOVIE NIIIIGHT!
WHAT ARE WE THINKING FIRST?
TNMS
CHEERLEADING
THE CASTLE LAKE DIAMONDS, OR THE MYSTERY AT PLUMFIELD?

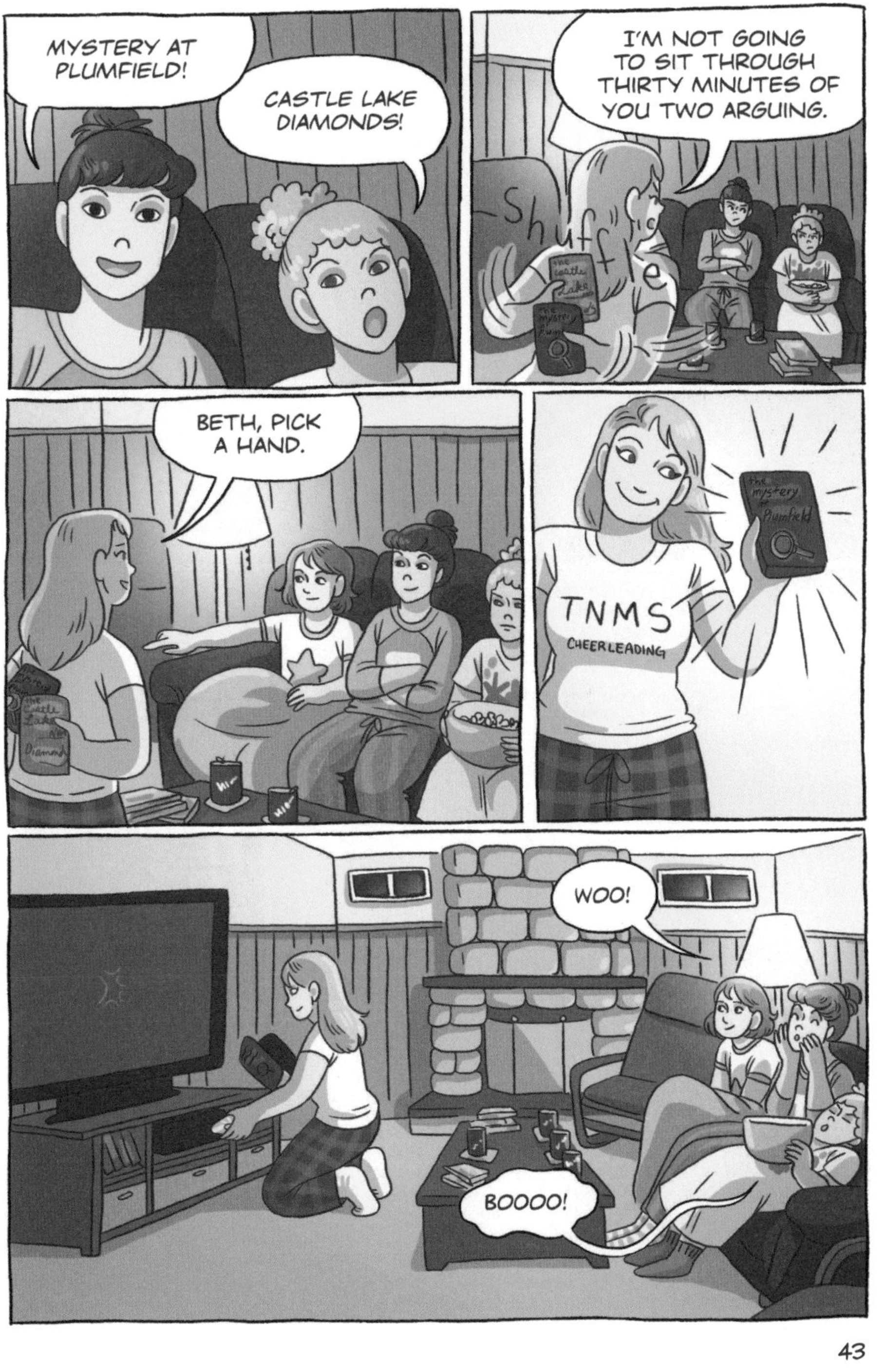

MYSTERY AT PLUMFIELD!
CASTLE LAKE DIAMONDS!
I'M NOT GOING TO SIT THROUGH THIRTY MINUTES OF YOU TWO ARGUING.
Shuffle
BETH, PICK A HAND.
the mystery of Plumfield
TNMS
CHEERLEADING
WOO!
BOOOO!

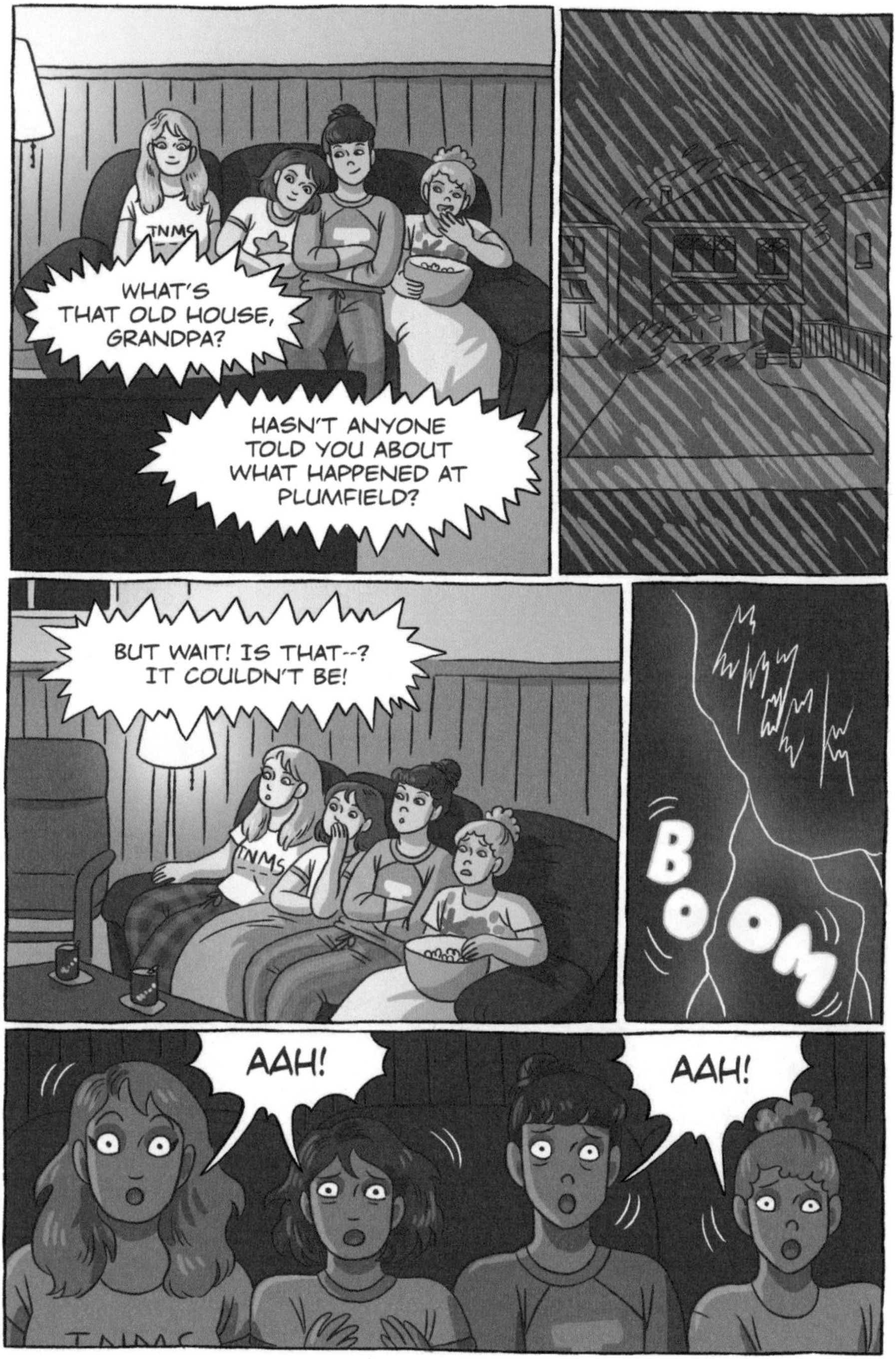
WHAT'S THAT OLD HOUSE, GRANDPA?
HASN'T ANYONE TOLD YOU ABOUT WHAT HAPPENED AT PLUMFIELD?
TNMS
BUT WAIT! IS THAT--? IT COULDN'T BE!
BOOM
AAH!
AAH!

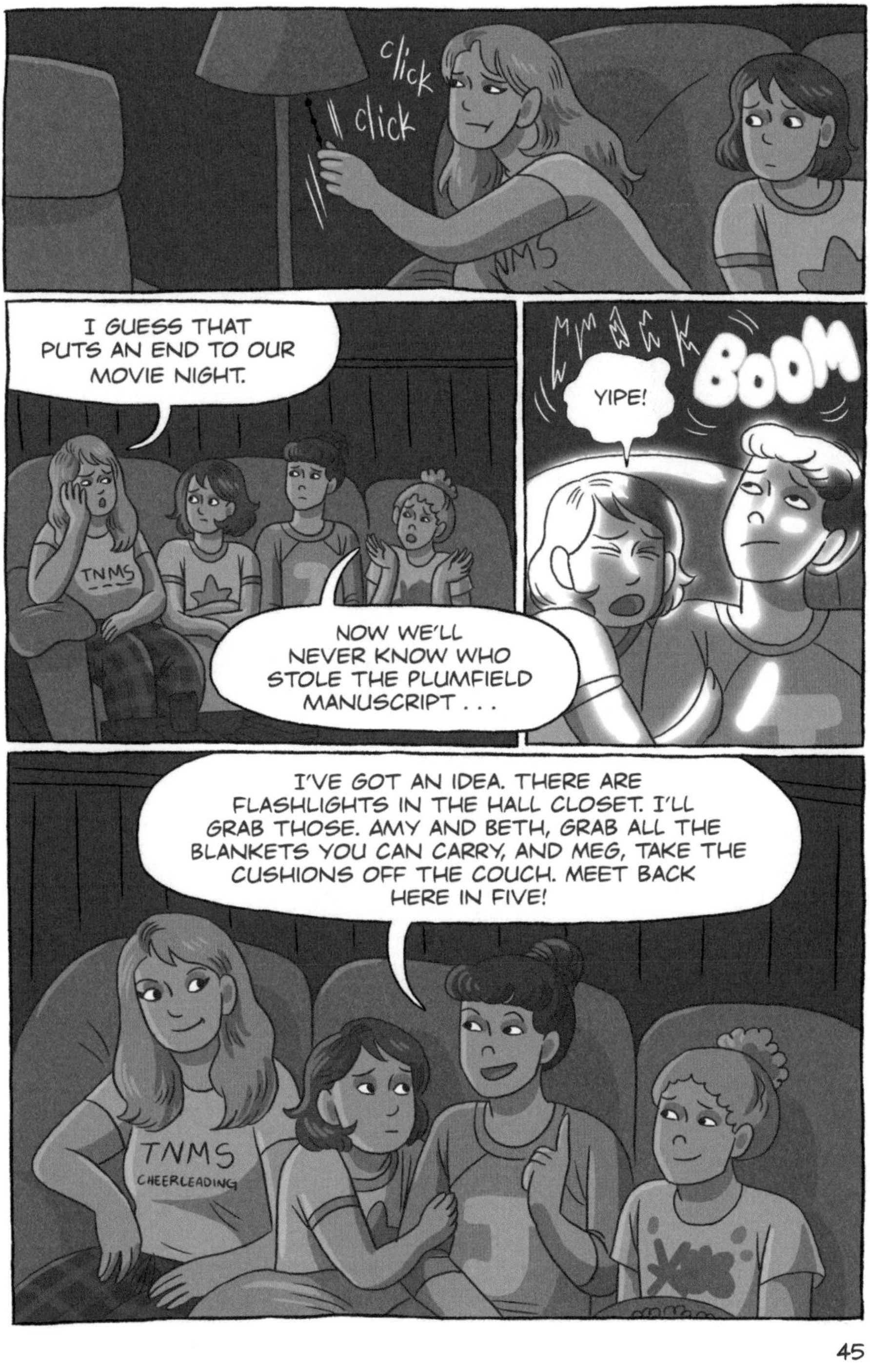
click
click
I GUESS THAT PUTS AN END TO OUR MOVIE NIGHT.
TNMS
NOW WE'LL NEVER KNOW WHO STOLE THE PLUMFIELD MANUSCRIPT . . .
CRACK
BOOM
YIPE!
I'VE GOT AN IDEA. THERE ARE FLASHLIGHTS IN THE HALL CLOSET. I'LL GRAB THOSE. AMY AND BETH, GRAB ALL THE BLANKETS YOU CAN CARRY, AND MEG, TAKE THE CUSHIONS OFF THE COUCH. MEET BACK HERE IN FIVE!
TNMS
CHEERLEADING

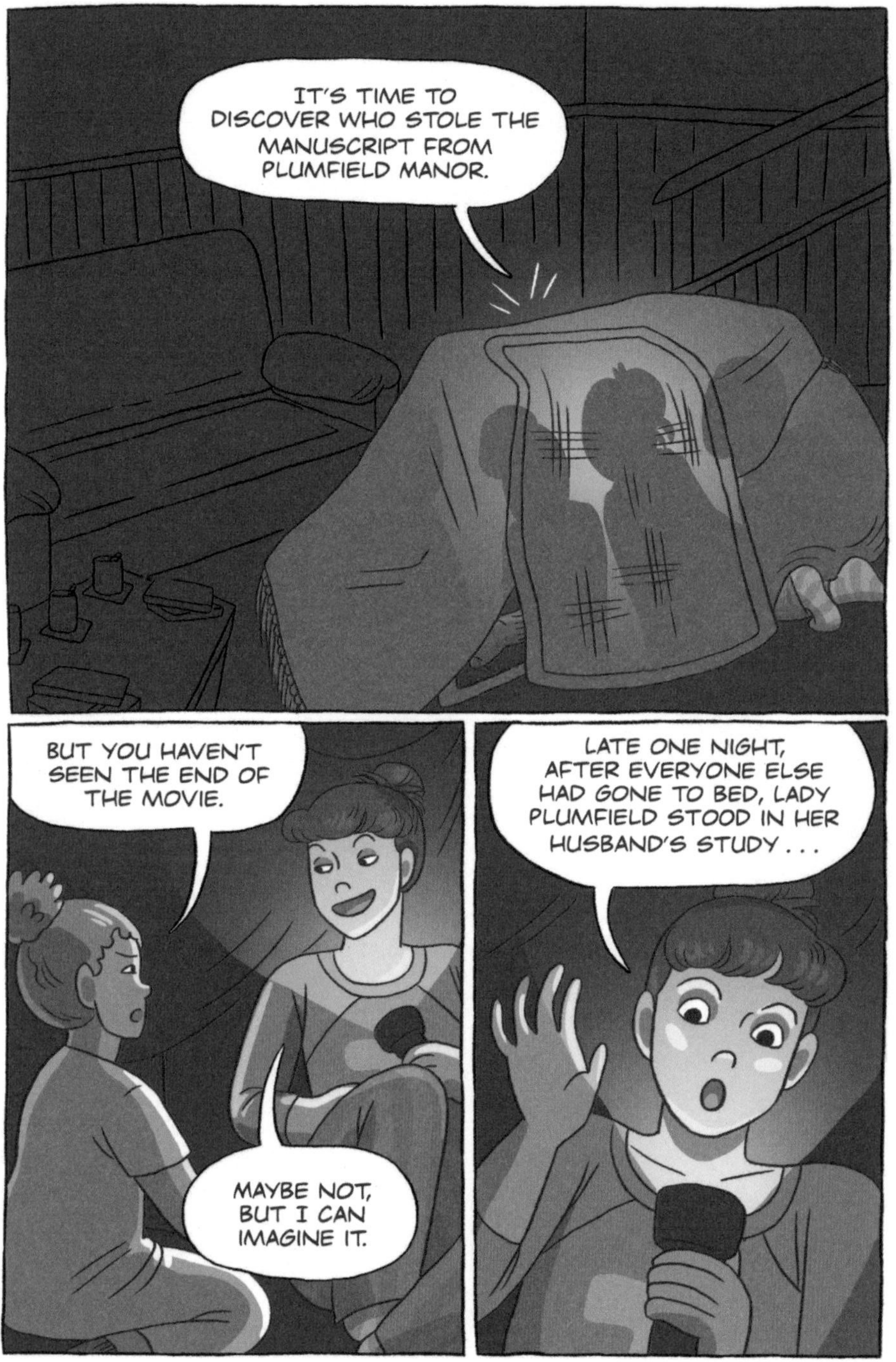
IT'S TIME TO DISCOVER WHO STOLE THE MANUSCRIPT FROM PLUMFIELD MANOR.
BUT YOU HAVEN'T SEEN THE END OF THE MOVIE.
MAYBE NOT, BUT I CAN IMAGINE IT.
LATE ONE NIGHT, AFTER EVERYONE ELSE HAD GONE TO BED, LADY PLUMFIELD STOOD IN HER HUSBAND'S STUDY . . .

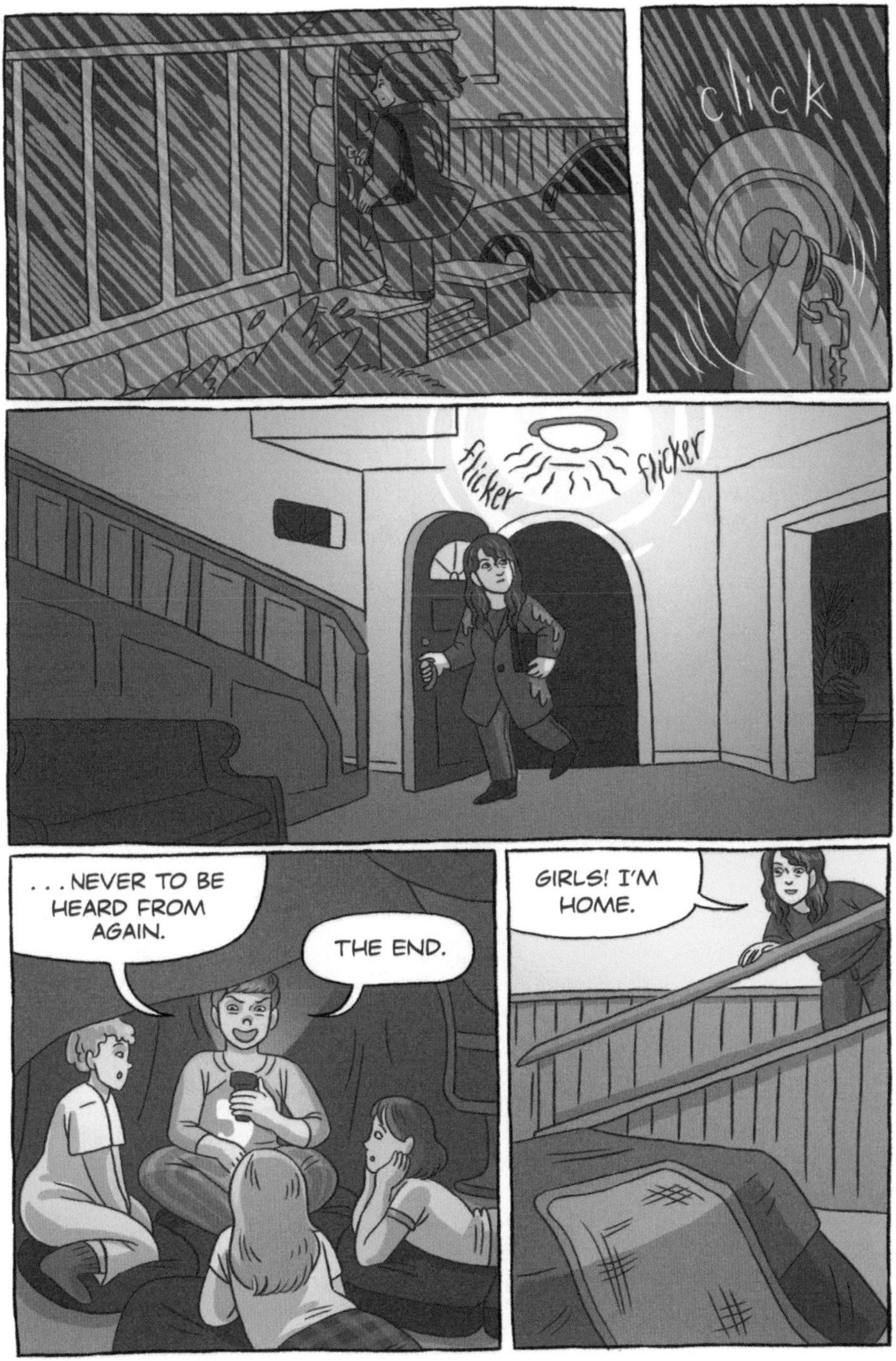
click
flicker
flicker
. . .NEVER TO BE HEARD FROM AGAIN.
THE END.
GIRLS! I'M HOME.

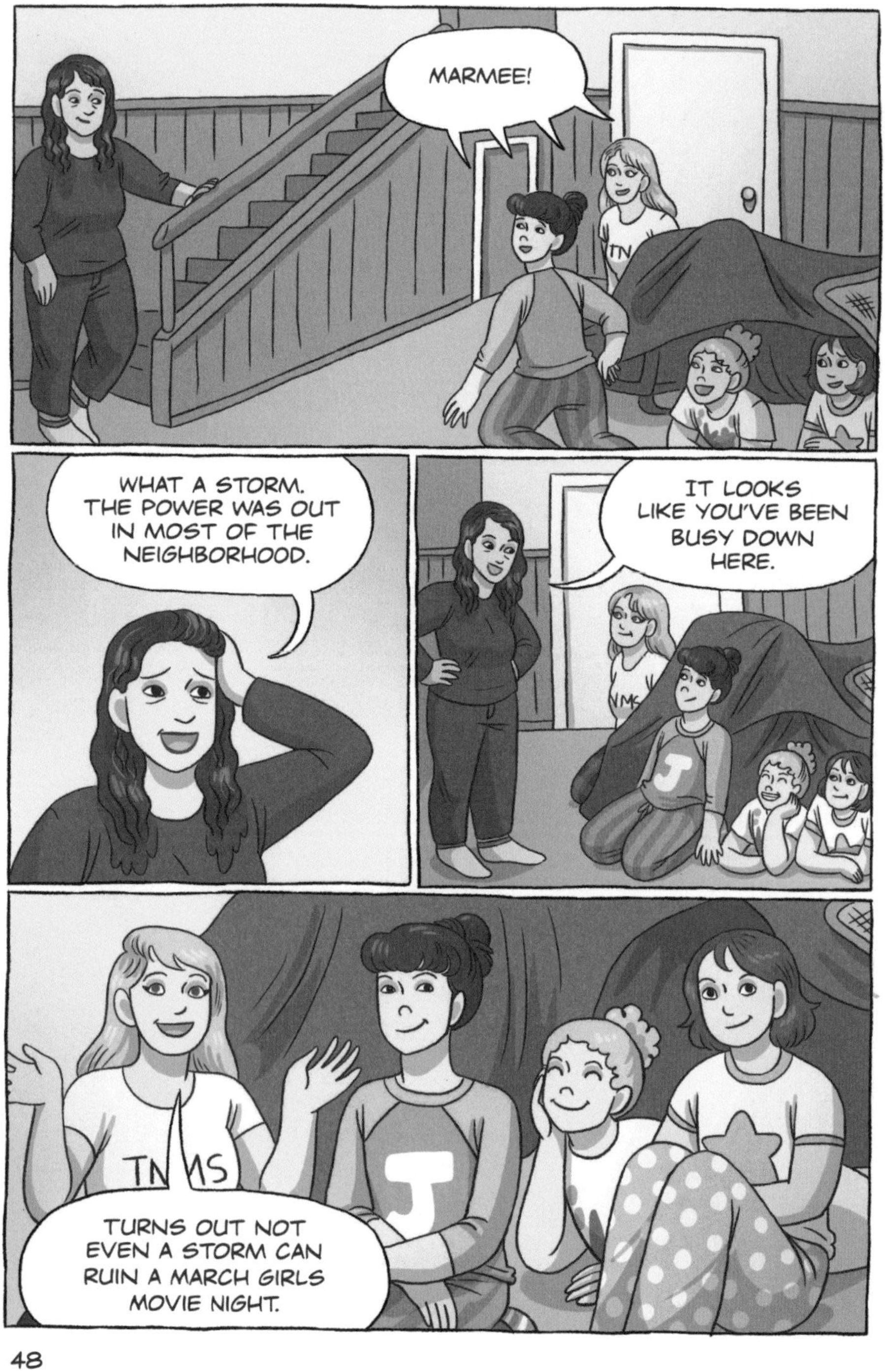
MARMEE!
TN
WHAT A STORM. THE POWER WAS OUT IN MOST OF THE NEIGHBORHOOD.
IT LOOKS LIKE YOU'VE BEEN BUSY DOWN HERE.
NMS
J
TNMS
TURNS OUT NOT EVEN A STORM CAN RUIN A MARCH GIRLS MOVIE NIGHT.
J

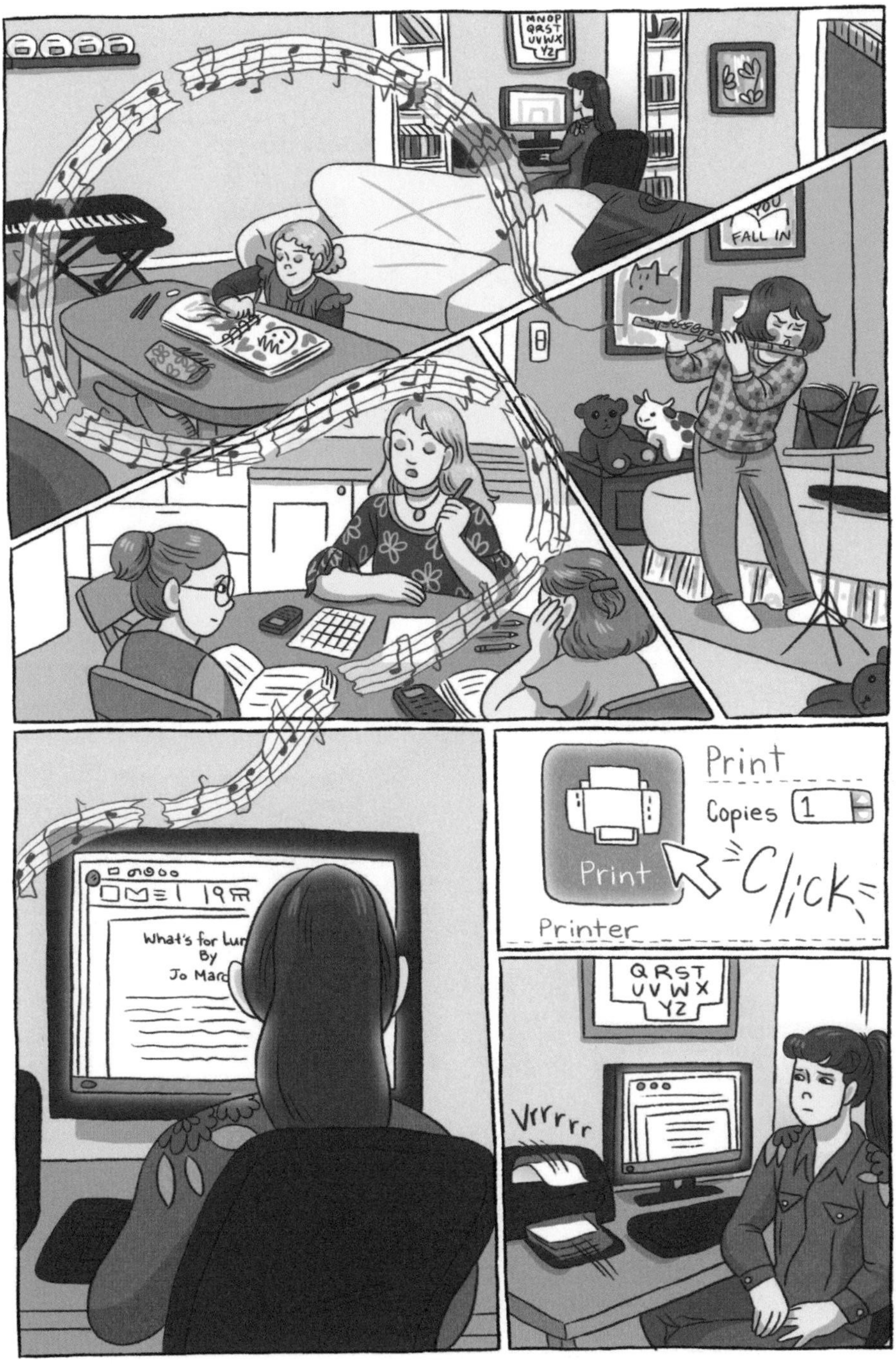
MNOP
QRST
UVWX
YZ
YOU
FALL IN
What's for Lun
By
Jo Marc
Print
Copies 1
Print
Printer
Click
QRST
UVWX
YZ
Vrrrrr

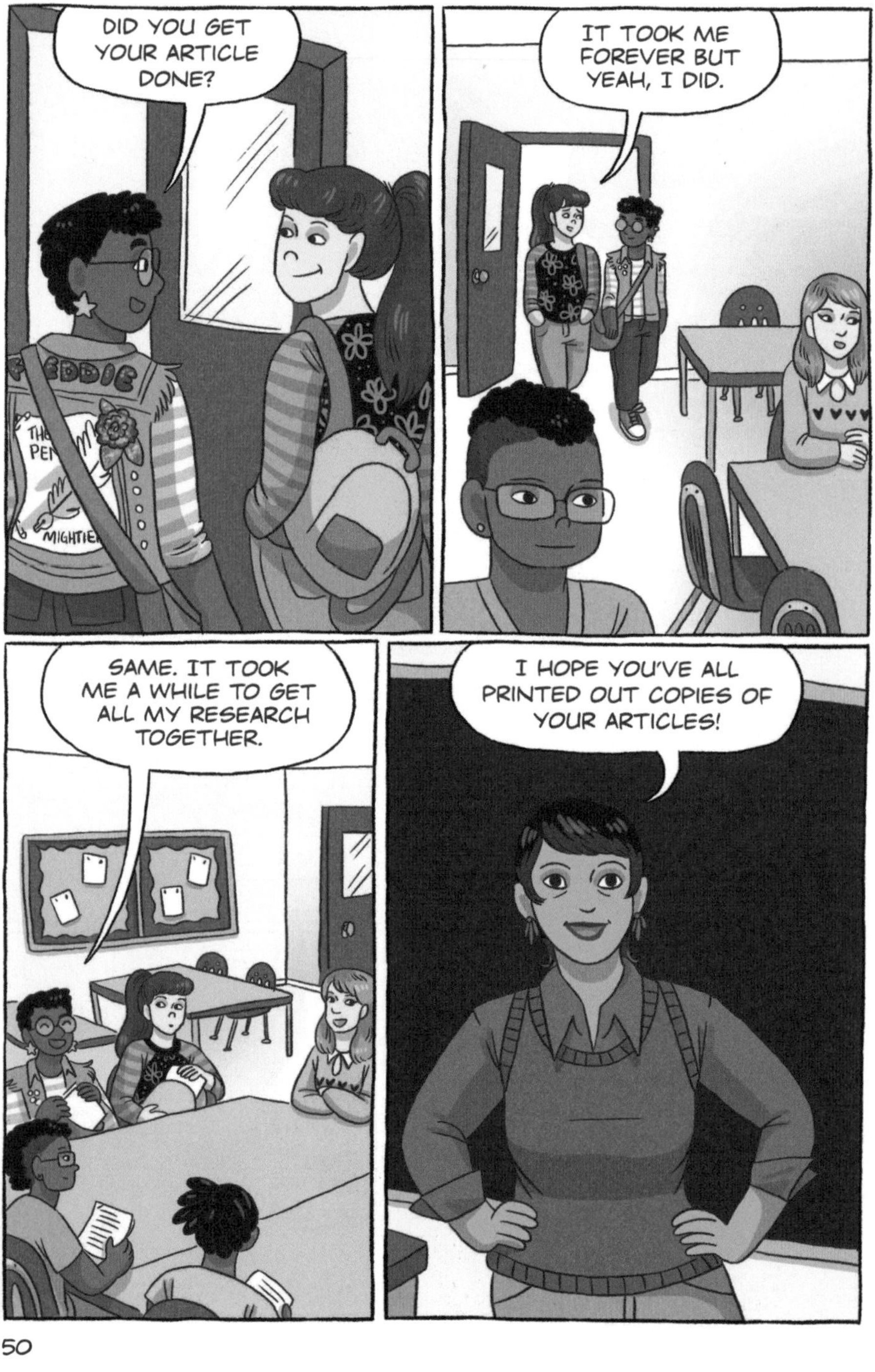
DID YOU GET YOUR ARTICLE DONE?
IT TOOK ME FOREVER BUT YEAH, I DID.
SAME. IT TOOK ME A WHILE TO GET ALL MY RESEARCH TOGETHER.
I HOPE YOU'VE ALL PRINTED OUT COPIES OF YOUR ARTICLES!

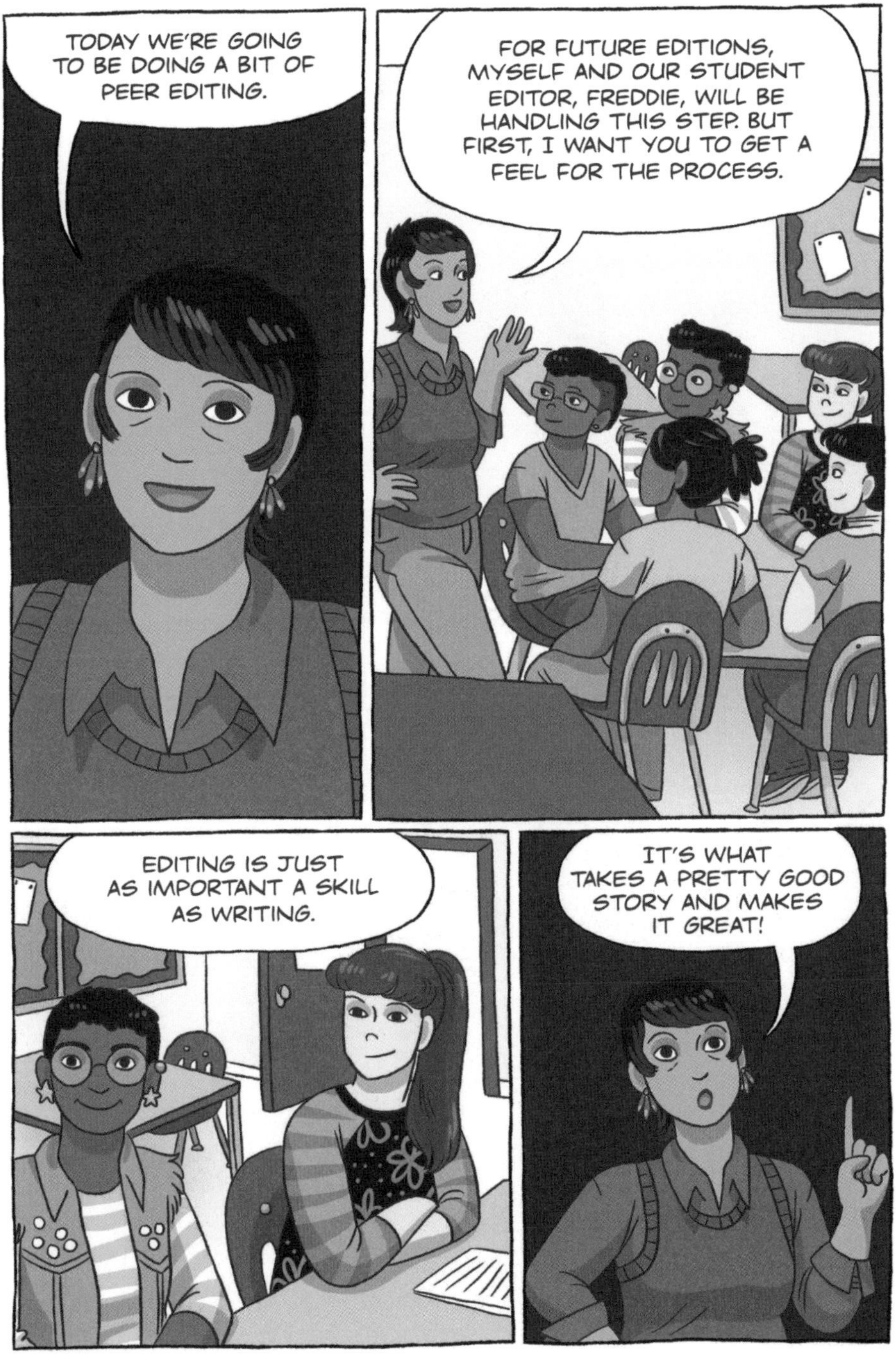
TODAY WE'RE GOING TO BE DOING A BIT OF PEER EDITING.
FOR FUTURE EDITIONS, MYSELF AND OUR STUDENT EDITOR, FREDDIE, WILL BE HANDLING THIS STEP. BUT FIRST, I WANT YOU TO GET A FEEL FOR THE PROCESS.
EDITING IS JUST AS IMPORTANT A SKILL AS WRITING.
IT'S WHAT TAKES A PRETTY GOOD STORY AND MAKES IT GREAT!

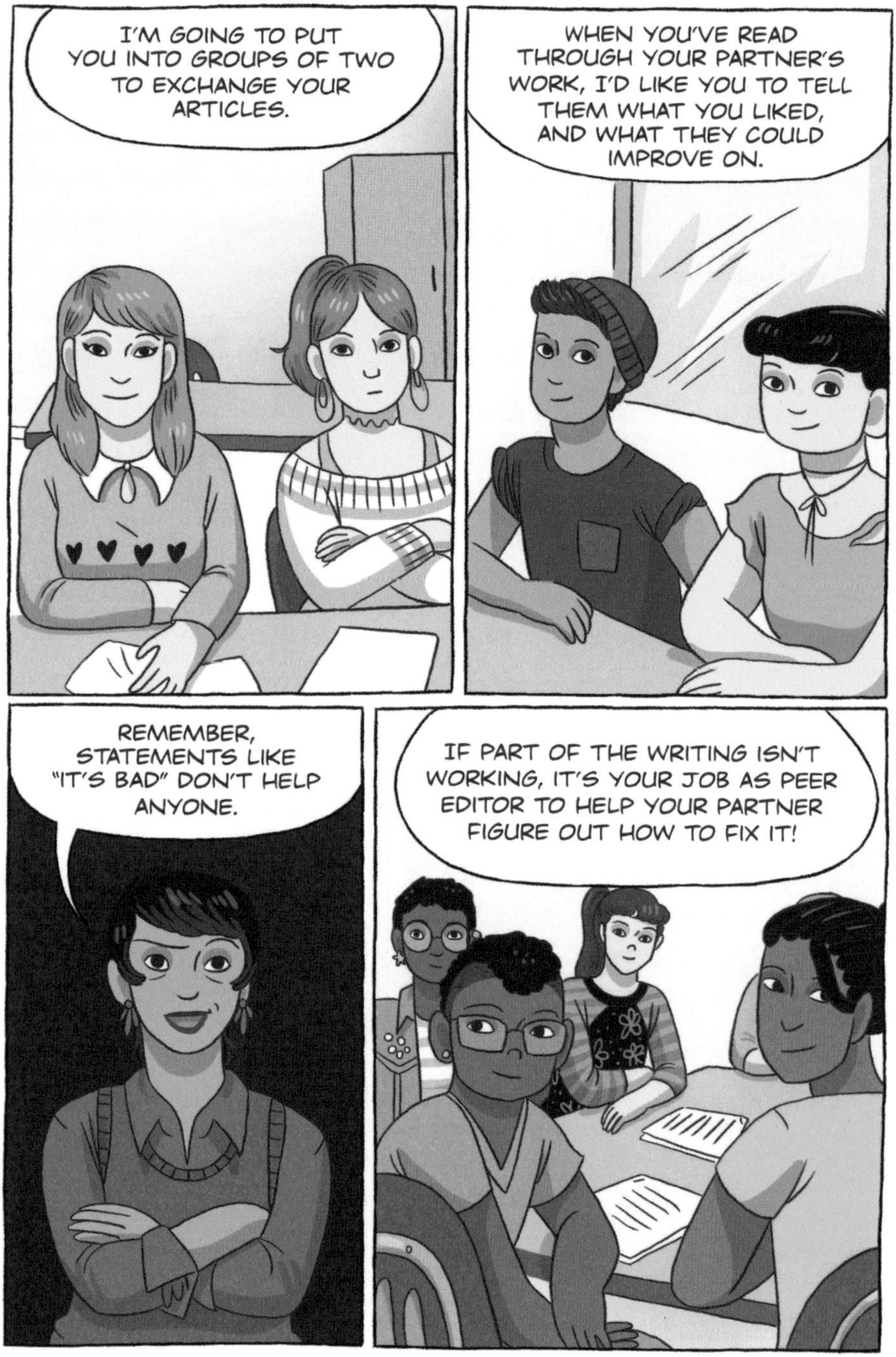
I'M GOING TO PUT YOU INTO GROUPS OF TWO TO EXCHANGE YOUR ARTICLES.
WHEN YOU'VE READ THROUGH YOUR PARTNER'S WORK, I'D LIKE YOU TO TELL THEM WHAT YOU LIKED, AND WHAT THEY COULD IMPROVE ON.
REMEMBER, STATEMENTS LIKE "IT'S BAD" DON'T HELP ANYONE.
IF PART OF THE WRITING ISN'T WORKING, IT'S YOUR JOB AS PEER EDITOR TO HELP YOUR PARTNER FIGURE OUT HOW TO FIX IT!

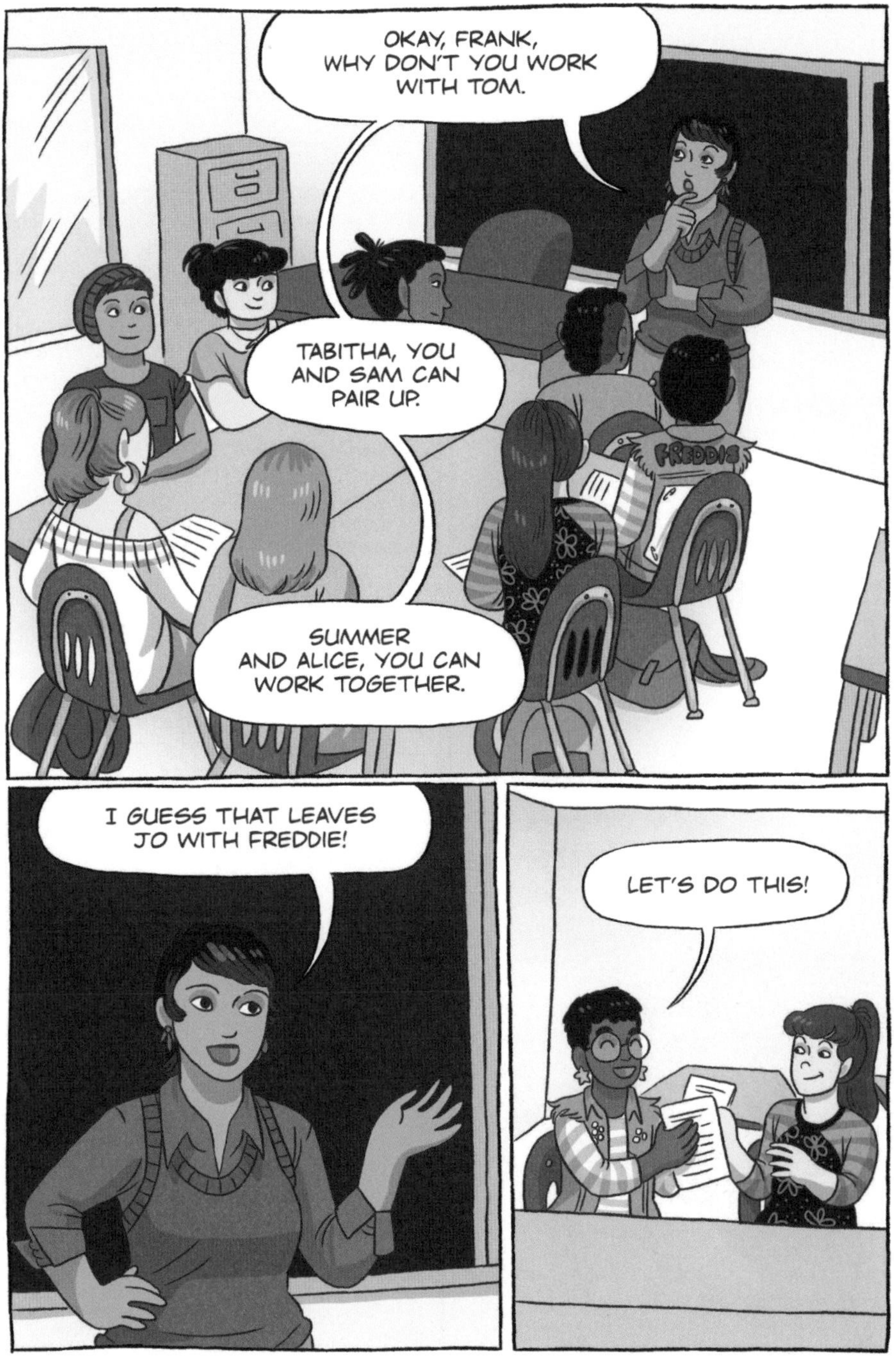
OKAY, FRANK, WHY DON'T YOU WORK WITH TOM.
TABITHA, YOU AND SAM CAN PAIR UP.
SUMMER AND ALICE, YOU CAN WORK TOGETHER.
FREDDIE
I GUESS THAT LEAVES JO WITH FREDDIE!
LET'S DO THIS!

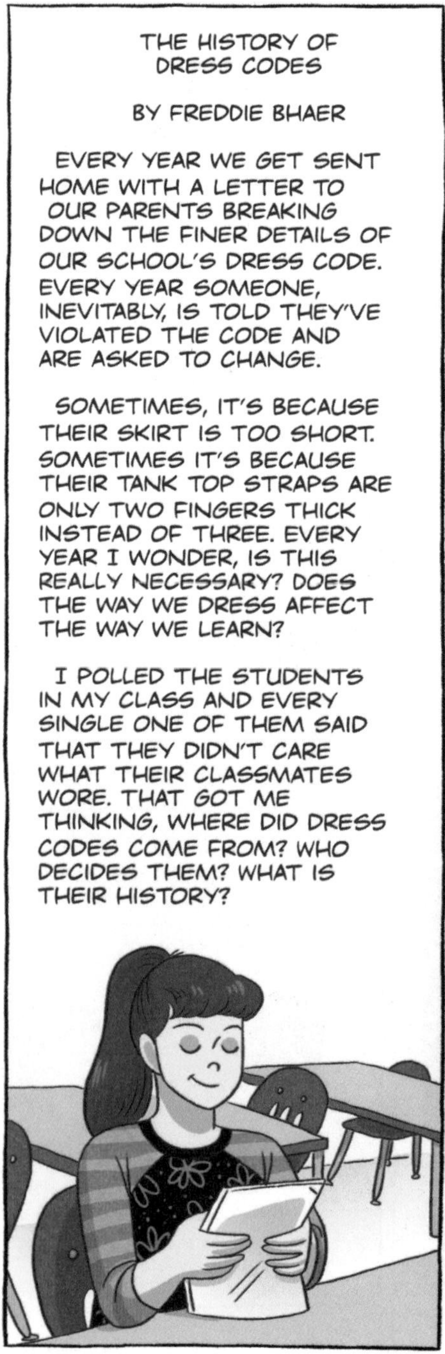
THE HISTORY OF DRESS CODES
BY FREDDIE BHAER
EVERY YEAR WE GET SENT HOME WITH A LETTER TO OUR PARENTS BREAKING DOWN THE FINER DETAILS OF OUR SCHOOL'S DRESS CODE. EVERY YEAR SOMEONE, INEVITABLY, IS TOLD THEY'VE VIOLATED THE CODE AND ARE ASKED TO CHANGE.
SOMETIMES, IT'S BECAUSE THEIR SKIRT IS TOO SHORT. SOMETIMES IT'S BECAUSE THEIR TANK TOP STRAPS ARE ONLY TWO FINGERS THICK INSTEAD OF THREE. EVERY YEAR I WONDER, IS THIS REALLY NECESSARY? DOES THE WAY WE DRESS AFFECT THE WAY WE LEARN?
I POLLED THE STUDENTS IN MY CLASS AND EVERY SINGLE ONE OF THEM SAID THAT THEY DIDN'T CARE WHAT THEIR CLASSMATES WORE. THAT GOT ME THINKING, WHERE DID DRESS CODES COME FROM? WHO DECIDES THEM? WHAT IS THEIR HISTORY?

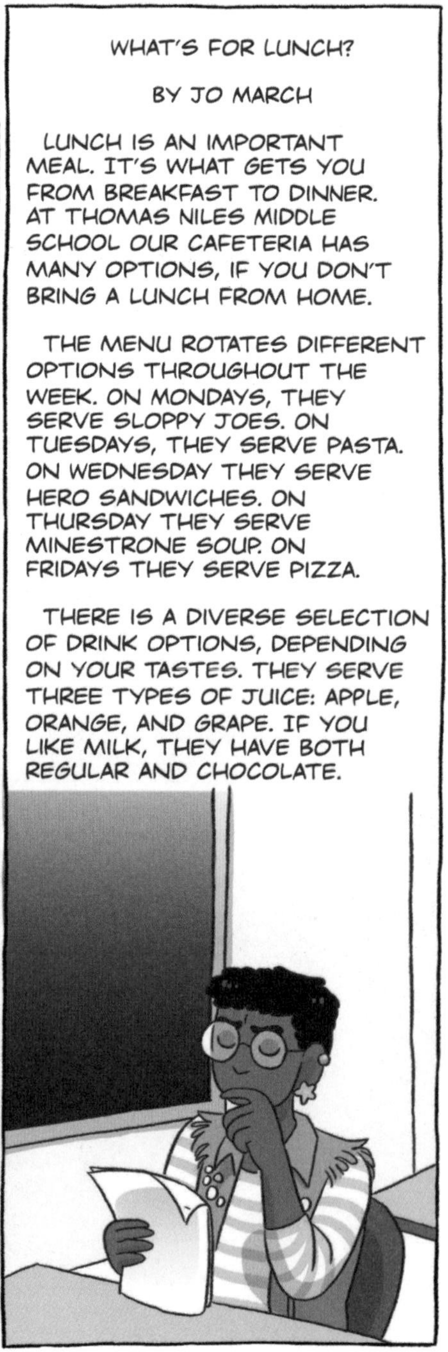
WHAT'S FOR LUNCH?
BY JO MARCH
LUNCH IS AN IMPORTANT MEAL. IT'S WHAT GETS YOU FROM BREAKFAST TO DINNER. AT THOMAS NILES MIDDLE SCHOOL OUR CAFETERIA HAS MANY OPTIONS, IF YOU DON'T BRING A LUNCH FROM HOME.
THE MENU ROTATES DIFFERENT OPTIONS THROUGHOUT THE WEEK. ON MONDAYS, THEY SERVE SLOPPY JOES. ON TUESDAYS, THEY SERVE PASTA. ON WEDNESDAY THEY SERVE HERO SANDWICHES. ON THURSDAY THEY SERVE MINESTRONE SOUP. ON FRIDAYS THEY SERVE PIZZA.
THERE IS A DIVERSE SELECTION OF DRINK OPTIONS, DEPENDING ON YOUR TASTES. THEY SERVE THREE TYPES OF JUICE: APPLE, ORANGE, AND GRAPE. IF YOU LIKE MILK, THEY HAVE BOTH REGULAR AND CHOCOLATE.

YOU DONE?

YEAH.

YOUR ARTICLE WAS SO INTERESTING, FREDDIE! I HAD NO IDEA SCHOOL DRESS CODES STARTED AS A REACTION AGAINST PROTESTS OF THE VIETNAM WAR.

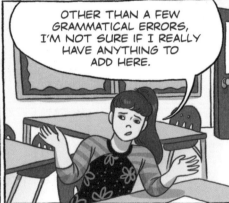

OTHER THAN A FEW GRAMMATICAL ERRORS, I'M NOT SURE IF I REALLY HAVE ANYTHING TO ADD HERE.

THANKS! DRESS CODES SEEMED LIKE A TOTALLY BORING TOPIC, BUT ONCE I STARTED RESEARCHING THEIR HISTORY, I WAS HOOKED.

I WISH I'D SEEN YOUR ARTICLE BEFORE WRITING MINE.

TO BE HONEST, IT WAS HARD TO FIND SOMETHING INTERESTING ABOUT SCHOOL LUNCHES. THIS ISN'T THE TYPE OF WRITING I USUALLY DO.

WHAT'S YOUR USUAL TYPE OF WRITING?

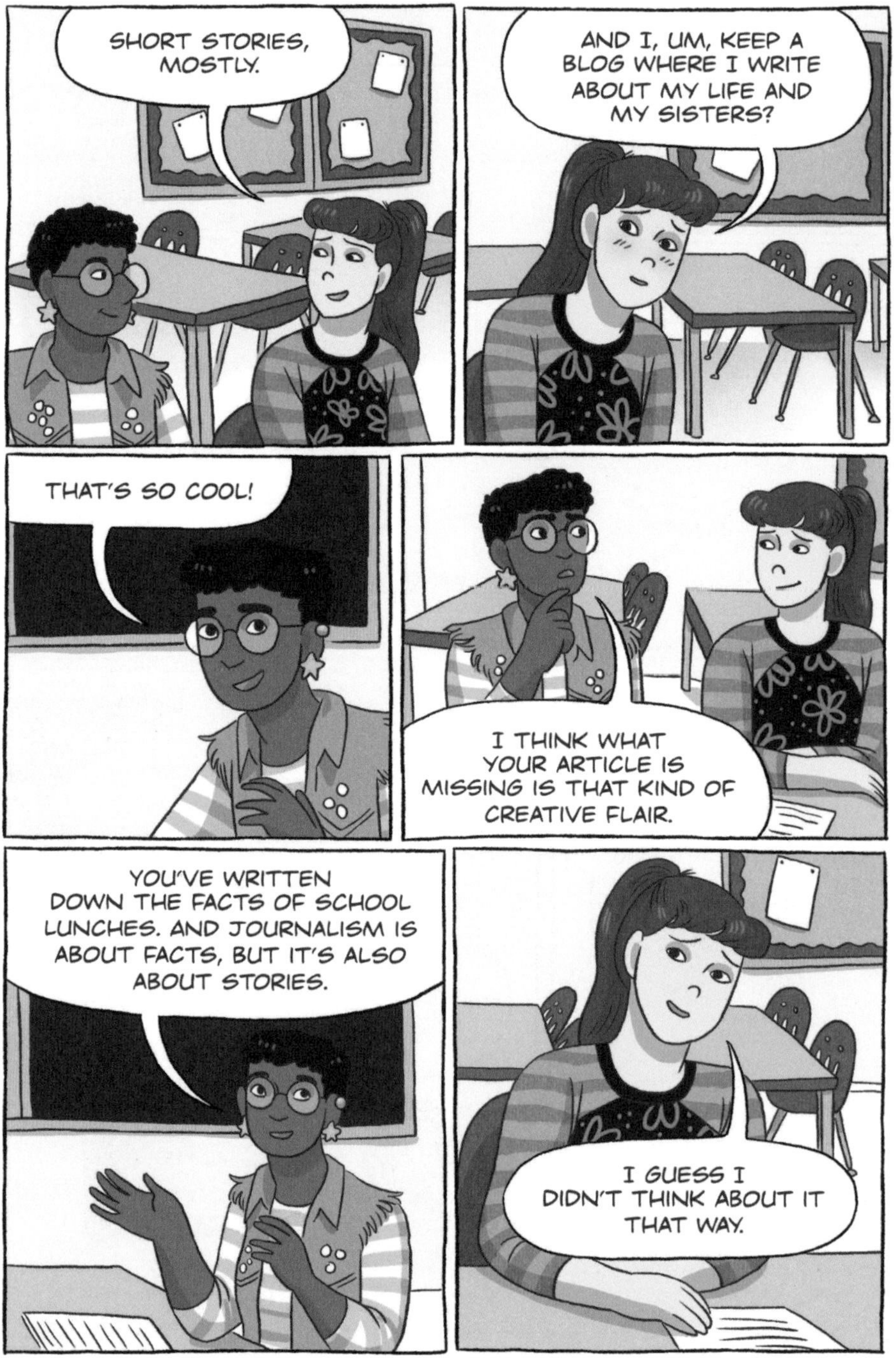
SHORT STORIES, MOSTLY.
AND I, UM, KEEP A BLOG WHERE I WRITE ABOUT MY LIFE AND MY SISTERS?
THAT'S SO COOL!
I THINK WHAT YOUR ARTICLE IS MISSING IS THAT KIND OF CREATIVE FLAIR.
YOU'VE WRITTEN DOWN THE FACTS OF SCHOOL LUNCHES. AND JOURNALISM IS ABOUT FACTS, BUT IT'S ALSO ABOUT STORIES.
I GUESS I DIDN'T THINK ABOUT IT THAT WAY.

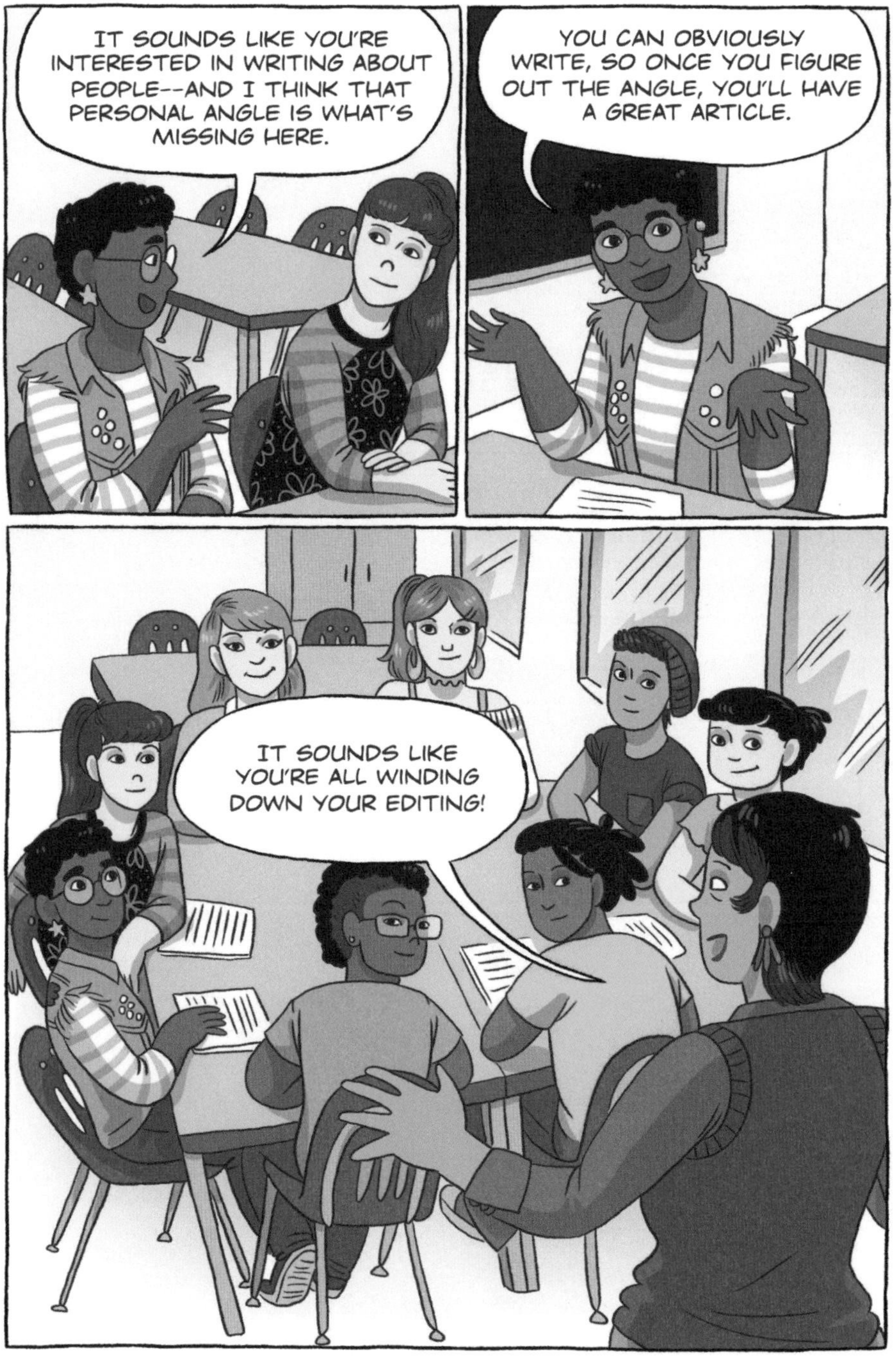
IT SOUNDS LIKE YOU'RE INTERESTED IN WRITING ABOUT PEOPLE--AND I THINK THAT PERSONAL ANGLE IS WHAT'S MISSING HERE.
YOU CAN OBVIOUSLY WRITE, SO ONCE YOU FIGURE OUT THE ANGLE, YOU'LL HAVE A GREAT ARTICLE.
IT SOUNDS LIKE YOU'RE ALL WINDING DOWN YOUR EDITING!

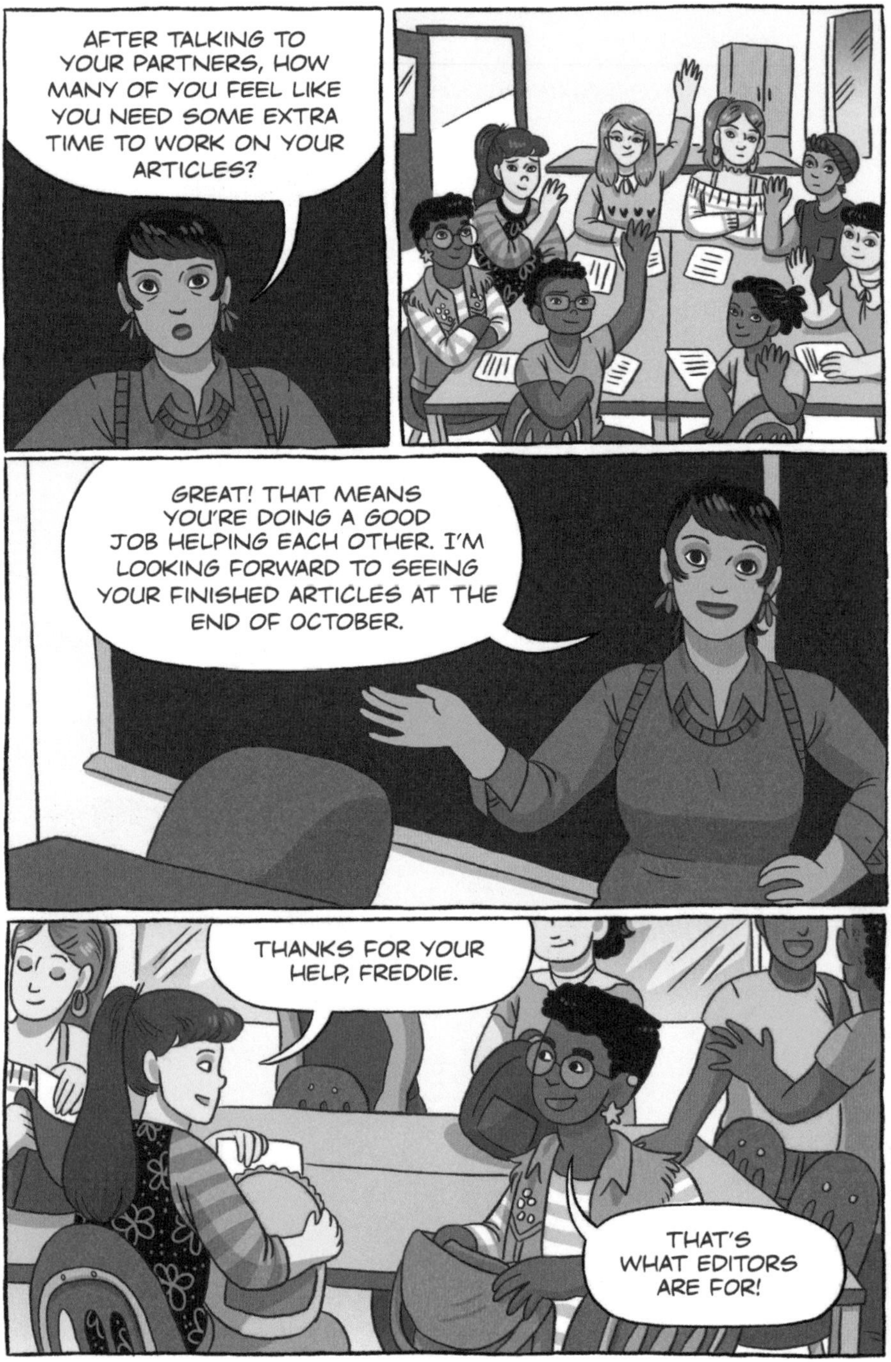
AFTER TALKING TO YOUR PARTNERS, HOW MANY OF YOU FEEL LIKE YOU NEED SOME EXTRA TIME TO WORK ON YOUR ARTICLES?
GREAT! THAT MEANS YOU'RE DOING A GOOD JOB HELPING EACH OTHER. I'M LOOKING FORWARD TO SEEING YOUR FINISHED ARTICLES AT THE END OF OCTOBER.
THANKS FOR YOUR HELP, FREDDIE.
THAT'S WHAT EDITORS ARE FOR!

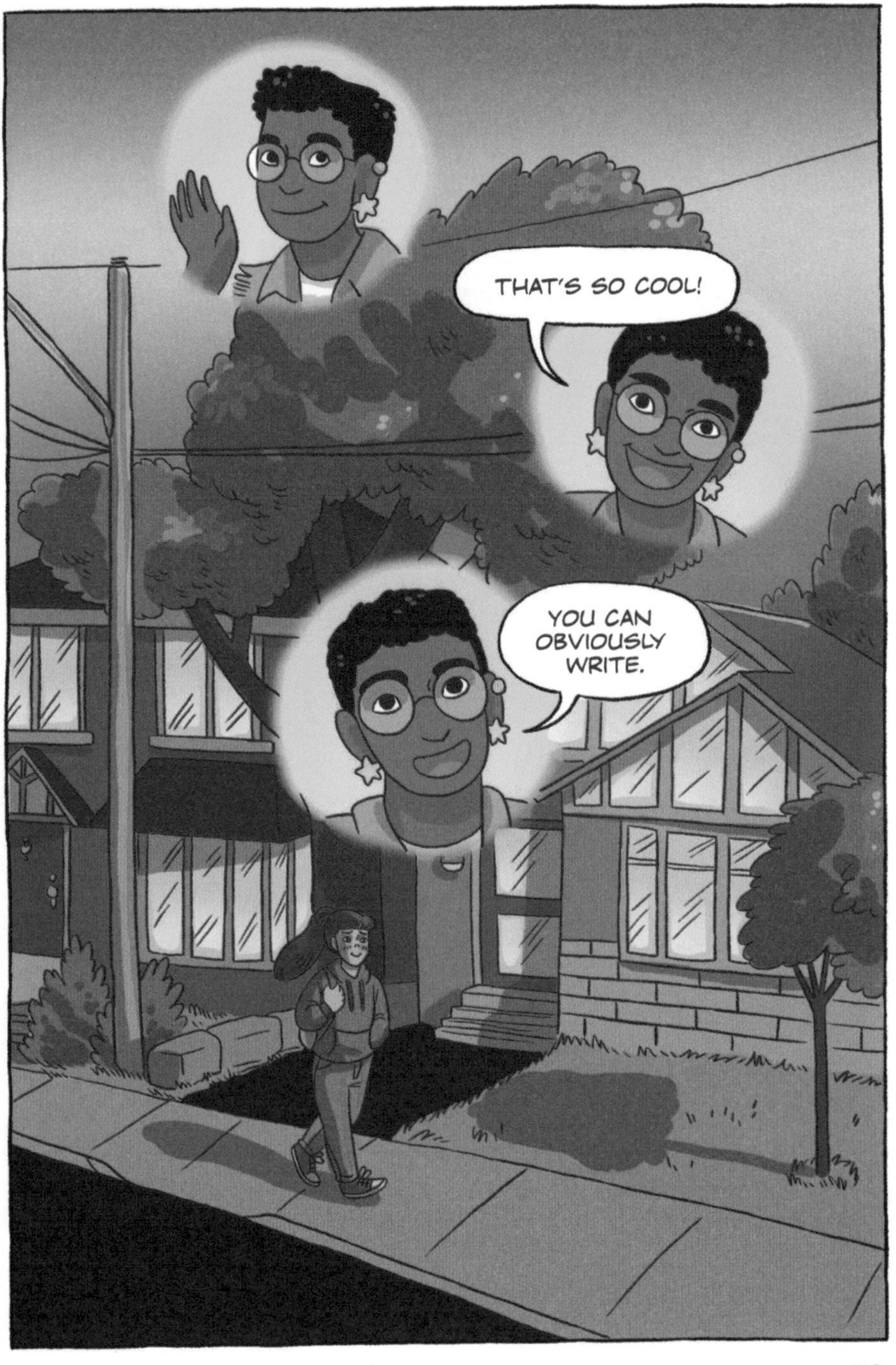
THAT'S SO COOL!
YOU CAN OBVIOUSLY WRITE.

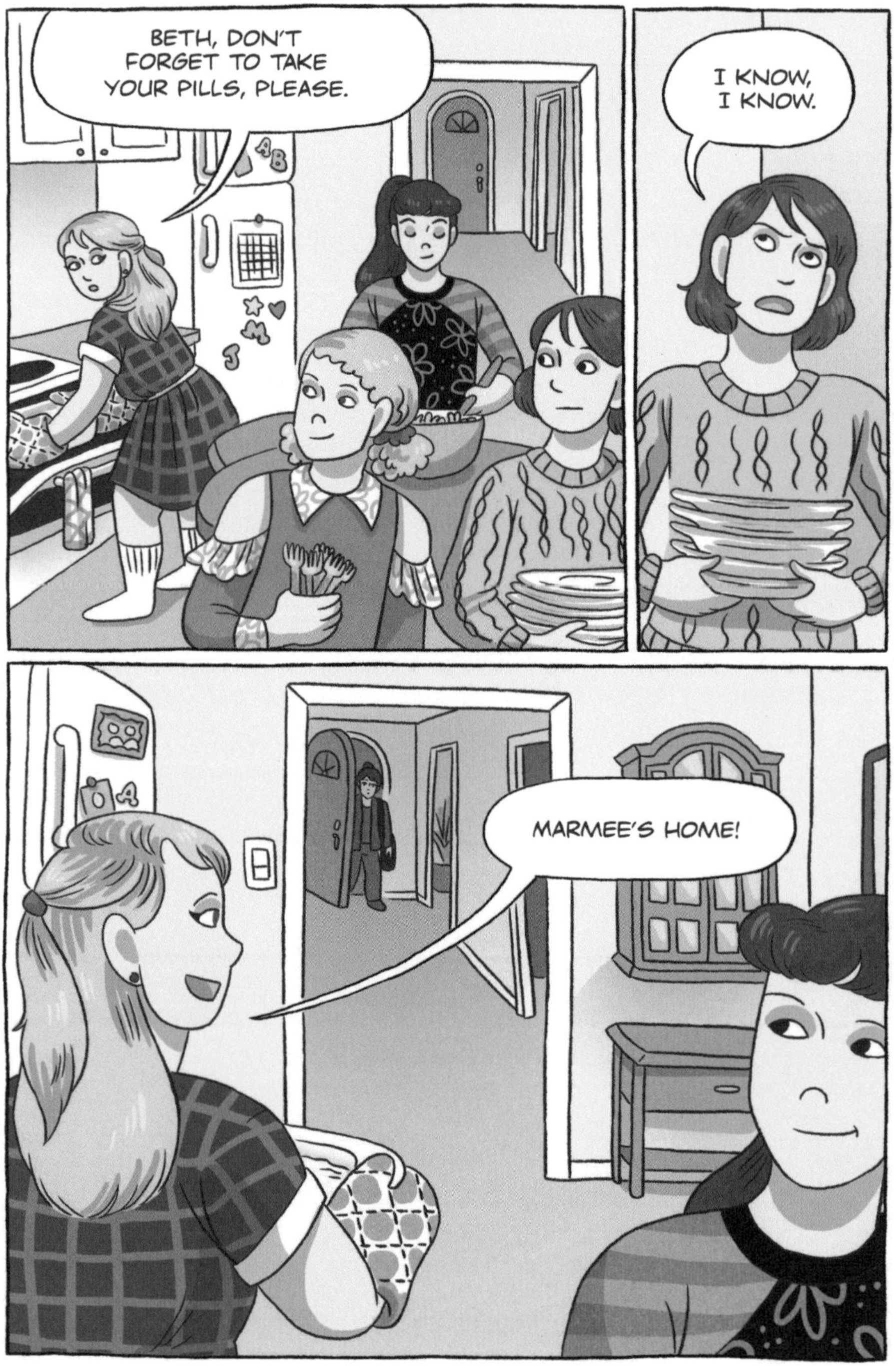
BETH, DON'T FORGET TO TAKE YOUR PILLS, PLEASE.
I KNOW, I KNOW.
MARMEE'S HOME!

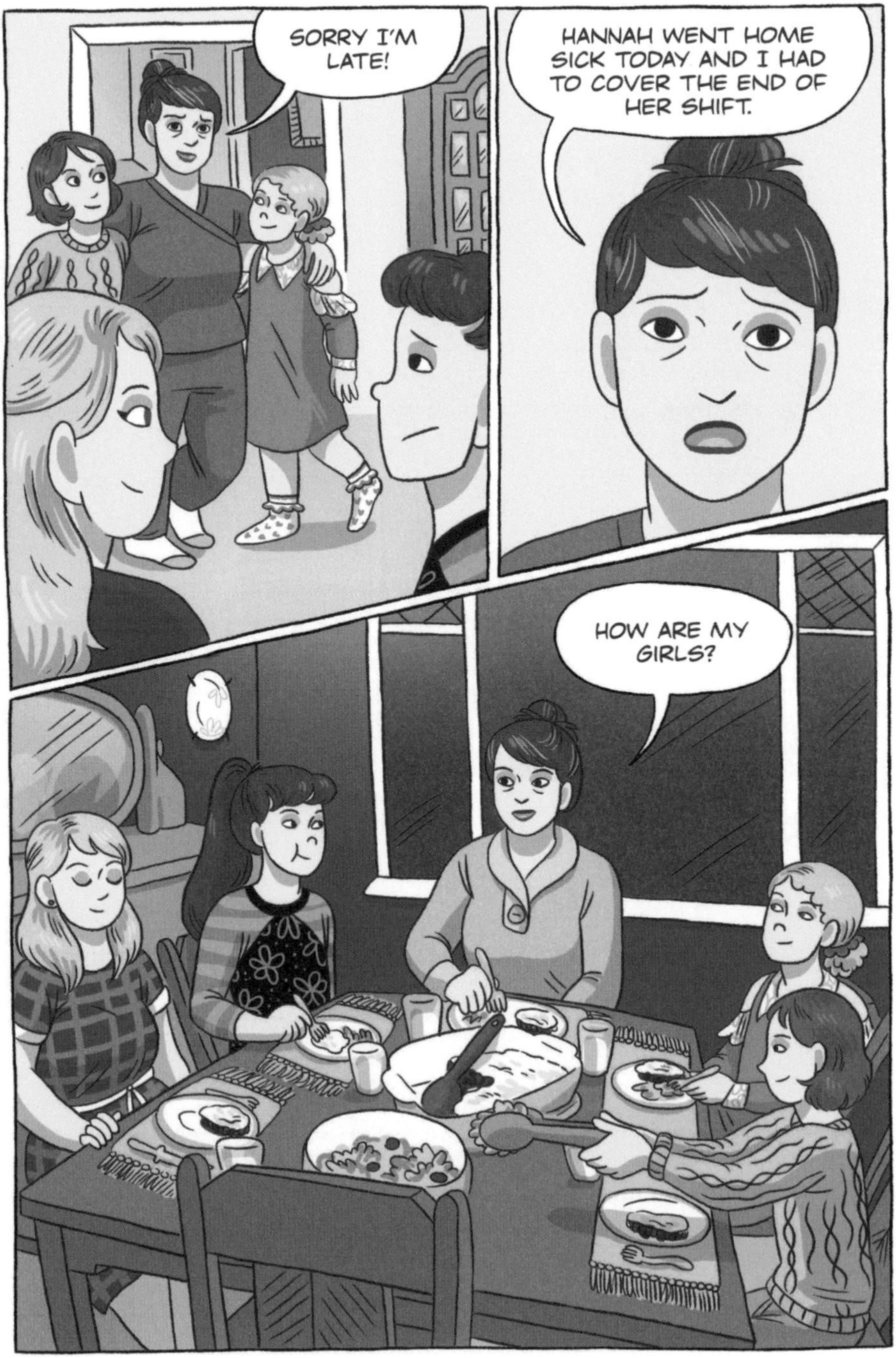
SORRY I'M LATE!
HANNAH WENT HOME SICK TODAY AND I HAD TO COVER THE END OF HER SHIFT.
HOW ARE MY GIRLS?

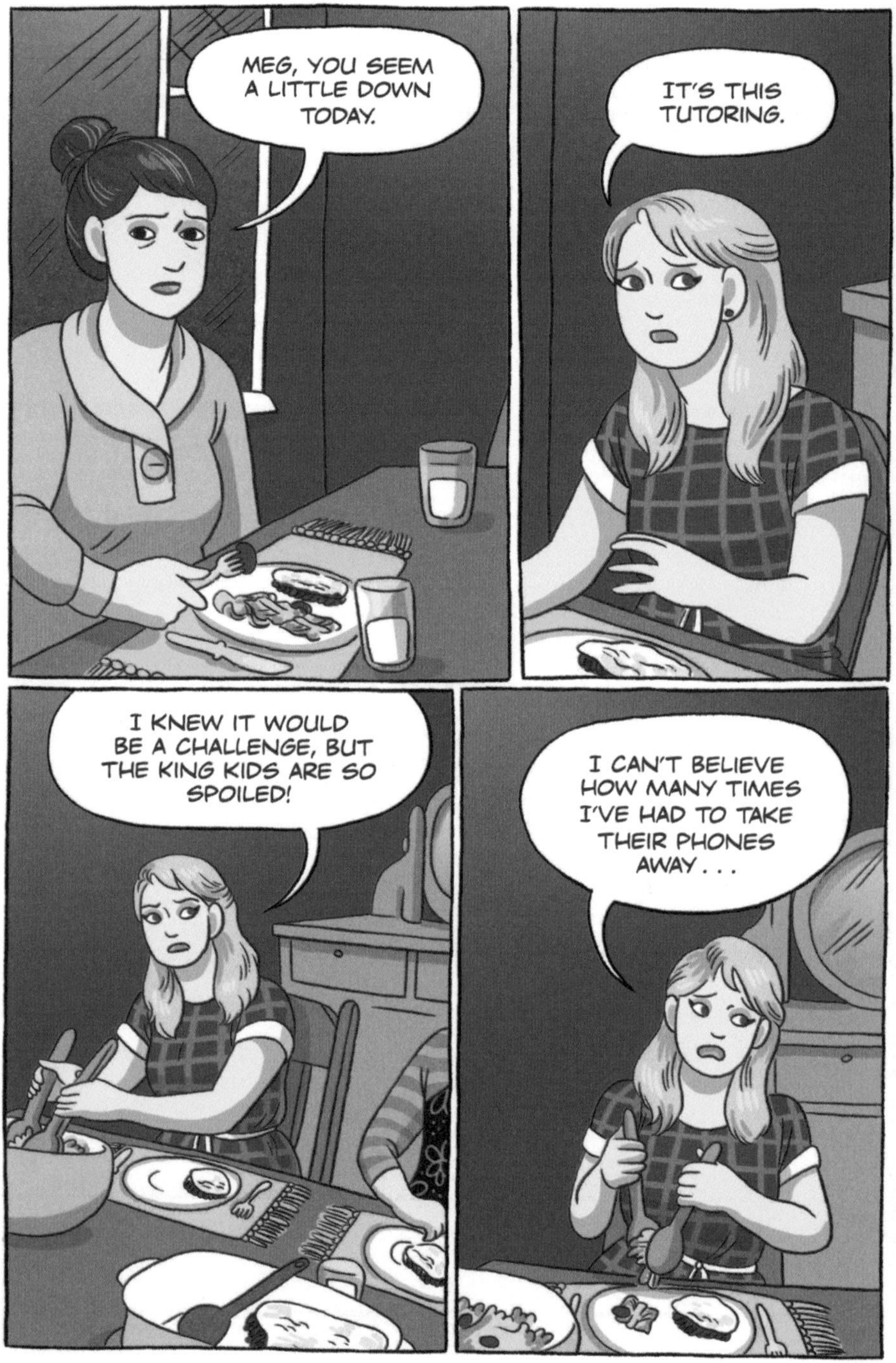
MEG, YOU SEEM A LITTLE DOWN TODAY.
IT'S THIS TUTORING.
I KNEW IT WOULD BE A CHALLENGE, BUT THE KING KIDS ARE SO SPOILED!
I CAN'T BELIEVE HOW MANY TIMES I'VE HAD TO TAKE THEIR PHONES AWAY . . .

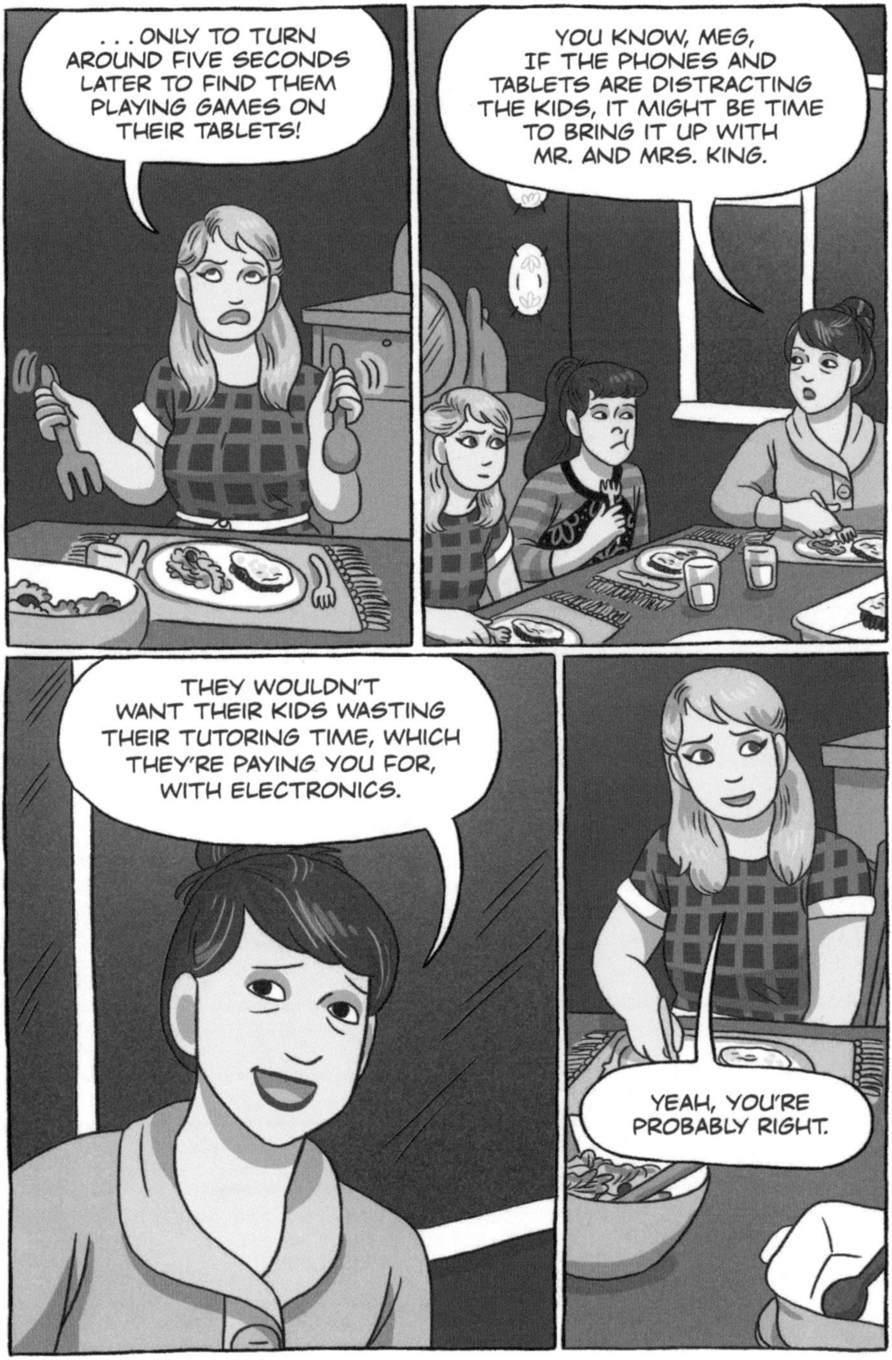
. . . ONLY TO TURN AROUND FIVE SECONDS LATER TO FIND THEM PLAYING GAMES ON THEIR TABLETS!
YOU KNOW, MEG, IF THE PHONES AND TABLETS ARE DISTRACTING THE KIDS, IT MIGHT BE TIME TO BRING IT UP WITH MR. AND MRS. KING.
THEY WOULDN'T WANT THEIR KIDS WASTING THEIR TUTORING TIME, WHICH THEY'RE PAYING YOU FOR, WITH ELECTRONICS.
YEAH, YOU'RE PROBABLY RIGHT.

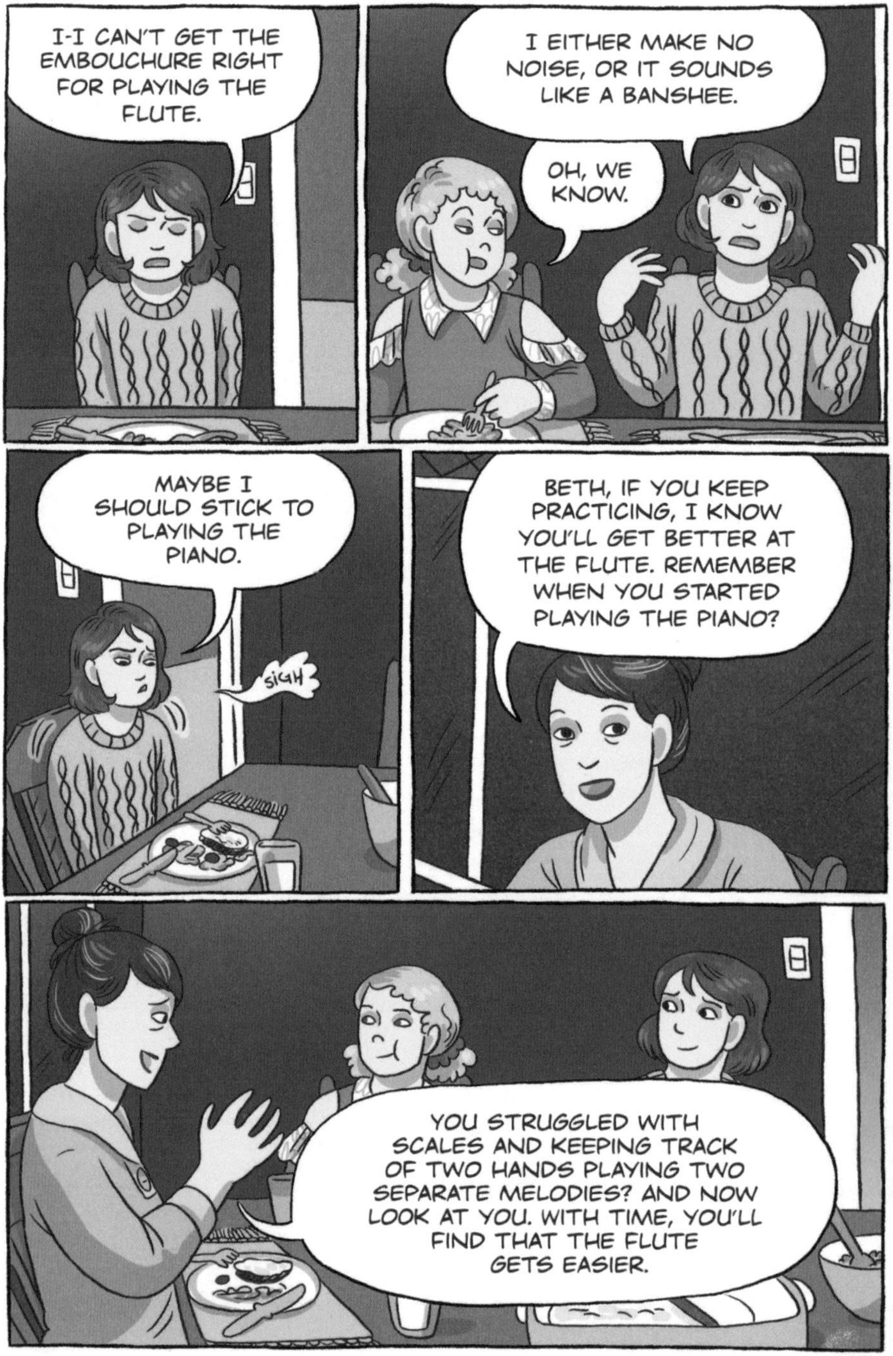
I-I CAN'T GET THE EMBOUCHURE RIGHT FOR PLAYING THE FLUTE.
I EITHER MAKE NO NOISE, OR IT SOUNDS LIKE A BANSHEE.
OH, WE KNOW.
MAYBE I SHOULD STICK TO PLAYING THE PIANO.
SIGH
BETH, IF YOU KEEP PRACTICING, I KNOW YOU'LL GET BETTER AT THE FLUTE. REMEMBER WHEN YOU STARTED PLAYING THE PIANO?
YOU STRUGGLED WITH SCALES AND KEEPING TRACK OF TWO HANDS PLAYING TWO SEPARATE MELODIES? AND NOW LOOK AT YOU. WITH TIME, YOU'LL FIND THAT THE FLUTE GETS EASIER.

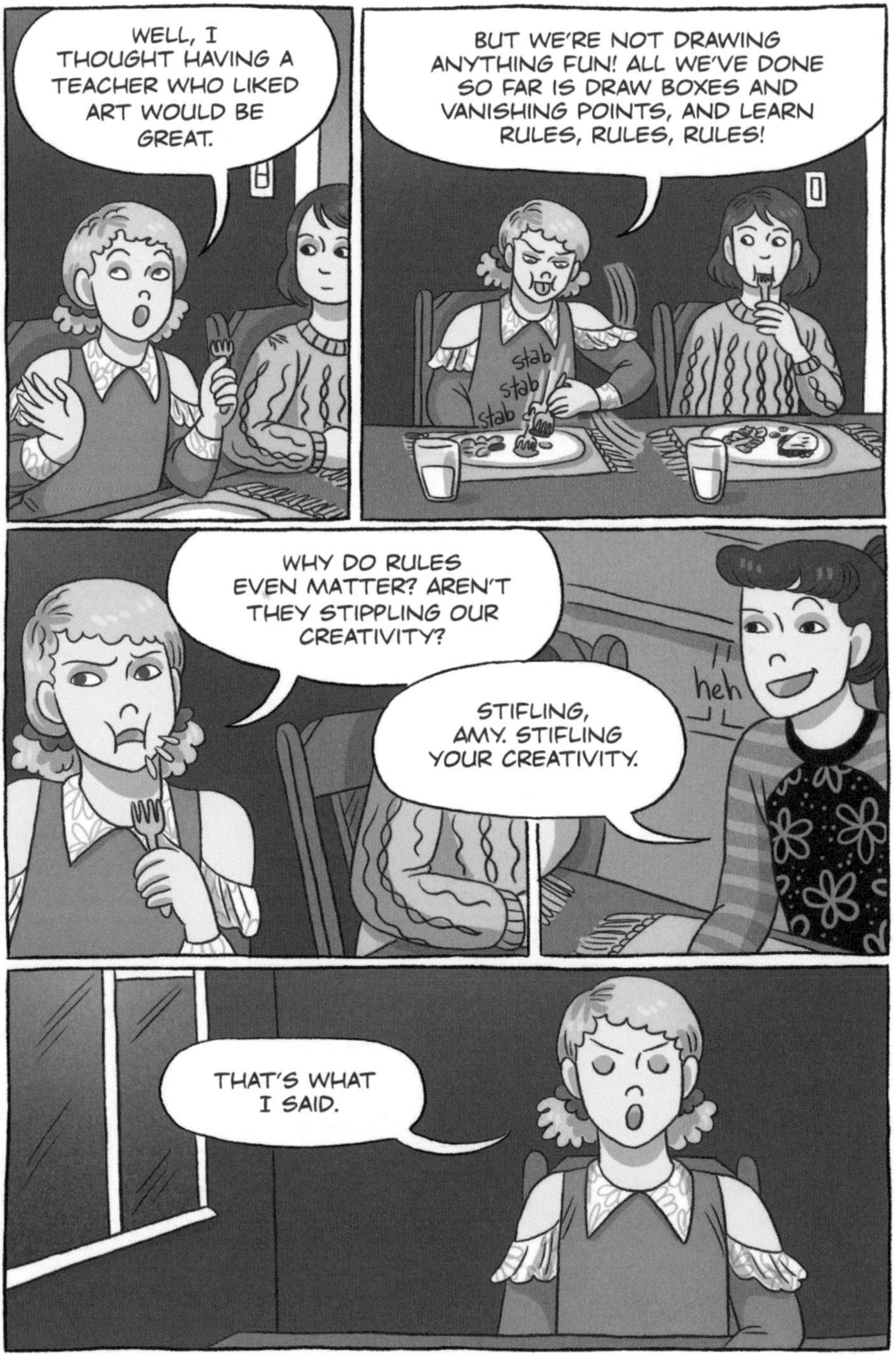
WELL, I THOUGHT HAVING A TEACHER WHO LIKED ART WOULD BE GREAT.
BUT WE'RE NOT DRAWING ANYTHING FUN! ALL WE'VE DONE SO FAR IS DRAW BOXES AND VANISHING POINTS, AND LEARN RULES, RULES, RULES!
stab
stab
stab
WHY DO RULES EVEN MATTER? AREN'T THEY STIPPLING OUR CREATIVITY?
heh
STIFLING, AMY. STIFLING YOUR CREATIVITY.
THAT'S WHAT I SAID.

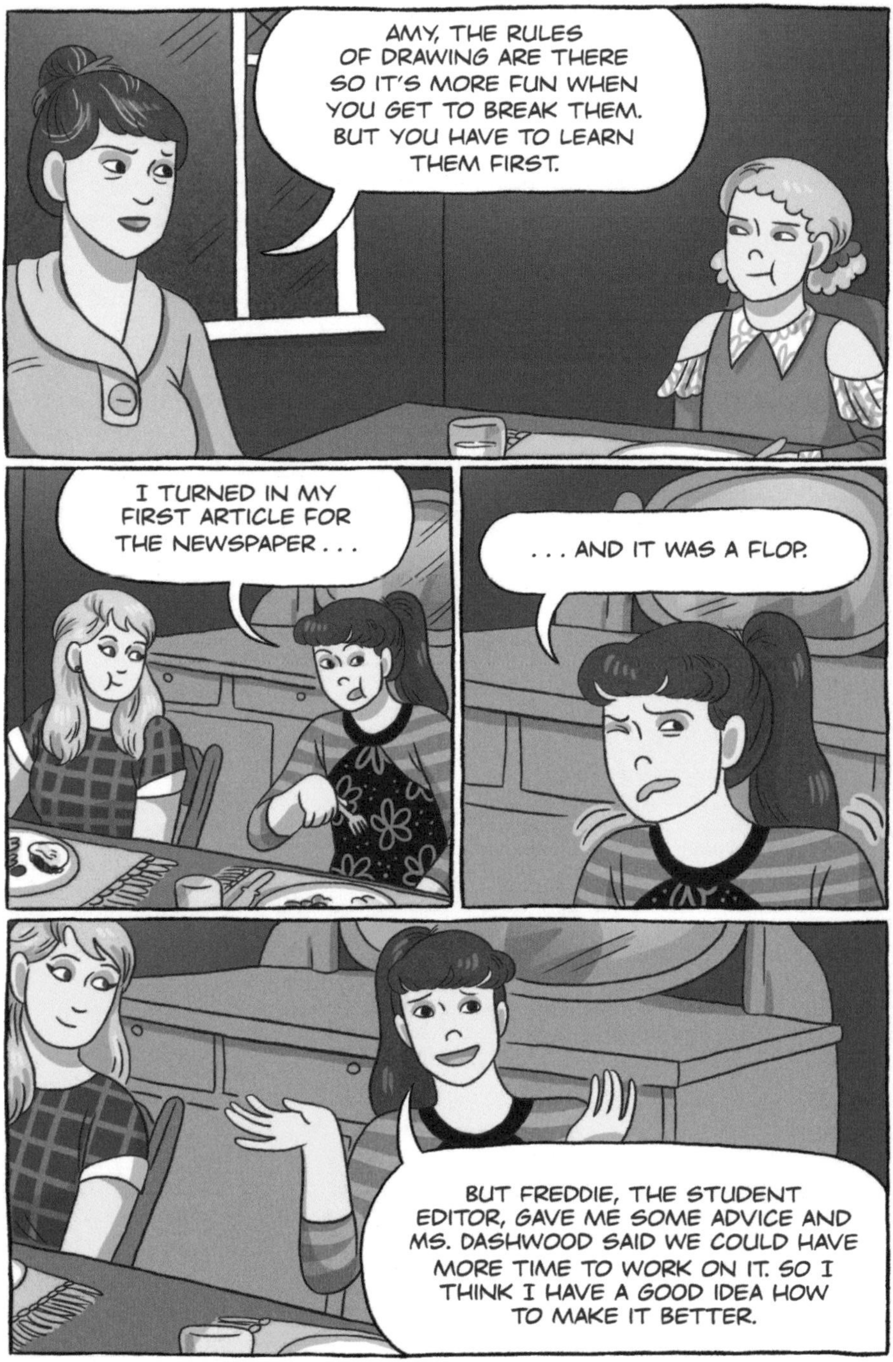
AMY, THE RULES OF DRAWING ARE THERE SO IT'S MORE FUN WHEN YOU GET TO BREAK THEM. BUT YOU HAVE TO LEARN THEM FIRST.
I TURNED IN MY FIRST ARTICLE FOR THE NEWSPAPER . . .
. . . AND IT WAS A FLOP.
BUT FREDDIE, THE STUDENT EDITOR, GAVE ME SOME ADVICE AND MS. DASHWOOD SAID WE COULD HAVE MORE TIME TO WORK ON IT. SO I THINK I HAVE A GOOD IDEA HOW TO MAKE IT BETTER.

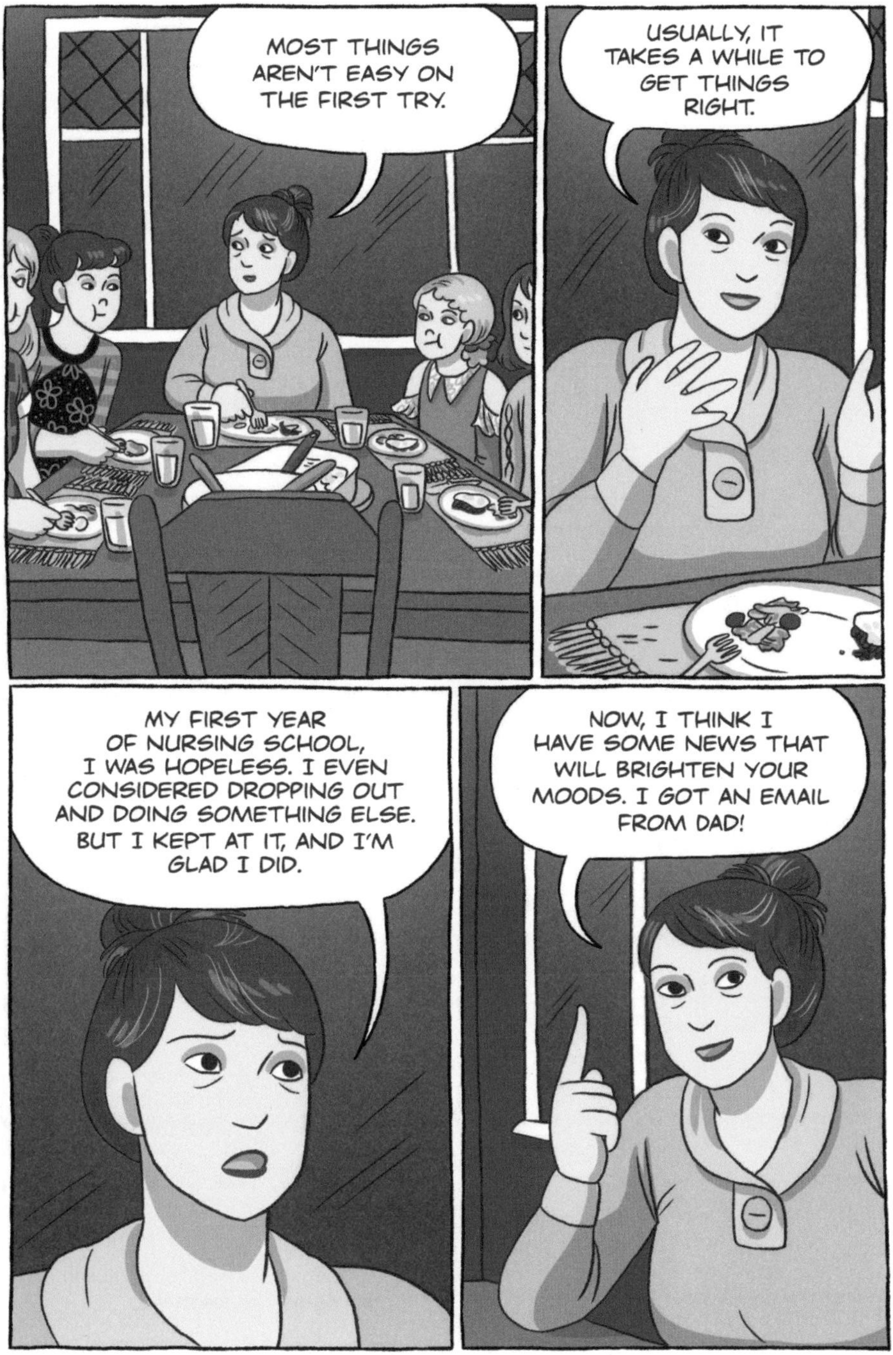
MOST THINGS AREN'T EASY ON THE FIRST TRY.
USUALLY, IT TAKES A WHILE TO GET THINGS RIGHT.
MY FIRST YEAR OF NURSING SCHOOL, I WAS HOPELESS. I EVEN CONSIDERED DROPPING OUT AND DOING SOMETHING ELSE. BUT I KEPT AT IT, AND I'M GLAD I DID.
NOW, I THINK I HAVE SOME NEWS THAT WILL BRIGHTEN YOUR MOODS. I GOT AN EMAIL FROM DAD!

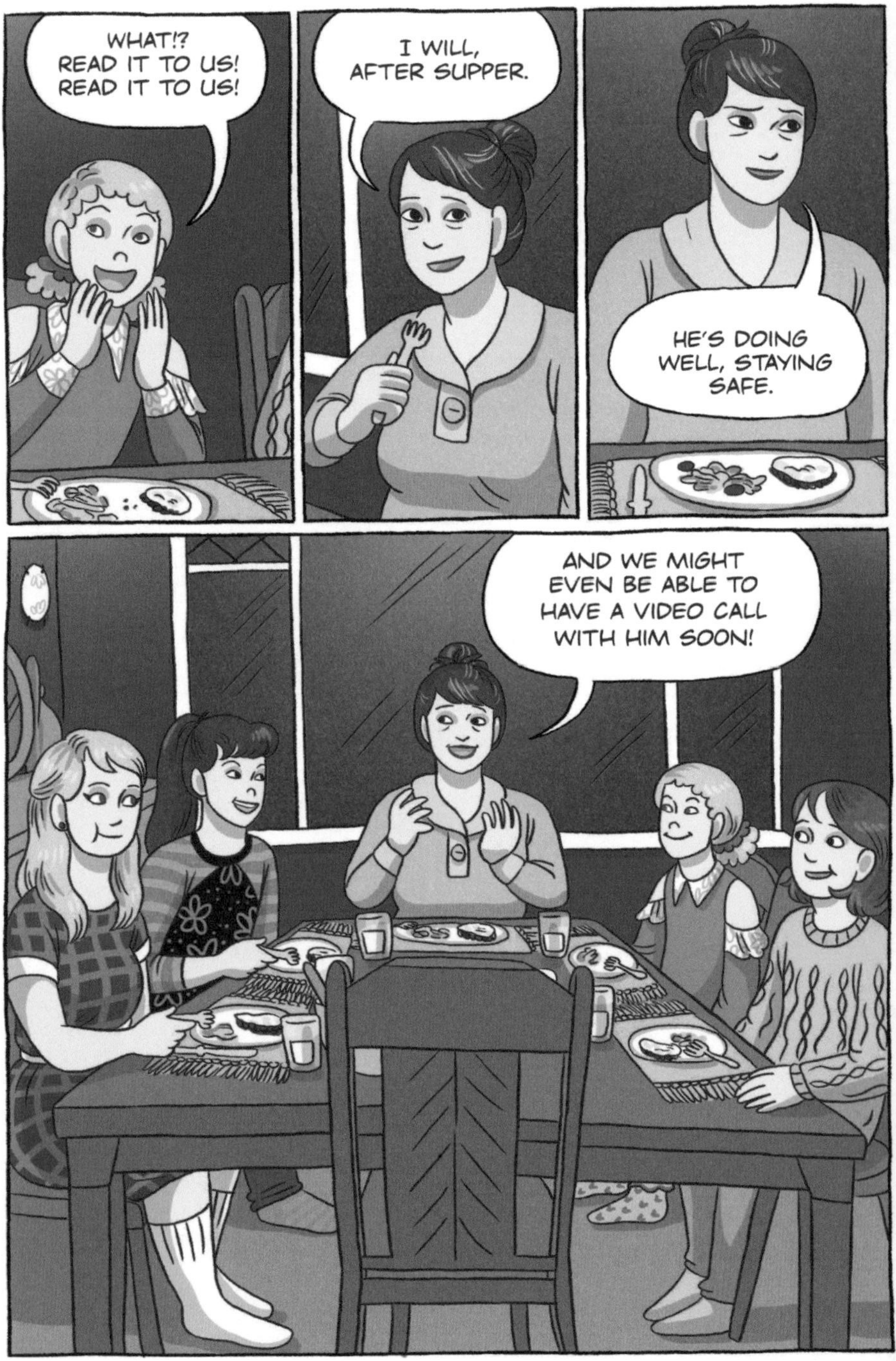
WHAT!? READ IT TO US! READ IT TO US!
I WILL, AFTER SUPPER.
HE'S DOING WELL, STAYING SAFE.
AND WE MIGHT EVEN BE ABLE TO HAVE A VIDEO CALL WITH HIM SOON!

CHAPTER 3

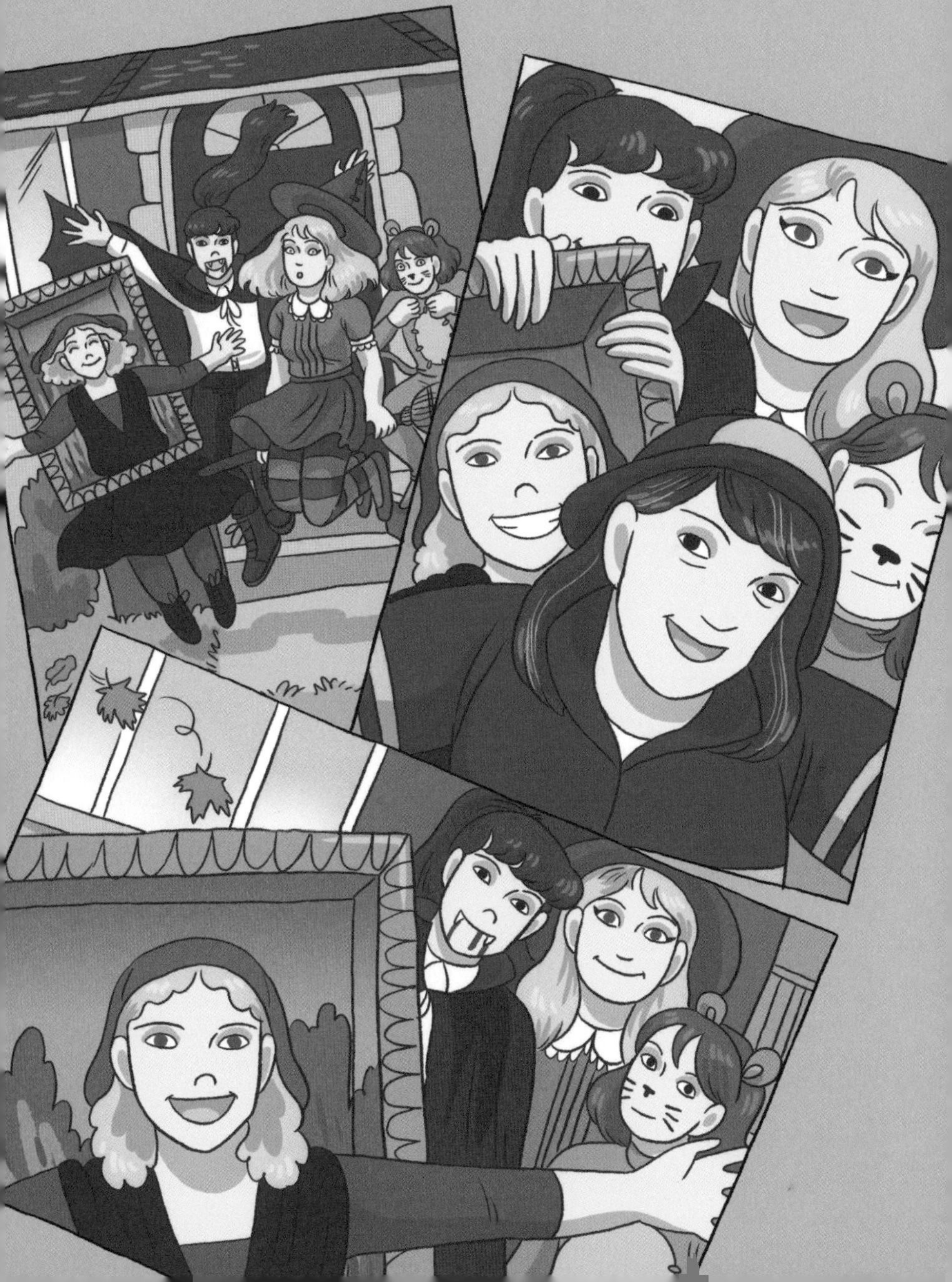

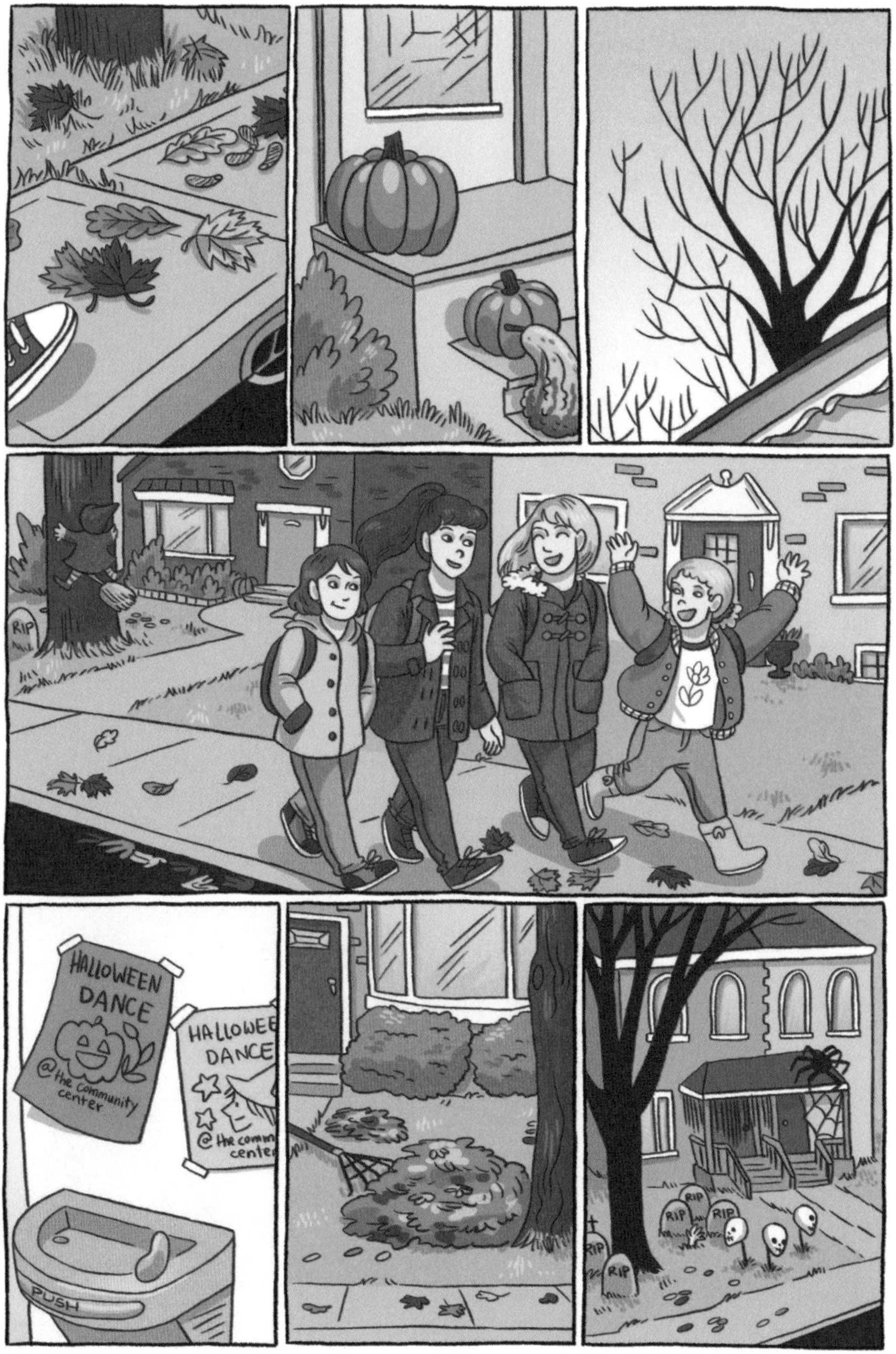
RIP
HALLOWEEN DANCE
@ the community center
HALLOWEE
DANCE
@ the comm
cente
PUSH
RIP
RIP
RIP
RIP
RIP

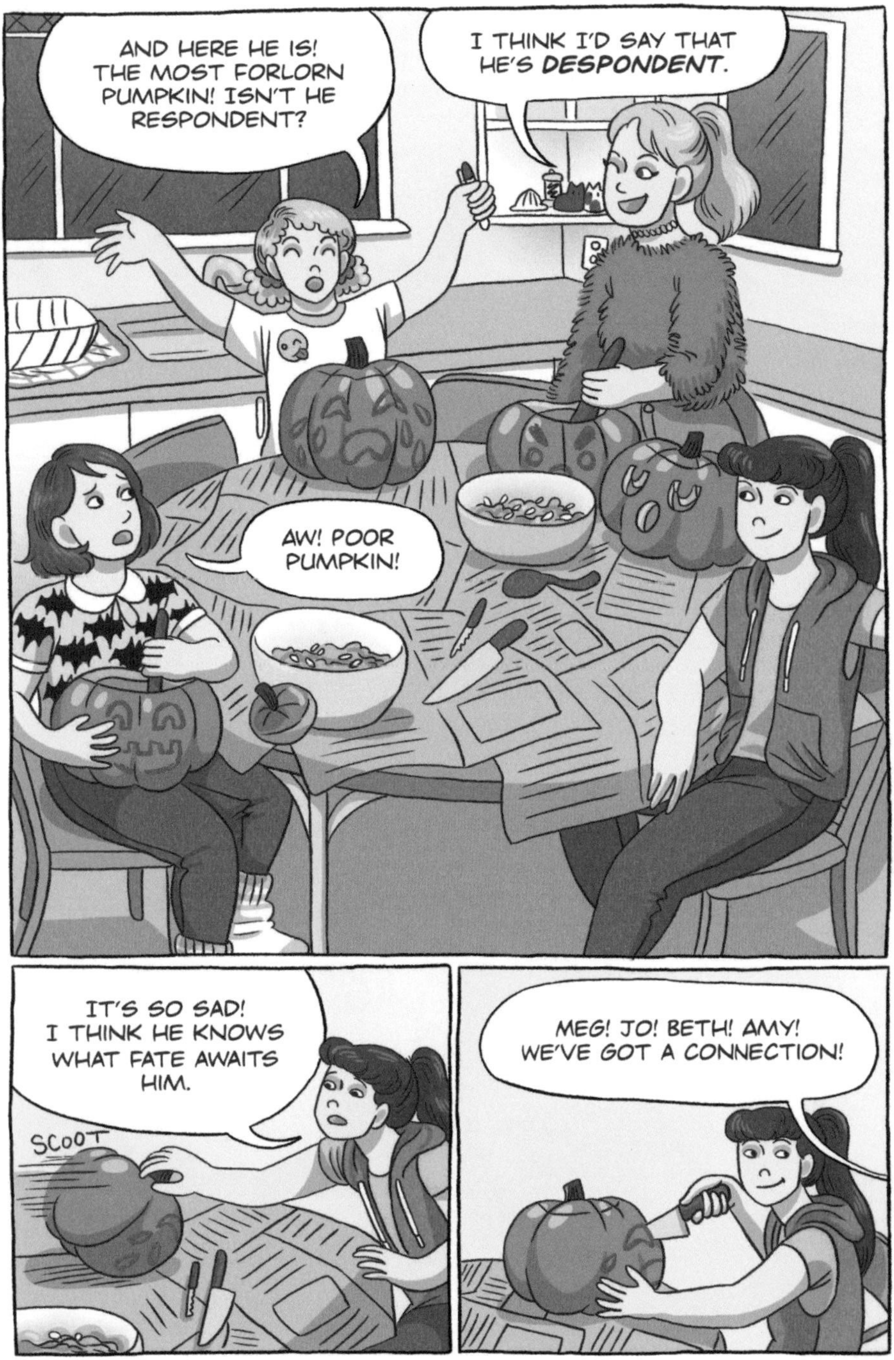
AND HERE HE IS! THE MOST FORLORN PUMPKIN! ISN'T HE RESPONDENT?
I THINK I'D SAY THAT HE'S **DESPONDENT**.
AW! POOR PUMPKIN!
IT'S SO SAD! I THINK HE KNOWS WHAT FATE AWAITS HIM.
SCOOT
MEG! JO! BETH! AMY! WE'VE GOT A CONNECTION!

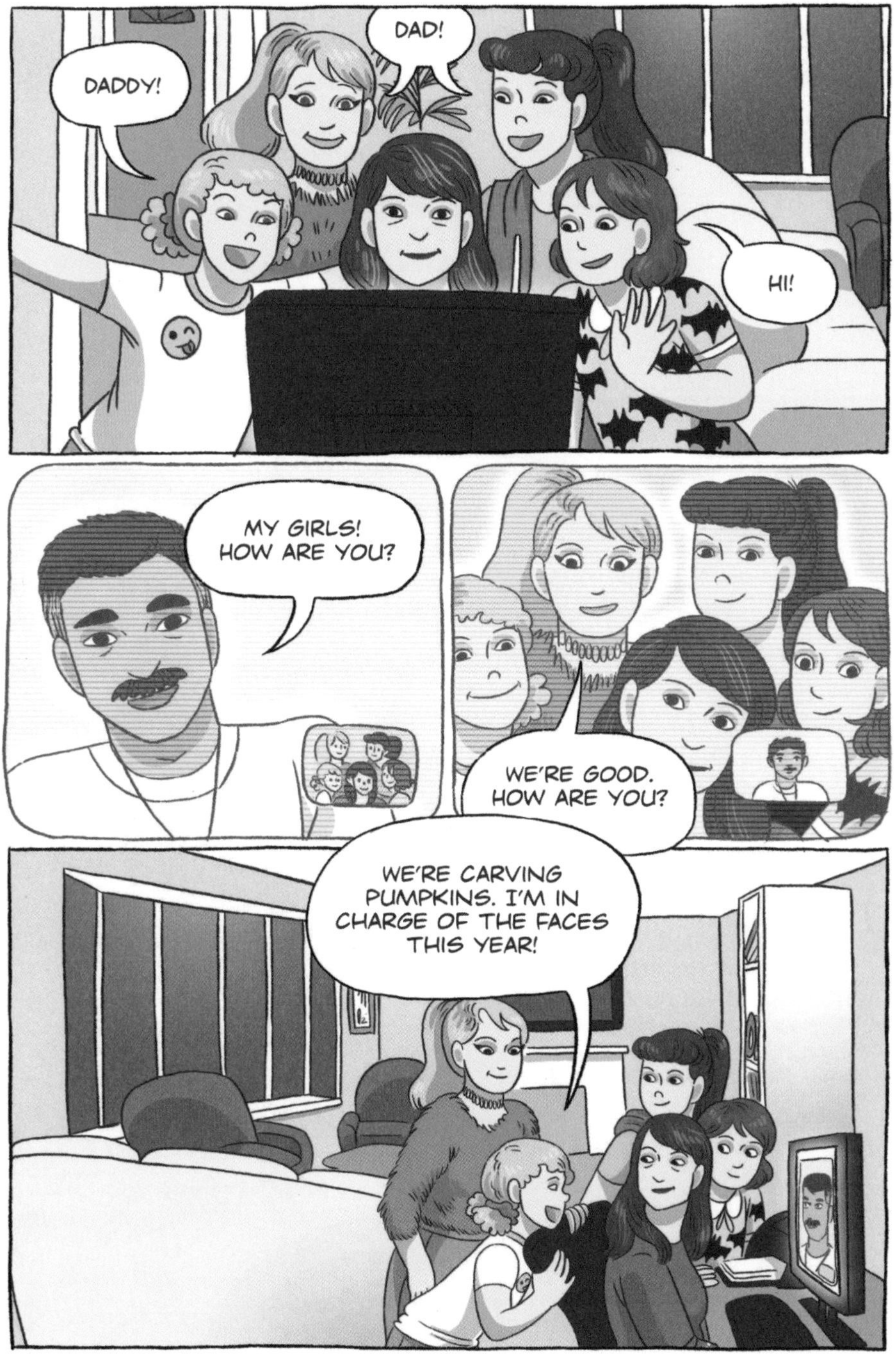
DADDY!
DAD!
HI!
MY GIRLS! HOW ARE YOU?
WE'RE GOOD. HOW ARE YOU?
WE'RE CARVING PUMPKINS. I'M IN CHARGE OF THE FACES THIS YEAR!

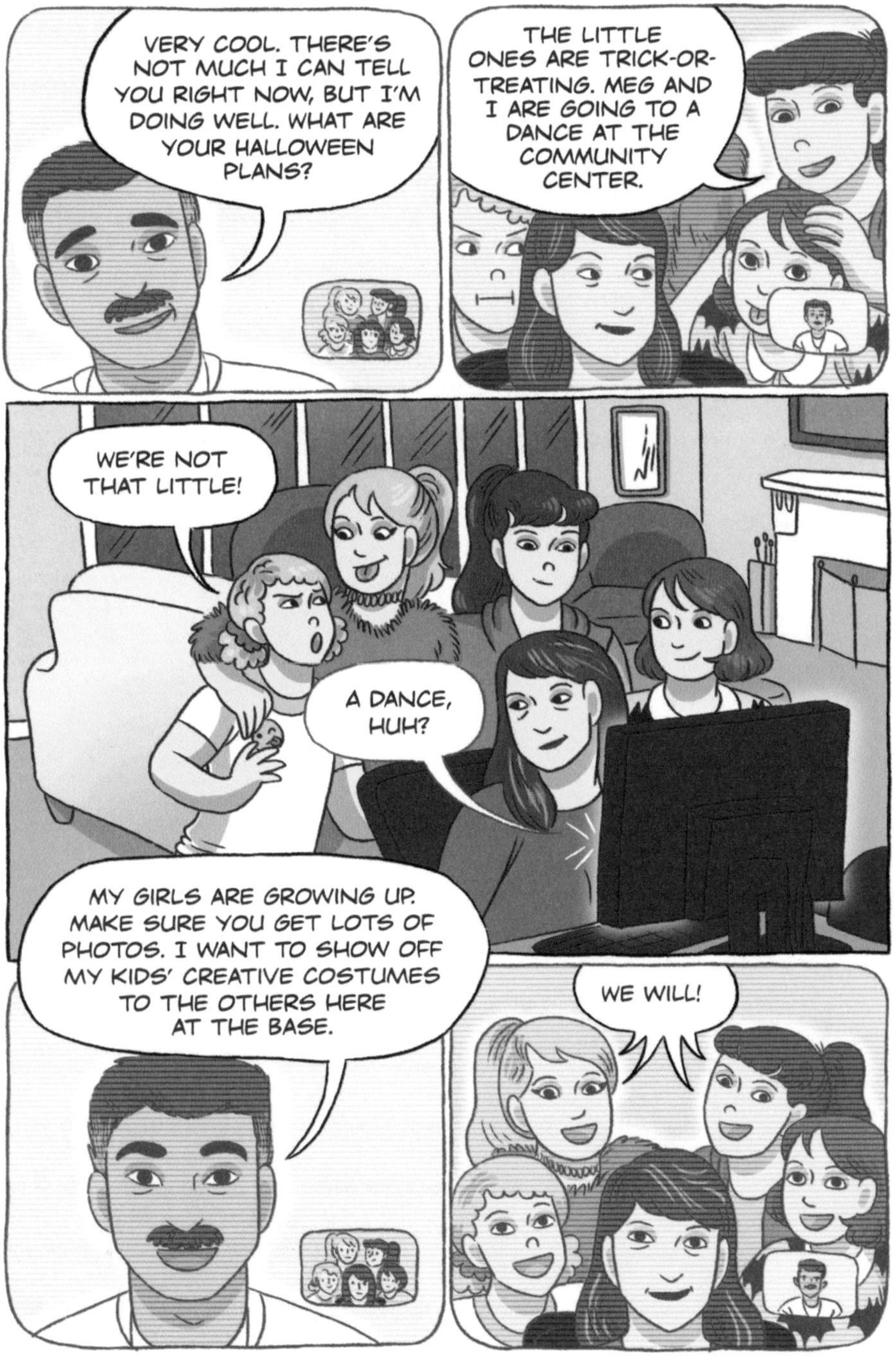
VERY COOL. THERE'S NOT MUCH I CAN TELL YOU RIGHT NOW, BUT I'M DOING WELL. WHAT ARE YOUR HALLOWEEN PLANS?
THE LITTLE ONES ARE TRICK-OR-TREATING. MEG AND I ARE GOING TO A DANCE AT THE COMMUNITY CENTER.
WE'RE NOT THAT LITTLE!
A DANCE, HUH?
MY GIRLS ARE GROWING UP. MAKE SURE YOU GET LOTS OF PHOTOS. I WANT TO SHOW OFF MY KIDS' CREATIVE COSTUMES TO THE OTHERS HERE AT THE BASE.
WE WILL!

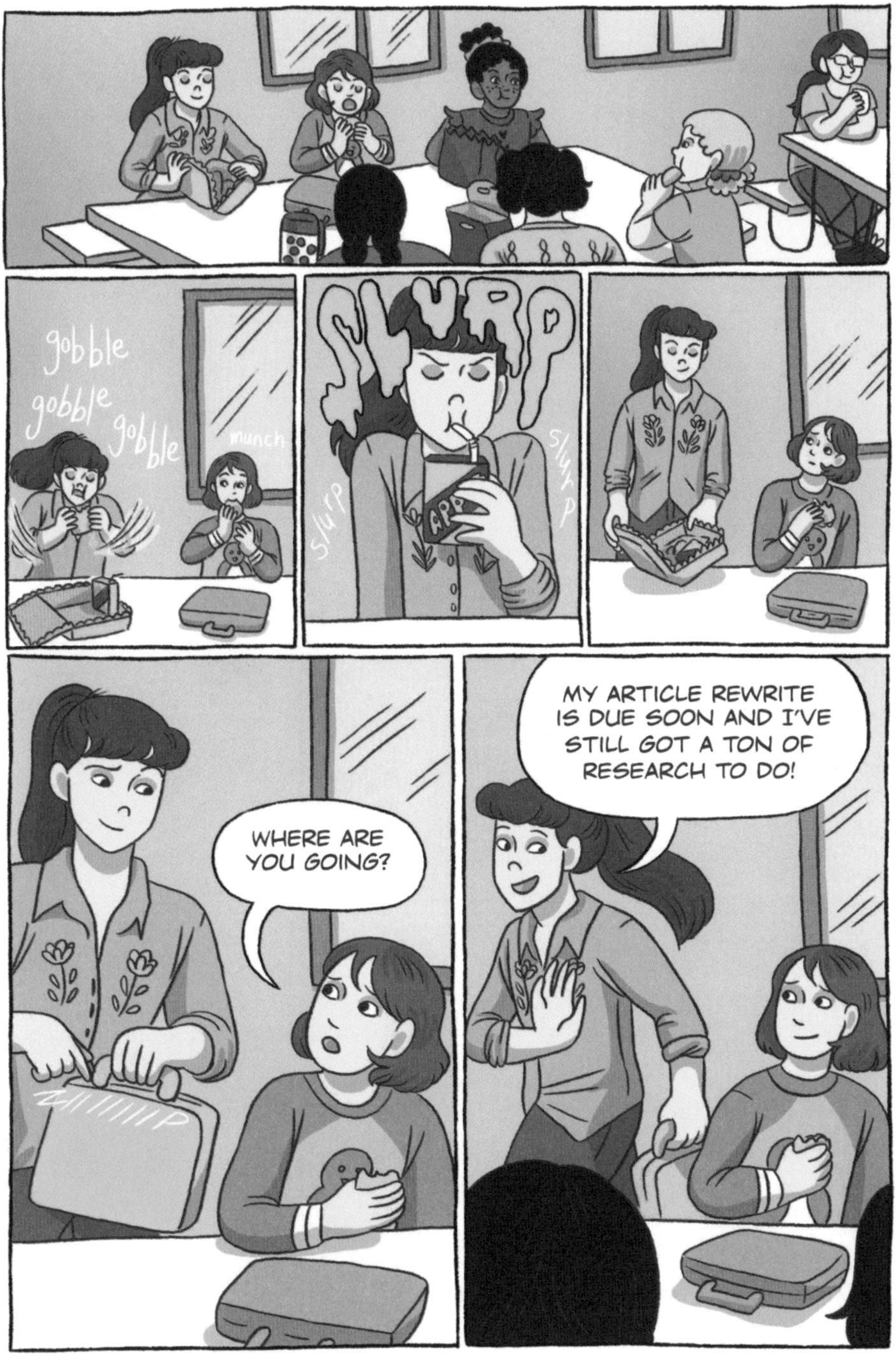
gobble
gobble
gobble
munch
SLURP
slurp
slurp
ZIIIIIIIP
WHERE ARE YOU GOING?
MY ARTICLE REWRITE IS DUE SOON AND I'VE STILL GOT A TON OF RESEARCH TO DO!

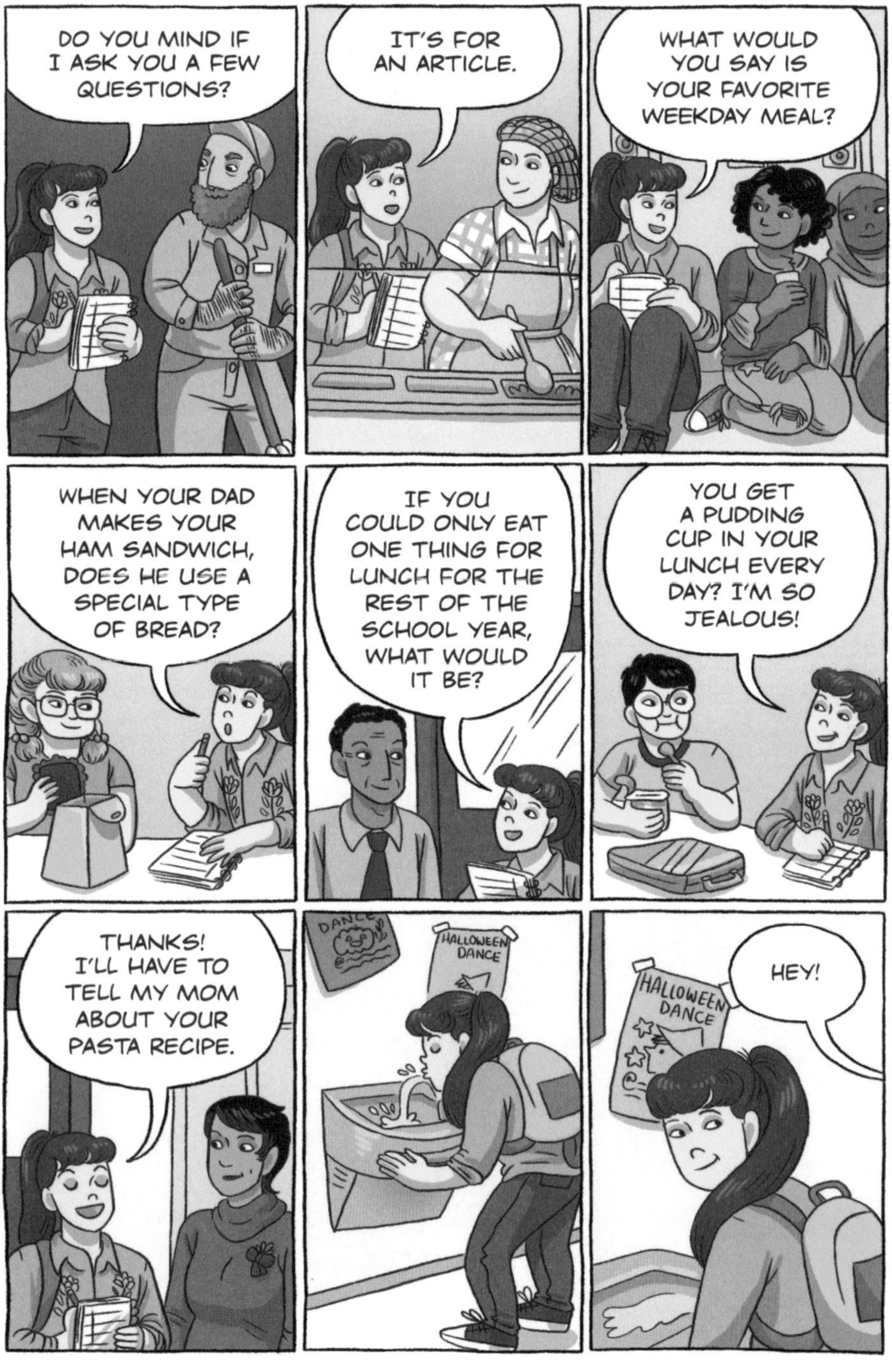
DO YOU MIND IF I ASK YOU A FEW QUESTIONS?
IT'S FOR AN ARTICLE.
WHAT WOULD YOU SAY IS YOUR FAVORITE WEEKDAY MEAL?
WHEN YOUR DAD MAKES YOUR HAM SANDWICH, DOES HE USE A SPECIAL TYPE OF BREAD?
IF YOU COULD ONLY EAT ONE THING FOR LUNCH FOR THE REST OF THE SCHOOL YEAR, WHAT WOULD IT BE?
YOU GET A PUDDING CUP IN YOUR LUNCH EVERY DAY? I'M SO JEALOUS!
THANKS! I'LL HAVE TO TELL MY MOM ABOUT YOUR PASTA RECIPE.
DANCE
HALLOWEEN DANCE
HALLOWEEN DANCE
HEY!

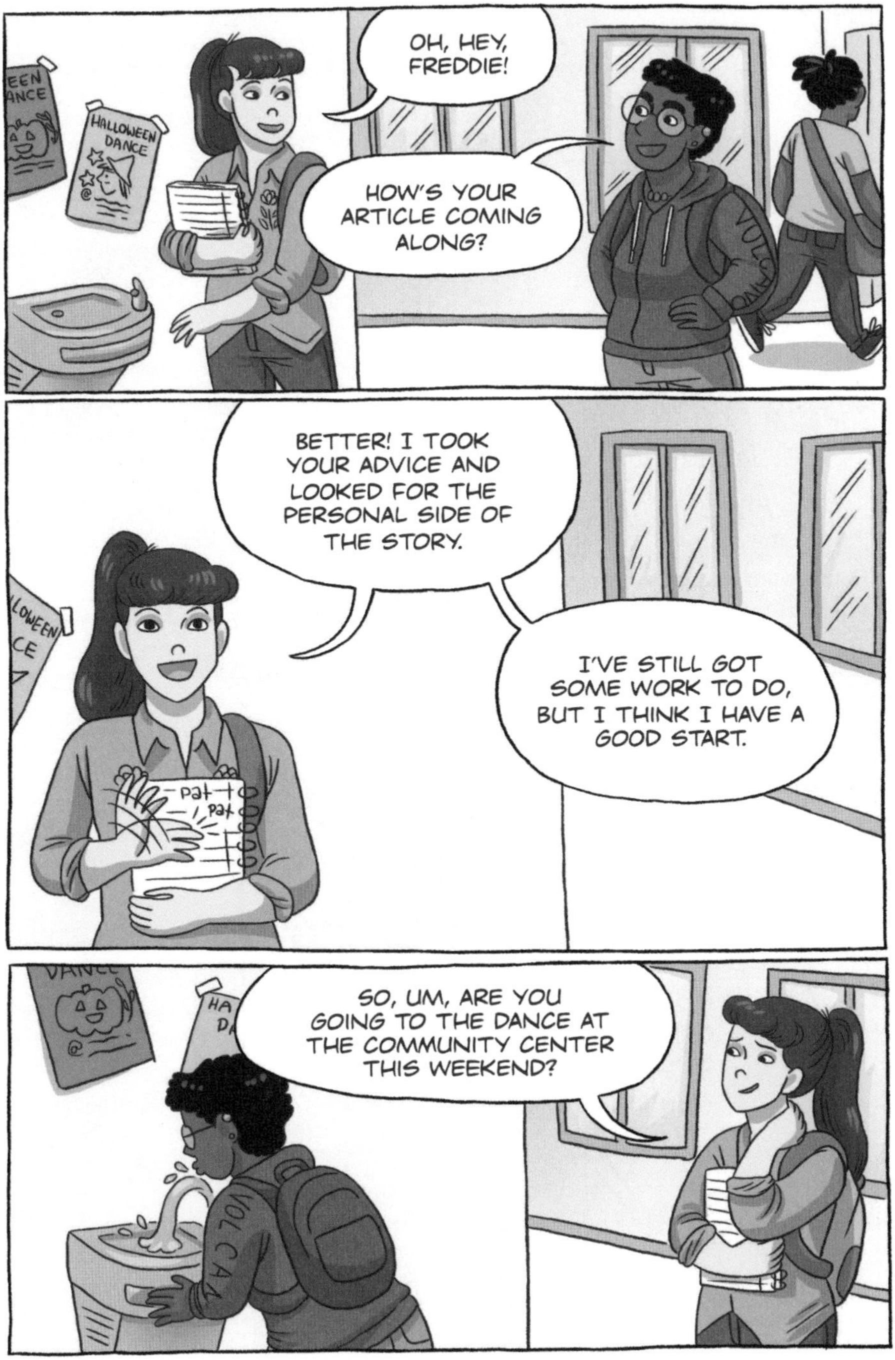
OH, HEY, FREDDIE!
HOW'S YOUR ARTICLE COMING ALONG?
HALLOWEEN DANCE
BETTER! I TOOK YOUR ADVICE AND LOOKED FOR THE PERSONAL SIDE OF THE STORY.
I'VE STILL GOT SOME WORK TO DO, BUT I THINK I HAVE A GOOD START.
pat
pat
SO, UM, ARE YOU GOING TO THE DANCE AT THE COMMUNITY CENTER THIS WEEKEND?

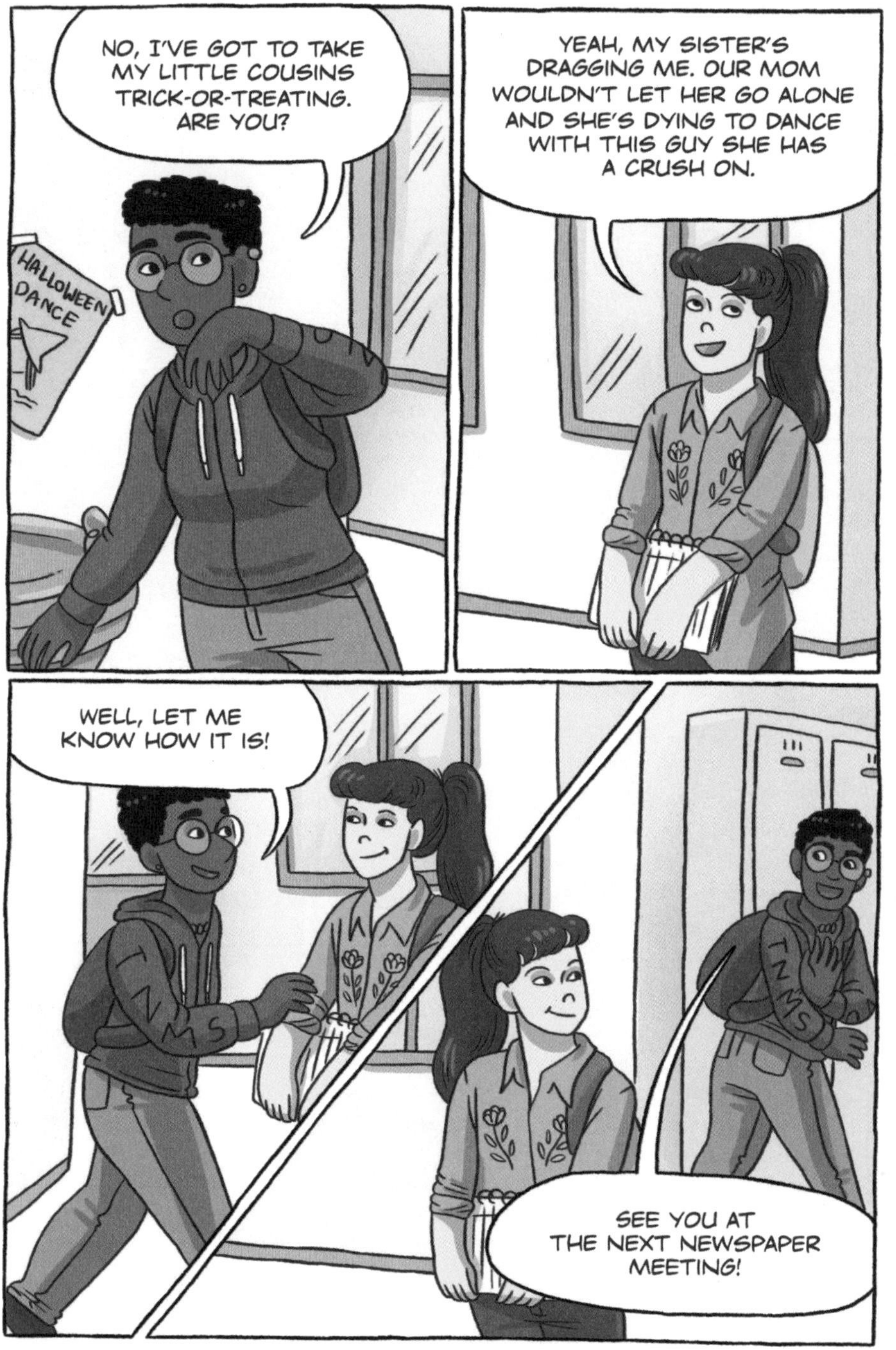
NO, I'VE GOT TO TAKE MY LITTLE COUSINS TRICK-OR-TREATING. ARE YOU?
HALLOWEEN DANCE
YEAH, MY SISTER'S DRAGGING ME. OUR MOM WOULDN'T LET HER GO ALONE AND SHE'S DYING TO DANCE WITH THIS GUY SHE HAS A CRUSH ON.
WELL, LET ME KNOW HOW IT IS!
TNMS
SEE YOU AT THE NEXT NEWSPAPER MEETING!

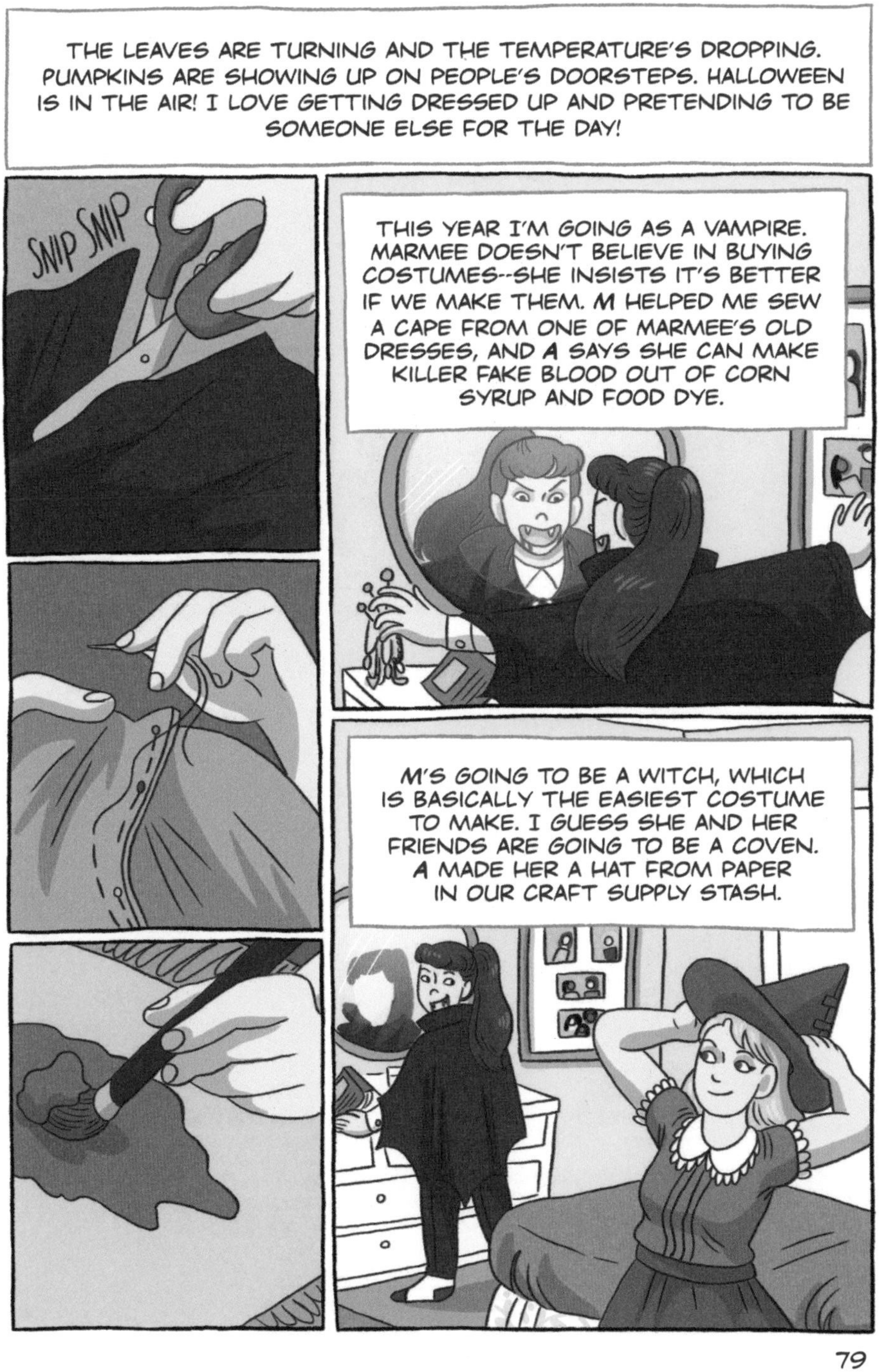
THE LEAVES ARE TURNING AND THE TEMPERATURE'S DROPPING. PUMPKINS ARE SHOWING UP ON PEOPLE'S DOORSTEPS. HALLOWEEN IS IN THE AIR! I LOVE GETTING DRESSED UP AND PRETENDING TO BE SOMEONE ELSE FOR THE DAY!
SNIP SNIP
THIS YEAR I'M GOING AS A VAMPIRE. MARMEE DOESN'T BELIEVE IN BUYING COSTUMES--SHE INSISTS IT'S BETTER IF WE MAKE THEM. M HELPED ME SEW A CAPE FROM ONE OF MARMEE'S OLD DRESSES, AND A SAYS SHE CAN MAKE KILLER FAKE BLOOD OUT OF CORN SYRUP AND FOOD DYE.
M'S GOING TO BE A WITCH, WHICH IS BASICALLY THE EASIEST COSTUME TO MAKE. I GUESS SHE AND HER FRIENDS ARE GOING TO BE A COVEN. A MADE HER A HAT FROM PAPER IN OUR CRAFT SUPPLY STASH.

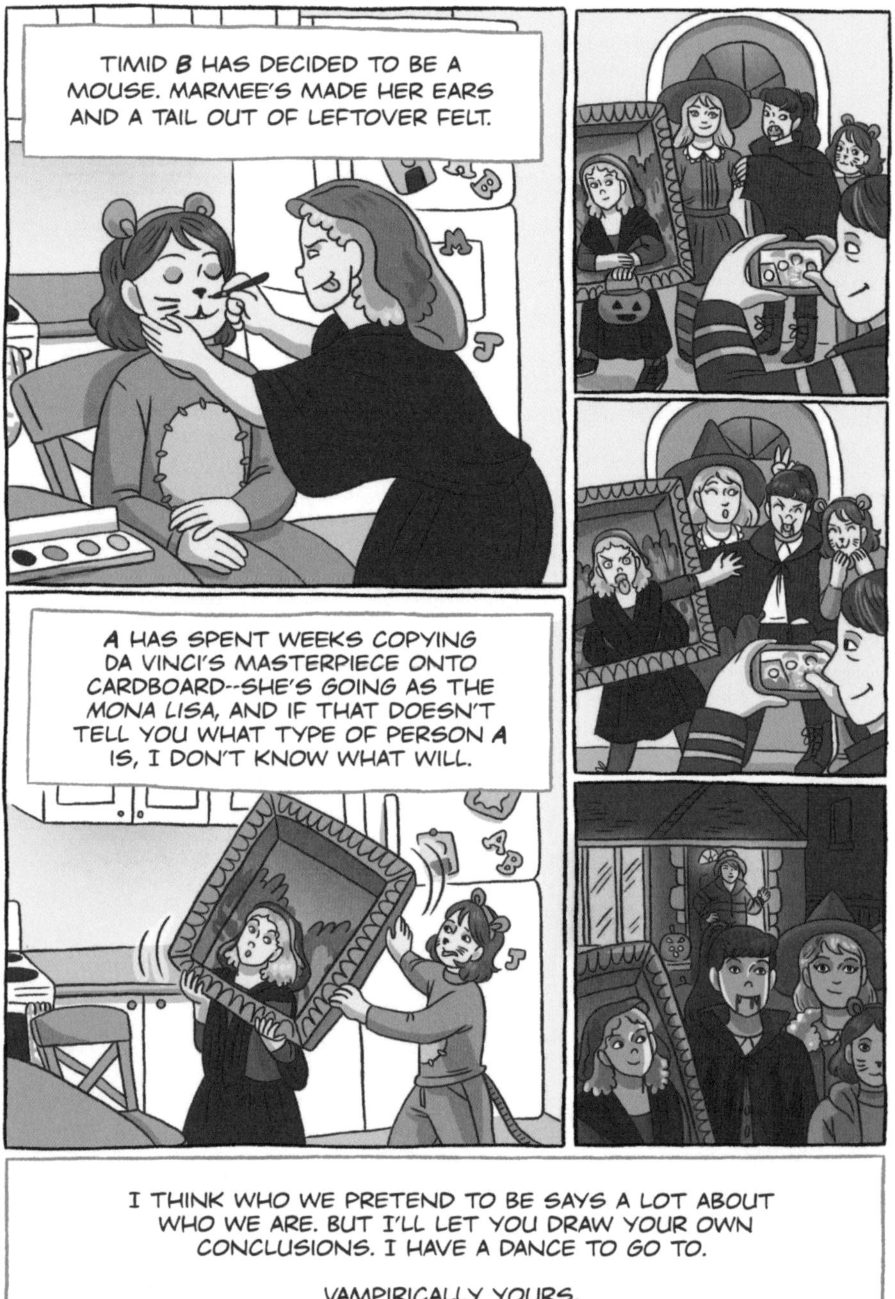
TIMID B HAS DECIDED TO BE A MOUSE. MARMEE'S MADE HER EARS AND A TAIL OUT OF LEFTOVER FELT.
A HAS SPENT WEEKS COPYING DA VINCI'S MASTERPIECE ONTO CARDBOARD--SHE'S GOING AS THE MONA LISA, AND IF THAT DOESN'T TELL YOU WHAT TYPE OF PERSON A IS, I DON'T KNOW WHAT WILL.
I THINK WHO WE PRETEND TO BE SAYS A LOT ABOUT WHO WE ARE. BUT I'LL LET YOU DRAW YOUR OWN CONCLUSIONS. I HAVE A DANCE TO GO TO.
VAMPIRICALLY YOURS,
J

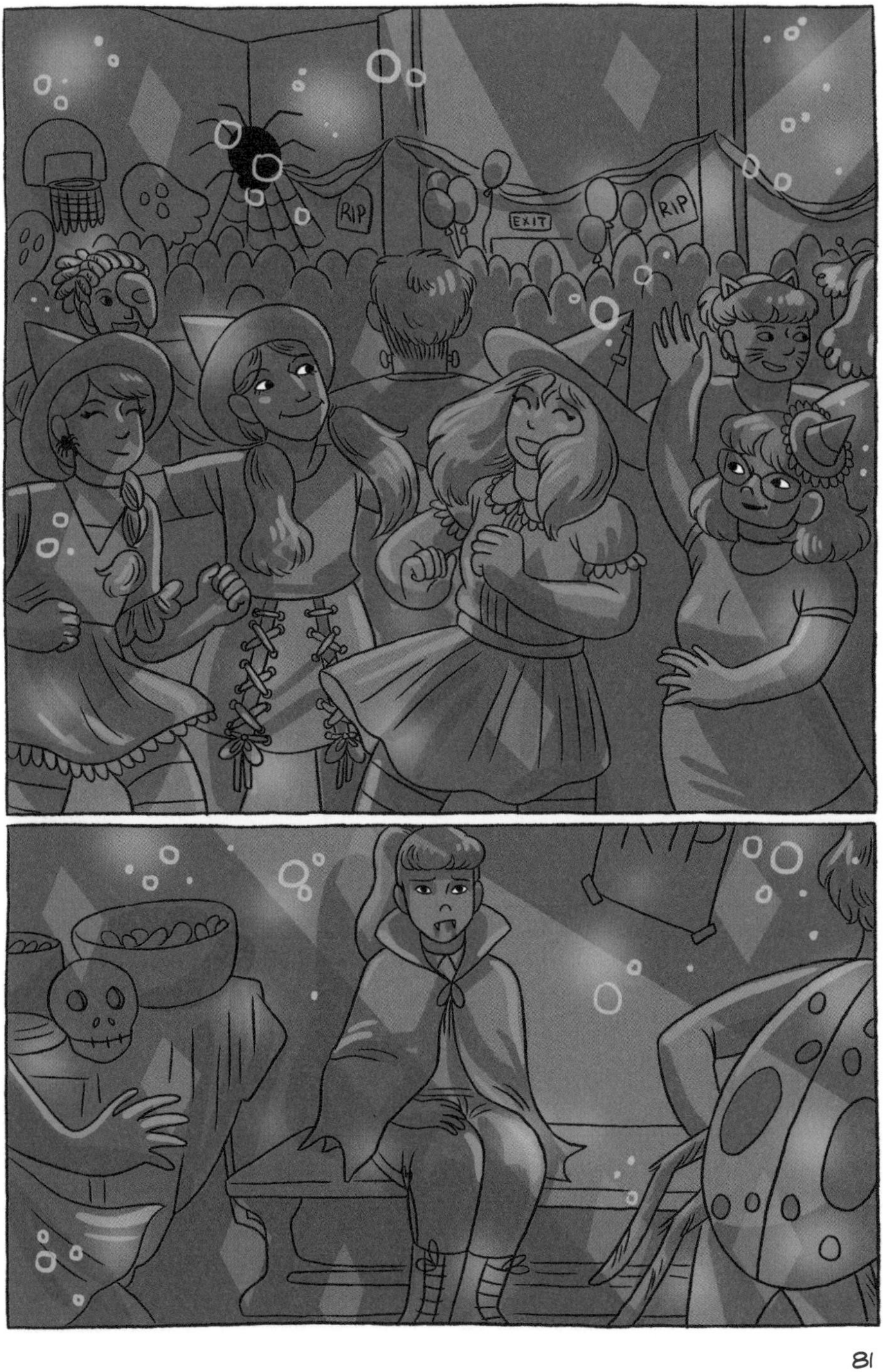
RIP
EXIT
RIP

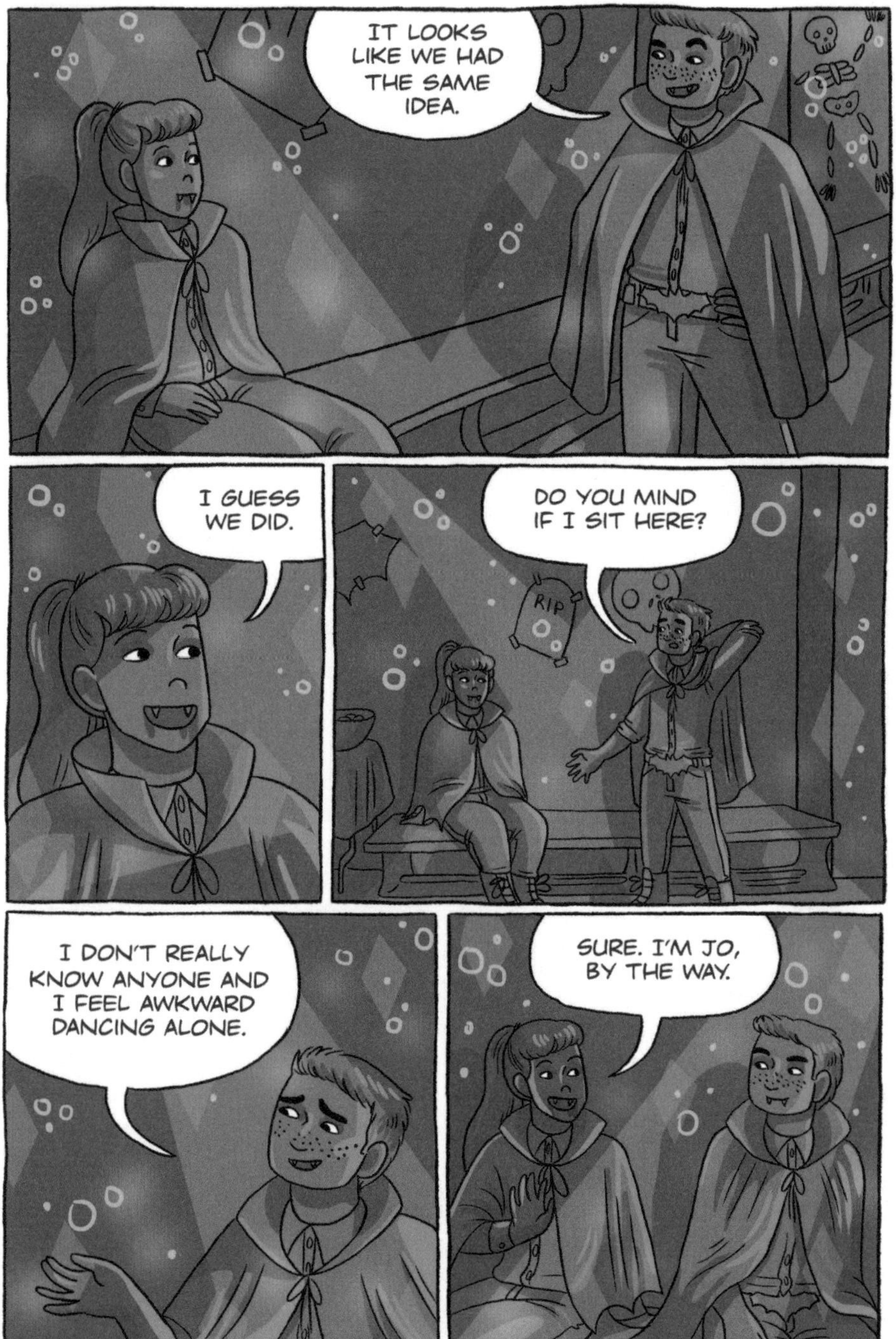
IT LOOKS LIKE WE HAD THE SAME IDEA.
I GUESS WE DID.
DO YOU MIND IF I SIT HERE?
RIP
I DON'T REALLY KNOW ANYONE AND I FEEL AWKWARD DANCING ALONE.
SURE. I'M JO, BY THE WAY.

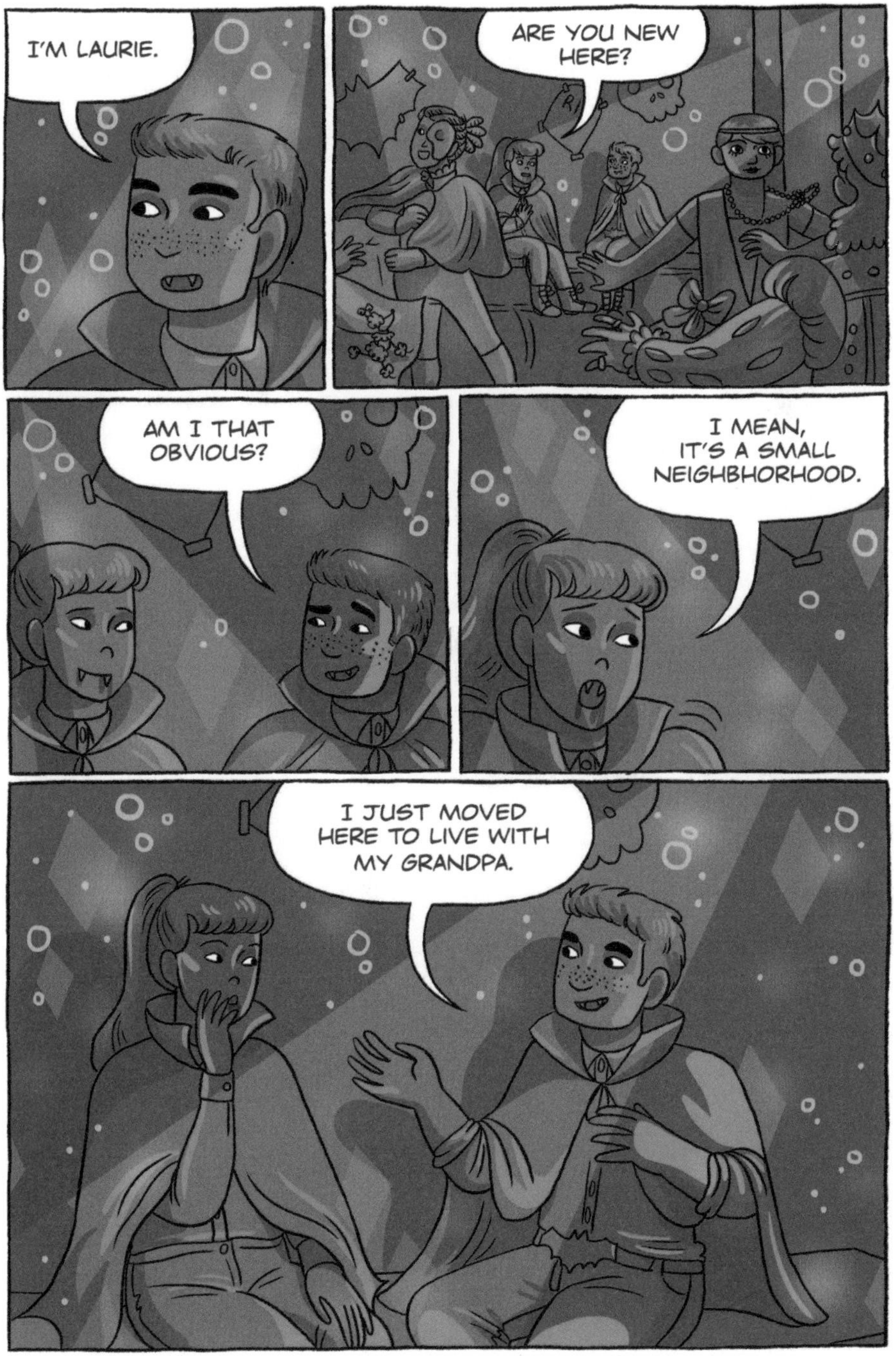
I'M LAURIE.
ARE YOU NEW HERE?
AM I THAT OBVIOUS?
I MEAN, IT'S A SMALL NEIGHBHORHOOD.
I JUST MOVED HERE TO LIVE WITH MY GRANDPA.

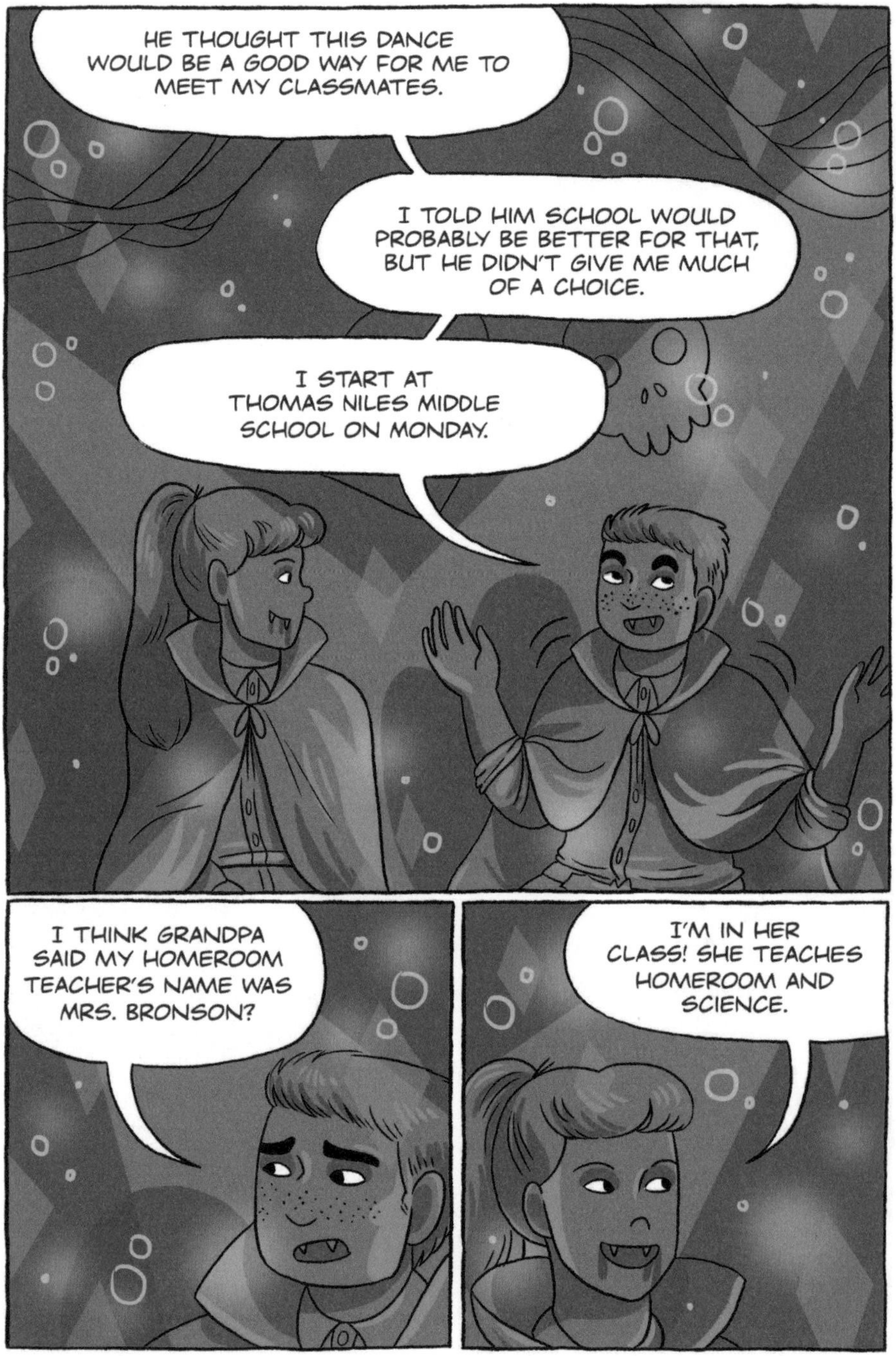
HE THOUGHT THIS DANCE WOULD BE A GOOD WAY FOR ME TO MEET MY CLASSMATES.
I TOLD HIM SCHOOL WOULD PROBABLY BE BETTER FOR THAT, BUT HE DIDN'T GIVE ME MUCH OF A CHOICE.
I START AT THOMAS NILES MIDDLE SCHOOL ON MONDAY.
I THINK GRANDPA SAID MY HOMEROOM TEACHER'S NAME WAS MRS. BRONSON?
I'M IN HER CLASS! SHE TEACHES HOMEROOM AND SCIENCE.

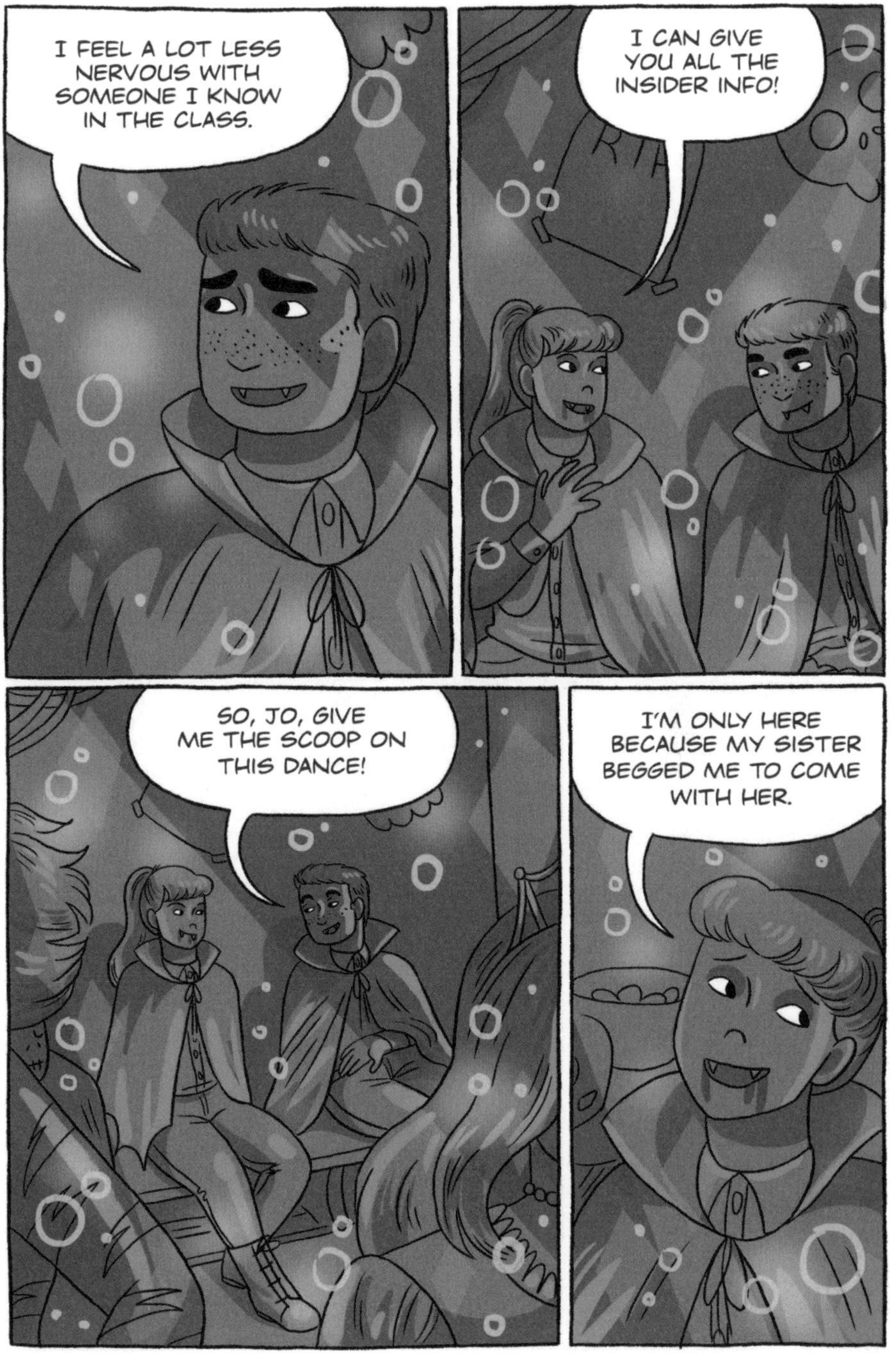
I FEEL A LOT LESS NERVOUS WITH SOMEONE I KNOW IN THE CLASS.
I CAN GIVE YOU ALL THE INSIDER INFO!
SO, JO, GIVE ME THE SCOOP ON THIS DANCE!
I'M ONLY HERE BECAUSE MY SISTER BEGGED ME TO COME WITH HER.

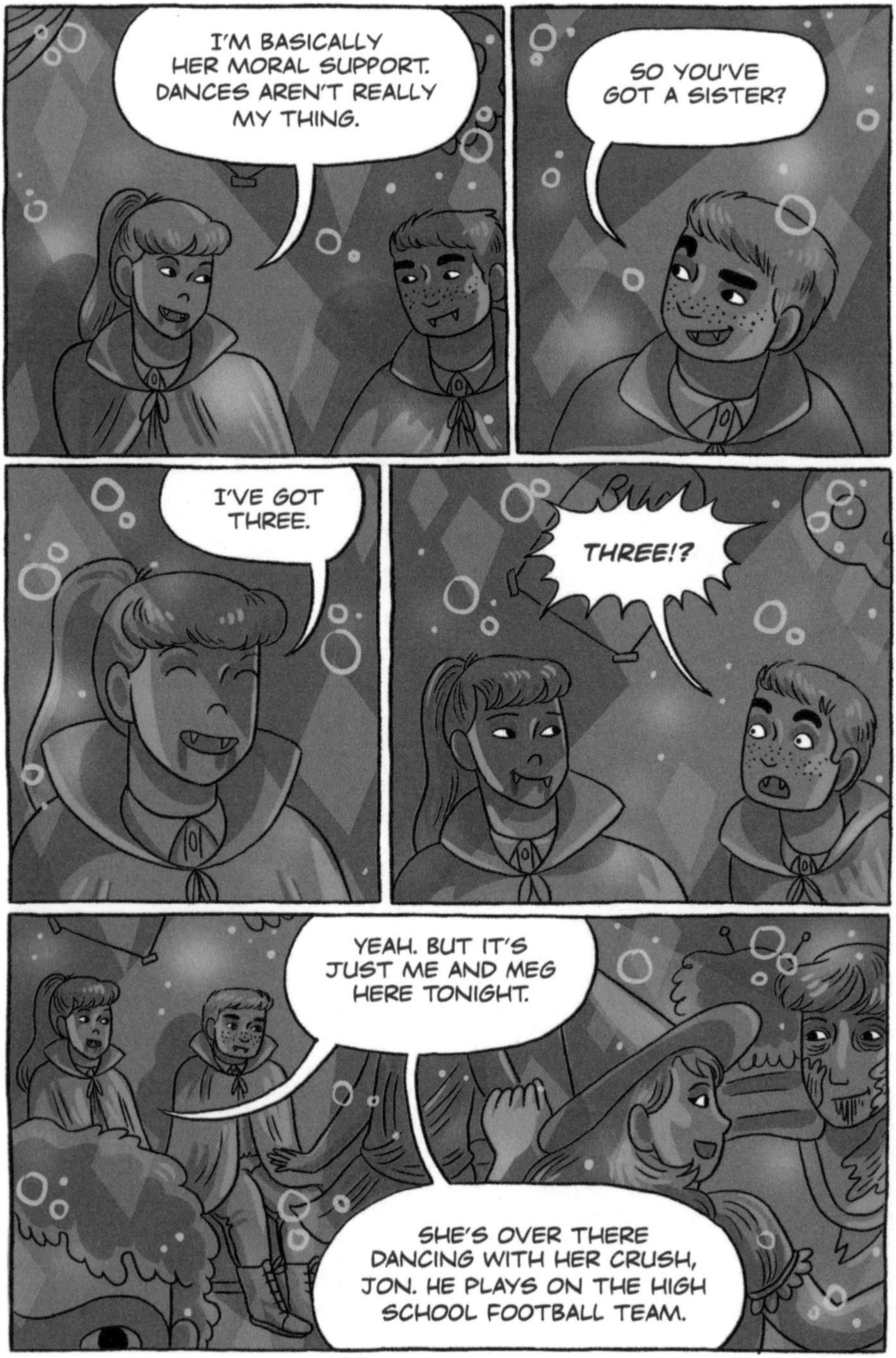
I'M BASICALLY HER MORAL SUPPORT. DANCES AREN'T REALLY MY THING.
SO YOU'VE GOT A SISTER?
I'VE GOT THREE.
THREE!?
YEAH. BUT IT'S JUST ME AND MEG HERE TONIGHT.
SHE'S OVER THERE DANCING WITH HER CRUSH, JON. HE PLAYS ON THE HIGH SCHOOL FOOTBALL TEAM.

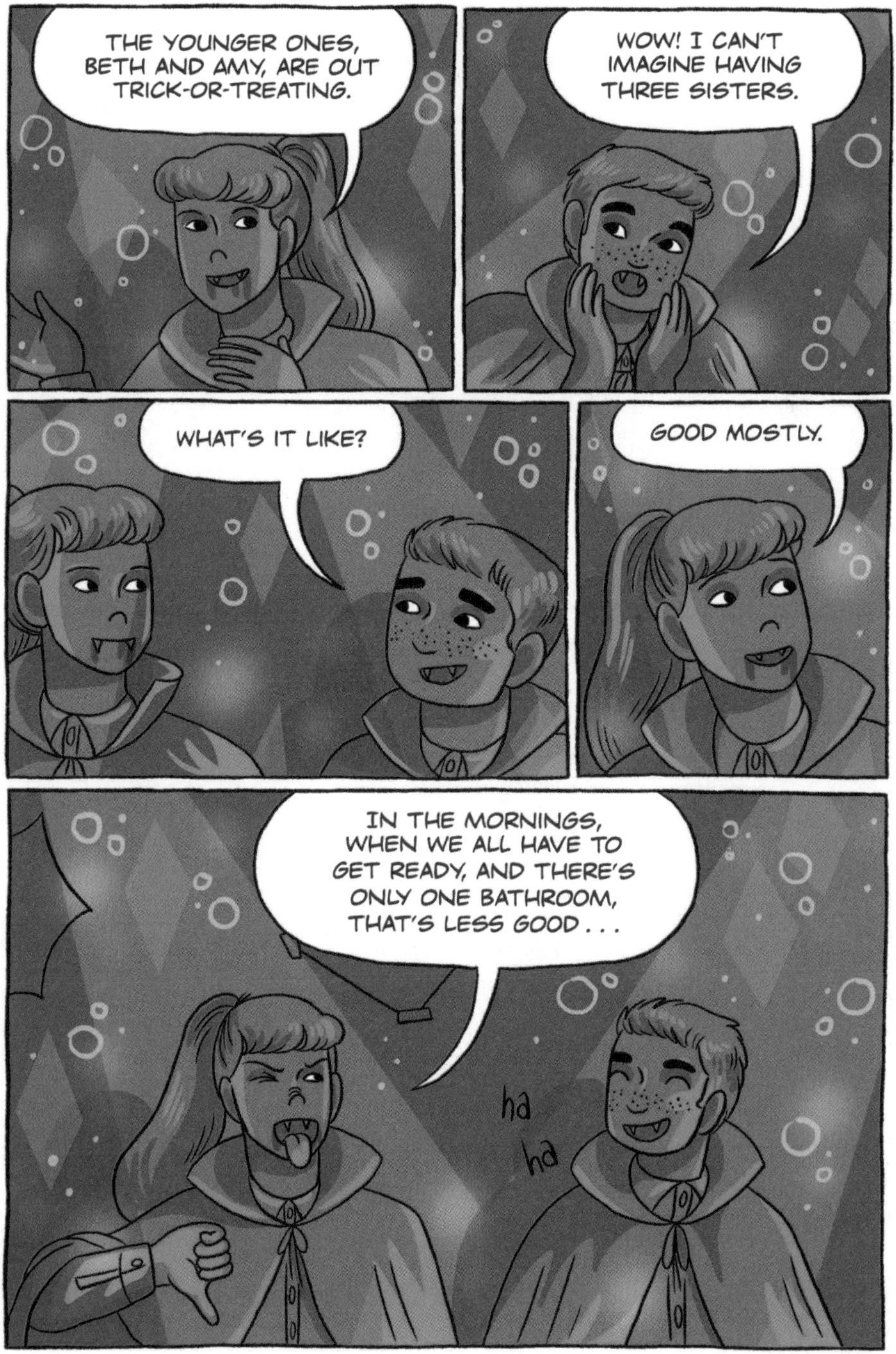
THE YOUNGER ONES, BETH AND AMY, ARE OUT TRICK-OR-TREATING.
WOW! I CAN'T IMAGINE HAVING THREE SISTERS.
WHAT'S IT LIKE?
GOOD MOSTLY.
IN THE MORNINGS, WHEN WE ALL HAVE TO GET READY, AND THERE'S ONLY ONE BATHROOM, THAT'S LESS GOOD . . .
ha
ha

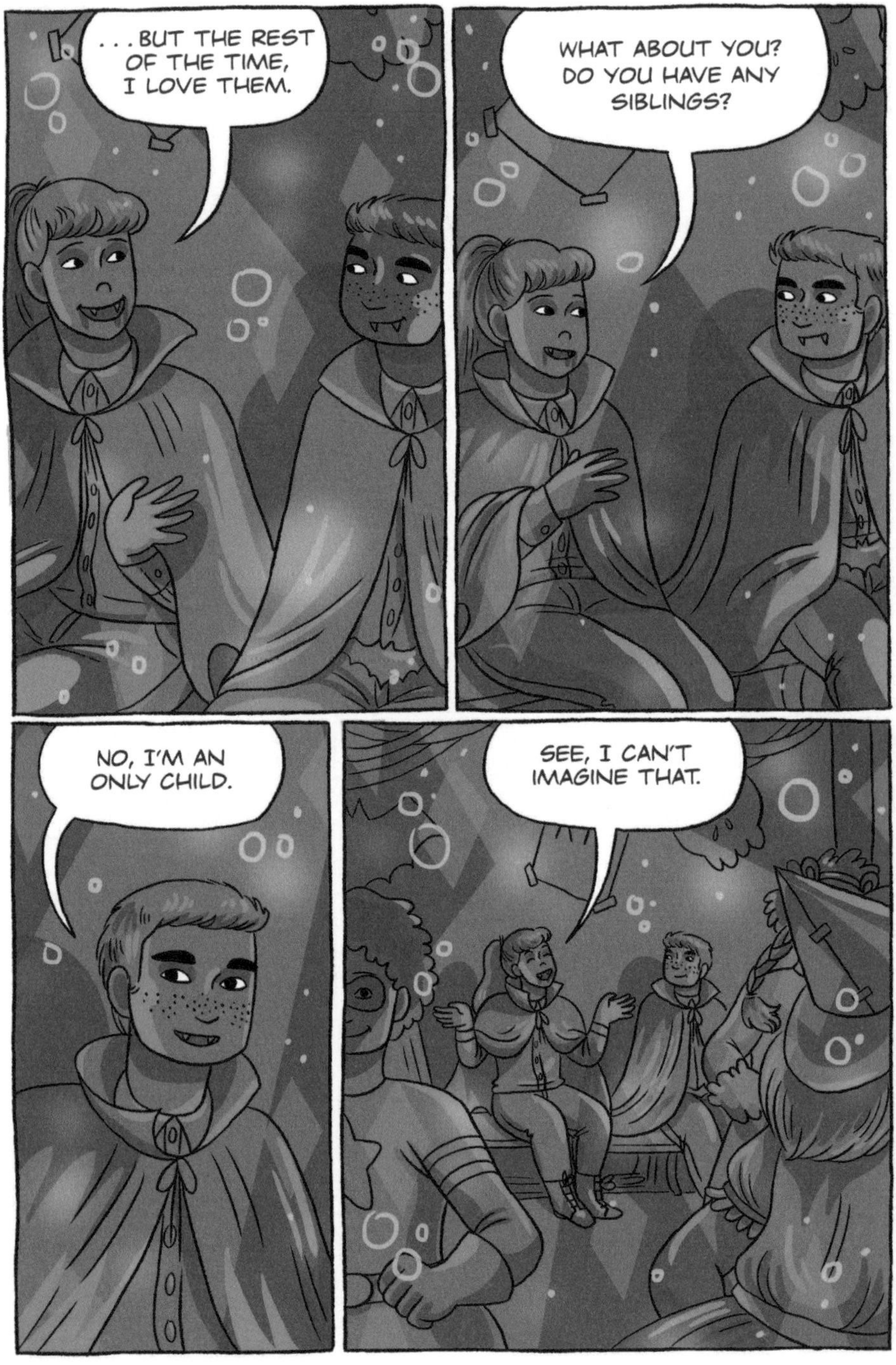
. . . BUT THE REST OF THE TIME, I LOVE THEM.
WHAT ABOUT YOU? DO YOU HAVE ANY SIBLINGS?
NO, I'M AN ONLY CHILD.
SEE, I CAN'T IMAGINE THAT.

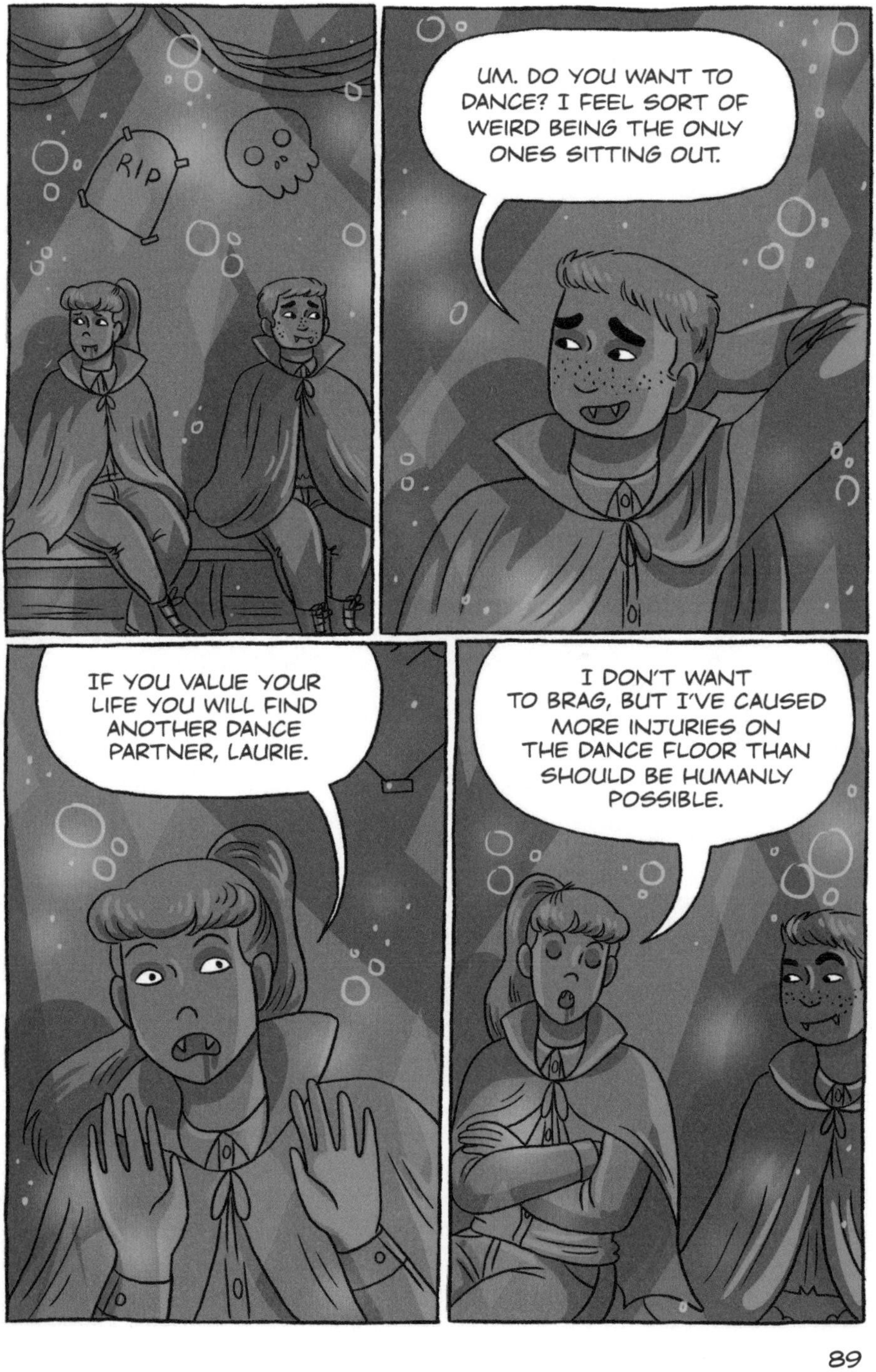
RIP
UM. DO YOU WANT TO DANCE? I FEEL SORT OF WEIRD BEING THE ONLY ONES SITTING OUT.
IF YOU VALUE YOUR LIFE YOU WILL FIND ANOTHER DANCE PARTNER, LAURIE.
I DON'T WANT TO BRAG, BUT I'VE CAUSED MORE INJURIES ON THE DANCE FLOOR THAN SHOULD BE HUMANLY POSSIBLE.

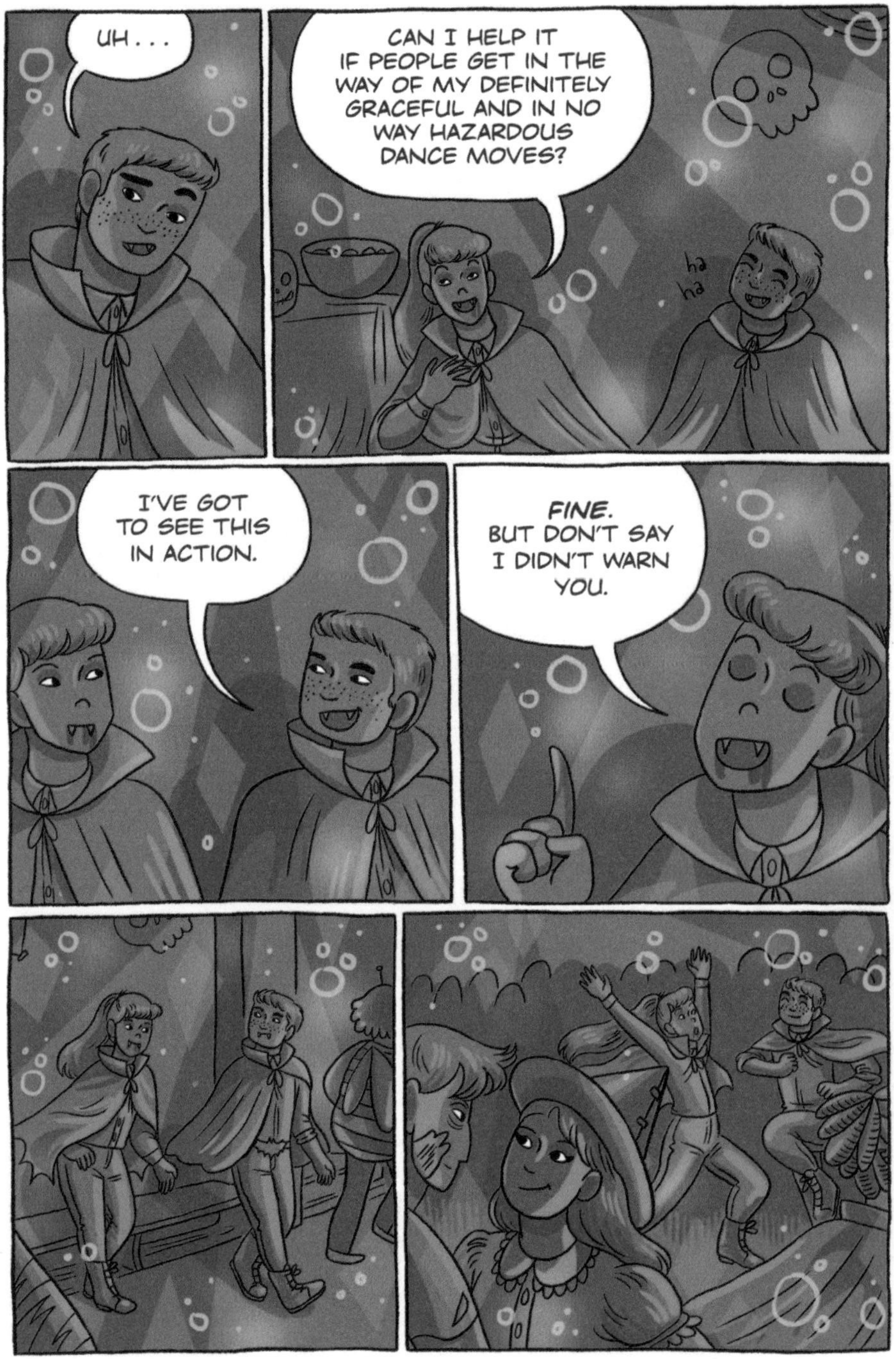
UH . . .
CAN I HELP IT IF PEOPLE GET IN THE WAY OF MY DEFINITELY GRACEFUL AND IN NO WAY HAZARDOUS DANCE MOVES?
ha ha
I'VE GOT TO SEE THIS IN ACTION.
FINE. BUT DON'T SAY I DIDN'T WARN YOU.

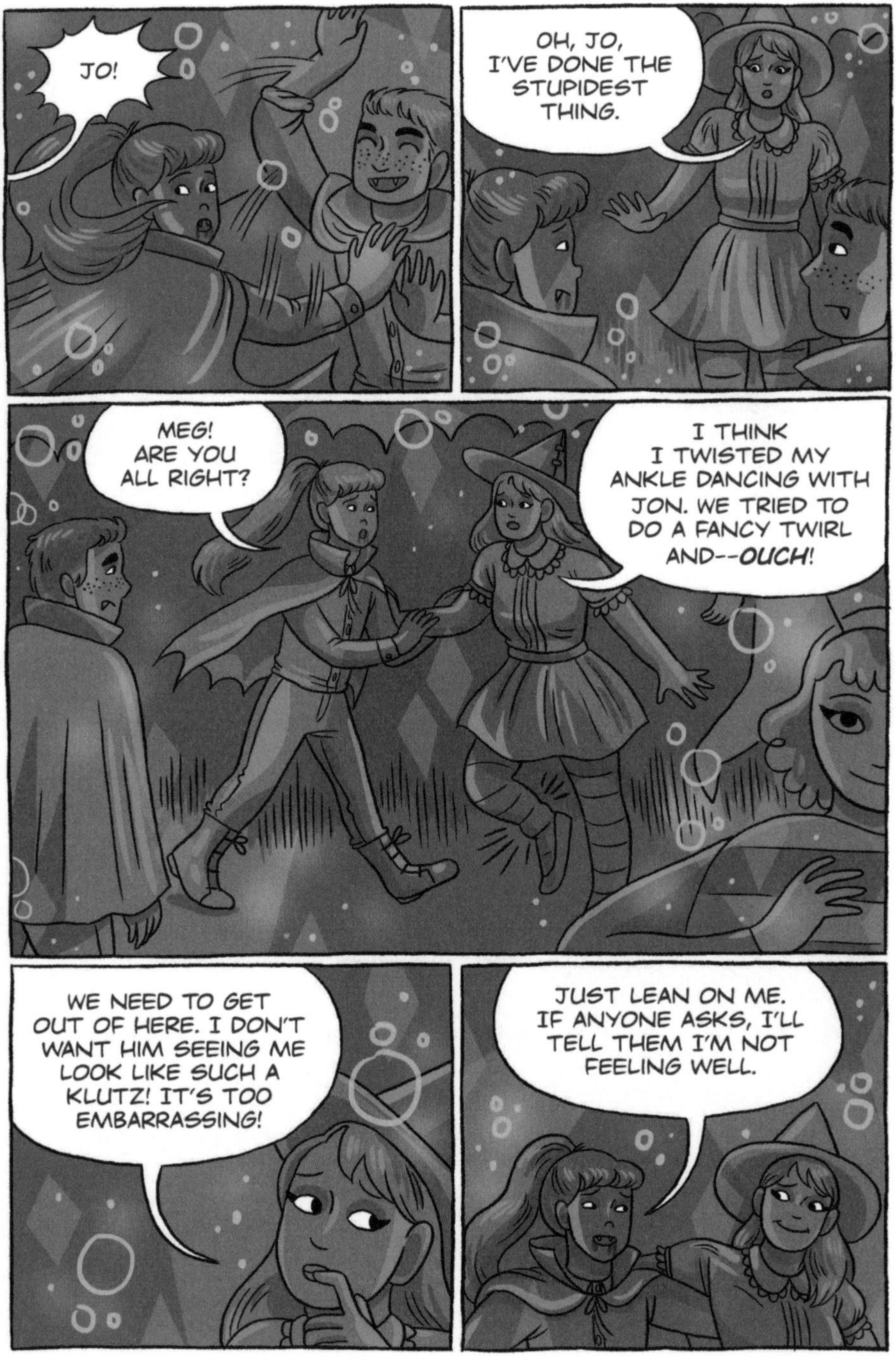
JO!
OH, JO, I'VE DONE THE STUPIDEST THING.
MEG! ARE YOU ALL RIGHT?
I THINK I TWISTED MY ANKLE DANCING WITH JON. WE TRIED TO DO A FANCY TWIRL AND--*OUCH*!
WE NEED TO GET OUT OF HERE. I DON'T WANT HIM SEEING ME LOOK LIKE SUCH A KLUTZ! IT'S TOO EMBARRASSING!
JUST LEAN ON ME. IF ANYONE ASKS, I'LL TELL THEM I'M NOT FEELING WELL.

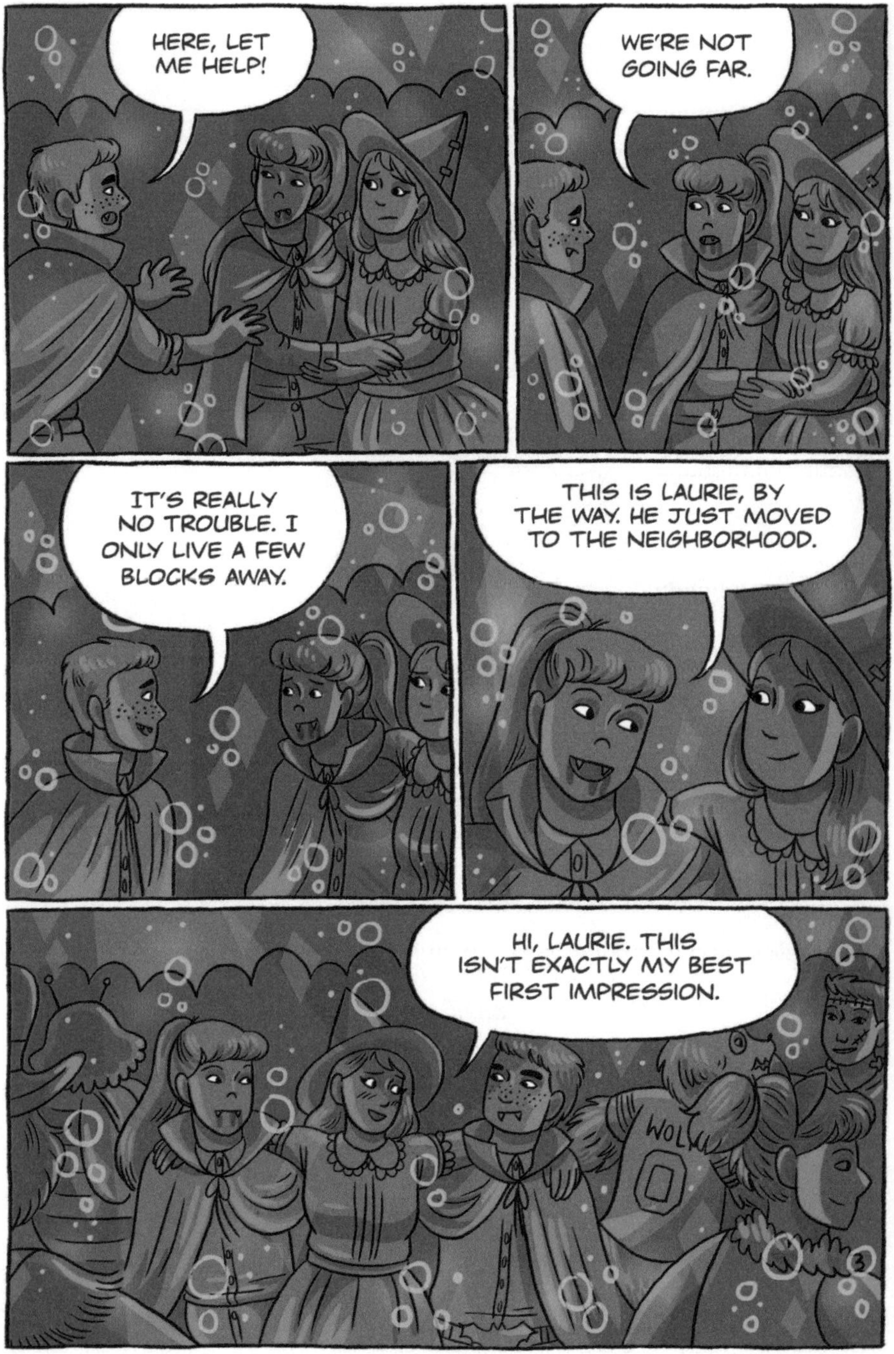
HERE, LET ME HELP!
WE'RE NOT GOING FAR.
IT'S REALLY NO TROUBLE. I ONLY LIVE A FEW BLOCKS AWAY.
THIS IS LAURIE, BY THE WAY. HE JUST MOVED TO THE NEIGHBORHOOD.
HI, LAURIE. THIS ISN'T EXACTLY MY BEST FIRST IMPRESSION.

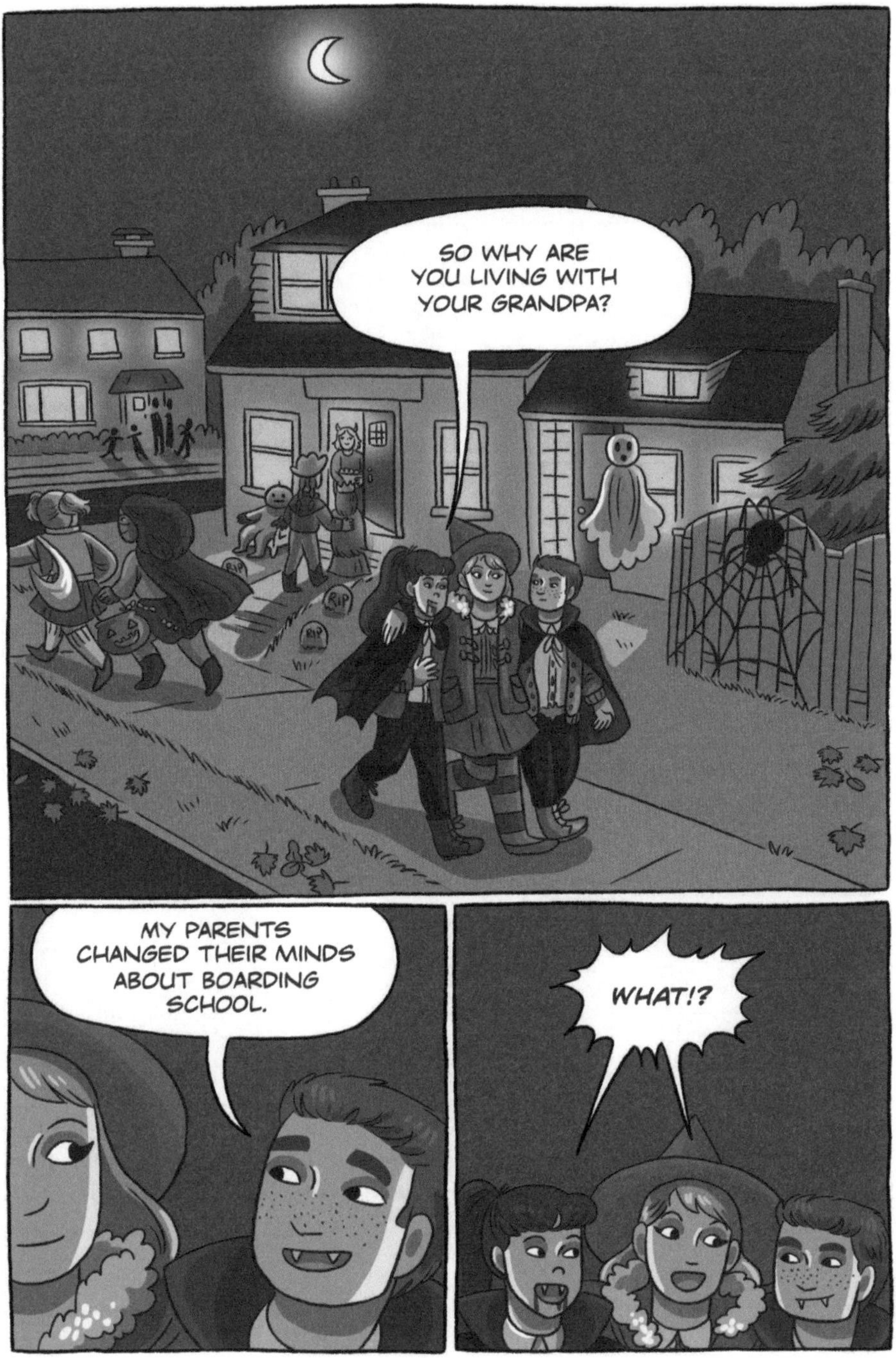
SO WHY ARE YOU LIVING WITH YOUR GRANDPA?
MY PARENTS CHANGED THEIR MINDS ABOUT BOARDING SCHOOL.
WHAT!?

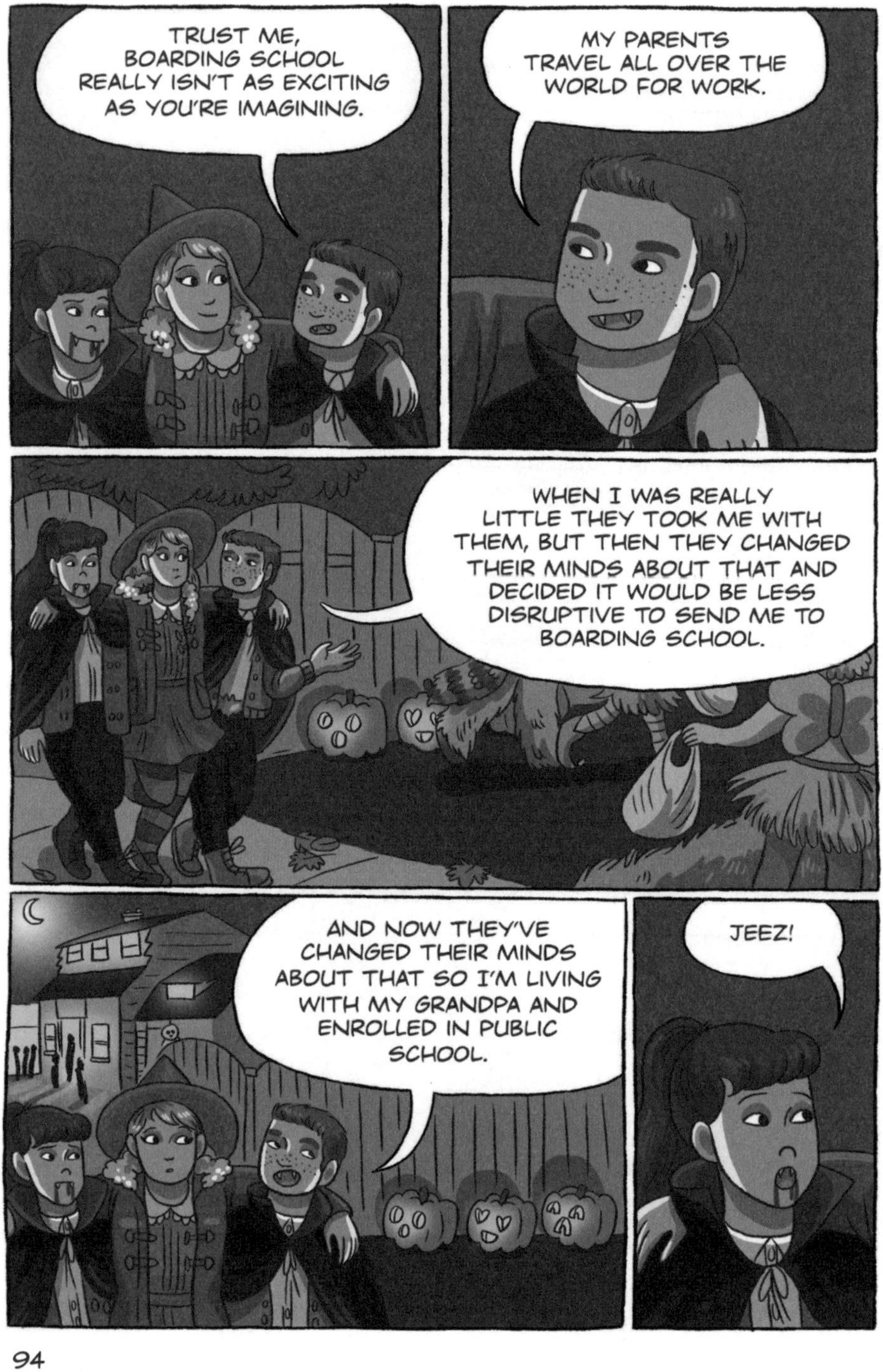
TRUST ME, BOARDING SCHOOL REALLY ISN'T AS EXCITING AS YOU'RE IMAGINING.
MY PARENTS TRAVEL ALL OVER THE WORLD FOR WORK.
WHEN I WAS REALLY LITTLE THEY TOOK ME WITH THEM, BUT THEN THEY CHANGED THEIR MINDS ABOUT THAT AND DECIDED IT WOULD BE LESS DISRUPTIVE TO SEND ME TO BOARDING SCHOOL.
AND NOW THEY'VE CHANGED THEIR MINDS ABOUT THAT SO I'M LIVING WITH MY GRANDPA AND ENROLLED IN PUBLIC SCHOOL.
JEEZ!

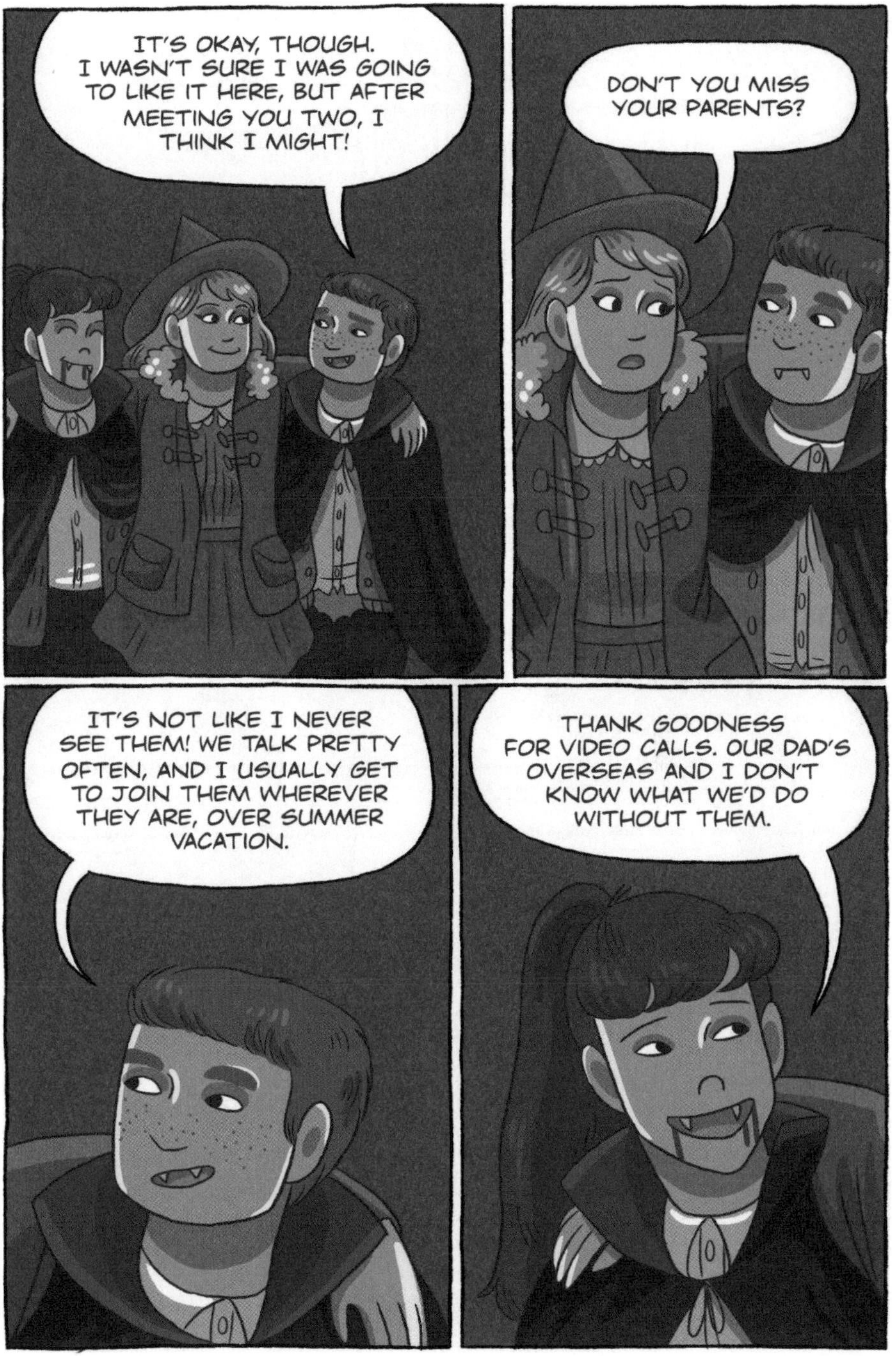
IT'S OKAY, THOUGH. I WASN'T SURE I WAS GOING TO LIKE IT HERE, BUT AFTER MEETING YOU TWO, I THINK I MIGHT!
DON'T YOU MISS YOUR PARENTS?
IT'S NOT LIKE I NEVER SEE THEM! WE TALK PRETTY OFTEN, AND I USUALLY GET TO JOIN THEM WHEREVER THEY ARE, OVER SUMMER VACATION.
THANK GOODNESS FOR VIDEO CALLS. OUR DAD'S OVERSEAS AND I DON'T KNOW WHAT WE'D DO WITHOUT THEM.

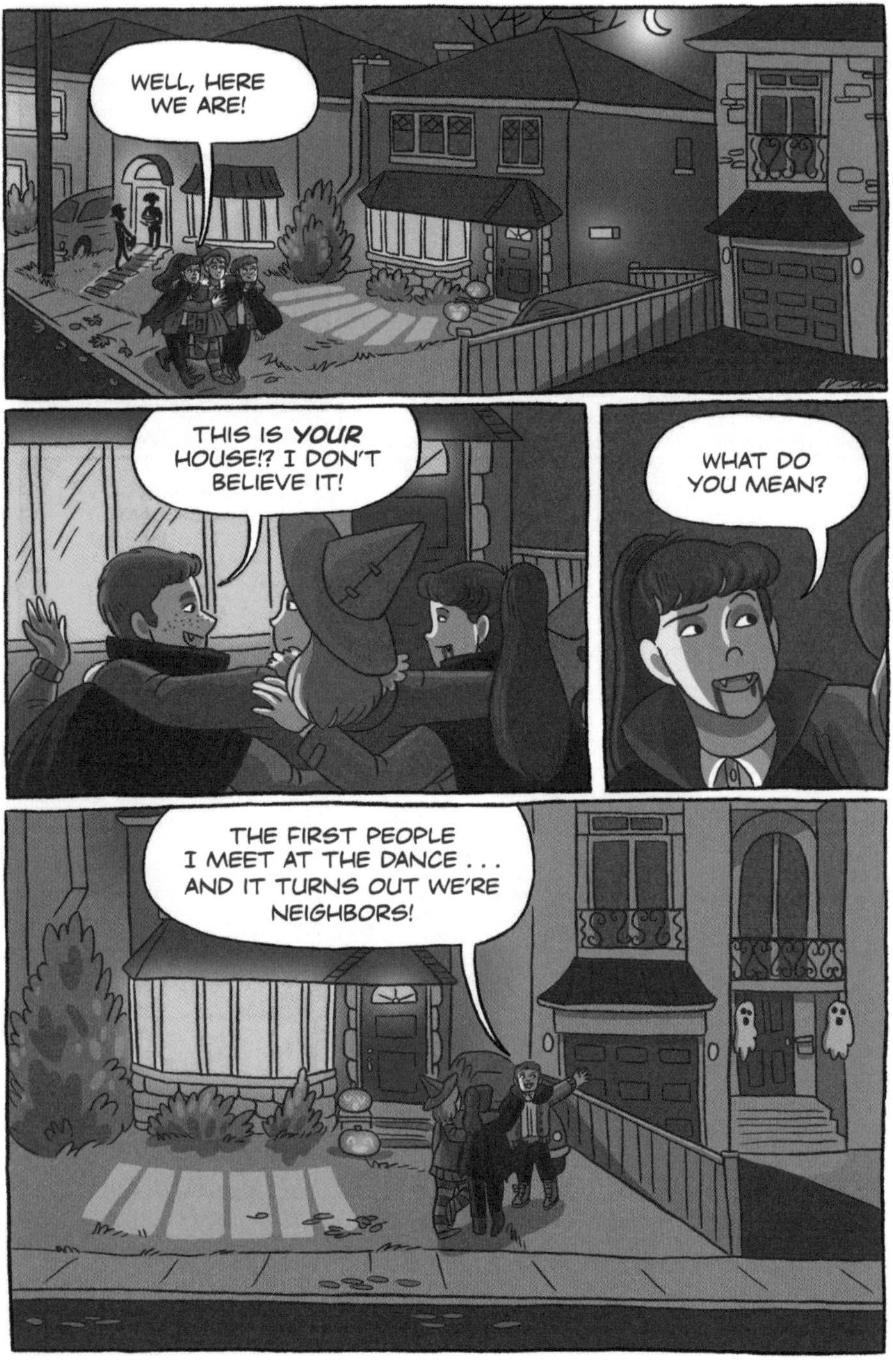
WELL, HERE WE ARE!
THIS IS YOUR HOUSE!? I DON'T BELIEVE IT!
WHAT DO YOU MEAN?
THE FIRST PEOPLE I MEET AT THE DANCE . . . AND IT TURNS OUT WE'RE NEIGHBORS!

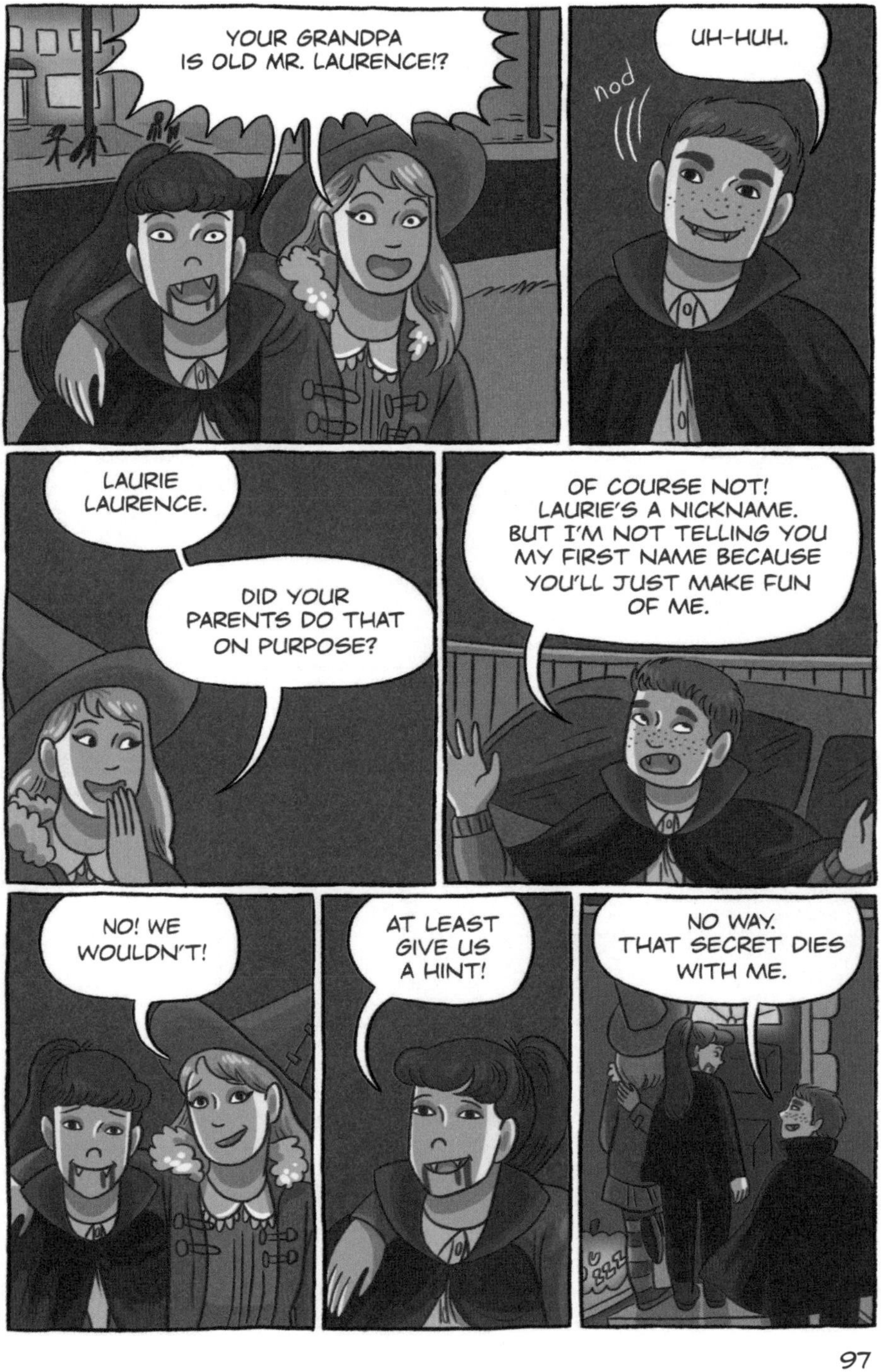
YOUR GRANDPA IS OLD MR. LAURENCE!?
nod
UH-HUH.
LAURIE LAURENCE.
DID YOUR PARENTS DO THAT ON PURPOSE?
OF COURSE NOT! LAURIE'S A NICKNAME. BUT I'M NOT TELLING YOU MY FIRST NAME BECAUSE YOU'LL JUST MAKE FUN OF ME.
NO! WE WOULDN'T!
AT LEAST GIVE US A HINT!
NO WAY. THAT SECRET DIES WITH ME.

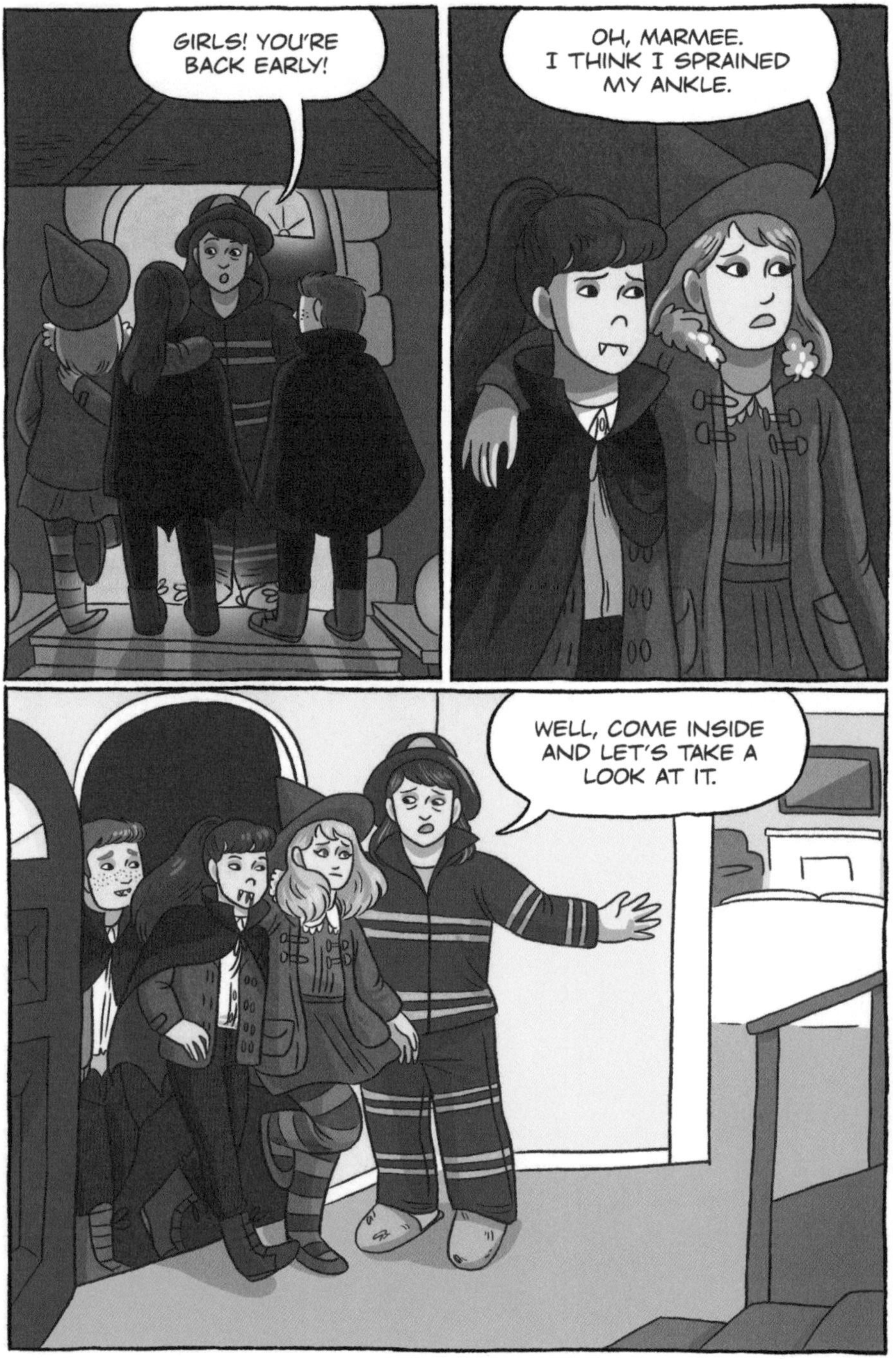
GIRLS! YOU'RE BACK EARLY!
OH, MARMEE. I THINK I SPRAINED MY ANKLE.
WELL, COME INSIDE AND LET'S TAKE A LOOK AT IT.

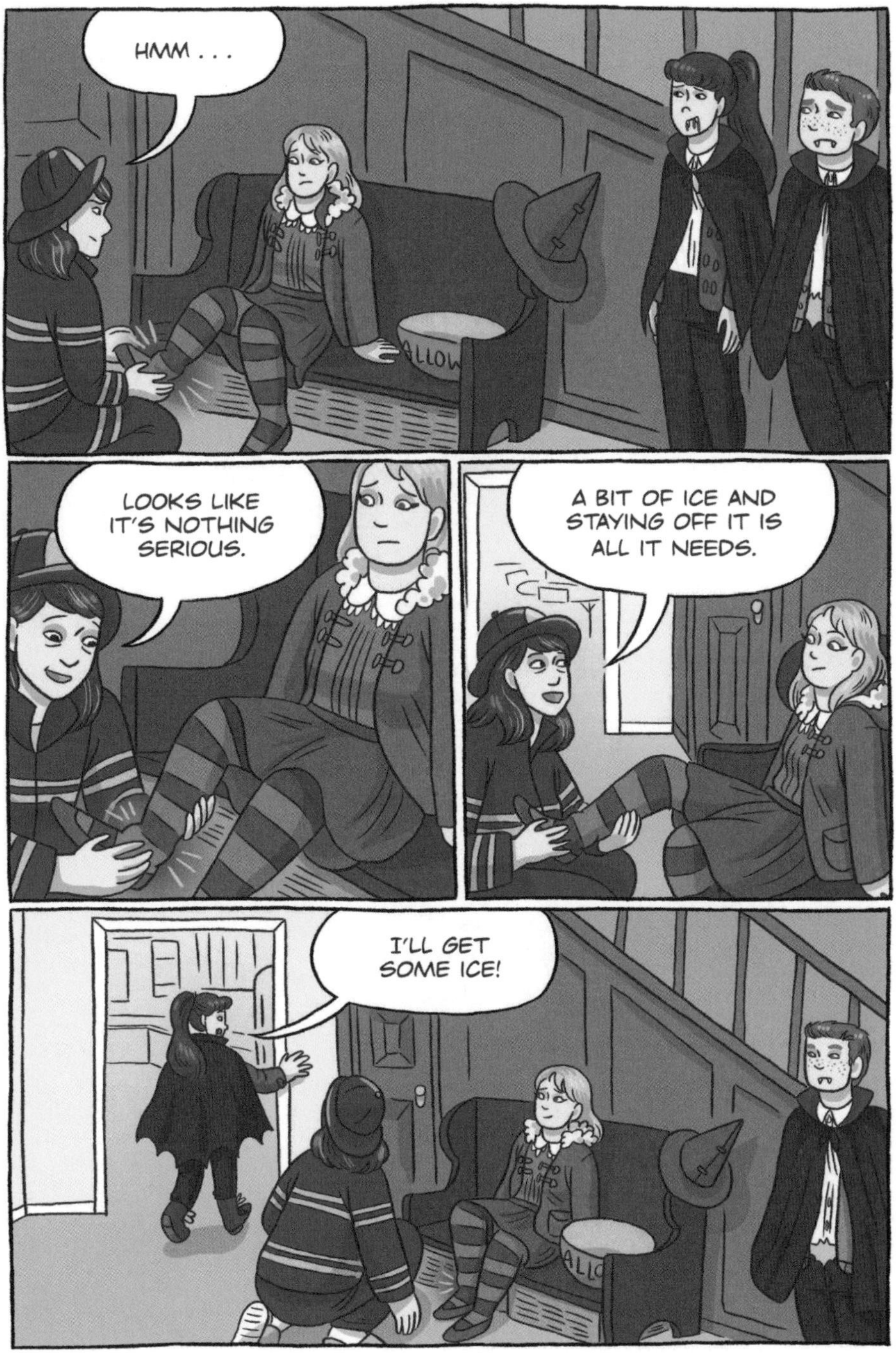
HMM . . .
LOOKS LIKE IT'S NOTHING SERIOUS.
A BIT OF ICE AND STAYING OFF IT IS ALL IT NEEDS.
I'LL GET SOME ICE!

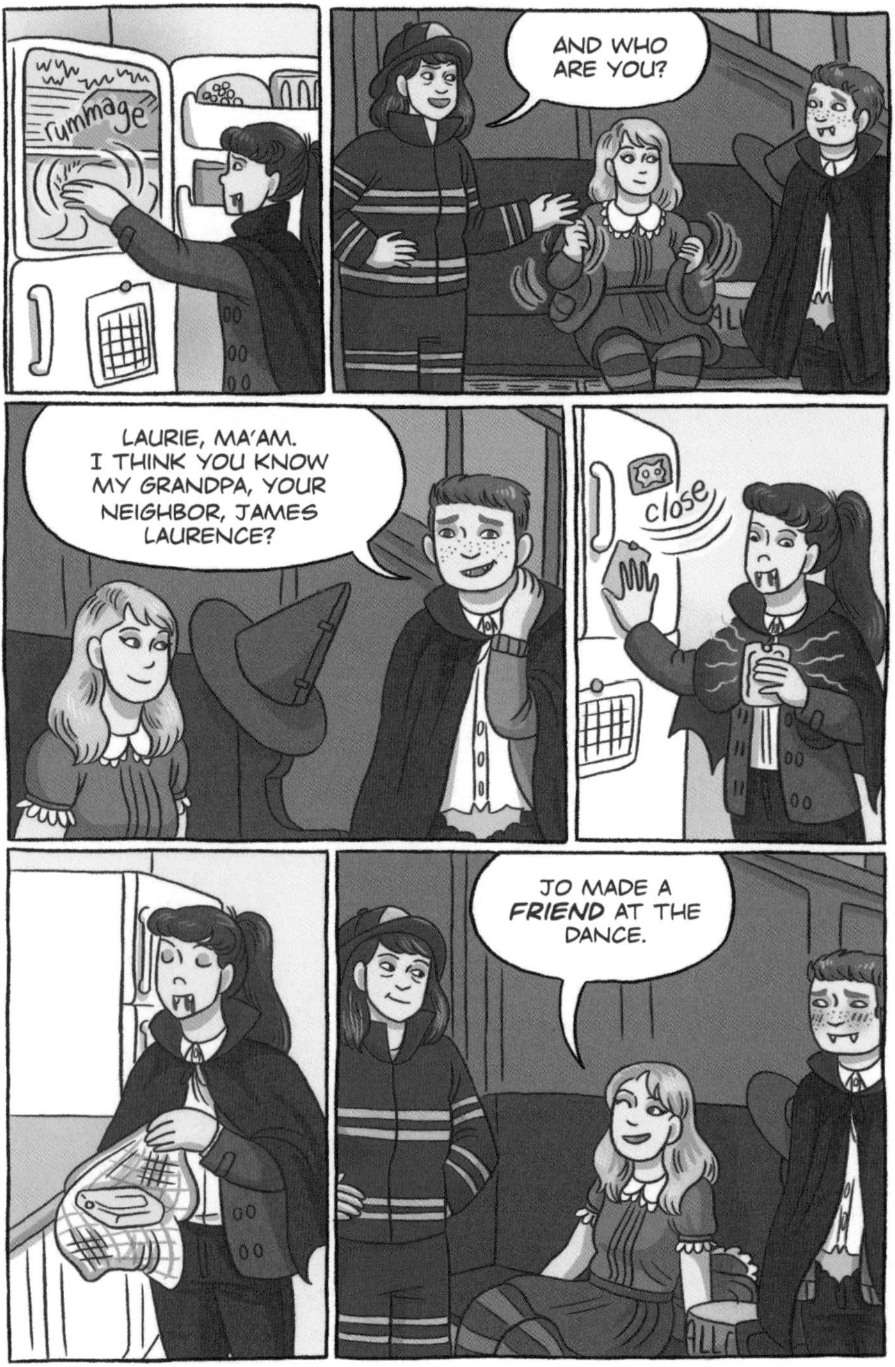
rummage
AND WHO ARE YOU?
LAURIE, MA'AM. I THINK YOU KNOW MY GRANDPA, YOUR NEIGHBOR, JAMES LAURENCE?
close
JO MADE A **FRIEND** AT THE DANCE.

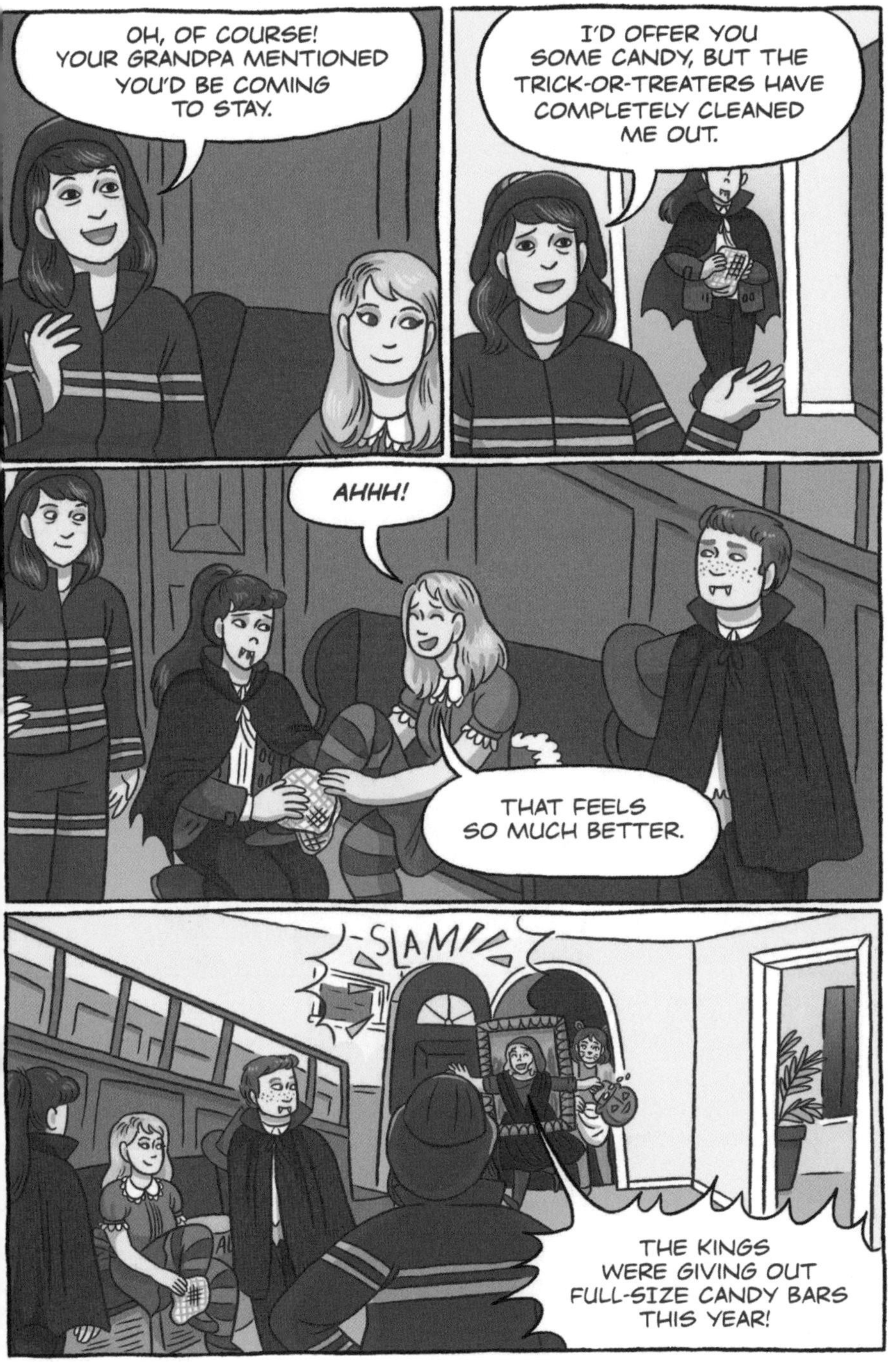
OH, OF COURSE! YOUR GRANDPA MENTIONED YOU'D BE COMING TO STAY.
I'D OFFER YOU SOME CANDY, BUT THE TRICK-OR-TREATERS HAVE COMPLETELY CLEANED ME OUT.
AHHH!
THAT FEELS SO MUCH BETTER.
SLAM!
THE KINGS WERE GIVING OUT FULL-SIZE CANDY BARS THIS YEAR!

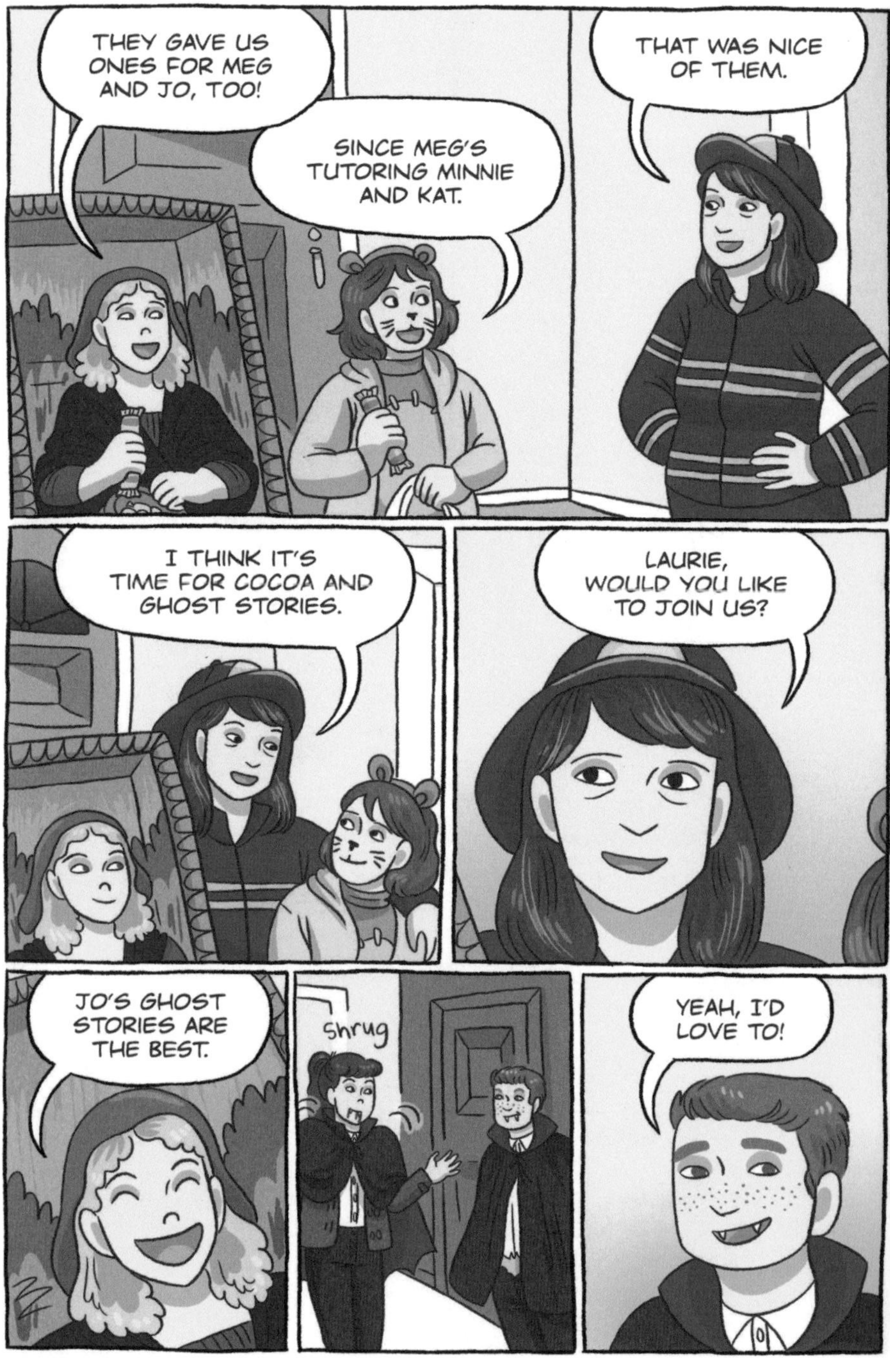
THEY GAVE US ONES FOR MEG AND JO, TOO!
SINCE MEG'S TUTORING MINNIE AND KAT.
THAT WAS NICE OF THEM.
I THINK IT'S TIME FOR COCOA AND GHOST STORIES.
LAURIE, WOULD YOU LIKE TO JOIN US?
JO'S GHOST STORIES ARE THE BEST.
shrug
YEAH, I'D LOVE TO!

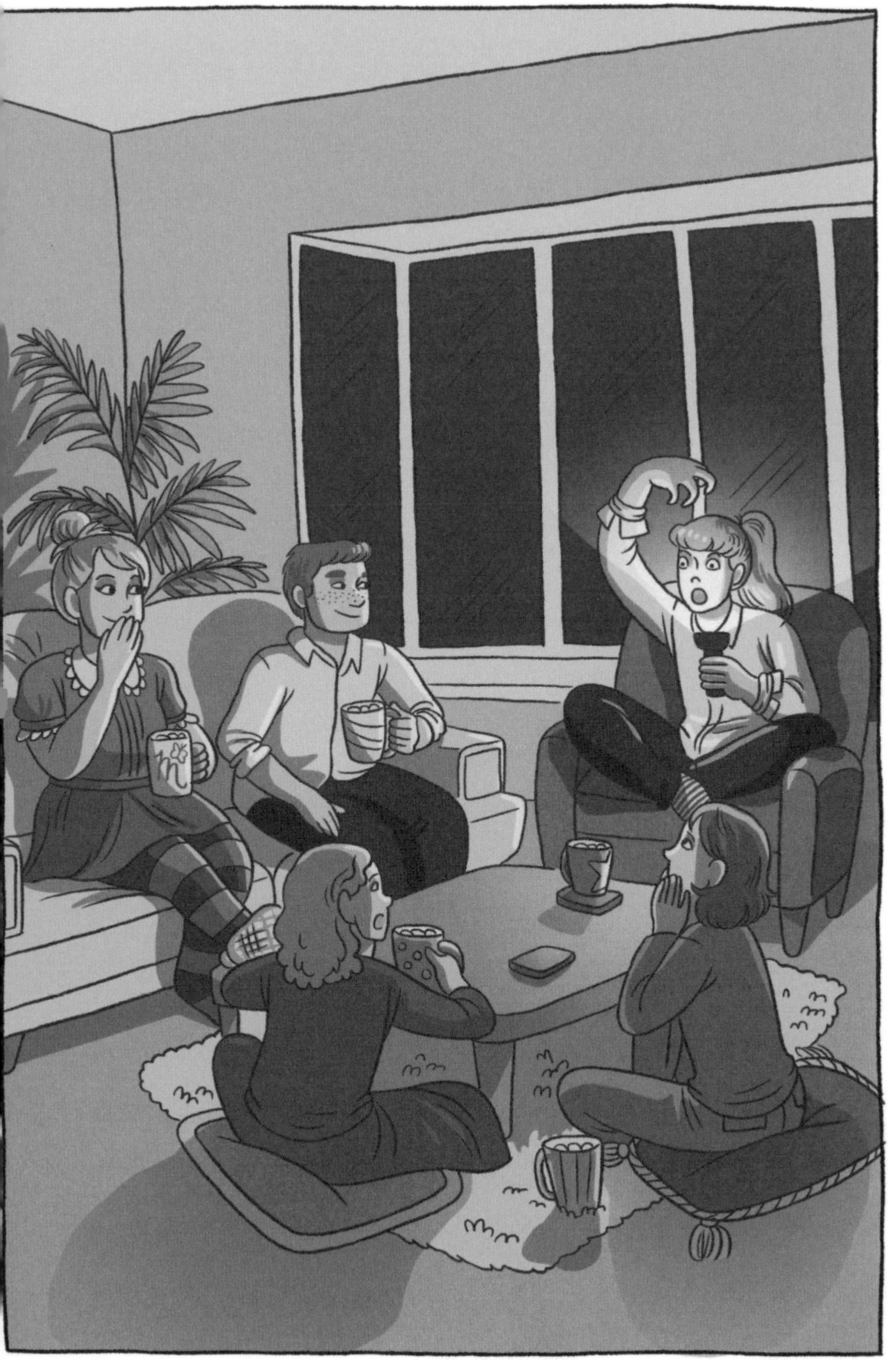

CHAPTER 4

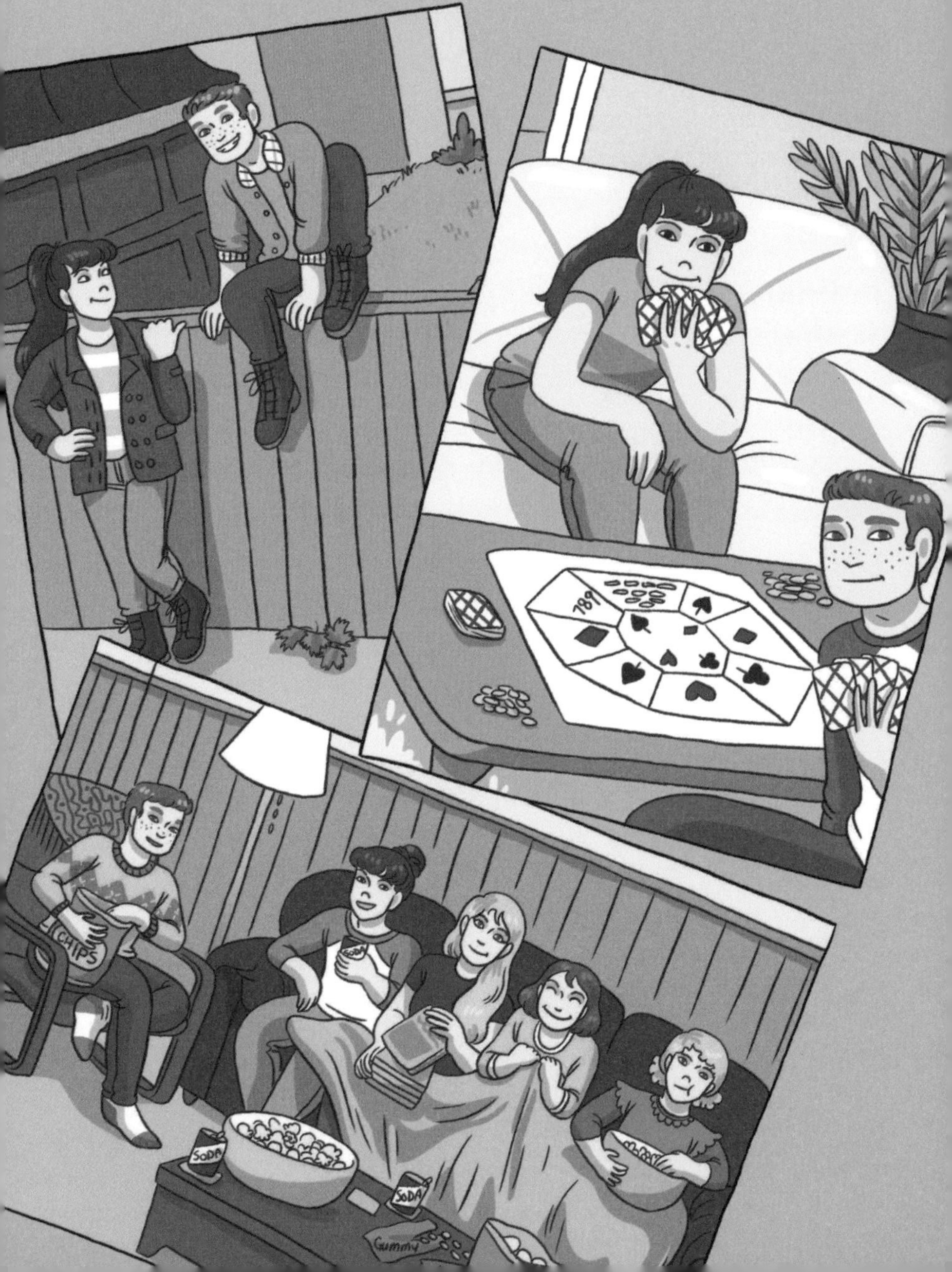
789
CHIPS
SODA
SODA
SODA
Gummy

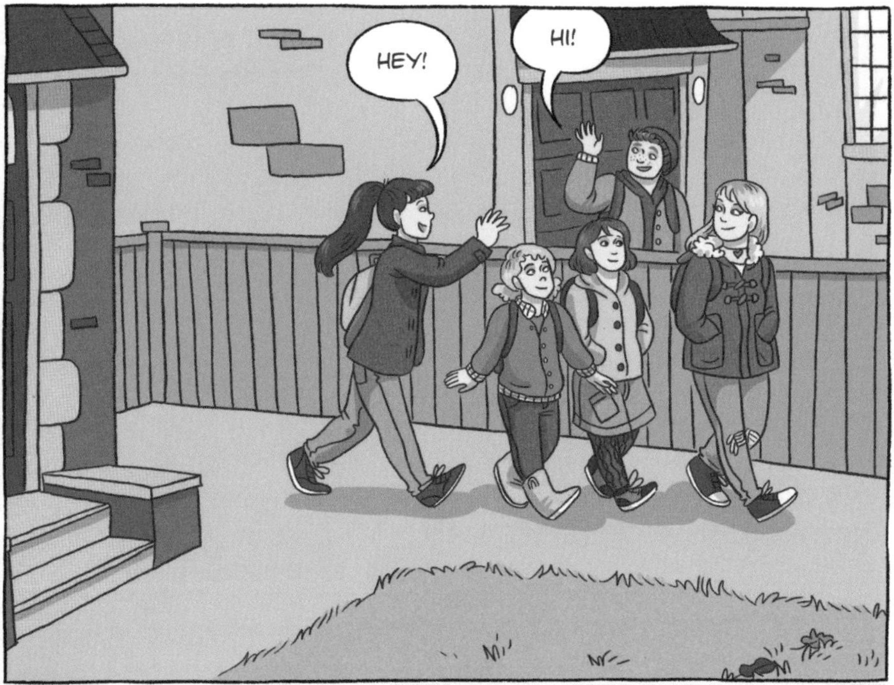
HEY!
HI!
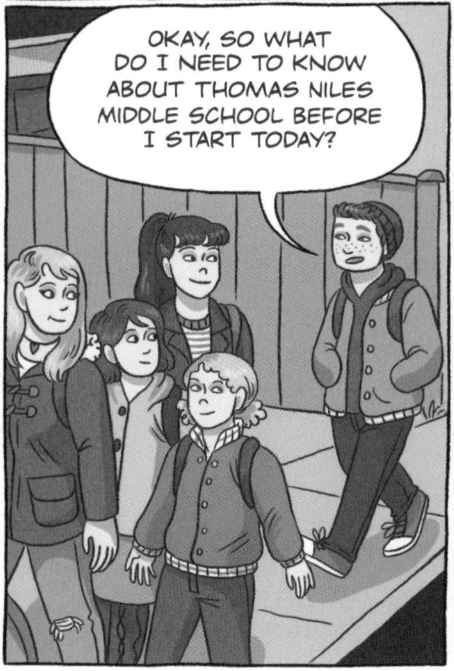
OKAY, SO WHAT DO I NEED TO KNOW ABOUT THOMAS NILES MIDDLE SCHOOL BEFORE I START TODAY?
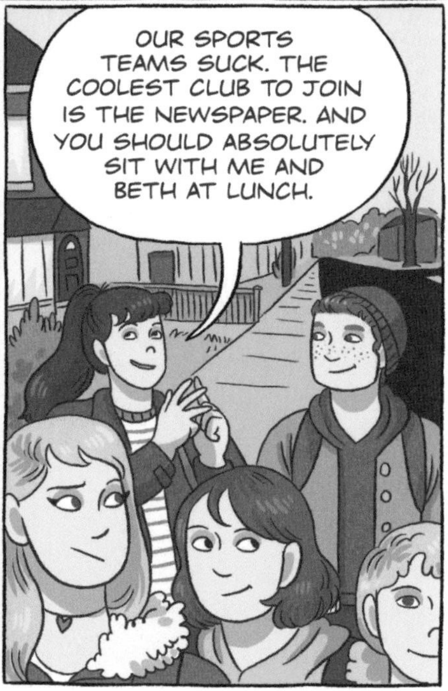
OUR SPORTS TEAMS SUCK. THE COOLEST CLUB TO JOIN IS THE NEWSPAPER. AND YOU SHOULD ABSOLUTELY SIT WITH ME AND BETH AT LUNCH.

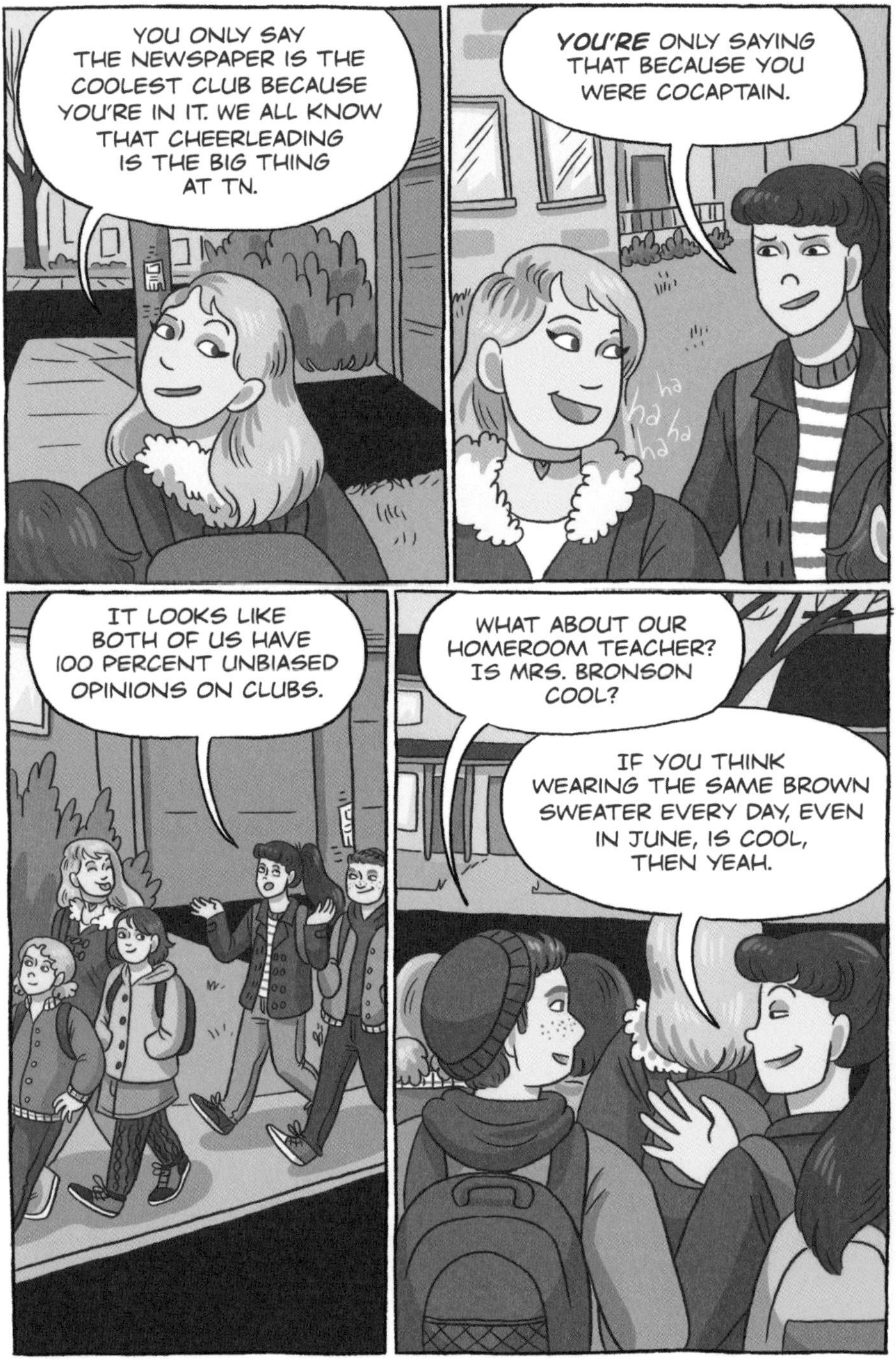
YOU ONLY SAY THE NEWSPAPER IS THE COOLEST CLUB BECAUSE YOU'RE IN IT. WE ALL KNOW THAT CHEERLEADING IS THE BIG THING AT TN.
YOU'RE ONLY SAYING THAT BECAUSE YOU WERE COCAPTAIN.
ha ha ha ha ha
IT LOOKS LIKE BOTH OF US HAVE 100 PERCENT UNBIASED OPINIONS ON CLUBS.
WHAT ABOUT OUR HOMEROOM TEACHER? IS MRS. BRONSON COOL?
IF YOU THINK WEARING THE SAME BROWN SWEATER EVERY DAY, EVEN IN JUNE, IS COOL, THEN YEAH.

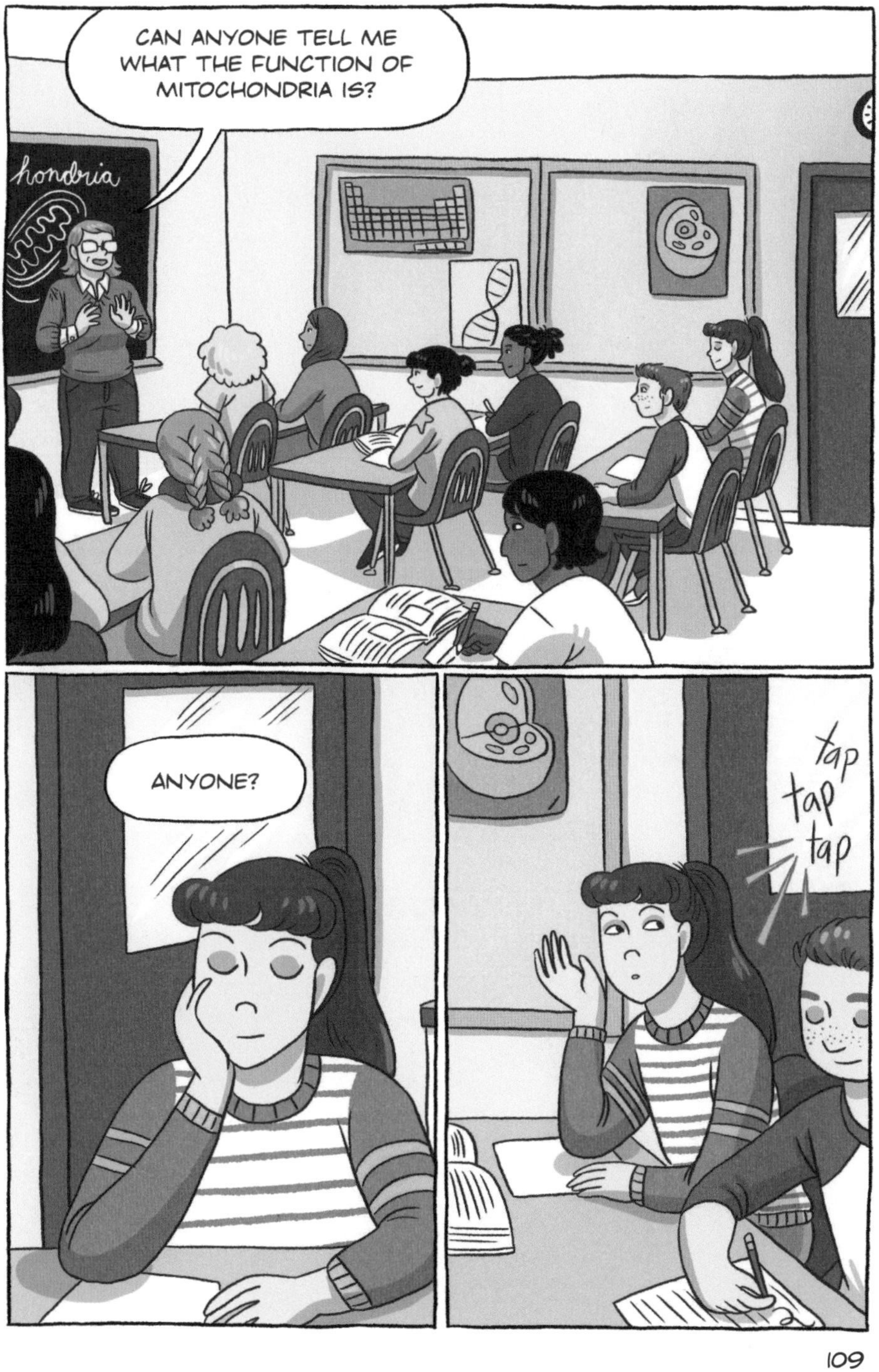
hondria
CAN ANYONE TELL ME WHAT THE FUNCTION OF MITOCHONDRIA IS?
ANYONE?
tap
tap
tap

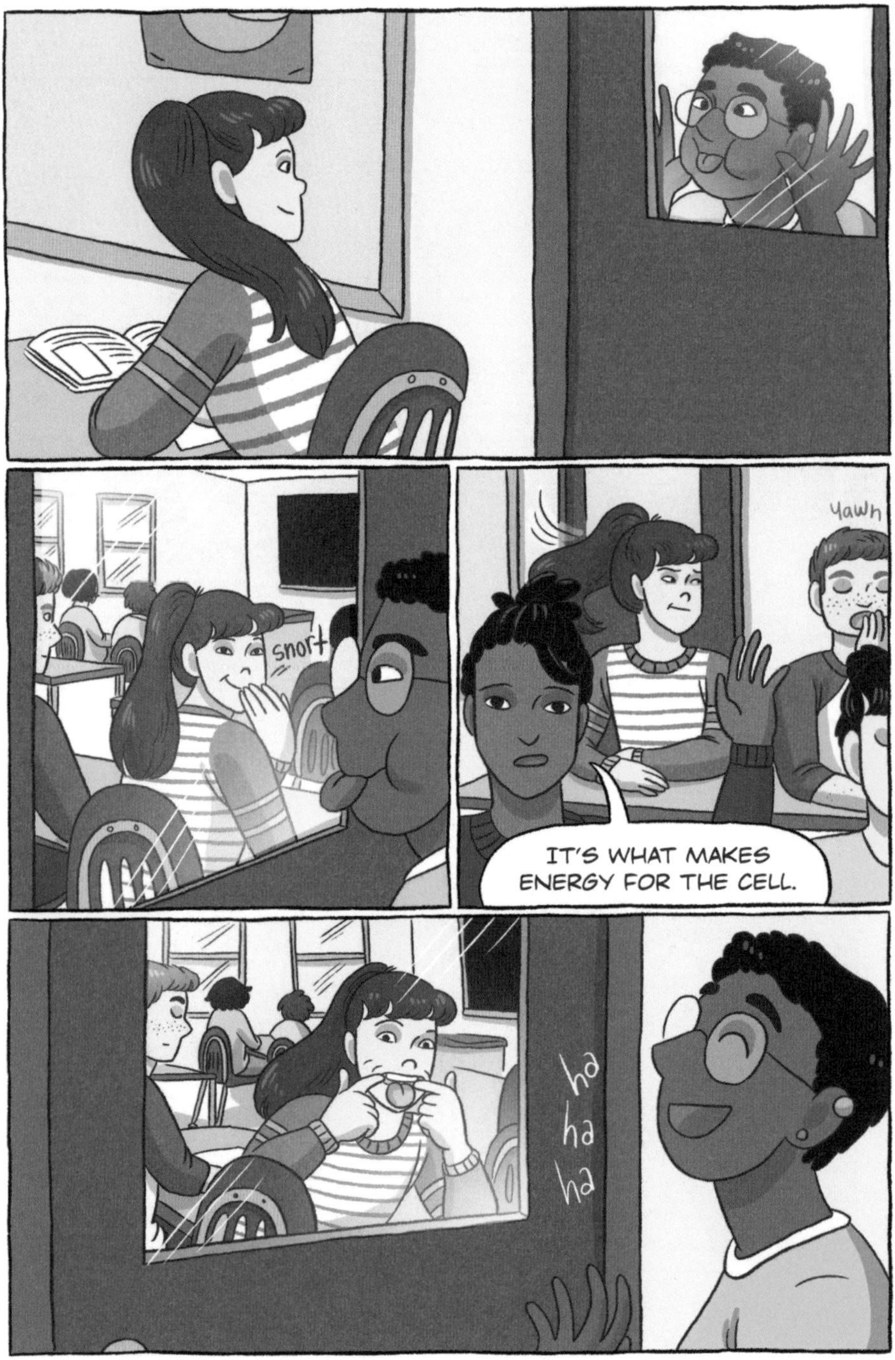
snort
yawn
IT'S WHAT MAKES ENERGY FOR THE CELL.
ha ha ha

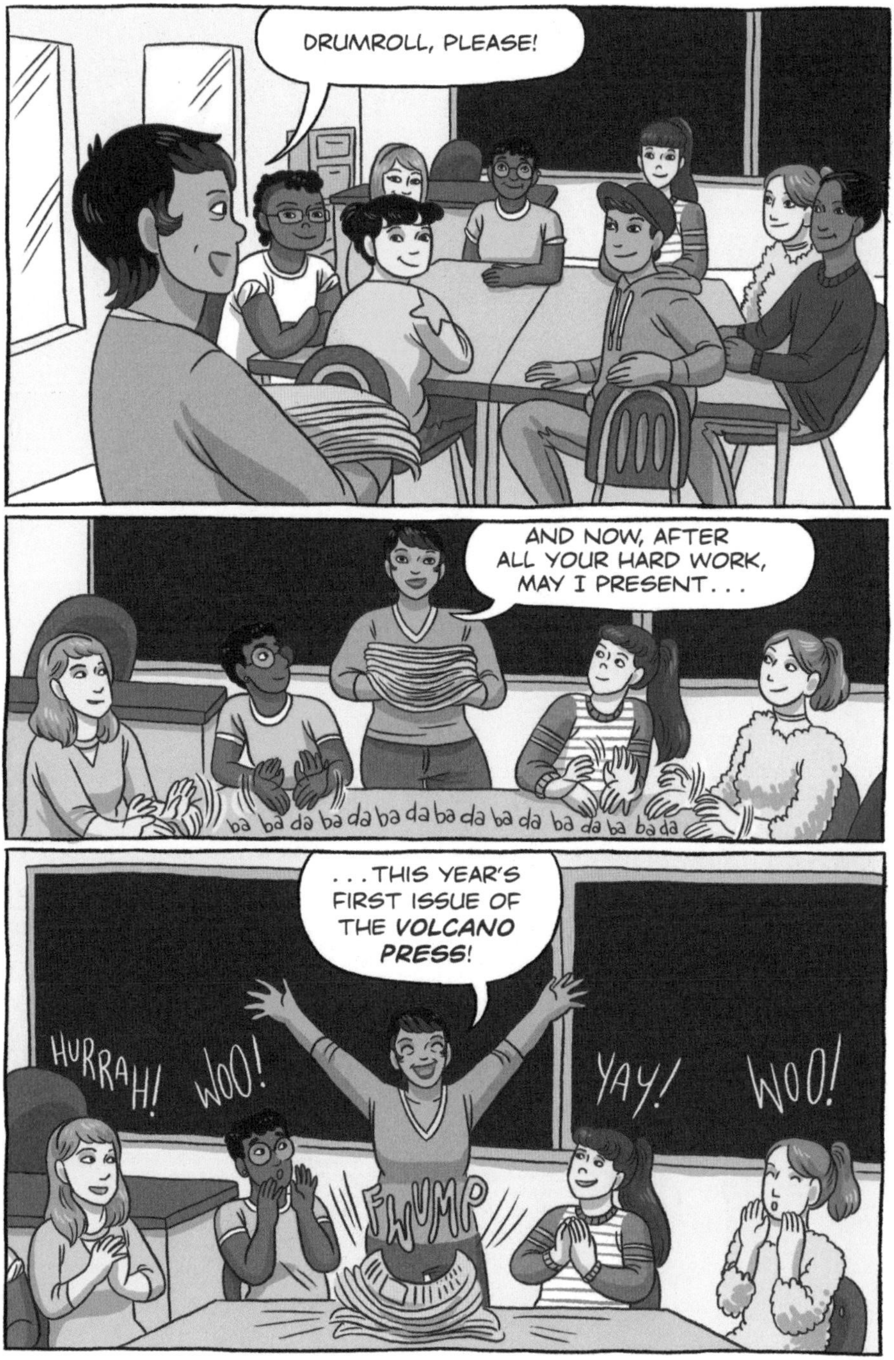
DRUMROLL, PLEASE!
AND NOW, AFTER ALL YOUR HARD WORK, MAY I PRESENT . . .
ba ba da ba da ba da ba da ba da ba da ba ba da
. . . THIS YEAR'S FIRST ISSUE OF THE *VOLCANO PRESS*!
HURRAH! WOO!
YAY! WOO!
FWUMP

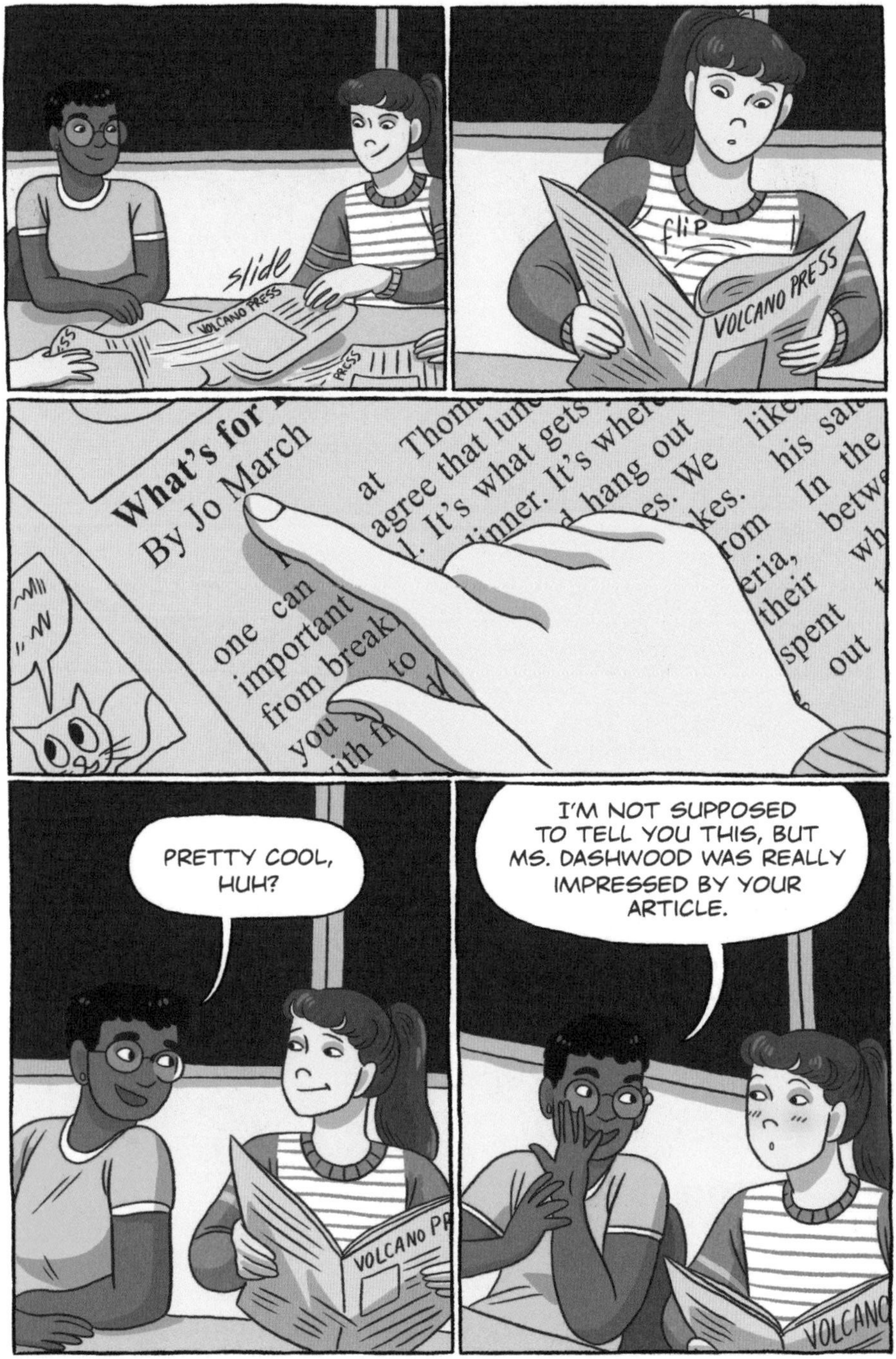
slide
VOLCANO PRESS
flip
VOLCANO PRESS
What's for
By Jo March
PRETTY COOL, HUH?
I'M NOT SUPPOSED TO TELL YOU THIS, BUT MS. DASHWOOD WAS REALLY IMPRESSED BY YOUR ARTICLE.
VOLCANO PR
VOLCANO

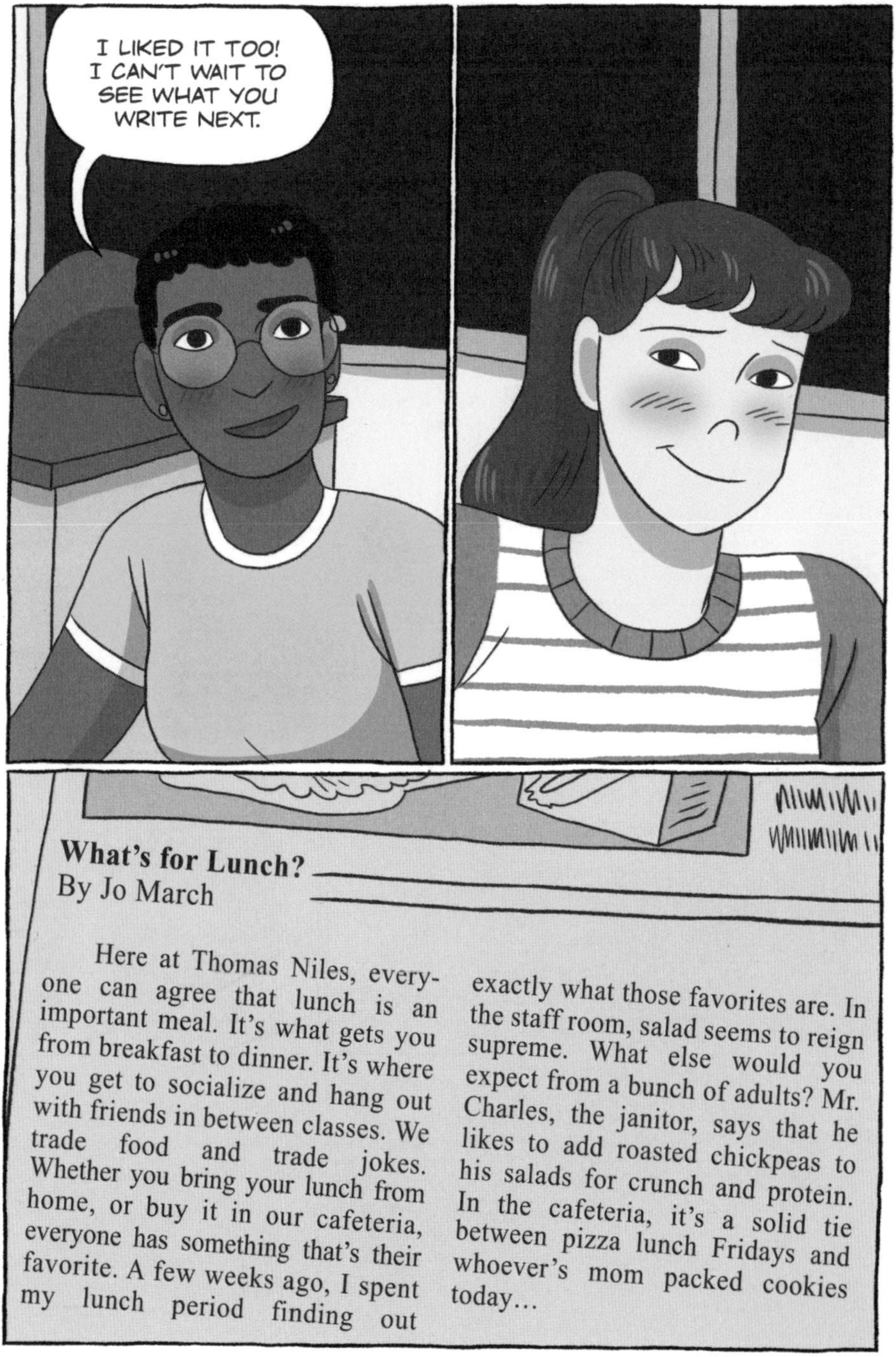
I LIKED IT TOO! I CAN'T WAIT TO SEE WHAT YOU WRITE NEXT.
What's for Lunch?
By Jo March
Here at Thomas Niles, everyone can agree that lunch is an important meal. It's what gets you from breakfast to dinner. It's where you get to socialize and hang out with friends in between classes. We trade food and trade jokes. Whether you bring your lunch from home, or buy it in our cafeteria, everyone has something that's their favorite. A few weeks ago, I spent my lunch period finding out exactly what those favorites are. In the staff room, salad seems to reign supreme. What else would you expect from a bunch of adults? Mr. Charles, the janitor, says that he likes to add roasted chickpeas to his salads for crunch and protein. In the cafeteria, it's a solid tie between pizza lunch Fridays and whoever's mom packed cookies today...

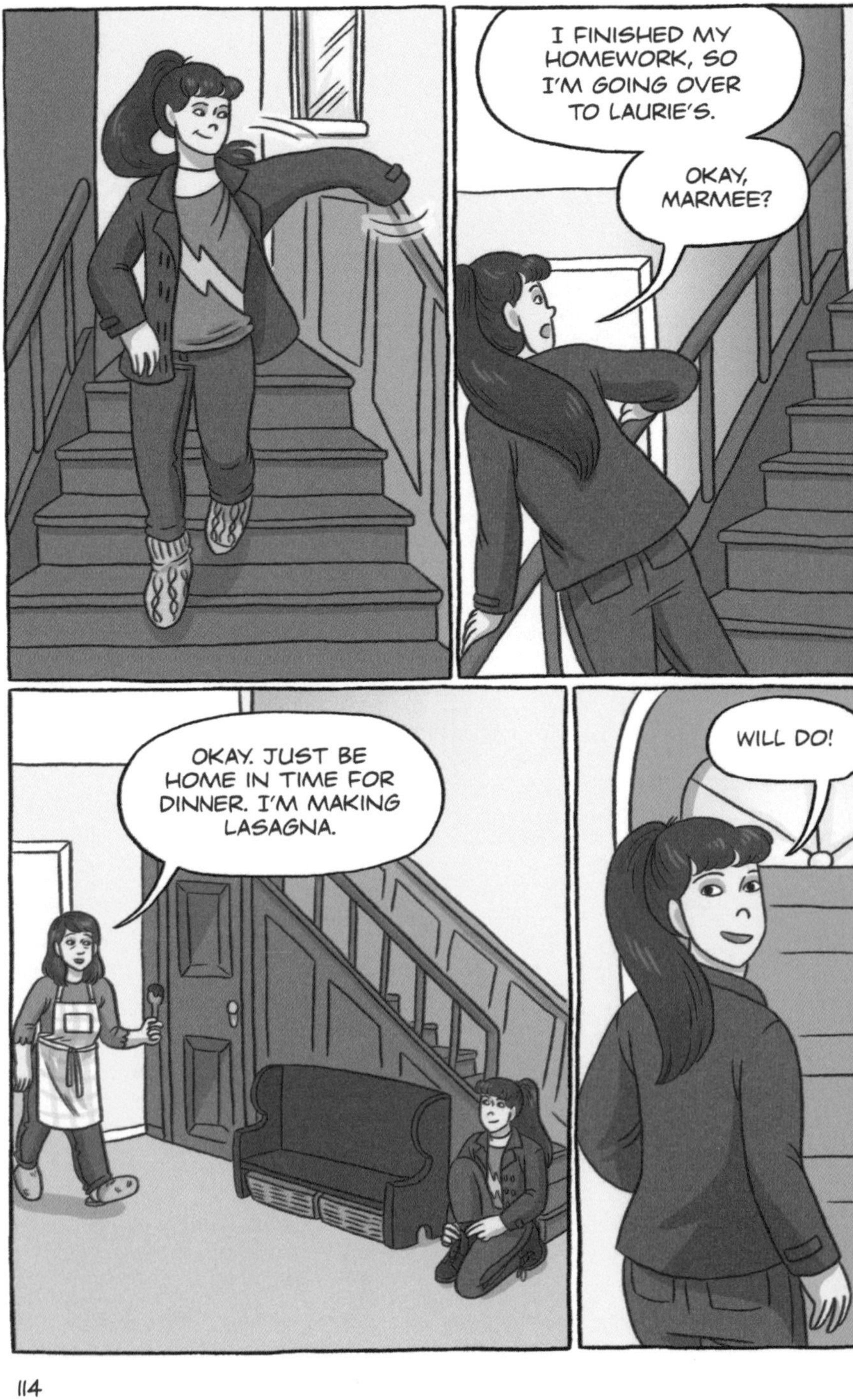
I FINISHED MY HOMEWORK, SO I'M GOING OVER TO LAURIE'S.
OKAY, MARMEE?
OKAY. JUST BE HOME IN TIME FOR DINNER. I'M MAKING LASAGNA.
WILL DO!

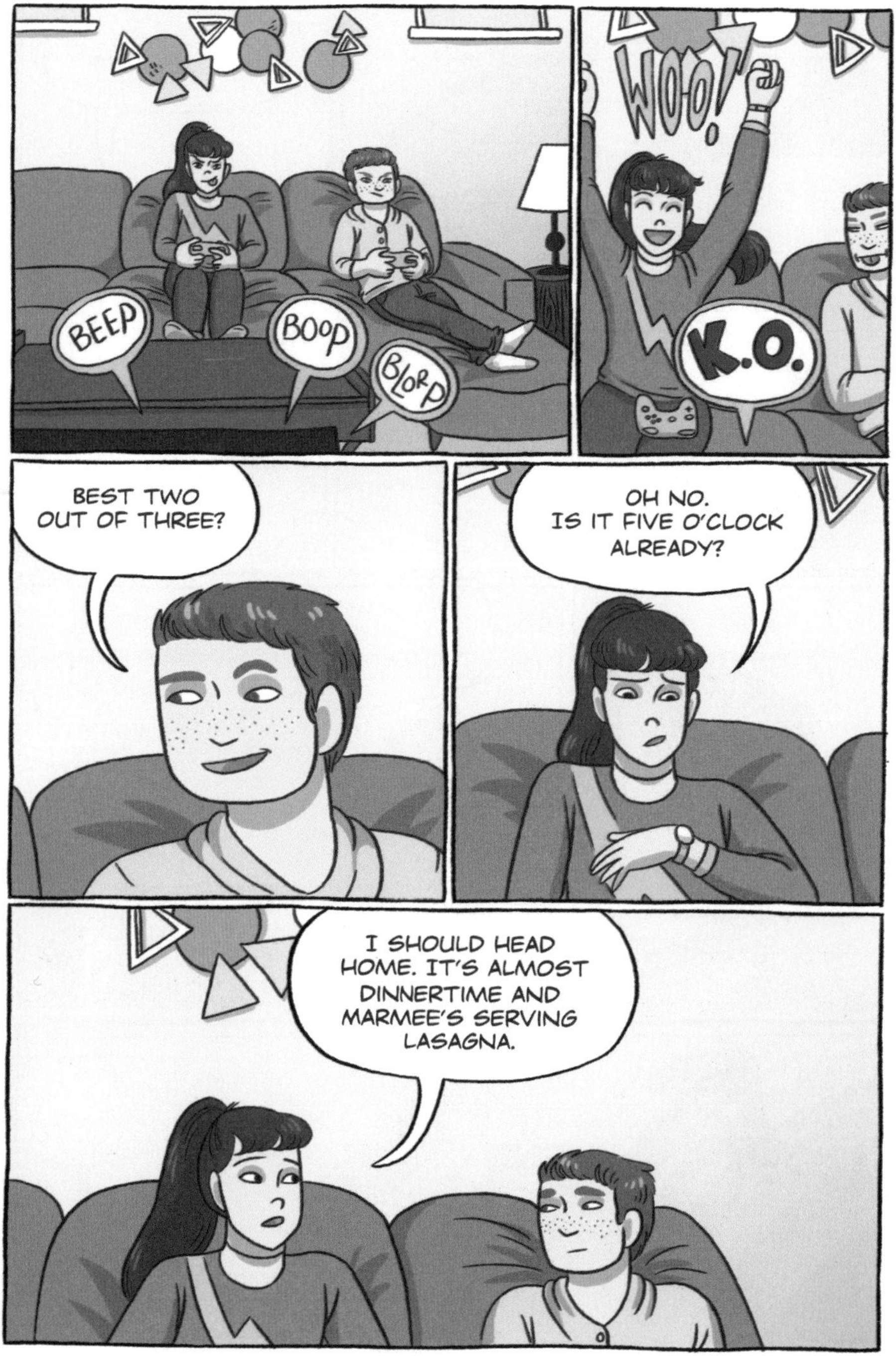
BEEP
BOOP
BLORP
WOO!
K.O.
BEST TWO OUT OF THREE?
OH NO. IS IT FIVE O'CLOCK ALREADY?
I SHOULD HEAD HOME. IT'S ALMOST DINNERTIME AND MARMEE'S SERVING LASAGNA.

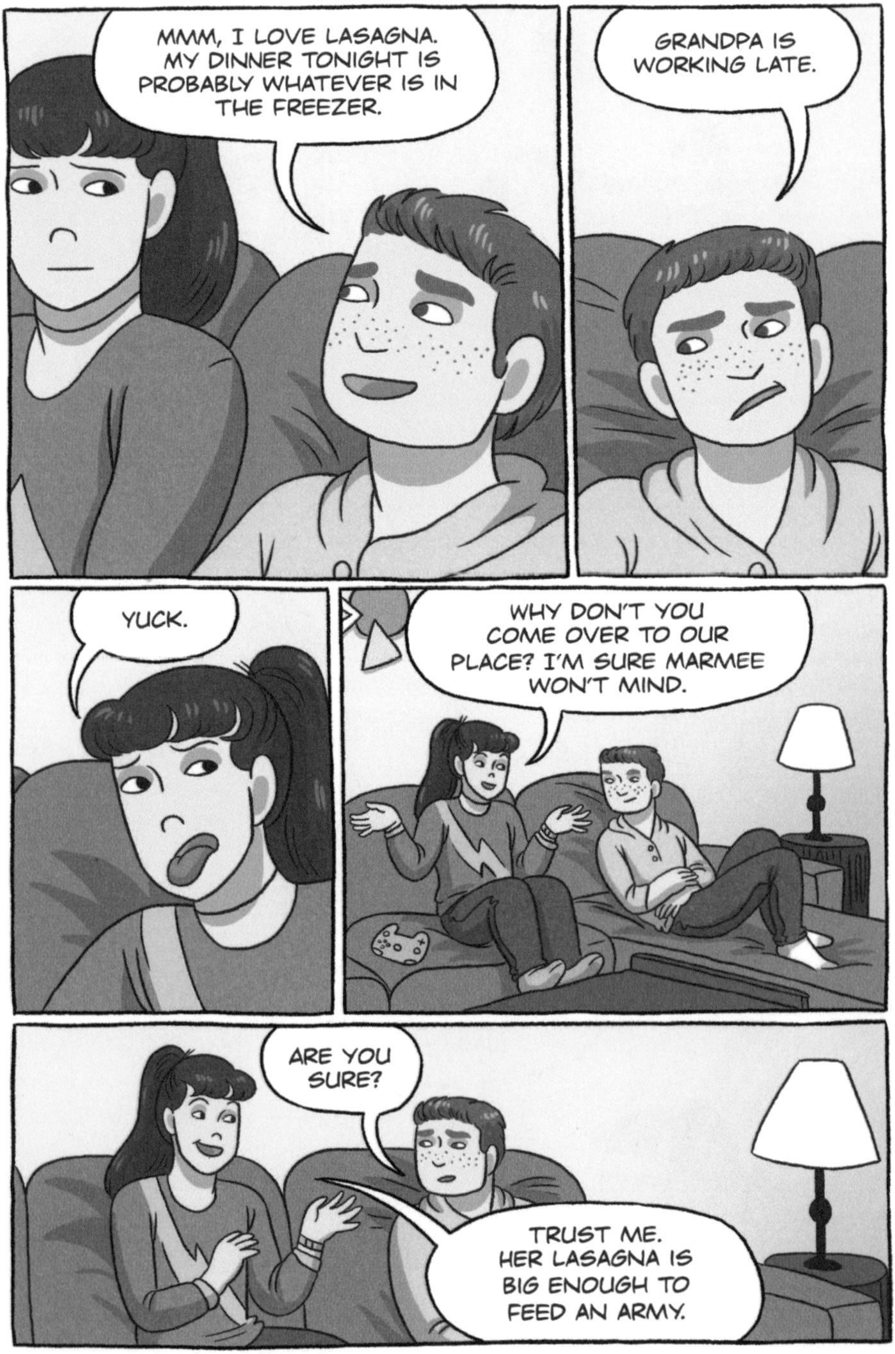
MMM, I LOVE LASAGNA. MY DINNER TONIGHT IS PROBABLY WHATEVER IS IN THE FREEZER.
GRANDPA IS WORKING LATE.
YUCK.
WHY DON'T YOU COME OVER TO OUR PLACE? I'M SURE MARMEE WON'T MIND.
ARE YOU SURE?
TRUST ME. HER LASAGNA IS BIG ENOUGH TO FEED AN ARMY.

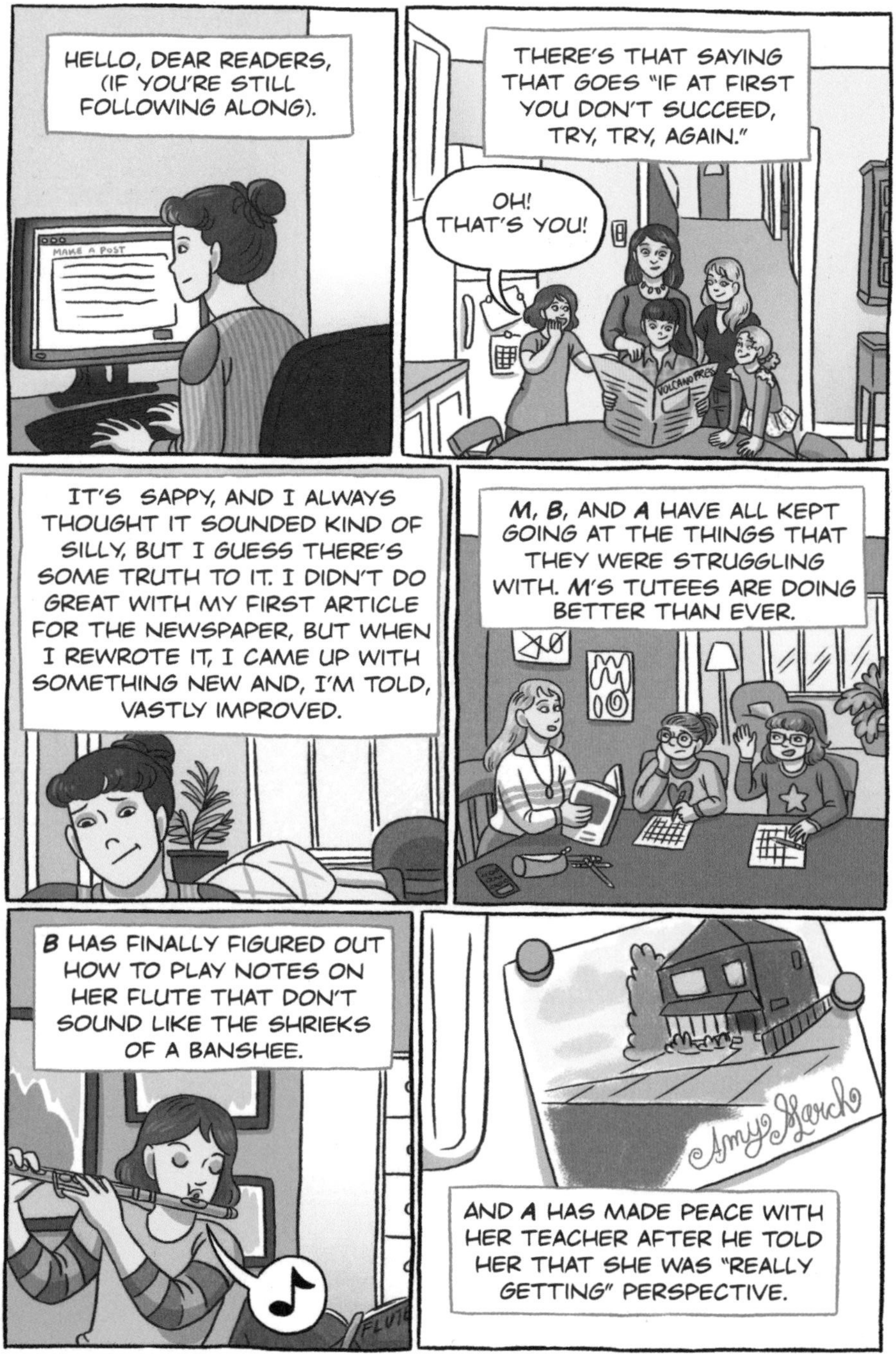
HELLO, DEAR READERS, (IF YOU'RE STILL FOLLOWING ALONG).
MAKE A POST
THERE'S THAT SAYING THAT GOES "IF AT FIRST YOU DON'T SUCCEED, TRY, TRY, AGAIN."
OH! THAT'S YOU!
VOLCANO PRESS
IT'S SAPPY, AND I ALWAYS THOUGHT IT SOUNDED KIND OF SILLY, BUT I GUESS THERE'S SOME TRUTH TO IT. I DIDN'T DO GREAT WITH MY FIRST ARTICLE FOR THE NEWSPAPER, BUT WHEN I REWROTE IT, I CAME UP WITH SOMETHING NEW AND, I'M TOLD, VASTLY IMPROVED.
M, B, AND A HAVE ALL KEPT GOING AT THE THINGS THAT THEY WERE STRUGGLING WITH. M'S TUTEES ARE DOING BETTER THAN EVER.
B HAS FINALLY FIGURED OUT HOW TO PLAY NOTES ON HER FLUTE THAT DON'T SOUND LIKE THE SHRIEKS OF A BANSHEE.
FLUTE
Amy March
AND A HAS MADE PEACE WITH HER TEACHER AFTER HE TOLD HER THAT SHE WAS "REALLY GETTING" PERSPECTIVE.

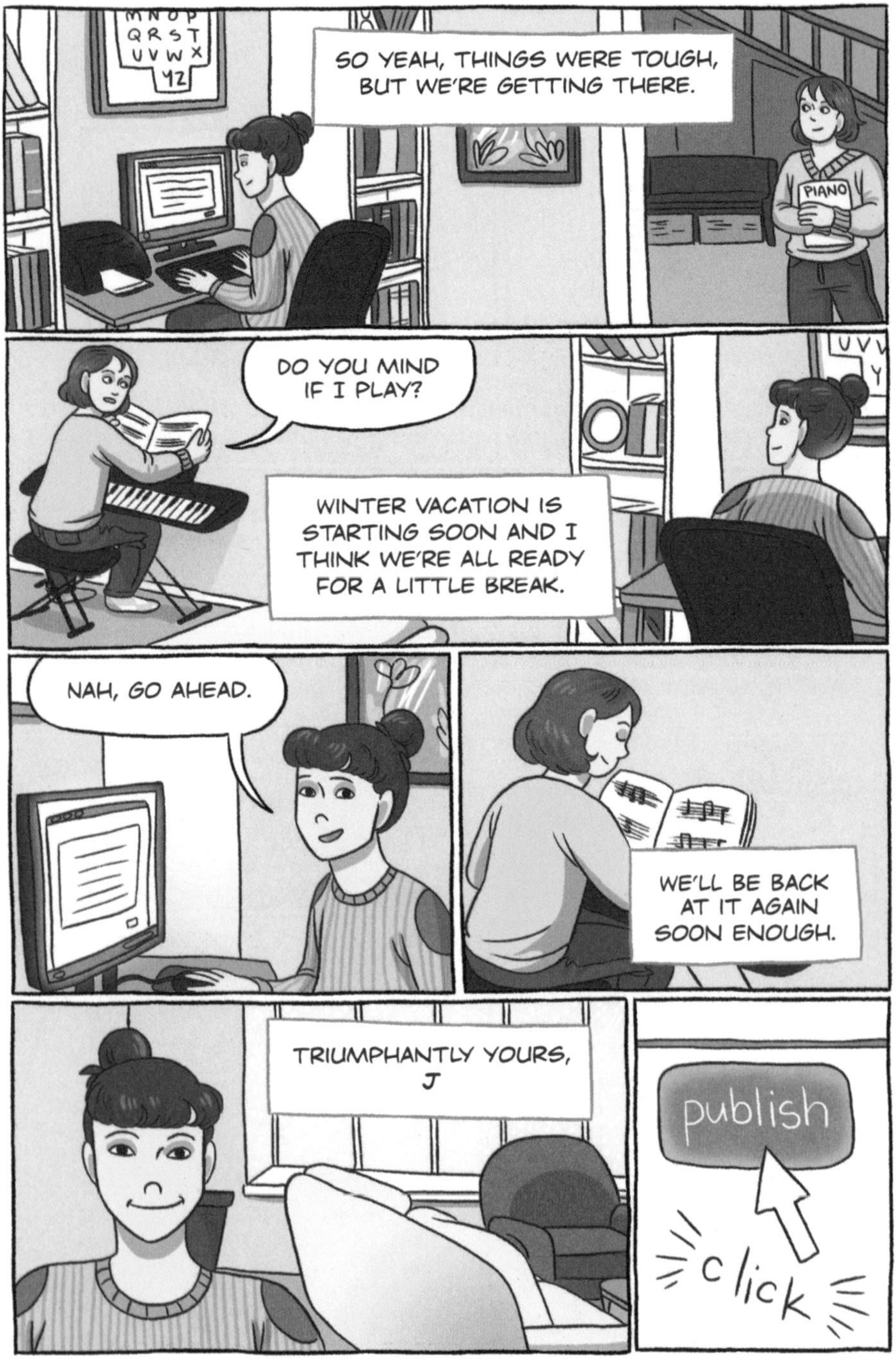
MNOP QRST UVWX YZ
SO YEAH, THINGS WERE TOUGH, BUT WE'RE GETTING THERE.
PIANO
DO YOU MIND IF I PLAY?
WINTER VACATION IS STARTING SOON AND I THINK WE'RE ALL READY FOR A LITTLE BREAK.
NAH, GO AHEAD.
WE'LL BE BACK AT IT AGAIN SOON ENOUGH.
TRIUMPHANTLY YOURS, J
publish
click

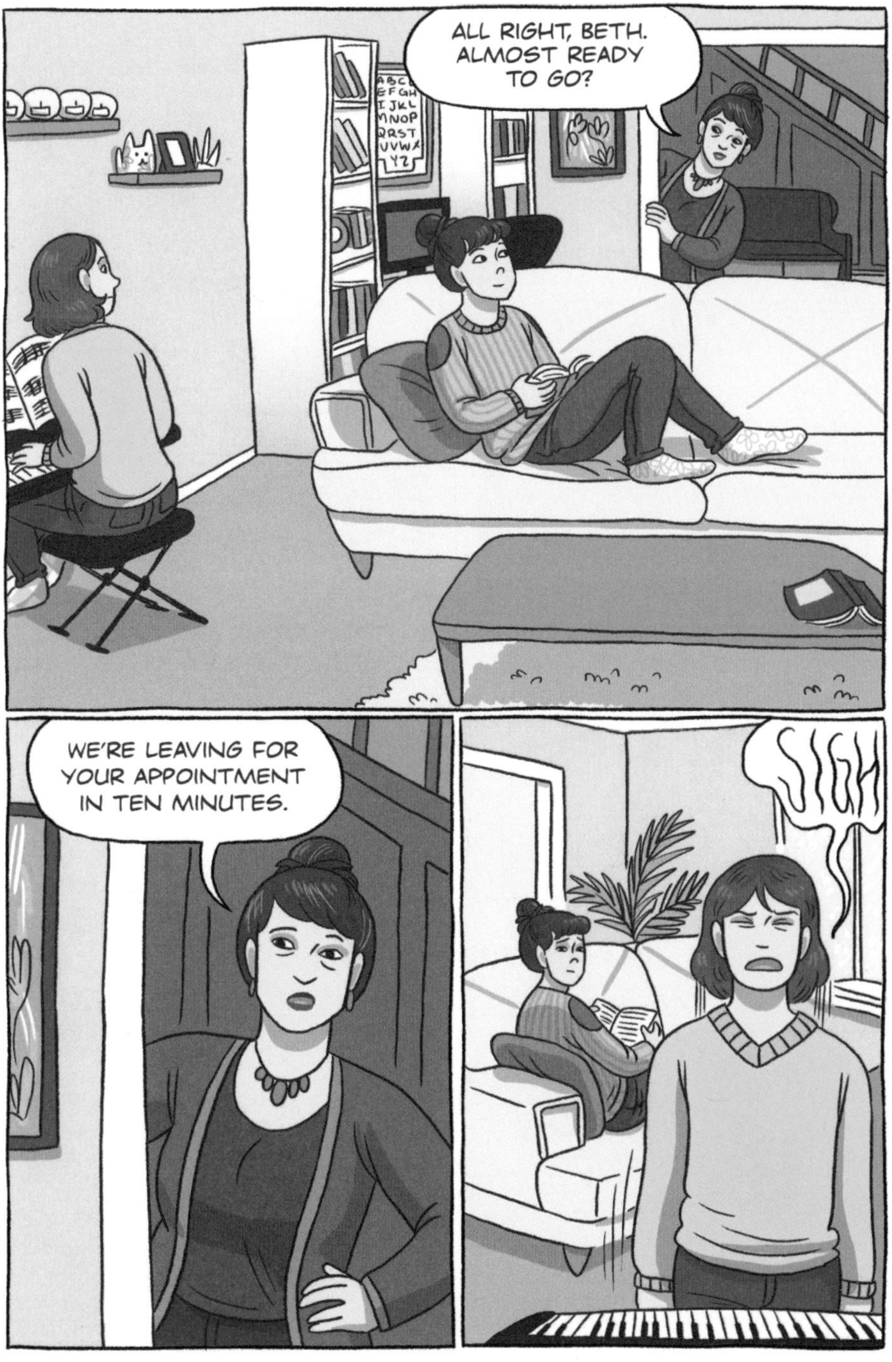
ALL RIGHT, BETH. ALMOST READY TO GO?
WE'RE LEAVING FOR YOUR APPOINTMENT IN TEN MINUTES.
SIGH

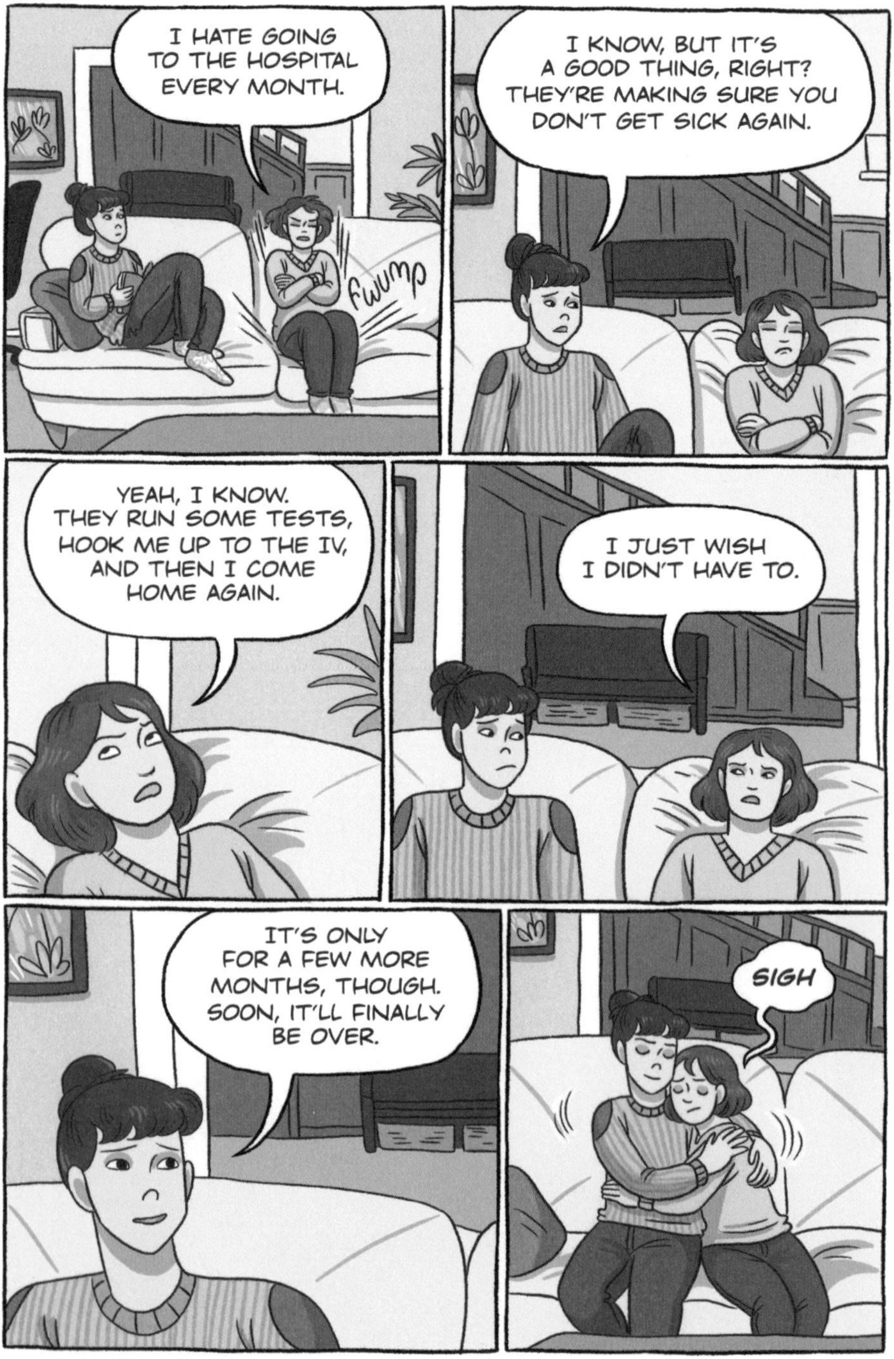
I HATE GOING TO THE HOSPITAL EVERY MONTH.
fwump
I KNOW, BUT IT'S A GOOD THING, RIGHT? THEY'RE MAKING SURE YOU DON'T GET SICK AGAIN.
YEAH, I KNOW. THEY RUN SOME TESTS, HOOK ME UP TO THE IV, AND THEN I COME HOME AGAIN.
I JUST WISH I DIDN'T HAVE TO.
IT'S ONLY FOR A FEW MORE MONTHS, THOUGH. SOON, IT'LL FINALLY BE OVER.
SIGH

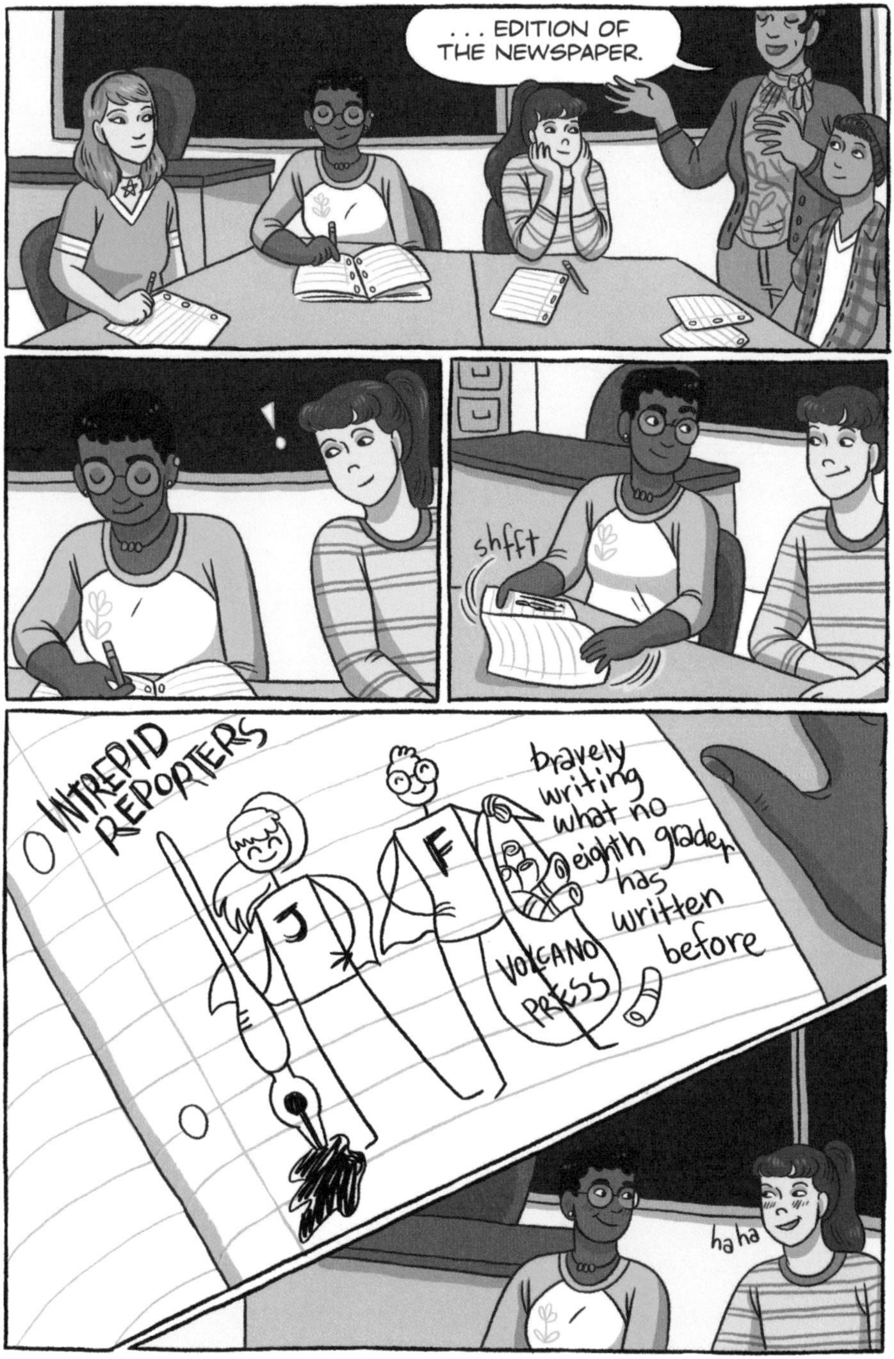
. . . EDITION OF THE NEWSPAPER.
!
shffT
INTREPID REPORTERS
J
F
VOLCANO PRESS
bravely writing what no eighth grader has written before
ha ha

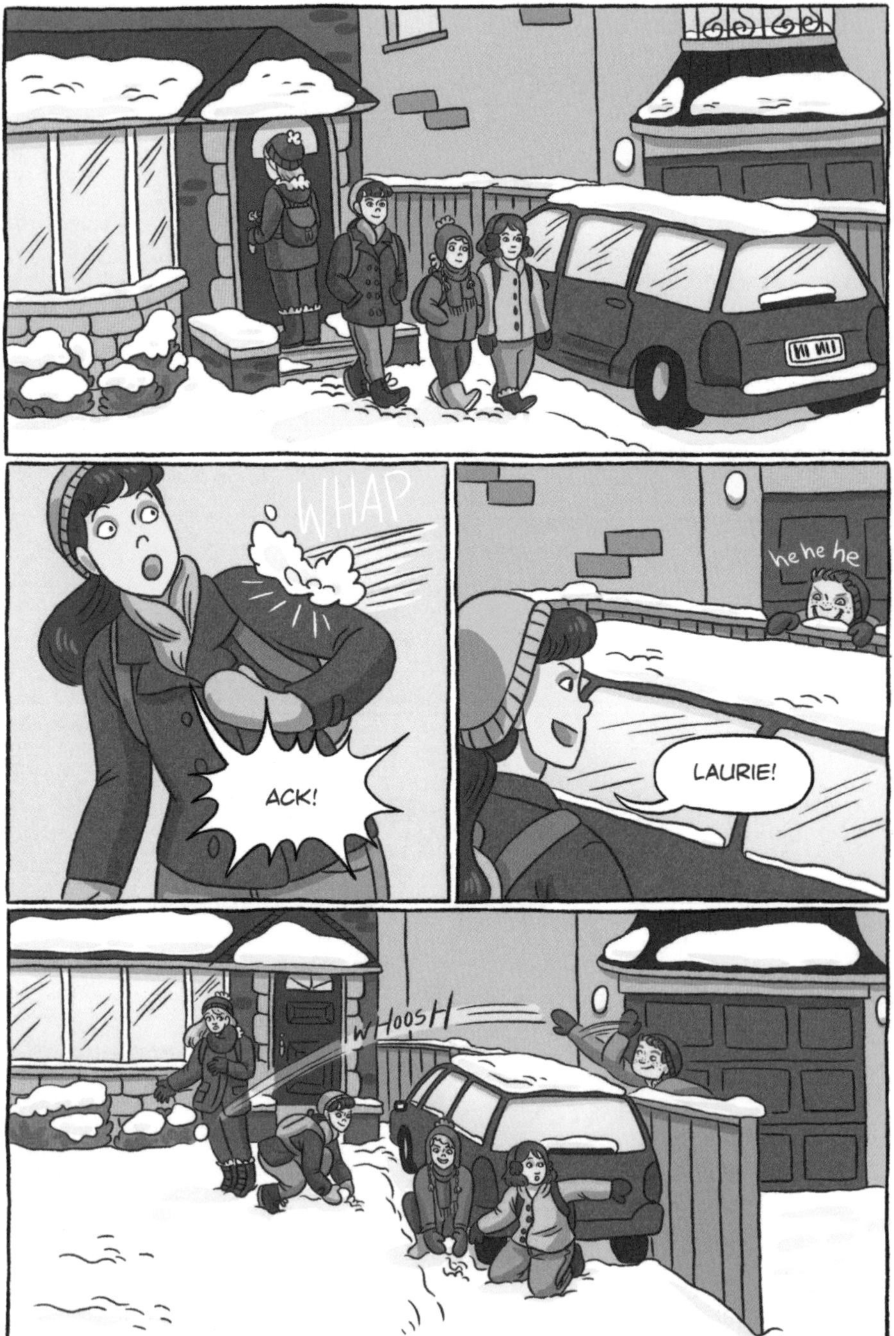
WHAP
ACK!
he he he
LAURIE!
WHOOSH

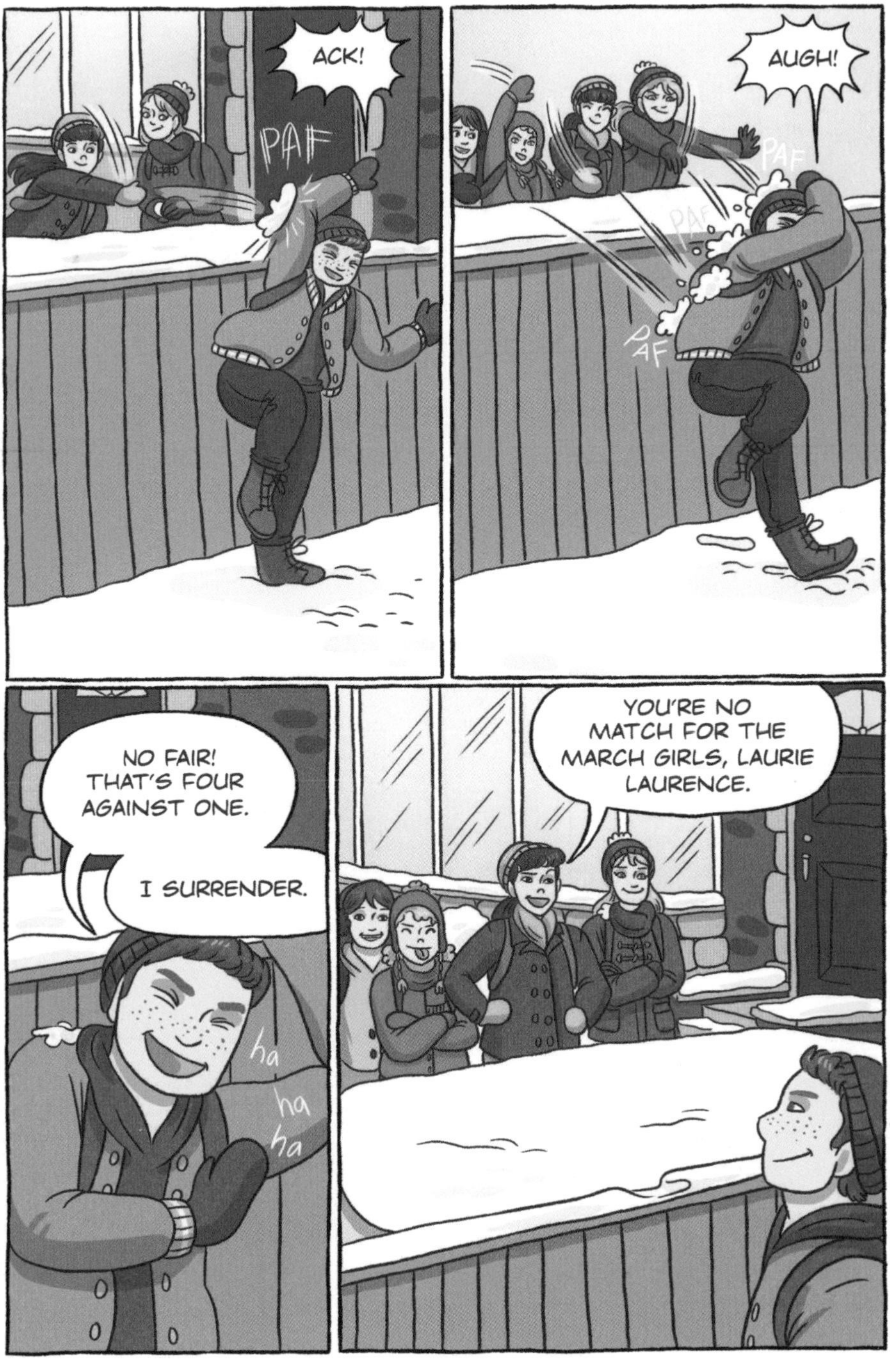
ACK!
PAF
AUGH!
PAF
PAF
PAF
NO FAIR! THAT'S FOUR AGAINST ONE.
I SURRENDER.
ha
ha
ha
YOU'RE NO MATCH FOR THE MARCH GIRLS, LAURIE LAURENCE.

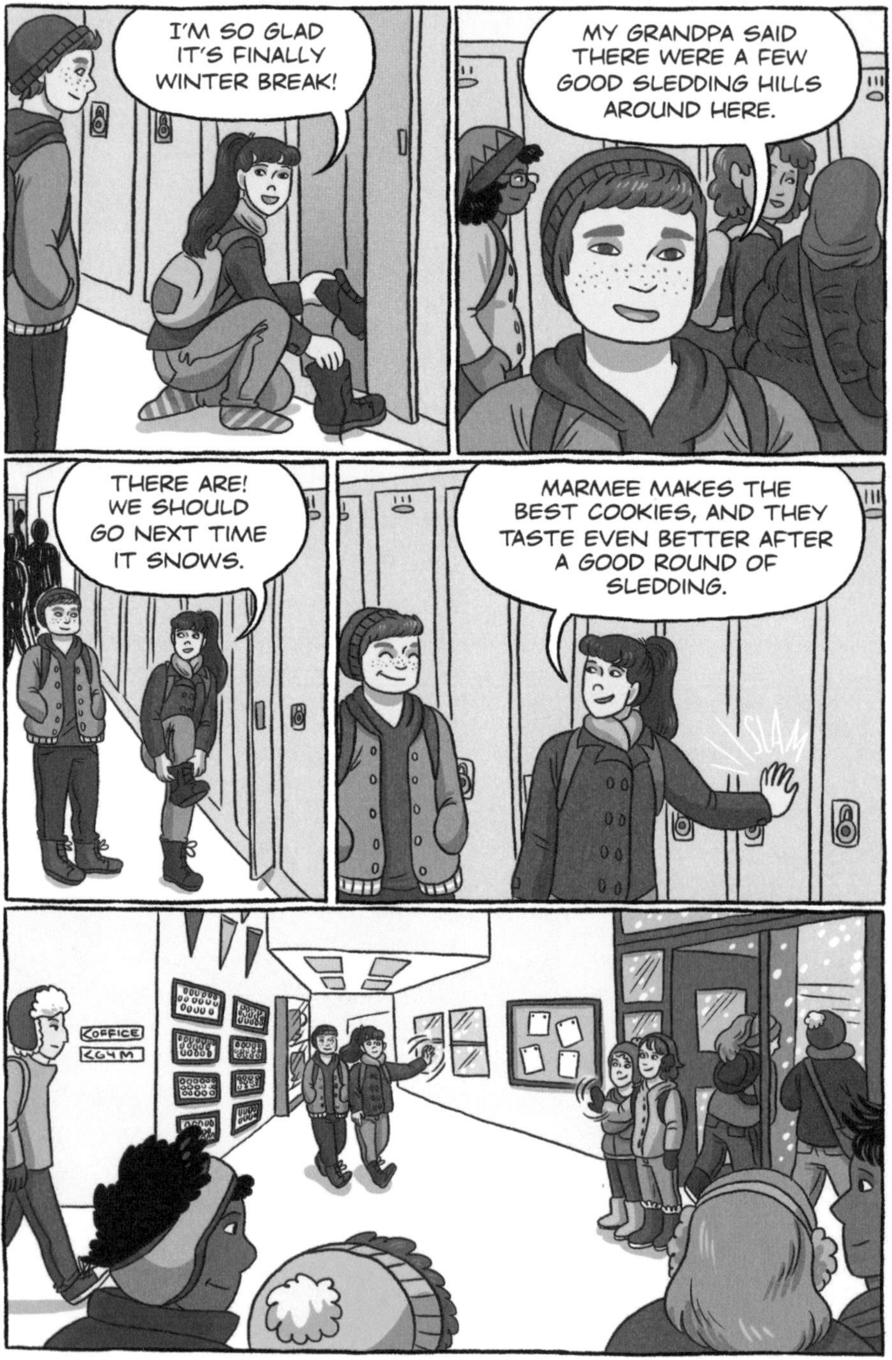
I'M SO GLAD IT'S FINALLY WINTER BREAK!
MY GRANDPA SAID THERE WERE A FEW GOOD SLEDDING HILLS AROUND HERE.
THERE ARE! WE SHOULD GO NEXT TIME IT SNOWS.
MARMEE MAKES THE BEST COOKIES, AND THEY TASTE EVEN BETTER AFTER A GOOD ROUND OF SLEDDING.
SLAM
<OFFICE
<GYM

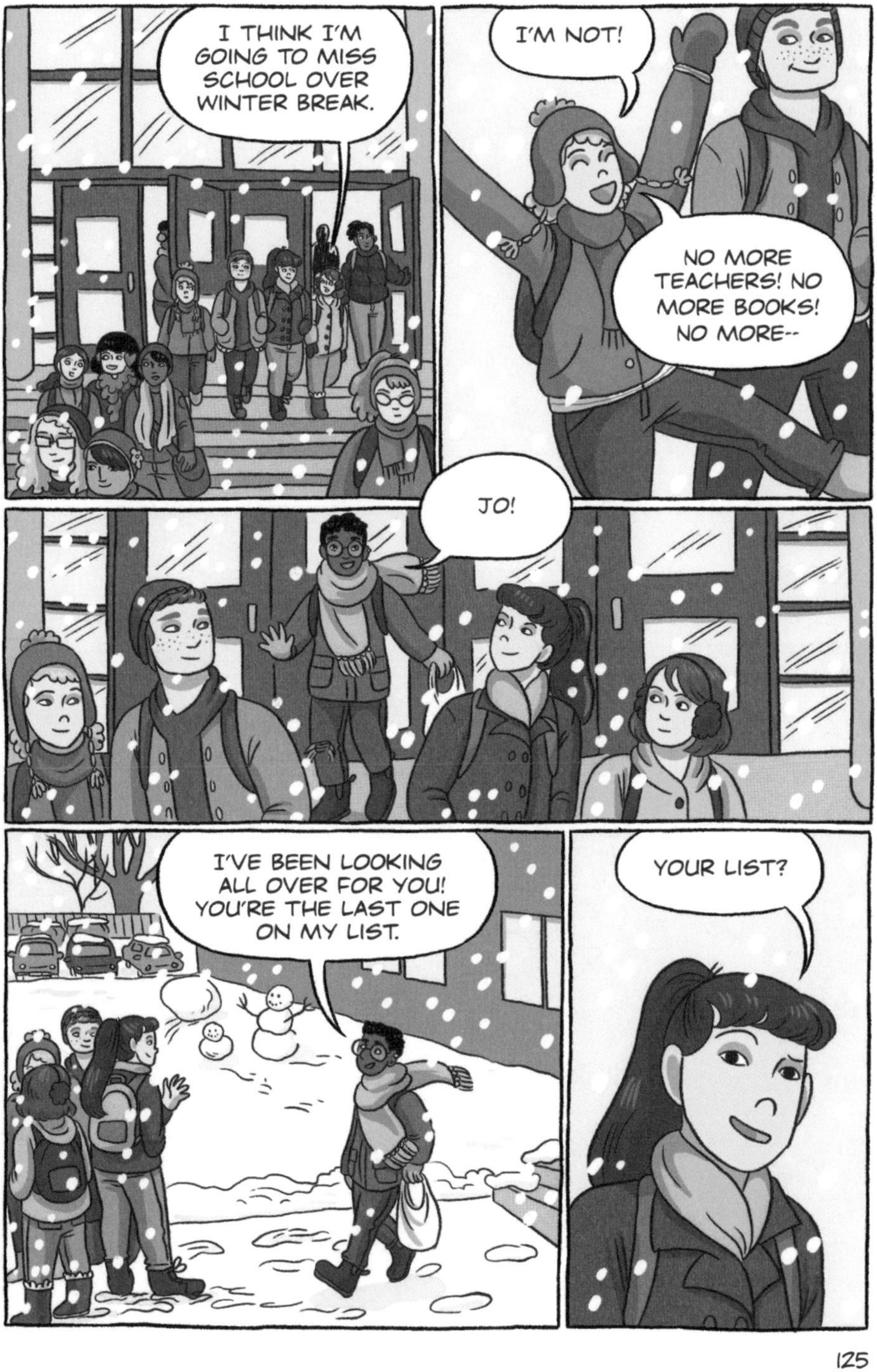
I THINK I'M GOING TO MISS SCHOOL OVER WINTER BREAK.
I'M NOT!
NO MORE TEACHERS! NO MORE BOOKS! NO MORE--
JO!
I'VE BEEN LOOKING ALL OVER FOR YOU! YOU'RE THE LAST ONE ON MY LIST.
YOUR LIST?

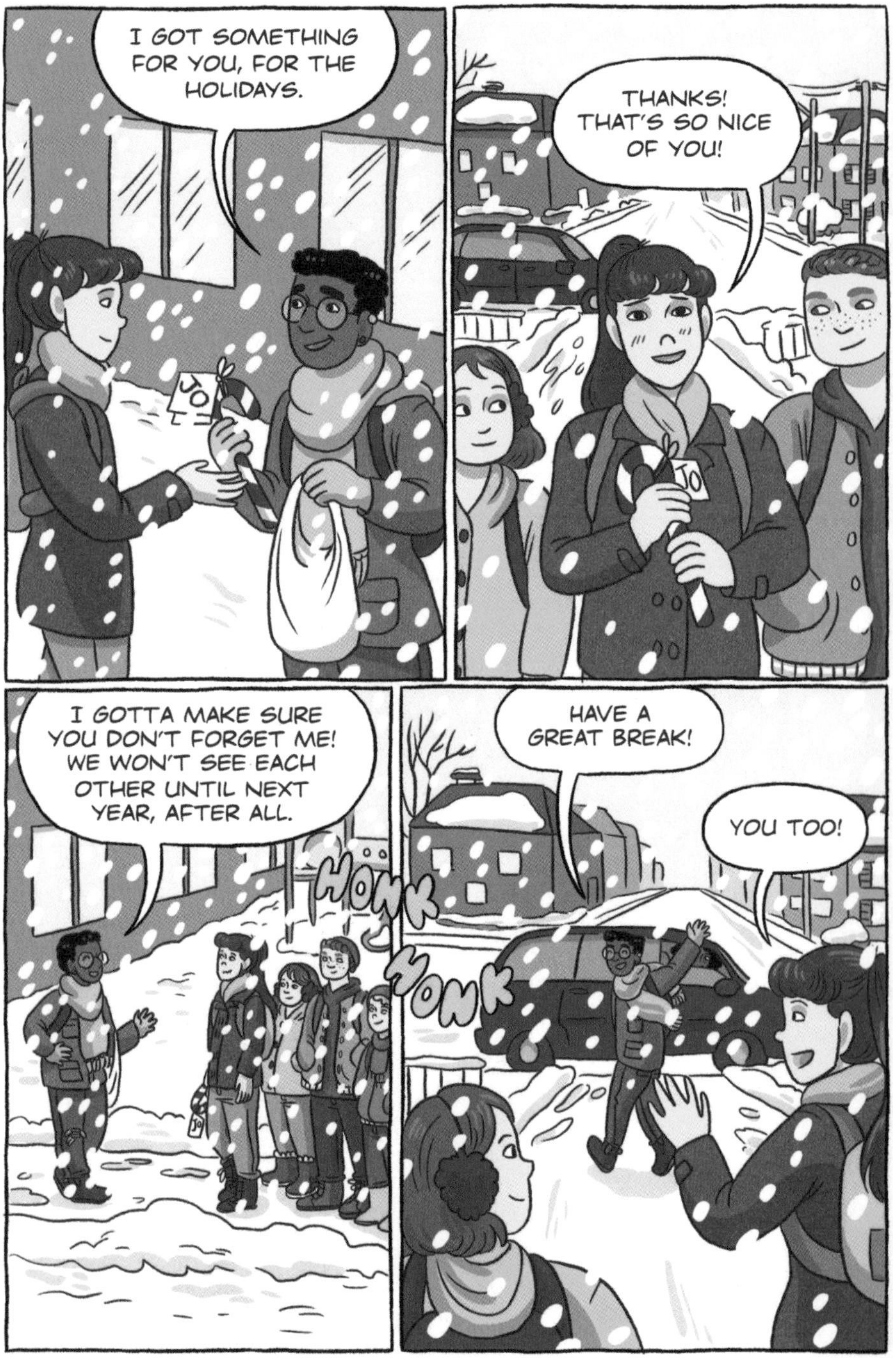
I GOT SOMETHING FOR YOU, FOR THE HOLIDAYS.
JO
THANKS! THAT'S SO NICE OF YOU!
JO
I GOTTA MAKE SURE YOU DON'T FORGET ME! WE WON'T SEE EACH OTHER UNTIL NEXT YEAR, AFTER ALL.
HONK
HONK
HAVE A GREAT BREAK!
YOU TOO!

CHAPTER 5

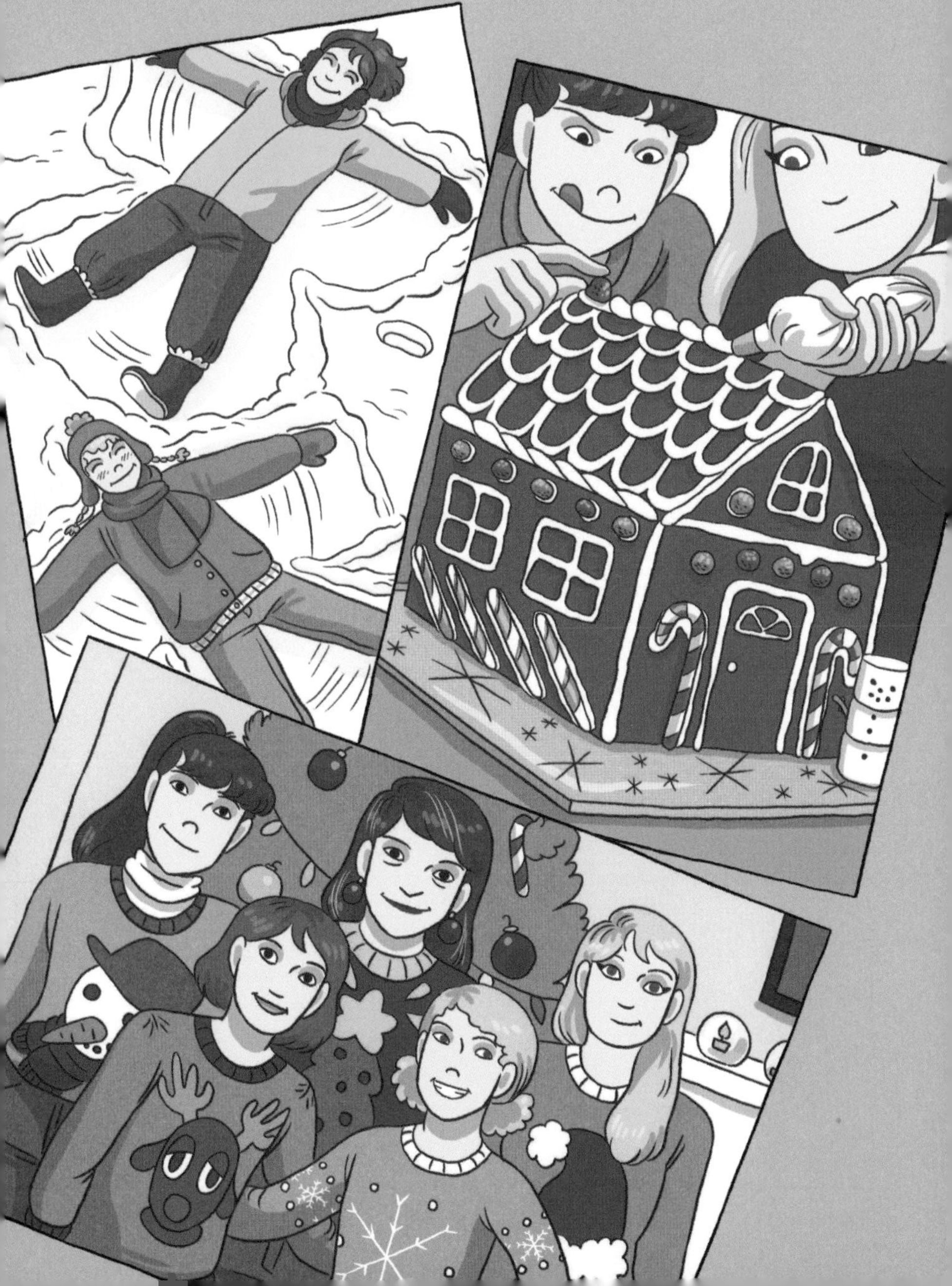

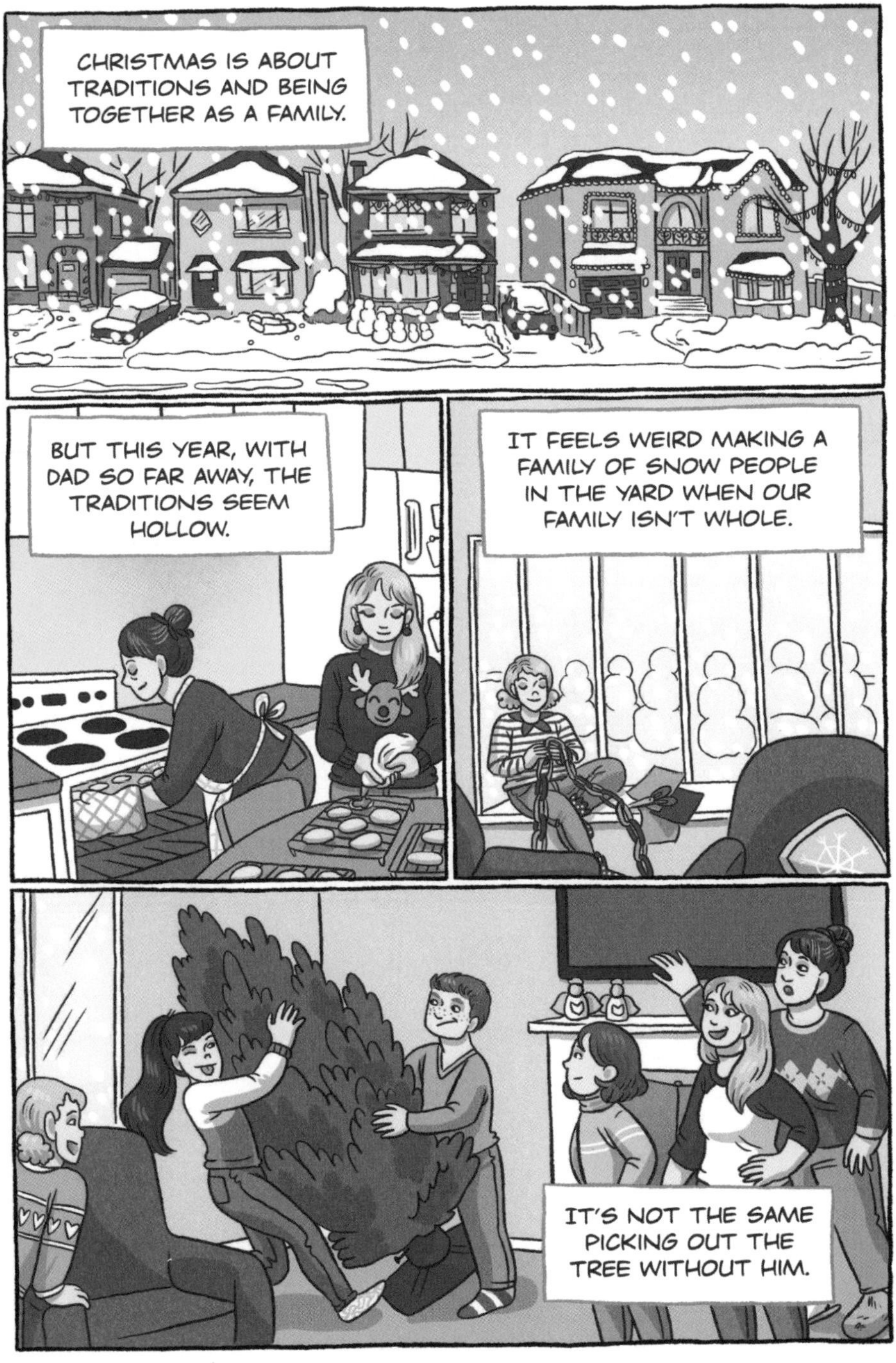
CHRISTMAS IS ABOUT TRADITIONS AND BEING TOGETHER AS A FAMILY.
BUT THIS YEAR, WITH DAD SO FAR AWAY, THE TRADITIONS SEEM HOLLOW.
IT FEELS WEIRD MAKING A FAMILY OF SNOW PEOPLE IN THE YARD WHEN OUR FAMILY ISN'T WHOLE.
IT'S NOT THE SAME PICKING OUT THE TREE WITHOUT HIM.

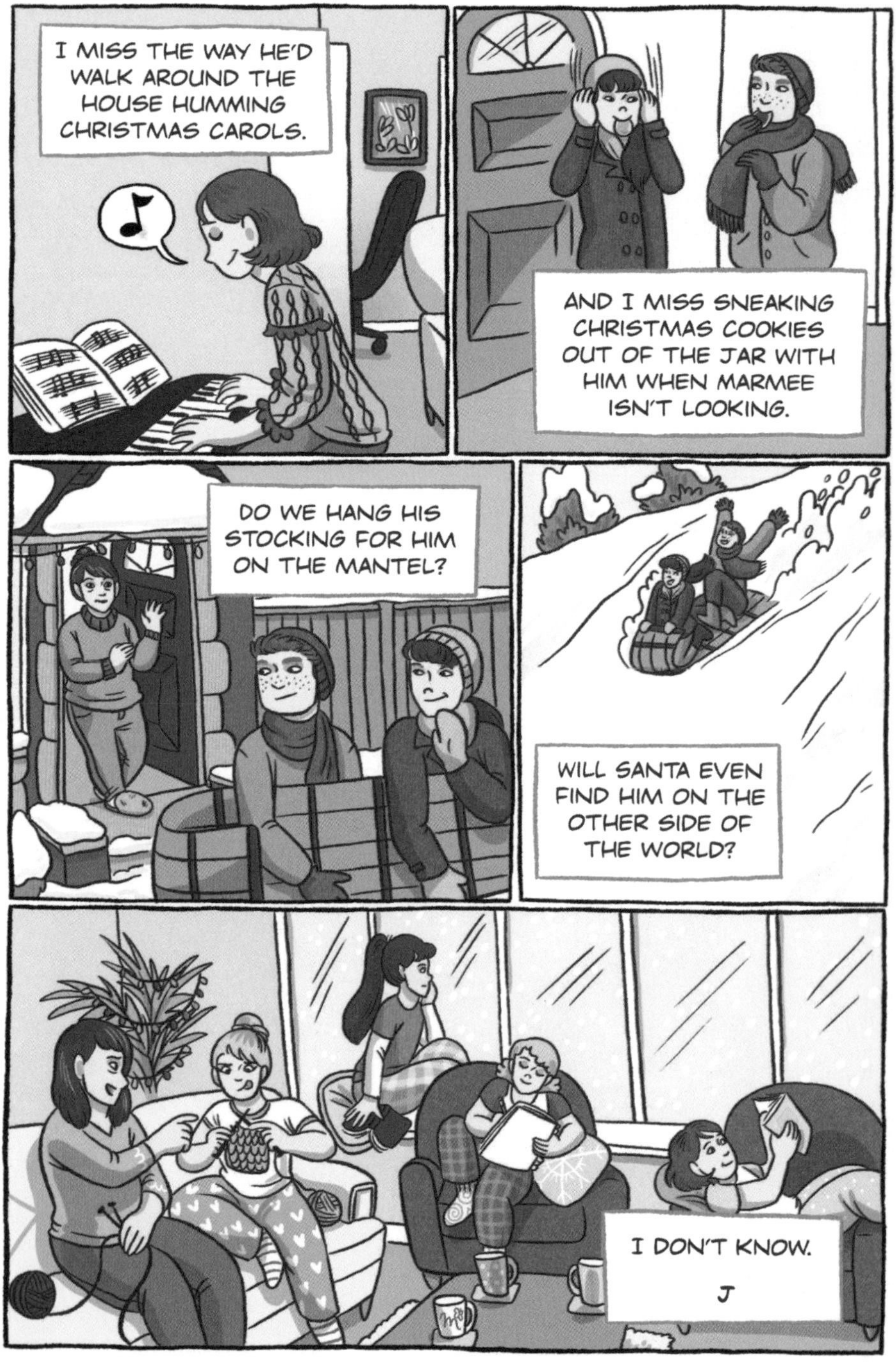
I MISS THE WAY HE'D WALK AROUND THE HOUSE HUMMING CHRISTMAS CAROLS.
AND I MISS SNEAKING CHRISTMAS COOKIES OUT OF THE JAR WITH HIM WHEN MARMEE ISN'T LOOKING.
DO WE HANG HIS STOCKING FOR HIM ON THE MANTEL?
WILL SANTA EVEN FIND HIM ON THE OTHER SIDE OF THE WORLD?
I DON'T KNOW.
J

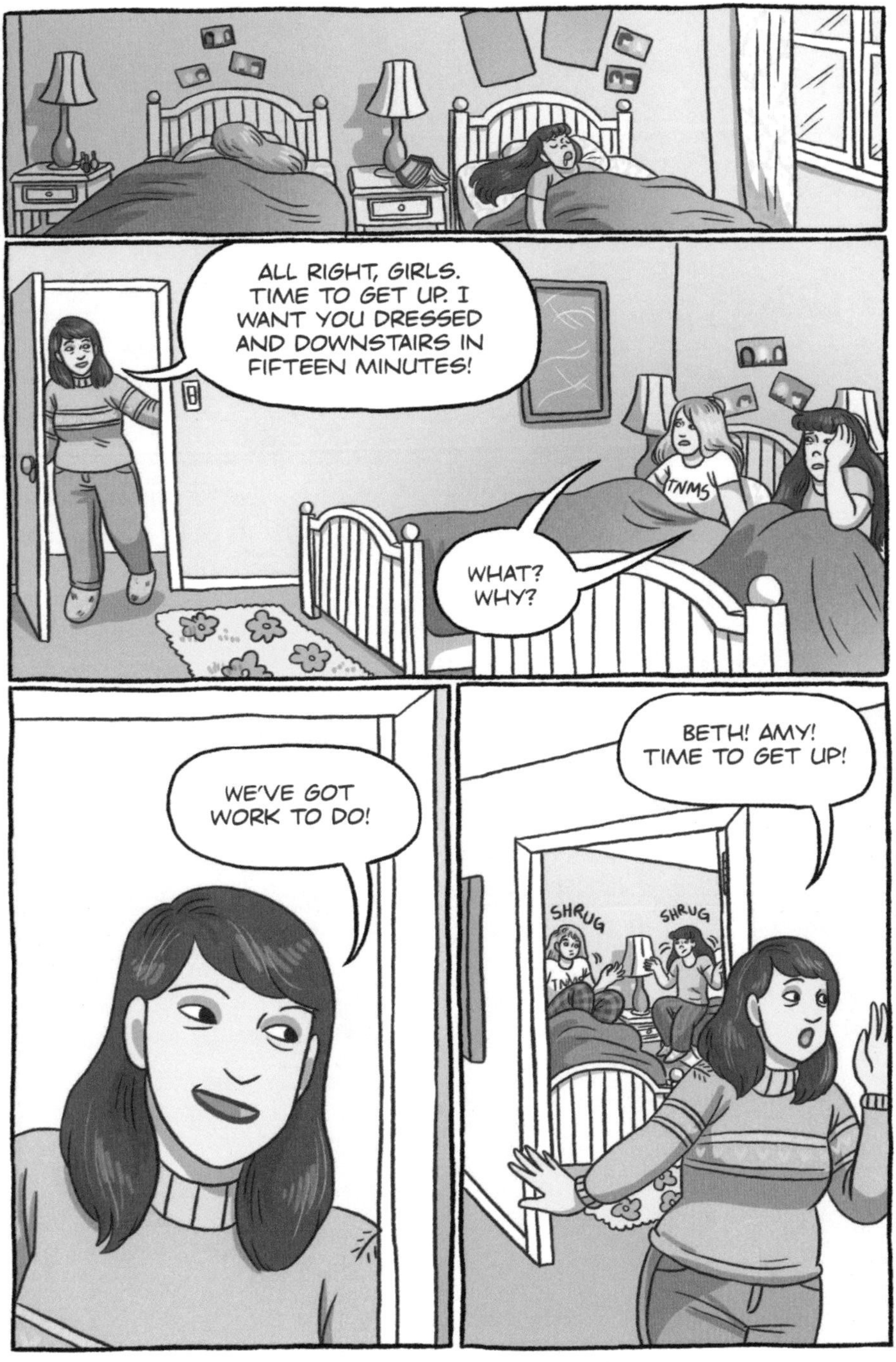
ALL RIGHT, GIRLS. TIME TO GET UP. I WANT YOU DRESSED AND DOWNSTAIRS IN FIFTEEN MINUTES!
TNMS
WHAT? WHY?
WE'VE GOT WORK TO DO!
BETH! AMY! TIME TO GET UP!
SHRUG
SHRUG

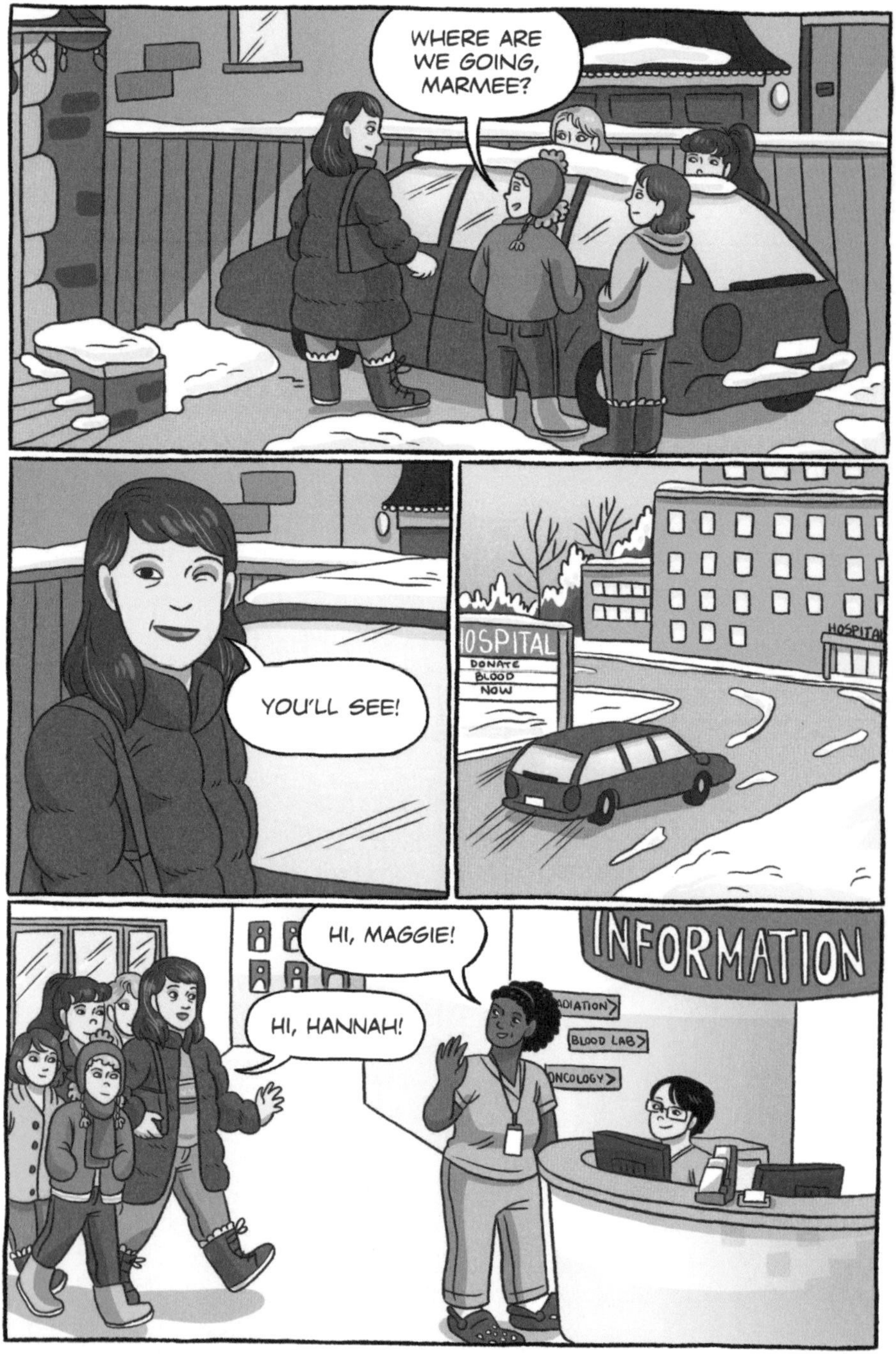
WHERE ARE WE GOING, MARMEE?
YOU'LL SEE!
HOSPITAL
DONATE BLOOD NOW
HOSPITAL
HI, MAGGIE!
HI, HANNAH!
INFORMATION
RADIATION
BLOOD LAB
ONCOLOGY

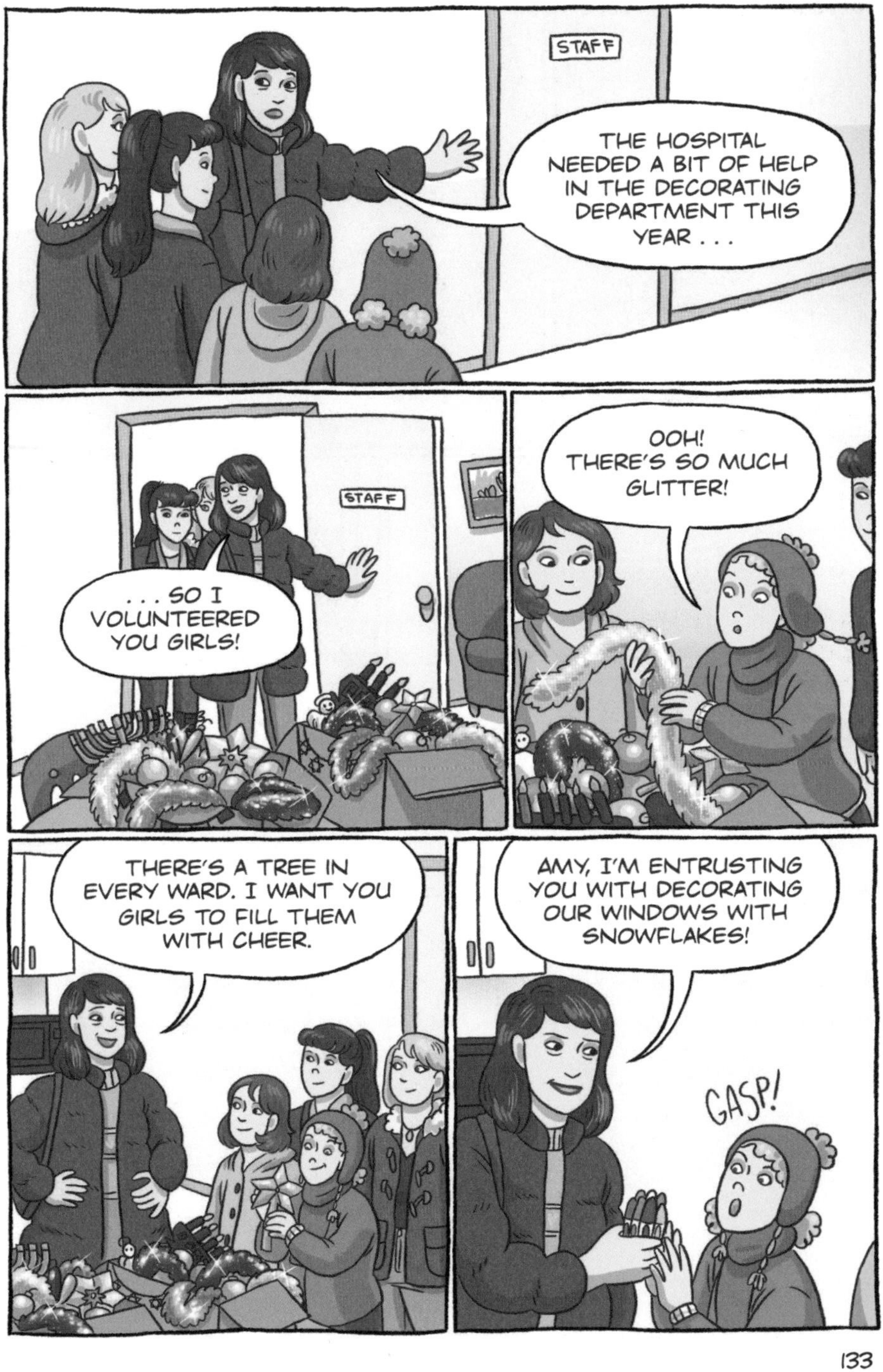
STAFF
THE HOSPITAL NEEDED A BIT OF HELP IN THE DECORATING DEPARTMENT THIS YEAR . . .
STAFF
. . . SO I VOLUNTEERED YOU GIRLS!
OOH! THERE'S SO MUCH GLITTER!
THERE'S A TREE IN EVERY WARD. I WANT YOU GIRLS TO FILL THEM WITH CHEER.
AMY, I'M ENTRUSTING YOU WITH DECORATING OUR WINDOWS WITH SNOWFLAKES!
GASP!

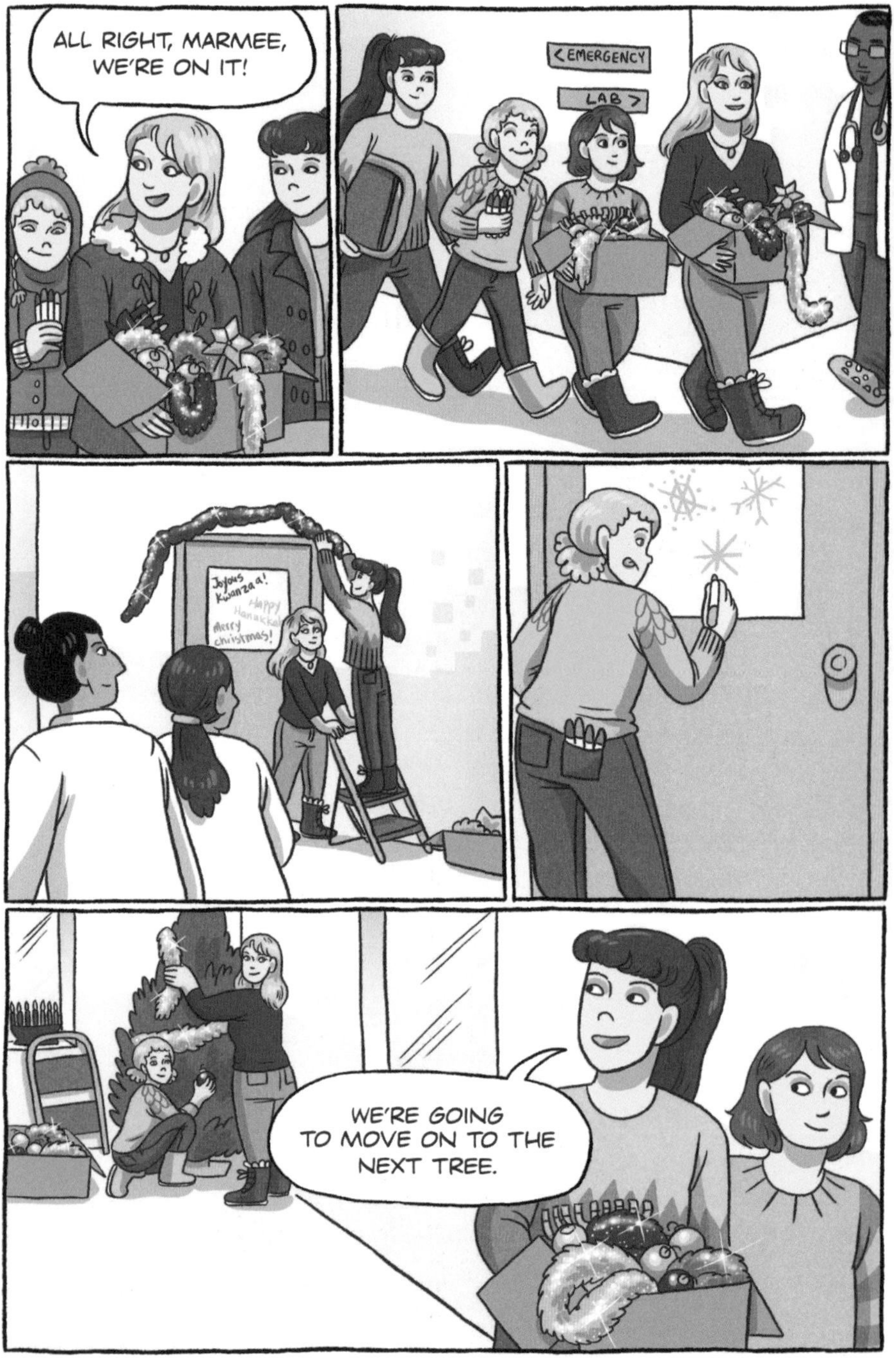
ALL RIGHT, MARMEE, WE'RE ON IT!
< EMERGENCY
LAB >
Joyous Kwanzaa!
Happy Hanukkah!
Merry christmas!
WE'RE GOING TO MOVE ON TO THE NEXT TREE.

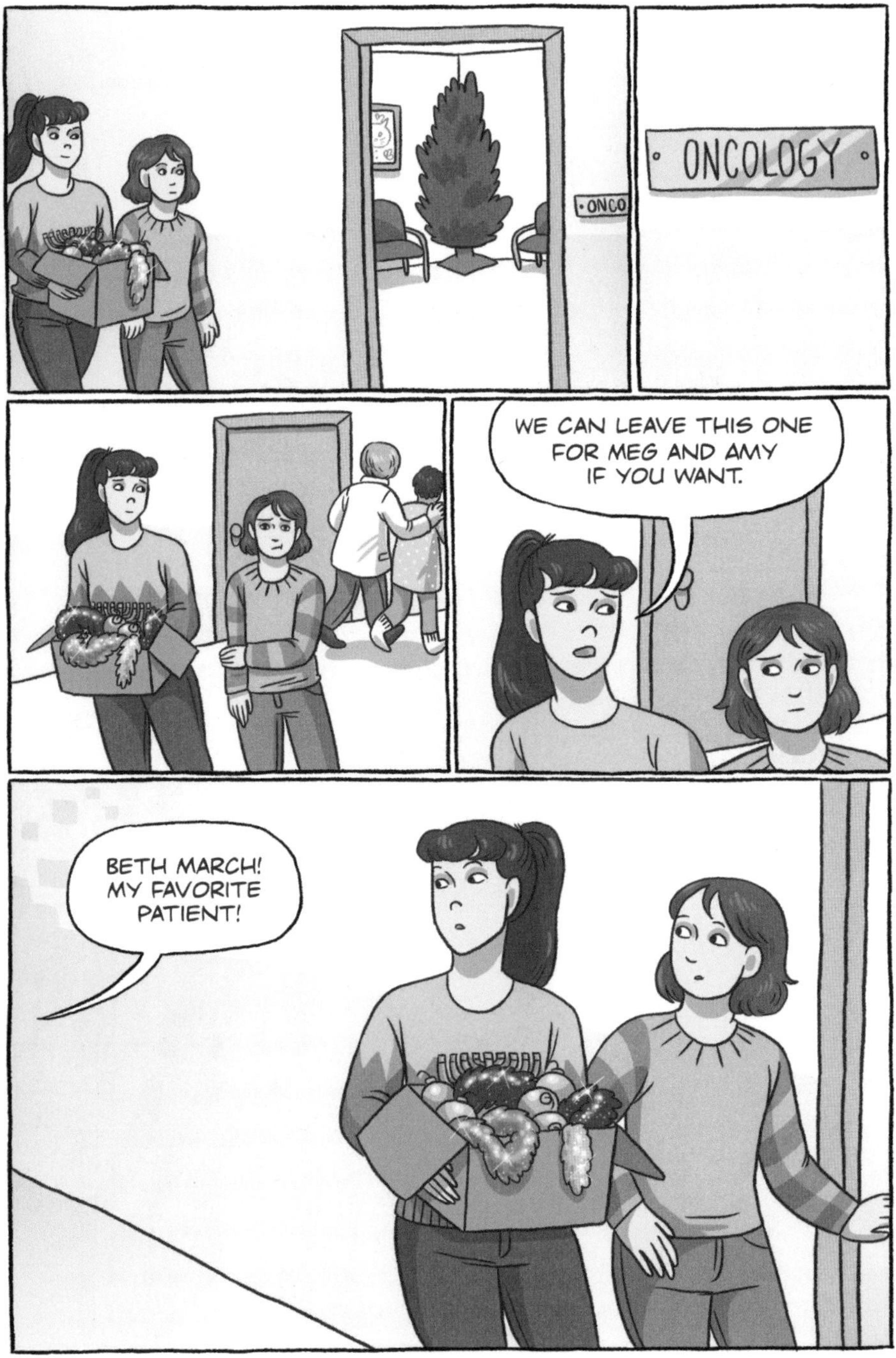
ONCO
ONCOLOGY
WE CAN LEAVE THIS ONE FOR MEG AND AMY IF YOU WANT.
BETH MARCH! MY FAVORITE PATIENT!

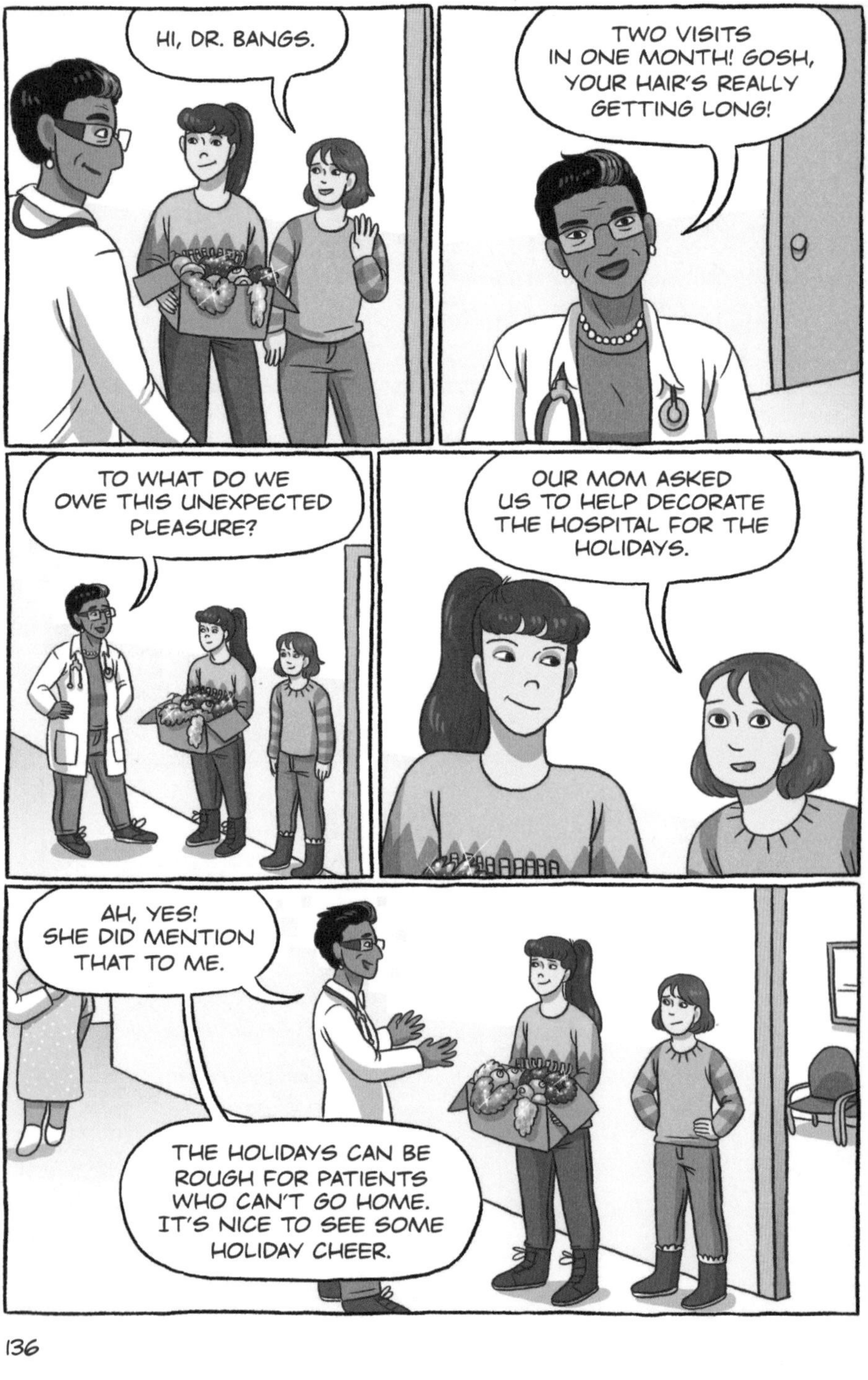
HI, DR. BANGS.
TWO VISITS IN ONE MONTH! GOSH, YOUR HAIR'S REALLY GETTING LONG!
TO WHAT DO WE OWE THIS UNEXPECTED PLEASURE?
OUR MOM ASKED US TO HELP DECORATE THE HOSPITAL FOR THE HOLIDAYS.
AH, YES! SHE DID MENTION THAT TO ME.
THE HOLIDAYS CAN BE ROUGH FOR PATIENTS WHO CAN'T GO HOME. IT'S NICE TO SEE SOME HOLIDAY CHEER.

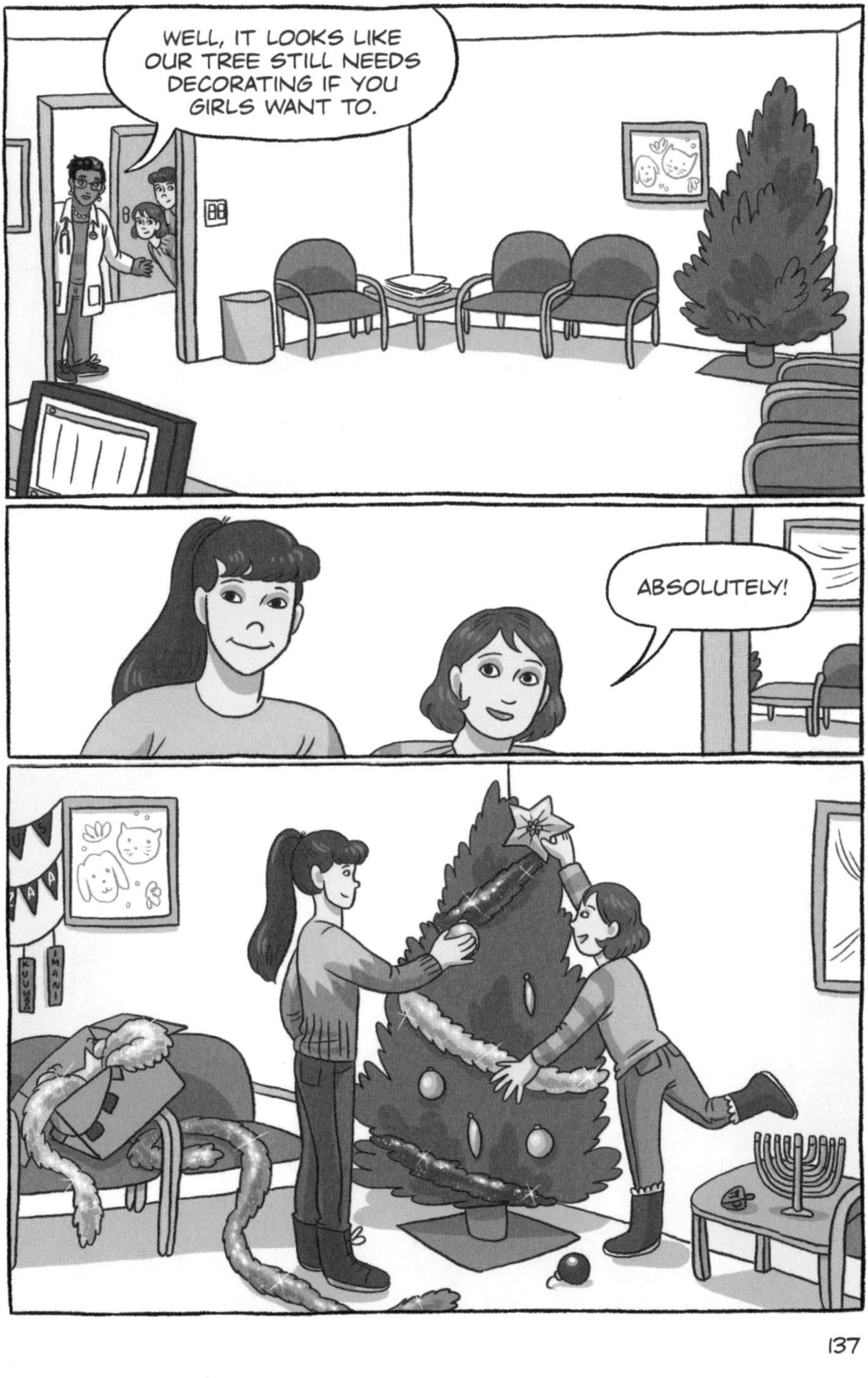
WELL, IT LOOKS LIKE OUR TREE STILL NEEDS DECORATING IF YOU GIRLS WANT TO.
ABSOLUTELY!

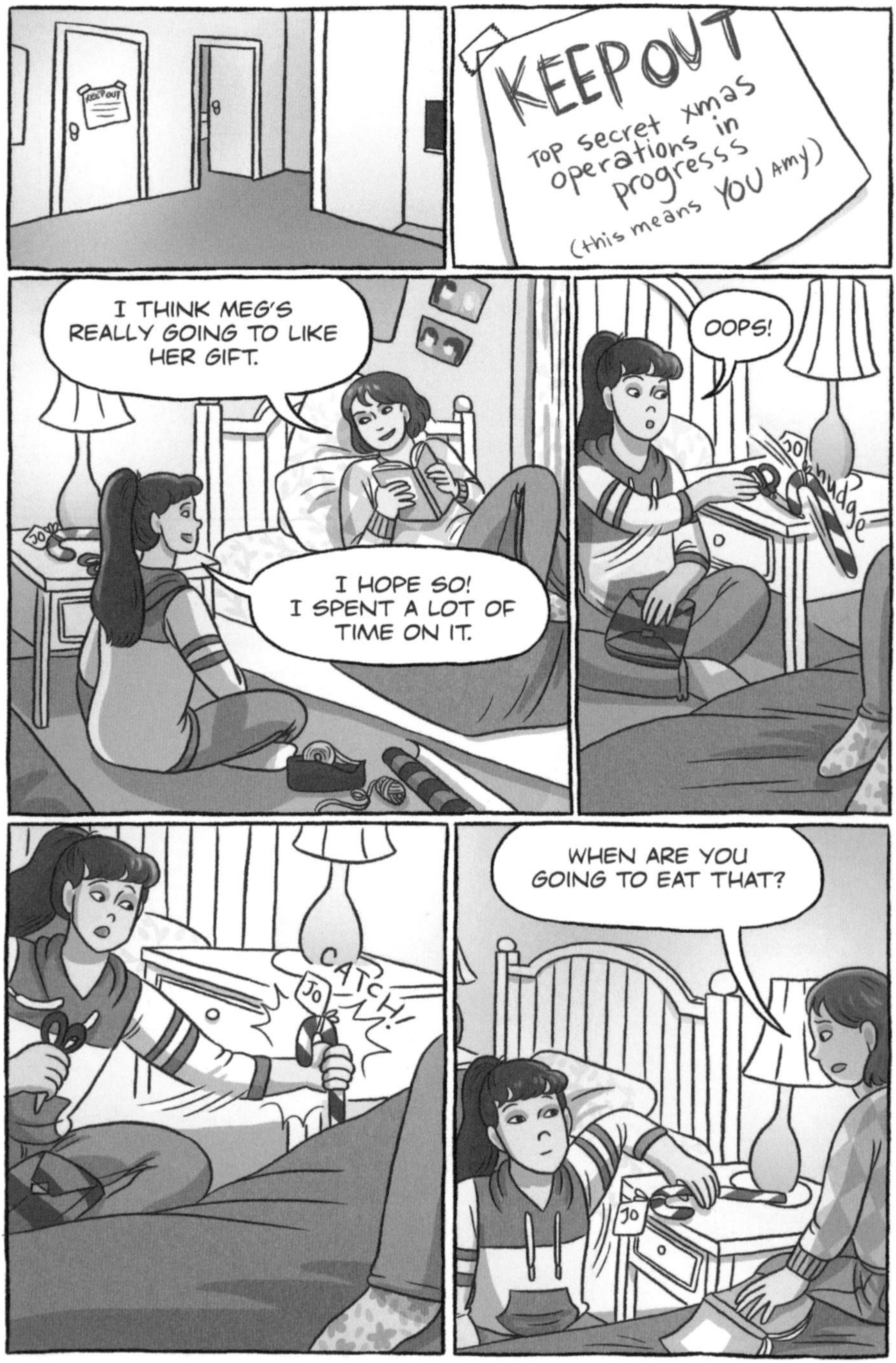
KEEP OUT
top secret xmas operations in progresss
(this means YOU Amy)
I THINK MEG'S REALLY GOING TO LIKE HER GIFT.
I HOPE SO! I SPENT A LOT OF TIME ON IT.
OOPS!
nudge
CATCH!
WHEN ARE YOU GOING TO EAT THAT?

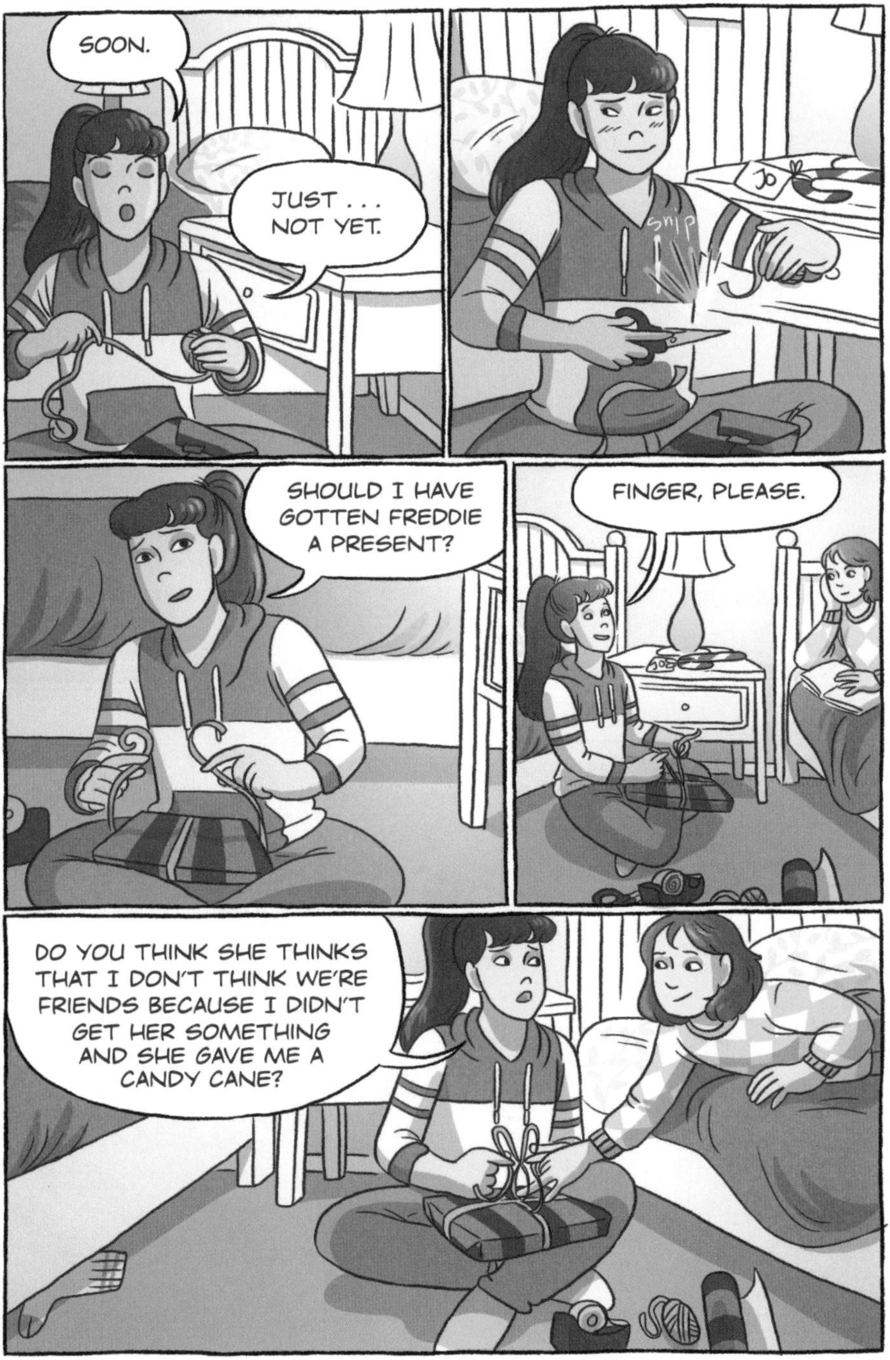
SOON.
JUST . . . NOT YET.
SNIP
JO
SHOULD I HAVE GOTTEN FREDDIE A PRESENT?
FINGER, PLEASE.
DO YOU THINK SHE THINKS THAT I DON'T THINK WE'RE FRIENDS BECAUSE I DIDN'T GET HER SOMETHING AND SHE GAVE ME A CANDY CANE?

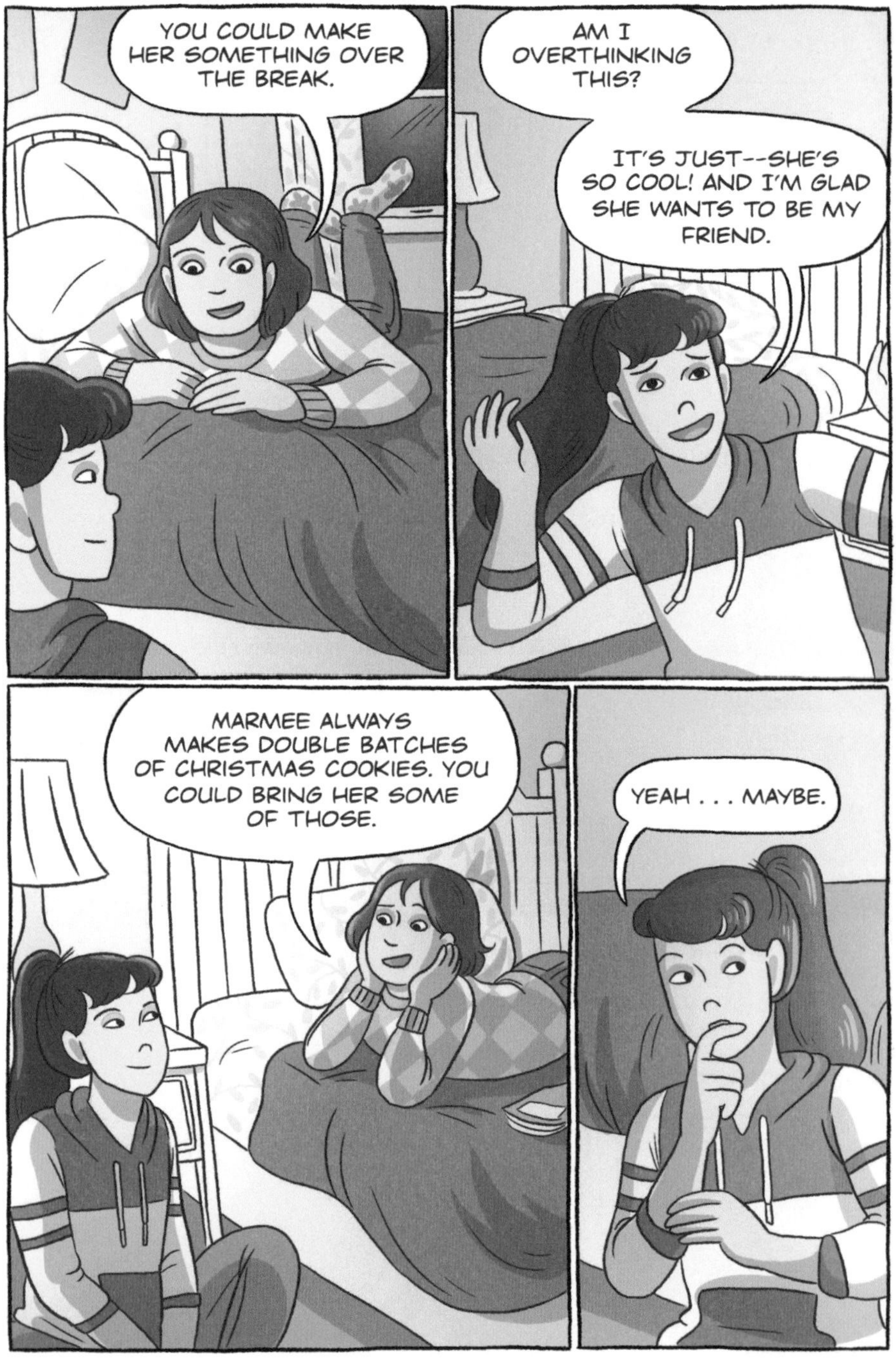
YOU COULD MAKE HER SOMETHING OVER THE BREAK.
AM I OVERTHINKING THIS?
IT'S JUST--SHE'S SO COOL! AND I'M GLAD SHE WANTS TO BE MY FRIEND.
MARMEE ALWAYS MAKES DOUBLE BATCHES OF CHRISTMAS COOKIES. YOU COULD BRING HER SOME OF THOSE.
YEAH . . . MAYBE.

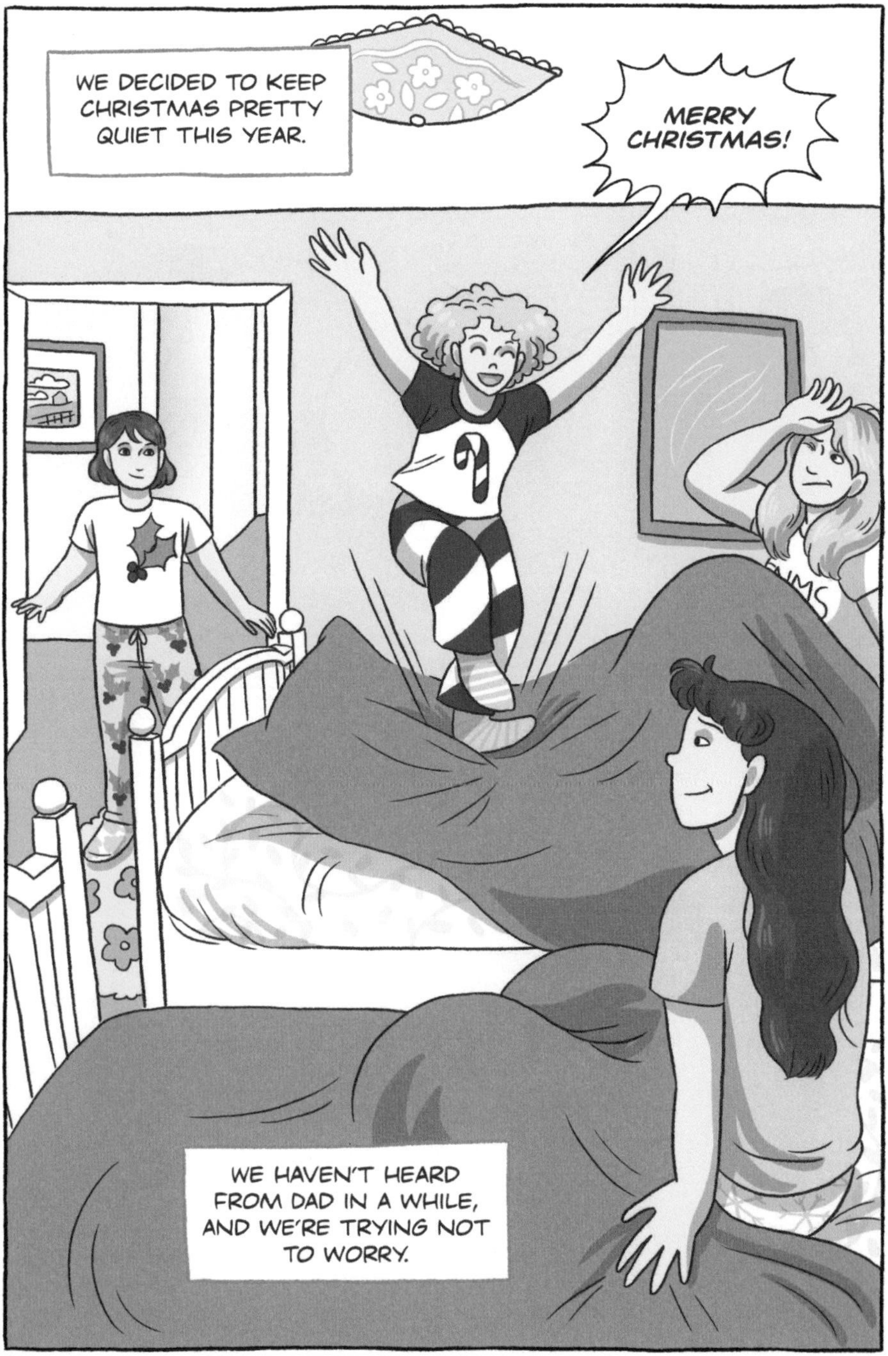
WE DECIDED TO KEEP CHRISTMAS PRETTY QUIET THIS YEAR.
MERRY CHRISTMAS!
WE HAVEN'T HEARD FROM DAD IN A WHILE, AND WE'RE TRYING NOT TO WORRY.

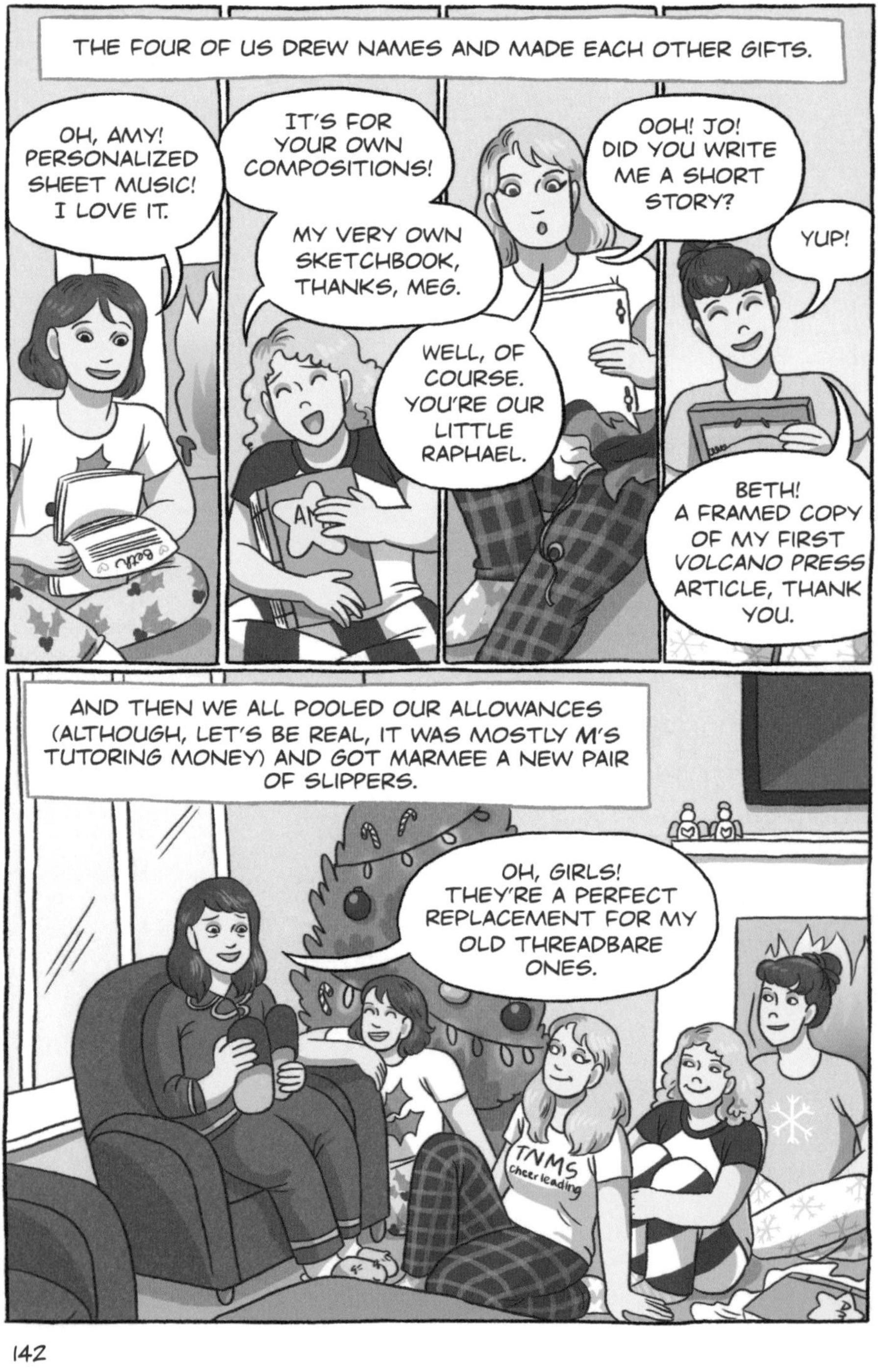
THE FOUR OF US DREW NAMES AND MADE EACH OTHER GIFTS.
OH, AMY! PERSONALIZED SHEET MUSIC! I LOVE IT.
IT'S FOR YOUR OWN COMPOSITIONS!
MY VERY OWN SKETCHBOOK, THANKS, MEG.
WELL, OF COURSE. YOU'RE OUR LITTLE RAPHAEL.
OOH! JO! DID YOU WRITE ME A SHORT STORY?
YUP!
BETH! A FRAMED COPY OF MY FIRST VOLCANO PRESS ARTICLE, THANK YOU.
AND THEN WE ALL POOLED OUR ALLOWANCES (ALTHOUGH, LET'S BE REAL, IT WAS MOSTLY M'S TUTORING MONEY) AND GOT MARMEE A NEW PAIR OF SLIPPERS.
OH, GIRLS! THEY'RE A PERFECT REPLACEMENT FOR MY OLD THREADBARE ONES.
TNMS cheerleading

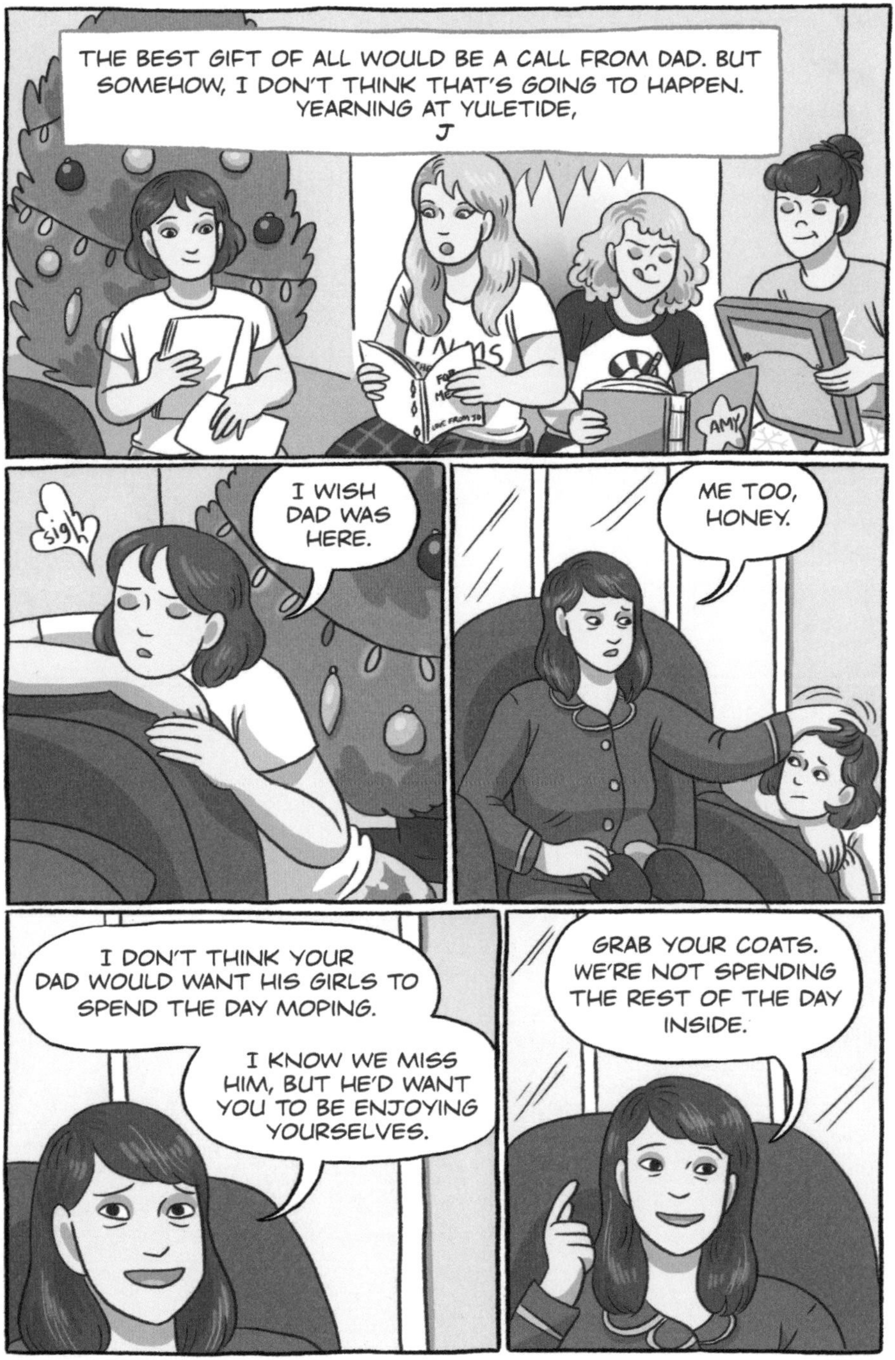
THE BEST GIFT OF ALL WOULD BE A CALL FROM DAD. BUT SOMEHOW, I DON'T THINK THAT'S GOING TO HAPPEN. YEARNING AT YULETIDE, J
AMY
sigh
I WISH DAD WAS HERE.
ME TOO, HONEY.
I DON'T THINK YOUR DAD WOULD WANT HIS GIRLS TO SPEND THE DAY MOPING.
I KNOW WE MISS HIM, BUT HE'D WANT YOU TO BE ENJOYING YOURSELVES.
GRAB YOUR COATS. WE'RE NOT SPENDING THE REST OF THE DAY INSIDE.

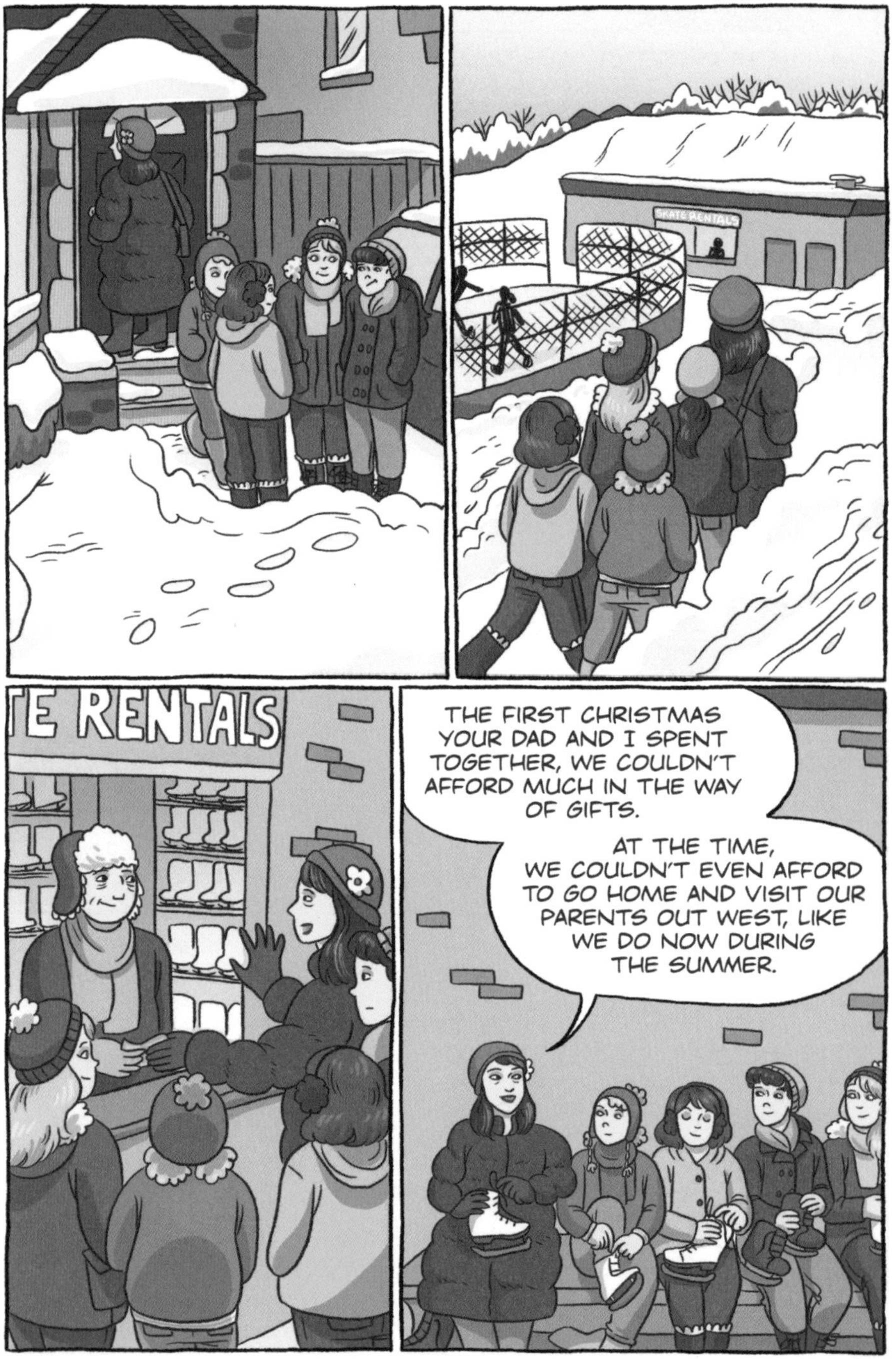
SKATE RENTALS
TE RENTALS
THE FIRST CHRISTMAS YOUR DAD AND I SPENT TOGETHER, WE COULDN'T AFFORD MUCH IN THE WAY OF GIFTS.
AT THE TIME, WE COULDN'T EVEN AFFORD TO GO HOME AND VISIT OUR PARENTS OUT WEST, LIKE WE DO NOW DURING THE SUMMER.

CHRISTMAS MORNING FELT LONELY WITHOUT THE REST OF OUR FAMILY, SO WE DECIDED TO FILL THE DAY WITH FUN. WE SPENT THE WHOLE AFTERNOON AT THE SKATING RINK.

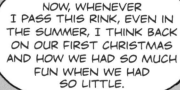
NOW, WHENEVER I PASS THIS RINK, EVEN IN THE SUMMER, I THINK BACK ON OUR FIRST CHRISTMAS AND HOW WE HAD SO MUCH FUN WHEN WE HAD SO LITTLE.

THAT'S SO ROMANTIC!

SO LET'S SKATE TODAY, AND THINK OF DAD. WHEREVER HE IS, I'M SURE IT'S NOT COLD ENOUGH TO SKATE. LET'S DO IT FOR HIM.

SKATE RENTALS

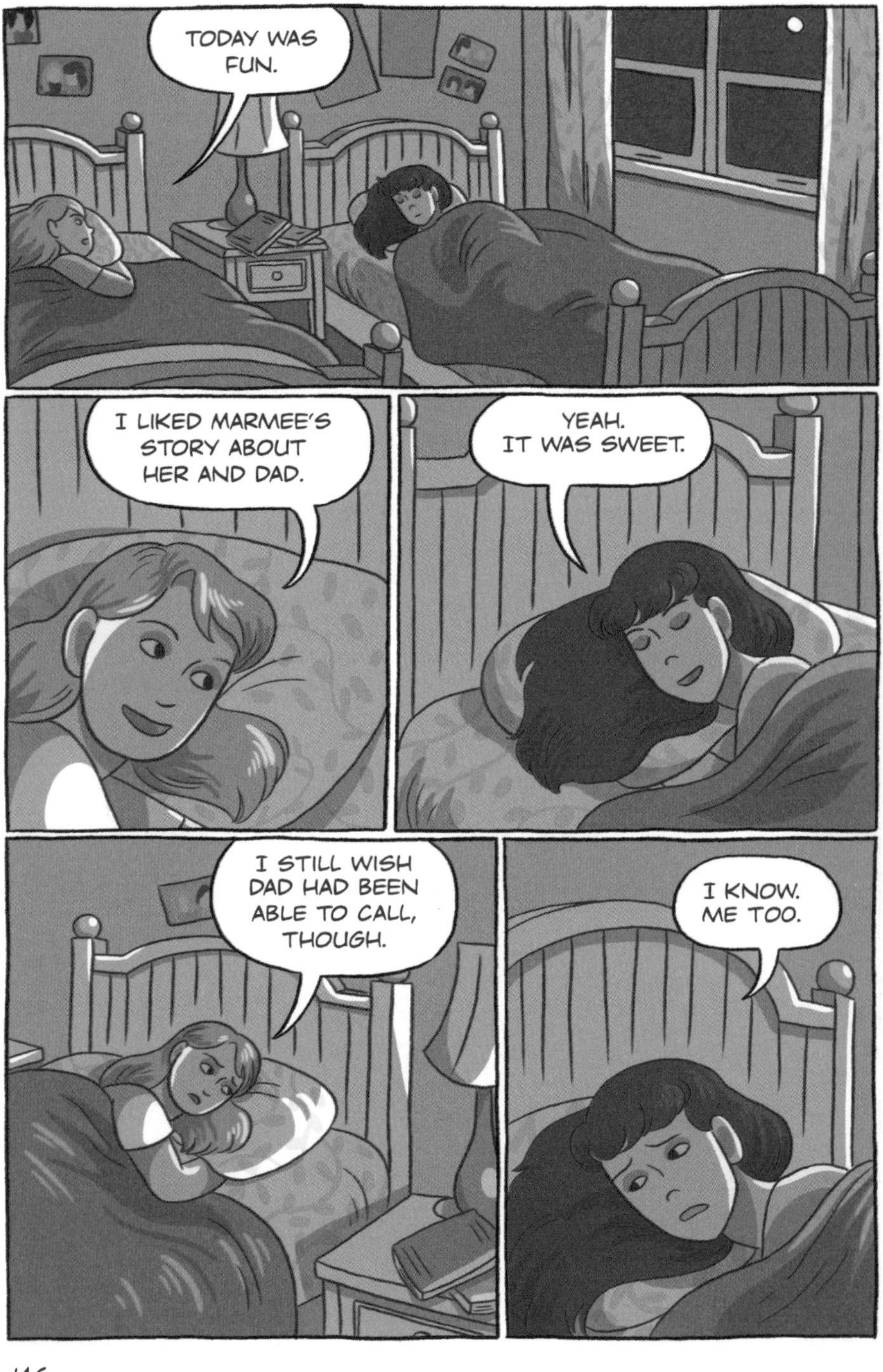
TODAY WAS FUN.
I LIKED MARMEE'S STORY ABOUT HER AND DAD.
YEAH. IT WAS SWEET.
I STILL WISH DAD HAD BEEN ABLE TO CALL, THOUGH.
I KNOW. ME TOO.

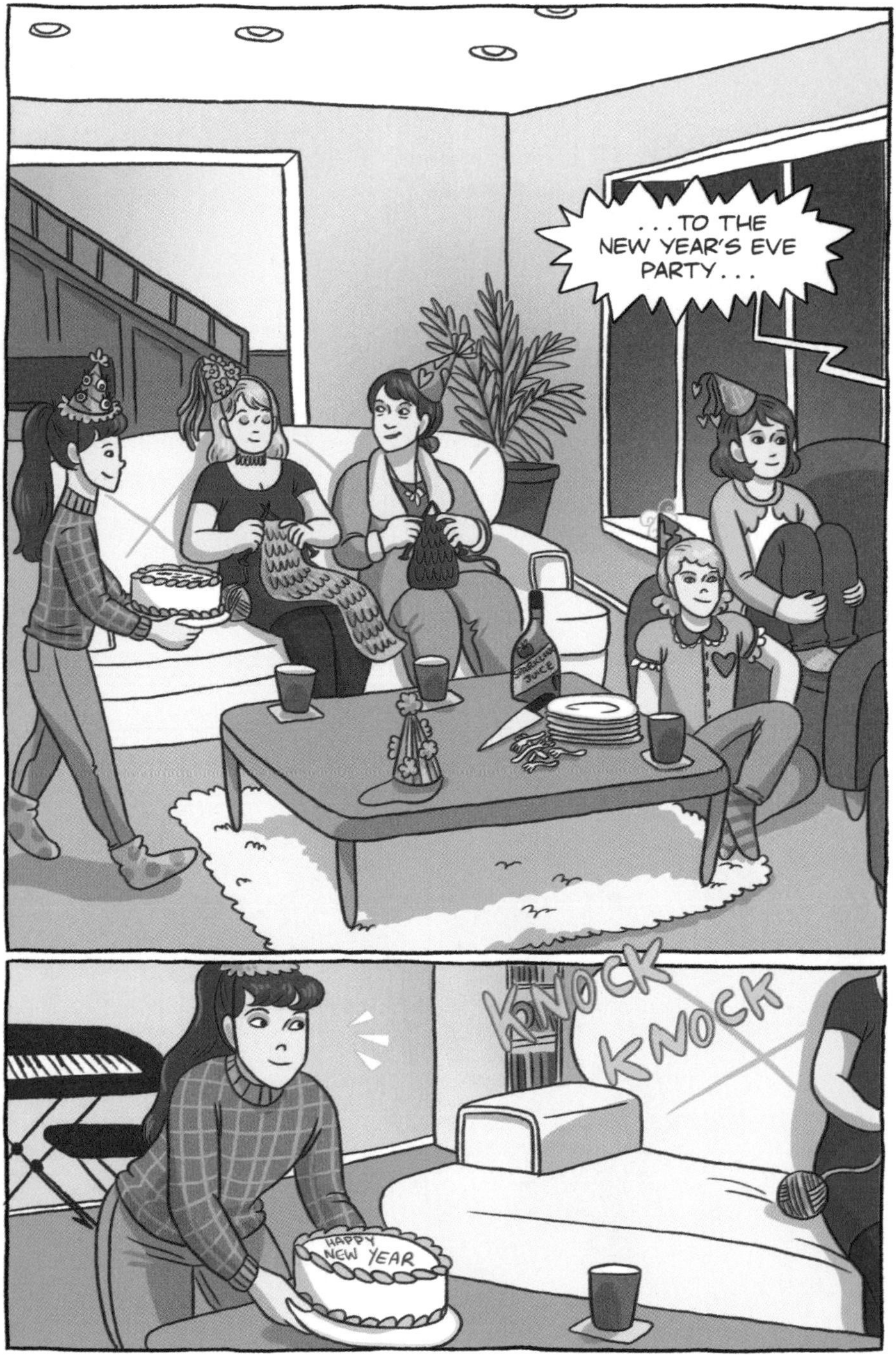
. . . TO THE NEW YEAR'S EVE PARTY . . .
SPARKLING JUICE
KNOCK KNOCK
HAPPY NEW YEAR

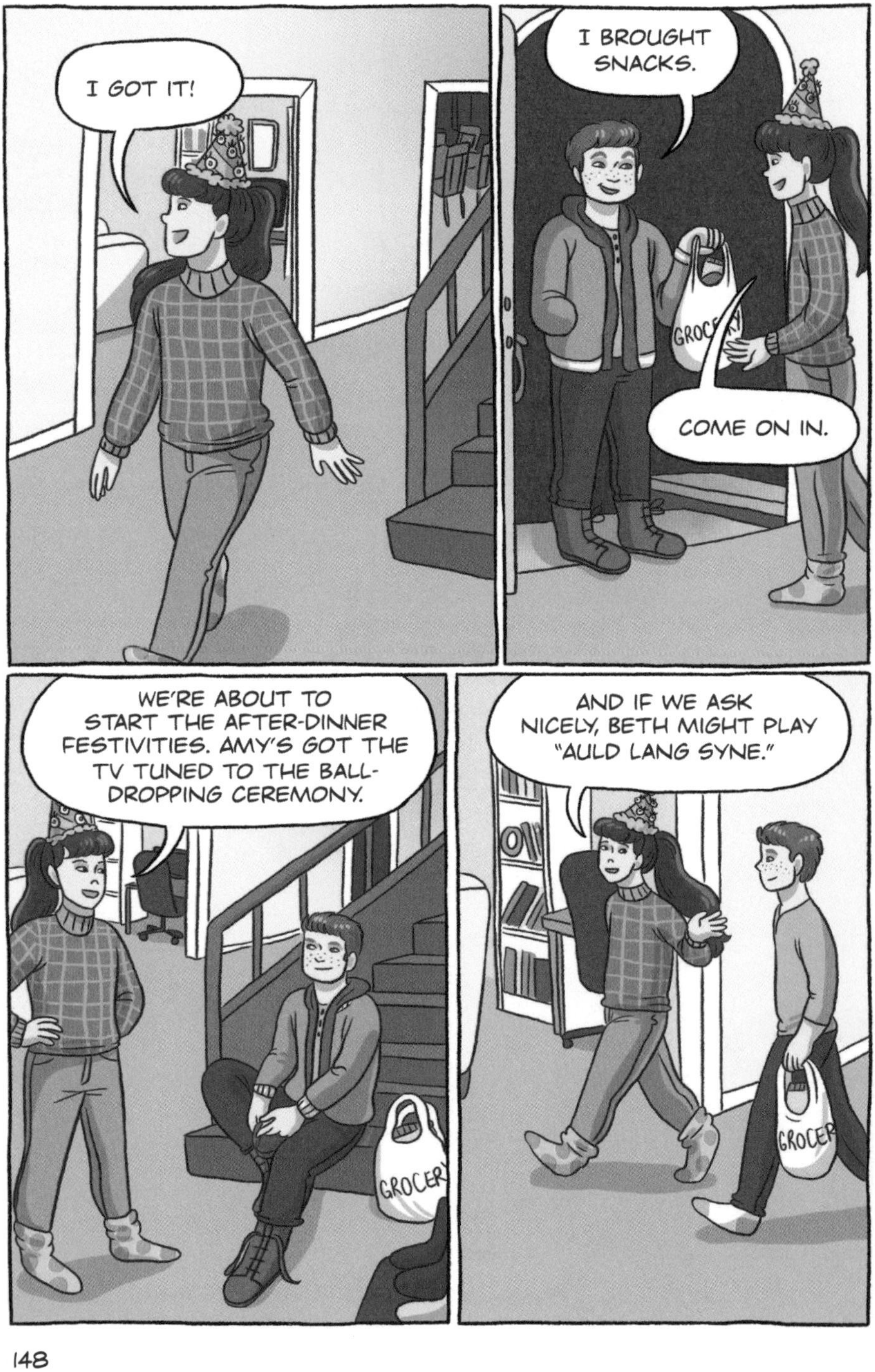
I GOT IT!
I BROUGHT SNACKS.
GROCERY
COME ON IN.
WE'RE ABOUT TO START THE AFTER-DINNER FESTIVITIES. AMY'S GOT THE TV TUNED TO THE BALL-DROPPING CEREMONY.
GROCERY
AND IF WE ASK NICELY, BETH MIGHT PLAY "AULD LANG SYNE."
GROCER

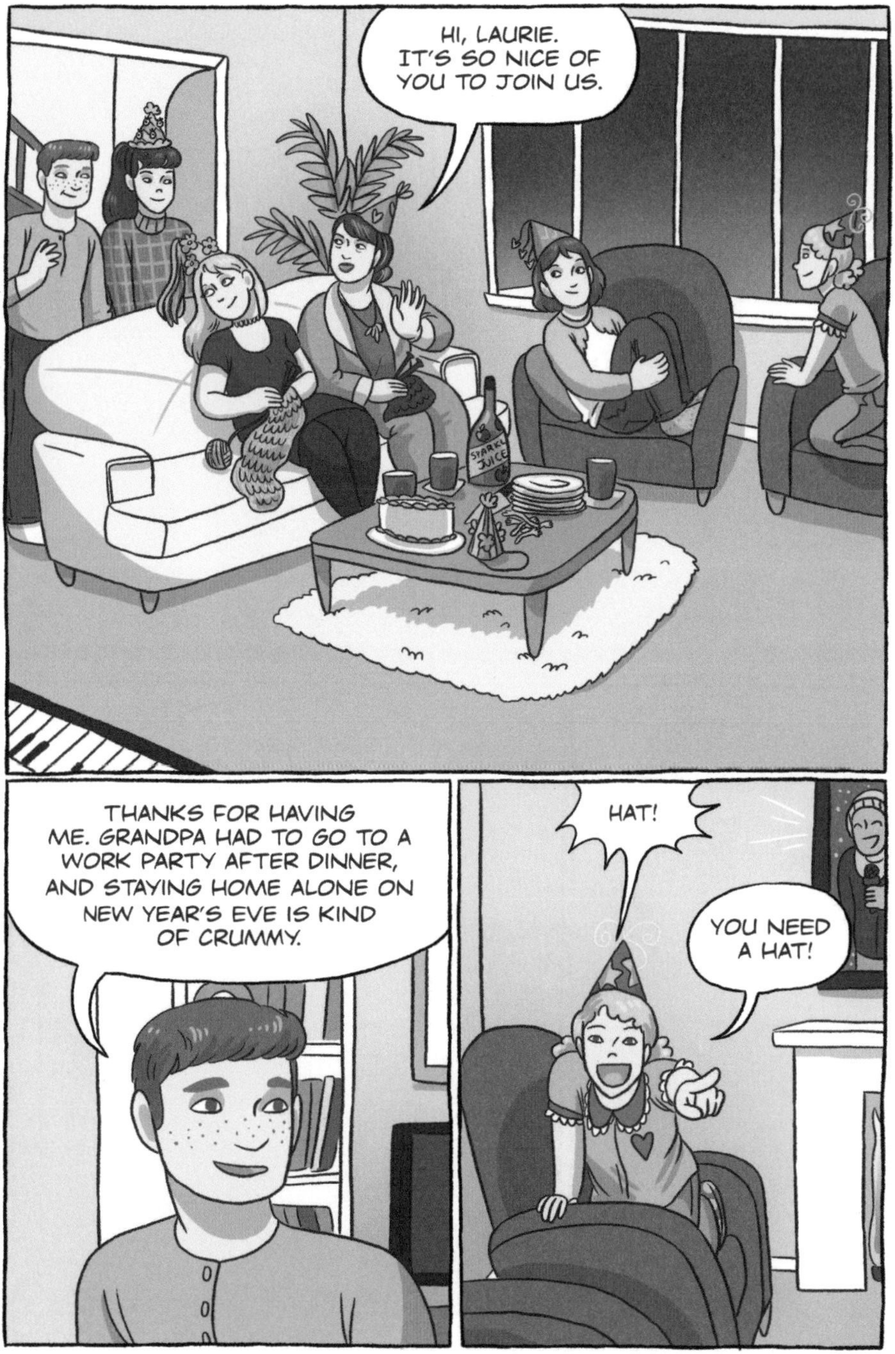
HI, LAURIE. IT'S SO NICE OF YOU TO JOIN US.
THANKS FOR HAVING ME. GRANDPA HAD TO GO TO A WORK PARTY AFTER DINNER, AND STAYING HOME ALONE ON NEW YEAR'S EVE IS KIND OF CRUMMY.
HAT!
YOU NEED A HAT!

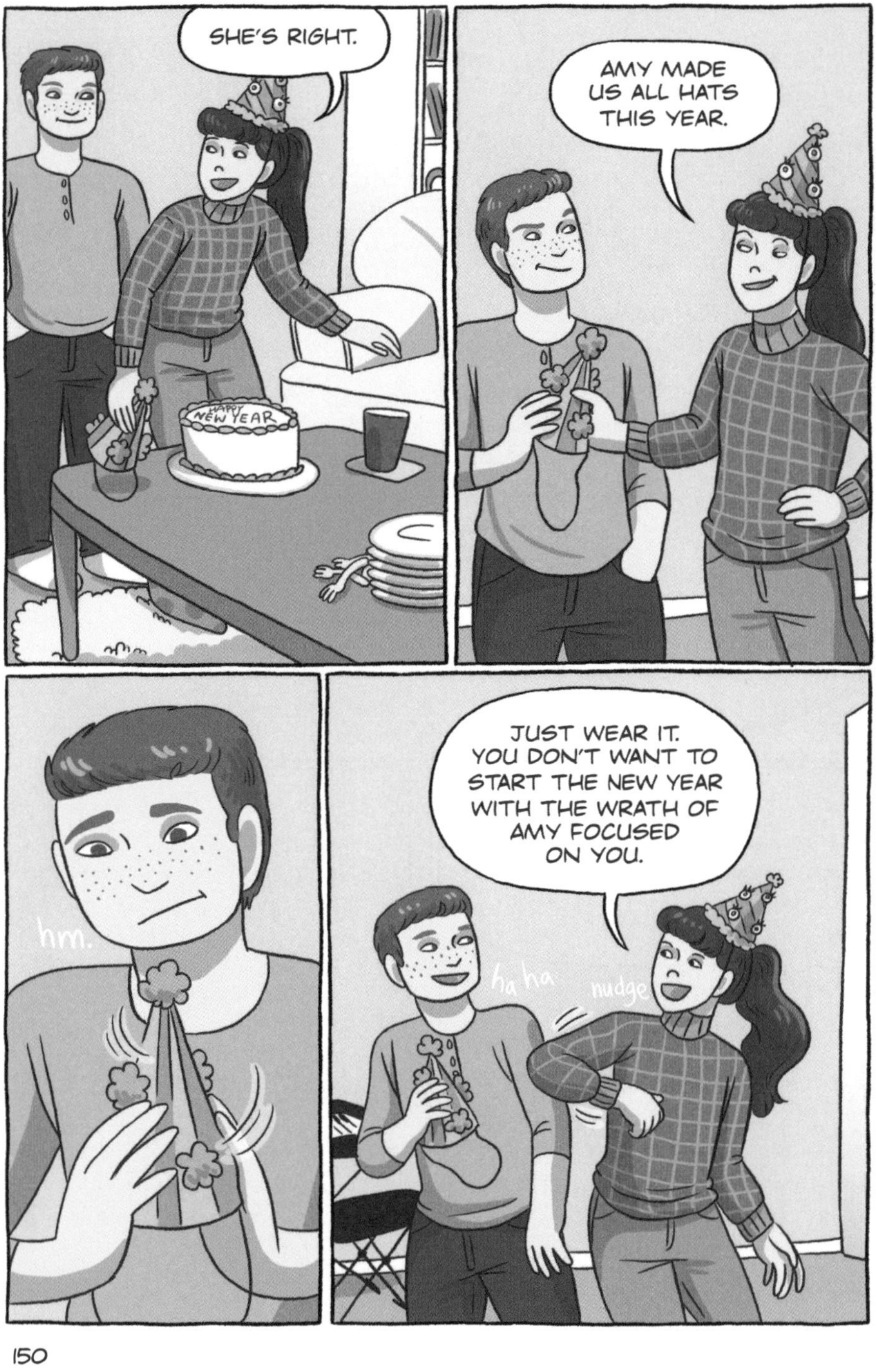
SHE'S RIGHT.
HAPPY NEW YEAR
AMY MADE US ALL HATS THIS YEAR.
hm.
JUST WEAR IT. YOU DON'T WANT TO START THE NEW YEAR WITH THE WRATH OF AMY FOCUSED ON YOU.
ha ha
nudge

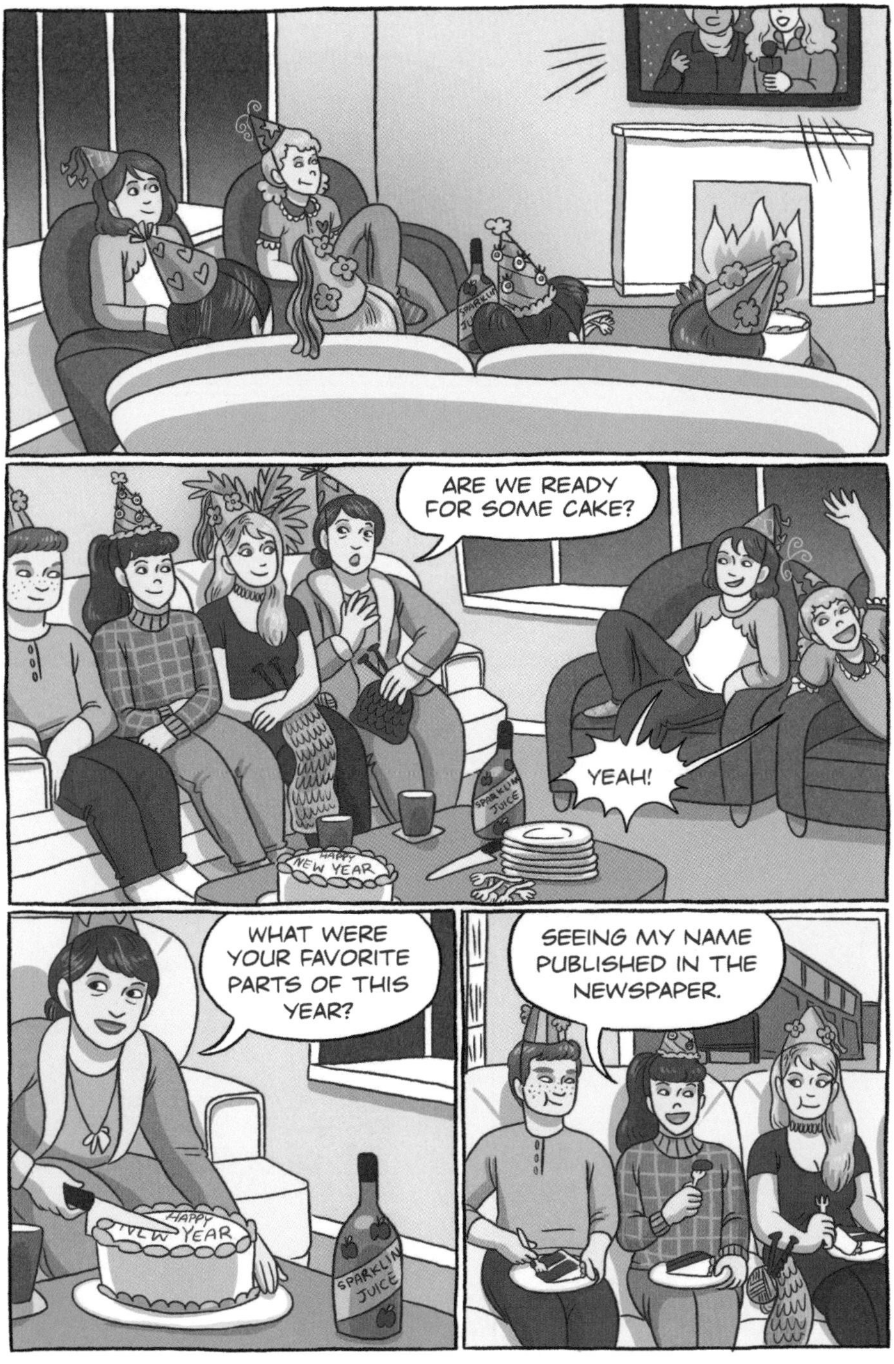
ARE WE READY FOR SOME CAKE?
YEAH!
SPARKLIN JUICE
HAPPY NEW YEAR
WHAT WERE YOUR FAVORITE PARTS OF THIS YEAR?
HAPPY NEW YEAR
SPARKLIN JUICE
SEEING MY NAME PUBLISHED IN THE NEWSPAPER.

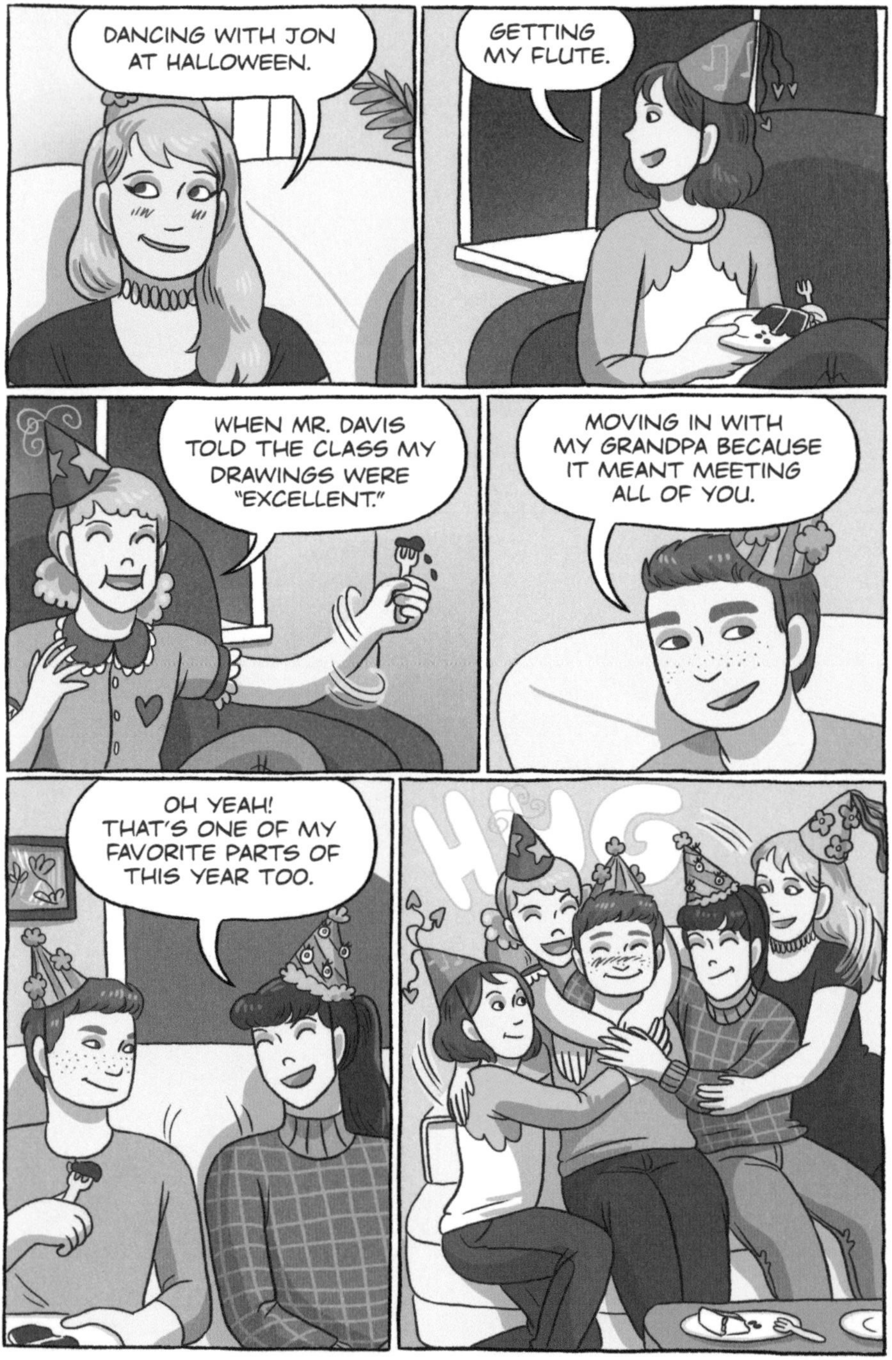
DANCING WITH JON AT HALLOWEEN.
GETTING MY FLUTE.
WHEN MR. DAVIS TOLD THE CLASS MY DRAWINGS WERE "EXCELLENT."
MOVING IN WITH MY GRANDPA BECAUSE IT MEANT MEETING ALL OF YOU.
OH YEAH! THAT'S ONE OF MY FAVORITE PARTS OF THIS YEAR TOO.
HUG

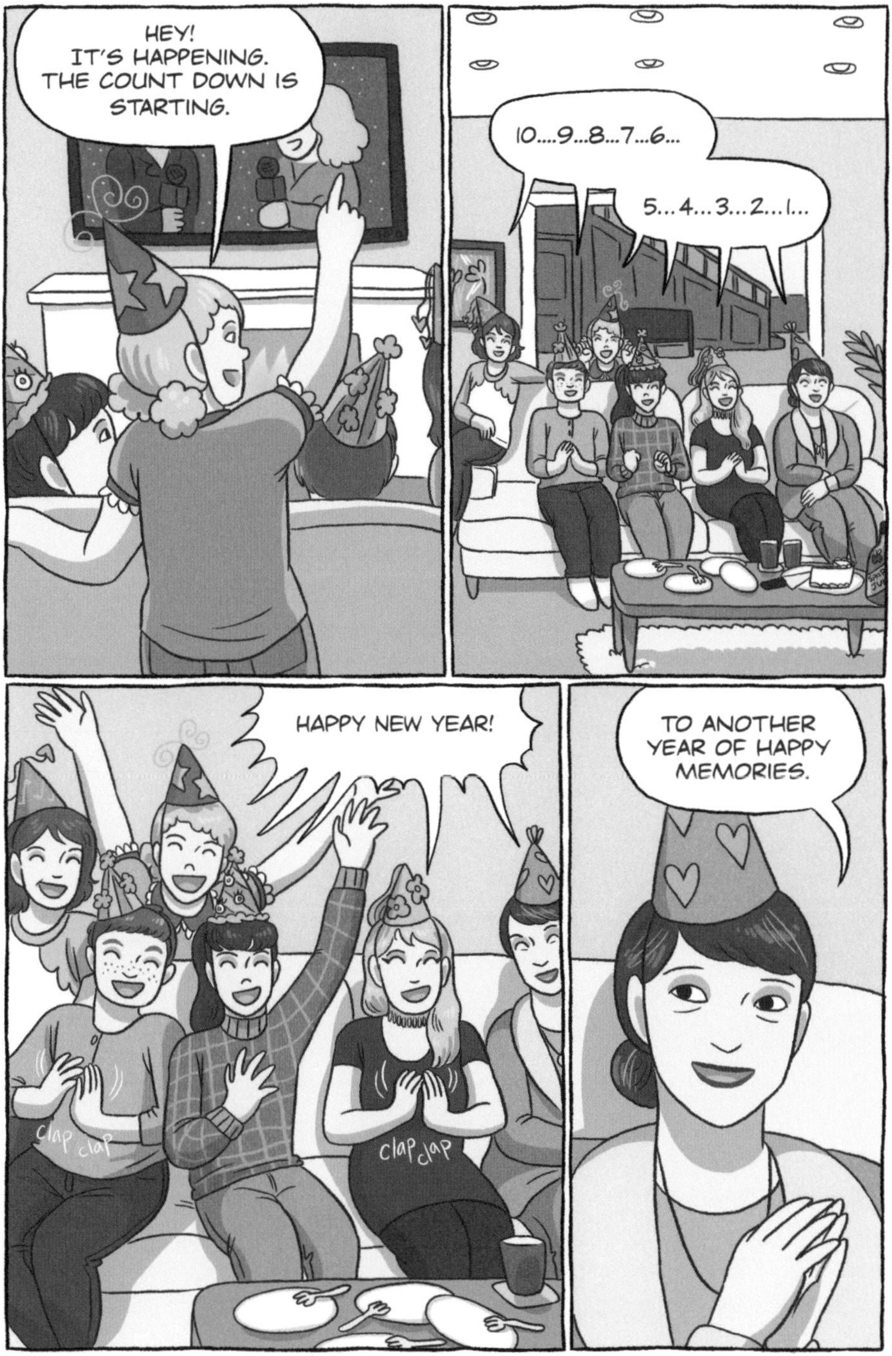
HEY! IT'S HAPPENING. THE COUNT DOWN IS STARTING.
10....9...8...7...6...
5... 4... 3... 2... 1...
HAPPY NEW YEAR!
clap clap
clap clap
TO ANOTHER YEAR OF HAPPY MEMORIES.

CHAPTER 6

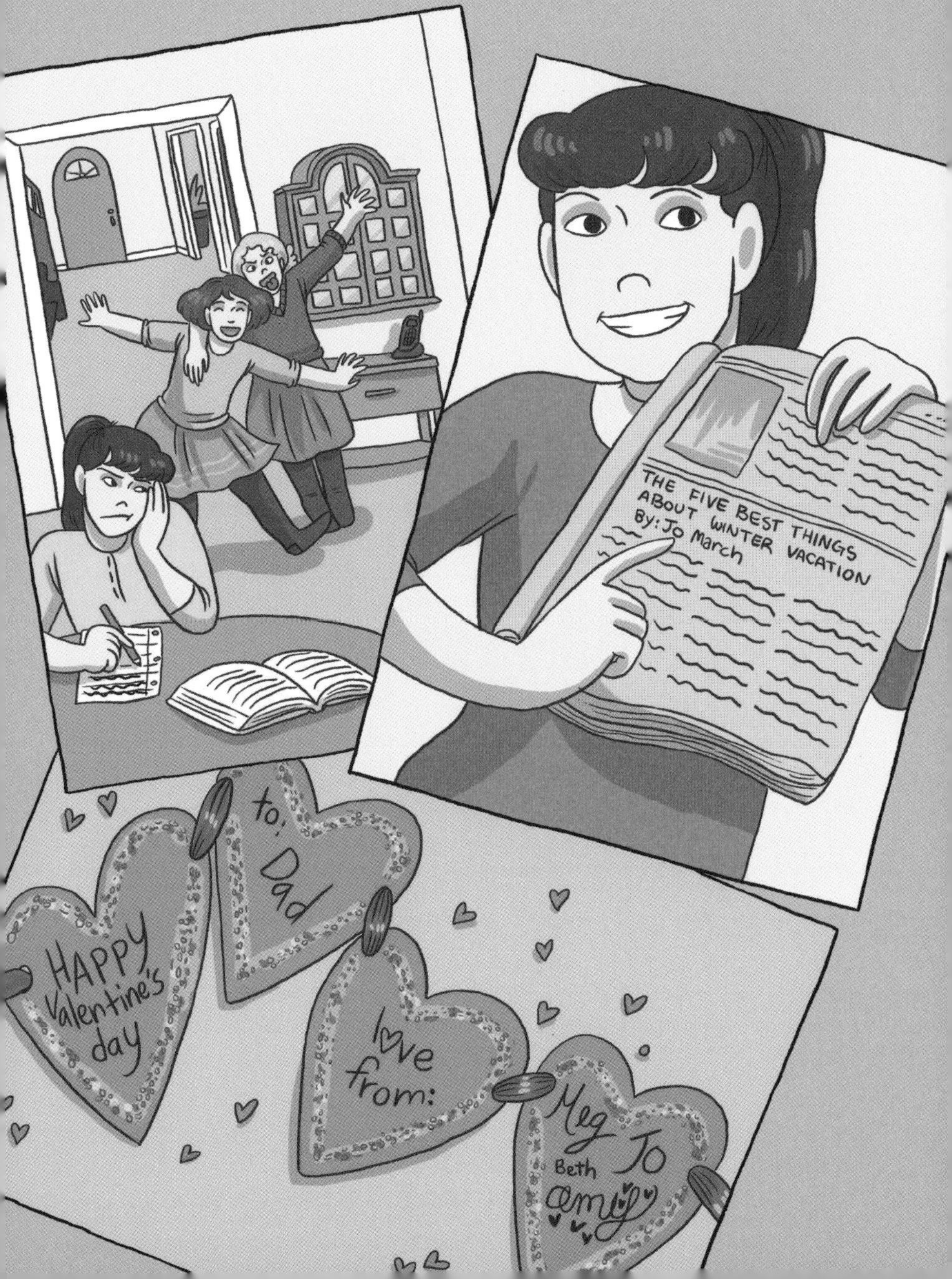
THE FIVE BEST THINGS ABOUT WINTER VACATION
By: Jo March
HAPPY Valentine's day
to: Dad
love from:
Meg
Jo
Beth
amy

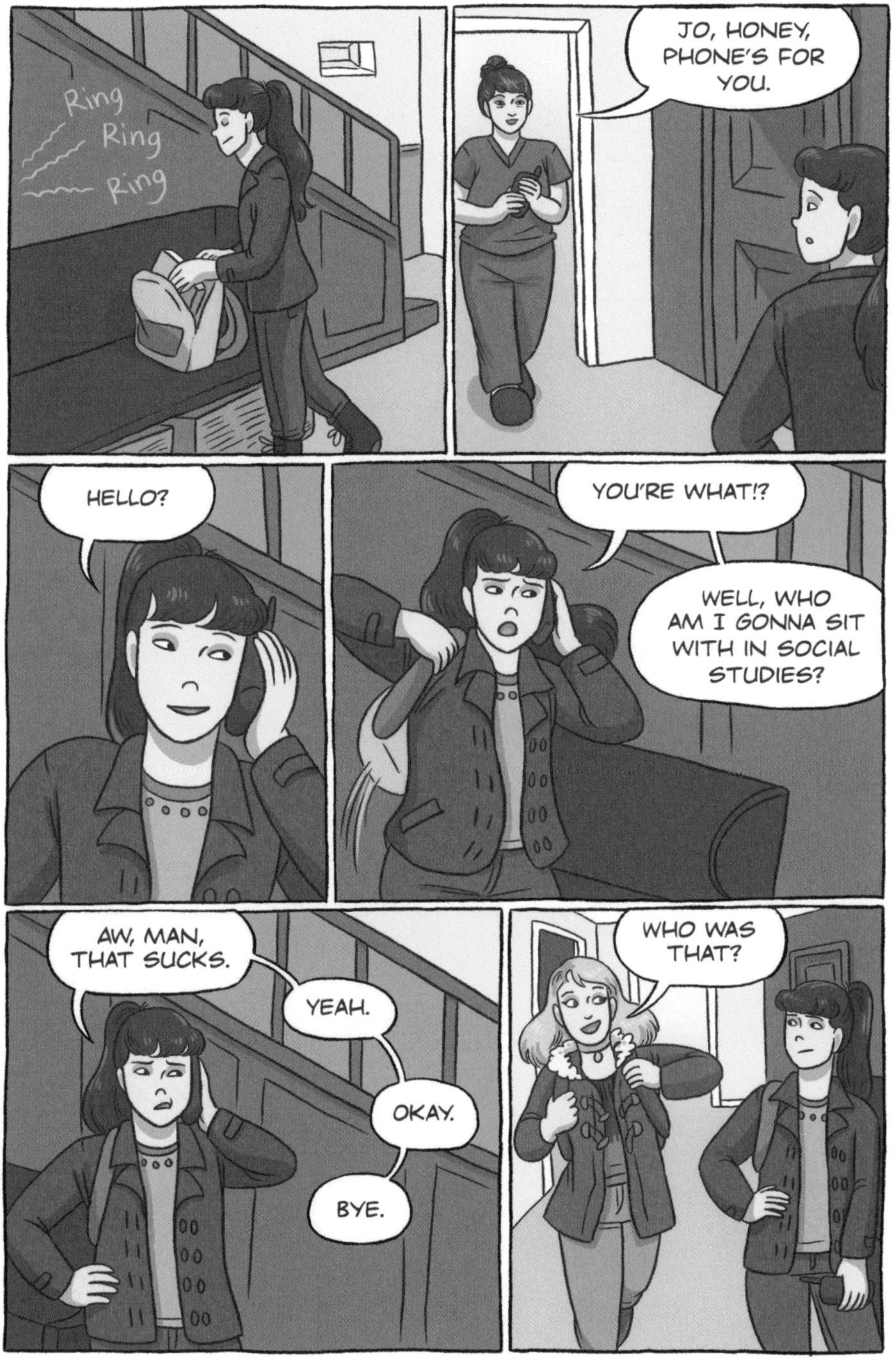

Ring
Ring
Ring
JO, HONEY, PHONE'S FOR YOU.
HELLO?
YOU'RE WHAT!?
WELL, WHO AM I GONNA SIT WITH IN SOCIAL STUDIES?
AW, MAN, THAT SUCKS.
YEAH.
OKAY.
BYE.
WHO WAS THAT?

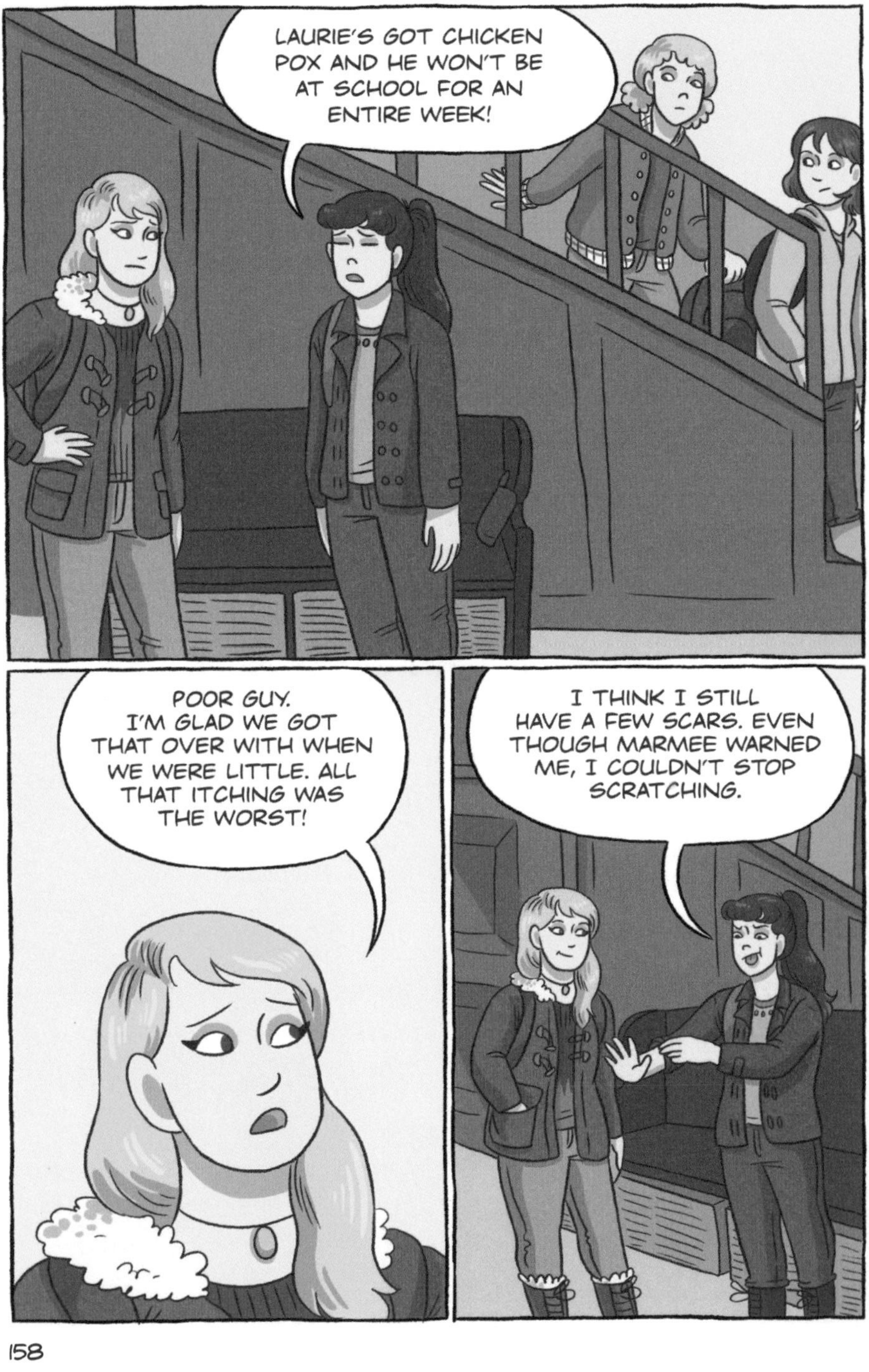
LAURIE'S GOT CHICKEN POX AND HE WON'T BE AT SCHOOL FOR AN ENTIRE WEEK!
POOR GUY. I'M GLAD WE GOT THAT OVER WITH WHEN WE WERE LITTLE. ALL THAT ITCHING WAS THE WORST!
I THINK I STILL HAVE A FEW SCARS. EVEN THOUGH MARMEE WARNED ME, I COULDN'T STOP SCRATCHING.

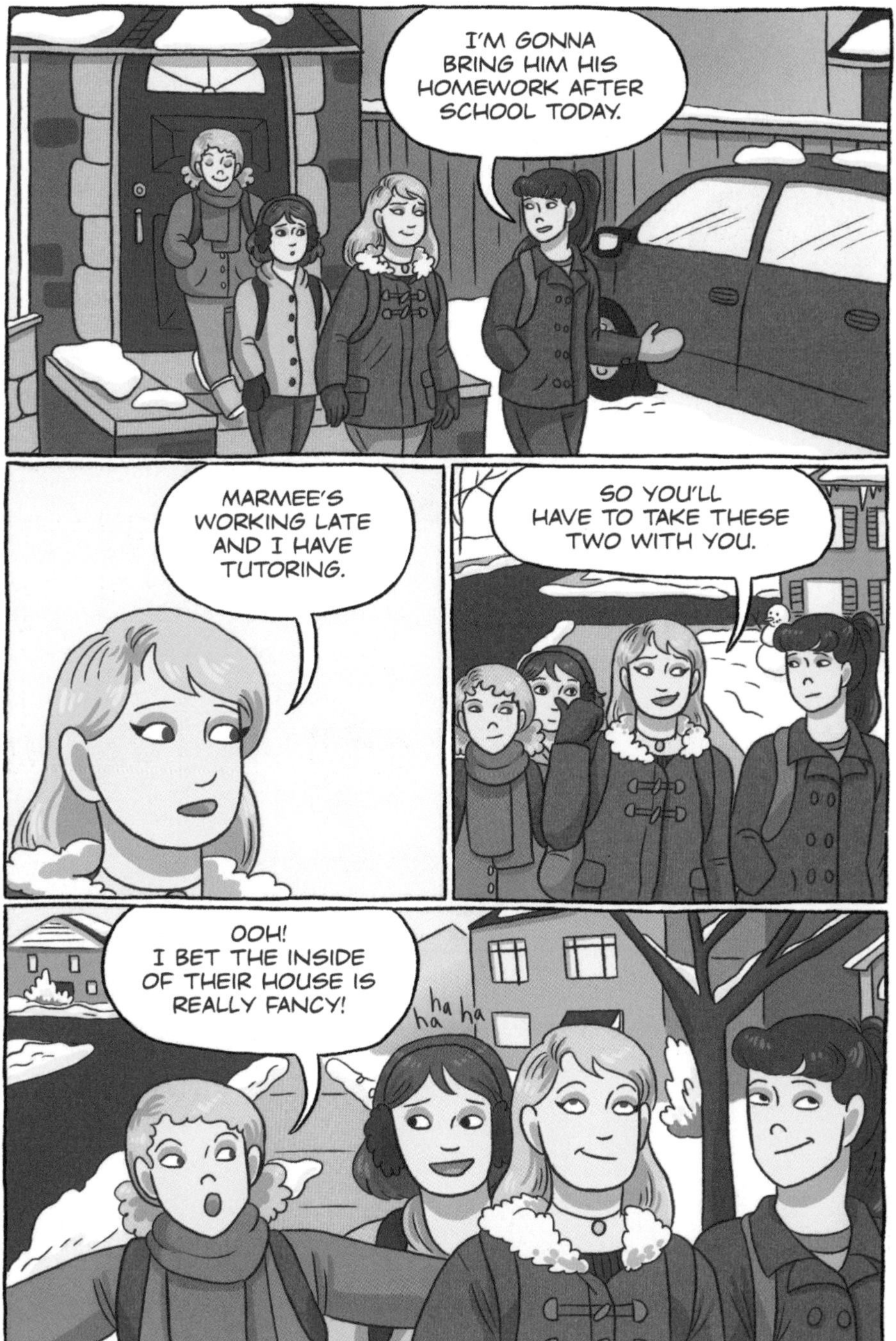
I'M GONNA BRING HIM HIS HOMEWORK AFTER SCHOOL TODAY.
MARMEE'S WORKING LATE AND I HAVE TUTORING.
SO YOU'LL HAVE TO TAKE THESE TWO WITH YOU.
OOH! I BET THE INSIDE OF THEIR HOUSE IS REALLY FANCY!
ha ha ha ha

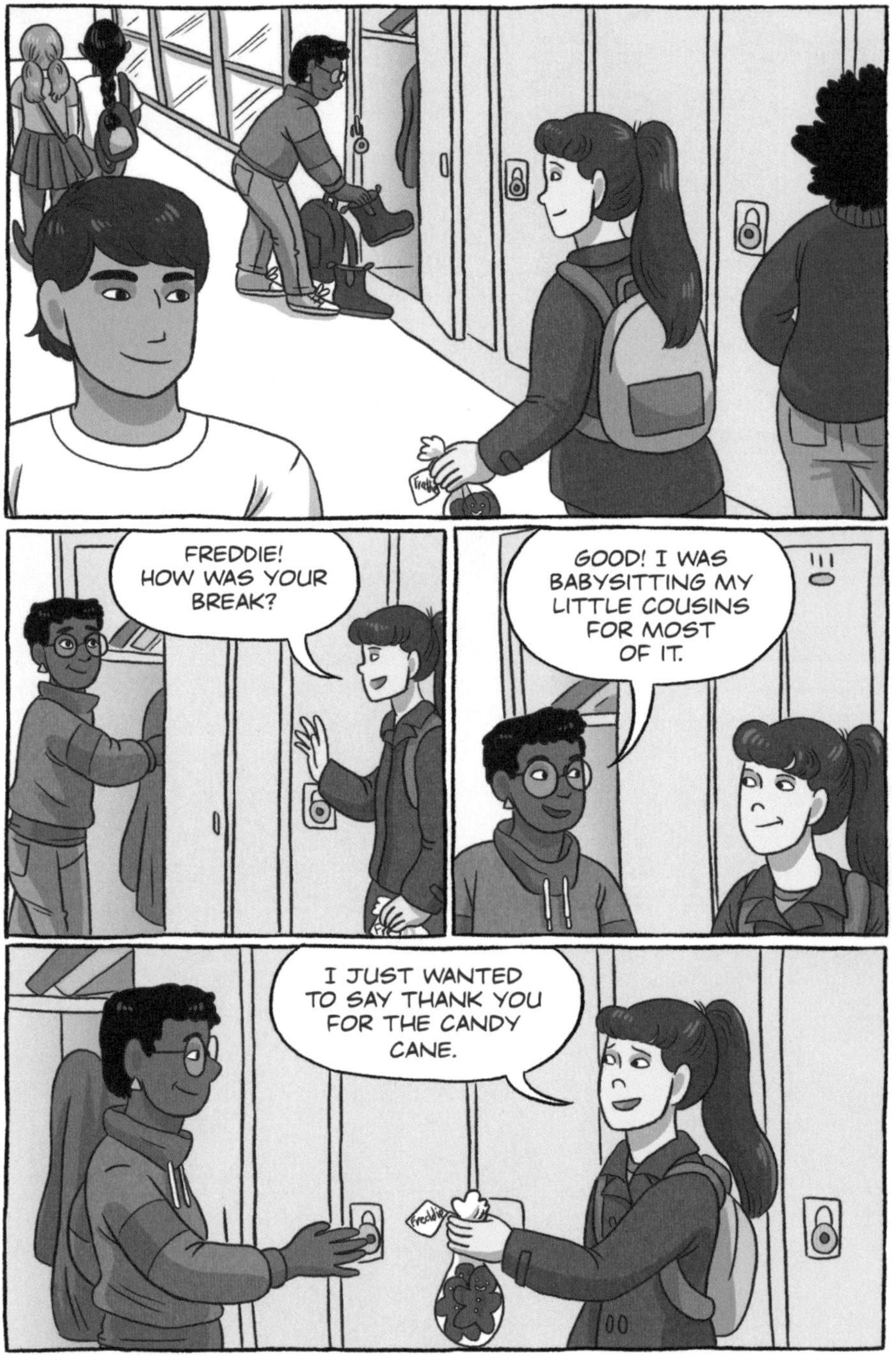

Freddie
FREDDIE! HOW WAS YOUR BREAK?
GOOD! I WAS BABYSITTING MY LITTLE COUSINS FOR MOST OF IT.
I JUST WANTED TO SAY THANK YOU FOR THE CANDY CANE.
Freddie

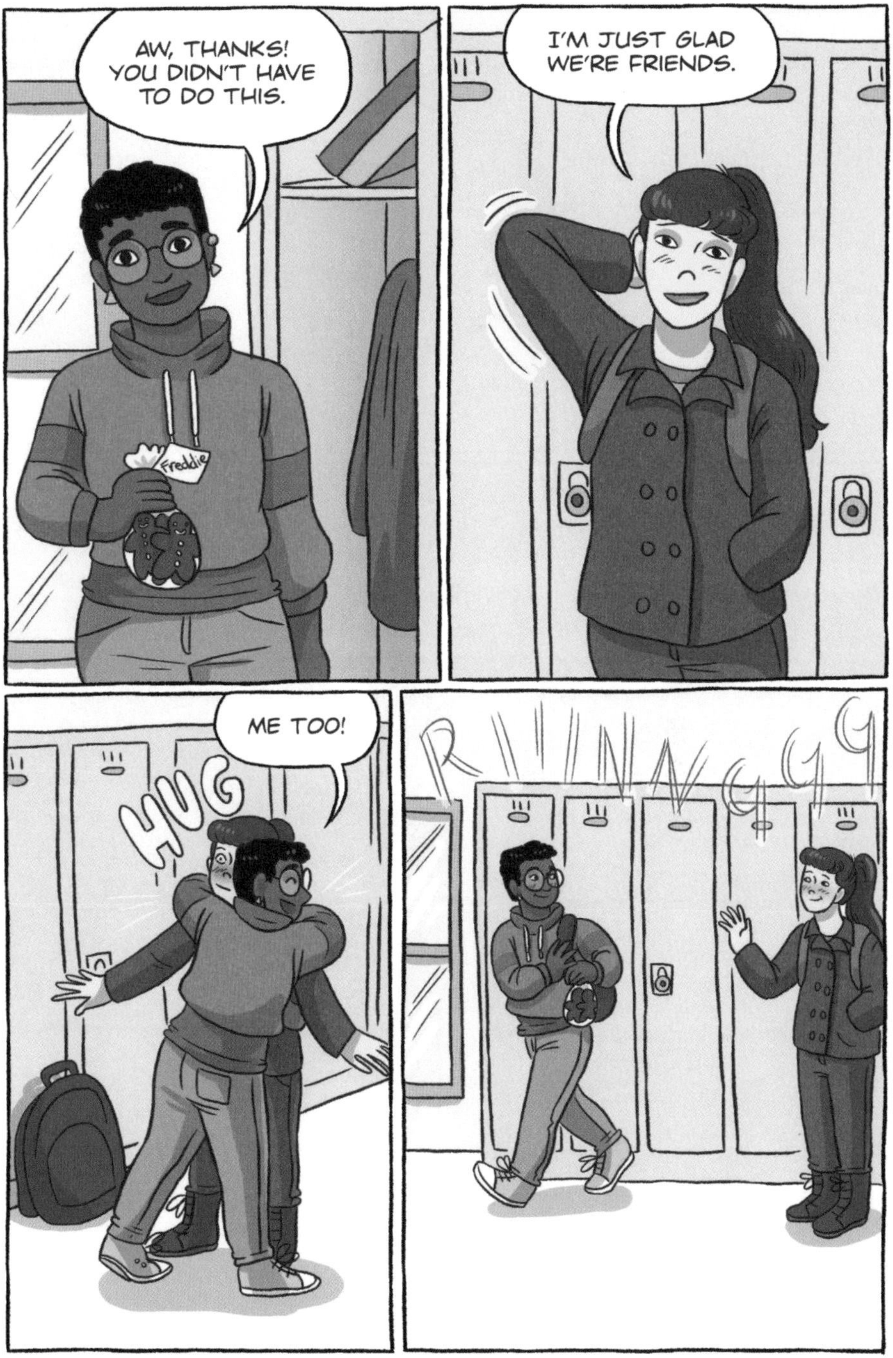
AW, THANKS! YOU DIDN'T HAVE TO DO THIS.
Freddie
I'M JUST GLAD WE'RE FRIENDS.
HUG
ME TOO!

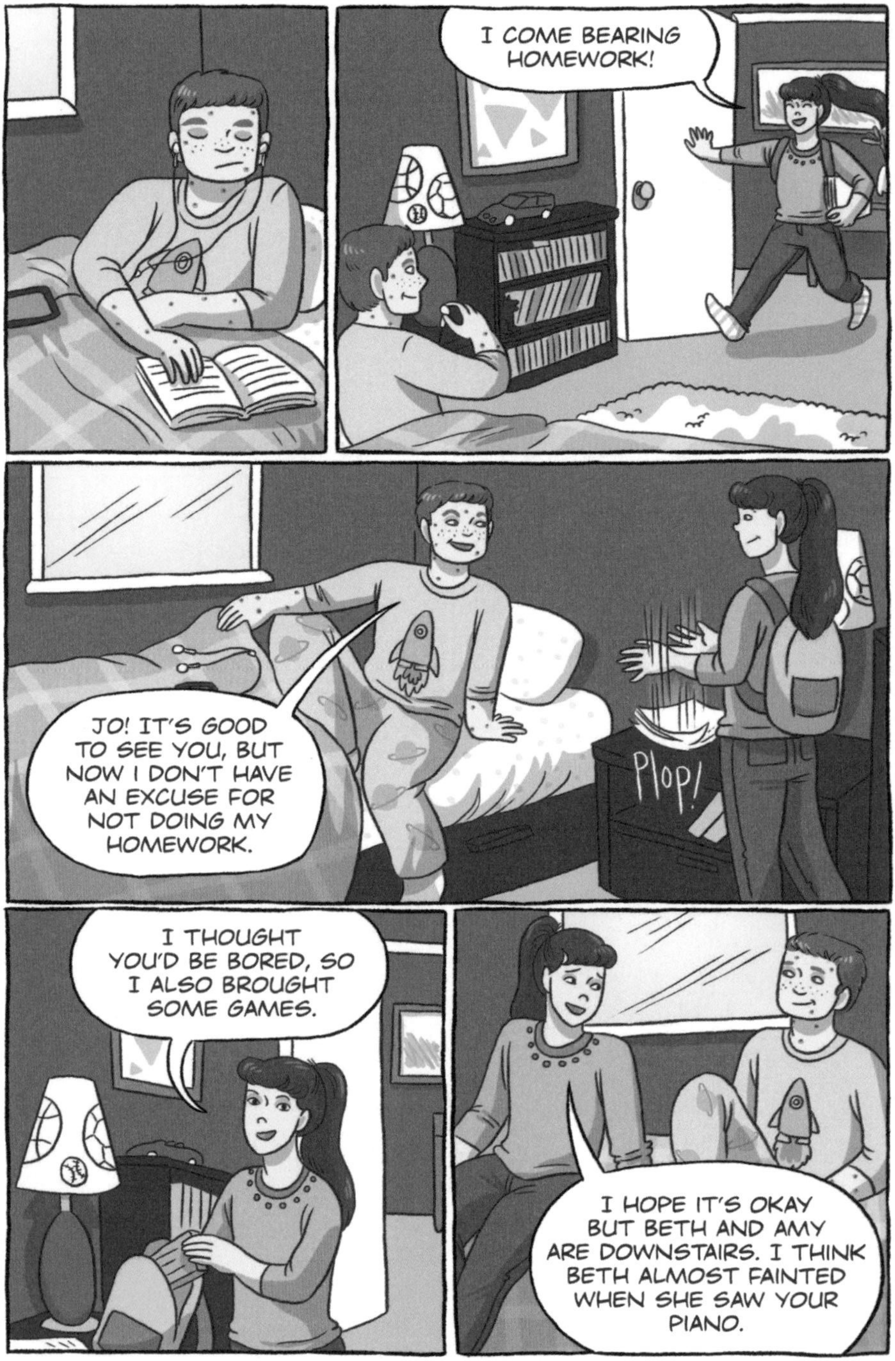
I COME BEARING HOMEWORK!
JO! IT'S GOOD TO SEE YOU, BUT NOW I DON'T HAVE AN EXCUSE FOR NOT DOING MY HOMEWORK.
PLOP!
I THOUGHT YOU'D BE BORED, SO I ALSO BROUGHT SOME GAMES.
I HOPE IT'S OKAY BUT BETH AND AMY ARE DOWNSTAIRS. I THINK BETH ALMOST FAINTED WHEN SHE SAW YOUR PIANO.

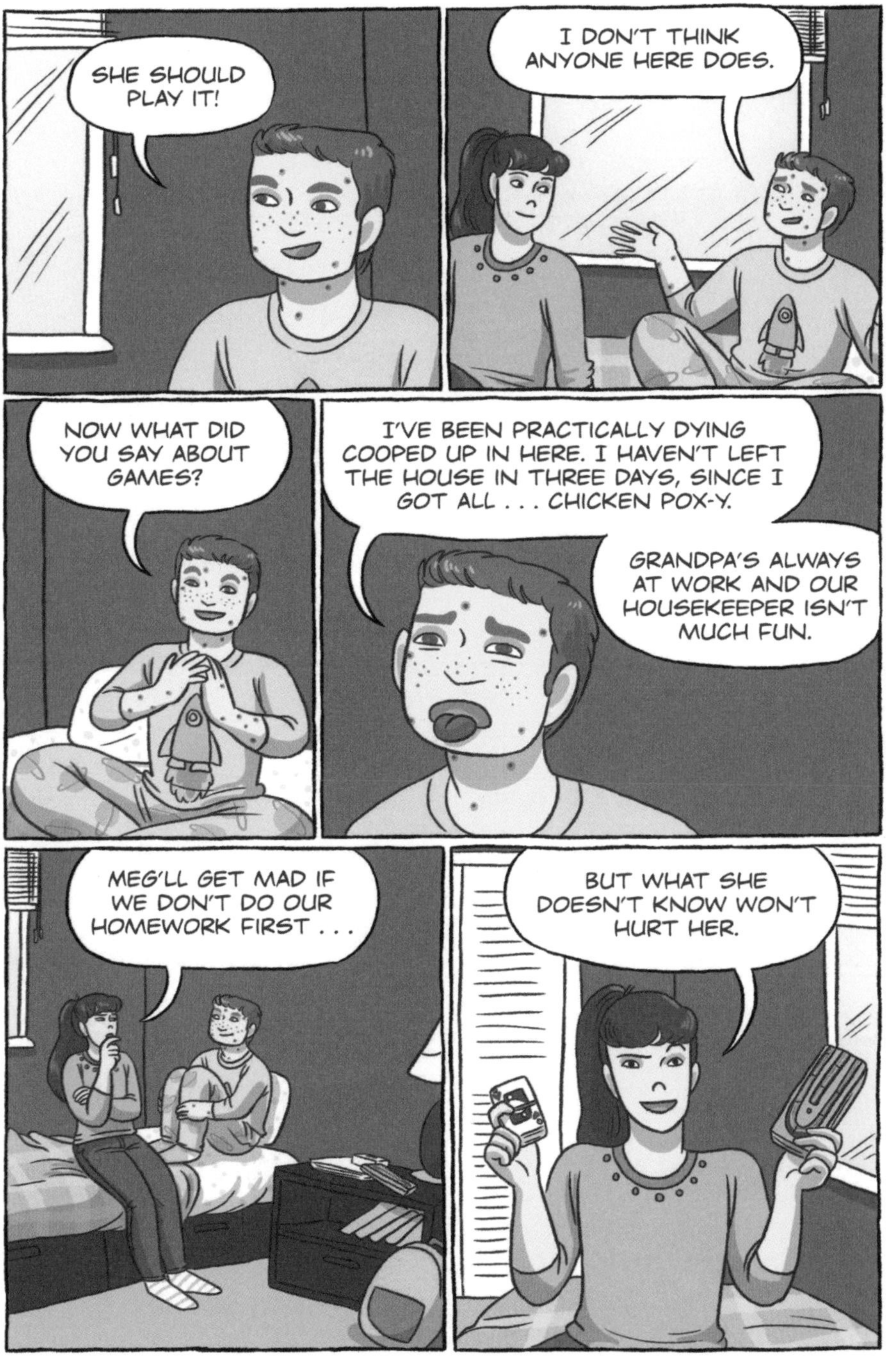
SHE SHOULD PLAY IT!
I DON'T THINK ANYONE HERE DOES.
NOW WHAT DID YOU SAY ABOUT GAMES?
I'VE BEEN PRACTICALLY DYING COOPED UP IN HERE. I HAVEN'T LEFT THE HOUSE IN THREE DAYS, SINCE I GOT ALL . . . CHICKEN POX-Y.
GRANDPA'S ALWAYS AT WORK AND OUR HOUSEKEEPER ISN'T MUCH FUN.
MEG'LL GET MAD IF WE DON'T DO OUR HOMEWORK FIRST . . .
BUT WHAT SHE DOESN'T KNOW WON'T HURT HER.

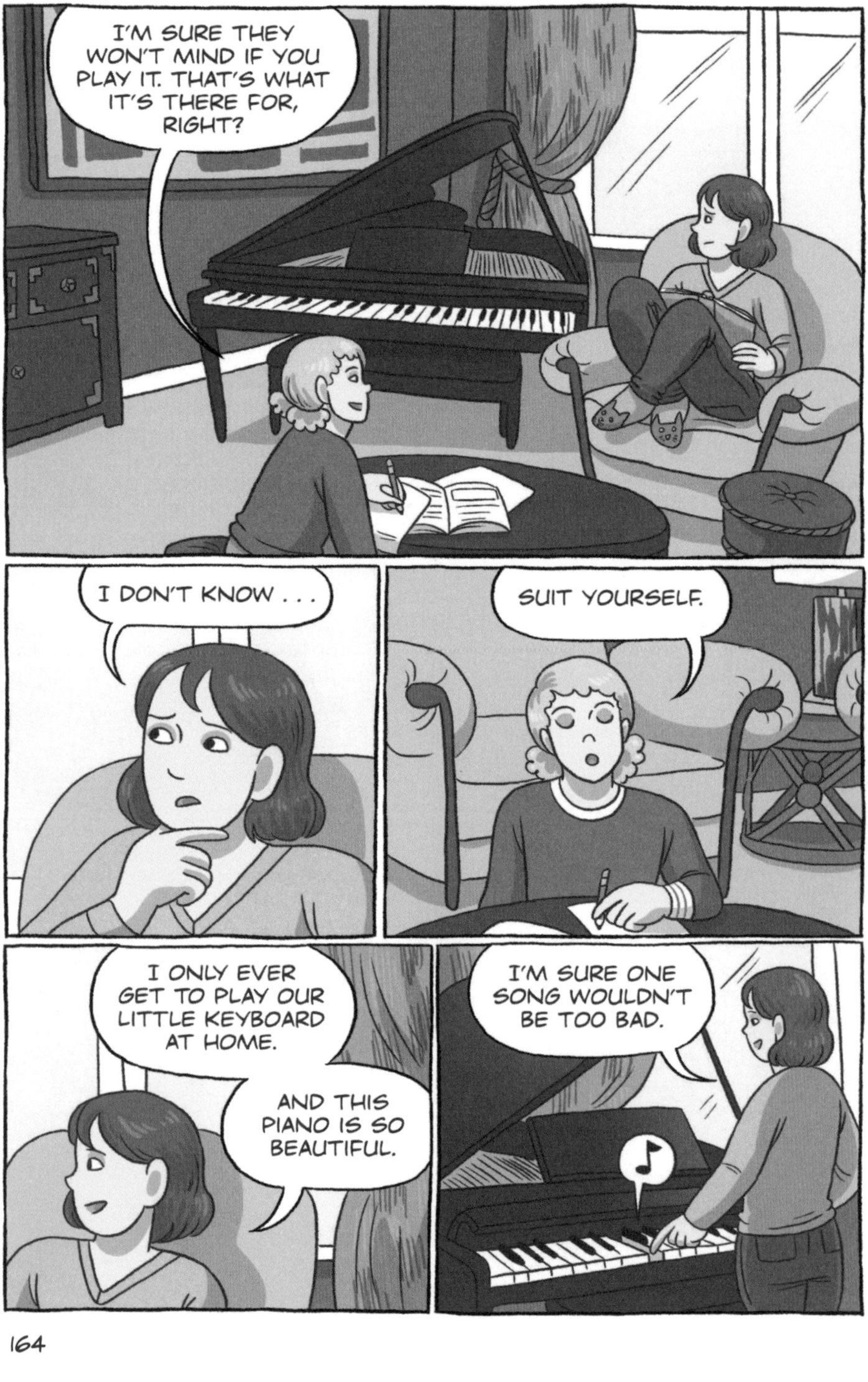
I'M SURE THEY WON'T MIND IF YOU PLAY IT. THAT'S WHAT IT'S THERE FOR, RIGHT?
I DON'T KNOW . . .
SUIT YOURSELF.
I ONLY EVER GET TO PLAY OUR LITTLE KEYBOARD AT HOME.
AND THIS PIANO IS SO BEAUTIFUL.
I'M SURE ONE SONG WOULDN'T BE TOO BAD.
♪

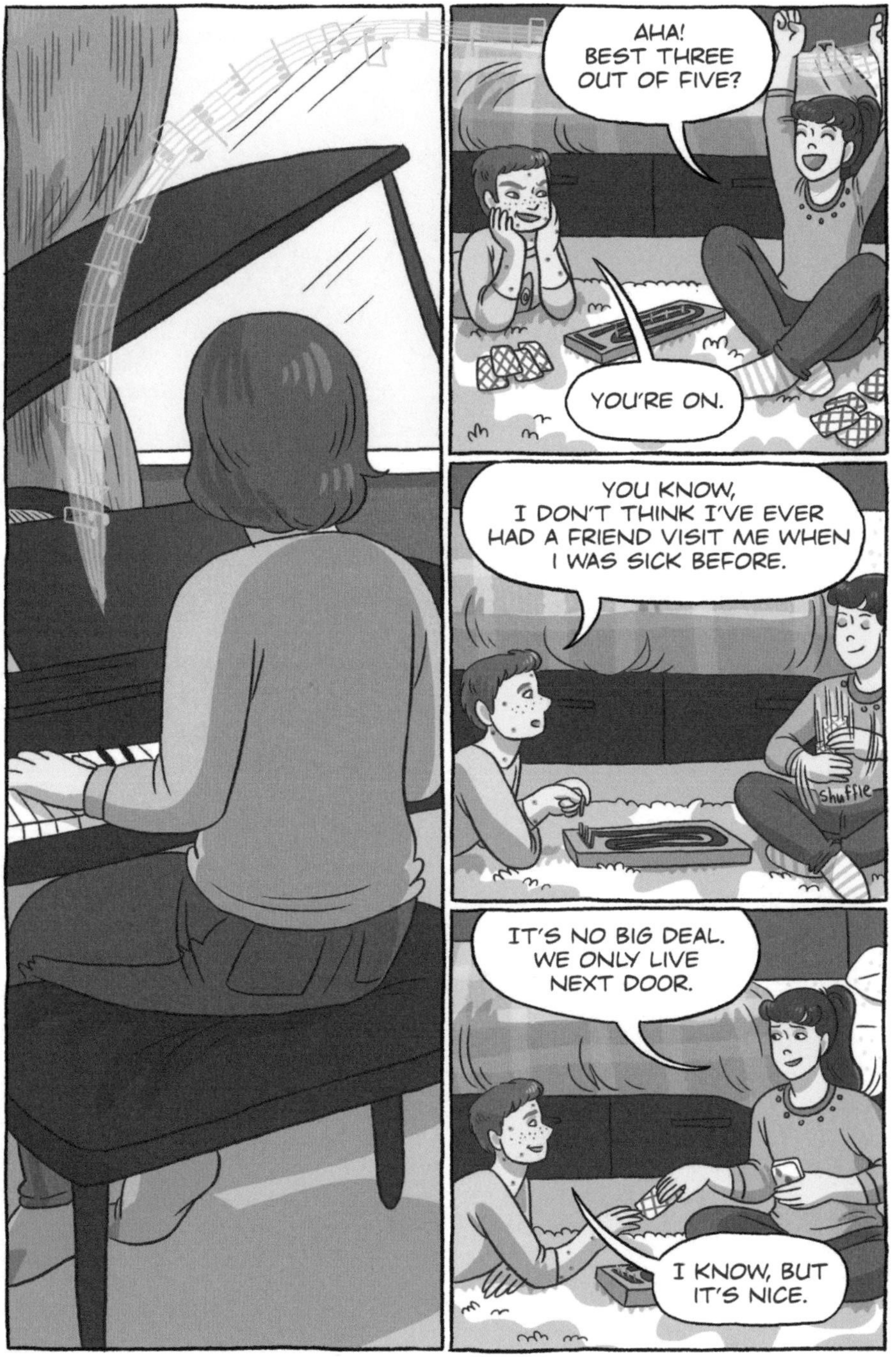
AHA! BEST THREE OUT OF FIVE?
YOU'RE ON.
YOU KNOW, I DON'T THINK I'VE EVER HAD A FRIEND VISIT ME WHEN I WAS SICK BEFORE.
Shuffle
IT'S NO BIG DEAL. WE ONLY LIVE NEXT DOOR.
I KNOW, BUT IT'S NICE.

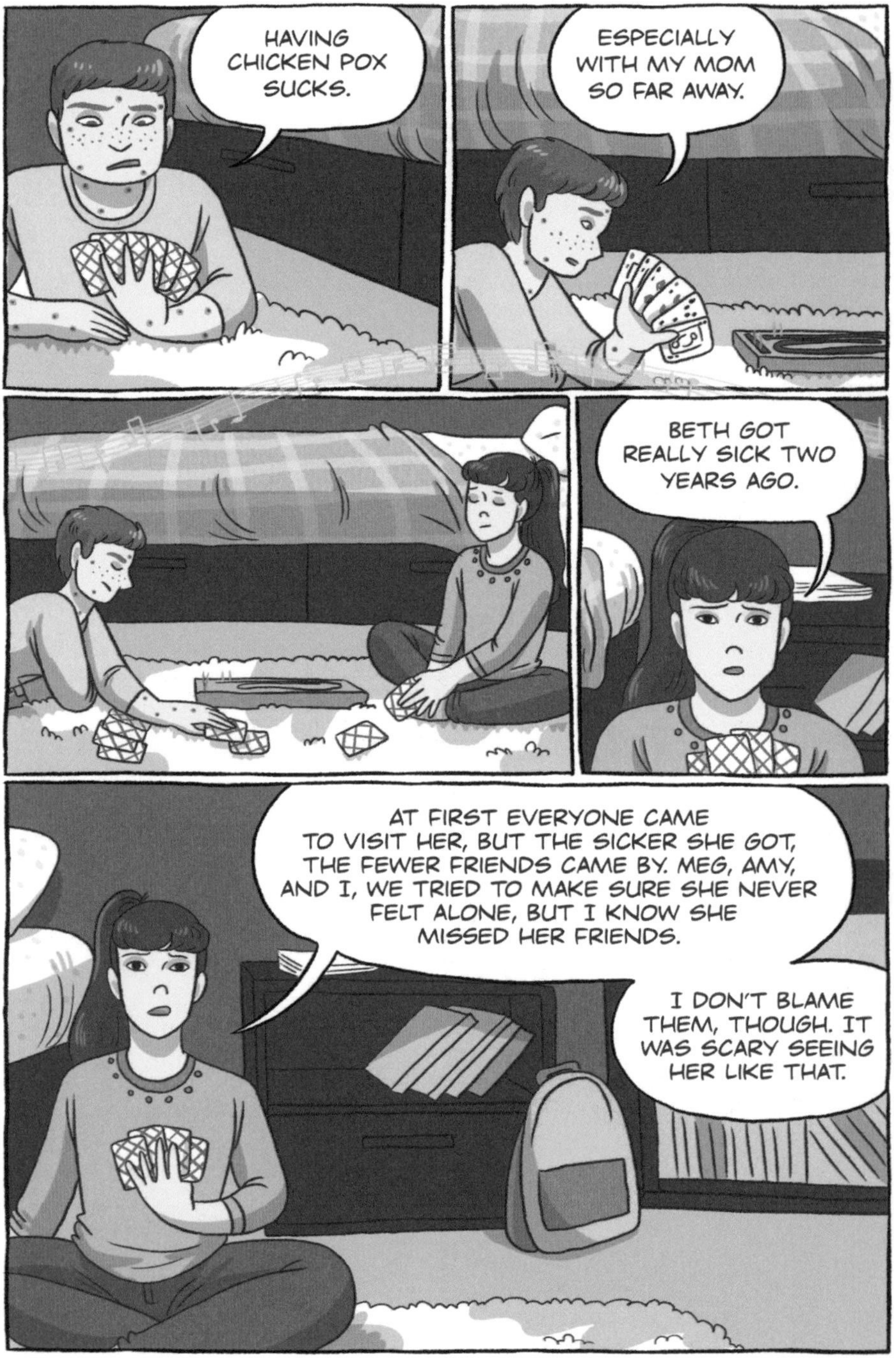
HAVING CHICKEN POX SUCKS.
ESPECIALLY WITH MY MOM SO FAR AWAY.
BETH GOT REALLY SICK TWO YEARS AGO.
AT FIRST EVERYONE CAME TO VISIT HER, BUT THE SICKER SHE GOT, THE FEWER FRIENDS CAME BY. MEG, AMY, AND I, WE TRIED TO MAKE SURE SHE NEVER FELT ALONE, BUT I KNOW SHE MISSED HER FRIENDS.
I DON'T BLAME THEM, THOUGH. IT WAS SCARY SEEING HER LIKE THAT.

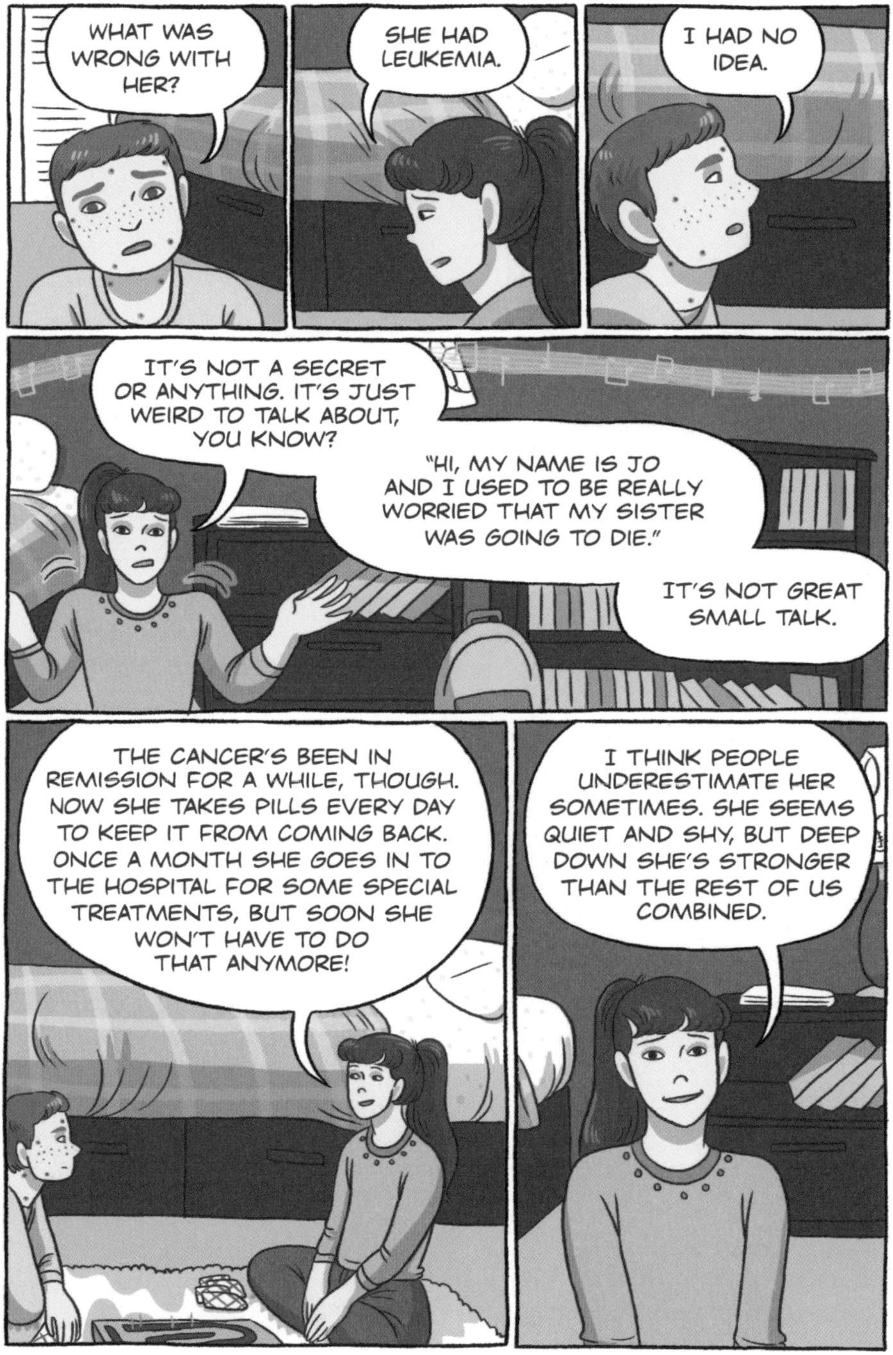
WHAT WAS WRONG WITH HER?
SHE HAD LEUKEMIA.
I HAD NO IDEA.
IT'S NOT A SECRET OR ANYTHING. IT'S JUST WEIRD TO TALK ABOUT, YOU KNOW?
"HI, MY NAME IS JO AND I USED TO BE REALLY WORRIED THAT MY SISTER WAS GOING TO DIE."
IT'S NOT GREAT SMALL TALK.
THE CANCER'S BEEN IN REMISSION FOR A WHILE, THOUGH. NOW SHE TAKES PILLS EVERY DAY TO KEEP IT FROM COMING BACK. ONCE A MONTH SHE GOES IN TO THE HOSPITAL FOR SOME SPECIAL TREATMENTS, BUT SOON SHE WON'T HAVE TO DO THAT ANYMORE!
I THINK PEOPLE UNDERESTIMATE HER SOMETIMES. SHE SEEMS QUIET AND SHY, BUT DEEP DOWN SHE'S STRONGER THAN THE REST OF US COMBINED.

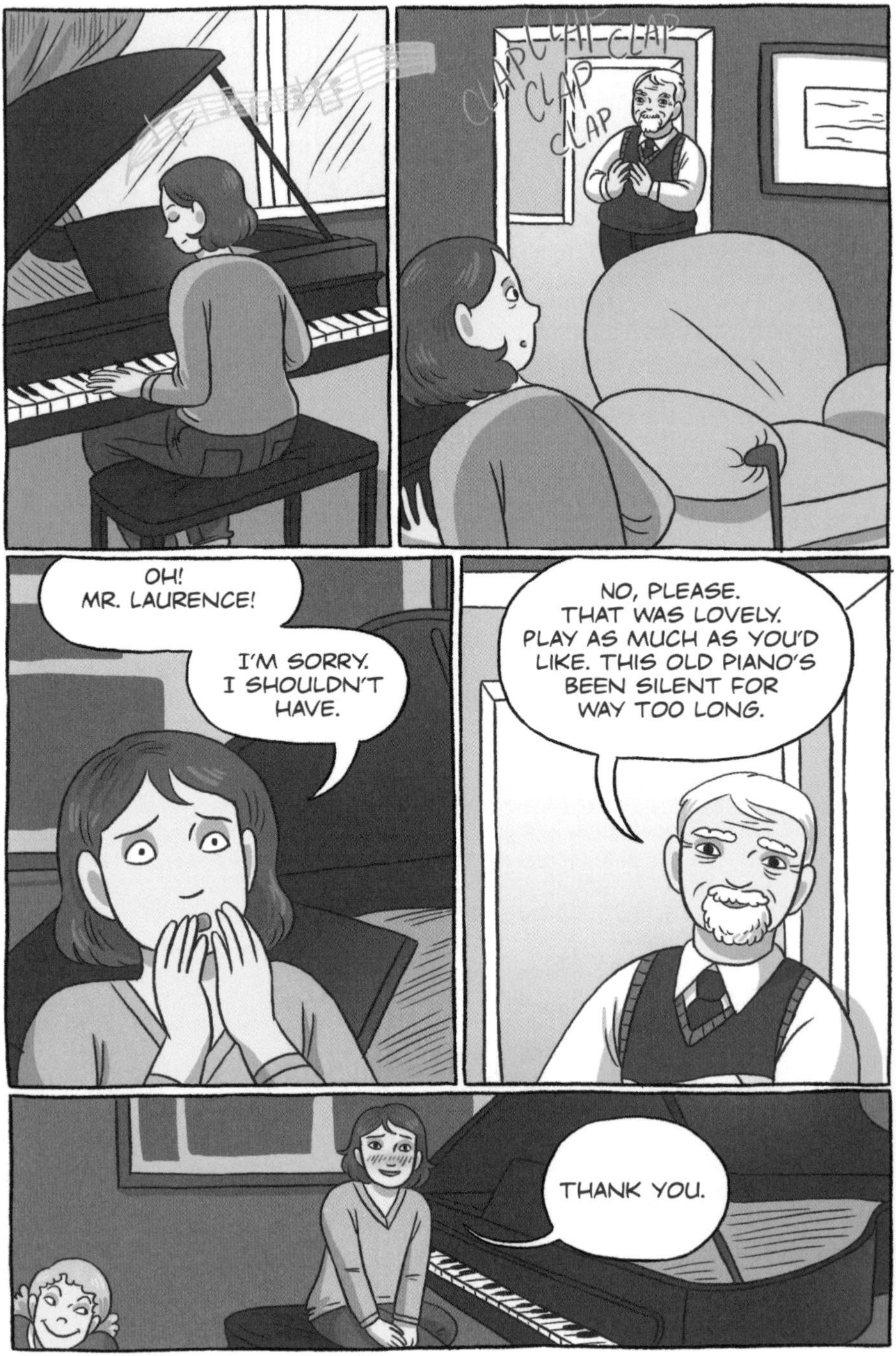
CLAP CLAP CLAP
CLAP
CLAP
OH! MR. LAURENCE!
I'M SORRY. I SHOULDN'T HAVE.
NO, PLEASE. THAT WAS LOVELY. PLAY AS MUCH AS YOU'D LIKE. THIS OLD PIANO'S BEEN SILENT FOR WAY TOO LONG.
THANK YOU.

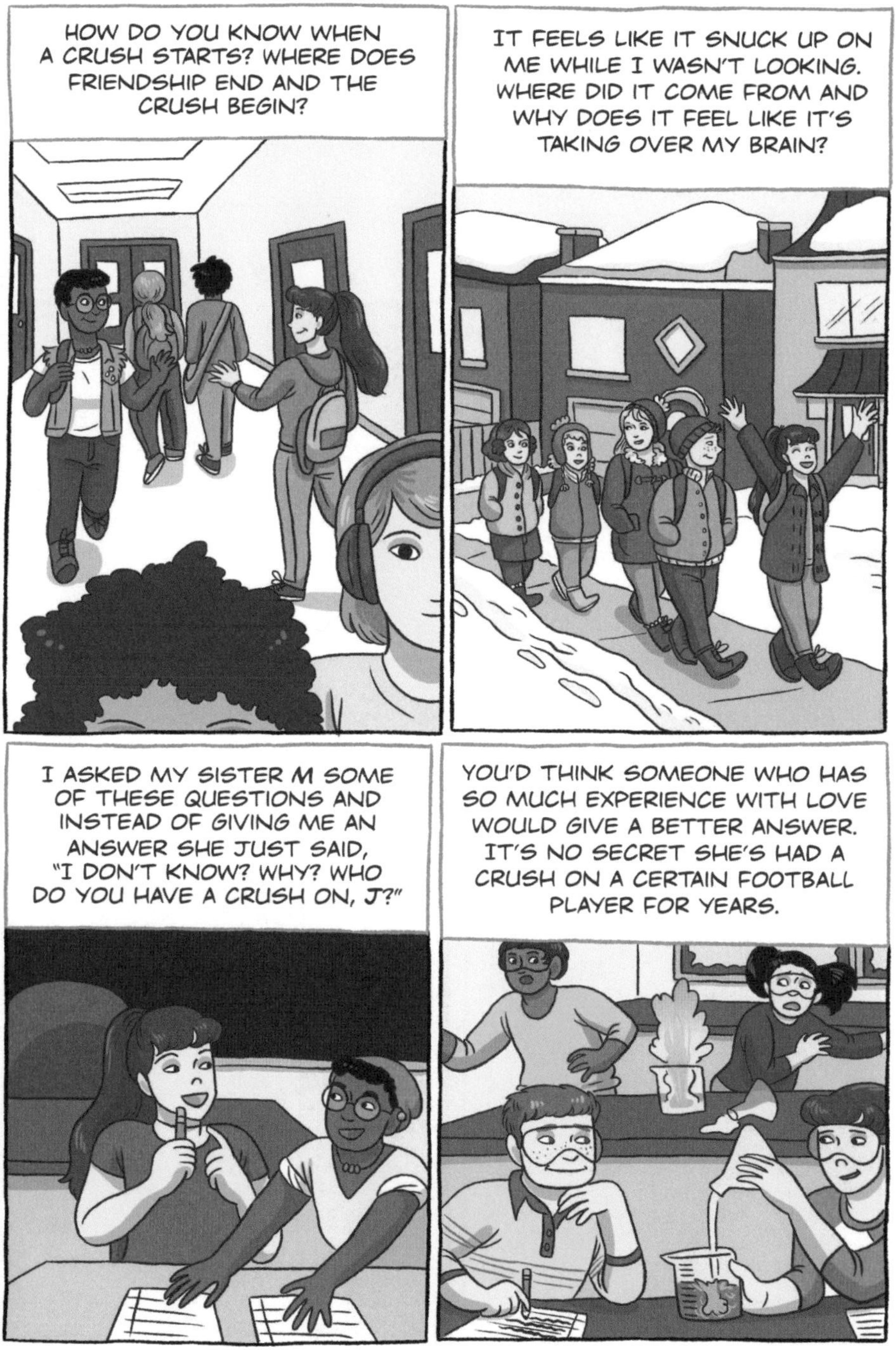
HOW DO YOU KNOW WHEN A CRUSH STARTS? WHERE DOES FRIENDSHIP END AND THE CRUSH BEGIN?
IT FEELS LIKE IT SNUCK UP ON ME WHILE I WASN'T LOOKING. WHERE DID IT COME FROM AND WHY DOES IT FEEL LIKE IT'S TAKING OVER MY BRAIN?
I ASKED MY SISTER M SOME OF THESE QUESTIONS AND INSTEAD OF GIVING ME AN ANSWER SHE JUST SAID, "I DON'T KNOW? WHY? WHO DO YOU HAVE A CRUSH ON, J?"
YOU'D THINK SOMEONE WHO HAS SO MUCH EXPERIENCE WITH LOVE WOULD GIVE A BETTER ANSWER. IT'S NO SECRET SHE'S HAD A CRUSH ON A CERTAIN FOOTBALL PLAYER FOR YEARS.

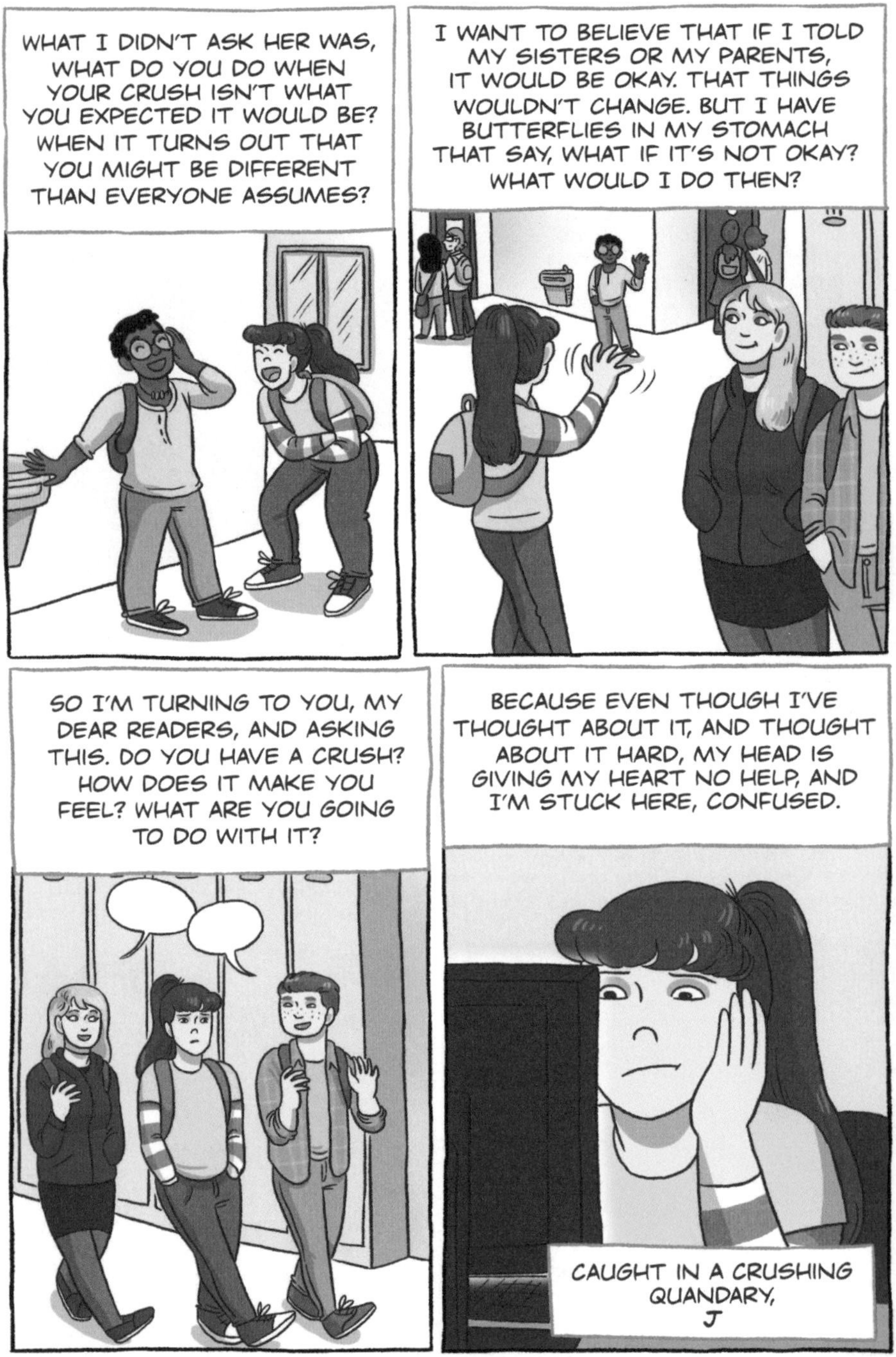
WHAT I DIDN'T ASK HER WAS, WHAT DO YOU DO WHEN YOUR CRUSH ISN'T WHAT YOU EXPECTED IT WOULD BE? WHEN IT TURNS OUT THAT YOU MIGHT BE DIFFERENT THAN EVERYONE ASSUMES?
I WANT TO BELIEVE THAT IF I TOLD MY SISTERS OR MY PARENTS, IT WOULD BE OKAY. THAT THINGS WOULDN'T CHANGE. BUT I HAVE BUTTERFLIES IN MY STOMACH THAT SAY, WHAT IF IT'S NOT OKAY? WHAT WOULD I DO THEN?
SO I'M TURNING TO YOU, MY DEAR READERS, AND ASKING THIS. DO YOU HAVE A CRUSH? HOW DOES IT MAKE YOU FEEL? WHAT ARE YOU GOING TO DO WITH IT?
BECAUSE EVEN THOUGH I'VE THOUGHT ABOUT IT, AND THOUGHT ABOUT IT HARD, MY HEAD IS GIVING MY HEART NO HELP, AND I'M STUCK HERE, CONFUSED.
CAUGHT IN A CRUSHING QUANDARY,
J

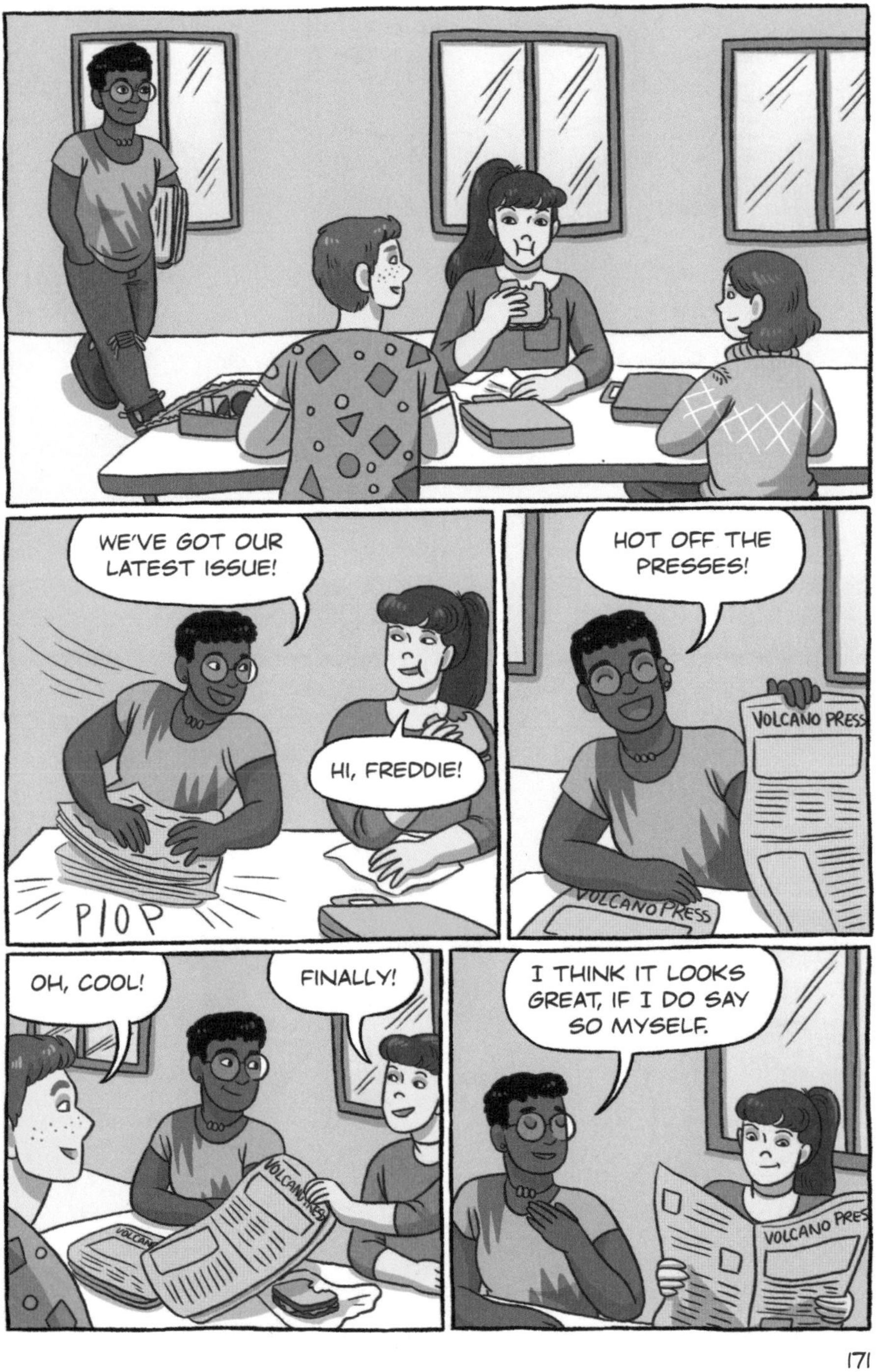
WE'VE GOT OUR LATEST ISSUE!
HI, FREDDIE!
PLOP
HOT OFF THE PRESSES!
VOLCANO PRESS
OH, COOL!
FINALLY!
I THINK IT LOOKS GREAT, IF I DO SAY SO MYSELF.

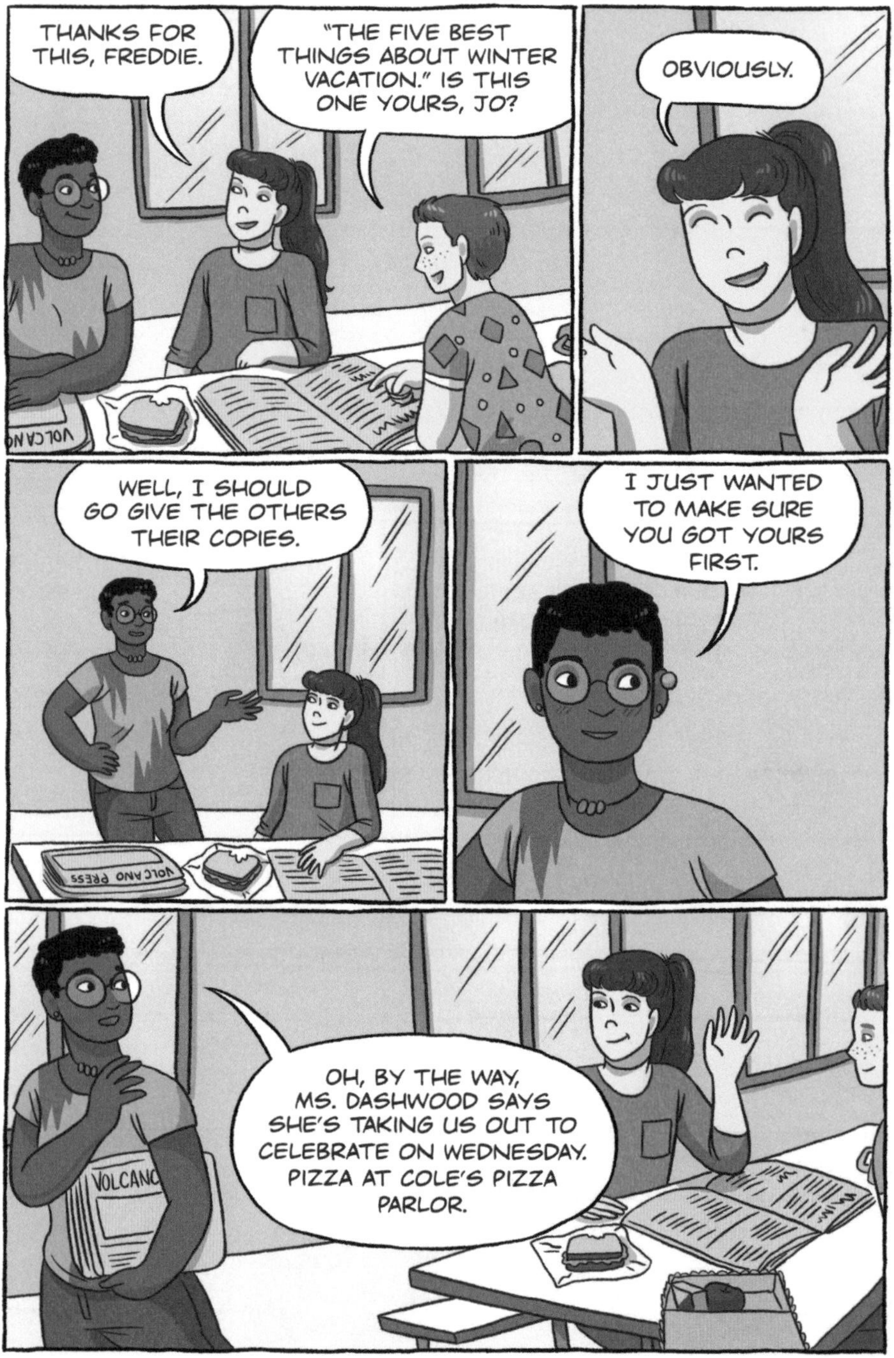
THANKS FOR THIS, FREDDIE.
"THE FIVE BEST THINGS ABOUT WINTER VACATION." IS THIS ONE YOURS, JO?
VOLCANO
OBVIOUSLY.
WELL, I SHOULD GO GIVE THE OTHERS THEIR COPIES.
VOLCANO PRESS
I JUST WANTED TO MAKE SURE YOU GOT YOURS FIRST.
VOLCANO
OH, BY THE WAY, MS. DASHWOOD SAYS SHE'S TAKING US OUT TO CELEBRATE ON WEDNESDAY. PIZZA AT COLE'S PIZZA PARLOR.

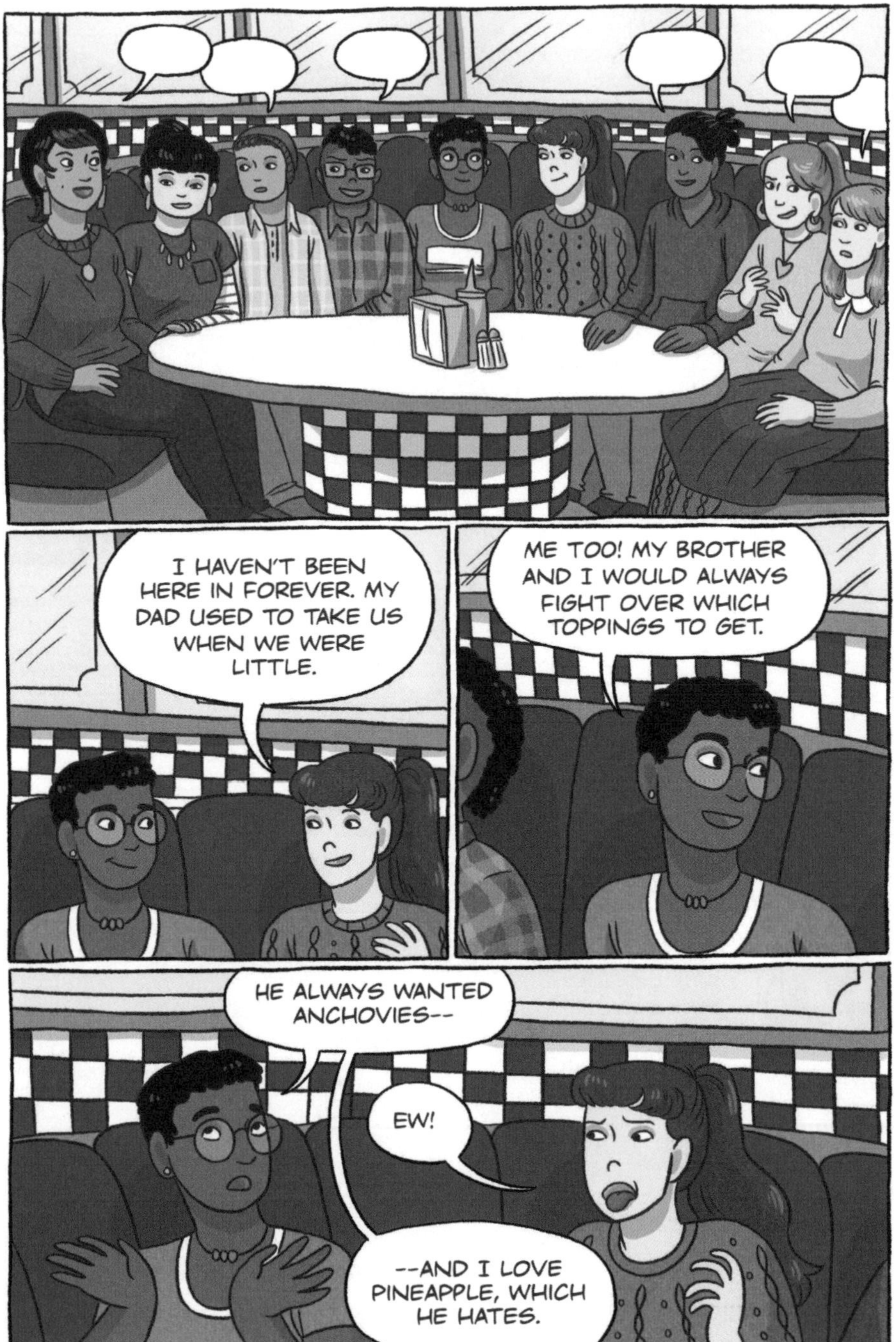
I HAVEN'T BEEN HERE IN FOREVER. MY DAD USED TO TAKE US WHEN WE WERE LITTLE.
ME TOO! MY BROTHER AND I WOULD ALWAYS FIGHT OVER WHICH TOPPINGS TO GET.
HE ALWAYS WANTED ANCHOVIES--
EW!
--AND I LOVE PINEAPPLE, WHICH HE HATES.

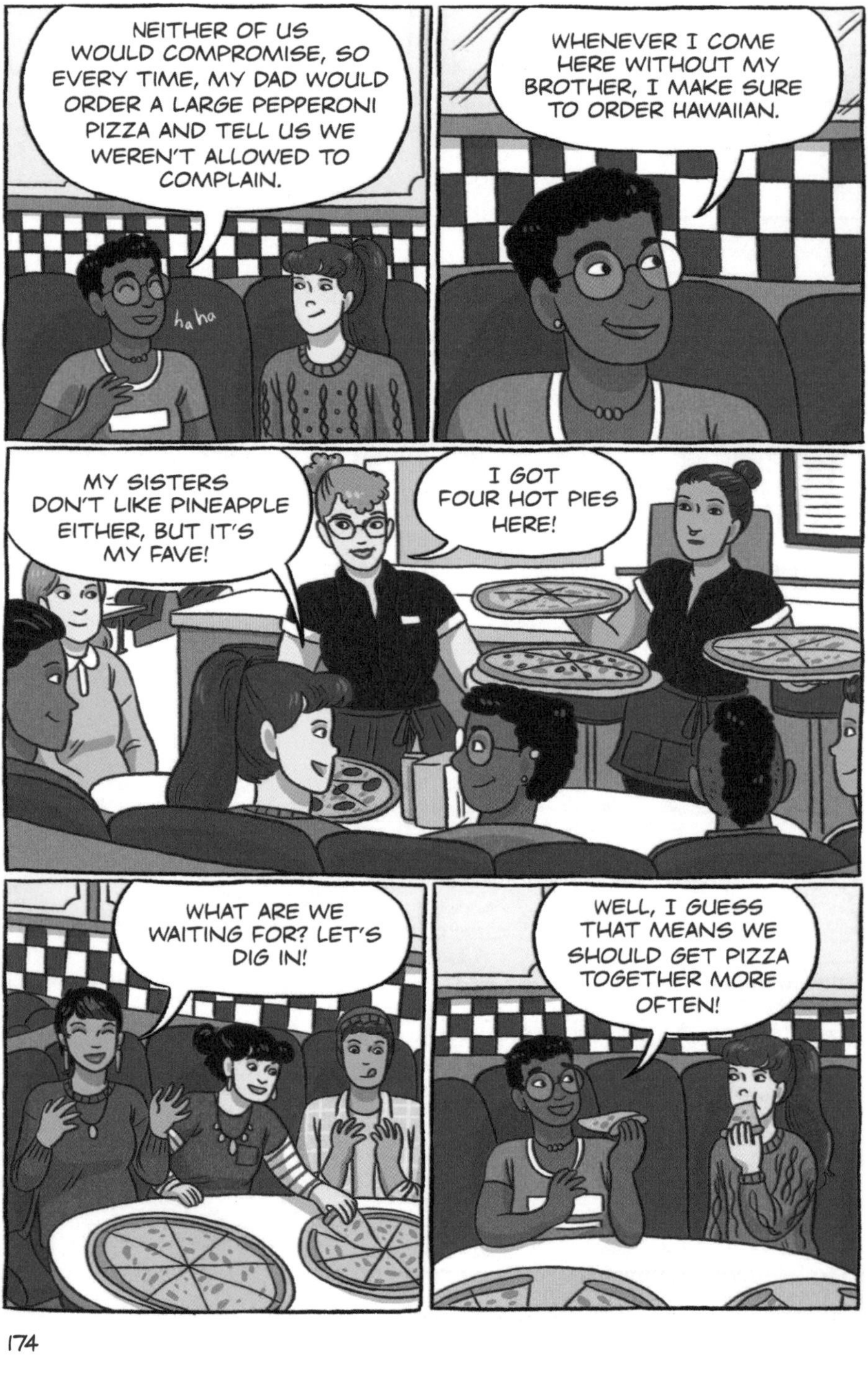
NEITHER OF US WOULD COMPROMISE, SO EVERY TIME, MY DAD WOULD ORDER A LARGE PEPPERONI PIZZA AND TELL US WE WEREN'T ALLOWED TO COMPLAIN.
haha
WHENEVER I COME HERE WITHOUT MY BROTHER, I MAKE SURE TO ORDER HAWAIIAN.
MY SISTERS DON'T LIKE PINEAPPLE EITHER, BUT IT'S MY FAVE!
I GOT FOUR HOT PIES HERE!
WHAT ARE WE WAITING FOR? LET'S DIG IN!
WELL, I GUESS THAT MEANS WE SHOULD GET PIZZA TOGETHER MORE OFTEN!

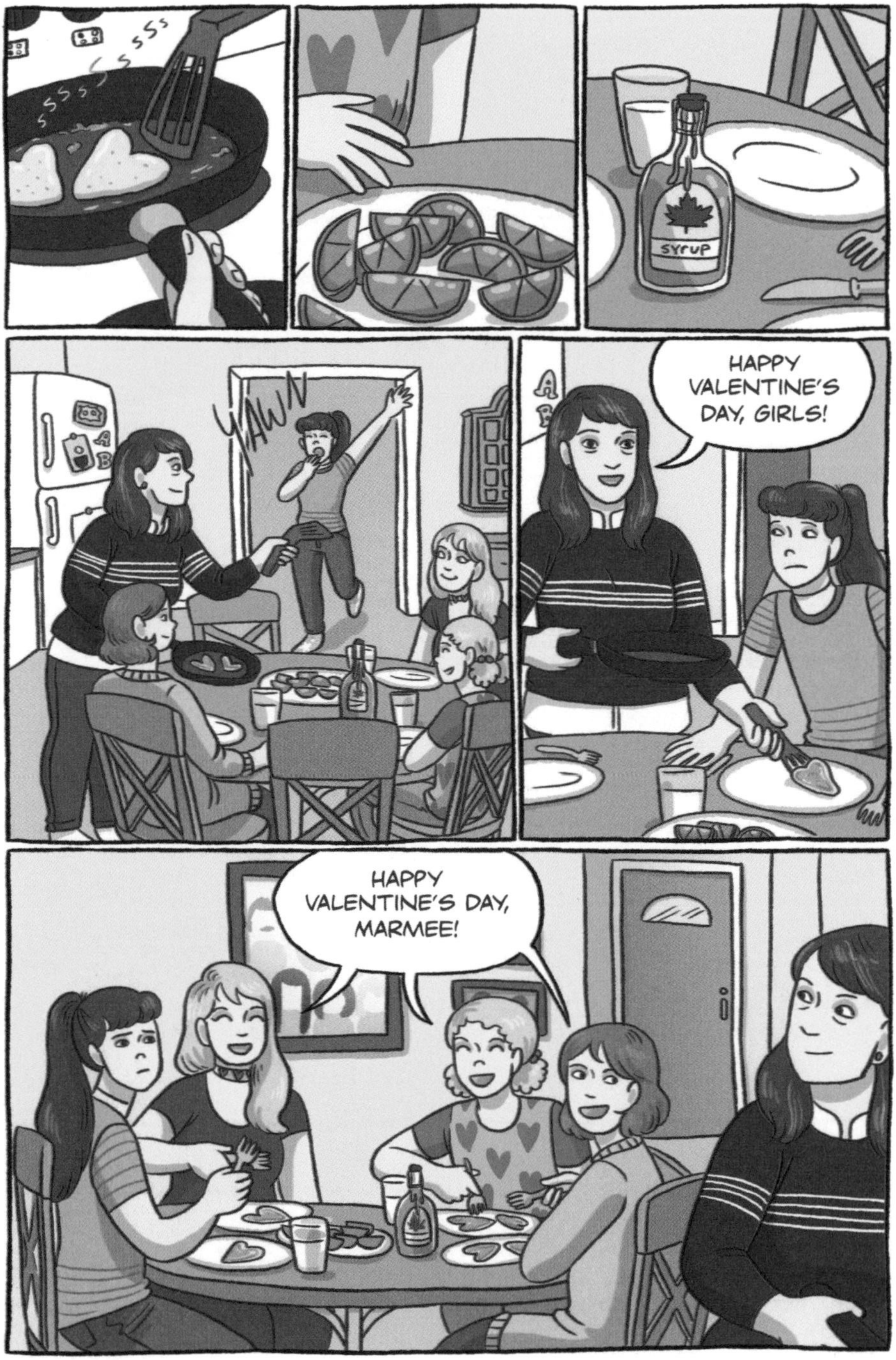

S S S S
S S S S
SYRUP
YAWN
HAPPY VALENTINE'S DAY, GIRLS!
HAPPY VALENTINE'S DAY, MARMEE!

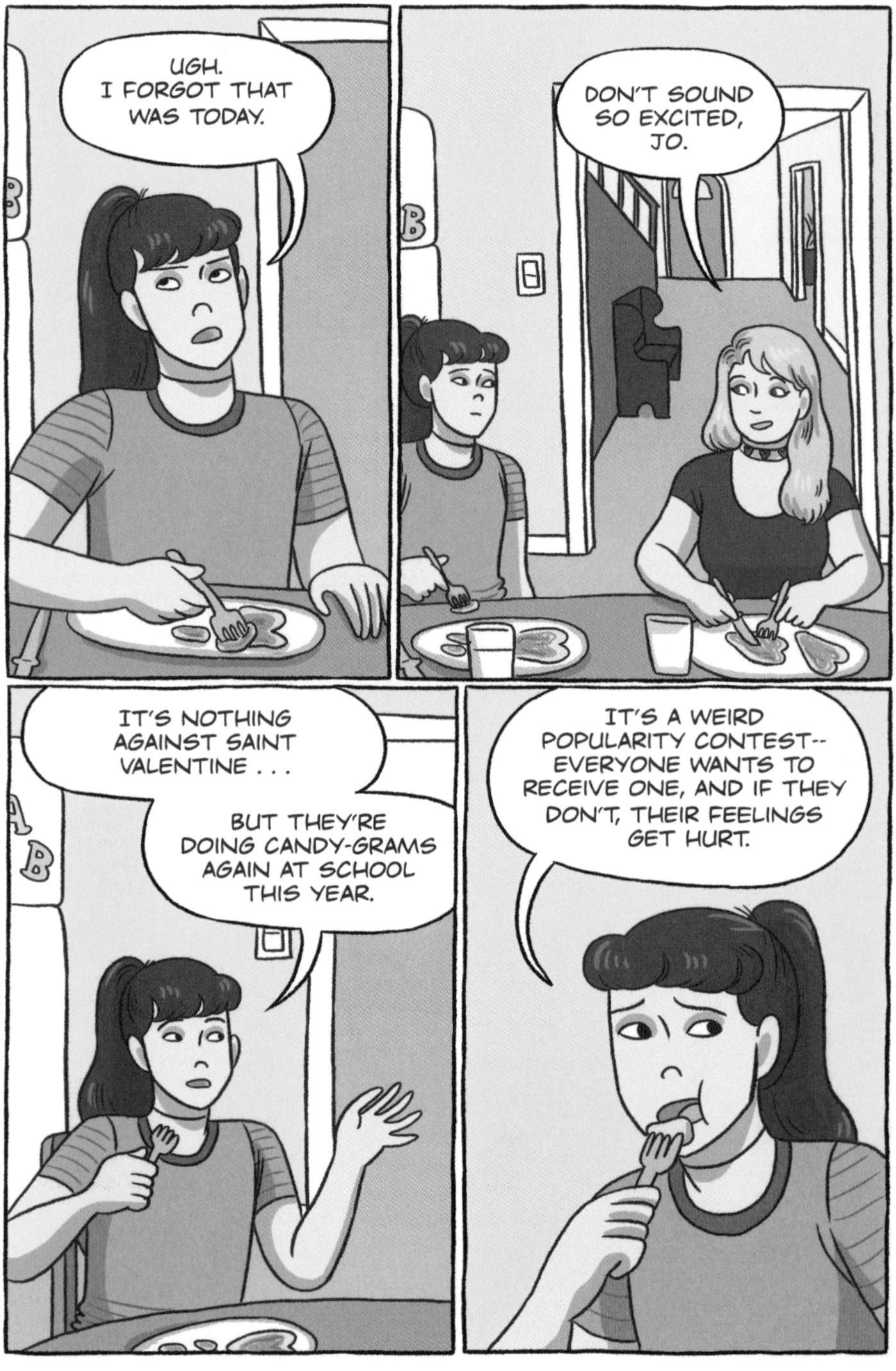
UGH.
I FORGOT THAT
WAS TODAY.
DON'T SOUND
SO EXCITED,
JO.
IT'S NOTHING
AGAINST SAINT
VALENTINE . . .
BUT THEY'RE
DOING CANDY-GRAMS
AGAIN AT SCHOOL
THIS YEAR.
IT'S A WEIRD
POPULARITY CONTEST--
EVERYONE WANTS TO
RECEIVE ONE, AND IF THEY
DON'T, THEIR FEELINGS
GET HURT.

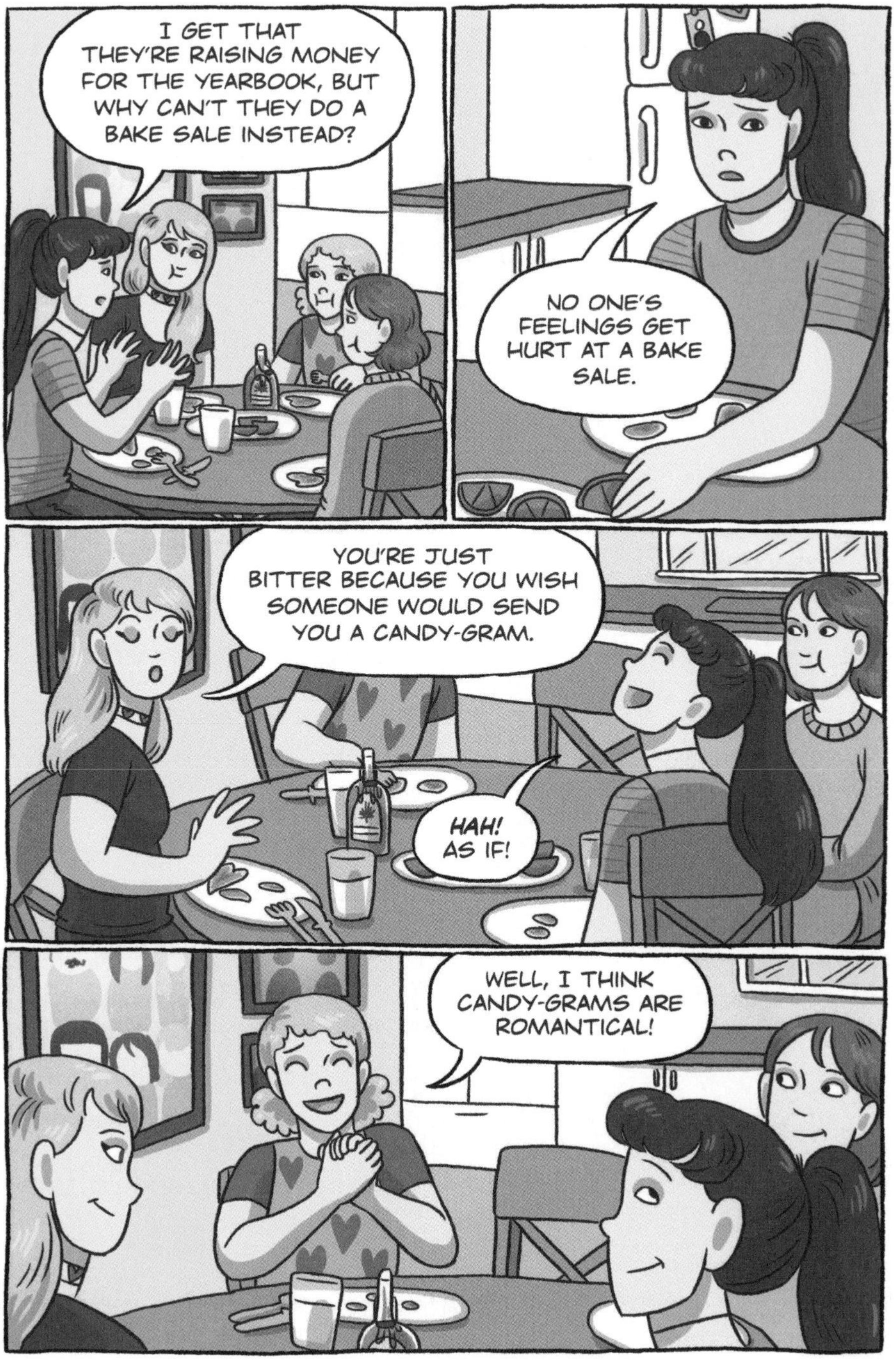

I GET THAT THEY'RE RAISING MONEY FOR THE YEARBOOK, BUT WHY CAN'T THEY DO A BAKE SALE INSTEAD?
NO ONE'S FEELINGS GET HURT AT A BAKE SALE.
YOU'RE JUST BITTER BECAUSE YOU WISH SOMEONE WOULD SEND YOU A CANDY-GRAM.
HAH! AS IF!
WELL, I THINK CANDY-GRAMS ARE ROMANTICAL!

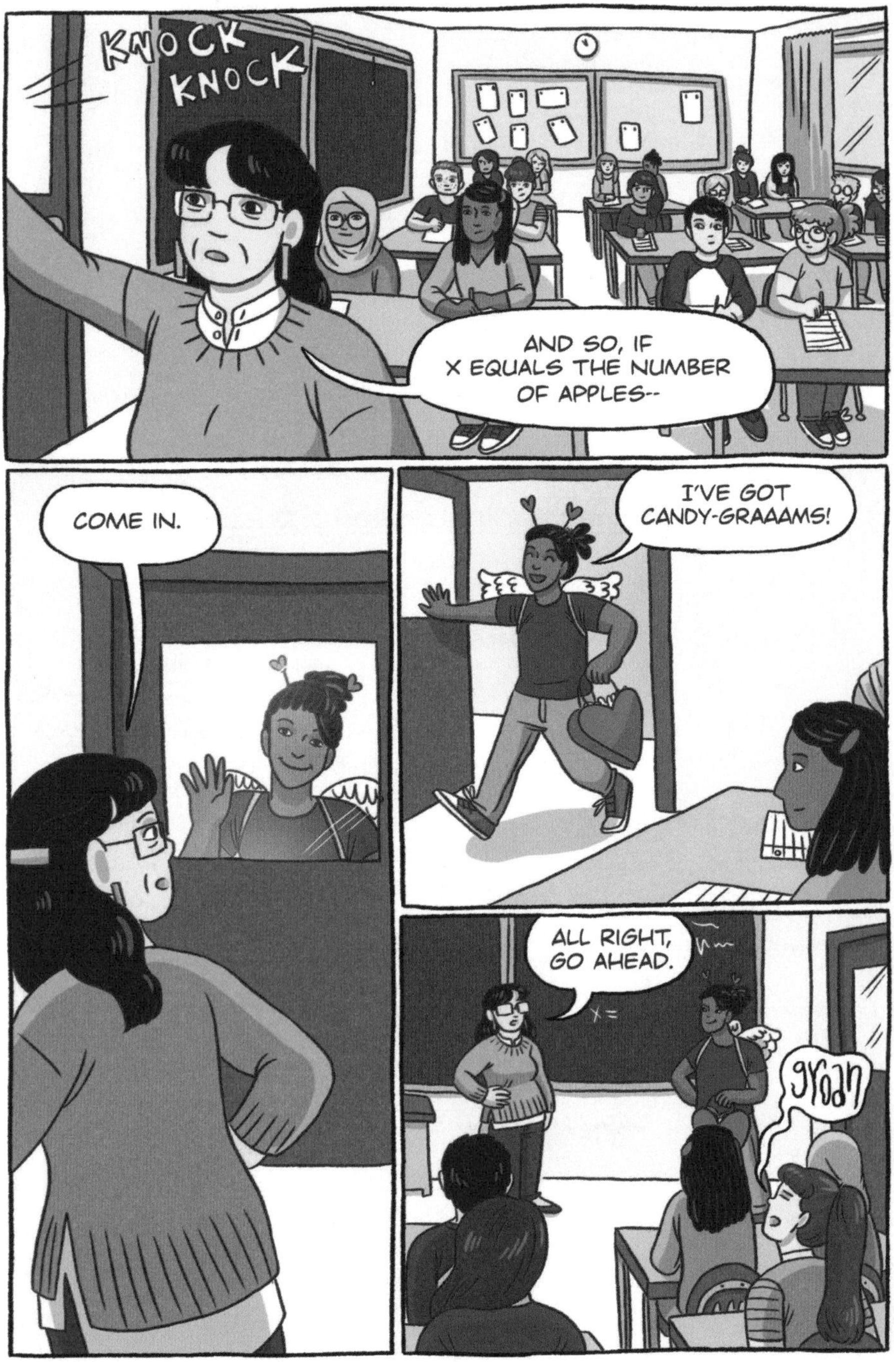

KNOCK KNOCK
AND SO, IF X EQUALS THE NUMBER OF APPLES--
COME IN.
I'VE GOT CANDY-GRAAAMS!
ALL RIGHT, GO AHEAD.
groan

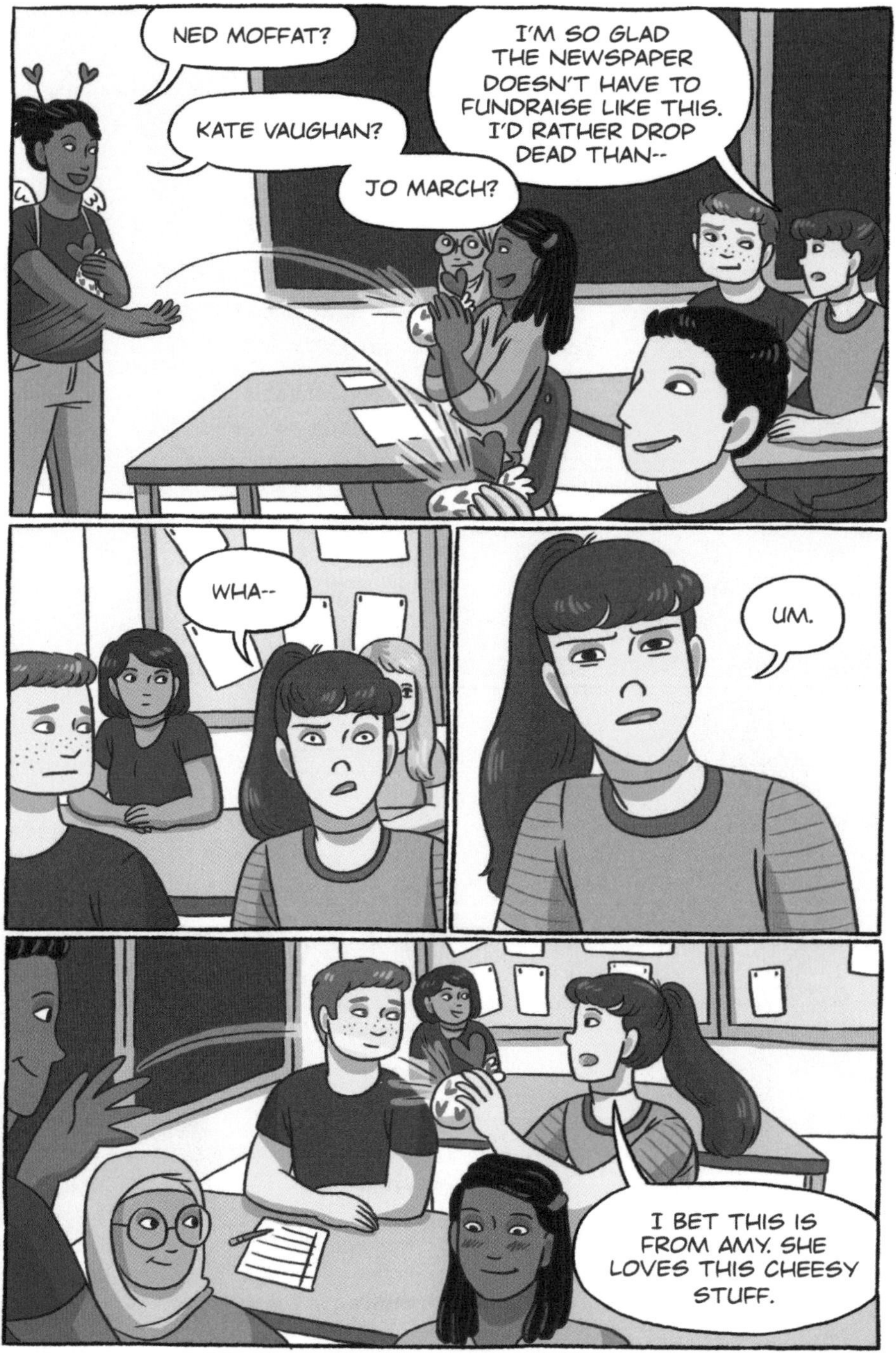
NED MOFFAT?
KATE VAUGHAN?
JO MARCH?
I'M SO GLAD THE NEWSPAPER DOESN'T HAVE TO FUNDRAISE LIKE THIS. I'D RATHER DROP DEAD THAN--
WHA--
UM.
I BET THIS IS FROM AMY. SHE LOVES THIS CHEESY STUFF.

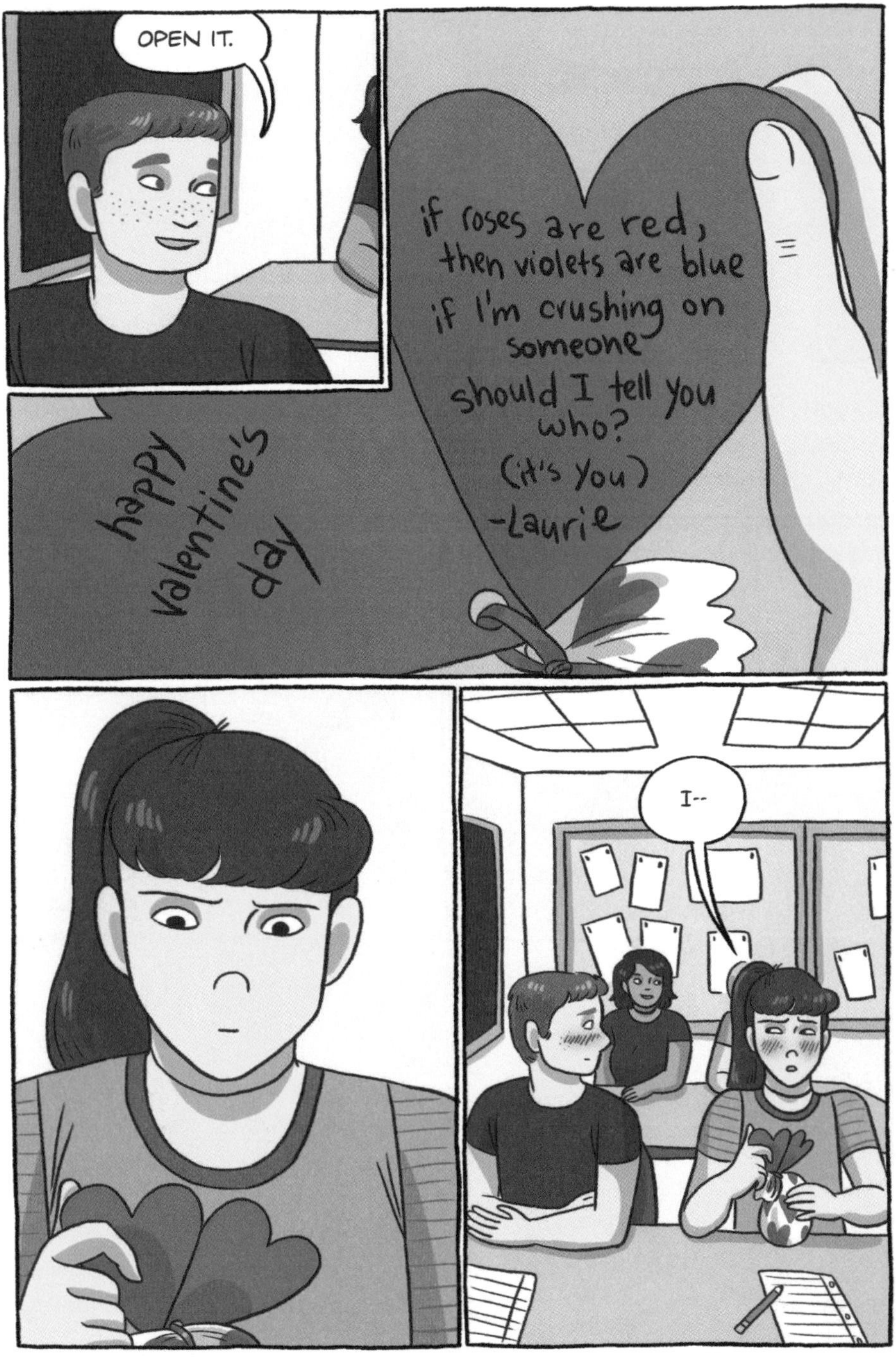
OPEN IT.
if roses are red, then violets are blue if I'm crushing on someone should I tell you who? (it's you) -Laurie
happy valentine's day
I--

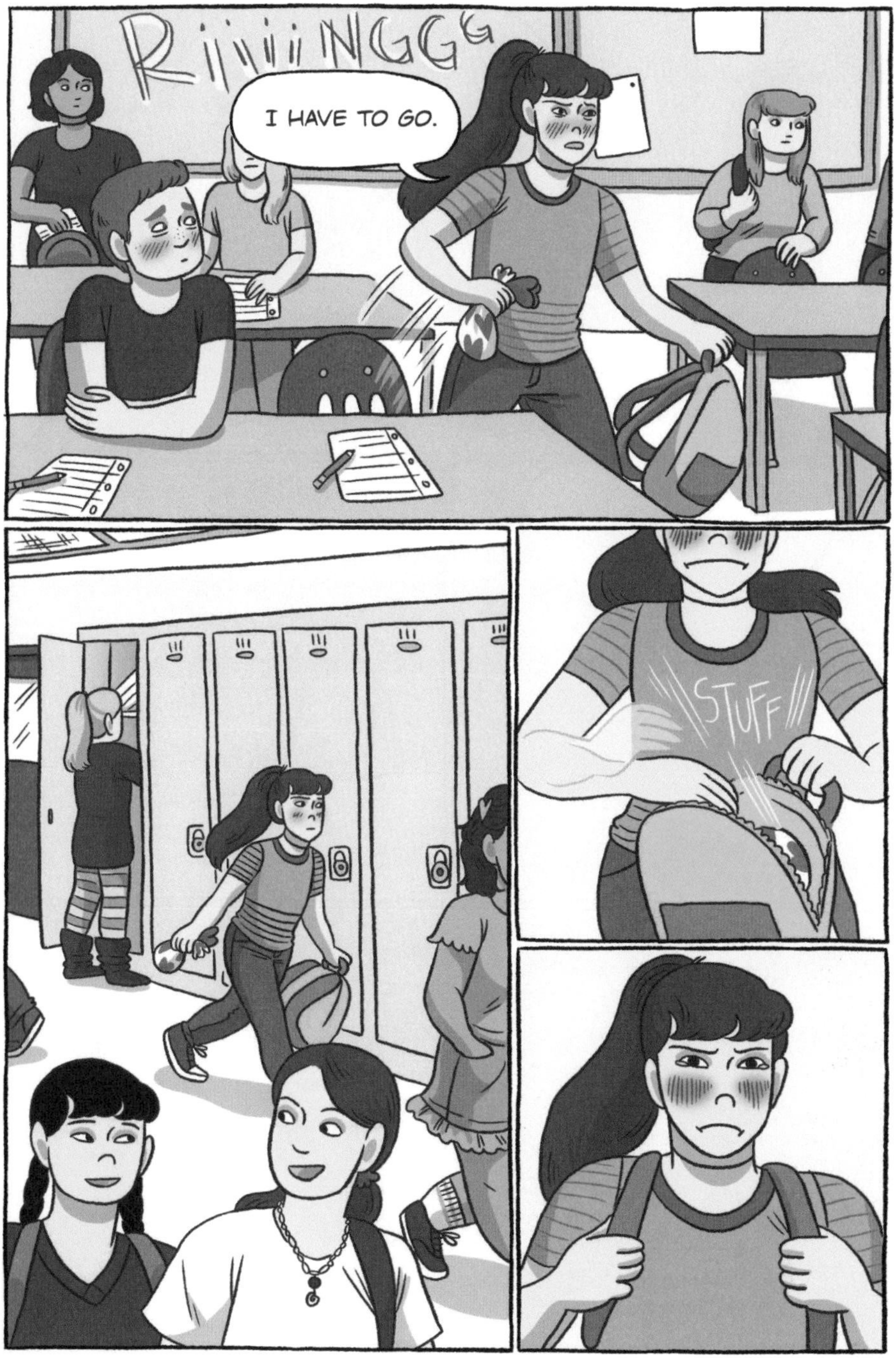
RIIIIINGGG
I HAVE TO GO.
STUFF

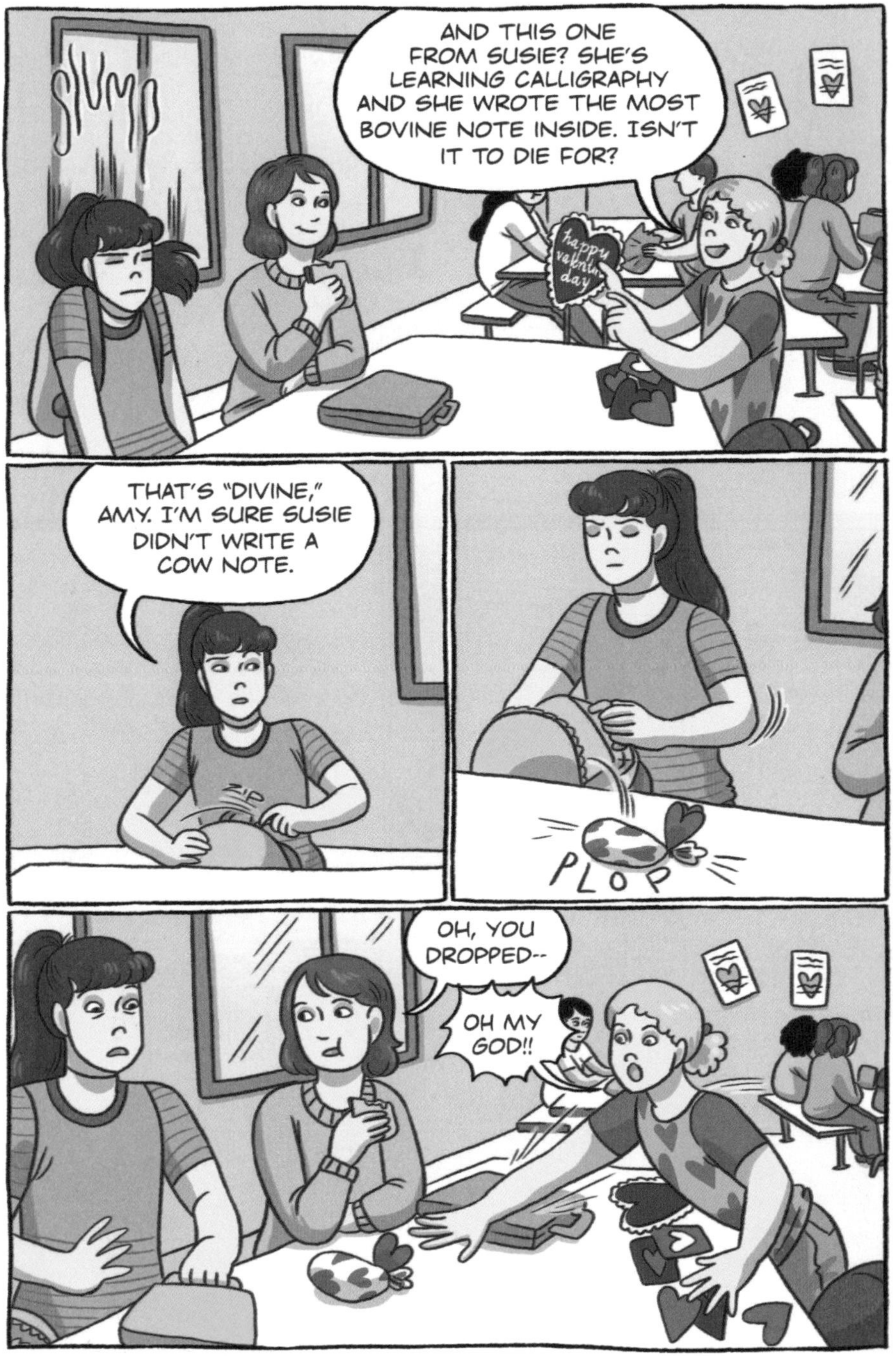
SLUMP
AND THIS ONE FROM SUSIE? SHE'S LEARNING CALLIGRAPHY AND SHE WROTE THE MOST BOVINE NOTE INSIDE. ISN'T IT TO DIE FOR?
happy valentine day
THAT'S "DIVINE," AMY. I'M SURE SUSIE DIDN'T WRITE A COW NOTE.
ZIP
PLOP
OH, YOU DROPPED--
OH MY GOD!!

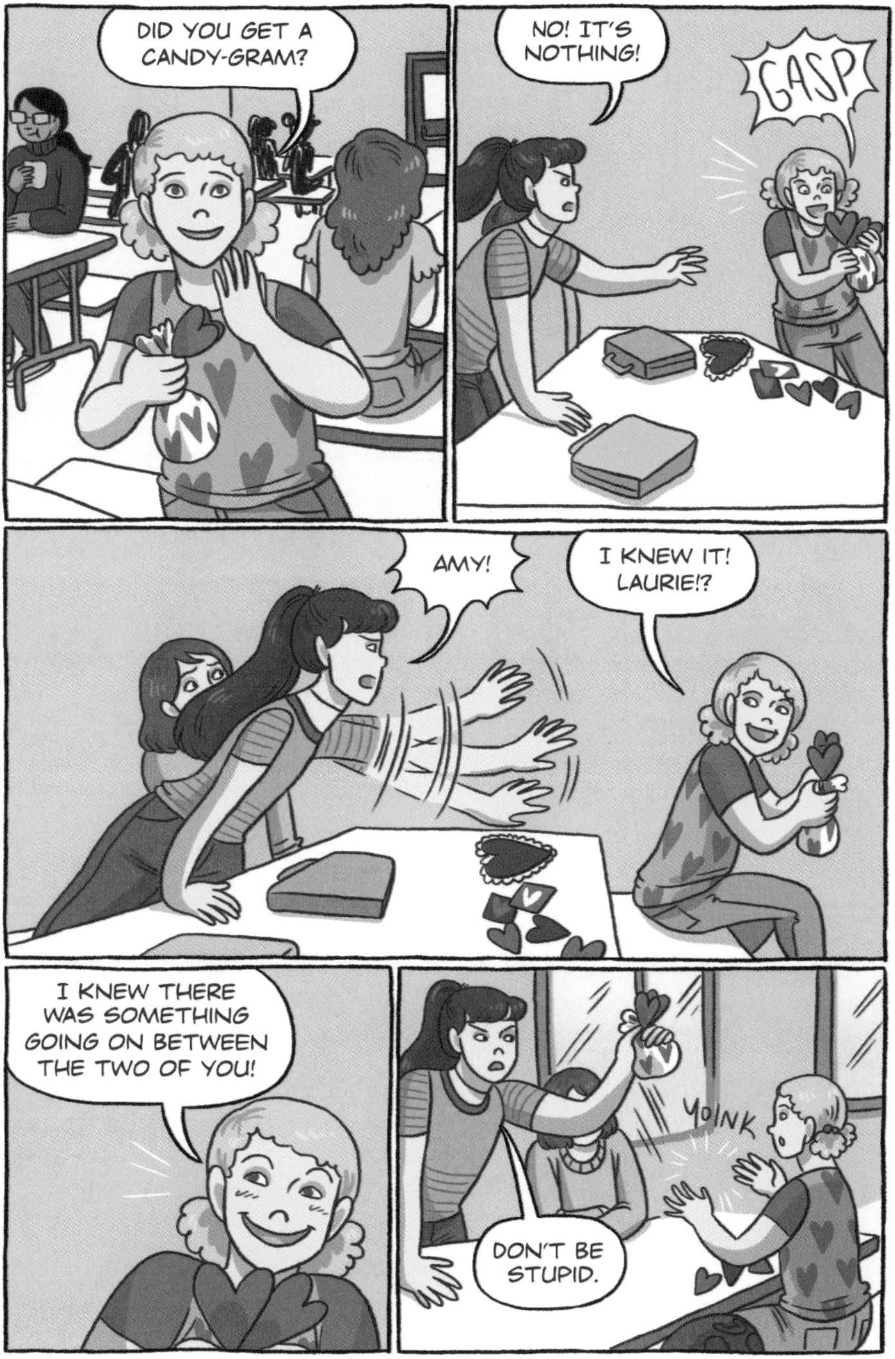
DID YOU GET A CANDY-GRAM?
NO! IT'S NOTHING!
GASP
AMY!
I KNEW IT! LAURIE!?
I KNEW THERE WAS SOMETHING GOING ON BETWEEN THE TWO OF YOU!
YOINK
DON'T BE STUPID.

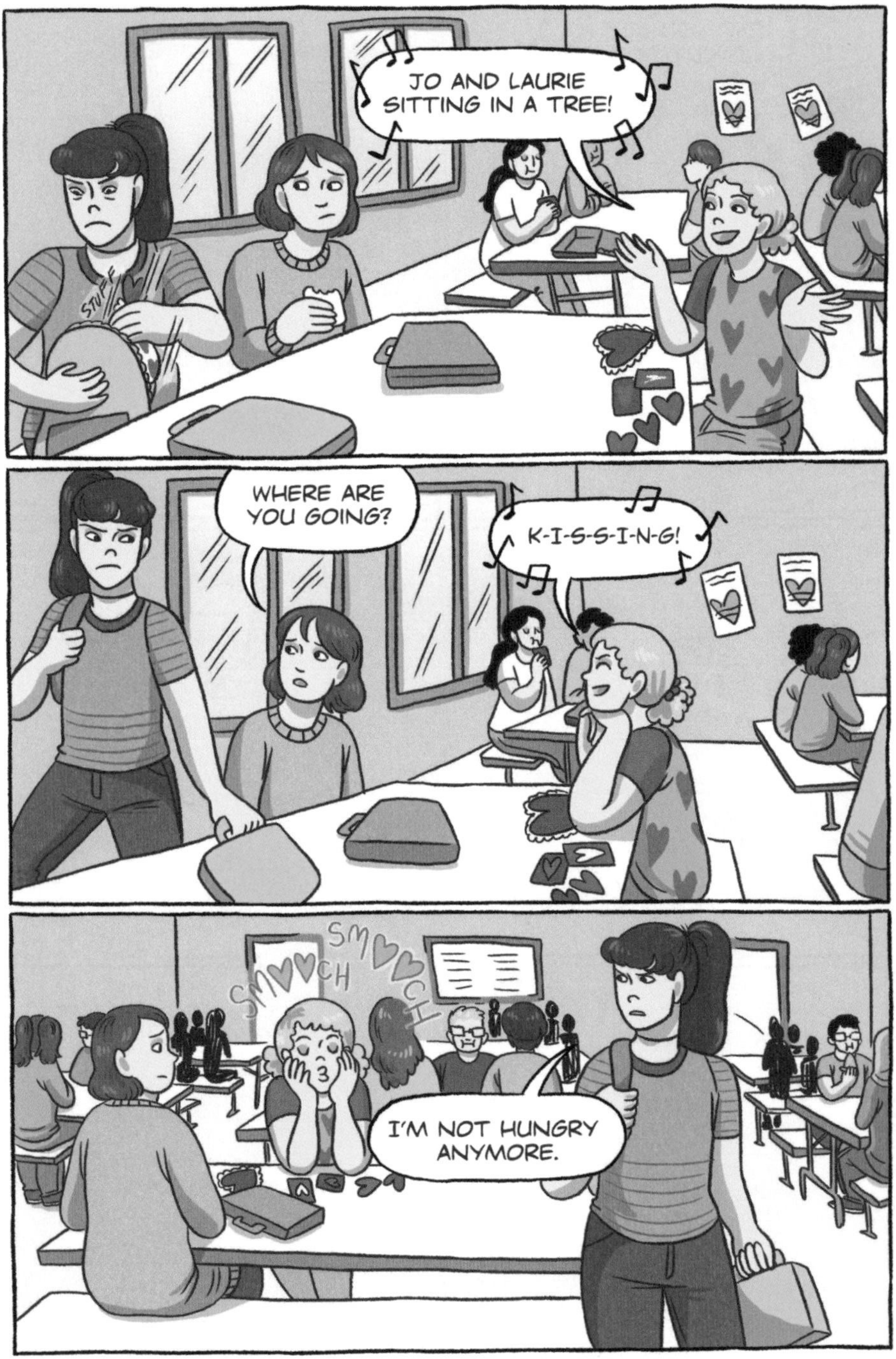
JO AND LAURIE
SITTING IN A TREE!
STUFF
WHERE ARE
YOU GOING?
K-I-S-S-I-N-G!
SMOOCH
SMOOCH
I'M NOT HUNGRY
ANYMORE.

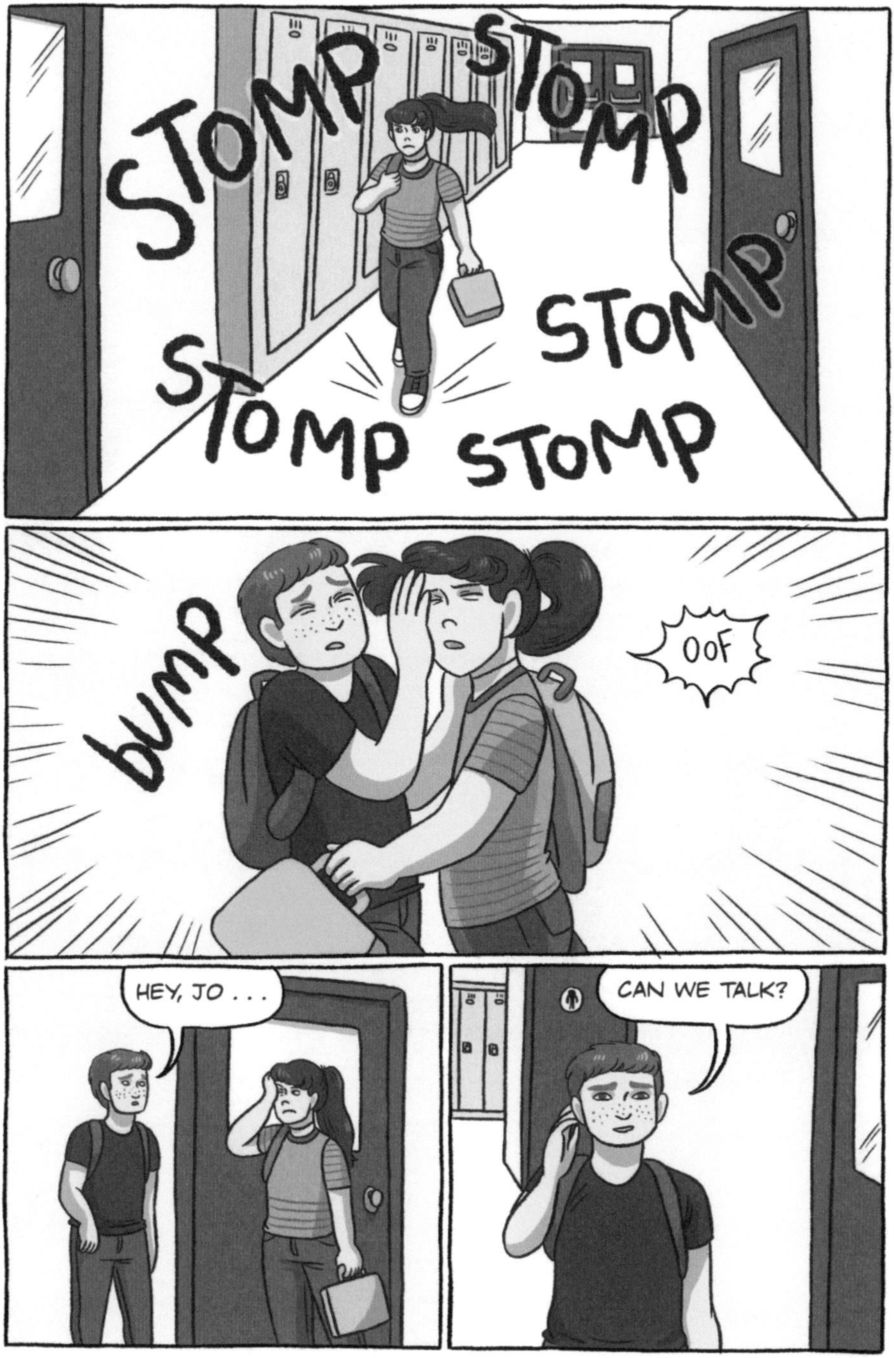
STOMP STOMP
STOMP
STOMP STOMP
bump
OOF
HEY, JO . . .
CAN WE TALK?

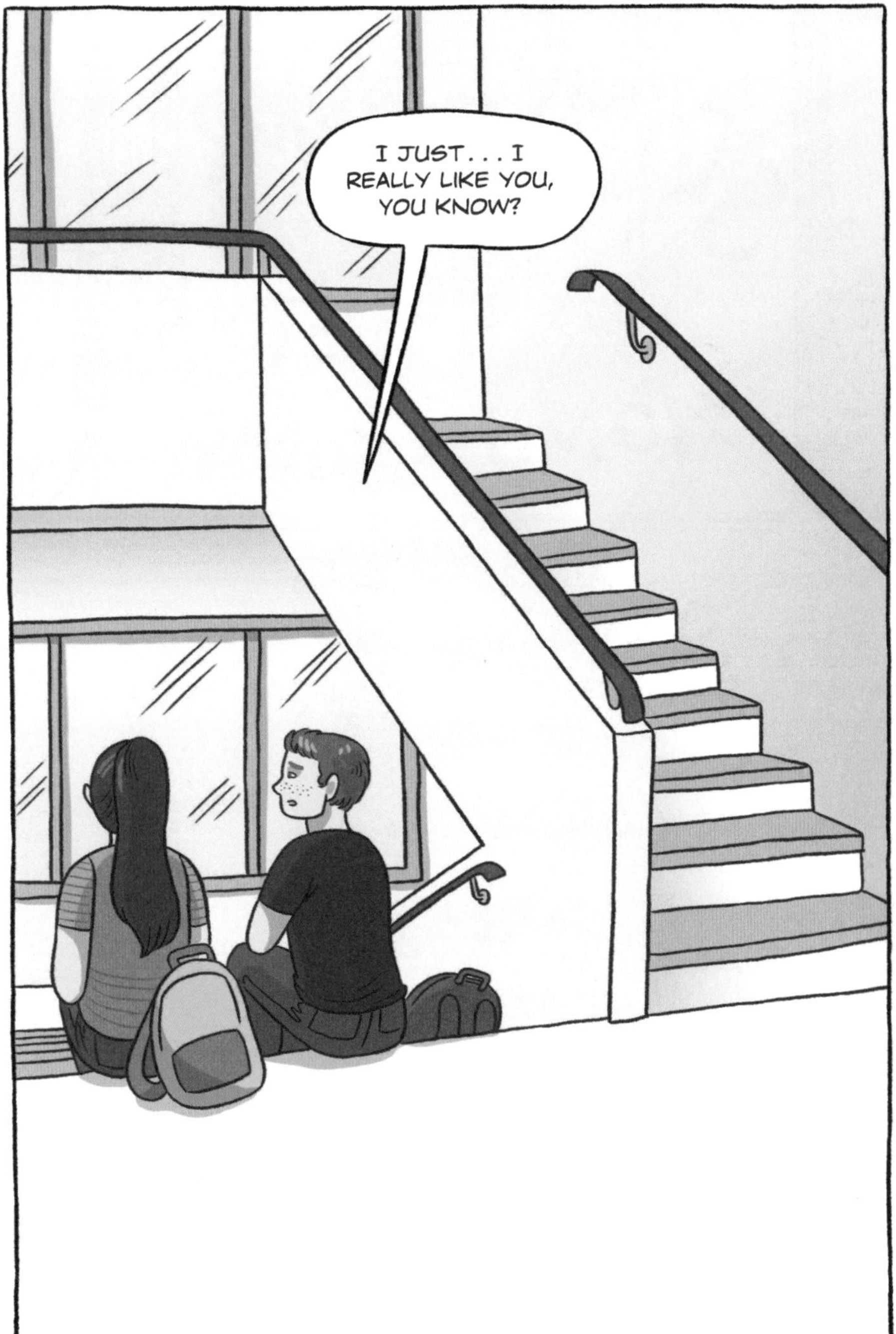
I JUST. . . I REALLY LIKE YOU, YOU KNOW?

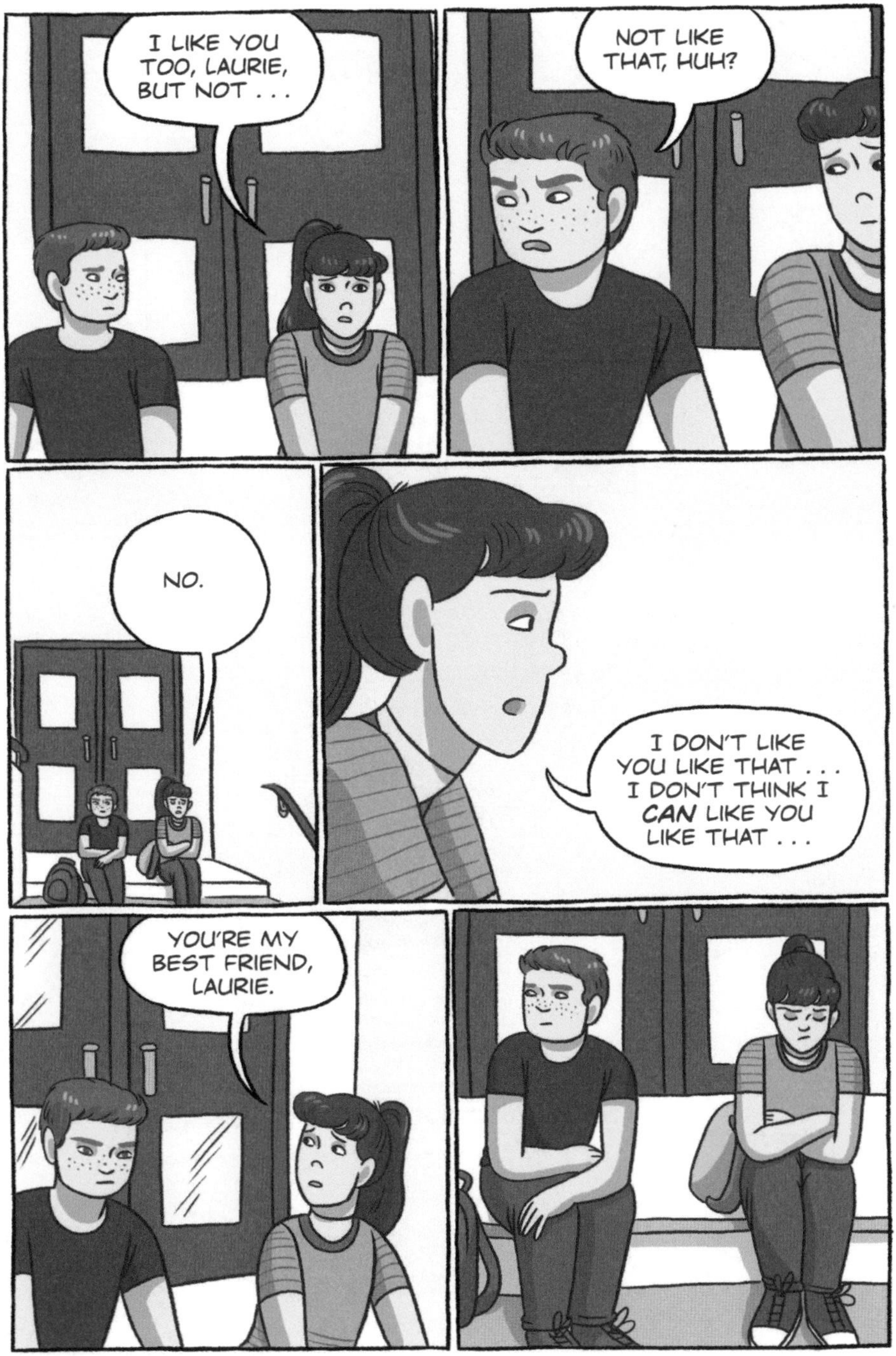
I LIKE YOU TOO, LAURIE, BUT NOT . . .
NOT LIKE THAT, HUH?
NO.
I DON'T LIKE YOU LIKE THAT . . . I DON'T THINK I **CAN** LIKE YOU LIKE THAT . . .
YOU'RE MY BEST FRIEND, LAURIE.

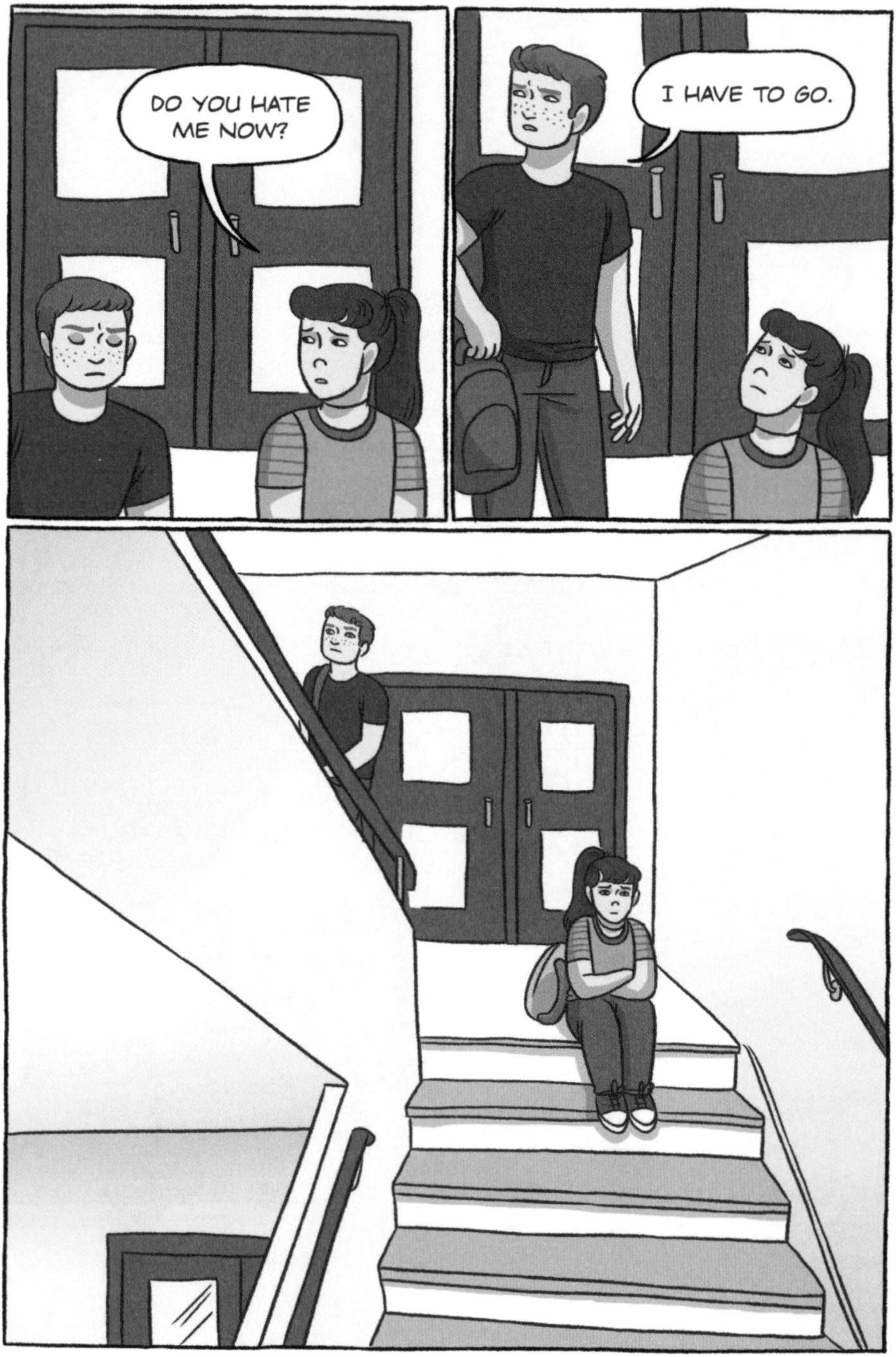
DO YOU HATE ME NOW?
I HAVE TO GO.

CHAPTER 7

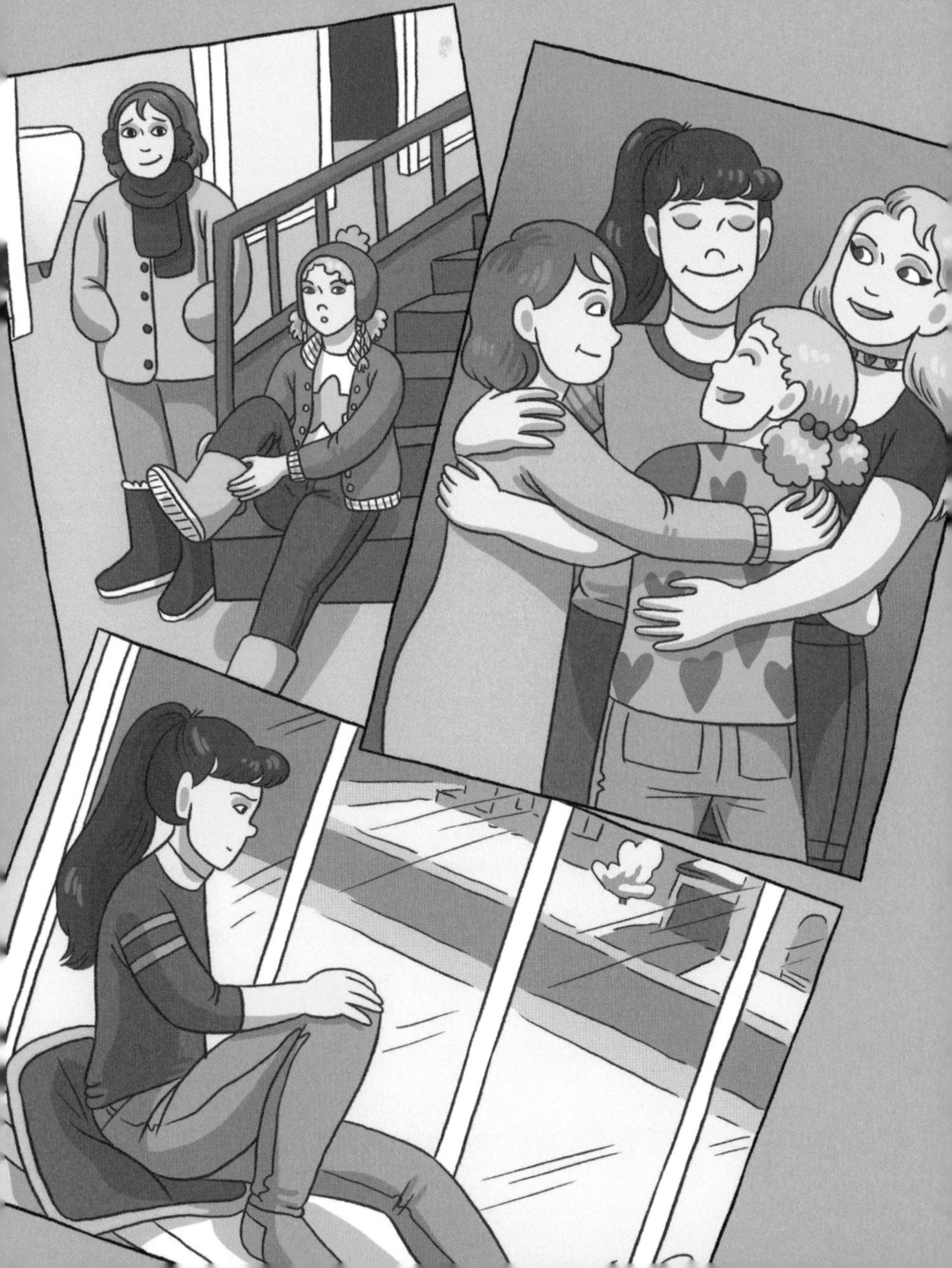

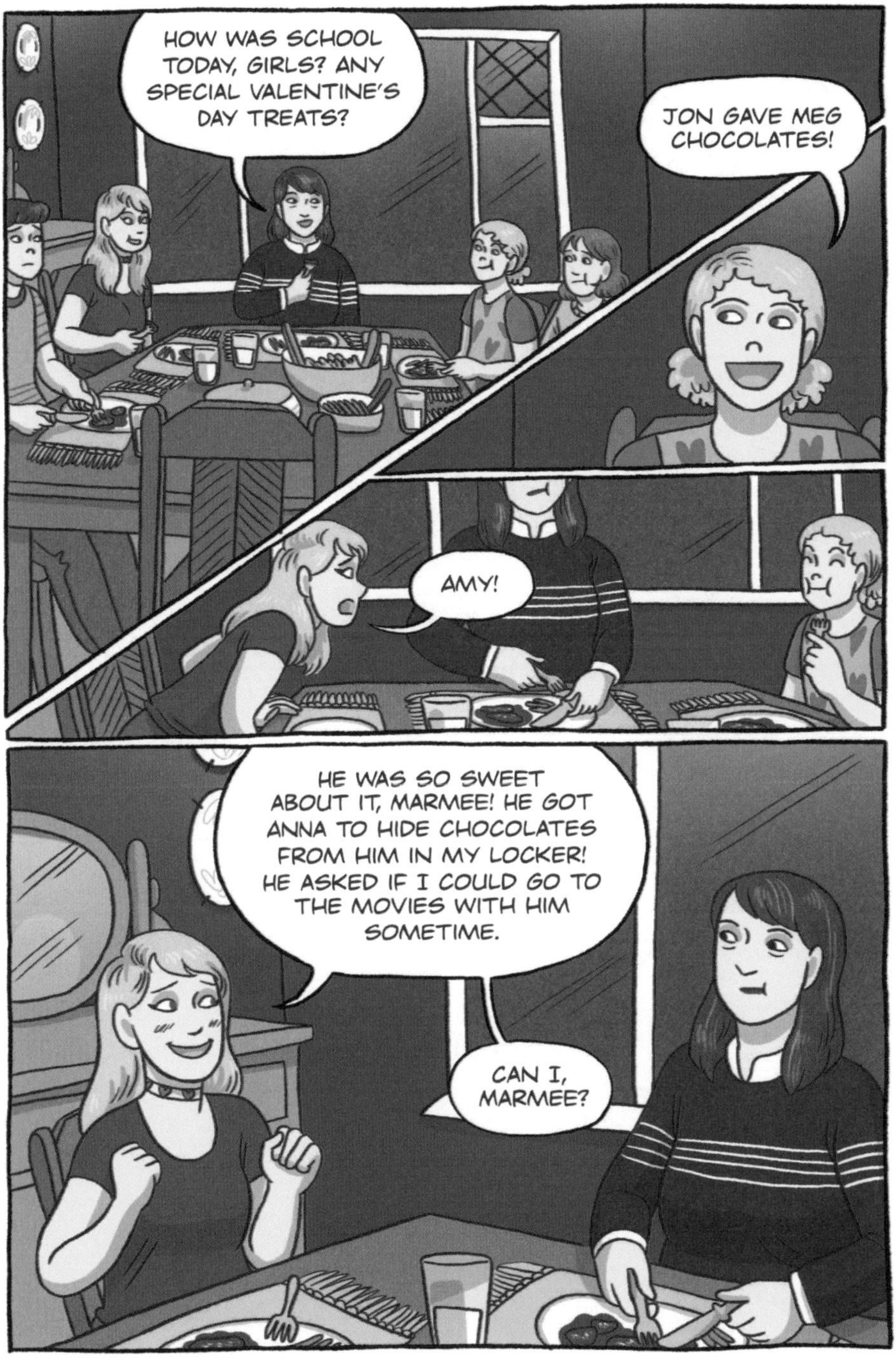
HOW WAS SCHOOL TODAY, GIRLS? ANY SPECIAL VALENTINE'S DAY TREATS?
JON GAVE MEG CHOCOLATES!
AMY!
HE WAS SO SWEET ABOUT IT, MARMEE! HE GOT ANNA TO HIDE CHOCOLATES FROM HIM IN MY LOCKER! HE ASKED IF I COULD GO TO THE MOVIES WITH HIM SOMETIME.
CAN I, MARMEE?

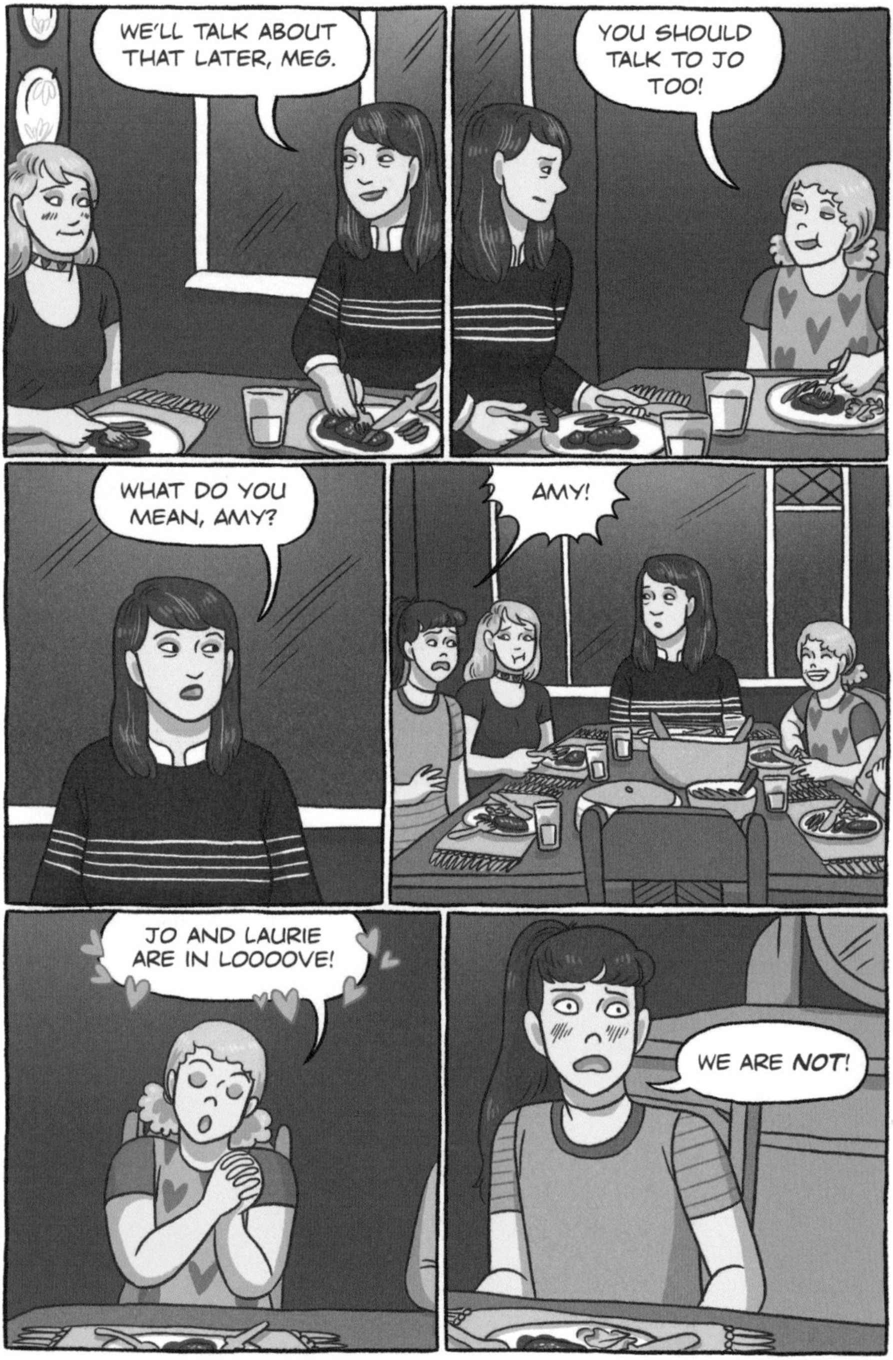
WE'LL TALK ABOUT THAT LATER, MEG.
YOU SHOULD TALK TO JO TOO!
WHAT DO YOU MEAN, AMY?
AMY!
JO AND LAURIE ARE IN LOOOOVE!
WE ARE NOT!

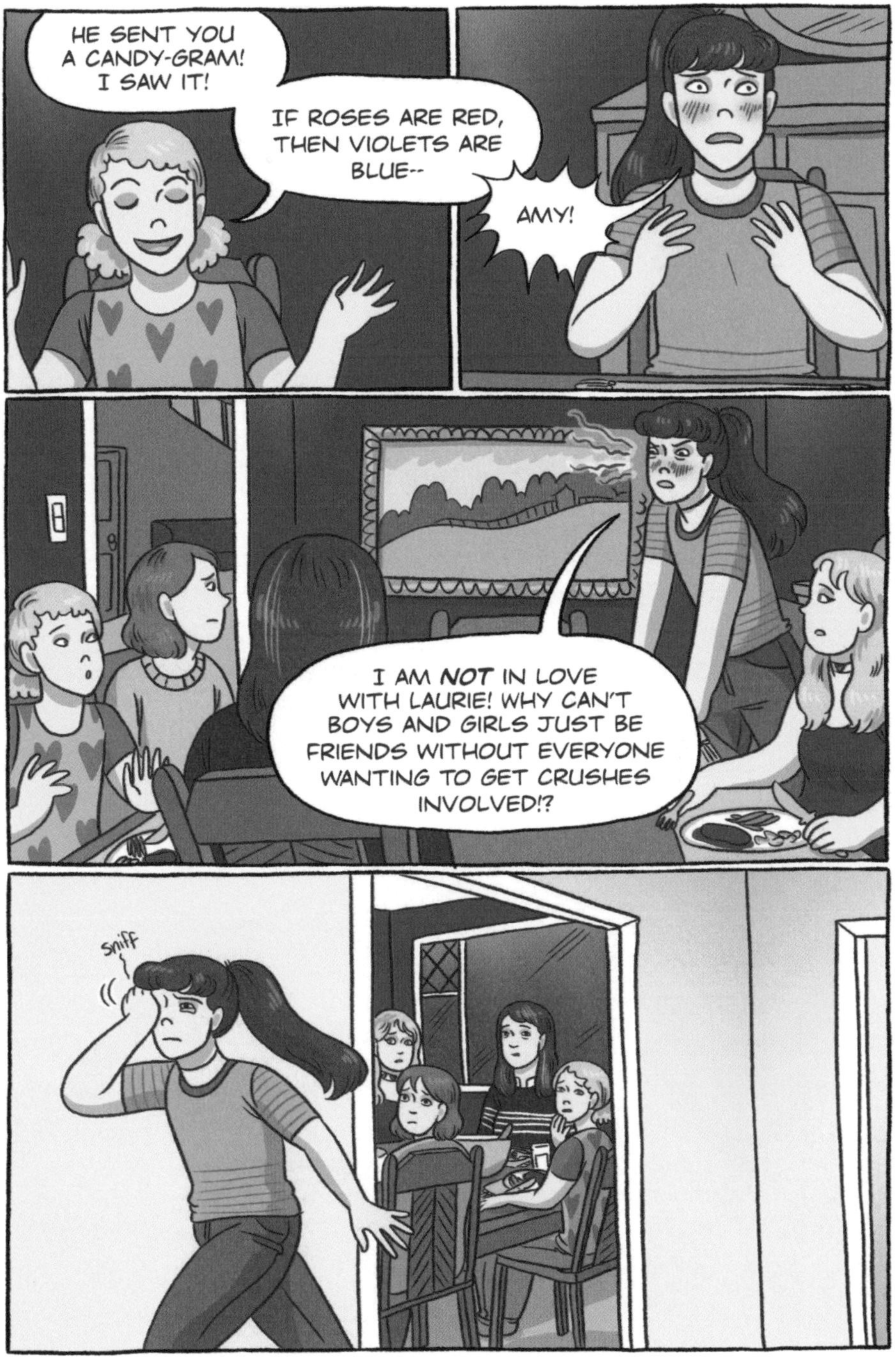
HE SENT YOU A CANDY-GRAM! I SAW IT!
IF ROSES ARE RED, THEN VIOLETS ARE BLUE--
AMY!
I AM NOT IN LOVE WITH LAURIE! WHY CAN'T BOYS AND GIRLS JUST BE FRIENDS WITHOUT EVERYONE WANTING TO GET CRUSHES INVOLVED!?
sniff

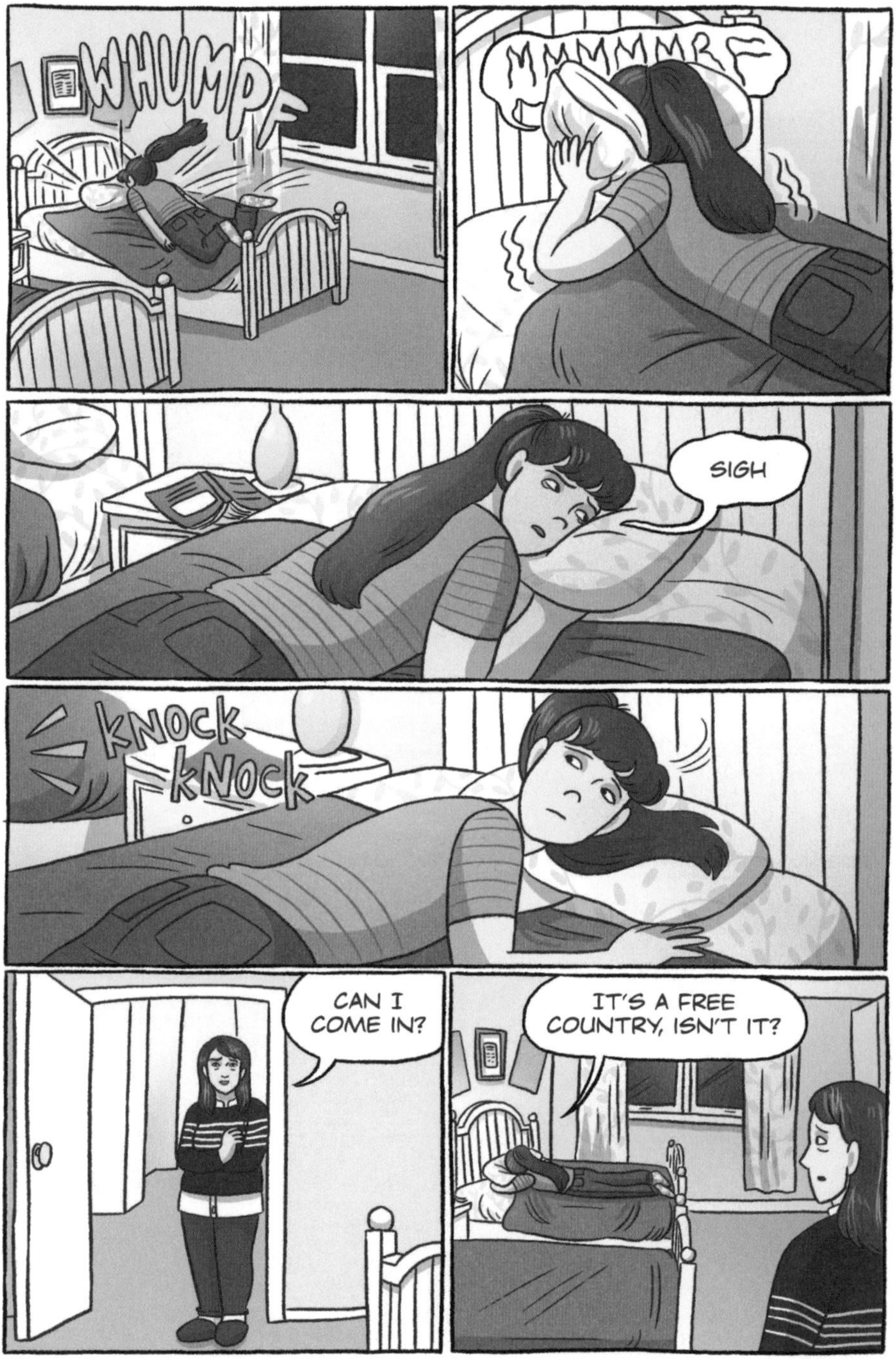
WHUMPF
MMMMMRF
SIGH
knock knock
CAN I COME IN?
IT'S A FREE COUNTRY, ISN'T IT?

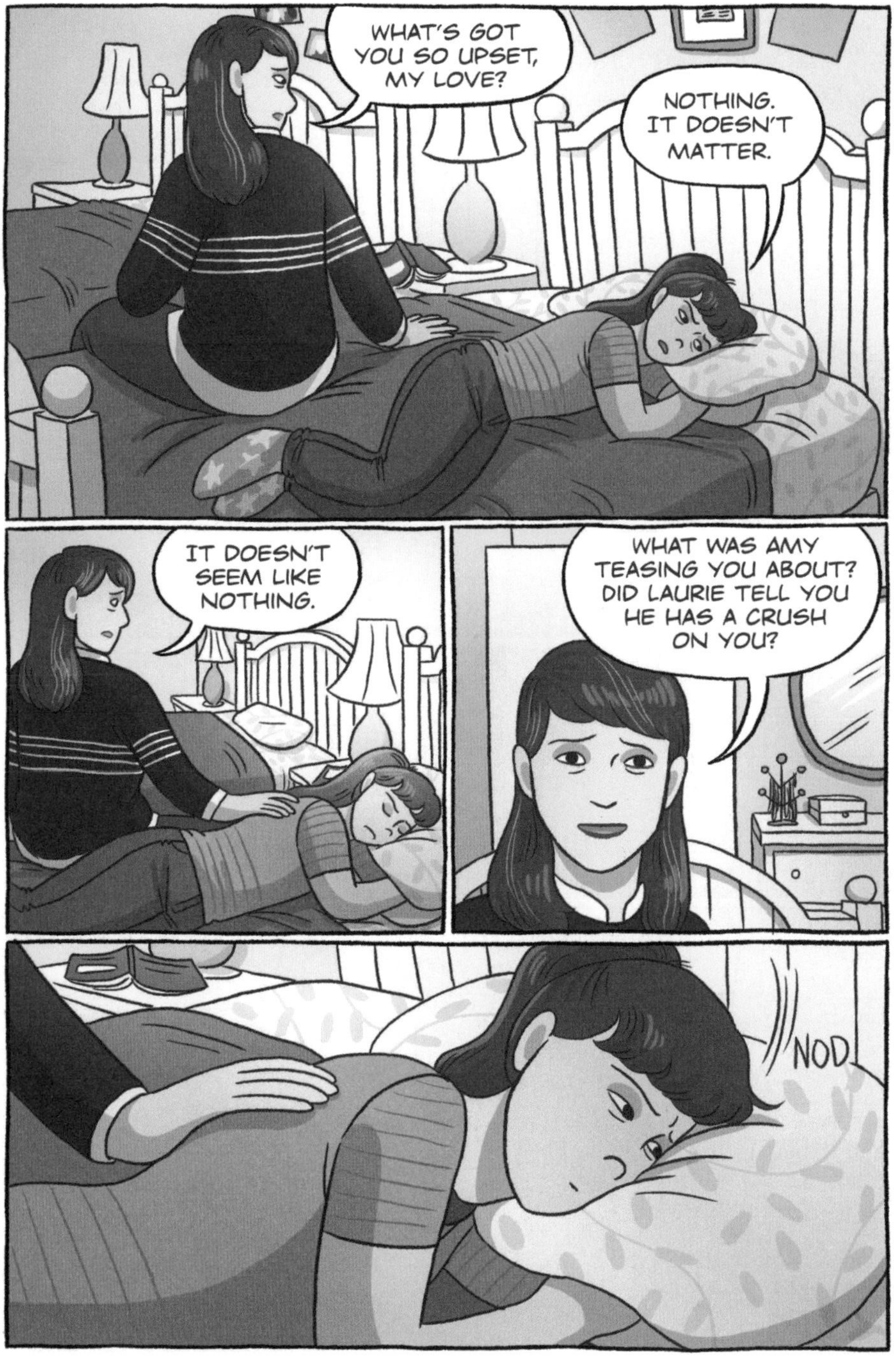
WHAT'S GOT YOU SO UPSET, MY LOVE?
NOTHING. IT DOESN'T MATTER.
IT DOESN'T SEEM LIKE NOTHING.
WHAT WAS AMY TEASING YOU ABOUT? DID LAURIE TELL YOU HE HAS A CRUSH ON YOU?
NOD

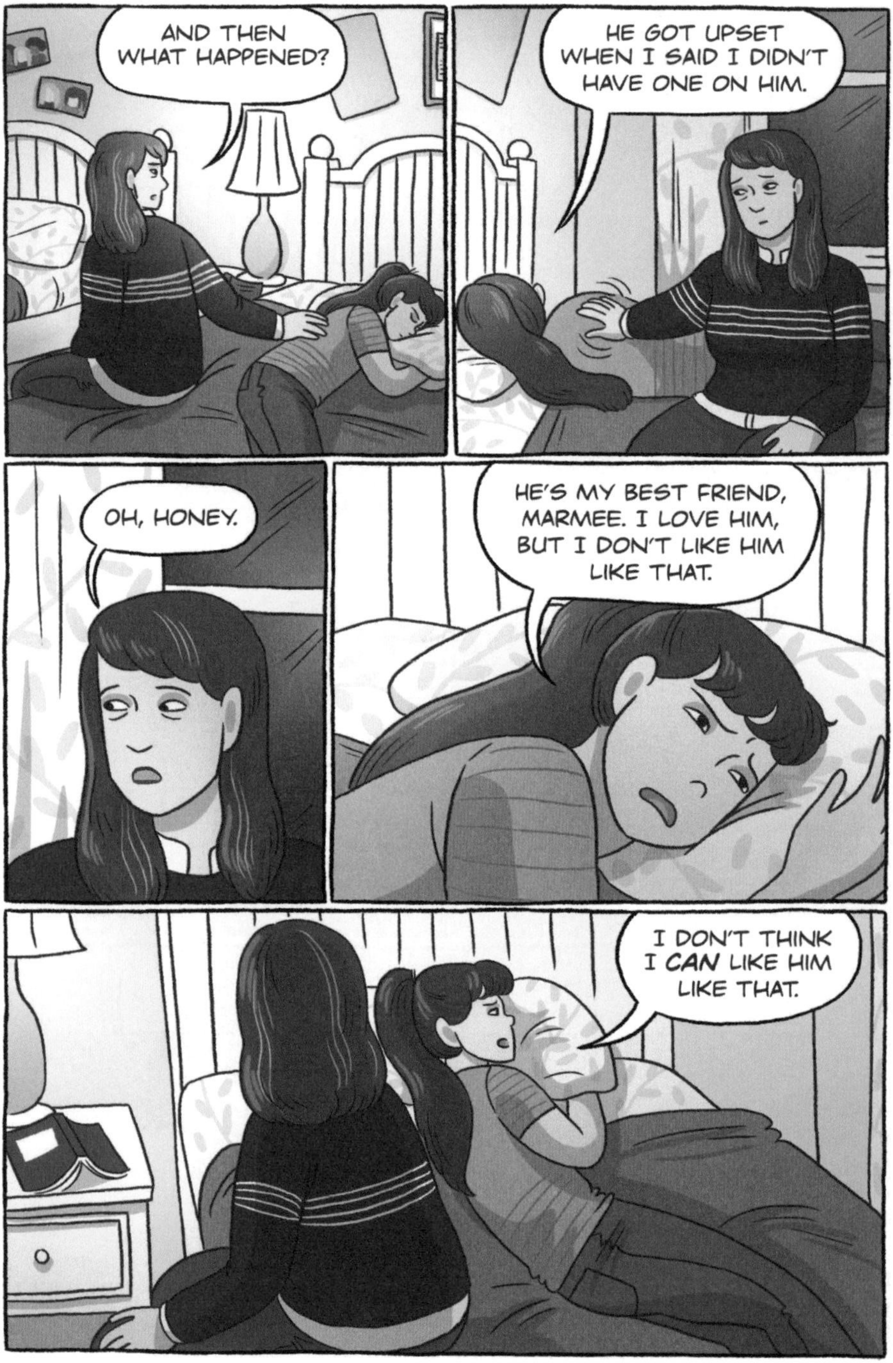
AND THEN WHAT HAPPENED?
HE GOT UPSET WHEN I SAID I DIDN'T HAVE ONE ON HIM.
OH, HONEY.
HE'S MY BEST FRIEND, MARMEE. I LOVE HIM, BUT I DON'T LIKE HIM LIKE THAT.
I DON'T THINK I **CAN** LIKE HIM LIKE THAT.

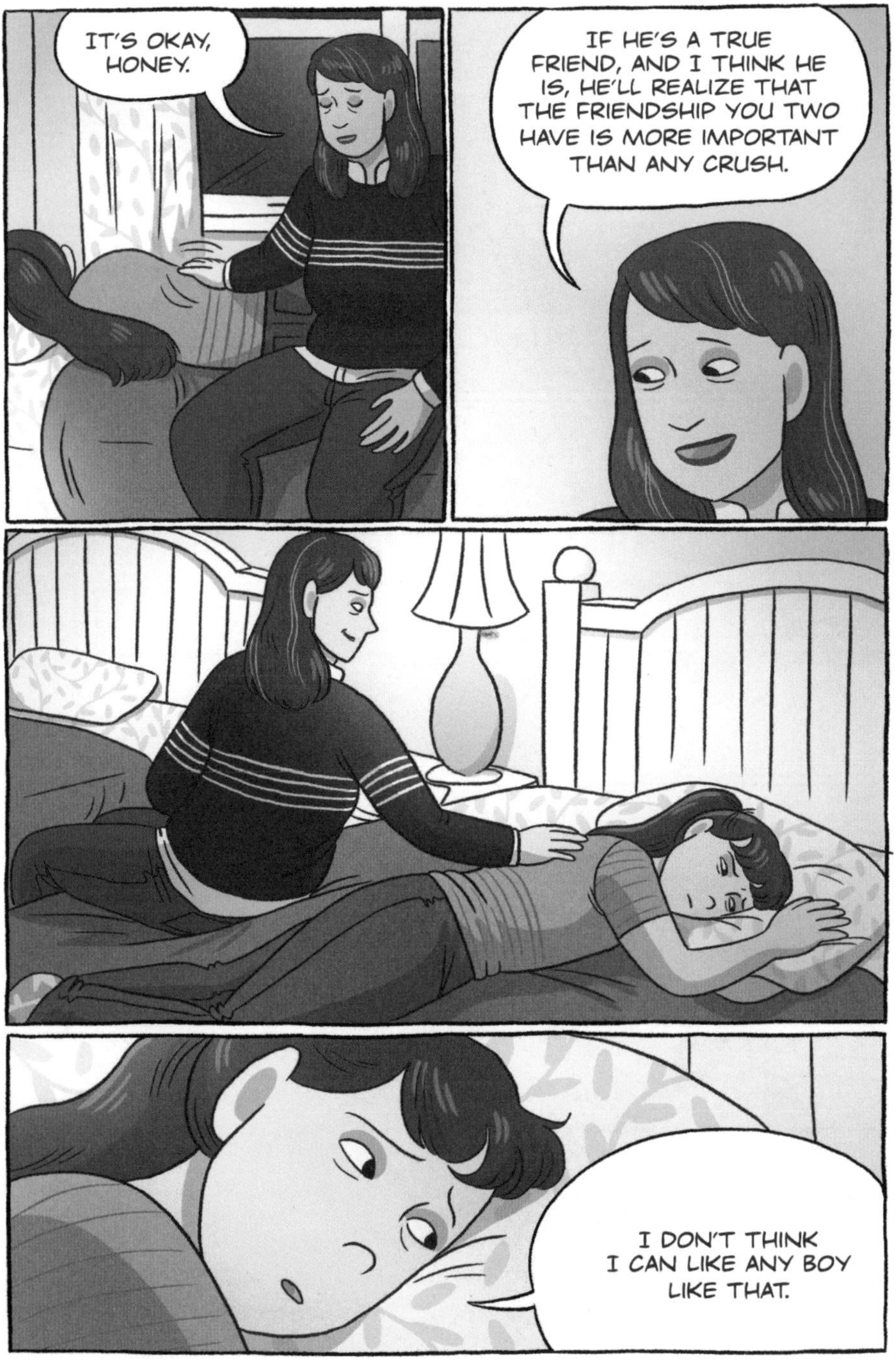
IT'S OKAY, HONEY.
IF HE'S A TRUE FRIEND, AND I THINK HE IS, HE'LL REALIZE THAT THE FRIENDSHIP YOU TWO HAVE IS MORE IMPORTANT THAN ANY CRUSH.
I DON'T THINK I CAN LIKE ANY BOY LIKE THAT.

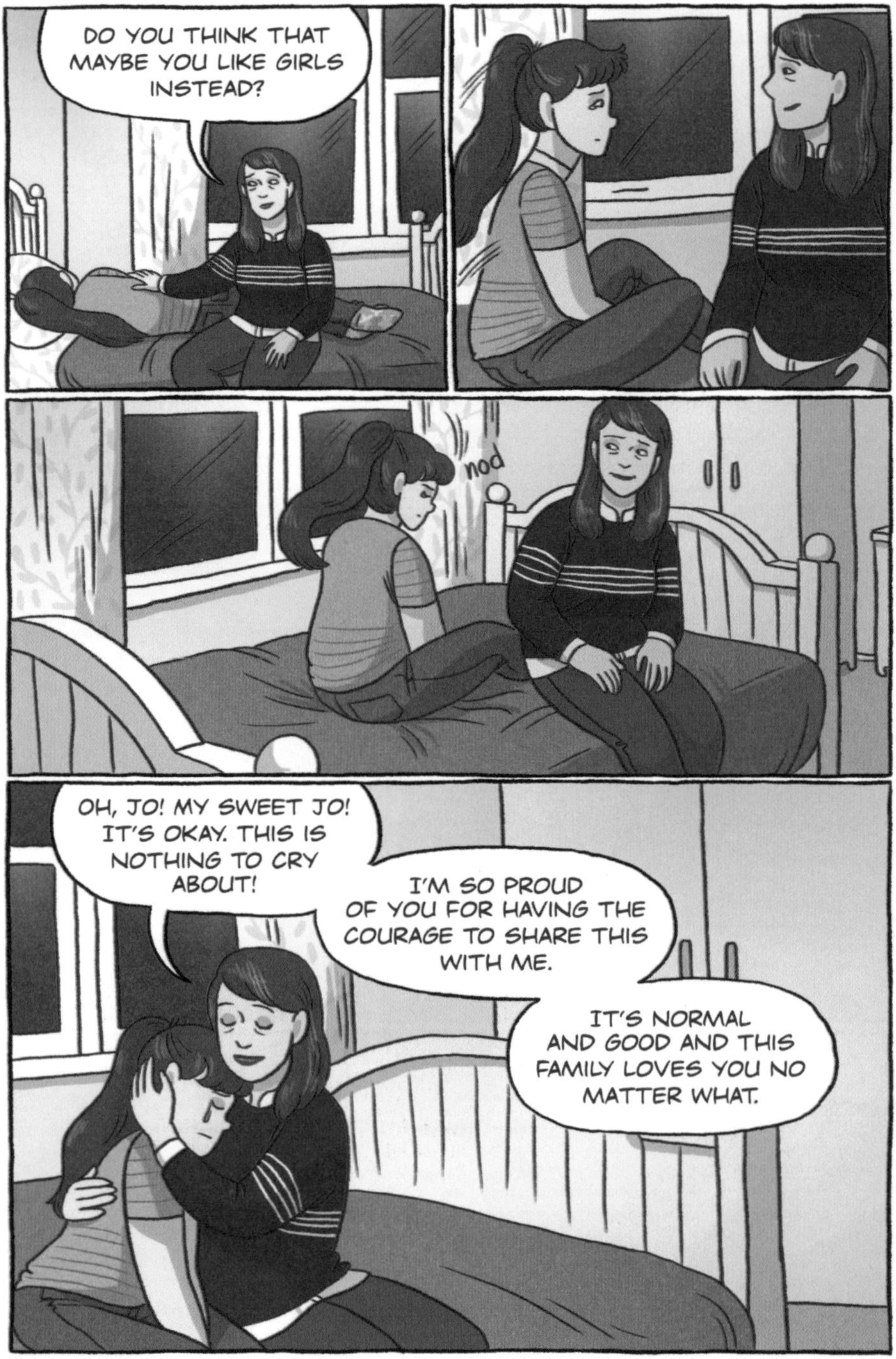
DO YOU THINK THAT MAYBE YOU LIKE GIRLS INSTEAD?
nod
OH, JO! MY SWEET JO! IT'S OKAY. THIS IS NOTHING TO CRY ABOUT!
I'M SO PROUD OF YOU FOR HAVING THE COURAGE TO SHARE THIS WITH ME.
IT'S NORMAL AND GOOD AND THIS FAMILY LOVES YOU NO MATTER WHAT.

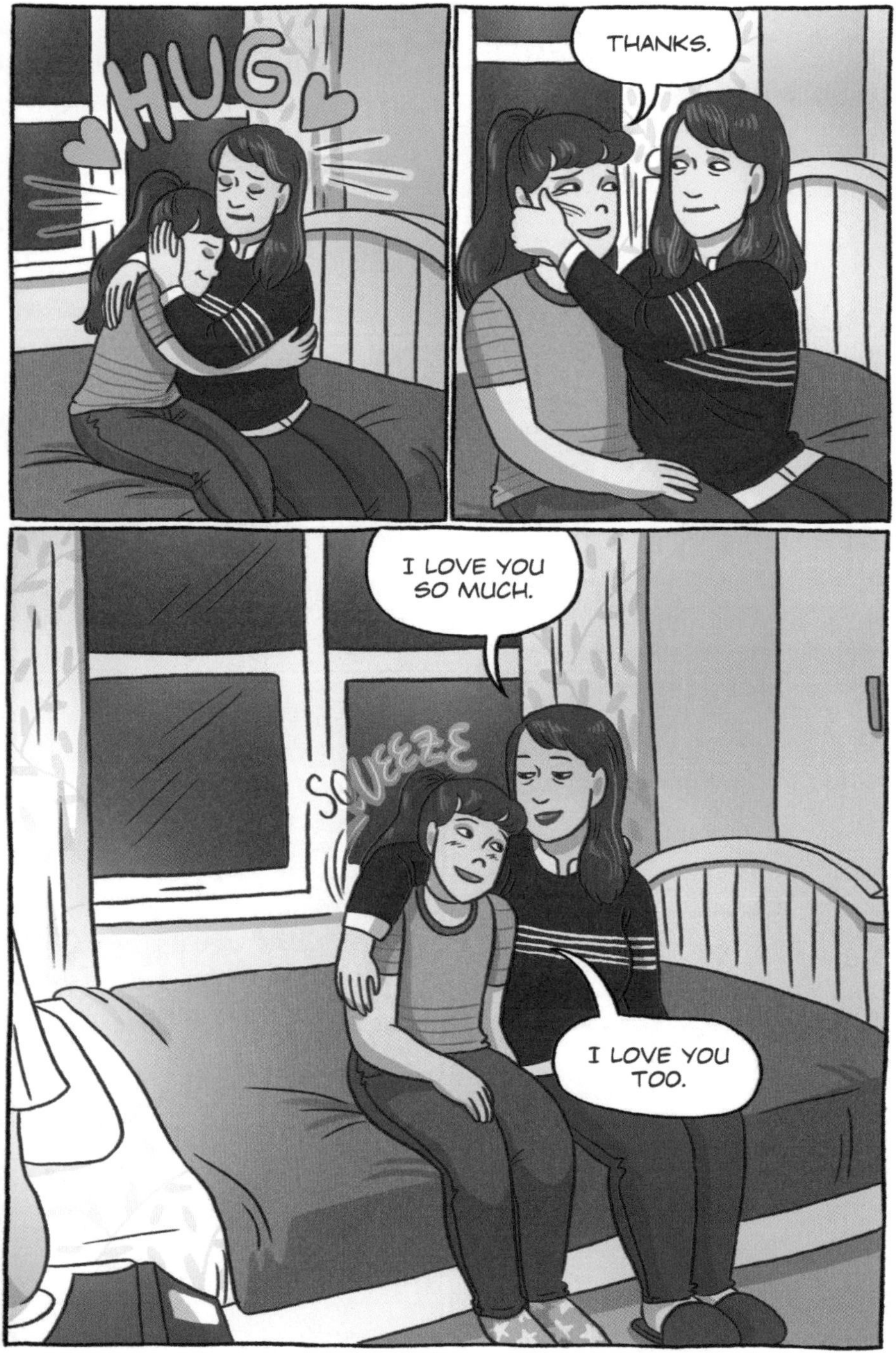
HUG
THANKS.
I LOVE YOU SO MUCH.
SQUEEZE
I LOVE YOU TOO.

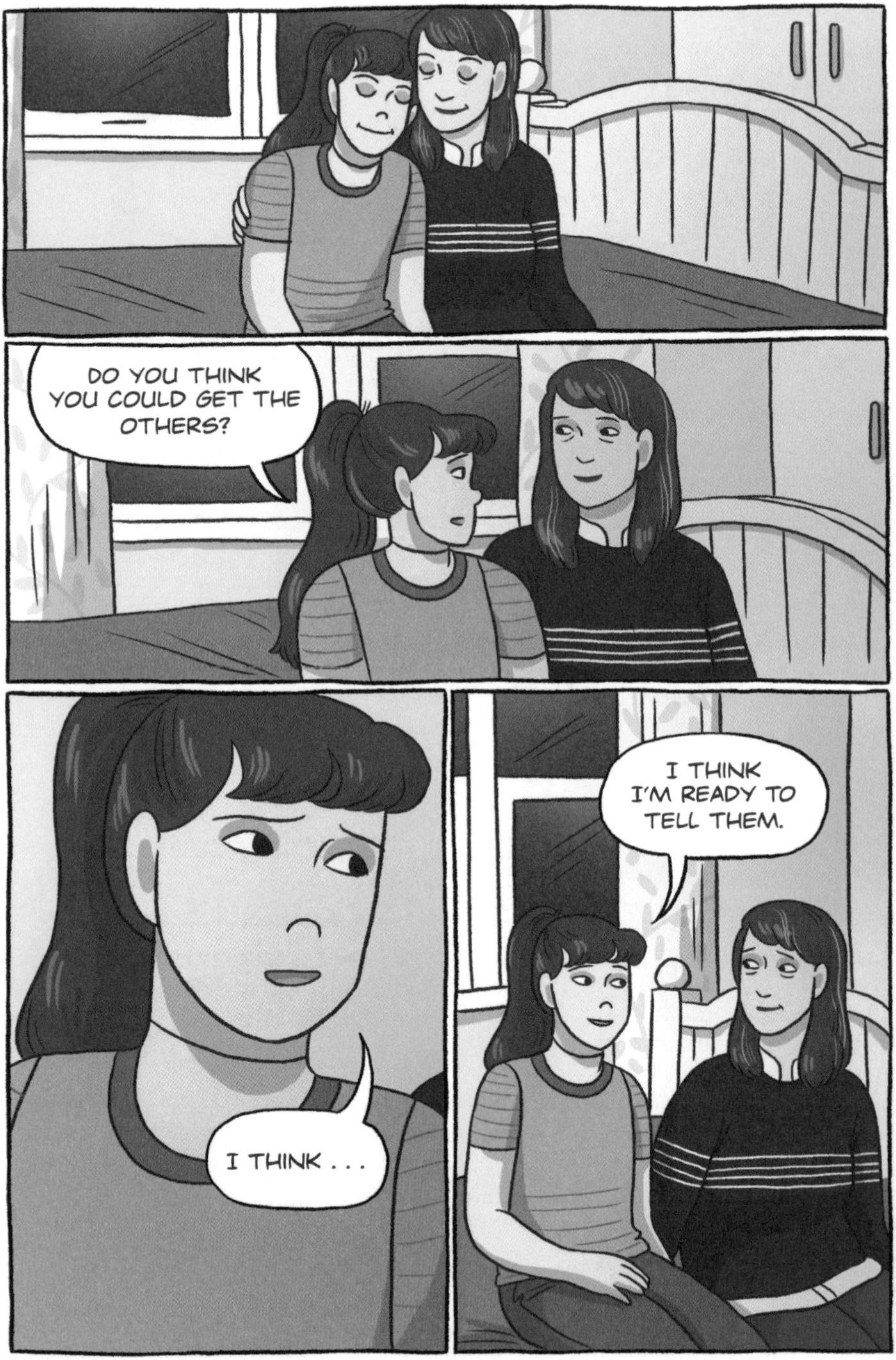
DO YOU THINK YOU COULD GET THE OTHERS?
I THINK . . .
I THINK I'M READY TO TELL THEM.

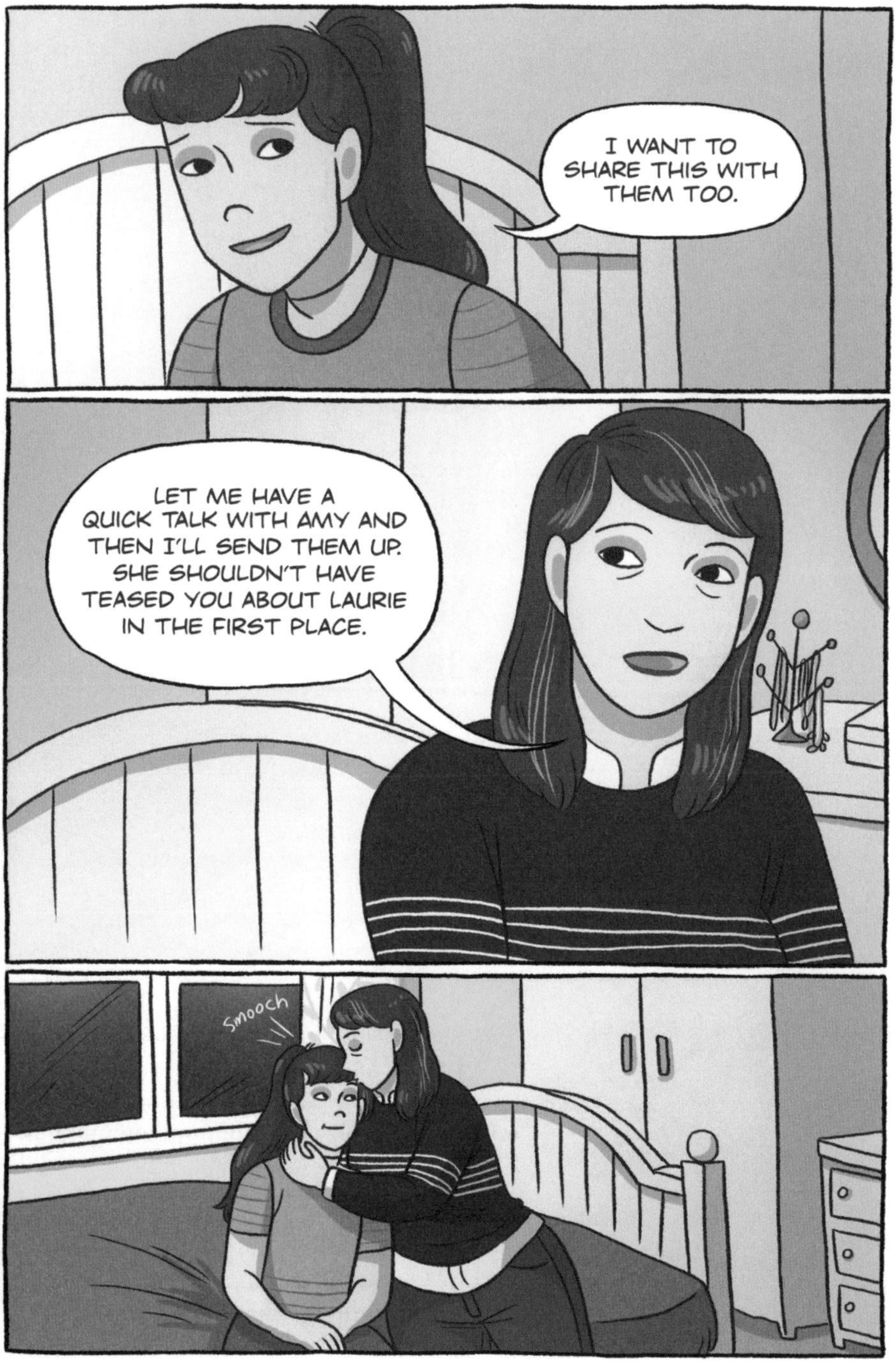
I WANT TO SHARE THIS WITH THEM TOO.
LET ME HAVE A QUICK TALK WITH AMY AND THEN I'LL SEND THEM UP. SHE SHOULDN'T HAVE TEASED YOU ABOUT LAURIE IN THE FIRST PLACE.
smooch

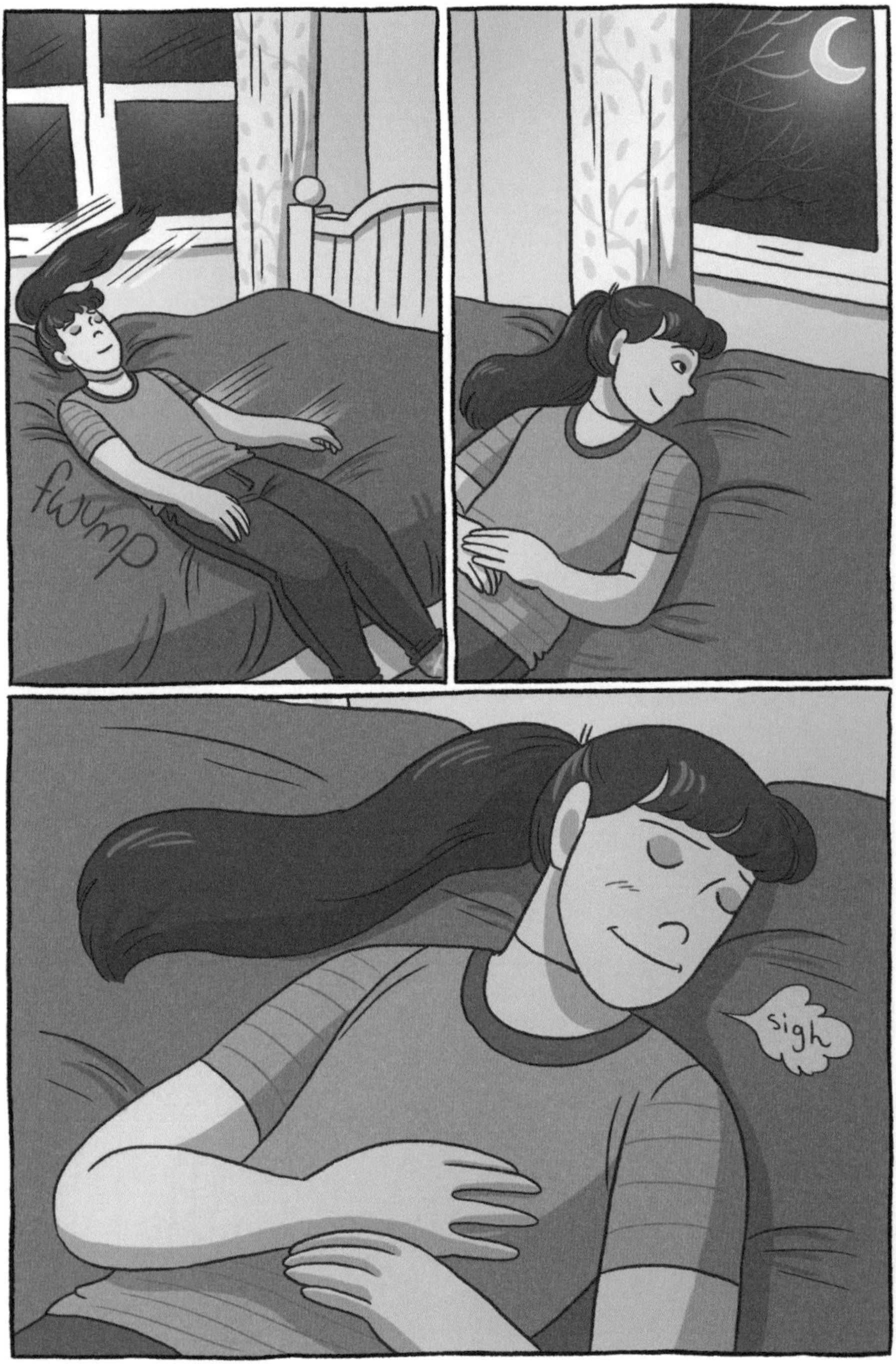
fwump
sigh

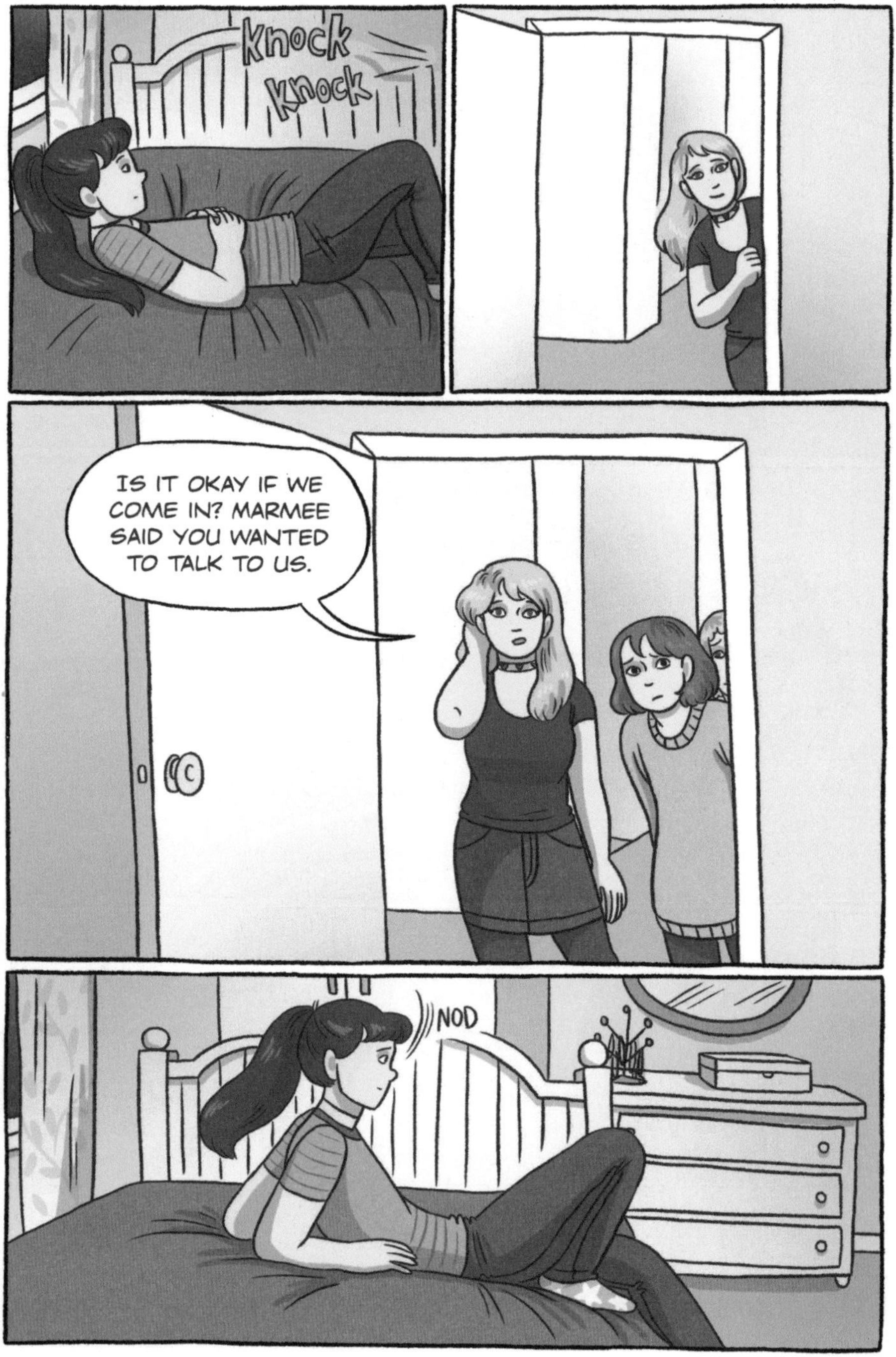
Knock Knock
IS IT OKAY IF WE COME IN? MARMEE SAID YOU WANTED TO TALK TO US.
NOD

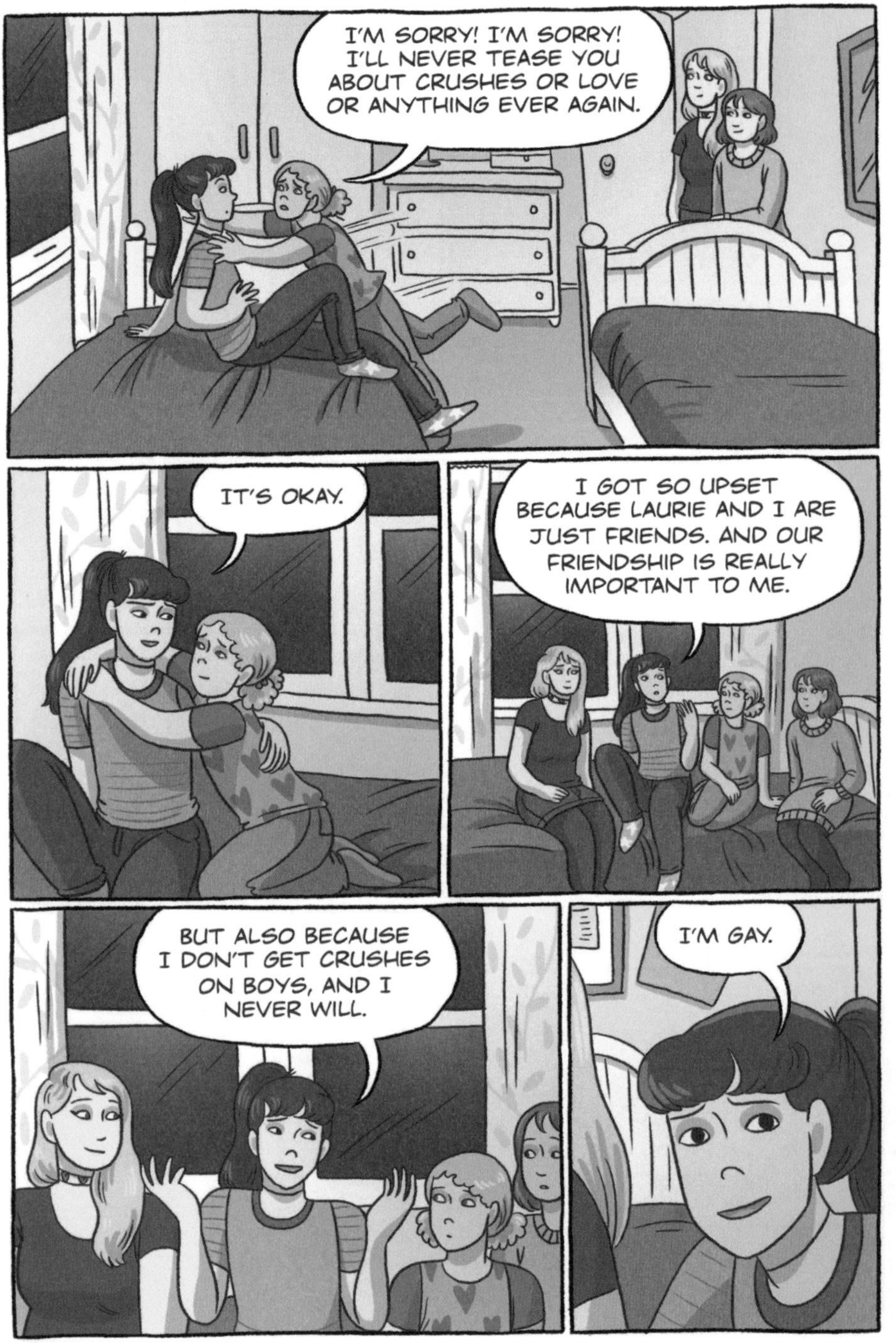
I'M SORRY! I'M SORRY! I'LL NEVER TEASE YOU ABOUT CRUSHES OR LOVE OR ANYTHING EVER AGAIN.
IT'S OKAY.
I GOT SO UPSET BECAUSE LAURIE AND I ARE JUST FRIENDS. AND OUR FRIENDSHIP IS REALLY IMPORTANT TO ME.
BUT ALSO BECAUSE I DON'T GET CRUSHES ON BOYS, AND I NEVER WILL.
I'M GAY.

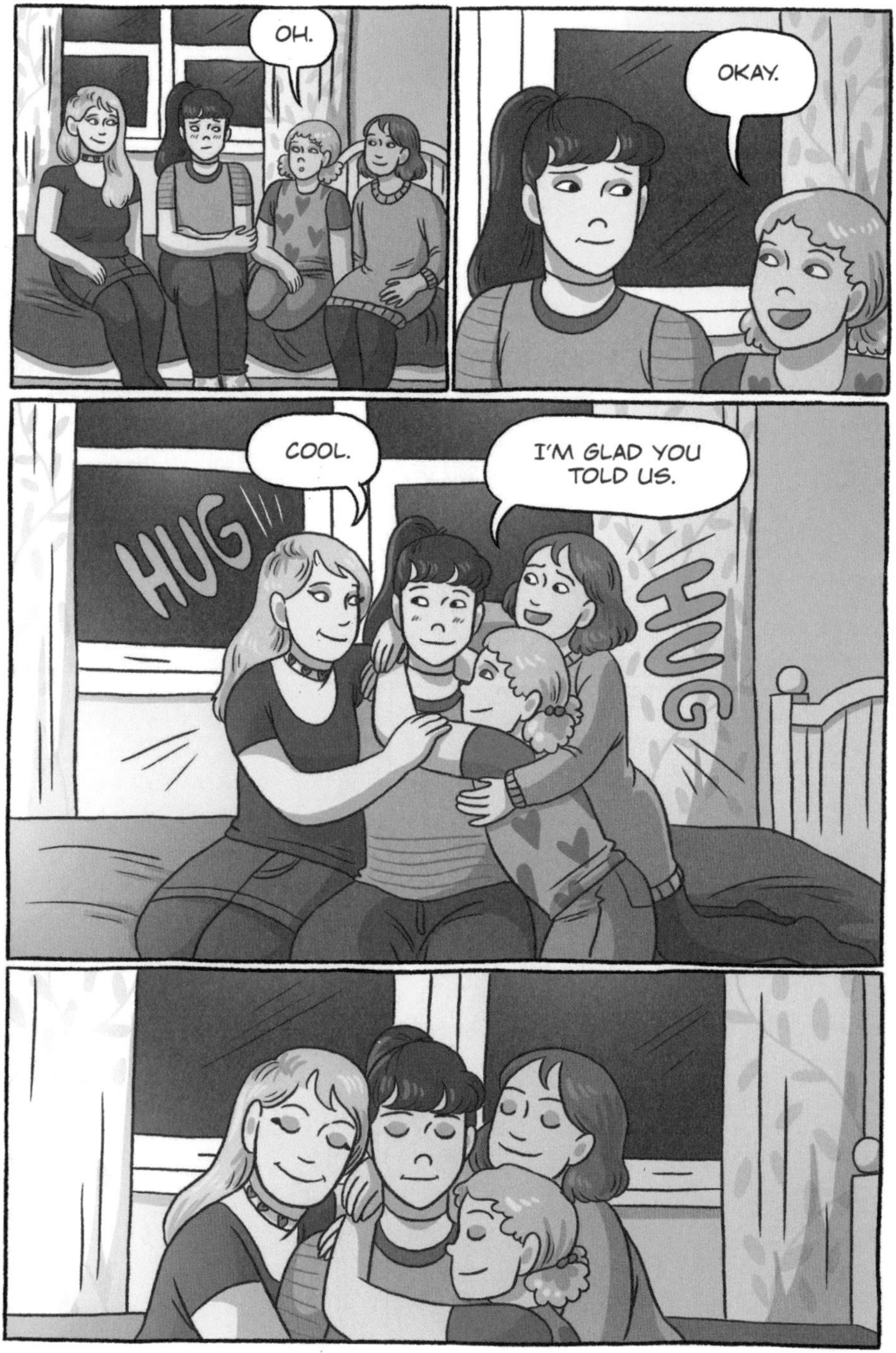
OH.
OKAY.
COOL.
HUG
I'M GLAD YOU TOLD US.
HUG

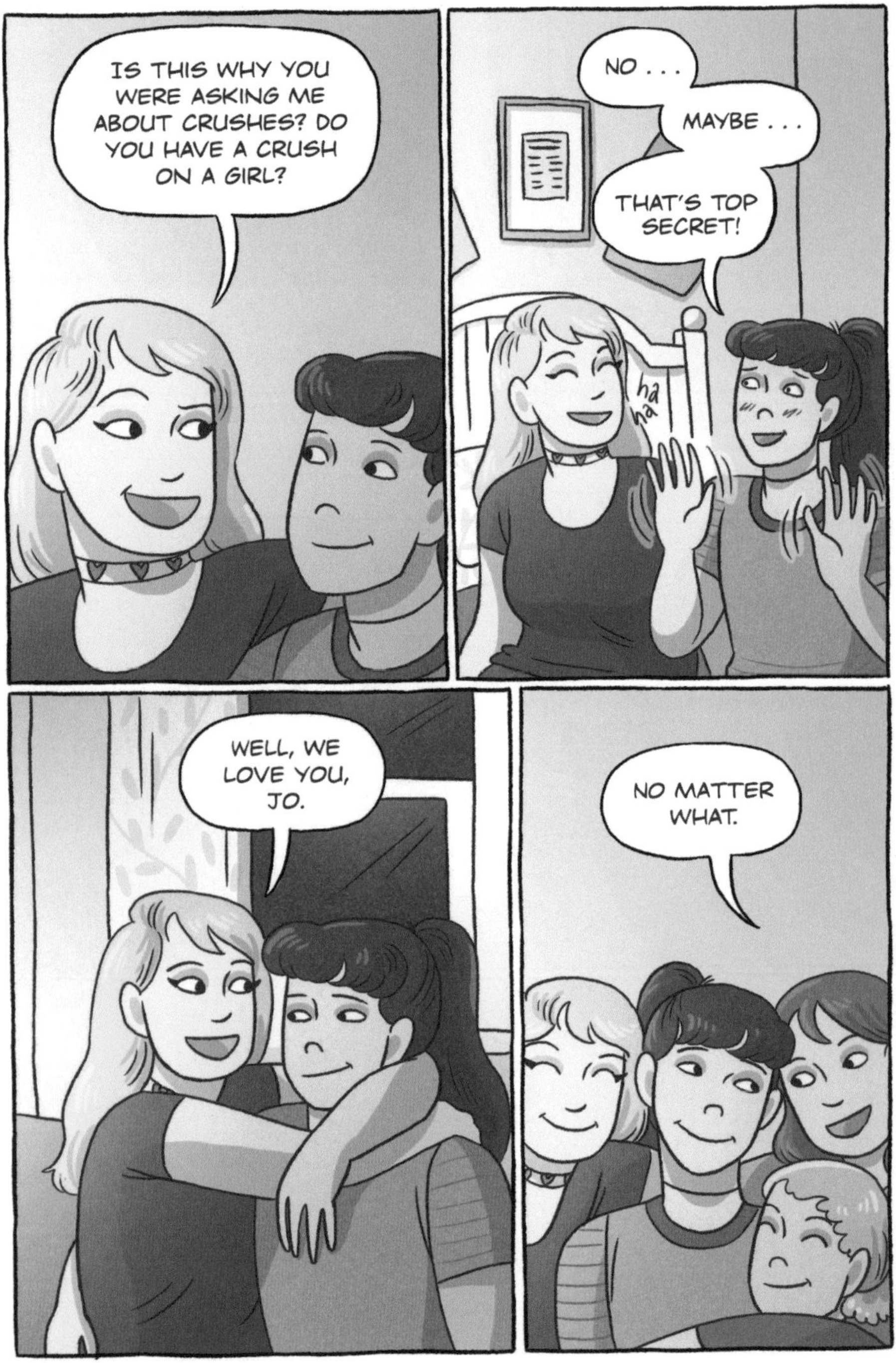
IS THIS WHY YOU WERE ASKING ME ABOUT CRUSHES? DO YOU HAVE A CRUSH ON A GIRL?
NO . . .
MAYBE . . .
THAT'S TOP SECRET!
ha ha
WELL, WE LOVE YOU, JO.
NO MATTER WHAT.

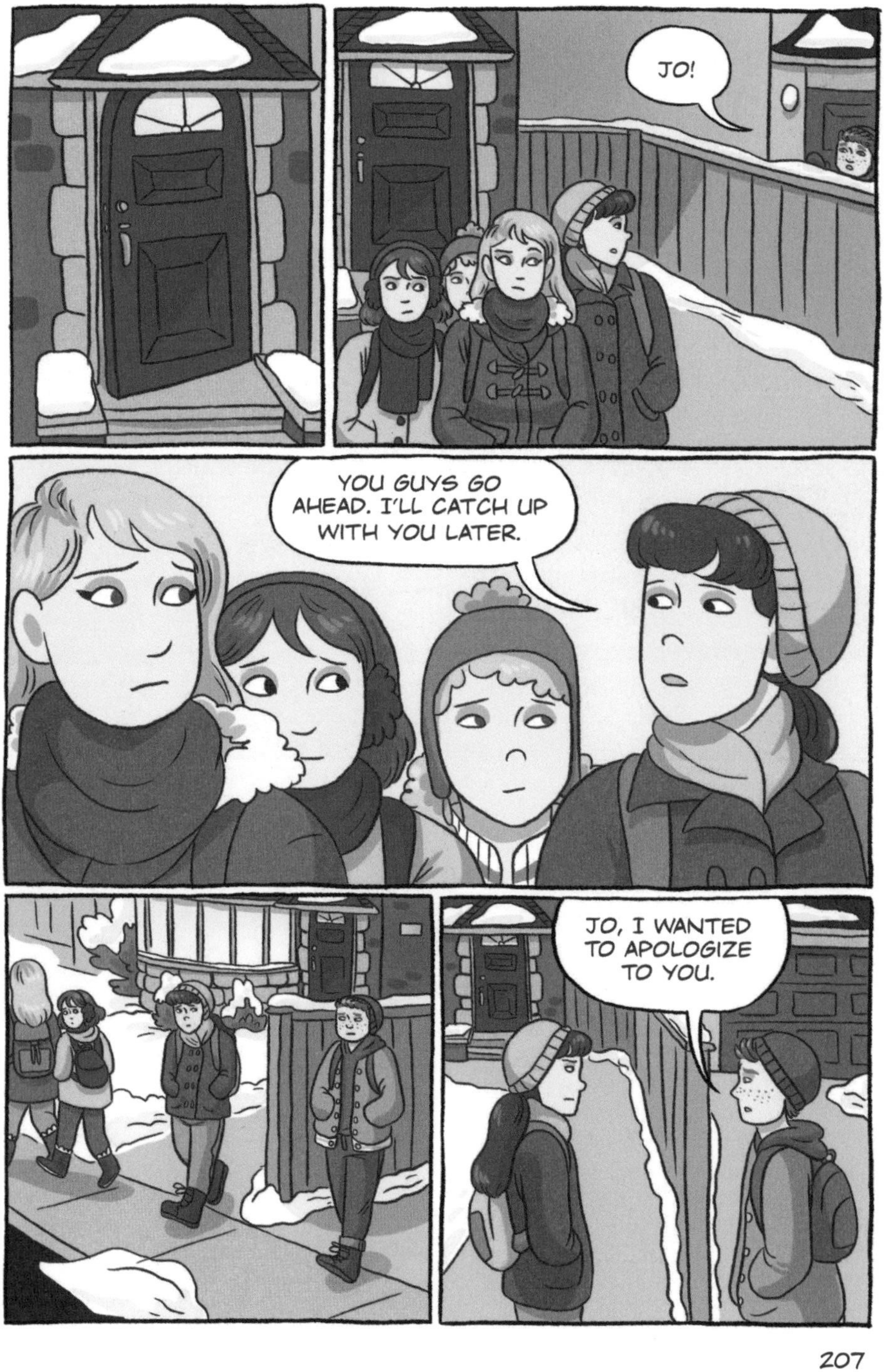
JO!
YOU GUYS GO AHEAD. I'LL CATCH UP WITH YOU LATER.
JO, I WANTED TO APOLOGIZE TO YOU.

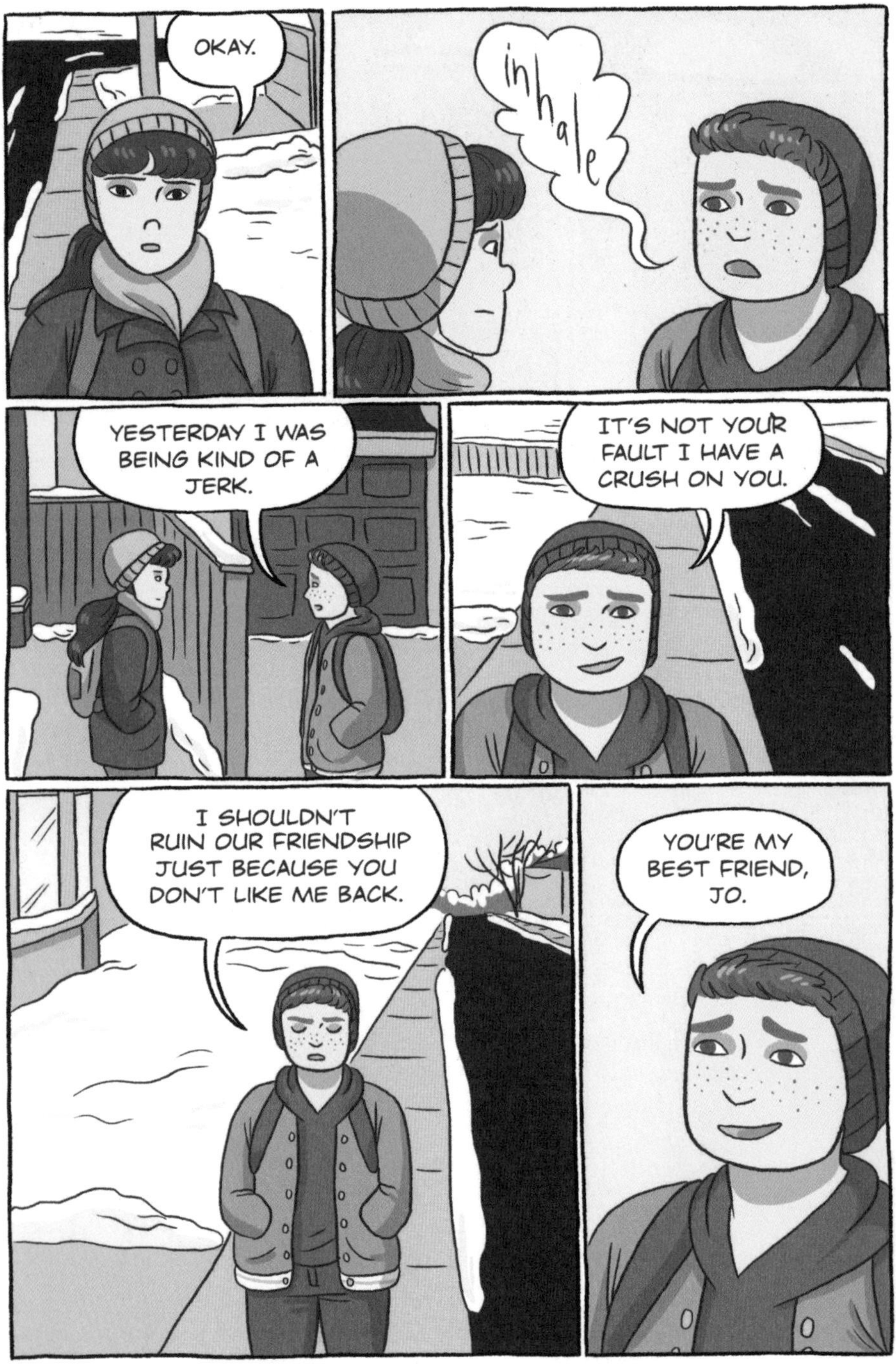
OKAY.
inhale
YESTERDAY I WAS BEING KIND OF A JERK.
IT'S NOT YOUR FAULT I HAVE A CRUSH ON YOU.
I SHOULDN'T RUIN OUR FRIENDSHIP JUST BECAUSE YOU DON'T LIKE ME BACK.
YOU'RE MY BEST FRIEND, JO.

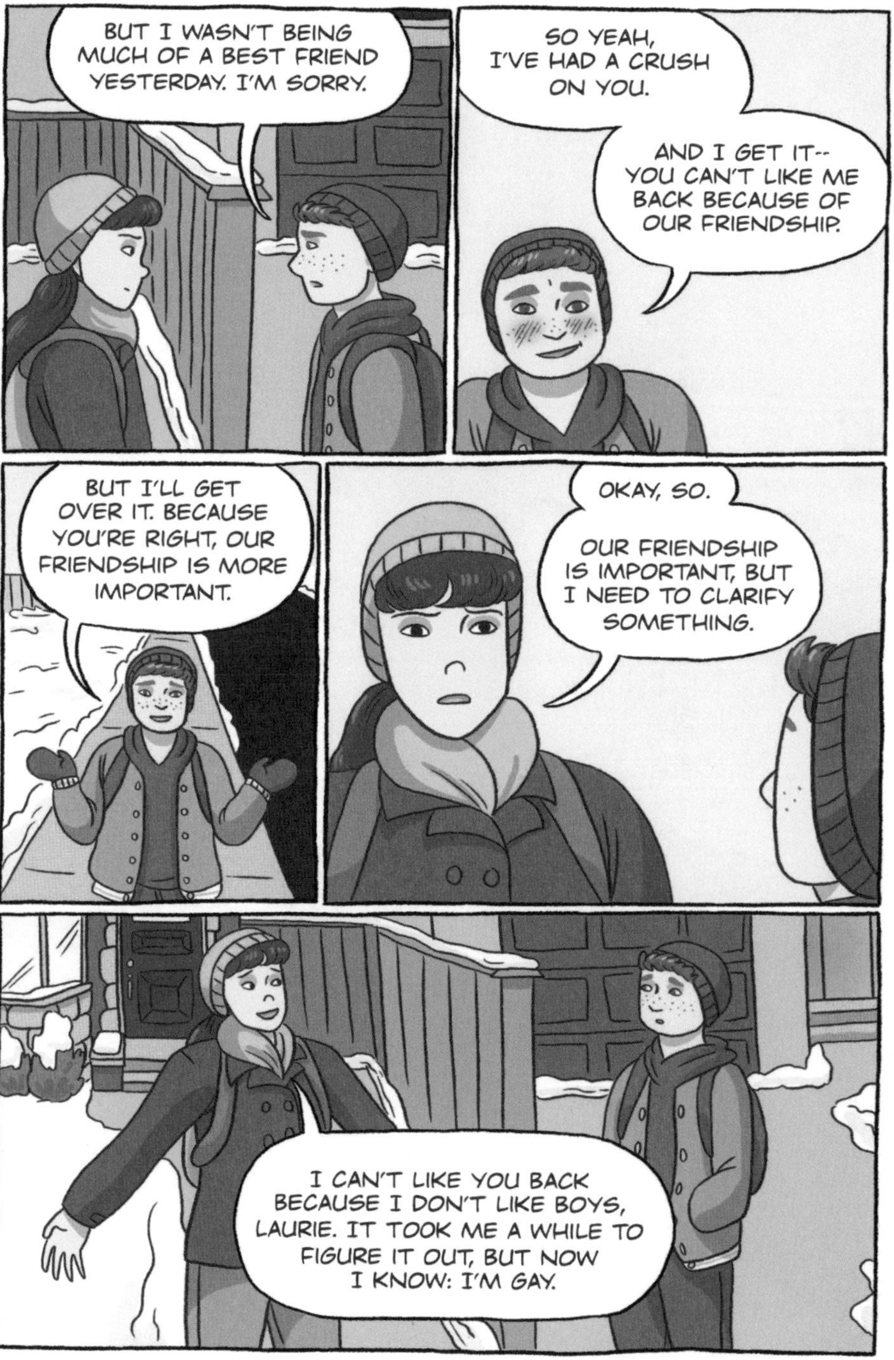
BUT I WASN'T BEING MUCH OF A BEST FRIEND YESTERDAY. I'M SORRY.
SO YEAH, I'VE HAD A CRUSH ON YOU.
AND I GET IT-- YOU CAN'T LIKE ME BACK BECAUSE OF OUR FRIENDSHIP.
BUT I'LL GET OVER IT. BECAUSE YOU'RE RIGHT, OUR FRIENDSHIP IS MORE IMPORTANT.
OKAY, SO.
OUR FRIENDSHIP IS IMPORTANT, BUT I NEED TO CLARIFY SOMETHING.
I CAN'T LIKE YOU BACK BECAUSE I DON'T LIKE BOYS, LAURIE. IT TOOK ME A WHILE TO FIGURE IT OUT, BUT NOW I KNOW: I'M GAY.

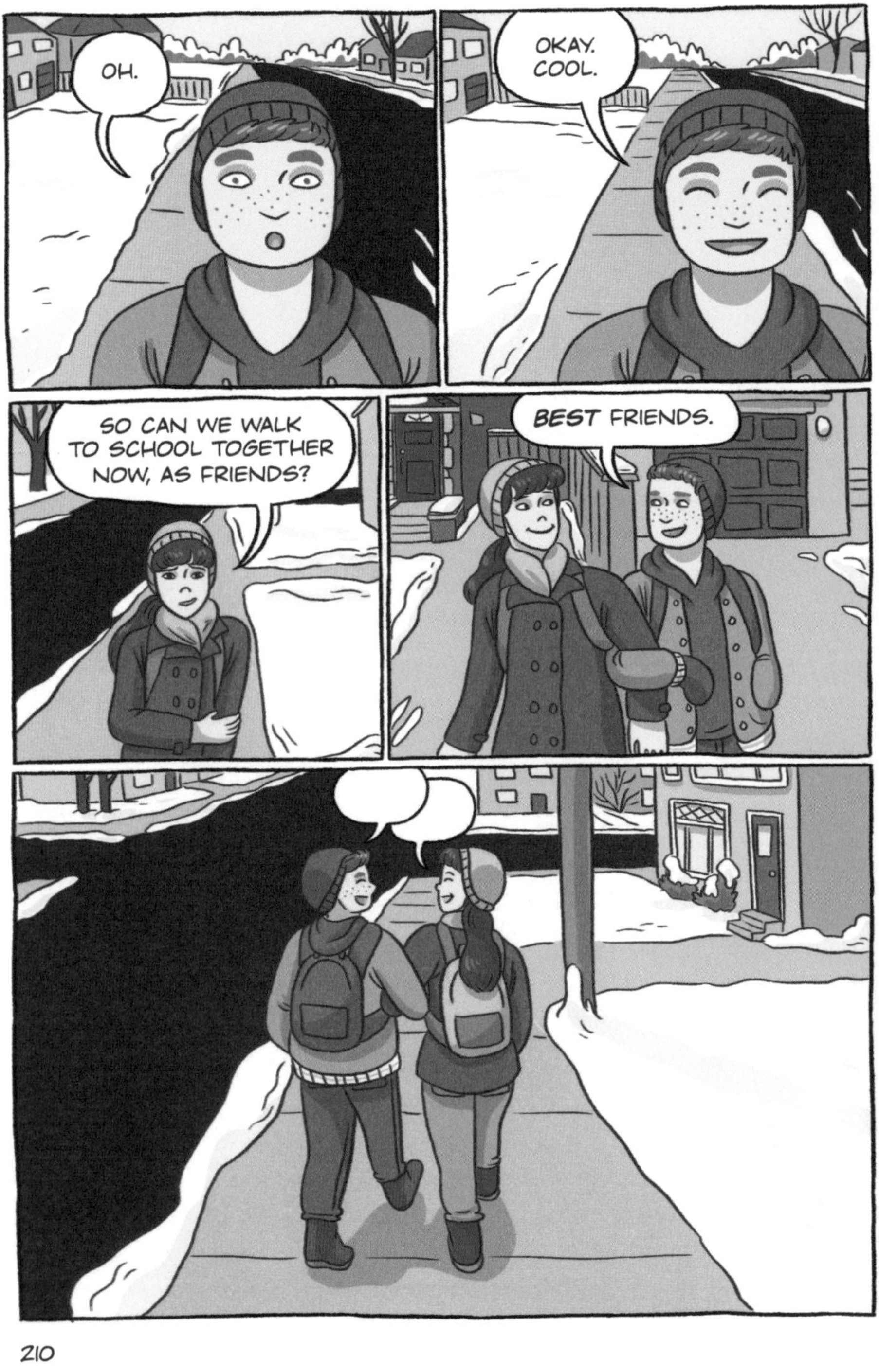
OH.
OKAY. COOL.
SO CAN WE WALK TO SCHOOL TOGETHER NOW, AS FRIENDS?
BEST FRIENDS.

CHAPTER 8

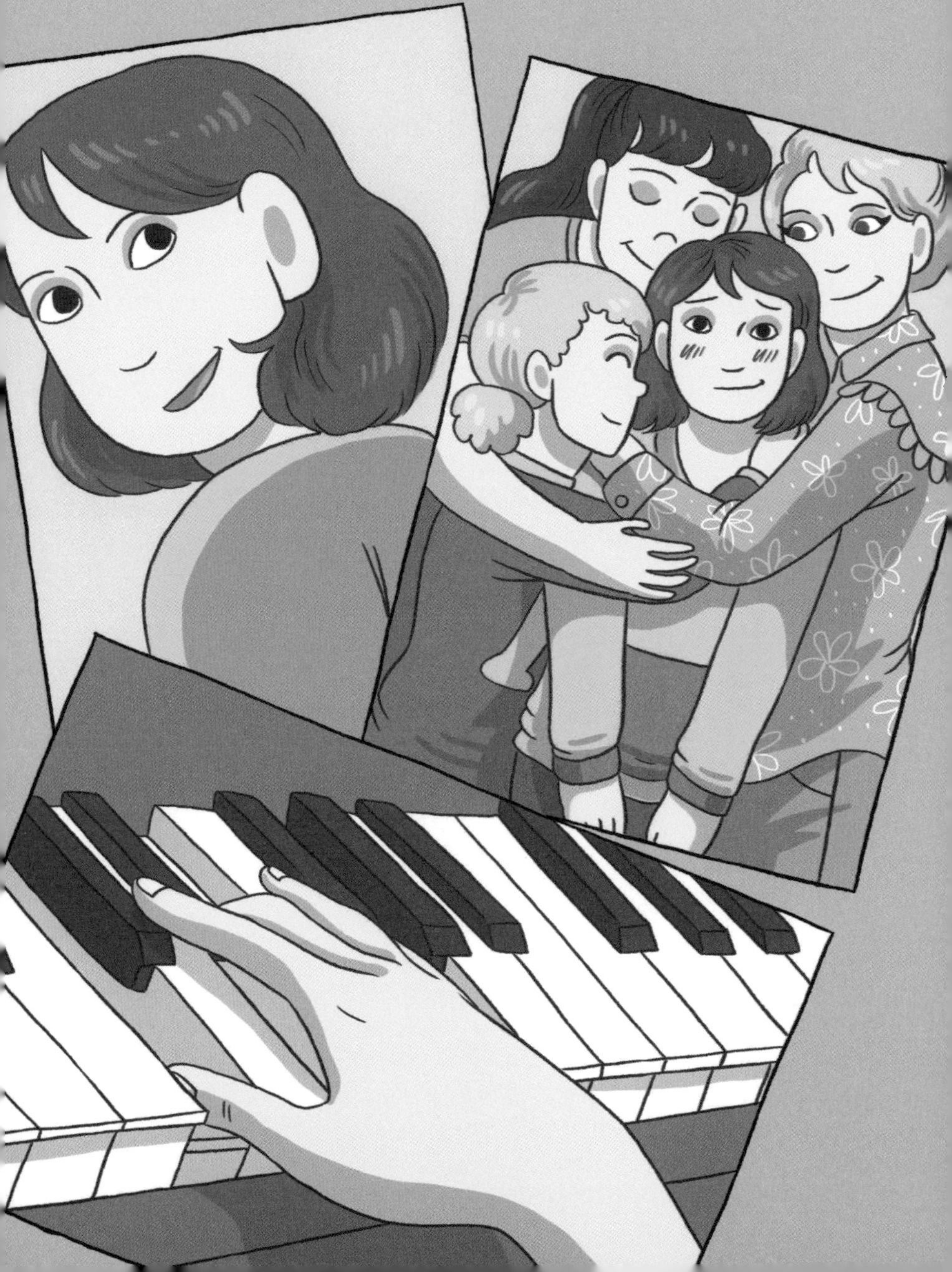

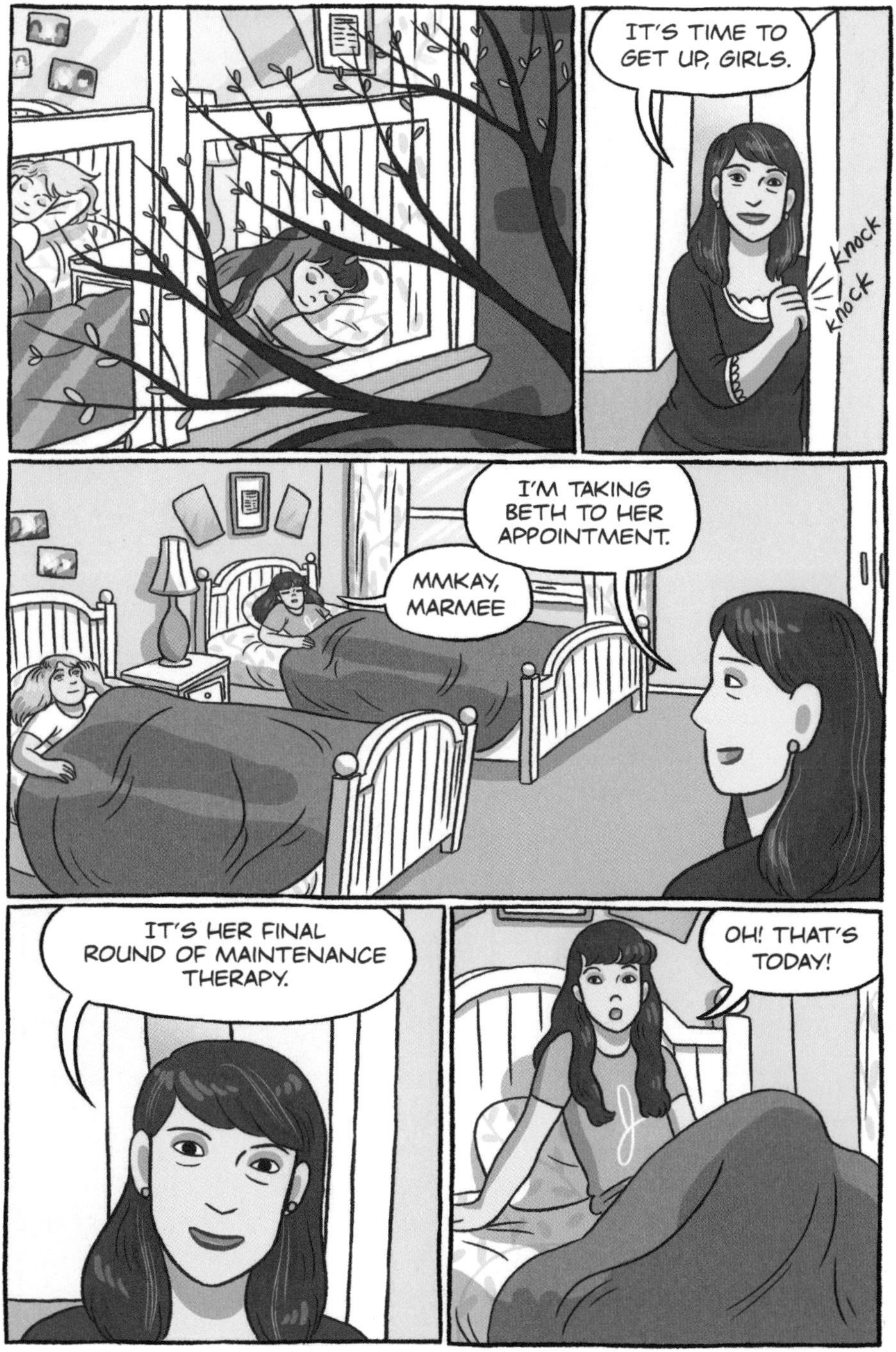
IT'S TIME TO GET UP, GIRLS.
knock knock
I'M TAKING BETH TO HER APPOINTMENT.
MMKAY, MARMEE
IT'S HER FINAL ROUND OF MAINTENANCE THERAPY.
OH! THAT'S TODAY!

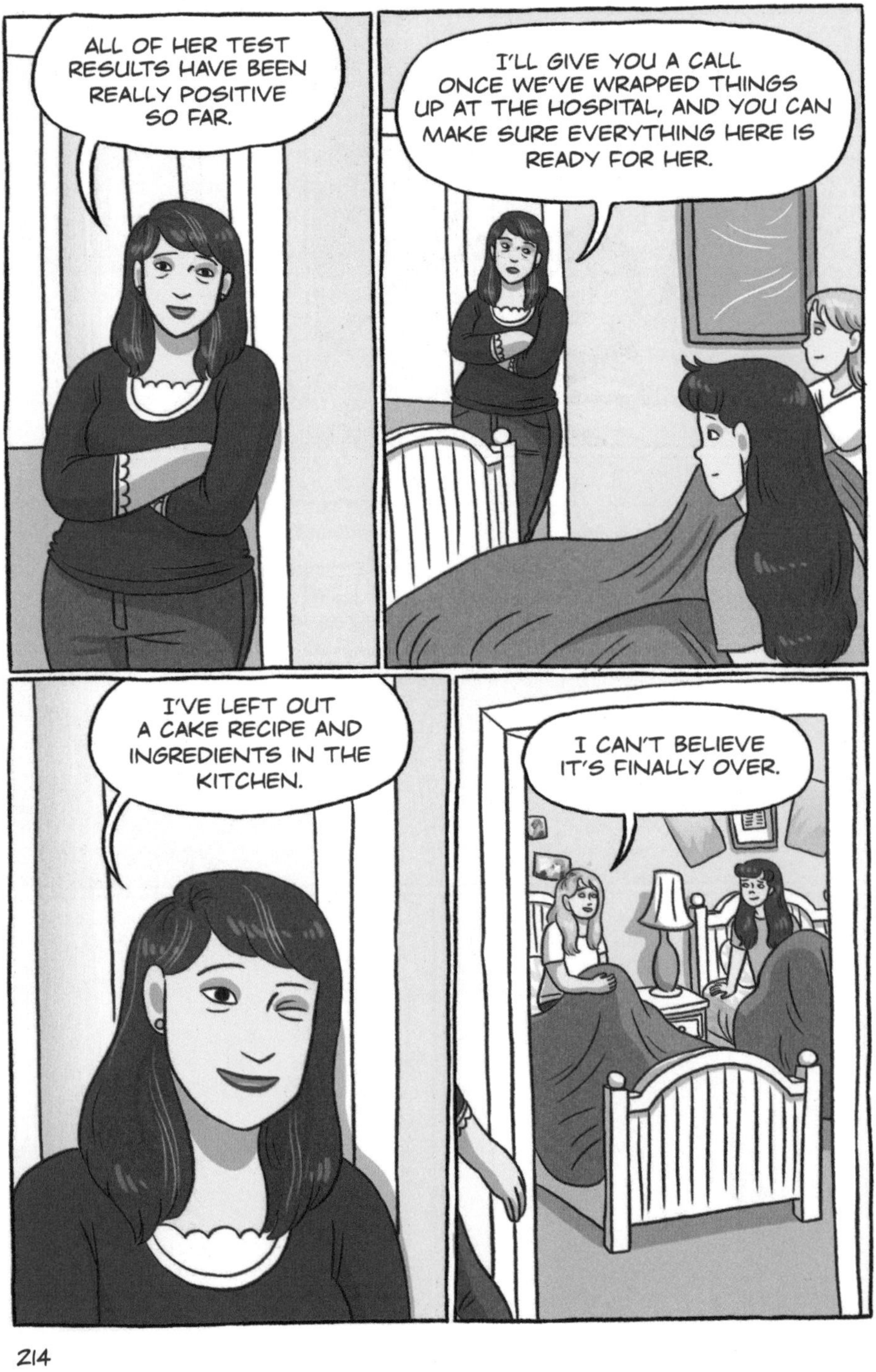
ALL OF HER TEST RESULTS HAVE BEEN REALLY POSITIVE SO FAR.
I'LL GIVE YOU A CALL ONCE WE'VE WRAPPED THINGS UP AT THE HOSPITAL, AND YOU CAN MAKE SURE EVERYTHING HERE IS READY FOR HER.
I'VE LEFT OUT A CAKE RECIPE AND INGREDIENTS IN THE KITCHEN.
I CAN'T BELIEVE IT'S FINALLY OVER.

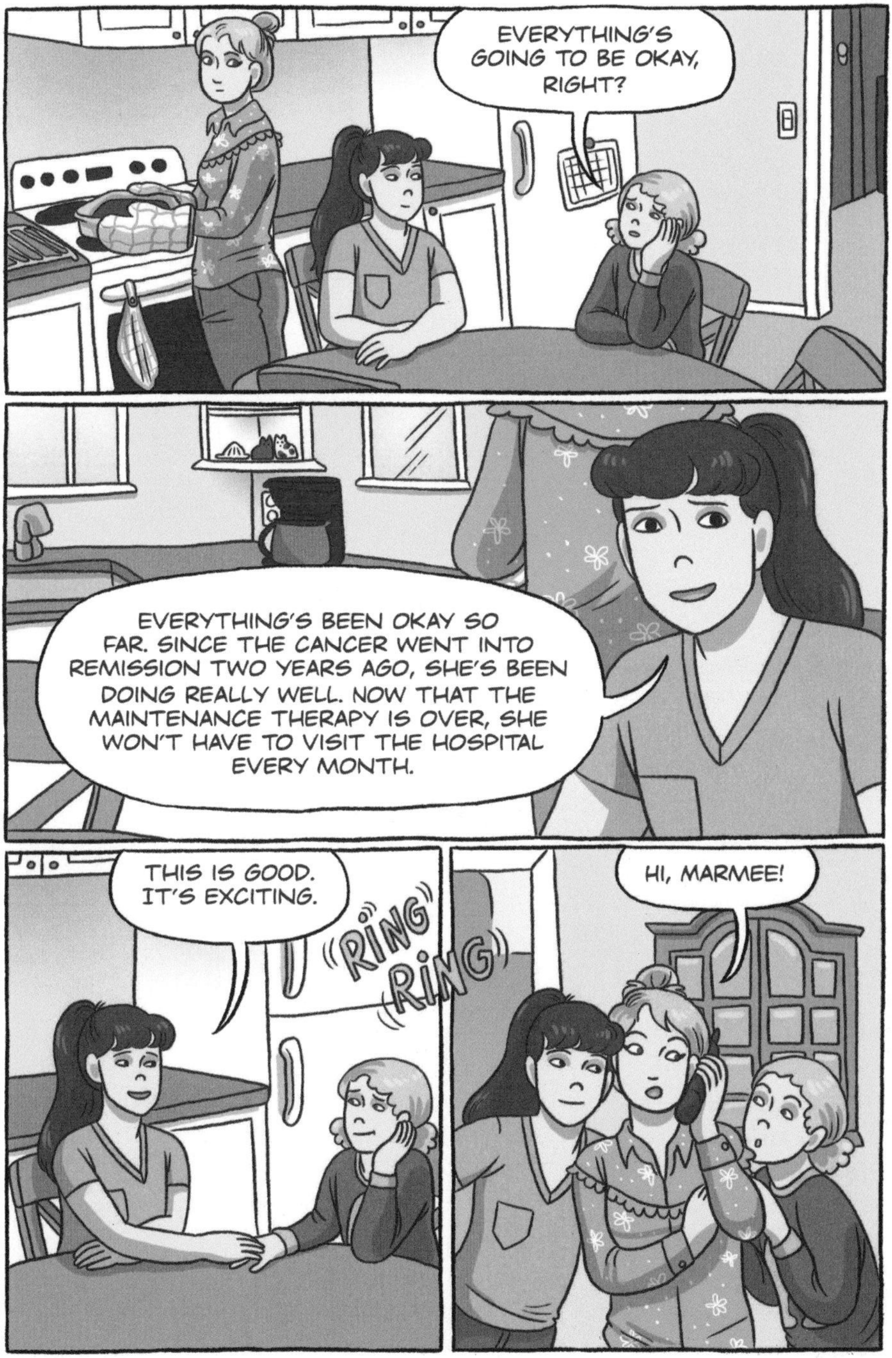
EVERYTHING'S GOING TO BE OKAY, RIGHT?
EVERYTHING'S BEEN OKAY SO FAR. SINCE THE CANCER WENT INTO REMISSION TWO YEARS AGO, SHE'S BEEN DOING REALLY WELL. NOW THAT THE MAINTENANCE THERAPY IS OVER, SHE WON'T HAVE TO VISIT THE HOSPITAL EVERY MONTH.
THIS IS GOOD. IT'S EXCITING.
RING
RING
HI, MARMEE!

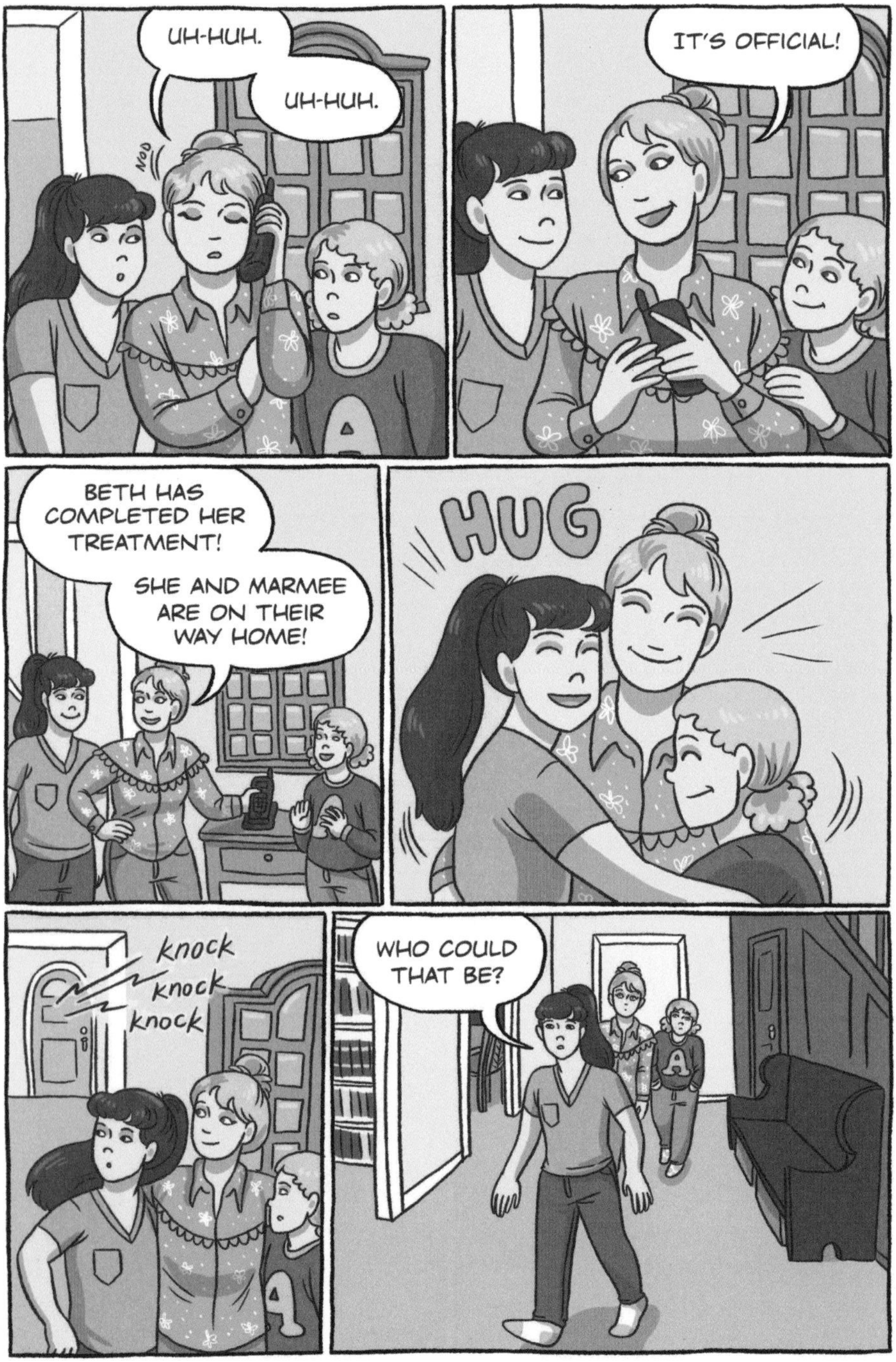
UH-HUH.
UH-HUH.
NOD
IT'S OFFICIAL!
BETH HAS COMPLETED HER TREATMENT!
SHE AND MARMEE ARE ON THEIR WAY HOME!
HUG
knock
knock
knock
WHO COULD THAT BE?

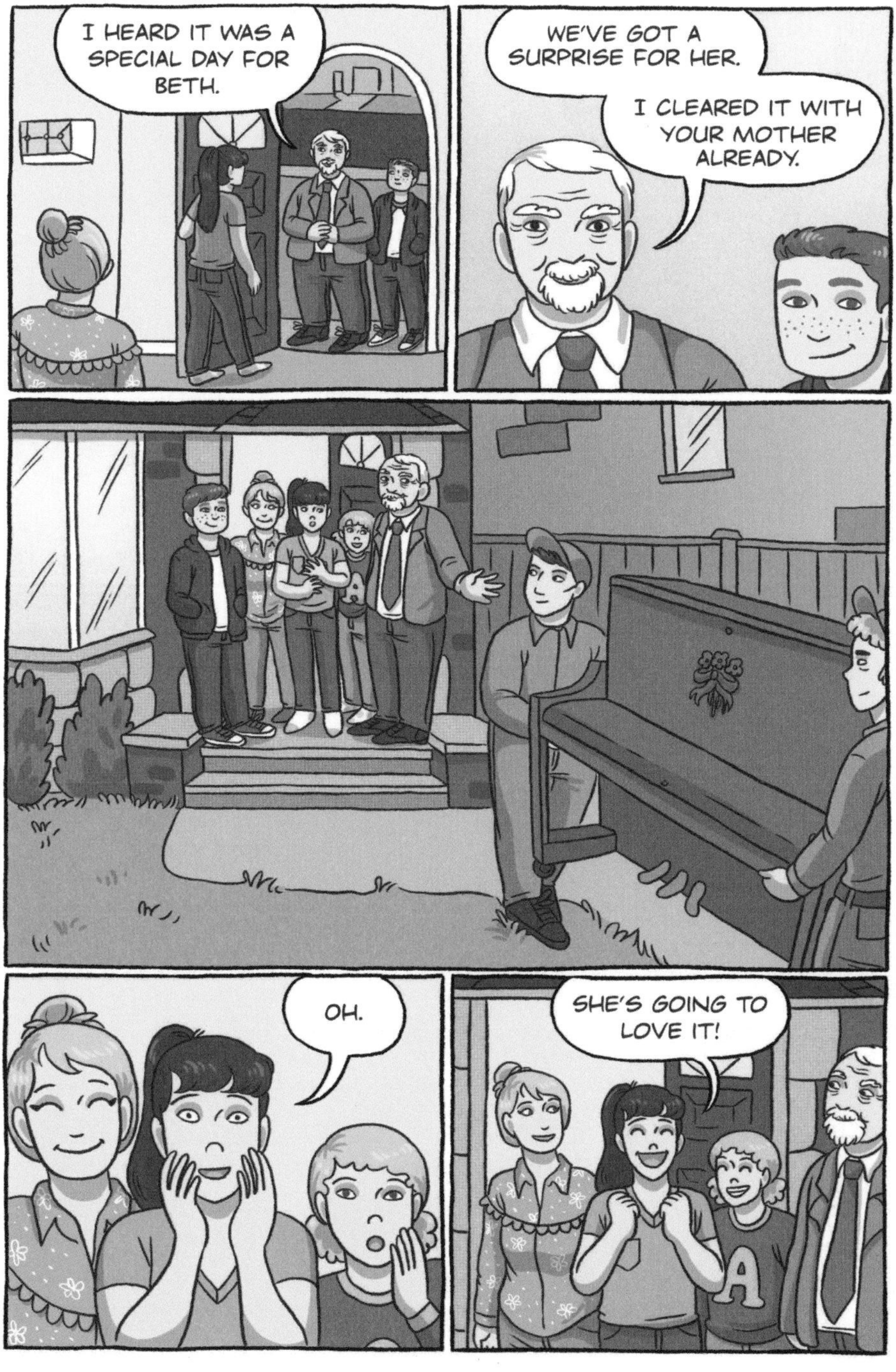
I HEARD IT WAS A SPECIAL DAY FOR BETH.
WE'VE GOT A SURPRISE FOR HER.
I CLEARED IT WITH YOUR MOTHER ALREADY.
OH.
SHE'S GOING TO LOVE IT!

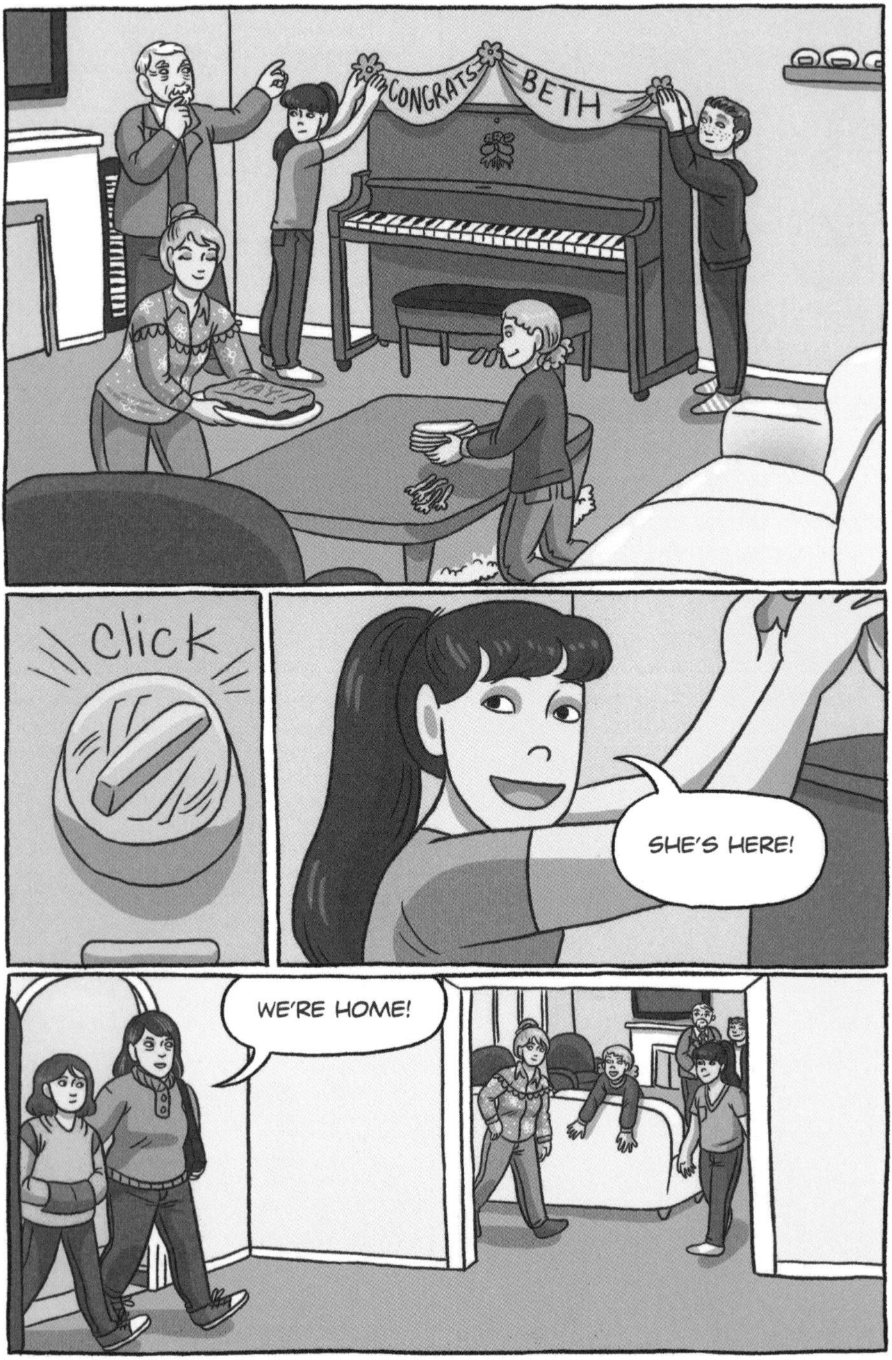
CONGRATS BETH
YAY!
click
SHE'S HERE!
WE'RE HOME!

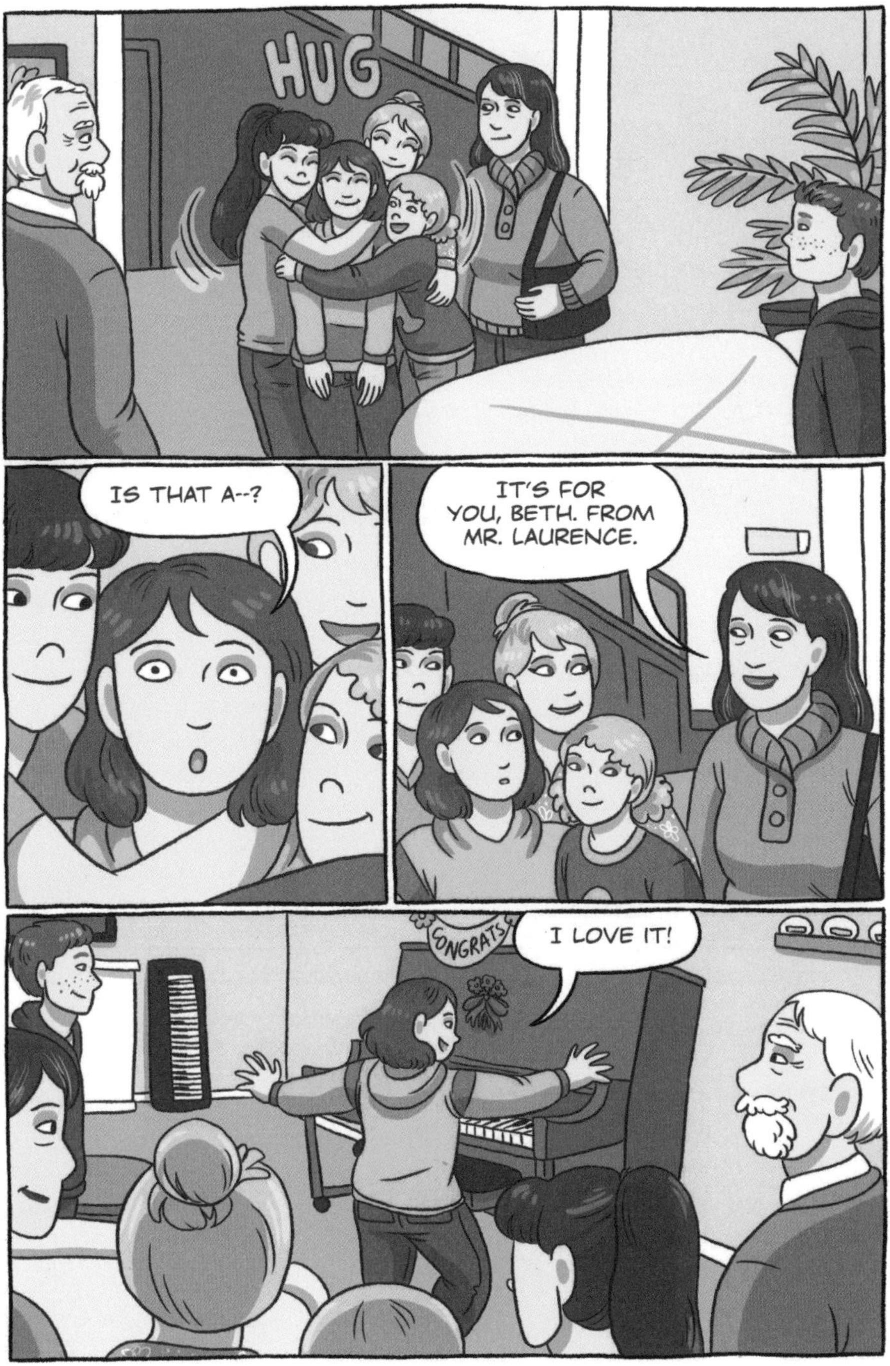
HUG
IS THAT A--?
IT'S FOR YOU, BETH. FROM MR. LAURENCE.
CONGRATS
I LOVE IT!

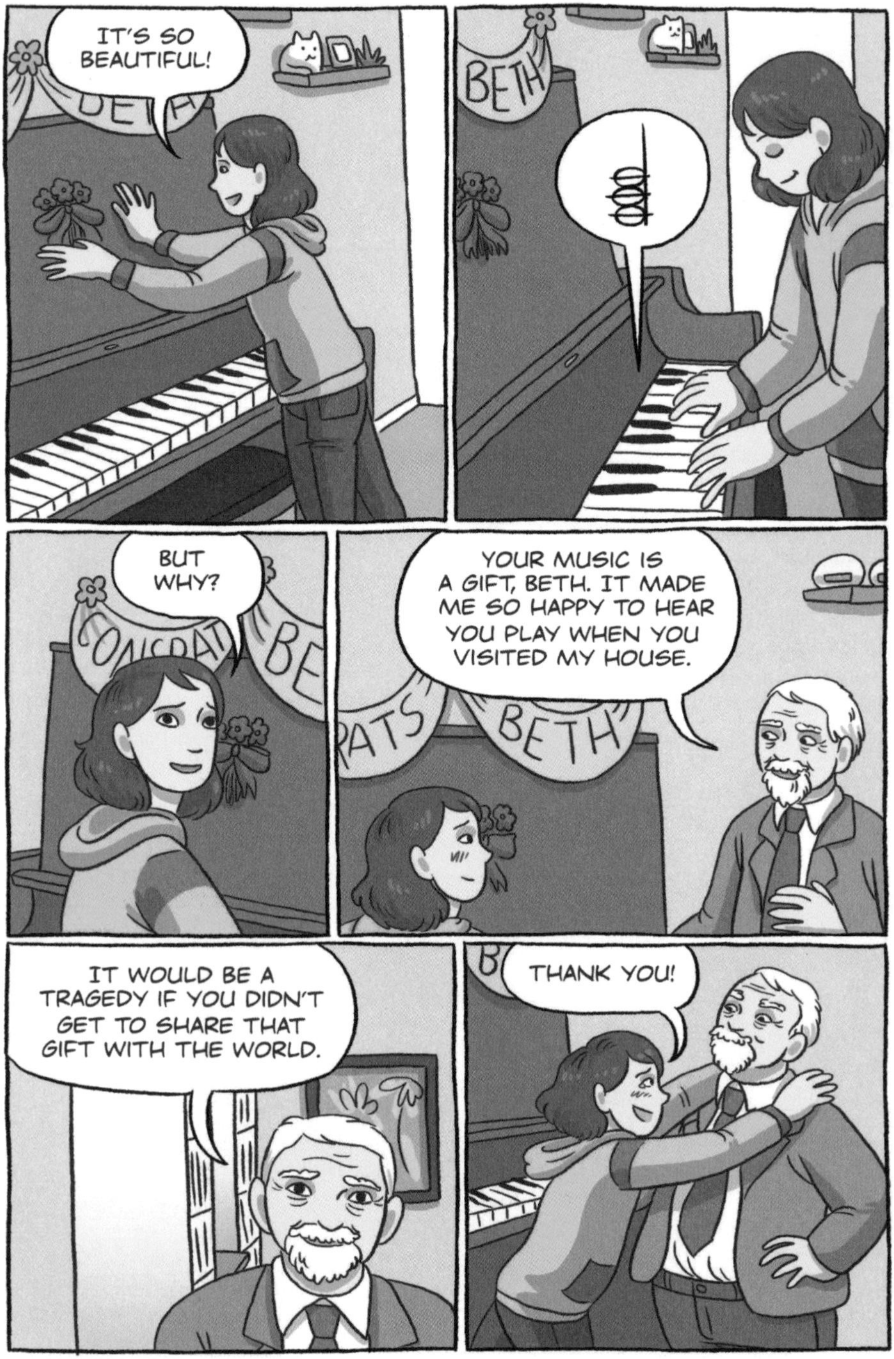
IT'S SO BEAUTIFUL!
BETH
BUT WHY?
YOUR MUSIC IS A GIFT, BETH. IT MADE ME SO HAPPY TO HEAR YOU PLAY WHEN YOU VISITED MY HOUSE.
BETH
IT WOULD BE A TRAGEDY IF YOU DIDN'T GET TO SHARE THAT GIFT WITH THE WORLD.
THANK YOU!

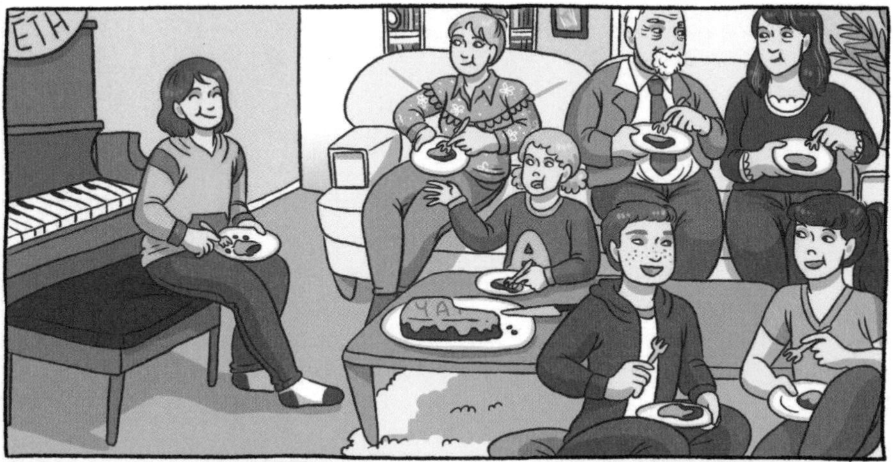

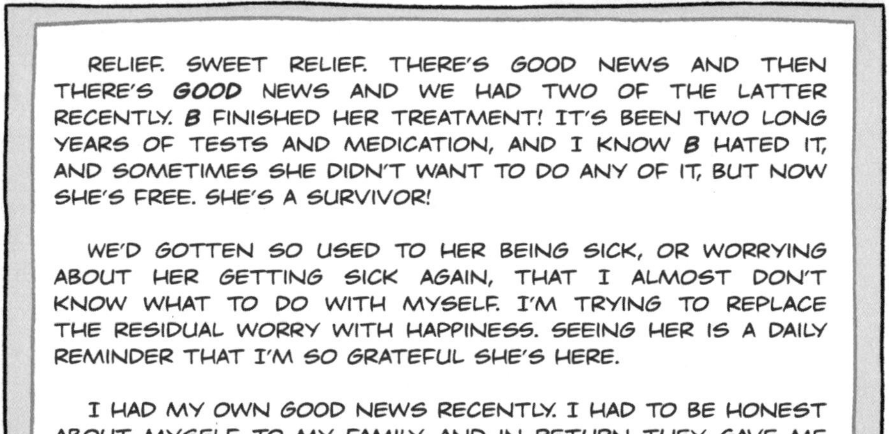
RELIEF. SWEET RELIEF. THERE'S GOOD NEWS AND THEN THERE'S ***GOOD*** NEWS AND WE HAD TWO OF THE LATTER RECENTLY. ***B*** FINISHED HER TREATMENT! IT'S BEEN TWO LONG YEARS OF TESTS AND MEDICATION, AND I KNOW ***B*** HATED IT, AND SOMETIMES SHE DIDN'T WANT TO DO ANY OF IT, BUT NOW SHE'S FREE. SHE'S A SURVIVOR!
WE'D GOTTEN SO USED TO HER BEING SICK, OR WORRYING ABOUT HER GETTING SICK AGAIN, THAT I ALMOST DON'T KNOW WHAT TO DO WITH MYSELF. I'M TRYING TO REPLACE THE RESIDUAL WORRY WITH HAPPINESS. SEEING HER IS A DAILY REMINDER THAT I'M SO GRATEFUL SHE'S HERE.
I HAD MY OWN GOOD NEWS RECENTLY. I HAD TO BE HONEST ABOUT MYSELF TO MY FAMILY, AND IN RETURN THEY GAVE ME NOTHING BUT LOVE AND SUPPORT. I'M NOT SURE IF I'M READY TO TALK ABOUT IT HERE YET--BUT WHEN I AM, YOU'LL KNOW.
RELIEVED! RELIEVED! RELIEVED!
J
type type

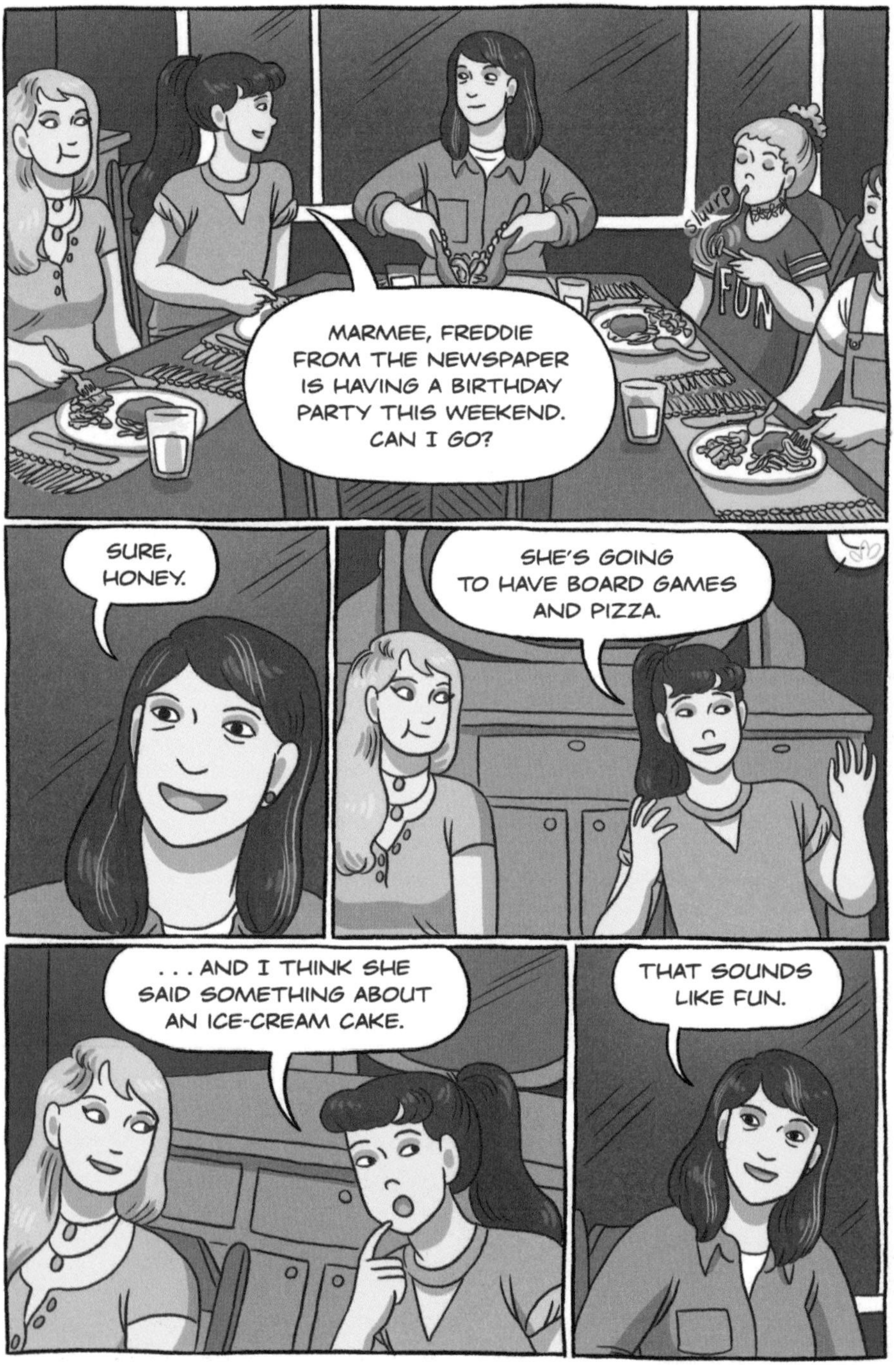
slurrP
FUN
MARMEE, FREDDIE FROM THE NEWSPAPER IS HAVING A BIRTHDAY PARTY THIS WEEKEND. CAN I GO?
SURE, HONEY.
SHE'S GOING TO HAVE BOARD GAMES AND PIZZA.
. . . AND I THINK SHE SAID SOMETHING ABOUT AN ICE-CREAM CAKE.
THAT SOUNDS LIKE FUN.

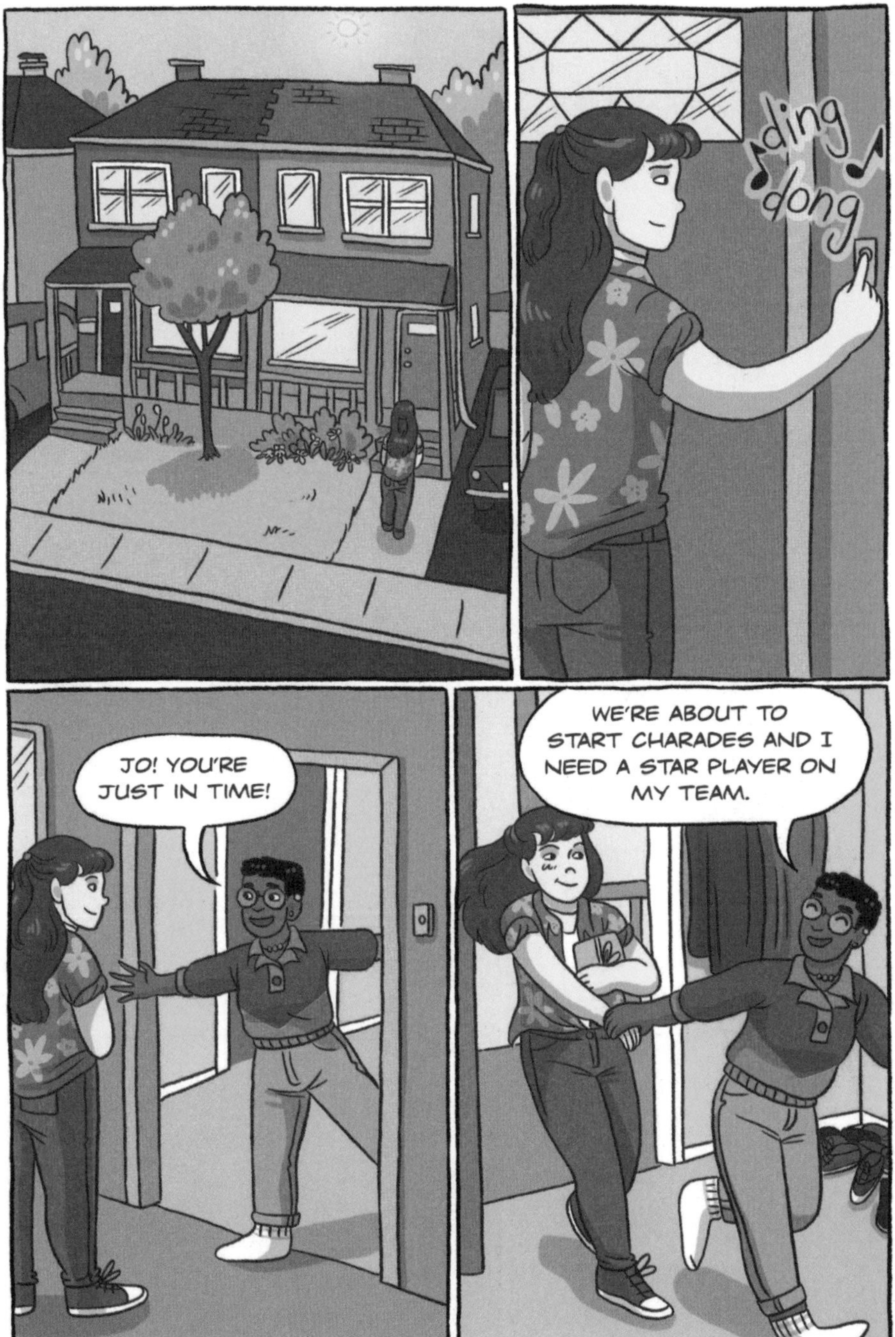
ding dong
JO! YOU'RE JUST IN TIME!
WE'RE ABOUT TO START CHARADES AND I NEED A STAR PLAYER ON MY TEAM.

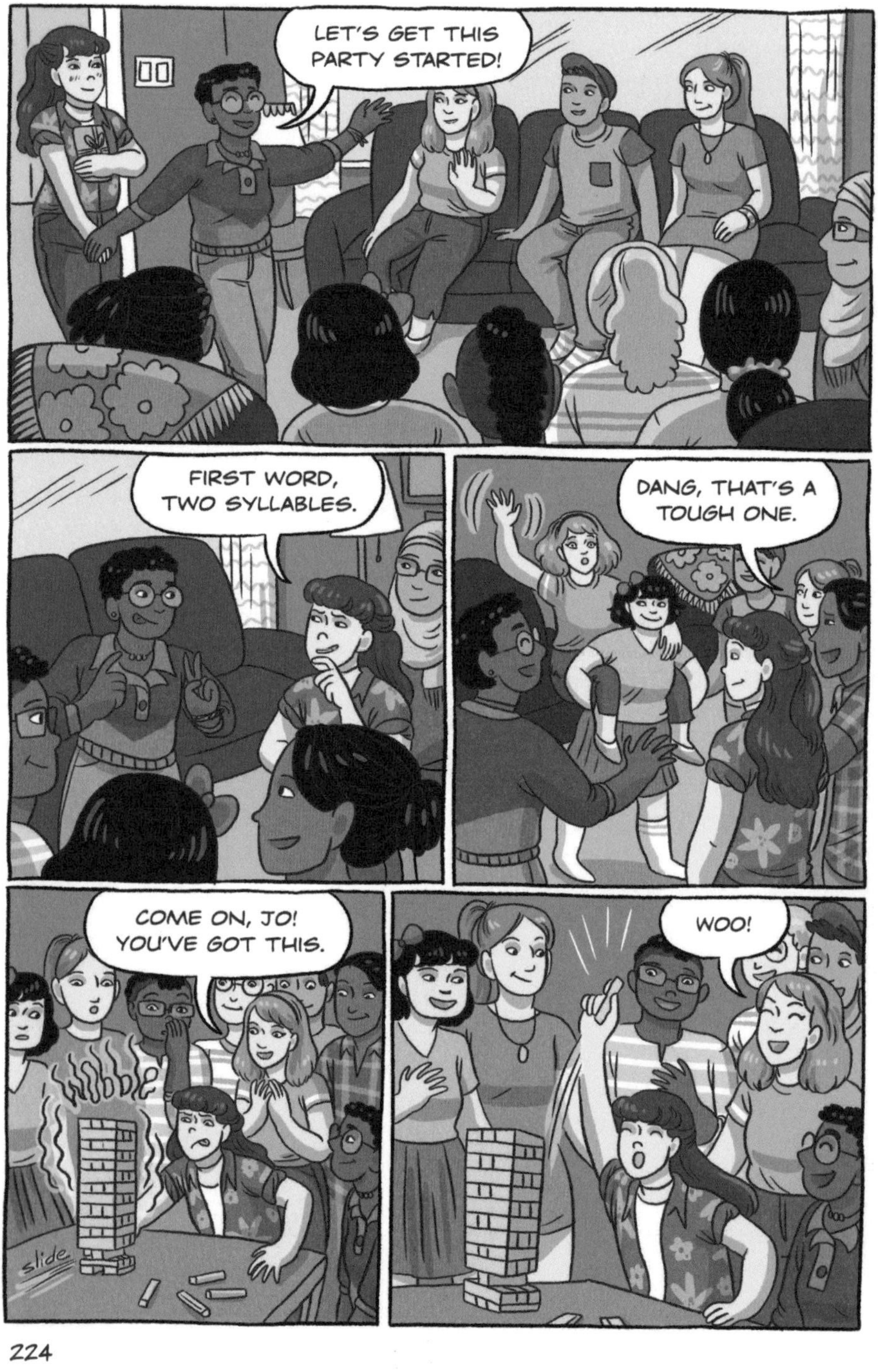
LET'S GET THIS PARTY STARTED!
FIRST WORD, TWO SYLLABLES.
DANG, THAT'S A TOUGH ONE.
COME ON, JO! YOU'VE GOT THIS.
slide
WOO!

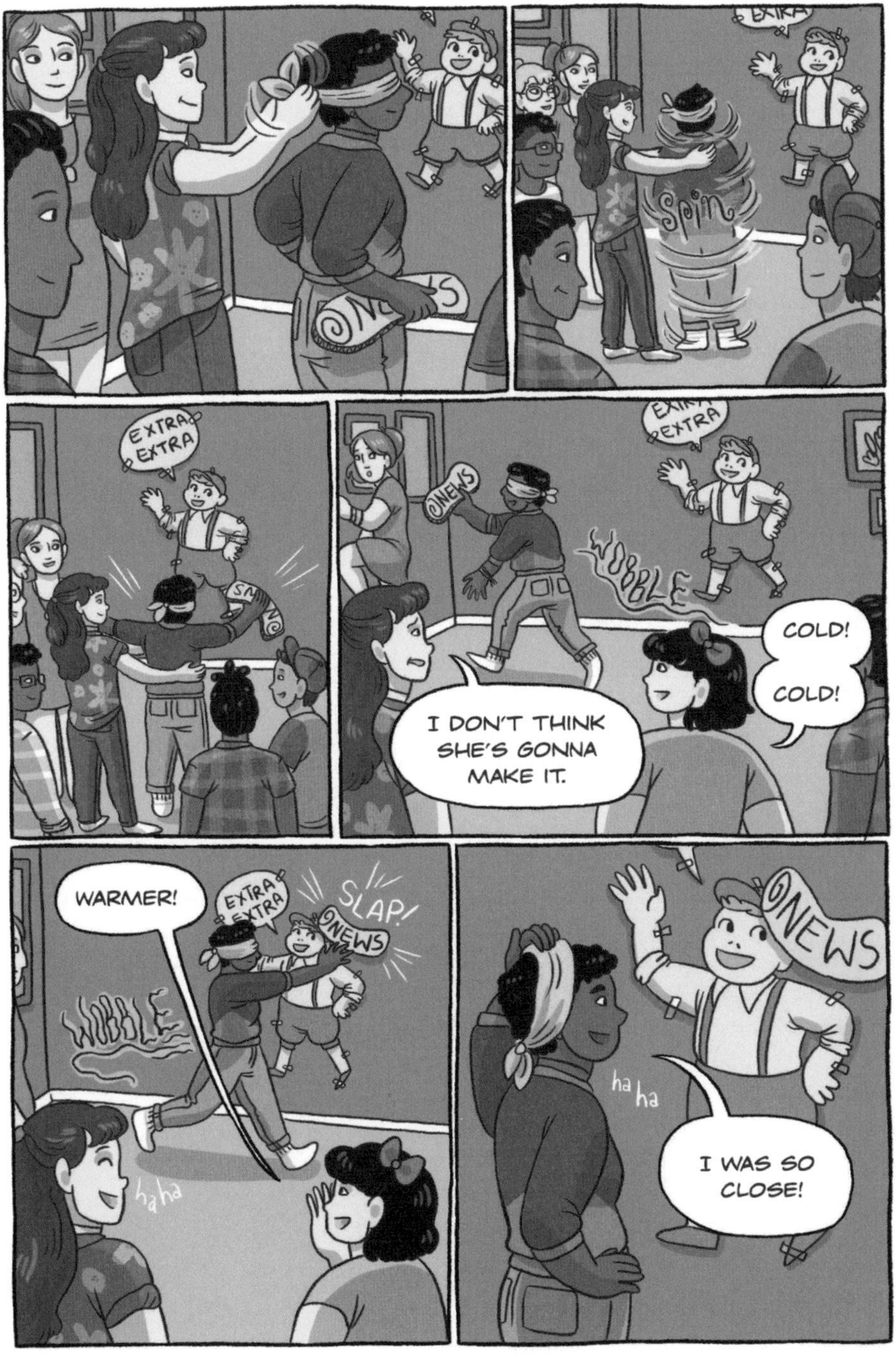
EXTRA
NEWS
SPIN
EXTRA EXTRA
SMACK
EXTRA EXTRA
NEWS
WOBBLE
COLD!
COLD!
I DON'T THINK SHE'S GONNA MAKE IT.
WARMER!
EXTRA EXTRA
SLAP!
NEWS
WOBBLE
haha
NEWS
haha
I WAS SO CLOSE!

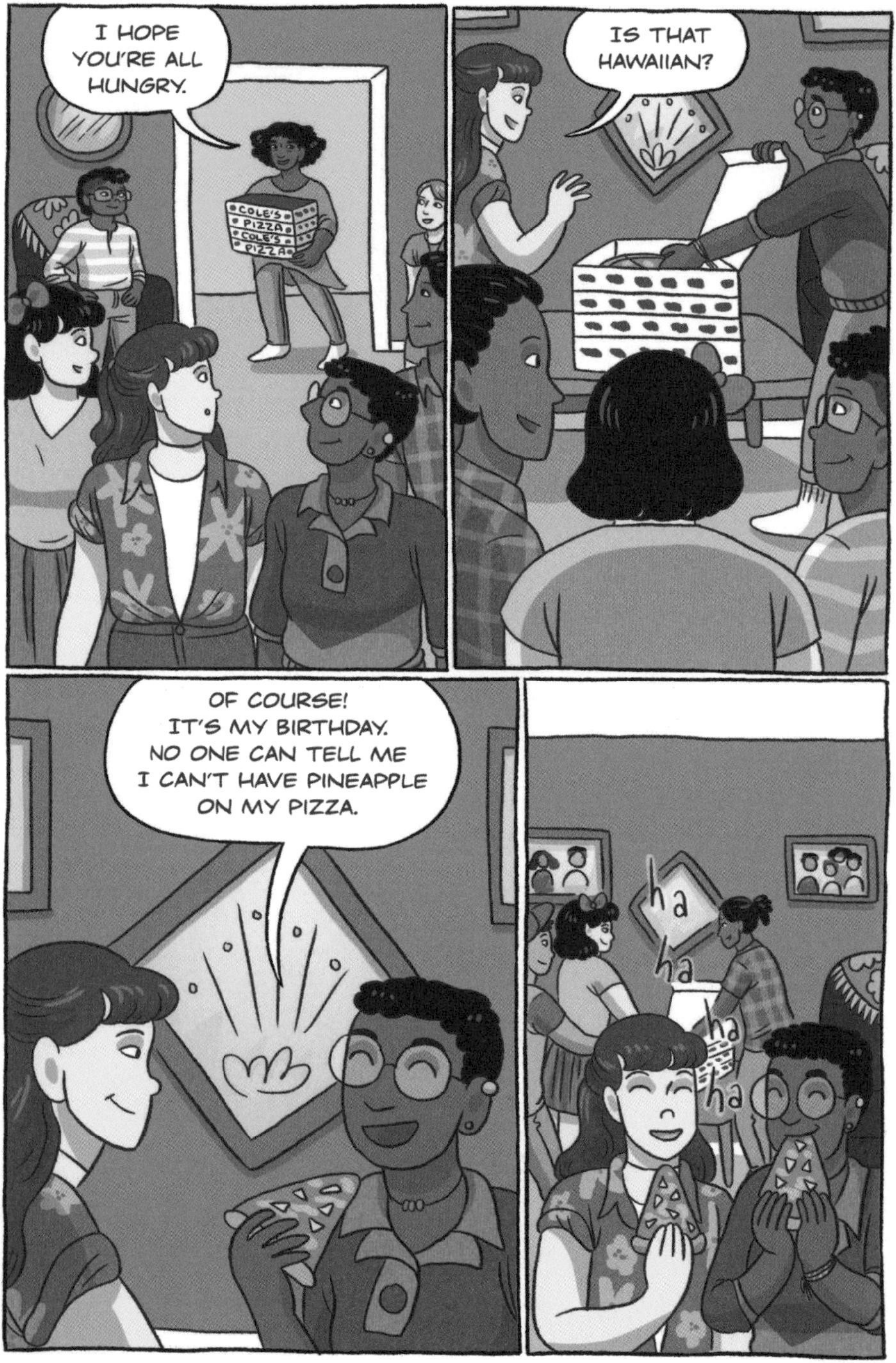
I HOPE YOU'RE ALL HUNGRY.
COLE'S PIZZA
COLE'S PIZZA
IS THAT HAWAIIAN?
OF COURSE! IT'S MY BIRTHDAY. NO ONE CAN TELL ME I CAN'T HAVE PINEAPPLE ON MY PIZZA.
ha ha ha ha

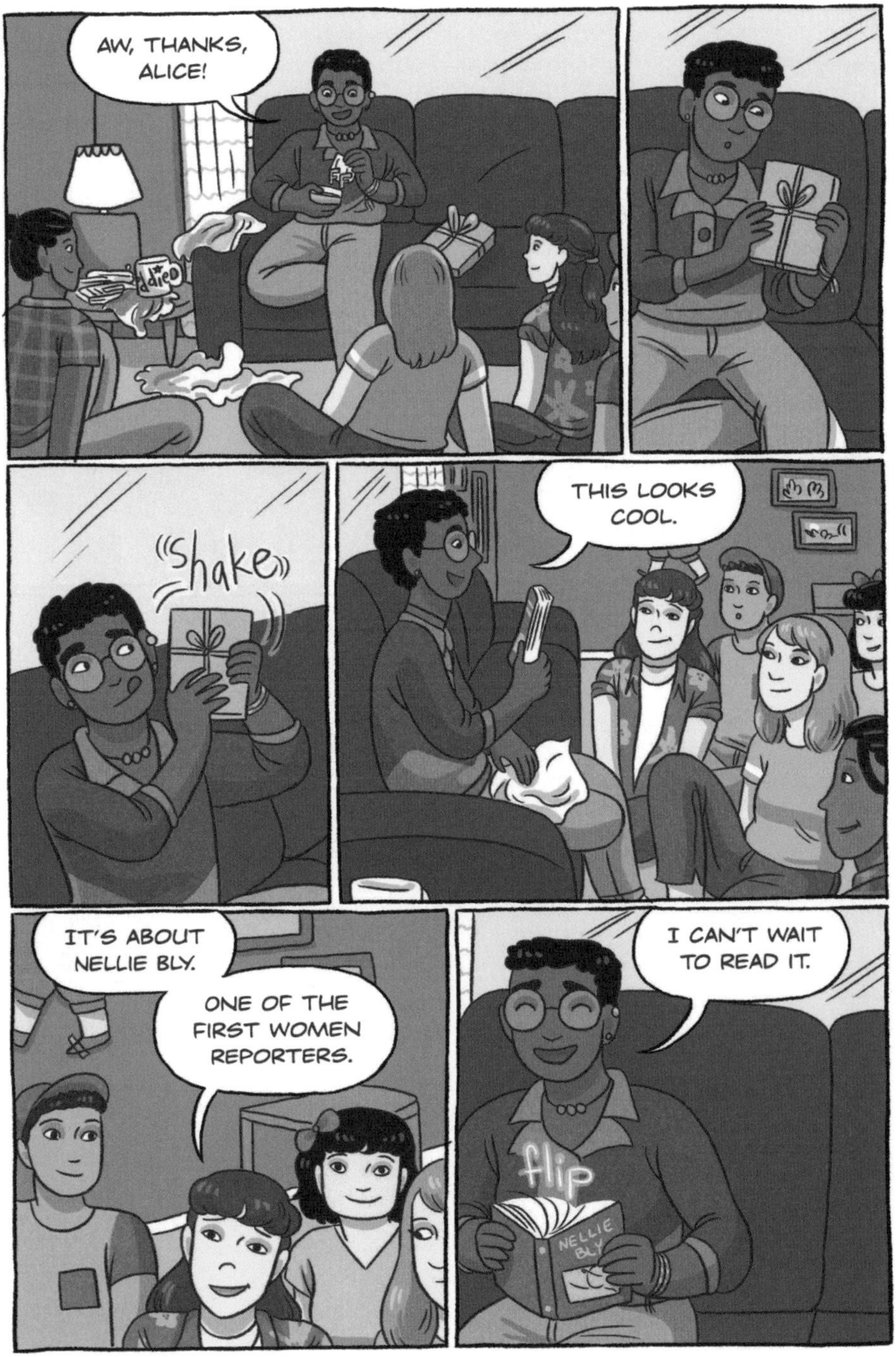
AW, THANKS, ALICE!
Shake
THIS LOOKS COOL.
IT'S ABOUT NELLIE BLY.
ONE OF THE FIRST WOMEN REPORTERS.
I CAN'T WAIT TO READ IT.
flip
NELLIE BLY

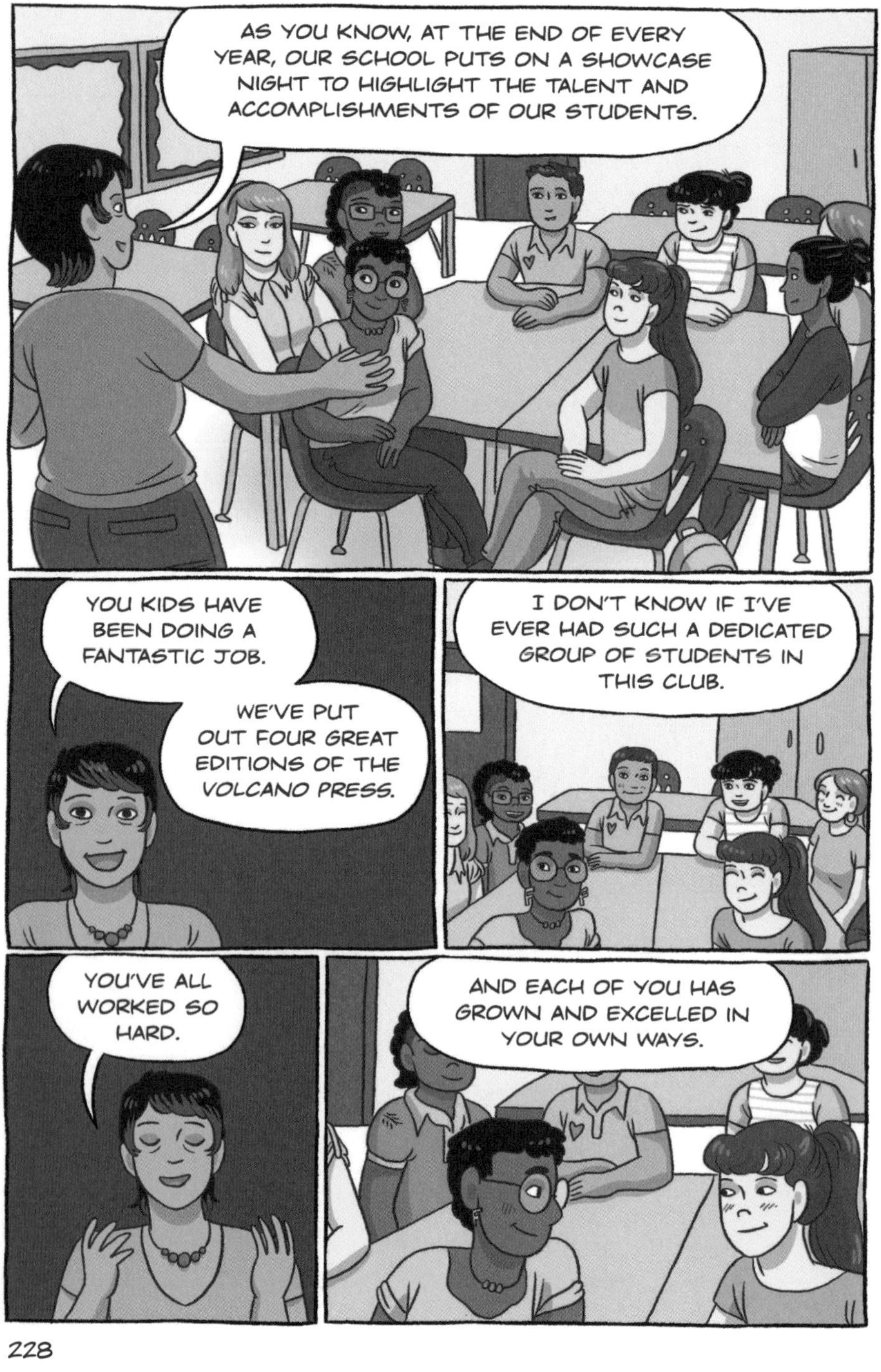
AS YOU KNOW, AT THE END OF EVERY YEAR, OUR SCHOOL PUTS ON A SHOWCASE NIGHT TO HIGHLIGHT THE TALENT AND ACCOMPLISHMENTS OF OUR STUDENTS.
YOU KIDS HAVE BEEN DOING A FANTASTIC JOB.
WE'VE PUT OUT FOUR GREAT EDITIONS OF THE VOLCANO PRESS.
I DON'T KNOW IF I'VE EVER HAD SUCH A DEDICATED GROUP OF STUDENTS IN THIS CLUB.
YOU'VE ALL WORKED SO HARD.
AND EACH OF YOU HAS GROWN AND EXCELLED IN YOUR OWN WAYS.

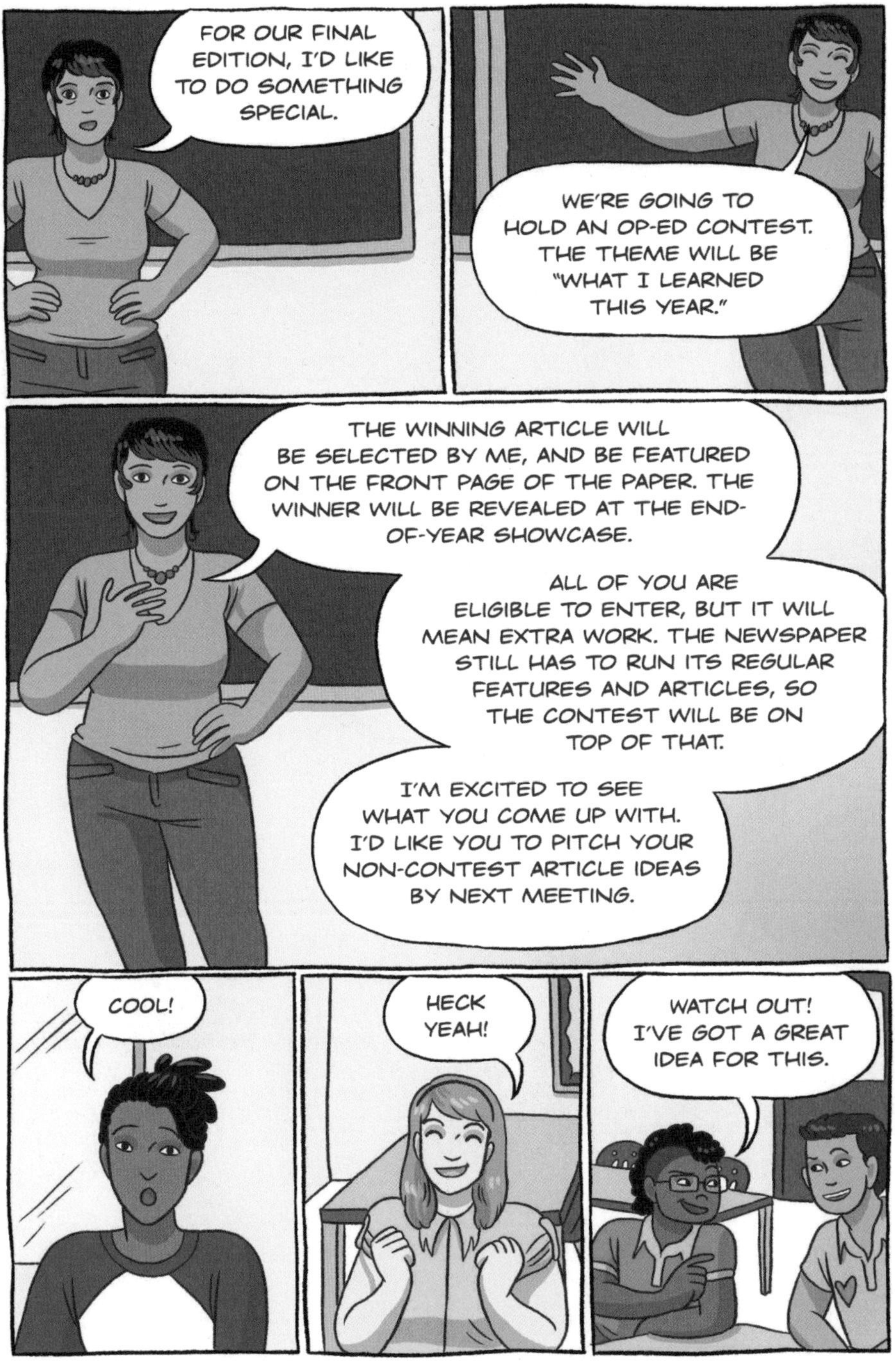
FOR OUR FINAL EDITION, I'D LIKE TO DO SOMETHING SPECIAL.
WE'RE GOING TO HOLD AN OP-ED CONTEST. THE THEME WILL BE "WHAT I LEARNED THIS YEAR."
THE WINNING ARTICLE WILL BE SELECTED BY ME, AND BE FEATURED ON THE FRONT PAGE OF THE PAPER. THE WINNER WILL BE REVEALED AT THE END-OF-YEAR SHOWCASE.
ALL OF YOU ARE ELIGIBLE TO ENTER, BUT IT WILL MEAN EXTRA WORK. THE NEWSPAPER STILL HAS TO RUN ITS REGULAR FEATURES AND ARTICLES, SO THE CONTEST WILL BE ON TOP OF THAT.
I'M EXCITED TO SEE WHAT YOU COME UP WITH. I'D LIKE YOU TO PITCH YOUR NON-CONTEST ARTICLE IDEAS BY NEXT MEETING.
COOL!
HECK YEAH!
WATCH OUT! I'VE GOT A GREAT IDEA FOR THIS.

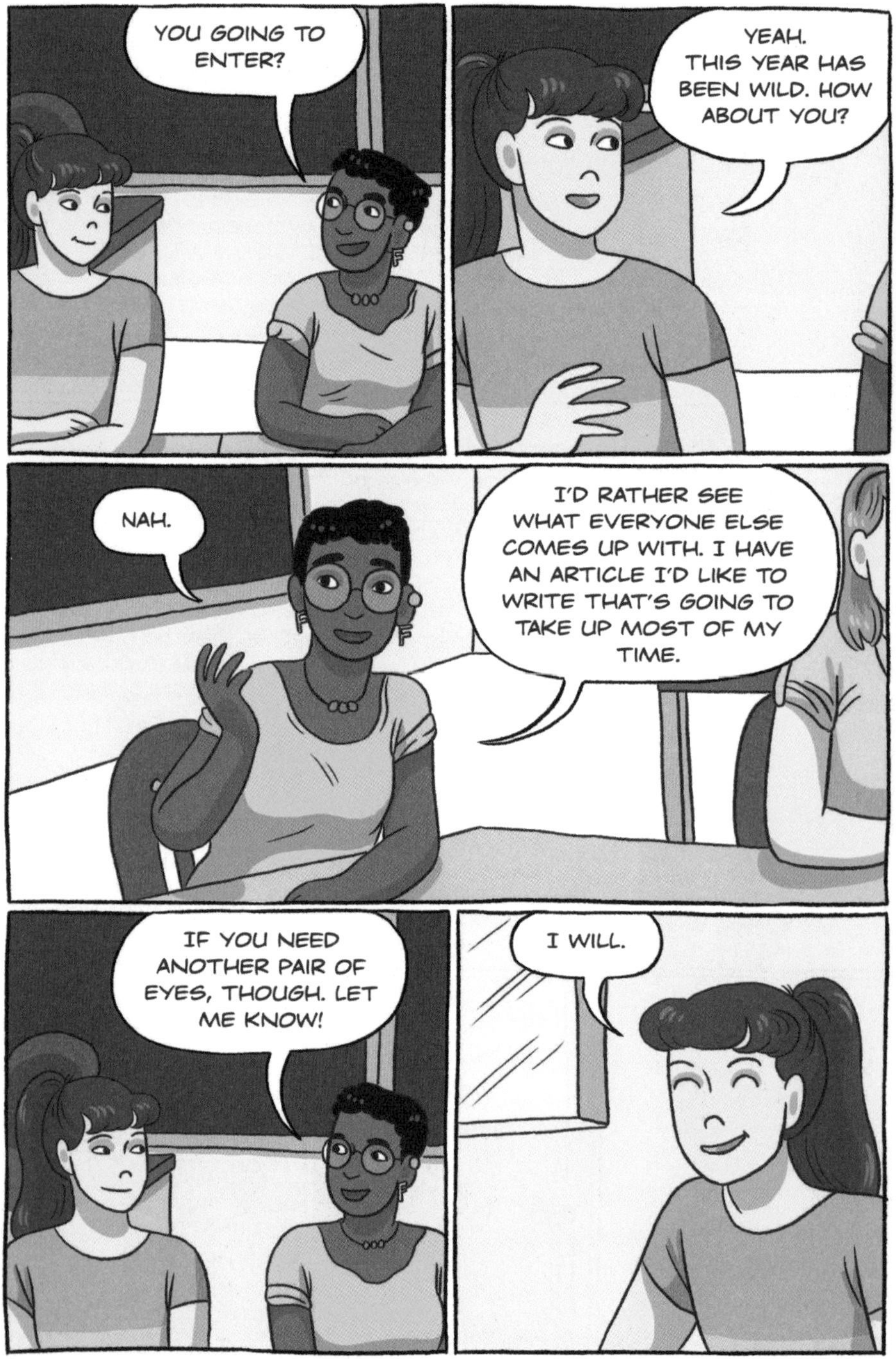
YOU GOING TO ENTER?
YEAH. THIS YEAR HAS BEEN WILD. HOW ABOUT YOU?
NAH.
I'D RATHER SEE WHAT EVERYONE ELSE COMES UP WITH. I HAVE AN ARTICLE I'D LIKE TO WRITE THAT'S GOING TO TAKE UP MOST OF MY TIME.
IF YOU NEED ANOTHER PAIR OF EYES, THOUGH. LET ME KNOW!
I WILL.

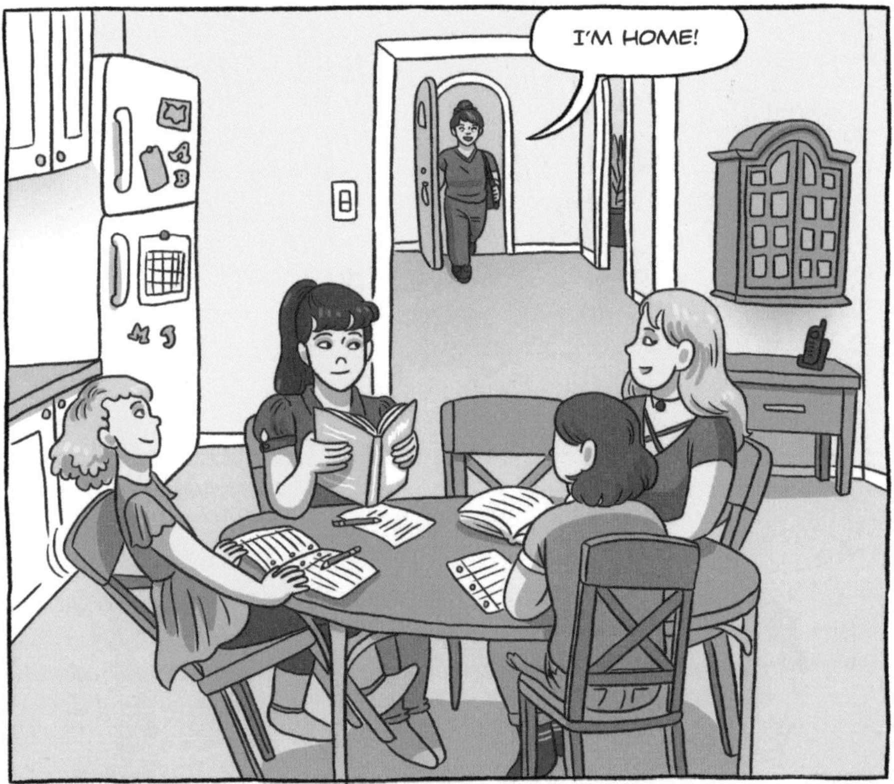
I'M HOME!

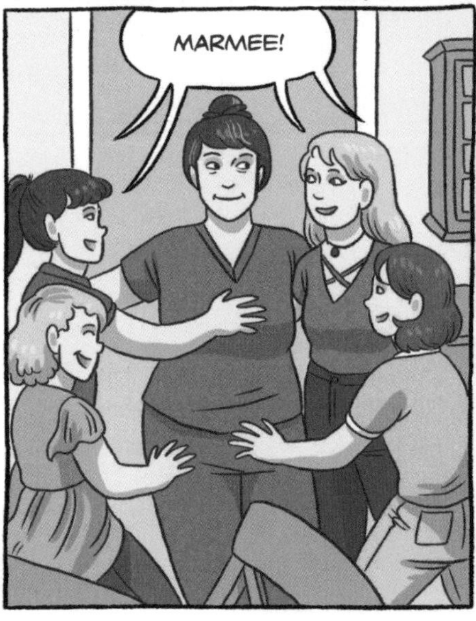
MARMEE!

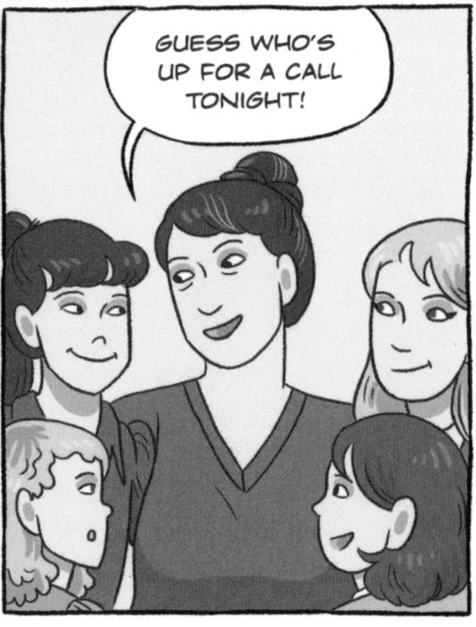
GUESS WHO'S UP FOR A CALL TONIGHT!

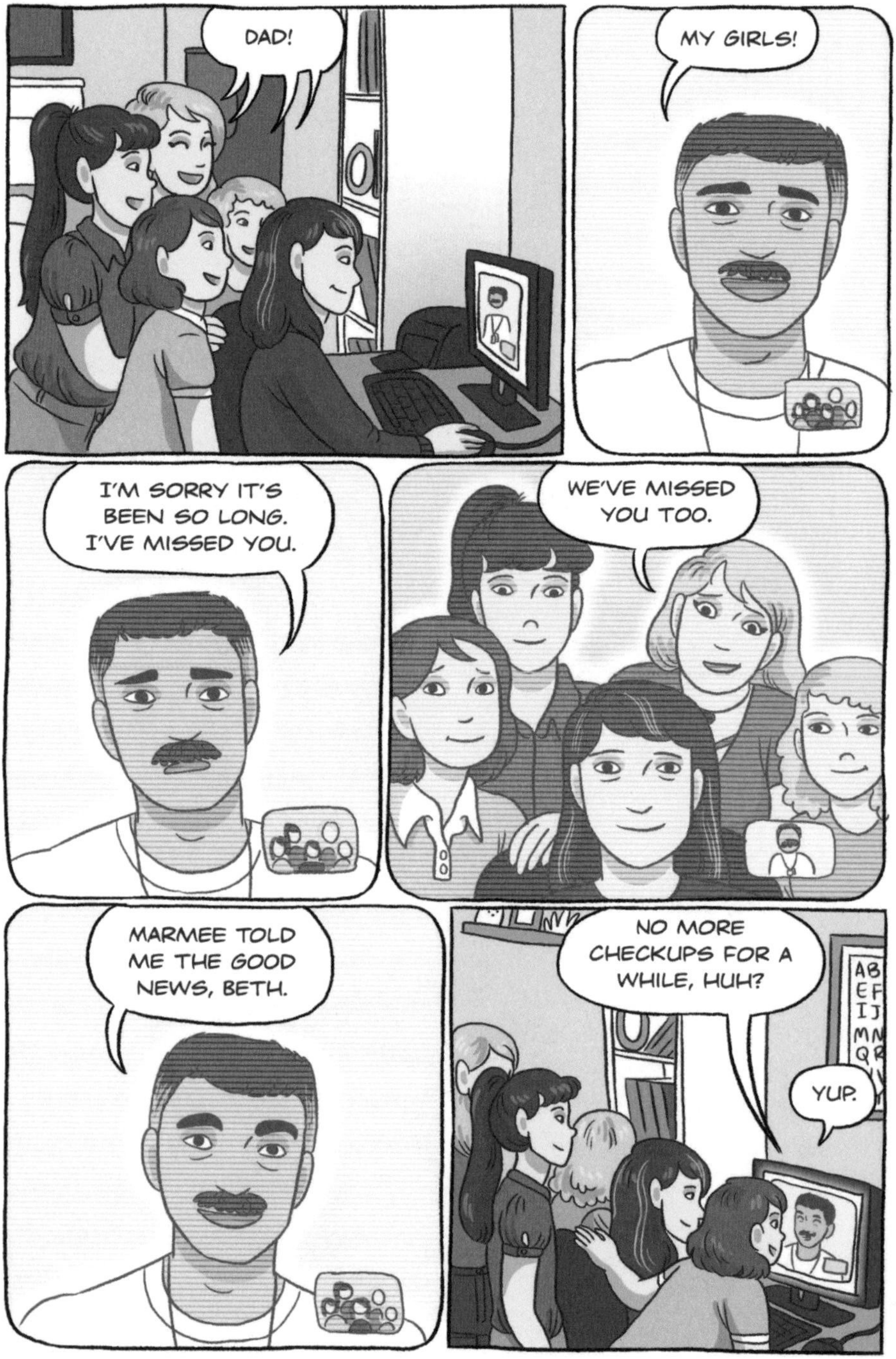
DAD!
MY GIRLS!
I'M SORRY IT'S BEEN SO LONG. I'VE MISSED YOU.
WE'VE MISSED YOU TOO.
MARMEE TOLD ME THE GOOD NEWS, BETH.
NO MORE CHECKUPS FOR A WHILE, HUH?
YUP.

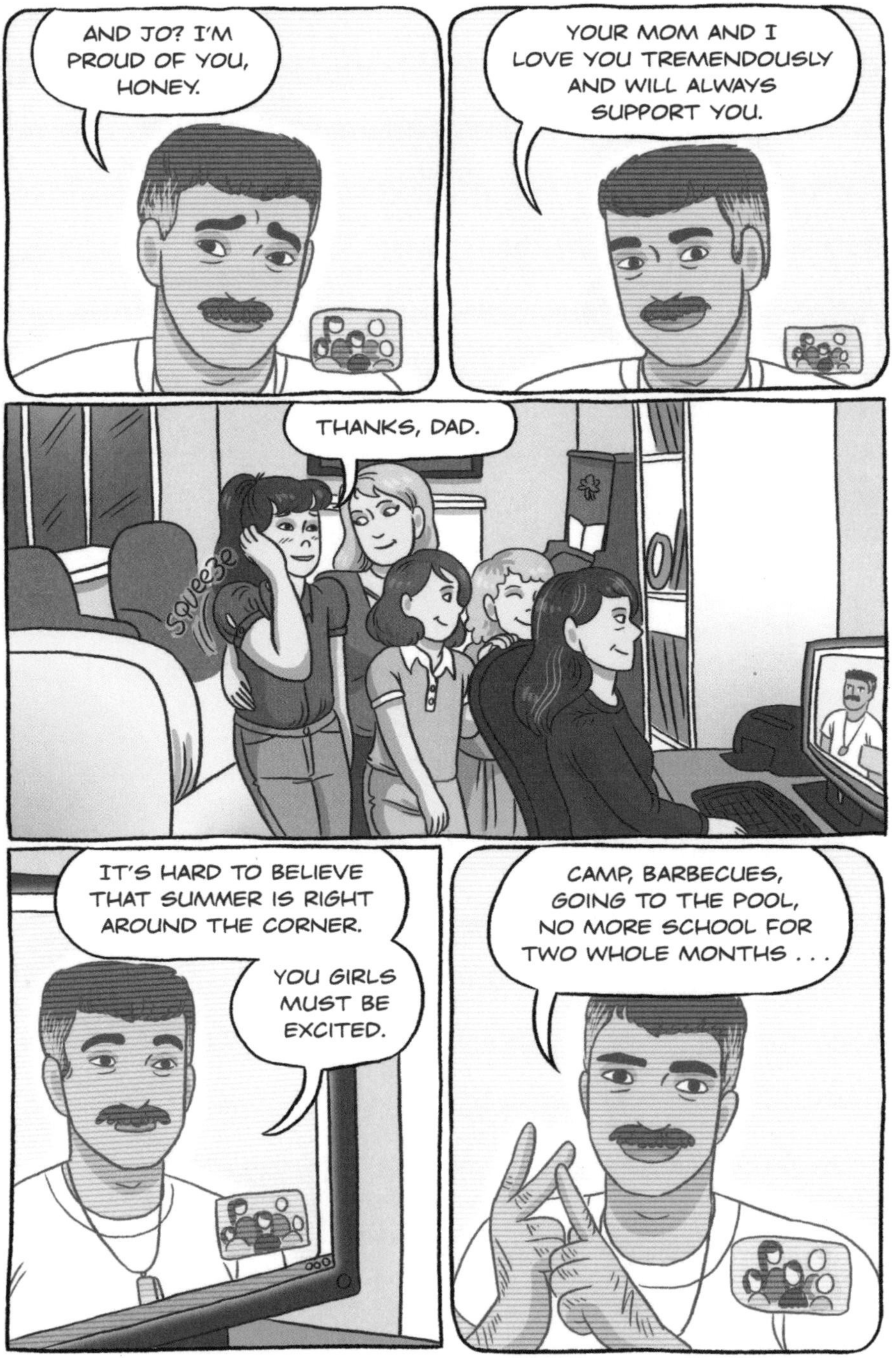
AND JO? I'M PROUD OF YOU, HONEY.
YOUR MOM AND I LOVE YOU TREMENDOUSLY AND WILL ALWAYS SUPPORT YOU.
THANKS, DAD.
squeeze
IT'S HARD TO BELIEVE THAT SUMMER IS RIGHT AROUND THE CORNER.
YOU GIRLS MUST BE EXCITED.
CAMP, BARBECUES, GOING TO THE POOL, NO MORE SCHOOL FOR TWO WHOLE MONTHS . . .

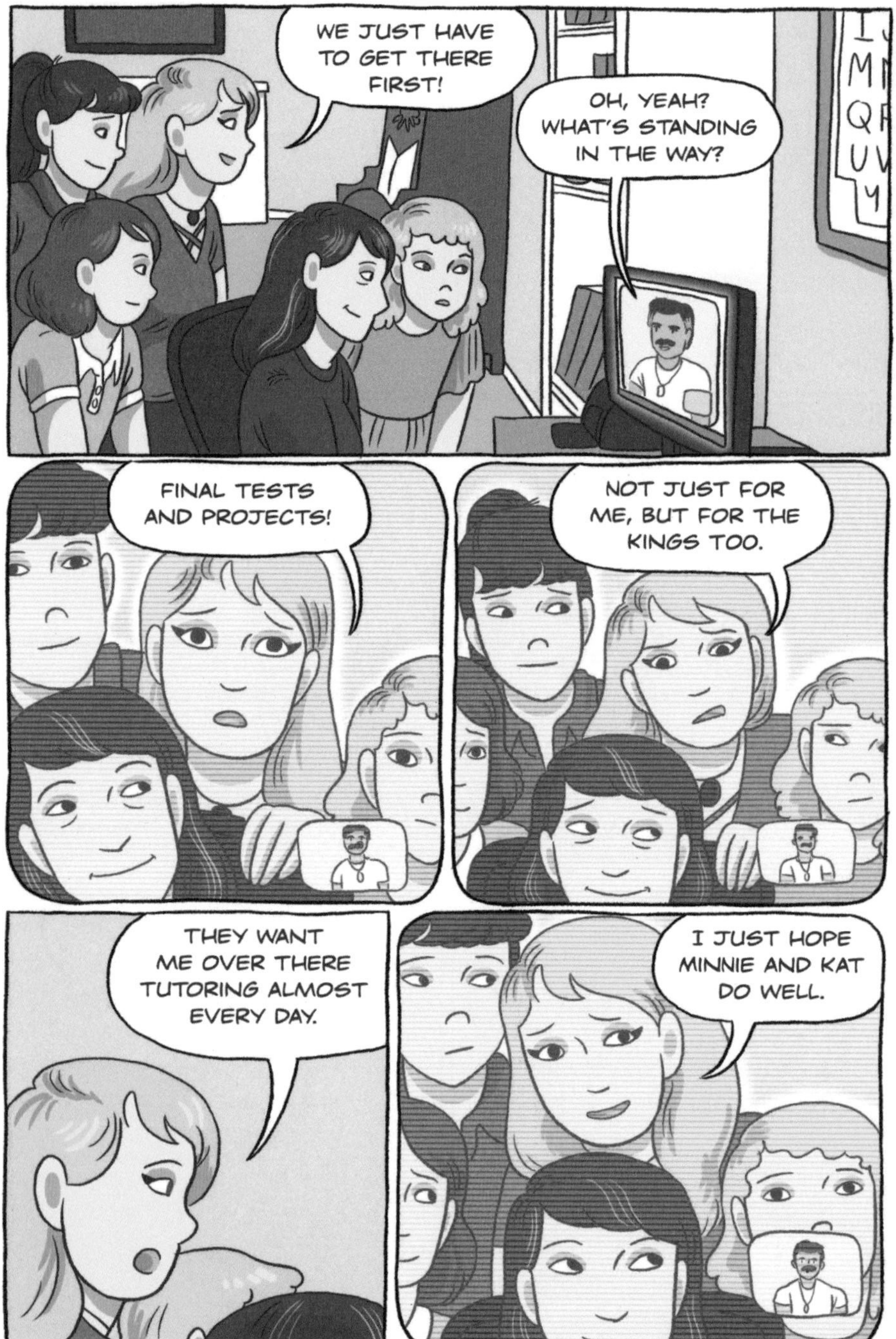
WE JUST HAVE TO GET THERE FIRST!
OH, YEAH? WHAT'S STANDING IN THE WAY?
FINAL TESTS AND PROJECTS!
NOT JUST FOR ME, BUT FOR THE KINGS TOO.
THEY WANT ME OVER THERE TUTORING ALMOST EVERY DAY.
I JUST HOPE MINNIE AND KAT DO WELL.

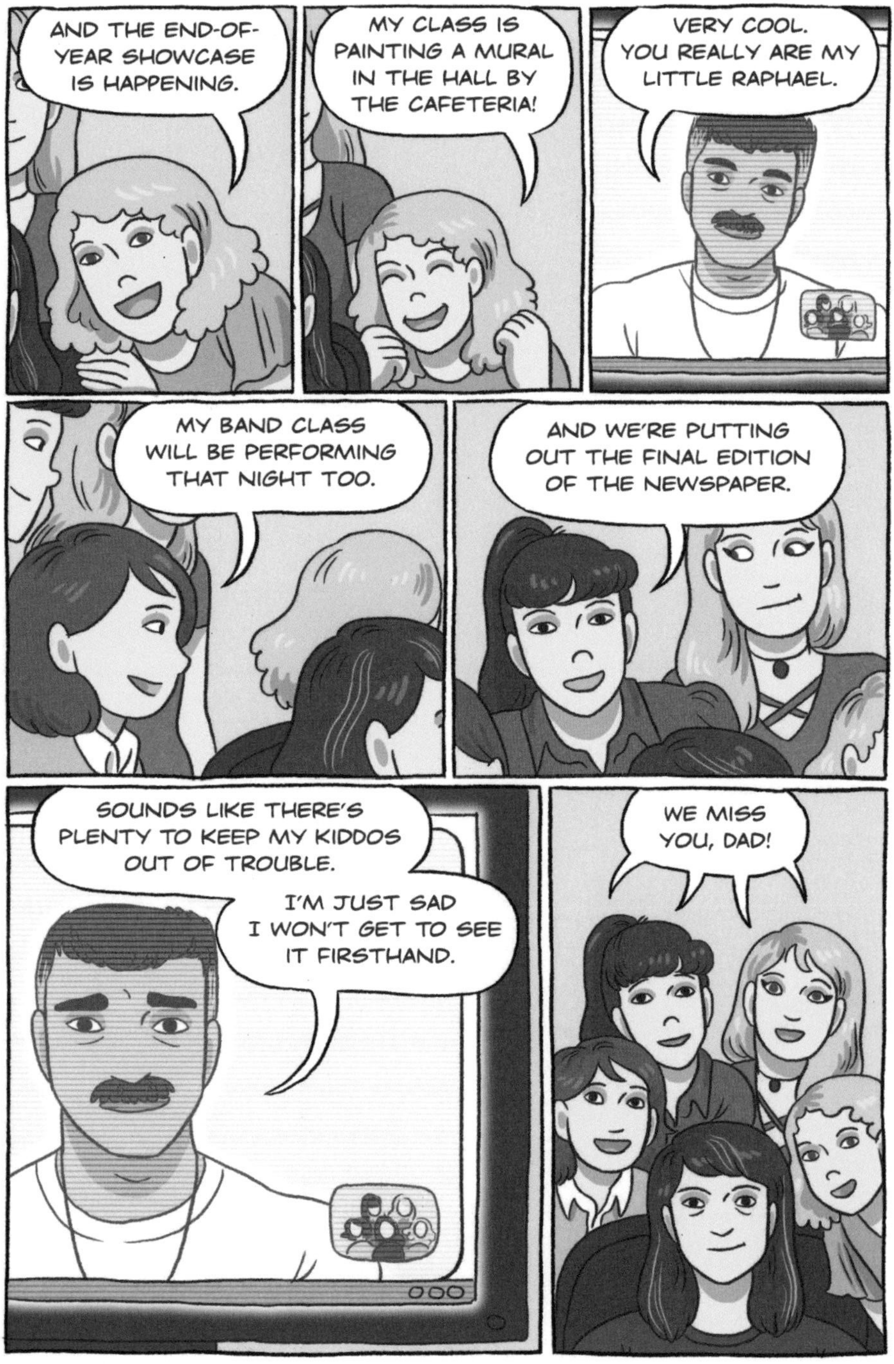
AND THE END-OF-YEAR SHOWCASE IS HAPPENING.
MY CLASS IS PAINTING A MURAL IN THE HALL BY THE CAFETERIA!
VERY COOL. YOU REALLY ARE MY LITTLE RAPHAEL.
MY BAND CLASS WILL BE PERFORMING THAT NIGHT TOO.
AND WE'RE PUTTING OUT THE FINAL EDITION OF THE NEWSPAPER.
SOUNDS LIKE THERE'S PLENTY TO KEEP MY KIDDOS OUT OF TROUBLE.
I'M JUST SAD I WON'T GET TO SEE IT FIRSTHAND.
WE MISS YOU, DAD!

CHAPTER 9

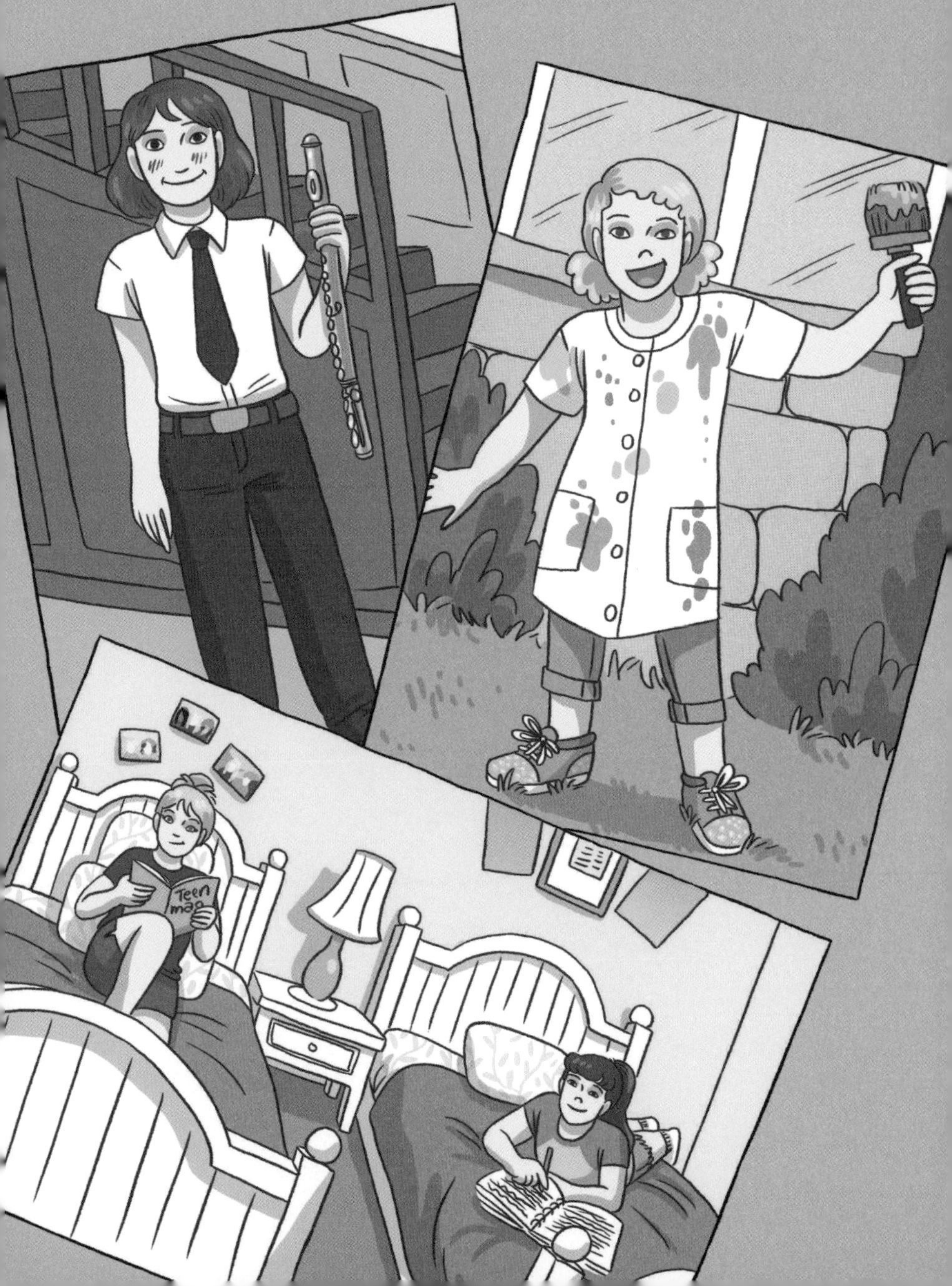
Teen mag

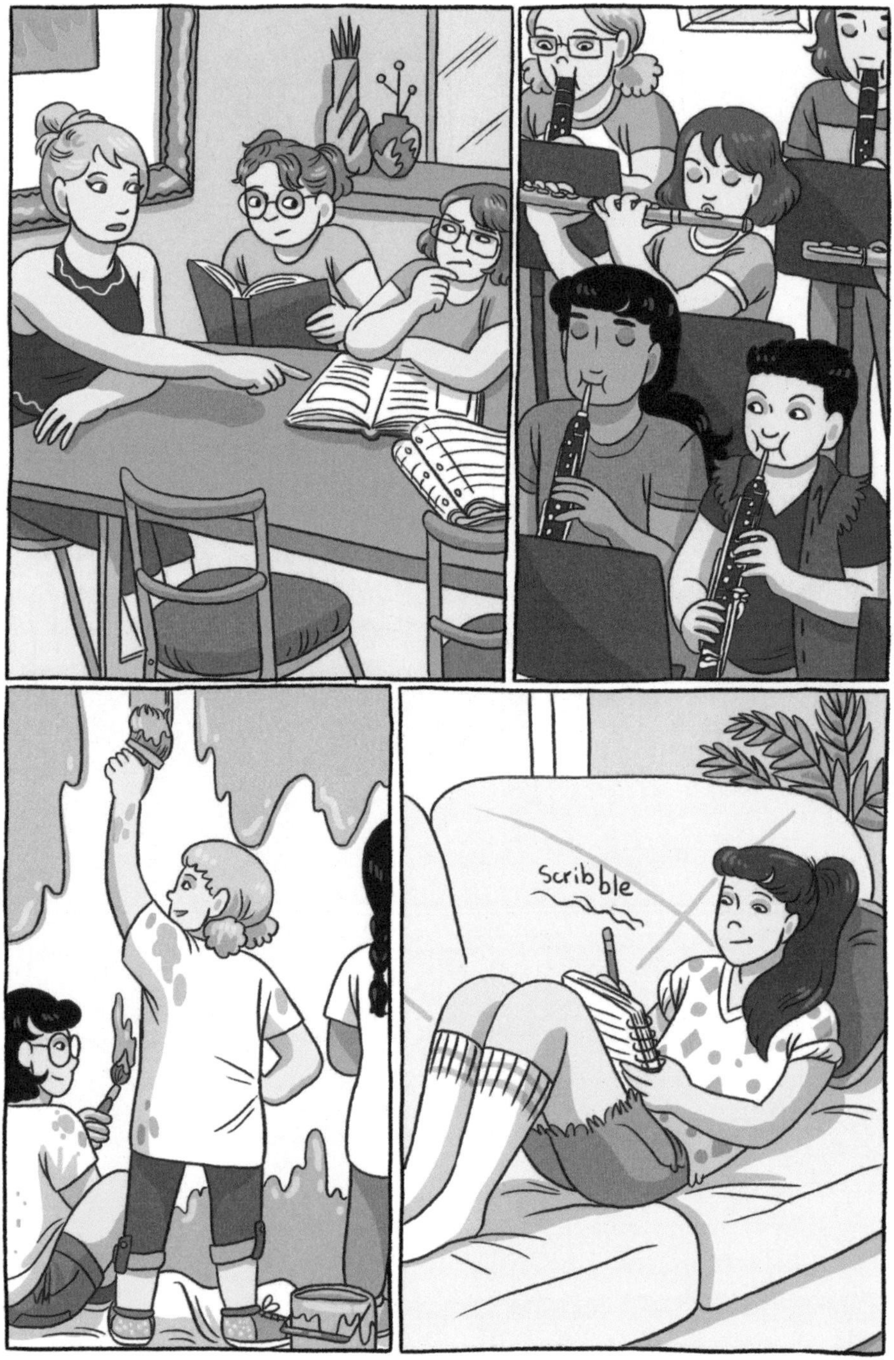
scribble

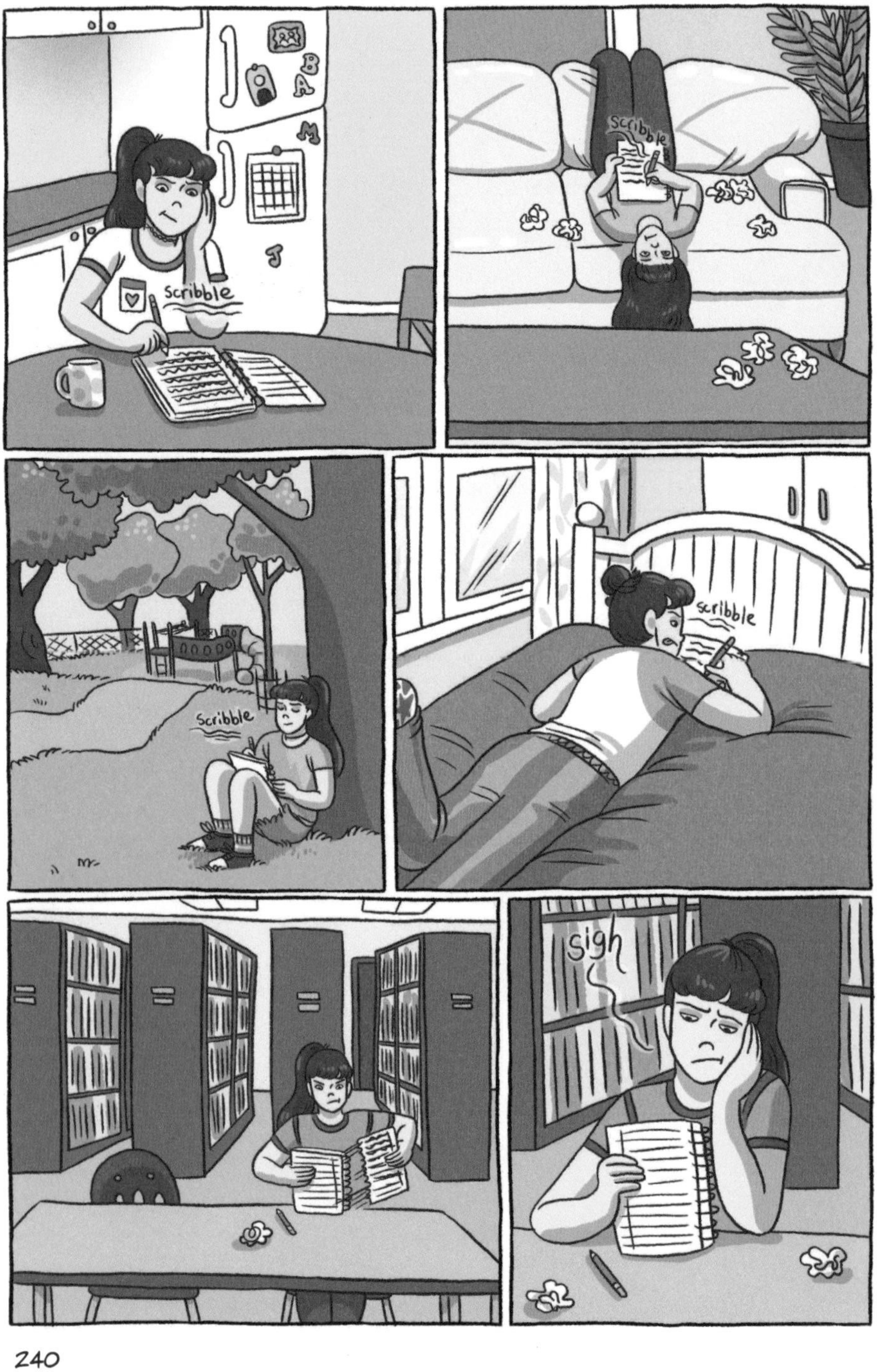
scribble
scribble
scribble
scribble
sigh

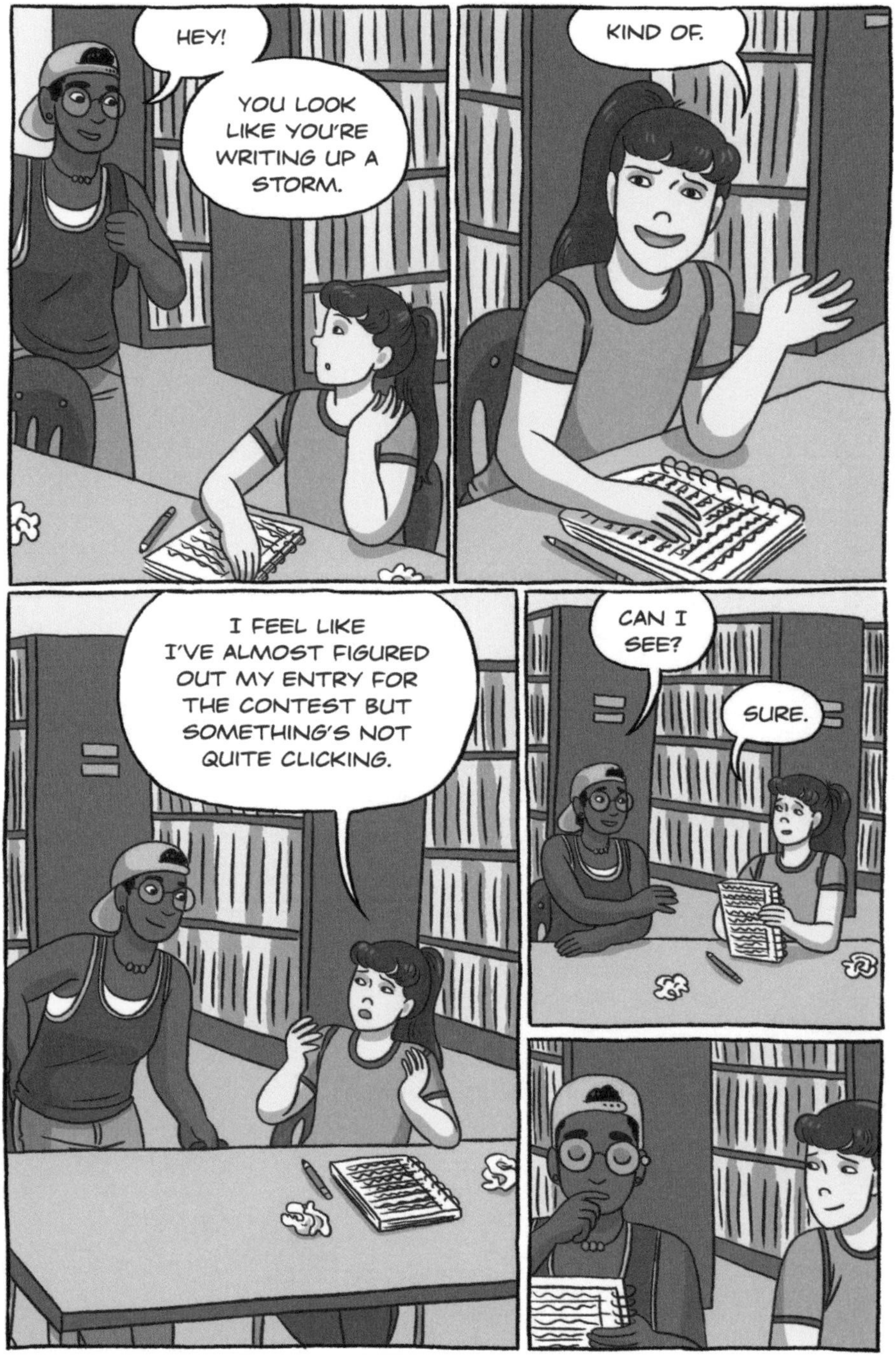
HEY!
YOU LOOK LIKE YOU'RE WRITING UP A STORM.
KIND OF.
I FEEL LIKE I'VE ALMOST FIGURED OUT MY ENTRY FOR THE CONTEST BUT SOMETHING'S NOT QUITE CLICKING.
CAN I SEE?
SURE.

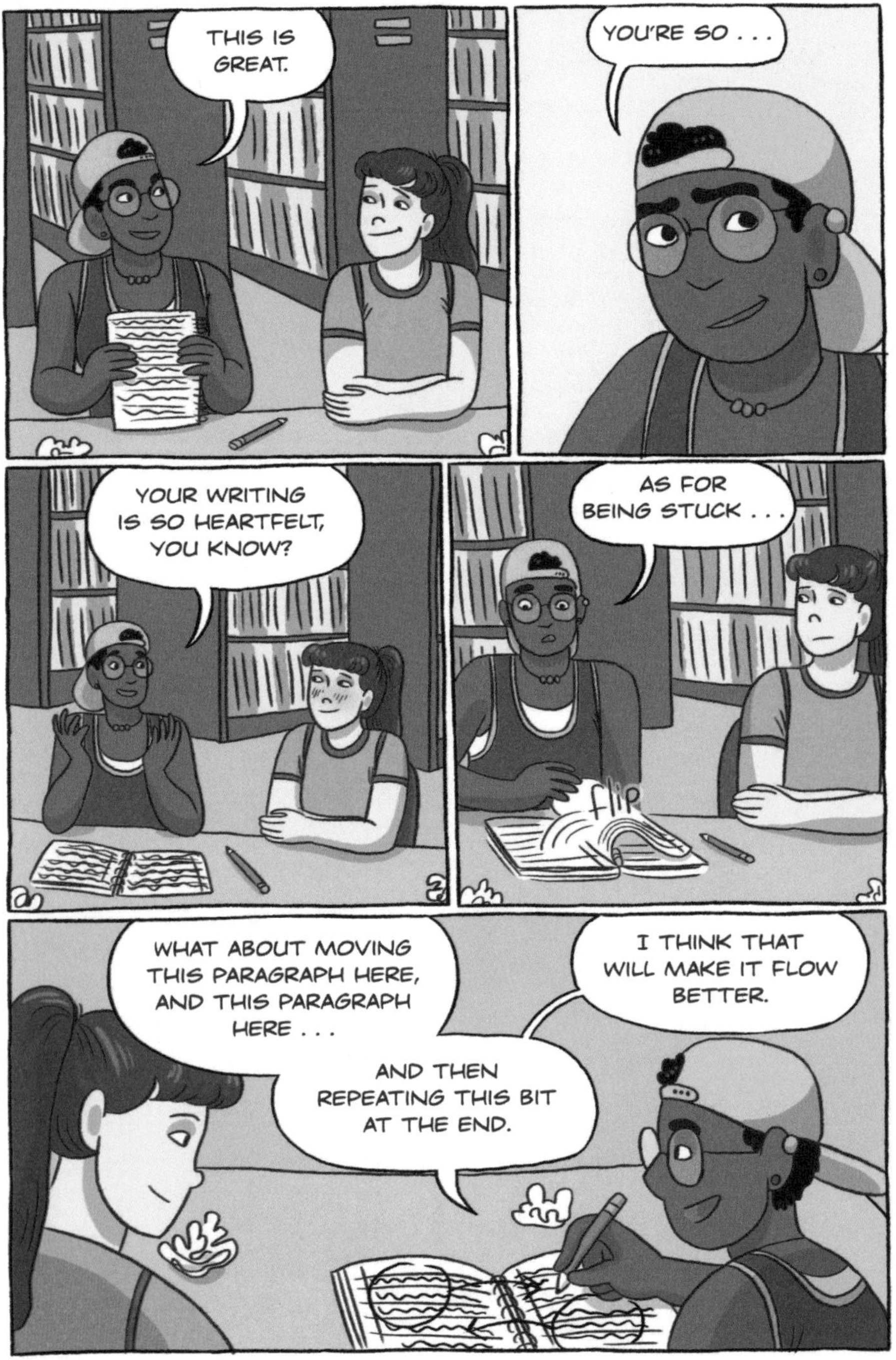
THIS IS GREAT.
YOU'RE SO . . .
YOUR WRITING IS SO HEARTFELT, YOU KNOW?
AS FOR BEING STUCK . . .
flip
WHAT ABOUT MOVING THIS PARAGRAPH HERE, AND THIS PARAGRAPH HERE . . .
AND THEN REPEATING THIS BIT AT THE END.
I THINK THAT WILL MAKE IT FLOW BETTER.

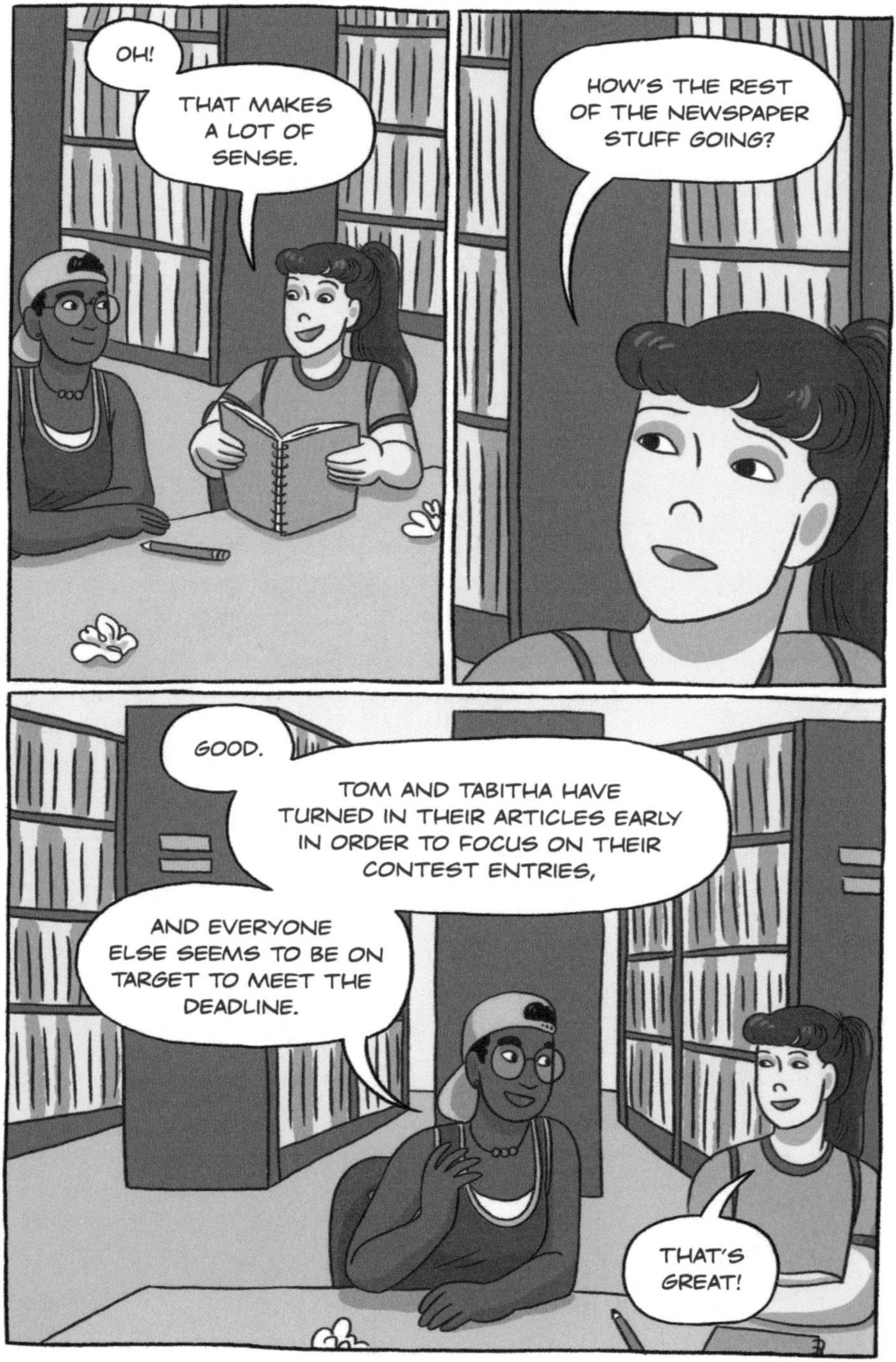
OH!
THAT MAKES A LOT OF SENSE.
HOW'S THE REST OF THE NEWSPAPER STUFF GOING?
GOOD.
TOM AND TABITHA HAVE TURNED IN THEIR ARTICLES EARLY IN ORDER TO FOCUS ON THEIR CONTEST ENTRIES,
AND EVERYONE ELSE SEEMS TO BE ON TARGET TO MEET THE DEADLINE.
THAT'S GREAT!

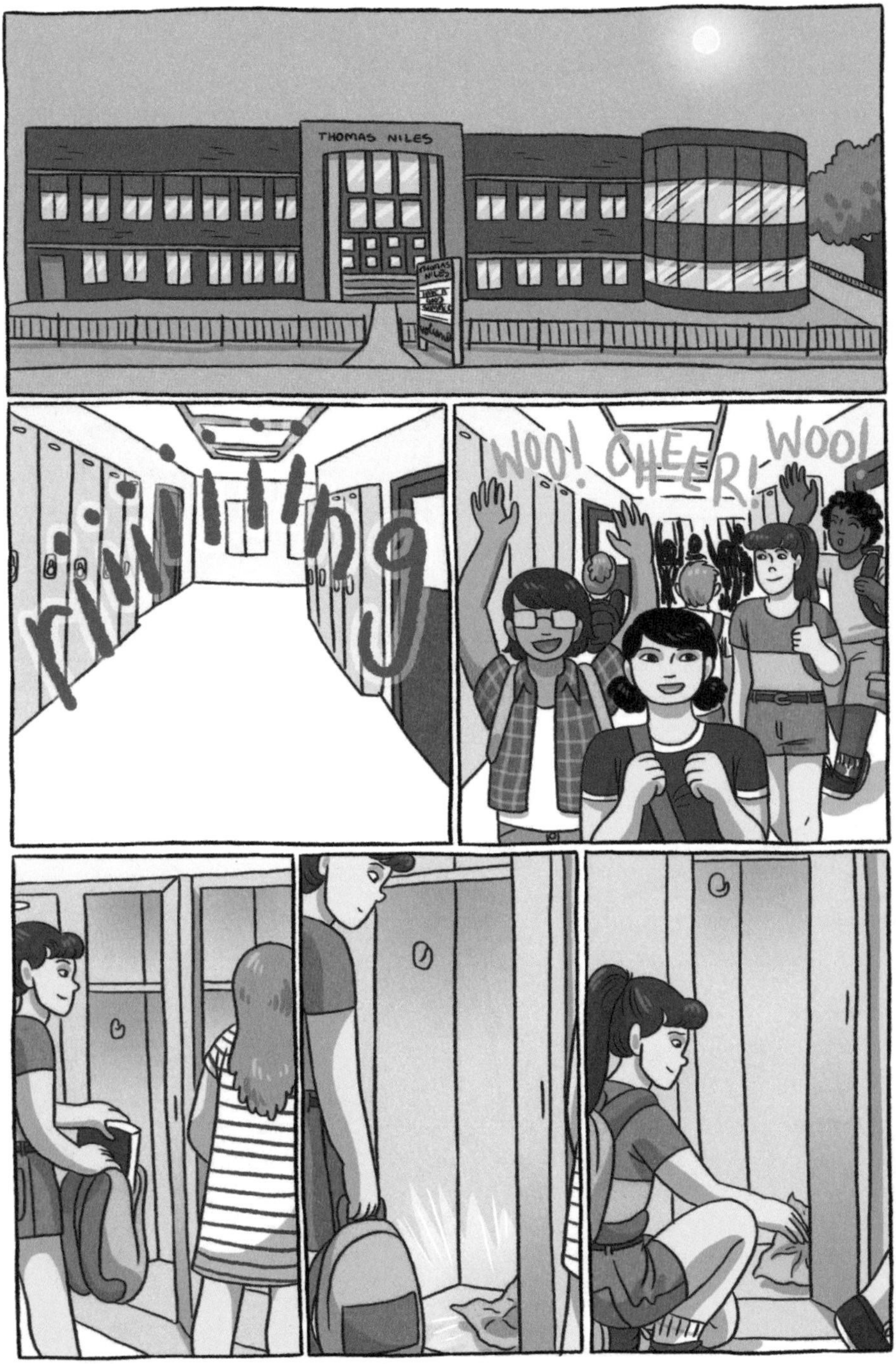
THOMAS NILES
riiiiiing
WOO! CHEER! WOO!

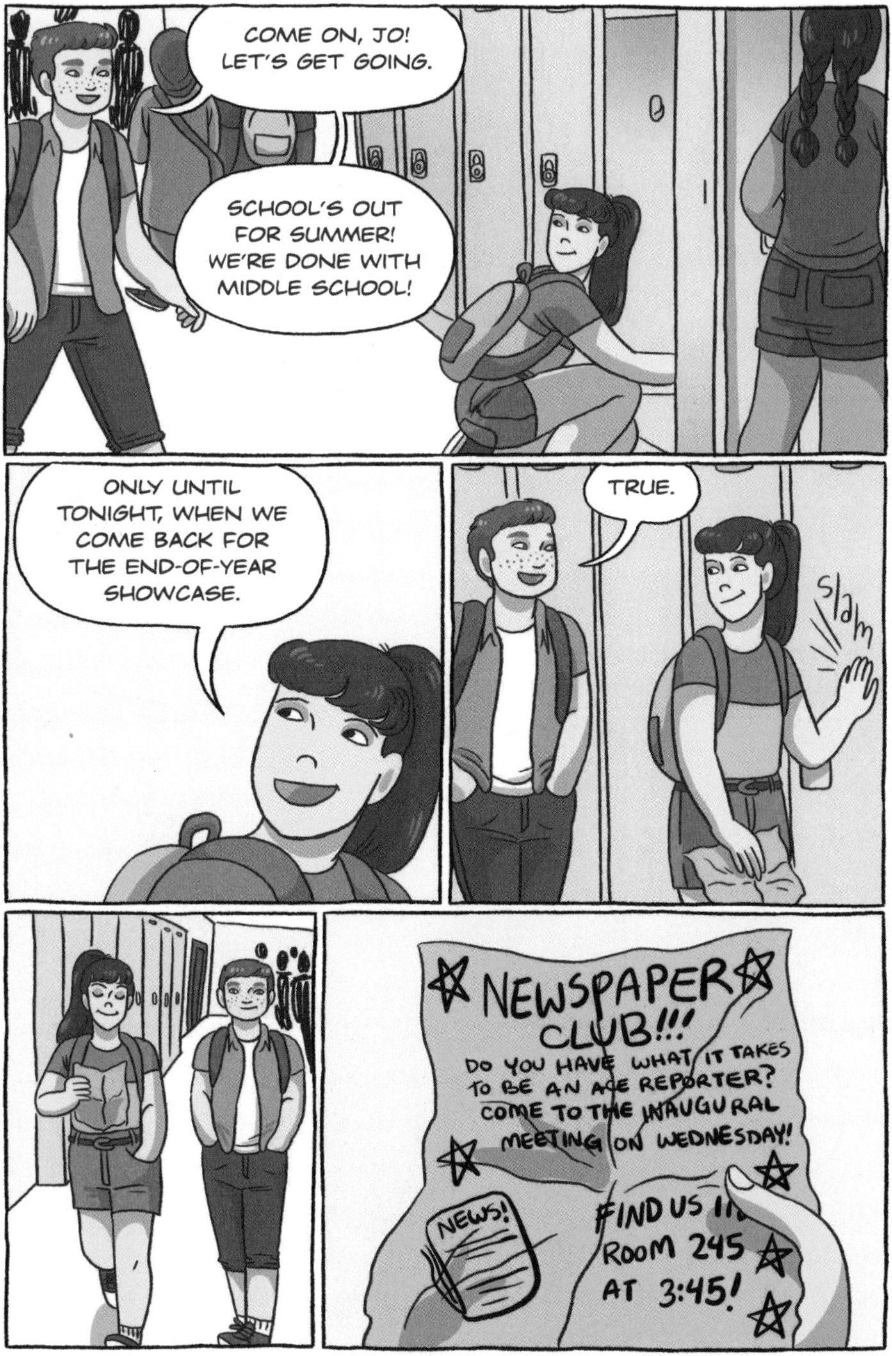
COME ON, JO! LET'S GET GOING.
SCHOOL'S OUT FOR SUMMER! WE'RE DONE WITH MIDDLE SCHOOL!
ONLY UNTIL TONIGHT, WHEN WE COME BACK FOR THE END-OF-YEAR SHOWCASE.
TRUE.
slam
NEWSPAPER CLUB!!!
DO YOU HAVE WHAT IT TAKES TO BE AN ACE REPORTER?
COME TO THE INAUGURAL MEETING ON WEDNESDAY!
NEWS!
ROOM 245
AT 3:45!

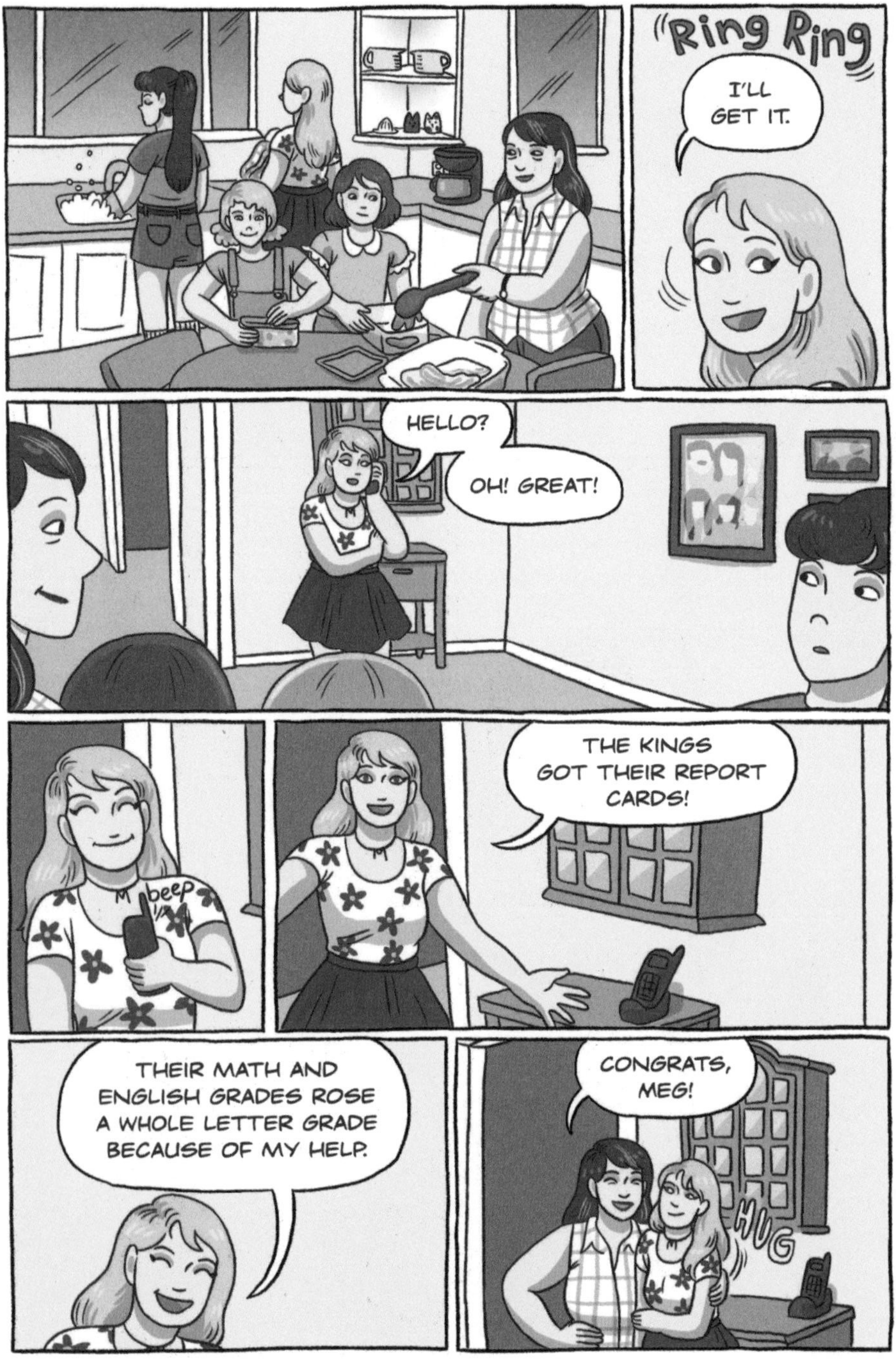
Ring Ring
I'LL GET IT.
HELLO?
OH! GREAT!
beep
THE KINGS GOT THEIR REPORT CARDS!
THEIR MATH AND ENGLISH GRADES ROSE A WHOLE LETTER GRADE BECAUSE OF MY HELP.
CONGRATS, MEG!
HUG

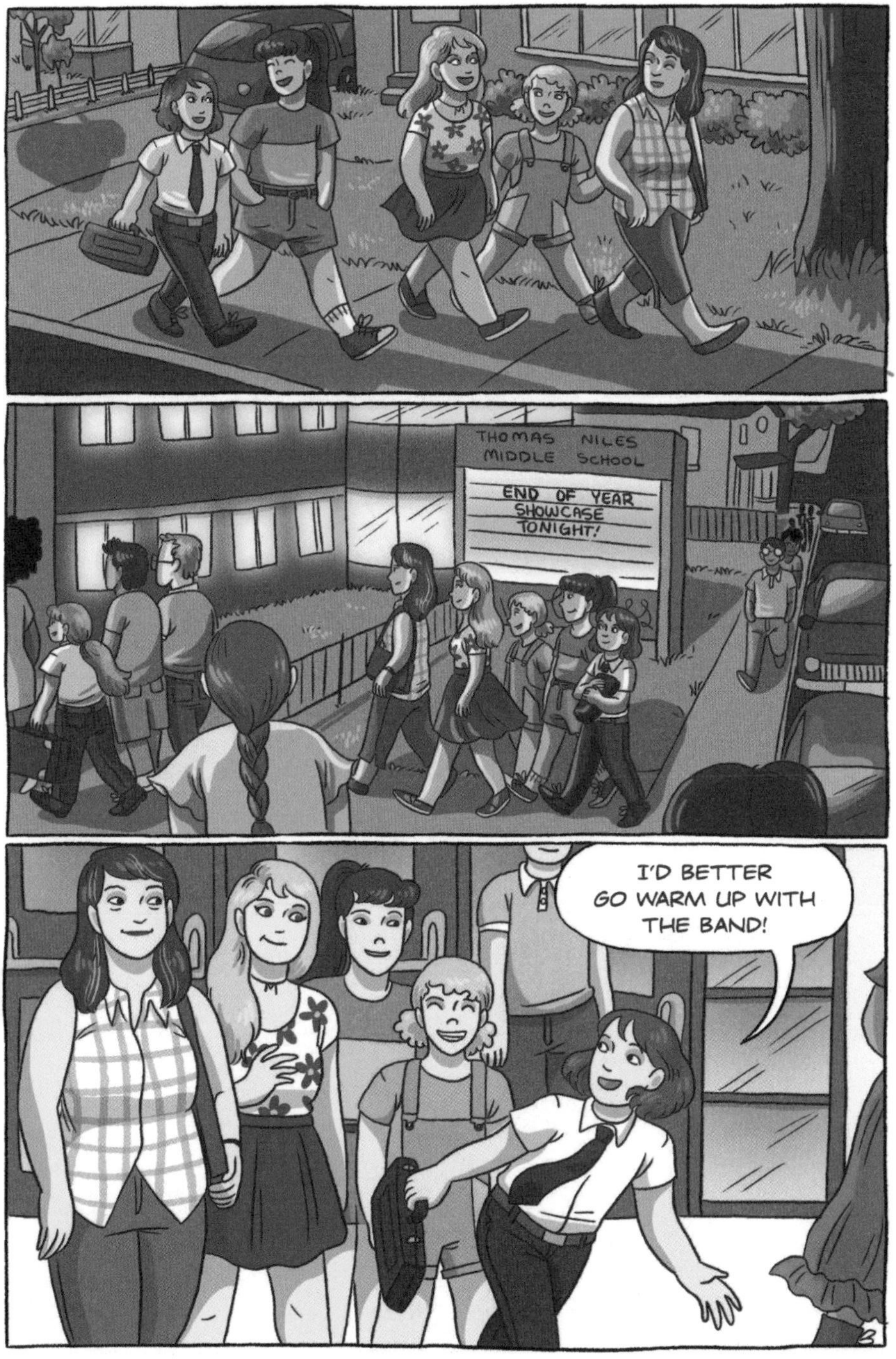
THOMAS NILES MIDDLE SCHOOL
END OF YEAR SHOWCASE TONIGHT!
I'D BETTER GO WARM UP WITH THE BAND!

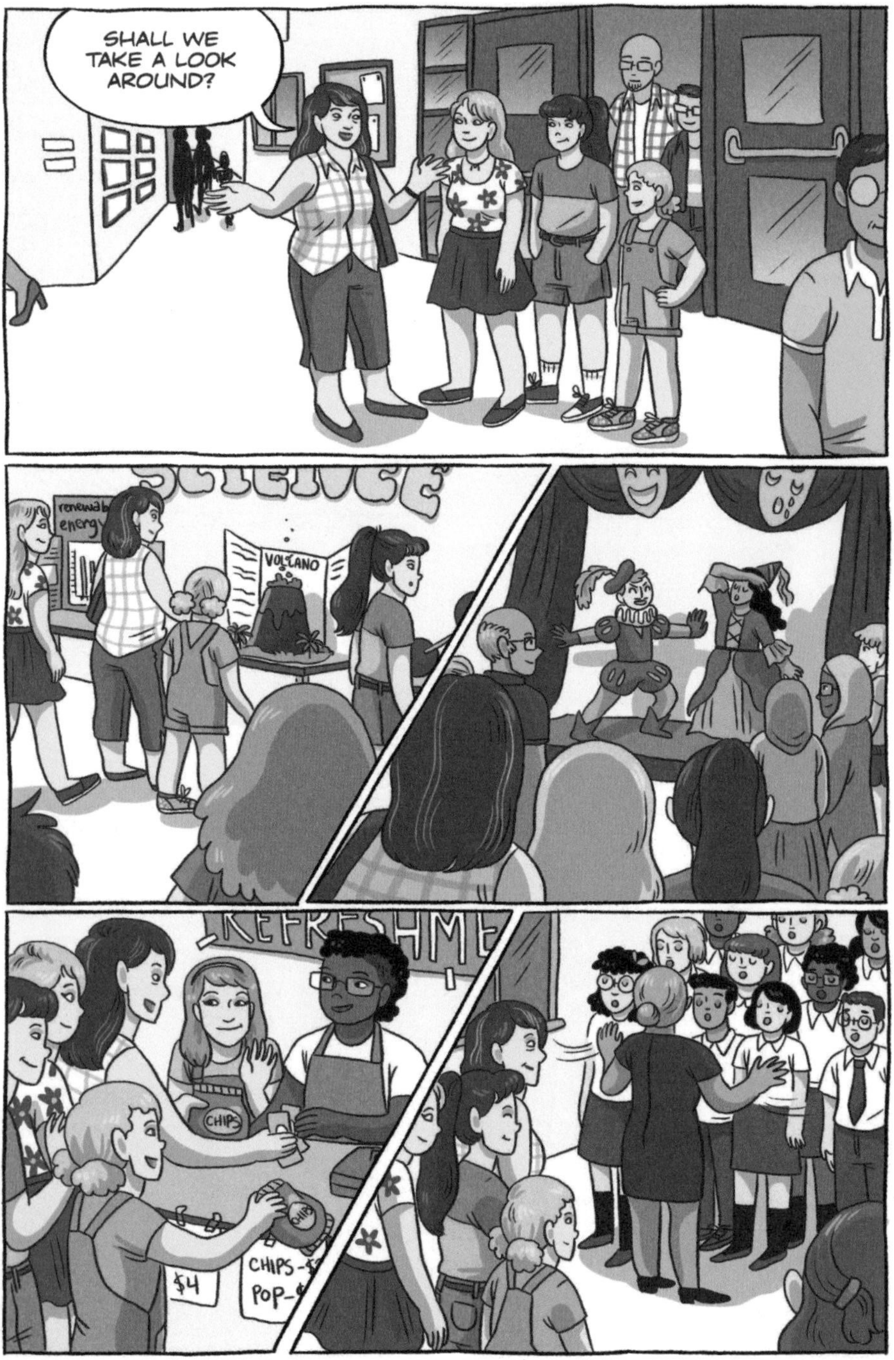

SHALL WE TAKE A LOOK AROUND?
SCIENCE
VOLCANO
REFRESHME
CHIPS
$4

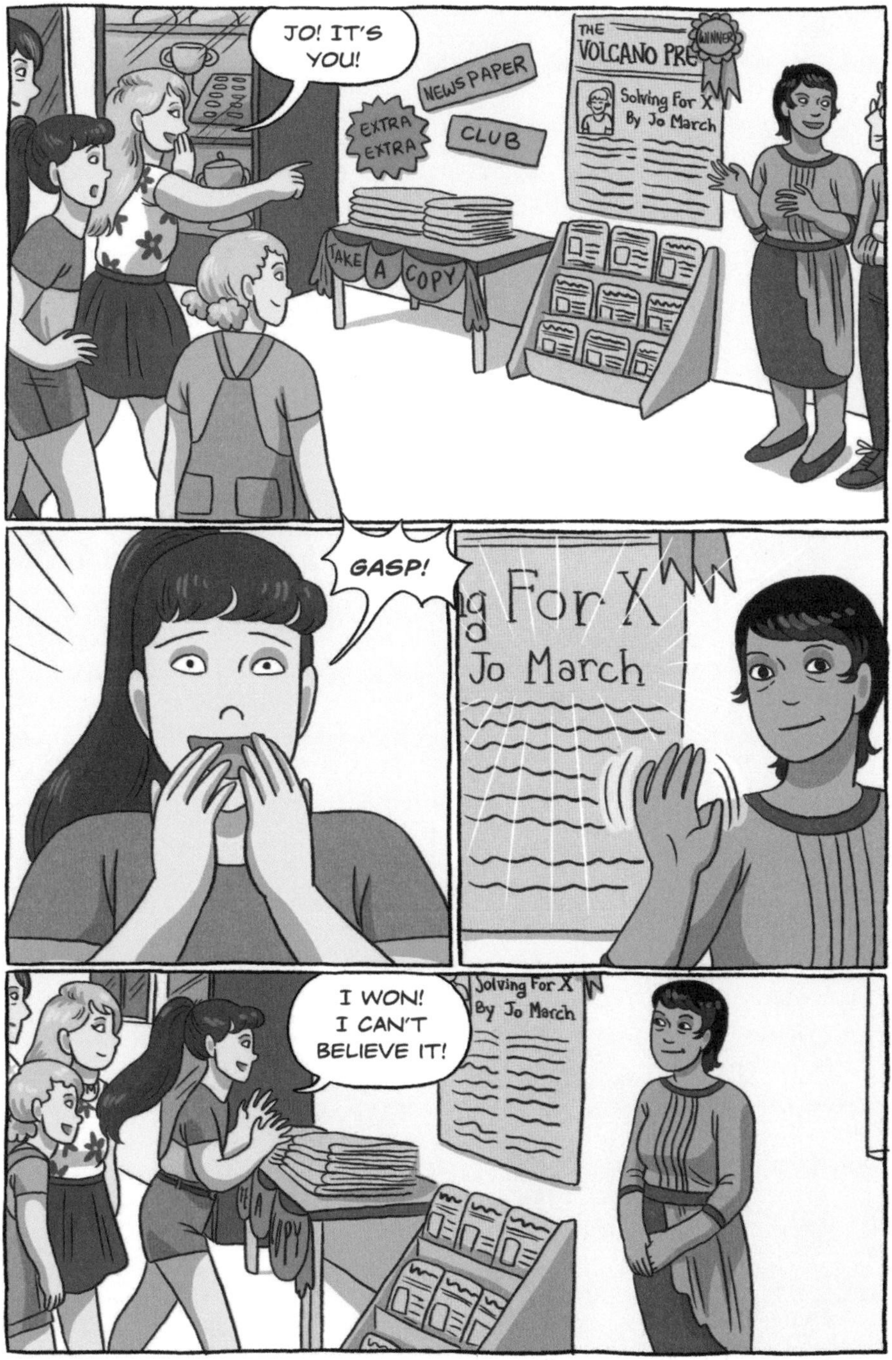
JO! IT'S YOU!
NEWSPAPER
EXTRA EXTRA
CLUB
THE VOLCANO PRE
WINNER
Solving For X
By Jo March
TAKE A COPY
GASP!
g For X
Jo March
I WON! I CAN'T BELIEVE IT!
Solving For X
By Jo March

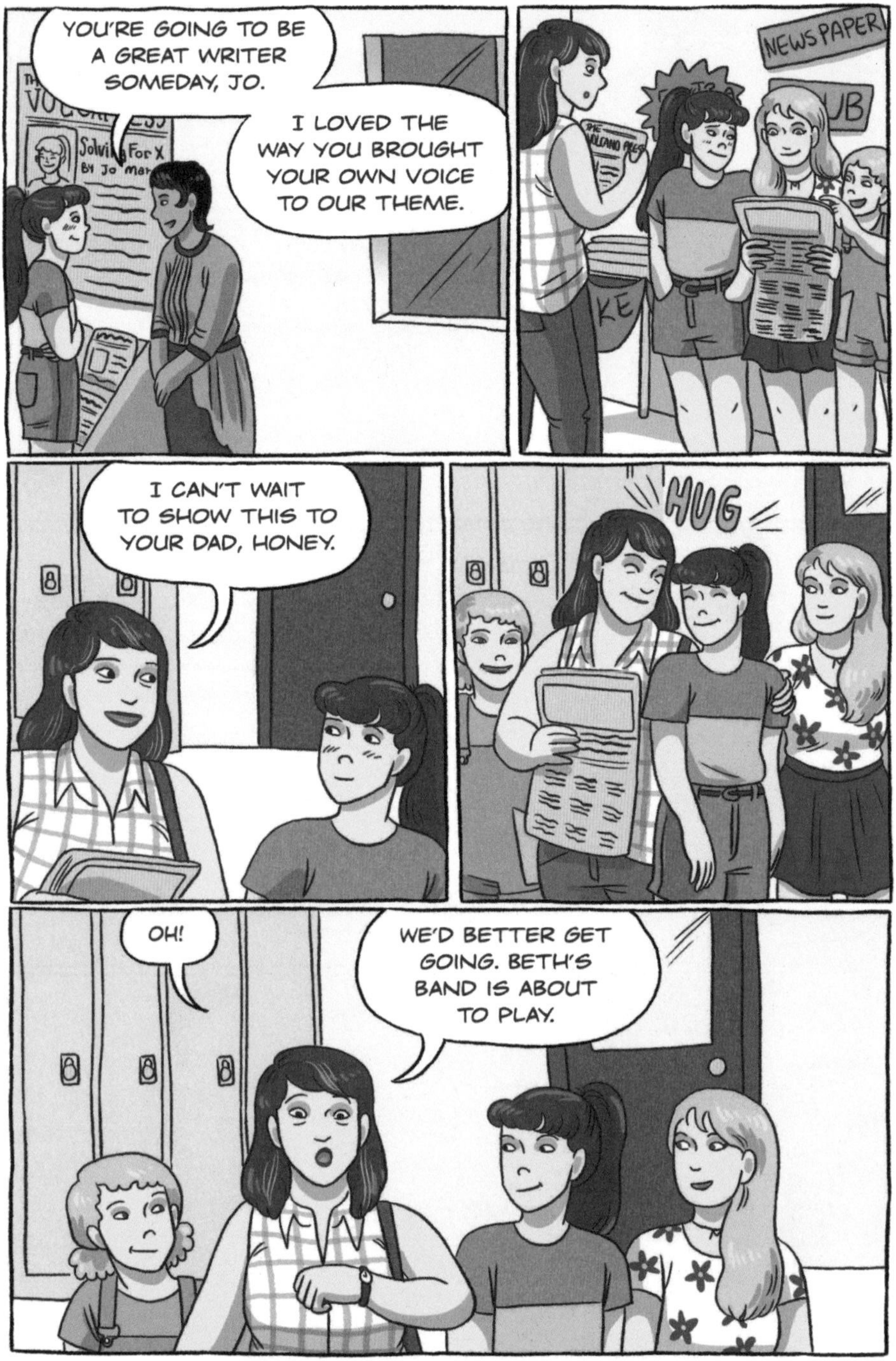
THE VOLCANO PRESS
Solving For X
BY Jo Mar
YOU'RE GOING TO BE A GREAT WRITER SOMEDAY, JO.
I LOVED THE WAY YOU BROUGHT YOUR OWN VOICE TO OUR THEME.
NEWSPAPER
CLUB
I CAN'T WAIT TO SHOW THIS TO YOUR DAD, HONEY.
HUG
OH!
WE'D BETTER GET GOING. BETH'S BAND IS ABOUT TO PLAY.

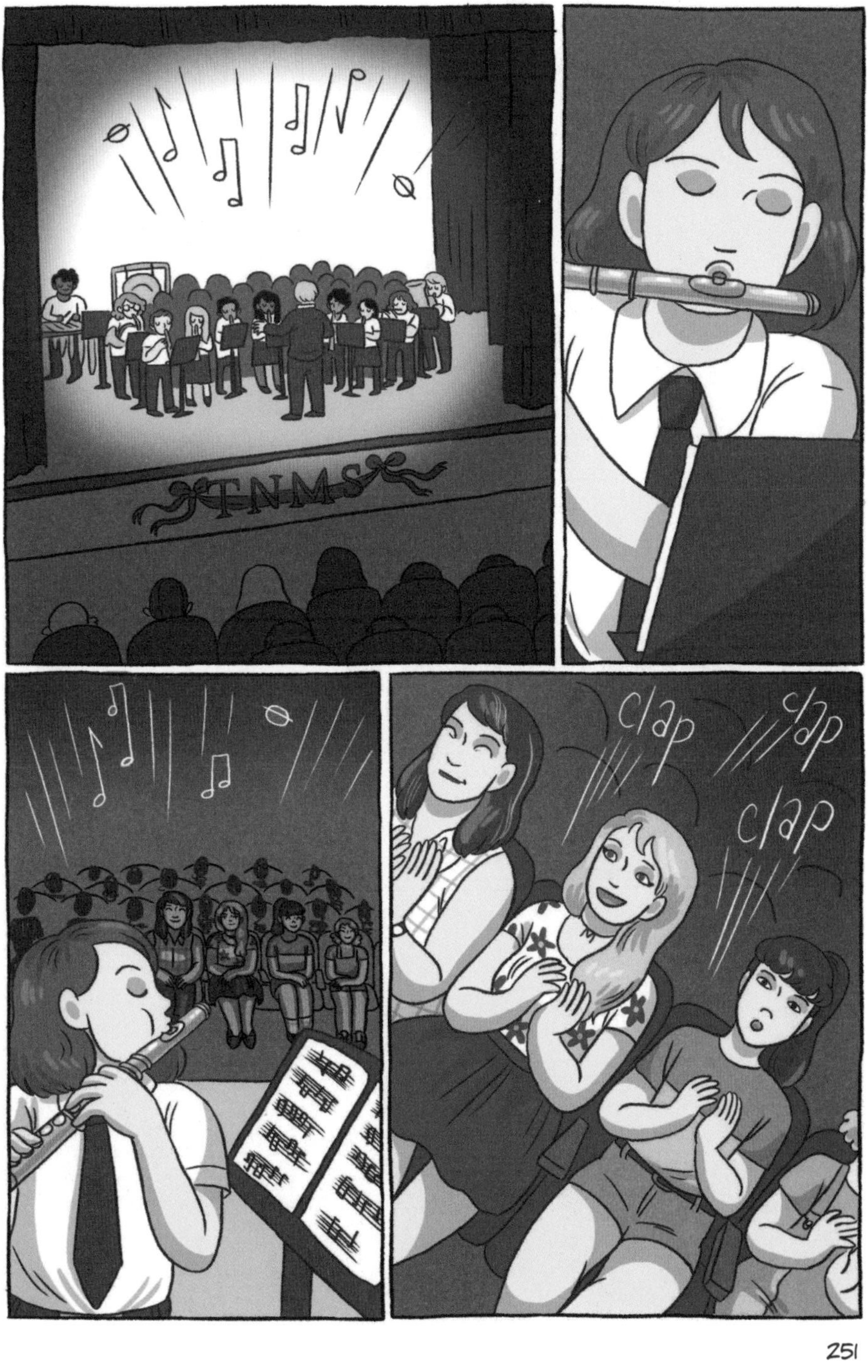
TNMS
clap
clap
clap

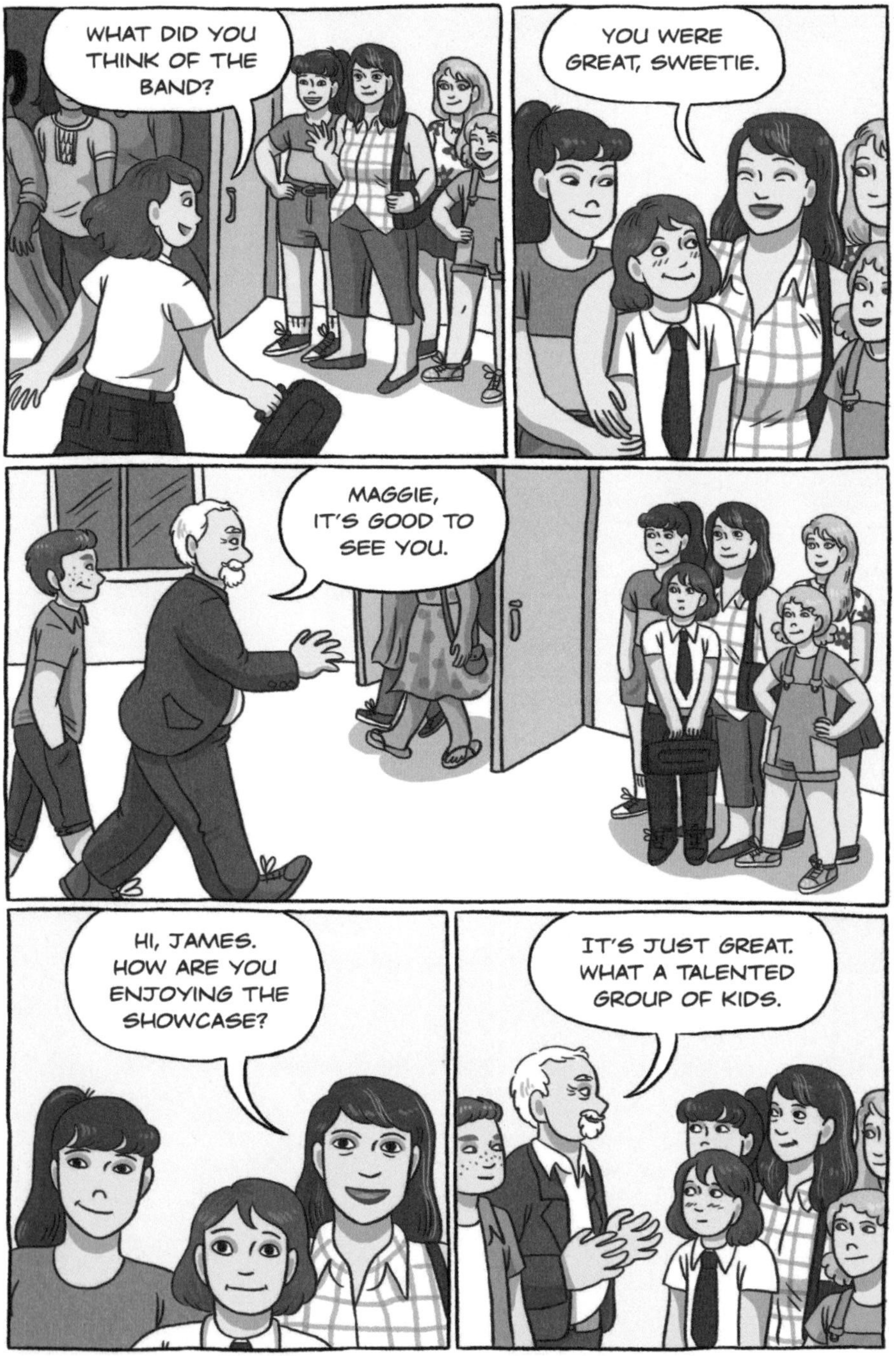

WHAT DID YOU THINK OF THE BAND?
YOU WERE GREAT, SWEETIE.
MAGGIE, IT'S GOOD TO SEE YOU.
HI, JAMES. HOW ARE YOU ENJOYING THE SHOWCASE?
IT'S JUST GREAT. WHAT A TALENTED GROUP OF KIDS.

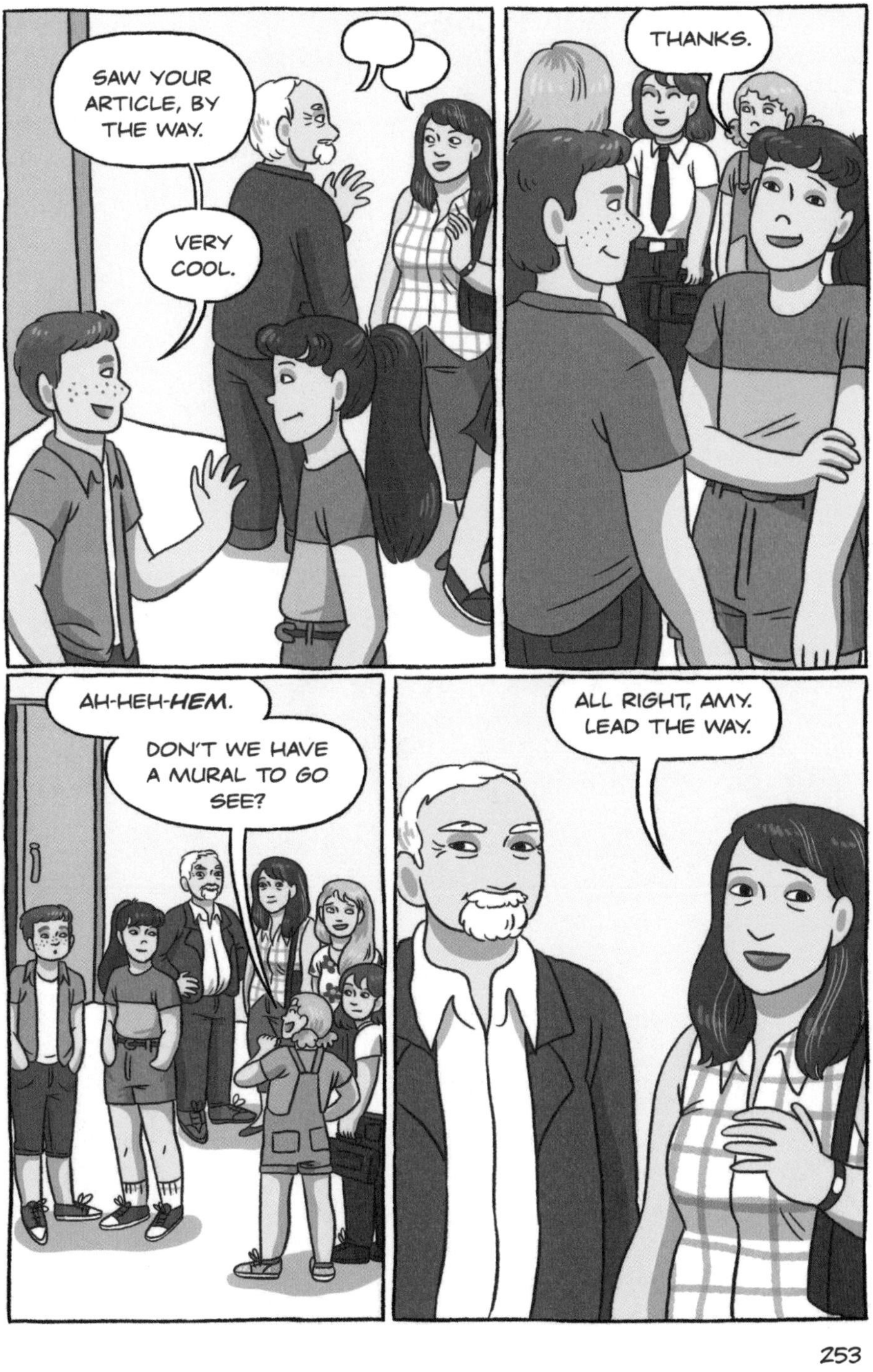
SAW YOUR ARTICLE, BY THE WAY.
VERY COOL.
THANKS.
AH-HEH-**HEM**.
DON'T WE HAVE A MURAL TO GO SEE?
ALL RIGHT, AMY. LEAD THE WAY.

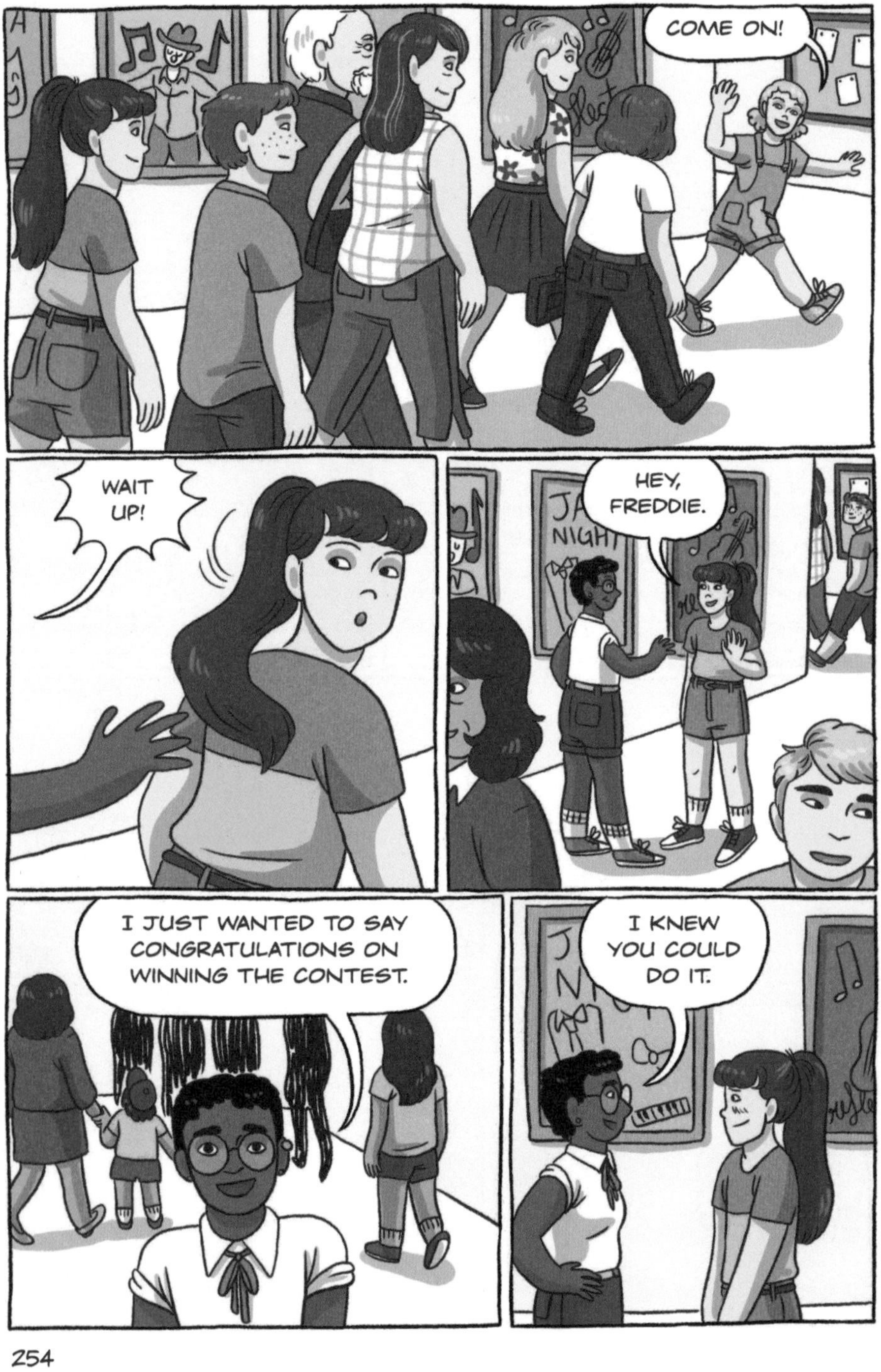
COME ON!
WAIT UP!
HEY, FREDDIE.
I JUST WANTED TO SAY CONGRATULATIONS ON WINNING THE CONTEST.
I KNEW YOU COULD DO IT.

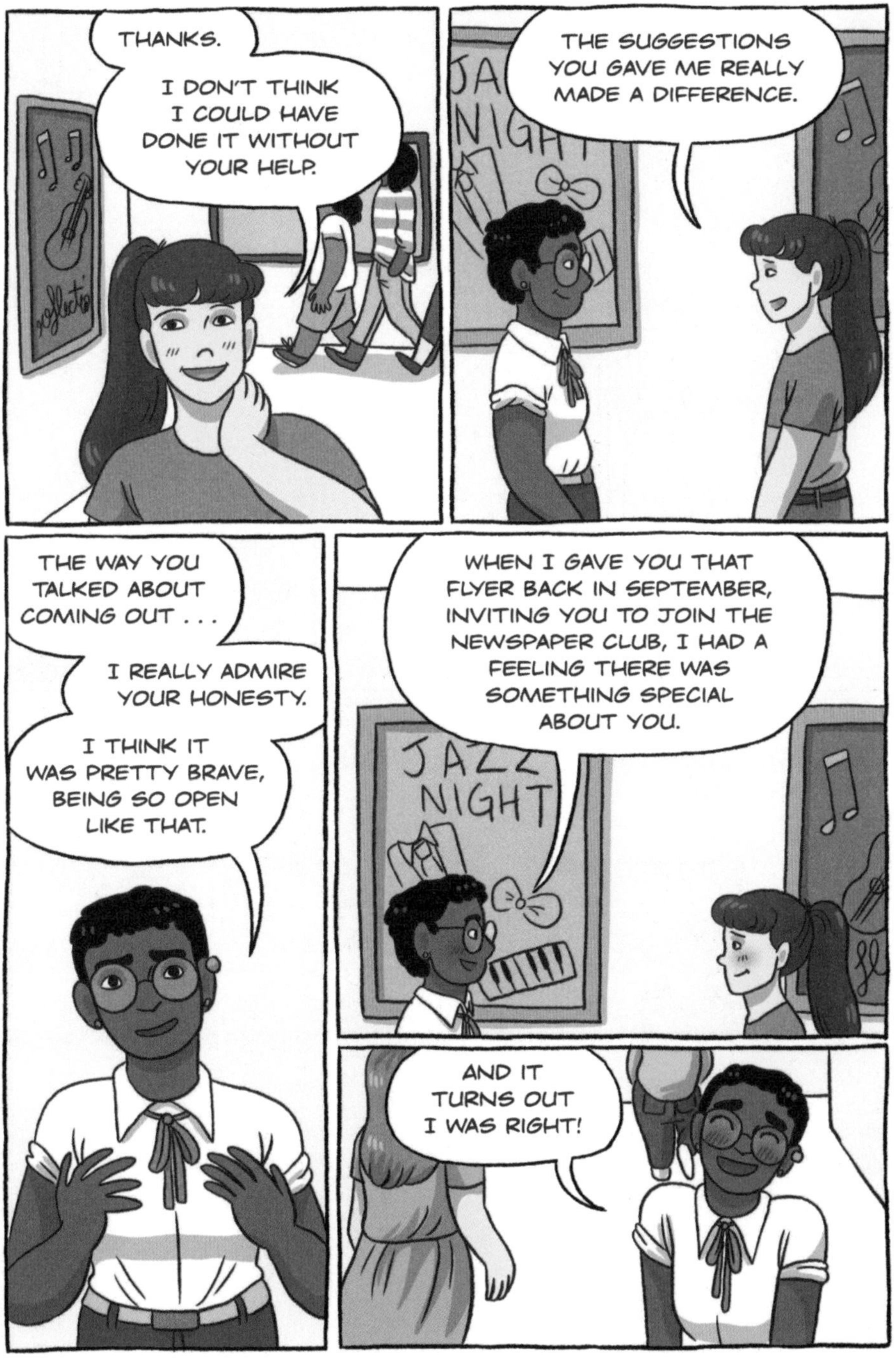
THANKS.
I DON'T THINK I COULD HAVE DONE IT WITHOUT YOUR HELP.
THE SUGGESTIONS YOU GAVE ME REALLY MADE A DIFFERENCE.
THE WAY YOU TALKED ABOUT COMING OUT . . .
I REALLY ADMIRE YOUR HONESTY.
I THINK IT WAS PRETTY BRAVE, BEING SO OPEN LIKE THAT.
JAZZ NIGHT
WHEN I GAVE YOU THAT FLYER BACK IN SEPTEMBER, INVITING YOU TO JOIN THE NEWSPAPER CLUB, I HAD A FEELING THERE WAS SOMETHING SPECIAL ABOUT YOU.
AND IT TURNS OUT I WAS RIGHT!

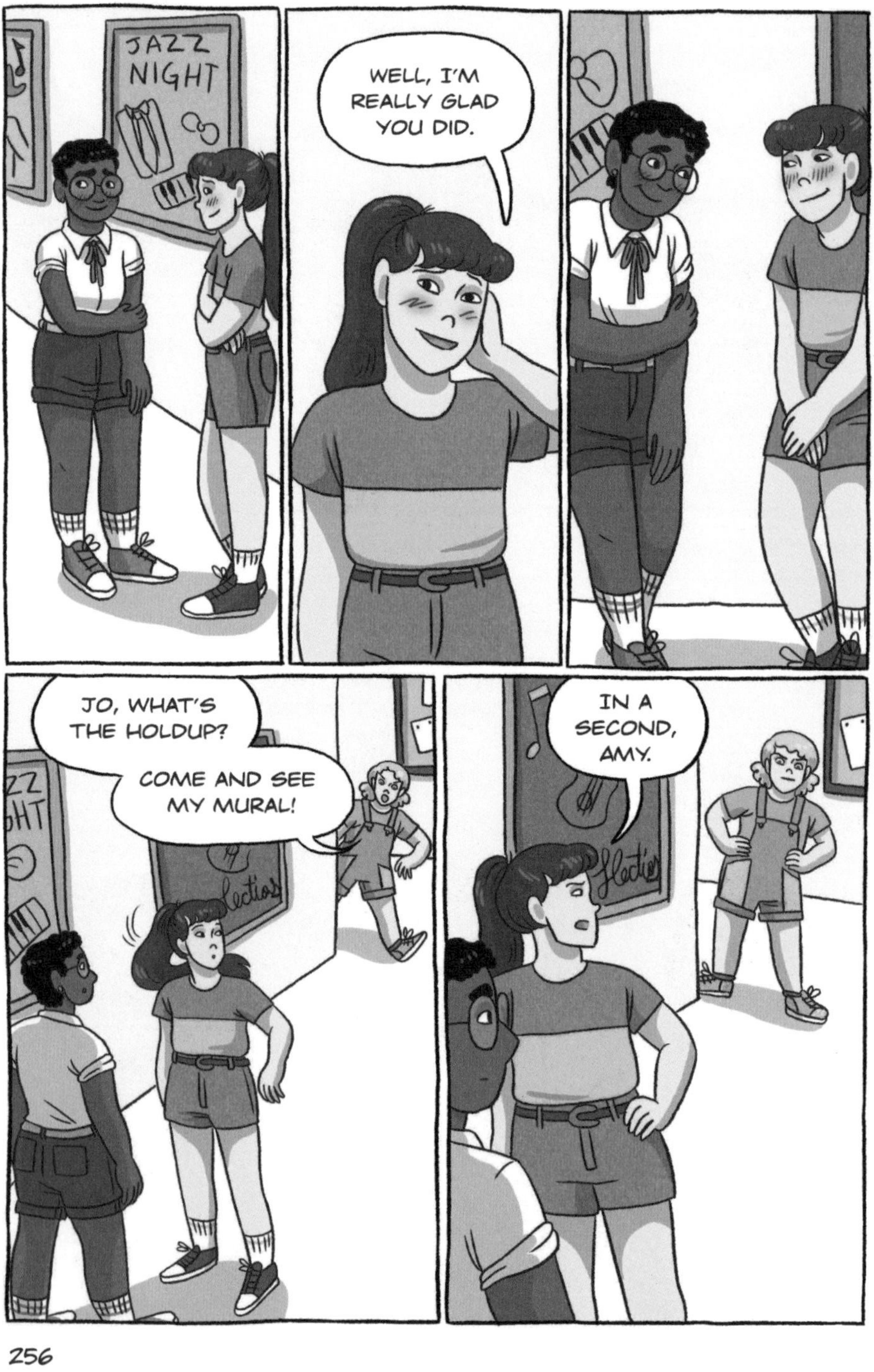
JAZZ NIGHT
WELL, I'M REALLY GLAD YOU DID.
JO, WHAT'S THE HOLDUP?
COME AND SEE MY MURAL!
IN A SECOND, AMY.

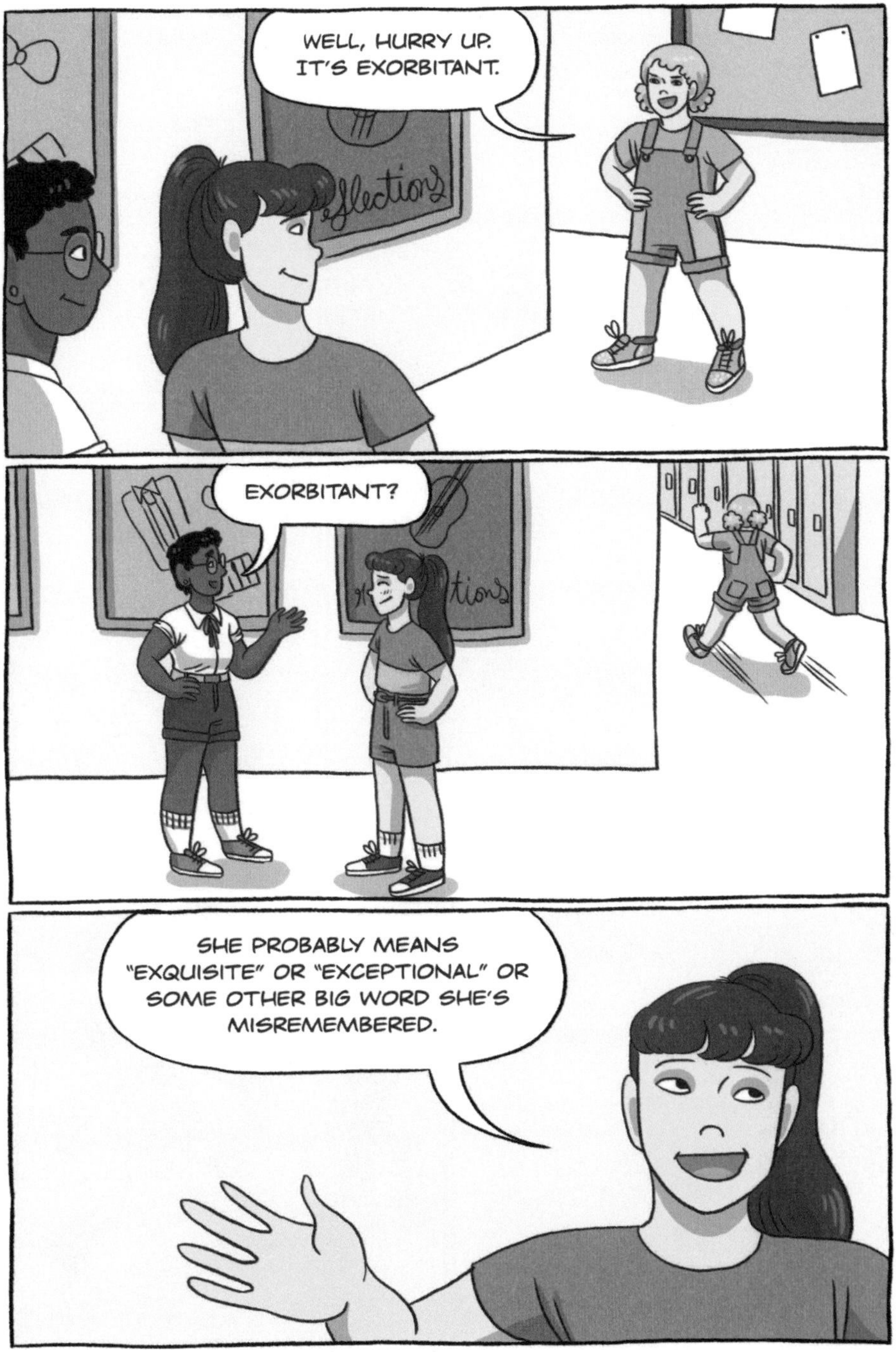
WELL, HURRY UP. IT'S EXORBITANT.
EXORBITANT?
SHE PROBABLY MEANS "EXQUISITE" OR "EXCEPTIONAL" OR SOME OTHER BIG WORD SHE'S MISREMEMBERED.

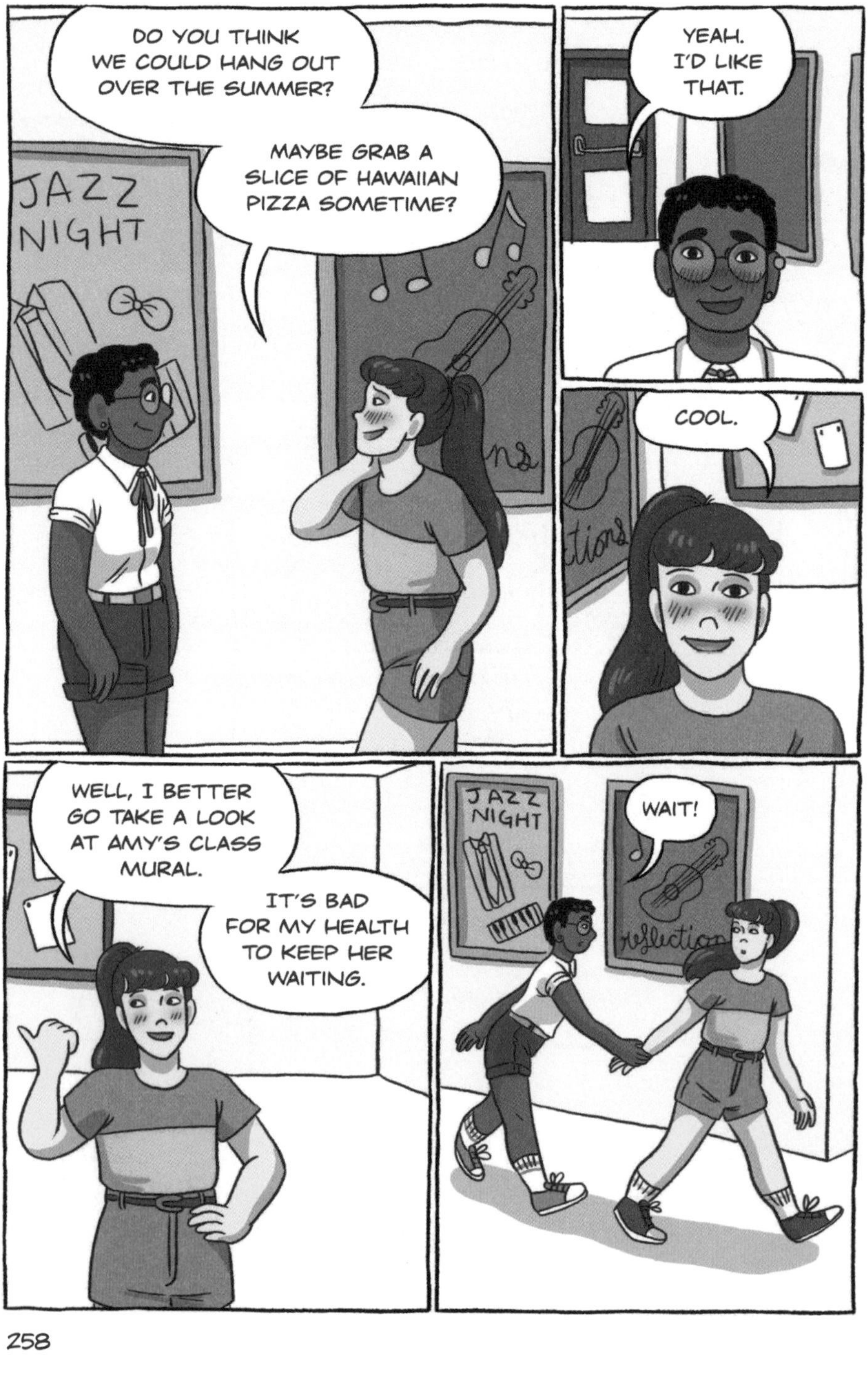
DO YOU THINK WE COULD HANG OUT OVER THE SUMMER?
MAYBE GRAB A SLICE OF HAWAIIAN PIZZA SOMETIME?
JAZZ NIGHT
YEAH. I'D LIKE THAT.
COOL.
WELL, I BETTER GO TAKE A LOOK AT AMY'S CLASS MURAL.
IT'S BAD FOR MY HEALTH TO KEEP HER WAITING.
JAZZ NIGHT
WAIT!

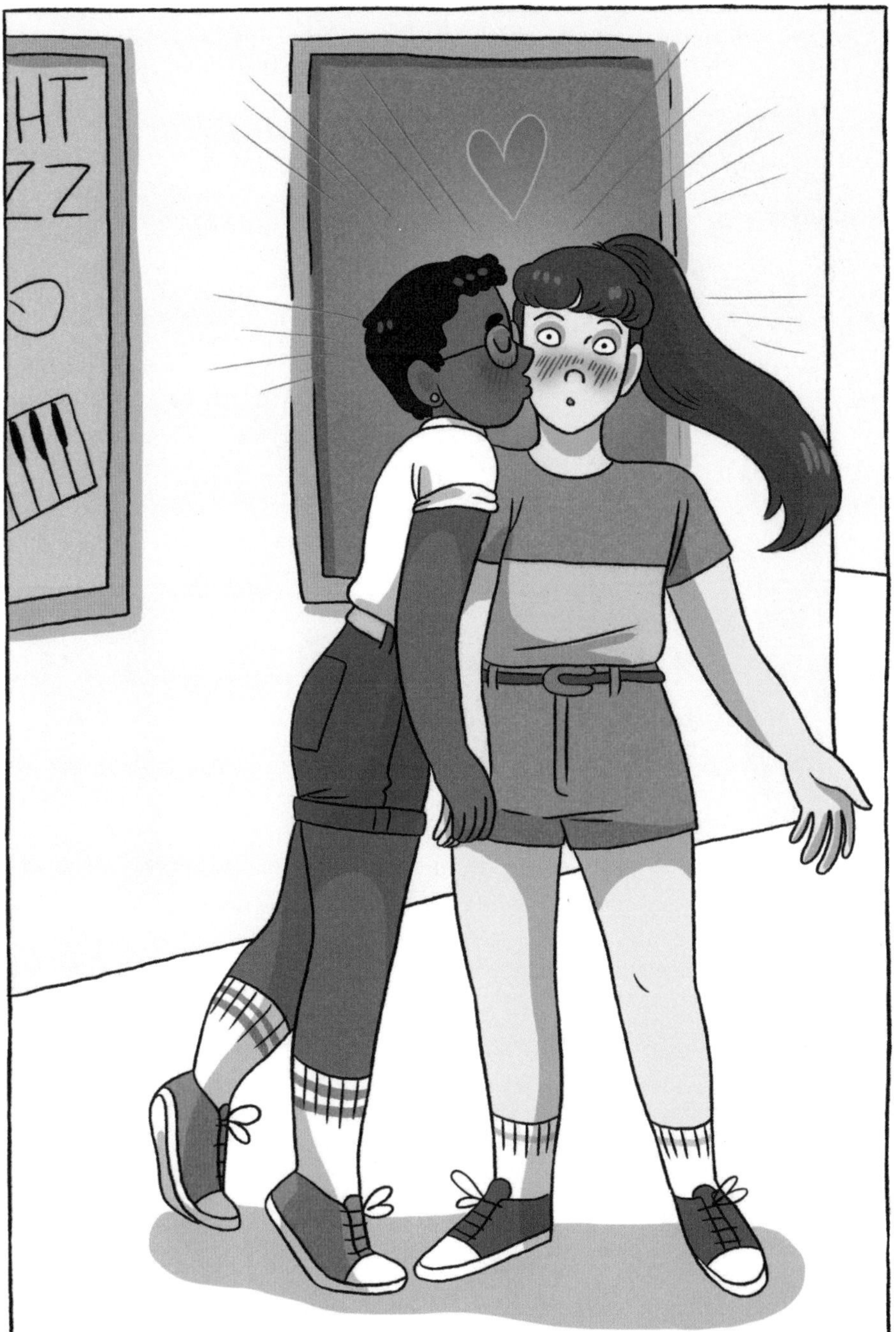

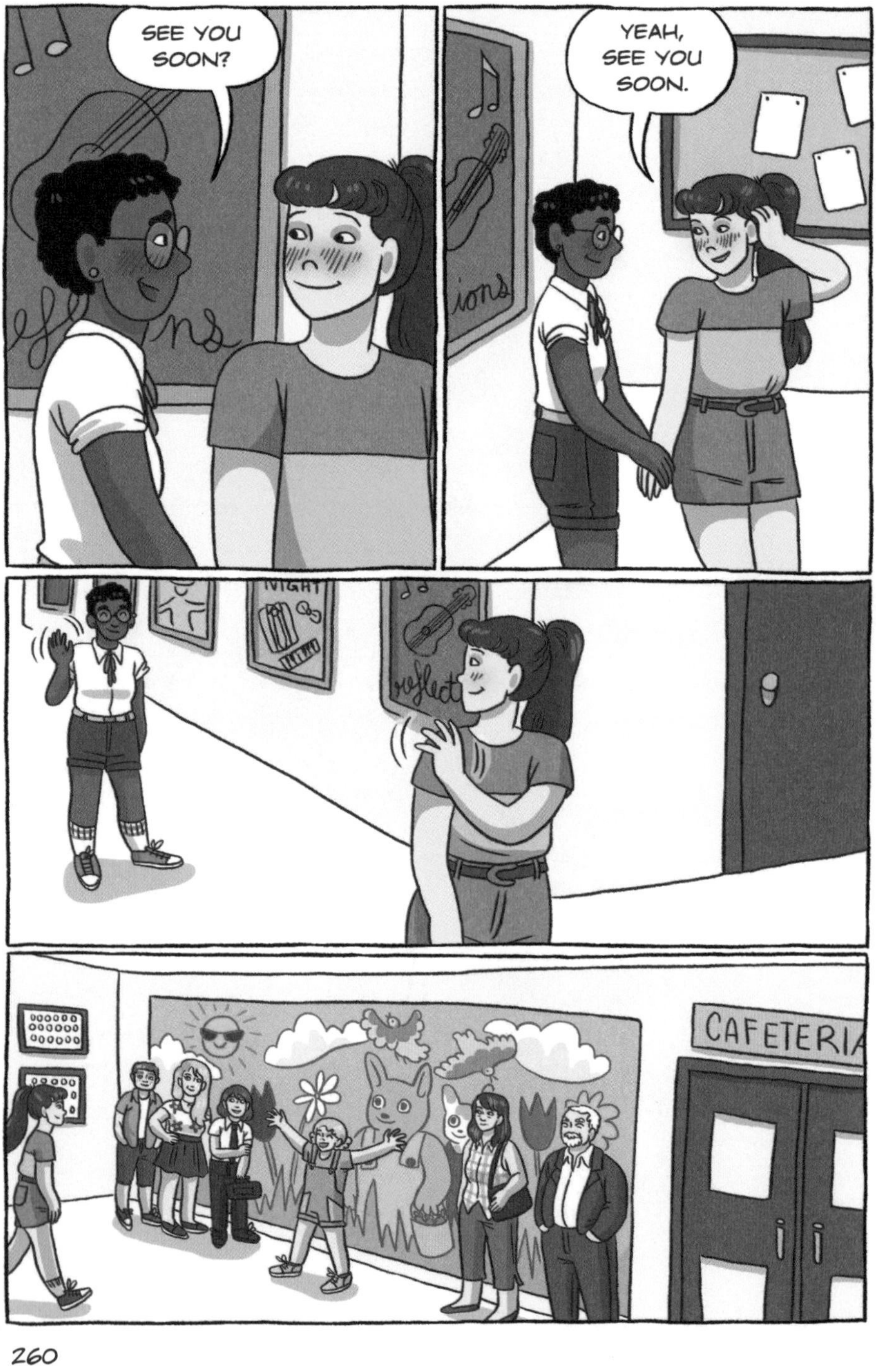
SEE YOU SOON?
YEAH, SEE YOU SOON.
CAFETERIA

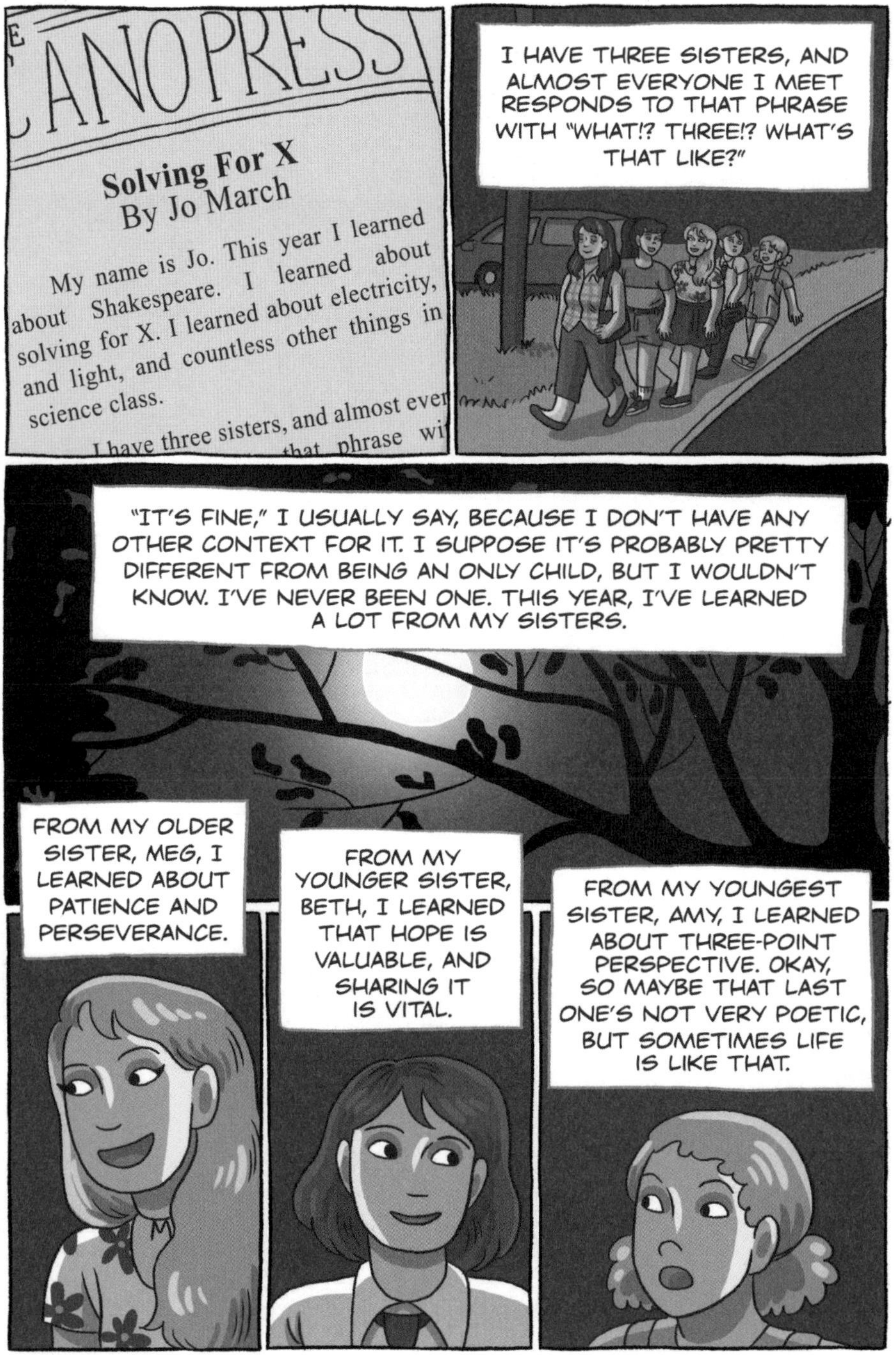
THE
ANO PRESS
Solving For X
By Jo March
My name is Jo. This year I learned about Shakespeare. I learned about solving for X. I learned about electricity, and light, and countless other things in science class.
I have three sisters, and almost ever
that phrase wi
I HAVE THREE SISTERS, AND ALMOST EVERYONE I MEET RESPONDS TO THAT PHRASE WITH "WHAT!? THREE!? WHAT'S THAT LIKE?"
"IT'S FINE," I USUALLY SAY, BECAUSE I DON'T HAVE ANY OTHER CONTEXT FOR IT. I SUPPOSE IT'S PROBABLY PRETTY DIFFERENT FROM BEING AN ONLY CHILD, BUT I WOULDN'T KNOW. I'VE NEVER BEEN ONE. THIS YEAR, I'VE LEARNED A LOT FROM MY SISTERS.
FROM MY OLDER SISTER, MEG, I LEARNED ABOUT PATIENCE AND PERSEVERANCE.
FROM MY YOUNGER SISTER, BETH, I LEARNED THAT HOPE IS VALUABLE, AND SHARING IT IS VITAL.
FROM MY YOUNGEST SISTER, AMY, I LEARNED ABOUT THREE-POINT PERSPECTIVE. OKAY, SO MAYBE THAT LAST ONE'S NOT VERY POETIC, BUT SOMETIMES LIFE IS LIKE THAT.

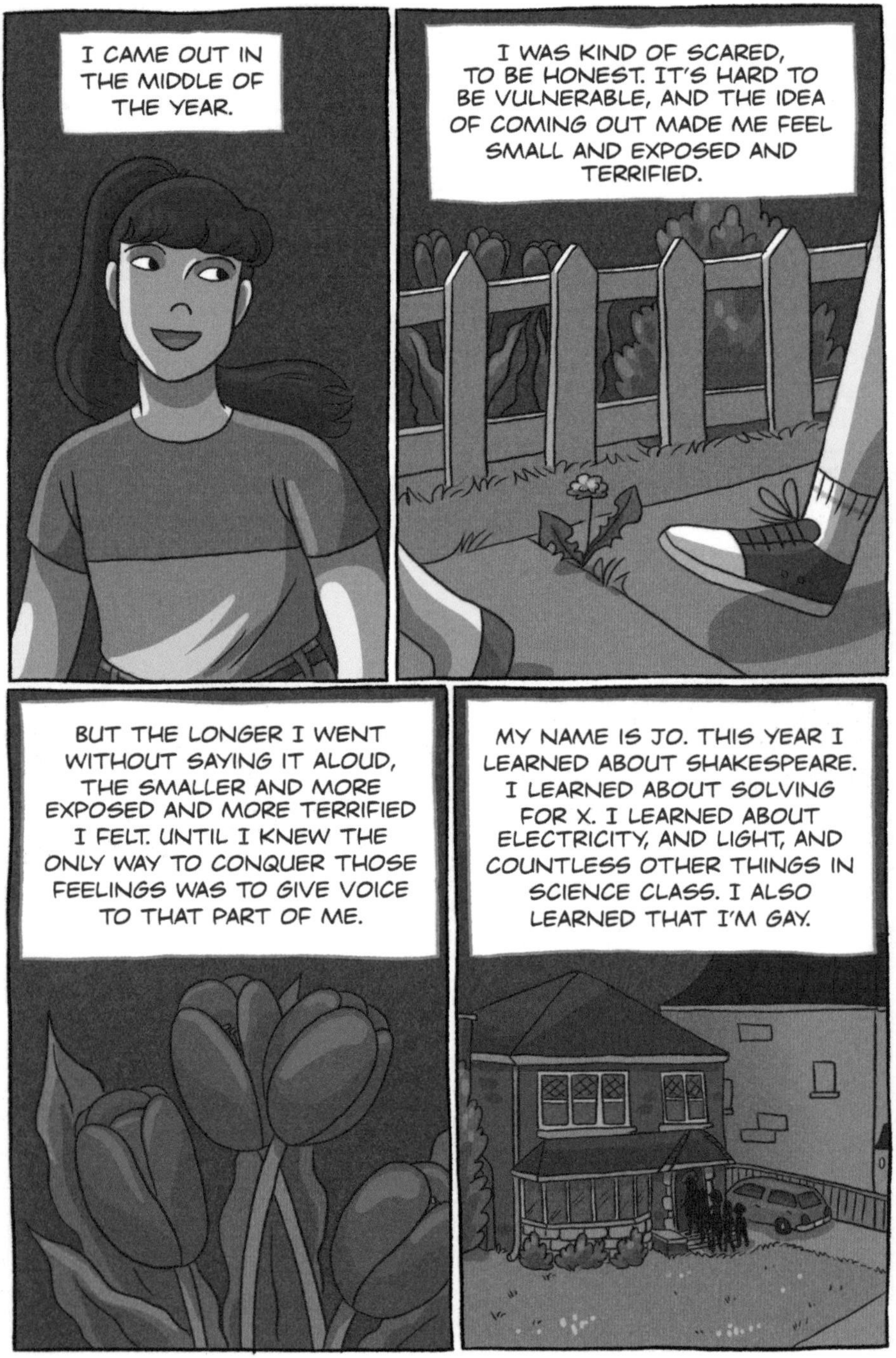
I CAME OUT IN THE MIDDLE OF THE YEAR.
I WAS KIND OF SCARED, TO BE HONEST. IT'S HARD TO BE VULNERABLE, AND THE IDEA OF COMING OUT MADE ME FEEL SMALL AND EXPOSED AND TERRIFIED.
BUT THE LONGER I WENT WITHOUT SAYING IT ALOUD, THE SMALLER AND MORE EXPOSED AND MORE TERRIFIED I FELT. UNTIL I KNEW THE ONLY WAY TO CONQUER THOSE FEELINGS WAS TO GIVE VOICE TO THAT PART OF ME.
MY NAME IS JO. THIS YEAR I LEARNED ABOUT SHAKESPEARE. I LEARNED ABOUT SOLVING FOR X. I LEARNED ABOUT ELECTRICITY, AND LIGHT, AND COUNTLESS OTHER THINGS IN SCIENCE CLASS. I ALSO LEARNED THAT I'M GAY.

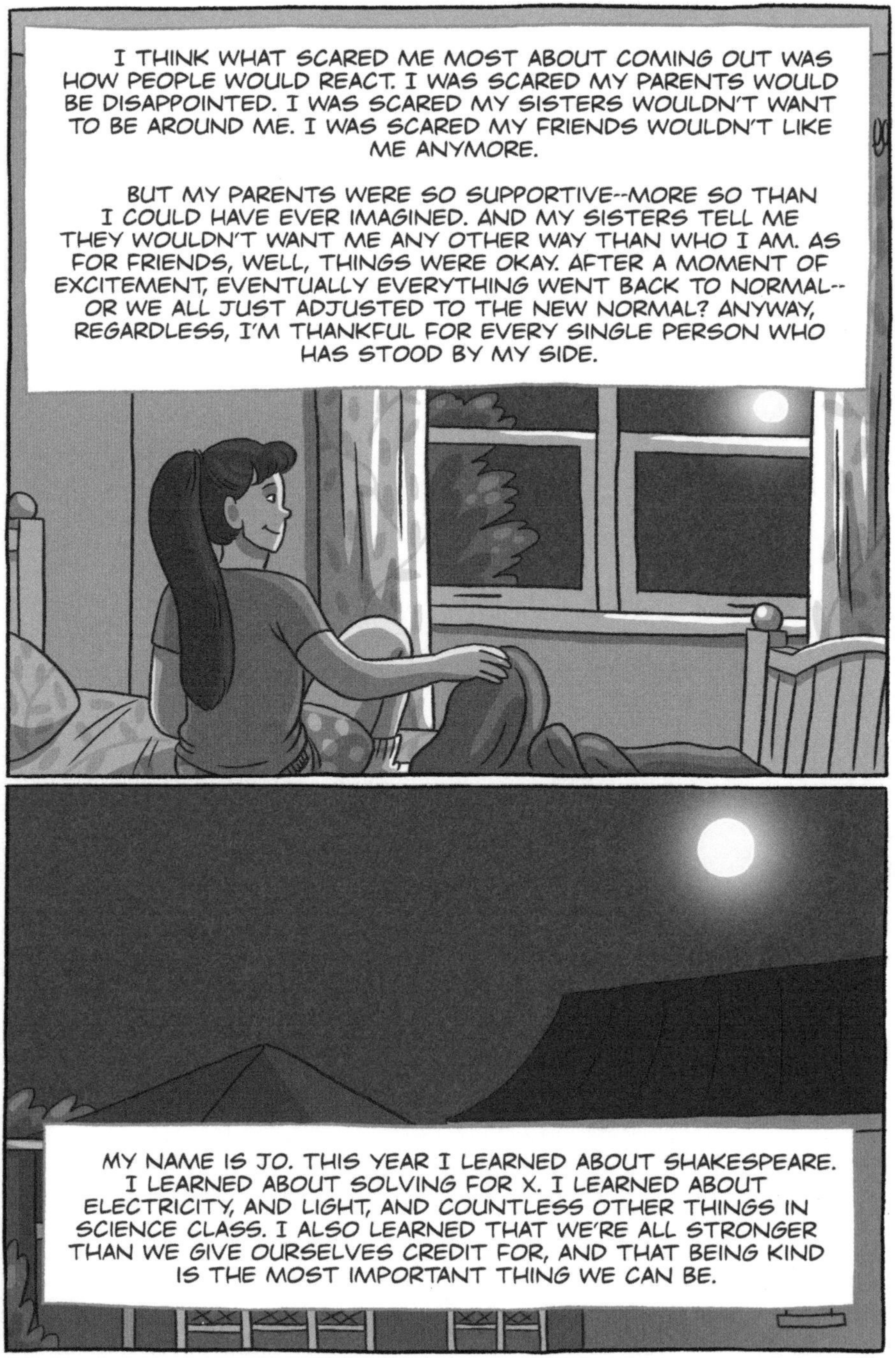
I THINK WHAT SCARED ME MOST ABOUT COMING OUT WAS HOW PEOPLE WOULD REACT. I WAS SCARED MY PARENTS WOULD BE DISAPPOINTED. I WAS SCARED MY SISTERS WOULDN'T WANT TO BE AROUND ME. I WAS SCARED MY FRIENDS WOULDN'T LIKE ME ANYMORE.
BUT MY PARENTS WERE SO SUPPORTIVE--MORE SO THAN I COULD HAVE EVER IMAGINED. AND MY SISTERS TELL ME THEY WOULDN'T WANT ME ANY OTHER WAY THAN WHO I AM. AS FOR FRIENDS, WELL, THINGS WERE OKAY. AFTER A MOMENT OF EXCITEMENT, EVENTUALLY EVERYTHING WENT BACK TO NORMAL--OR WE ALL JUST ADJUSTED TO THE NEW NORMAL? ANYWAY, REGARDLESS, I'M THANKFUL FOR EVERY SINGLE PERSON WHO HAS STOOD BY MY SIDE.
MY NAME IS JO. THIS YEAR I LEARNED ABOUT SHAKESPEARE. I LEARNED ABOUT SOLVING FOR X. I LEARNED ABOUT ELECTRICITY, AND LIGHT, AND COUNTLESS OTHER THINGS IN SCIENCE CLASS. I ALSO LEARNED THAT WE'RE ALL STRONGER THAN WE GIVE OURSELVES CREDIT FOR, AND THAT BEING KIND IS THE MOST IMPORTANT THING WE CAN BE.

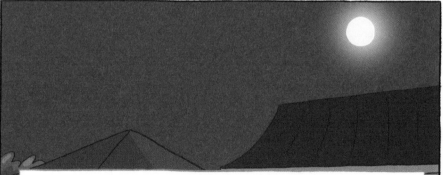

ACKNOWLEDGMENTS

Thank you to my agent, Elizabeth Bennett, for being the spark that ignited this project. Thank you to my editors, Jessica MacLeish and Alexandra Cooper, and the whole team at HC for pushing me to make my best work.

Thank you to James, Sfé, & Darren for cheering me on when I needed it, to the Wednesday-night pals at Cloudscape, and to my American friends for fielding all my questions about American vs. Canadian-isms.

And, of course, thank you to Louisa May Alcott.